Age of Tolerance

AGE

OF

TOLERANCE

A Novel of Alternate History
from Al to Allah

by Glen Reinsford

THE YUKON GROUP

Age of Tolerance
A Novel of Alternate History from Al to Allah

Published by
THE YUKON GROUP
Atlanta, Georgia

Copyright © 2005 by The Yukon Group
Cover Image © by The Yukon Group

Library of Congress Control Number
2005932447

ISBN 0-9772164-0-3
www.ageoftolerance.com
www.thereligionofpeace.com

Printed in the United States of America

To those who supported my writing, and to the many who inspired it.

Some who read this book may think that parts of it are too far-fetched as to be plausible. In fact, nearly everything in this story is based on events that have already occurred...

Glen Reinsford, 2005

Prelude

Monday, September 4th, 2051
New York, New York

Dust trickled down from the remaining tiles that dangled from the ceiling and onto Robert Danforth Jr.'s head, catching in his hair, just above his rapidly moistening brow. He didn't notice.

The long conference room was darker, not just from dust particles floating in the air but also from the loss of power, which coincided with the violent, unnatural impact that had shuddered through the building a few seconds before, softly swaying the pictures on the wall. Cups and mugs lay on the floor where they had been knocked off the table in the ensuing panic. The cups were already crushed, the mugs already stumbled on by people yelling and screaming.

Just a few moments earlier, he had been fighting a half-hearted battle to focus his attention away from the magnificent view of the harbor, with Staten and Ellis Islands framed in the background, and onto those who had invited him to this conference room, eighty-five floors off the ground. Now all he noticed outside was the mean crack that split the glass in a slight diagonal pattern from bottom to top. Black smoke rose slowly into view, along with the unmistakable stench of diesel fumes.

"What happened?" yelled the woman closest to him, whose heels didn't seem to be cooperating with her efforts to maintain balance. She was not the only one asking the question, which Danforth almost answered out of habit – after all he had been the center of attention just a few seconds earlier. But he knew that it wasn't asked of him, and that everyone probably knew as well as he did what had happened. Some of the most important names in Wall Street were experiencing immediate loss of prestige. Everyone was no one now. It didn't matter who you were five minutes ago.

The centrally located conference room was pandemonium. People were trying to get out, while others were trying to get in. Two double doors at either end led to two different corners of the building, each with stairwells. The word was shouted that the elevators weren't working and smoke was coming up from the stairs. Danforth may not have known how big the plane was that hit the Hope Tower and he certainly didn't know or care about how many people had already lost their lives that morning, but he did know that he needed to get himself down the stairs and out of that building.

He angled toward the side of the room, where he could see the closest exit. Smoke was indeed seeping around the stairwell door, indicating that it was probably blocked. Word was traveling back confirming this and he knew that he had to act quickly. Reversing direction and pushing past the bodies still streaming into the room from the opposite door, he raised his hands above his head and pointed back toward the hallway leading to the blocked stairwell. "Exit is clear! Head back over there!" he shouted.

Confused faces paused briefly on him then surged past, toward what little space remained on the other side of the room and into the small hallway beyond. This gave him a clearer path out and down the hallway and toward the opposite side of the tower, where he hoped the stairwell was truly clear. He repeated his words to anyone that he came across, sending them clawing desperately back into the growing mass of humanity pushing against each other as half were trying to get into a well that the other half knew was blocked. The shouting grew to a steady, incomprehensible roar behind him.

Even now, fifty years after 9/11, Danforth always made a habit of knowing where the exits were, just like his mother had taught him. The precious seconds that he had bought for himself could be the difference between life and death. Fewer people trying to get into the stairwell meant faster access for Danforth, and fewer people on the stairs meant a better possibility of getting out before the whole thing collapsed.

The long interior hallway was much different than he remembered from a few minutes before. Emergency spotlights pierced the dusk, with dazed figures stumbling in and out of the haze around the beams. An alarm blared with excruciating annoyance, punctuated every so often by a harsh voice that sounded as if it was coming through a bullhorn at a concentration camp. The words were all in Spanish, but *de Emergencia* needed no interpretation.

Danforth's tailored shirt was wet with perspiration by the time he reached the opposite end of the building. He was not encouraged by the fact that people were streaming past in the opposite direction. Finally, one young man clutched his arm and yelled in his ear that the stairwell was blocked with smoke and people.

Danforth knocked his hand away and staggered past without replying. If there were people in this stairwell, then it had to be better than the other. Why were there only two stairwells in a building that was constructed decades after 9/11?

The door to the stairs loomed ahead of him. True enough, there was black smoke oozing under the top of the frame. A small knot of people huddled around the entrance. Danforth shoved his way past and pulled the door open. It was like opening the oven to check on a casserole, only here the oven was filled with people. Blackened faces filled with shock stared back at him, part of a herd making its way up the stairs. They didn't stand a chance, he thought. To the top meant death. The only way out was to go down.

He dashed into the haze and mass of people, knocking several out of the way as he tried to reach the inside of the stairs. He quickly realized that he had to stay in the middle, however, as too many bodies were clutching the rails on each side for support. He didn't need the rails to go down, nor was it hard forcing his way past those coming up, since he had both the high ground and the element of surprise.

He pushed past them, hardly noticing the cursing or the occasional punch thrown at him, as he was driven by adrenaline and a pure animal desire to survive. A woman lost her balance and slipped under him. He was able to use her back quite adeptly and leapfrog the man bending over to help her, although knocking him down as well. To Danforth, these were no longer people – they were obstacles.

So intent was he in making his way past the others, that he was slow to realize the intensity of the smoke and heat, even as the desperate crowd thinned around him. When he finally broke out past the end, only a few stragglers remained. Some were trying to carry others, who looked badly burned or bloody. They parted for him as best they could and he scurried past, with his eyes stinging. It was only then, that he became aware of the flame directly below.

He plunged instinctively through the nearest exit door, held slightly ajar by a woman's purse, which he kicked aside. Pressure caused the door to slam behind him with such force that he worried it might not open again. He put his hand on the metal knob to see if he could pull it, but immediately recoiled in pain.

He hadn't realized how hot it was down here. His lungs felt singed, and he knew that he was now coughing just as heavily as anyone that he passed on the way down.

Visibility was reduced to little more than a few yards, but he could see that the paint was cracking on the near walls. What had he gotten himself into? He half expected his clothes to burst into flame at any moment. They felt scalding, as if he had put them on straight out of the dryer. He bent over in an effort to escape the heat, straining to see ahead. He knew the floor plan was different from the one upstairs, because he immediately saw a wall where he expected a hallway.

There weren't any emergency lights on this floor, but there was a dull glow from a few windowed offices. No people were in sight. Apparently everyone had fled up the stairs. He wasn't confident about finding his way across to the other stairwell. Somewhat absent-mindedly he turned back and grasped the door handle, burning his hand again. He tore his shirt off and wadded it up. He tried desperately to grip the knob with it, but it kept slipping. He then tried banging against the door, but to no avail.

His attention was drawn to an open office, two doors down, but he wasn't sure why. There seemed to be movement there, something that was making the daylight flicker. It was enough to prompt him to investigate. Walking through the door, however, he came upon a horrible scene. People in the building across the street were hanging out of broken windows with clothes wrapped around their heads. Smoke poured out behind them from jagged holes in the glass. Danforth's blood chilled as he saw one of the persons release their grip and drop out of view like a rock. More followed. It was unnatural, watching this occur so far off the ground. Danforth had never seen anyone jump to their death, though he had sometimes imagined what it had been like for his father and the other victims.

The reality was incomprehensible. He couldn't bear to look at the anguished, blackened faces that silently mouthed words then assumed determined expressions before jumping. If this had been photographed and shown fifty years ago, he wondered, would America have reacted differently? *Would this be happening to him now?*

The worst was yet to come, as Danforth grasped something not quite right about the scene as he turned away. Looking back, he peered closer through the drifting smoke, then had to grab onto a desk to keep from collapsing as he realized that what he was witnessing was not occurring in the building across the street. Rather it was a reflection, in the building's mirrored glass, of what was happening on the floors beneath him.

Danforth bolted back into the hallway and back to the same stairwell door. Steeling himself, he reached down as quickly as he could and twisted the knob with his bare hand, ignoring the sharp pain. The door pulled slightly open and he reached for the crack, but he couldn't get his fingers there in time. Hot ash flew into his face as the door fell shut. He screamed in frustration and pulled the knob again, burying the pain deep beneath anger and fear. This time he caught the edge of the door and pulled it open, even as his fingers seemed to melt on contact.

The scene had changed in just the last minute or two. There was an inferno of black debris mixed with sparks rushing up the stairs and through the door behind him. He took no interest in the charring body that was attempting to pull itself up from the floor below or the distant screams.

There was nothing to breath. He couldn't go down. Reluctantly, he made a quick decision to head up to the next floor. The handle there was no better than the one he had grappled with below.

At least the floor plan looked familiar, and there were a few emergency lights on as well. Though it probably wasn't meant to be the case, one shone down almost directly on a picture of an American President giving a State of the Union address to Congress. Though it was taken almost exactly fifty years ago, Danforth instantly recognized it. The banner at the bottom would say that Al Gore had been awarded the "Profiles in Courage" prize for that speech. Danforth's mother was in the chamber that day, an invited guest of the Gore Administration. The same picture had hung on the wall of her house for as long as he could remember.

He turned away and ran hunched over through the smoke, in the direction of the other stairwell. He heard occasional voices and coughing along the way, but there was no one at the other stairs when he got there. The door was closed and beginning to singe around the edges. Danforth slowed as he approached. This looked worse than what he had left. His lungs were aching. He put the shirt that was wrapped around his hand up to his mouth.

Groans were coming from the stairs on the other side of the door. Someone banged against it and the knob jiggled. He jammed his foot against the door to prevent it from opening. There was a horrible screaming on the other side then a second or two of absolute silence, followed by something that sounded like a gas fireplace being turned up. A pungent odor seeped through the door frame, mixing with the smoke.

Unnerved, Danforth backed away from the door. He was beginning to unravel.

Before he could collect himself, he was jarred by a woman's high-pitched voice. "Help me! Can you help me?" An older lady, perhaps in her seventies, with a gaudy choker around a thin, shriveled throat, came floating out of the haze toward him as he whirled around to face her.

The woman began to reach at him. "No!" he said, "Leave me alone!"

Before the woman could stop, Danforth stepped forward and hit her in the face with all he had, noting the confused look in her eyes just before he made contact. Her necklace flung apart, spinning into different pieces on the floor as she went down in a heap.

Danforth had not hit anyone since he was ten years old, and he had never hit anyone like that. He was surprised by his own fury. It shocked him. He wasn't a violent man, he told himself. He was just reacting to the situation. He was angry about what was happening, and he transferred that into action, just like in college when he and his friends used to throw food at the Nationalists that dared to speak on campus.

Danforth was in a fog. He was having trouble focusing. He kept hearing a noise, but couldn't place it until he looked down and saw that it was the old woman whimpering. She had curled into a fetal position, and was wrapped around his feet almost like a whipped dog. Gradually his senses returned.

Maybe he wasn't thinking clearly when he hit her, but now he realized that he had a new problem on his hands. If the woman survived, she would surely recognize him as the former CEO of CSR, and the newly appointed chairman of the Securities and Exchange Commission. If she talked, then it would jeopardize his fragile career. Danforth knew he wasn't a violent man. But this was an extraordinary situation. Sometimes people are forced to take drastic measures out of desperation.

The woman was clutching Danforth's foot, still crumpled on the floor beneath him. He tore himself out of her grasp, stepped a few feet away and bent down to see under the smoke. There was a fire extinguisher laying on the floor about ten yards down the hall. The woman was moaning louder. Danforth walked slowly down the hallway and reached for the heavy canister.

Time seemed to stand still.

He turned carefully as if in a trance, holding the newfound weapon in his hand, visualizing what he would do with it. He saw himself bringing it down on the woman's head. He saw himself killing another human being. Somehow it felt right. Not just right, but liberating.

He had not considered it to this point, but killing was the only rule that he hadn't broken, and it was bringing a sense of exhilaration that he had not felt in some time, even under the circumstances.

He recalled stealing when he was a boy, first from his family, then from his friends, then from his friends' families and finally from complete strangers, moving further and further out as he was caught and shamed. It was exciting to get something for nothing, certainly more so than working for it. Going to prostitutes had been like that as well, at least at first. Sharing physical intimacy without the traditional struggle to earn it, or bearing the obligation to protect and care for the woman, had a certain appeal. Then sex became so mundane for him that it wasn't worth the effort or health risk.

Danforth took steady, mechanical steps, crouching slightly to bring his watery eyes below the worst of the stinging haze. The woman was only a few feet away. She was still curled up, face to the ground... still moaning... just a few more steps...

"Yes... hey!"

The shouting jolted Danforth out of the bizarre little world that he was rapidly devolving into and back into focus. He dropped the fire extinguisher on his foot, almost certainly breaking at least one bone.

At first he couldn't see anything at all through the murky hallway. Slight movement gradually turned into a figure rushing directly toward him.

It turned out to be a black man about his age, perhaps younger, and bare from the waist up, save a tie that flapped ridiculously from his neck. He was holding what was probably his shirt to his face. In an instant he was kneeling over the woman, feeling her neck. Danforth noticed a large number of small scars on the man's left arm and side, from an injury apparently suffered years before. It reminded him of a photograph he had seen showing the back of a flogging victim from the slave era.

The man looked up triumphantly. "I knew it! I knew there was someone left down here. We can get her. We can get her off this floor! Come on!"

Let's get her, Danforth mouthed, still not understanding. The other man bent over the woman and looked up at Danforth. "Let's go. Grab her arms, I've got her ankles. That exit's jammed, but we can still get out the other way!"

He paused for a second and stuck out his hand. "My name's Ridley... Pat Ridley, although officially there's a 'junior' on the end, since I'm named after my father."

"Robert Dan... uh... Robert." Danforth gave a very weak handshake, followed by a coughing spasm. He couldn't care less about the man's family history.

There was no choice now. Danforth reluctantly picked up the canister and attempted to clench the hose with his teeth to free up his hands. Common sense was beginning to settle back into him. He felt like he was waking from a dream. The extinguisher slipped out of his mouth and fell onto his other foot. He yelped and tried to kick it out of the way.

"No, we'll need that," said the other man, who dropped one of the woman's legs and snatched up the extinguisher with his free hand. "Let's go!"

Danforth reached down and took the old woman's wrists in his hands. Her skin felt so loose that he thought it might pull right off the bone. Her body was twisted around and her head dangled back as she was carried. Danforth had to walk carefully to avoid kicking her face or stepping on her hair.

What a turn of events this was, he mused to himself – saving the person that he had almost killed. Perhaps the headlines might be kinder tomorrow than he had thought, although he doubted that any of them would survive. Still he held out hope that perhaps it was possible to get down the other stairwell

Pat Ridley Jr. seemed to know where he was going, and they made better time across the building, even bent over and burdened as they were. The smoke was thick and Danforth's mood sank even further upon seeing the paint bubbling around the edges of the stairwell door. Barely able to breath, he dropped the woman's wrists and fell to his knees, placing his hand against the wall and closing his eyes. How long before the building collapsed?

A sudden hissing caught his attention. It was the sound of the extinguisher, which Ridley was using to cool the door handle. He had torn some wallpaper from where it was literally curling from the heat, and evidently intended to try and manage the knob with it.

Danforth began to think. There was an extinguisher on the opposite wall that he hadn't even noticed before. Maybe it was his ticket down the stairs. He walked over and pulled it down. As Ridley worked the door, Danforth pulled the pin from the canister handle with an aching finger and stood with it in his hands for a few seconds, getting a good feel for how it worked. Once satisfied, he strode rapidly back toward the stairwell, arriving with perfect timing just as Ridley pulled open the door.

Danforth briefly turned his head to draw in a deep breath then hurtled past the other man, out into the stairwell and down the stairs, spraying wildly in front of him in a mad dash for life.

With his eyes barely open against the elements, he managed to reach the bottom and round the corner, but his last chance to make it down the remaining seventy-one floors fell short when he could no longer put off taking the next breath. Despite the chemicals that worked against the flames around him, he seemed to be inhaling lava. He may as well have been sealed inside a furnace.

He tripped over a corpse, probably the same wretch that he had seen earlier, attempting to crawl up the stairs. His head hit the wall and he collapsed near the blackened floor at the bottom of the steps. The skin on his bare arm sizzled against the metal lip that ran across the last concrete step. His eyes were now fully closed and he was fading to black. He knew it was over.

Instead of going out in a burst of flame as he expected, however, a trickle of coolness floated down on him, almost like snow. There was shouting. A hand grabbed at him, then another. He tried to open his eyes.

Ridley was lifting him onto his shoulders, coughing and muttering something about valiance. "Outstanding, valiant effort…"

"Hmm?" mumbled Danforth.

"You would give your life for me… for her… two people you don't even know!"

Ridley seemed inspired by Danforth's effort and Danforth wasn't going to correct him. If the man thought that the new SEC chairman had been beating back the flames on someone else's behalf, rather than staging a desperate effort to save his own skin, then so be it.

Danforth, who believed that the man carrying him was several years younger, felt like he had been redeemed. Rather than meeting his end on the steps, he was able to try once again at getting out of the hellhole. Ridley strained to make it up the last couple of steps and then slid Danforth off his back after they passed under the door frame. He kicked the fire door closed and they both collapsed on the floor next to the old woman.

After a few long seconds, Ridley pointed to her and said, "We need to get her up the stairs. We've got no time to lose."

"Oh no, no," Danforth growled through the pain in his throat. "We need to go down. We have to get out of the building. There's no other way."

Ridley was astonished. "We can't go down. There's no one left down there. The stairs are completely gone on the other side, and there's no getting through here either, until they come for us. You did your best, but the fire's just too hot."

It suddenly hit Danforth as hard as he had hit the woman next to him with his fist a few minutes earlier. He knew that the other man was right. It was true – hadn't he proved it? There was no way to get out of the building. His lungs were scorched. His hands were burned. He had been right earlier. It was over.

Very quickly he made a decision. He decided to trade certain death for thirty minutes of life. He decided to go up the stairs.

The last thing he did before following the other two out the door was to knock the picture of Al Gore down from the wall.

PART ONE

———

THE EXPERIMENT

1988

Sunday, September 4th, 1988
Washington, D.C.

Tension was as thick as the humidity on that hot afternoon at the Mall in Washington D.C. A sixteen-year-old girl stood in the sweltering heat next to her mother, watching a group of anti-choice protestors in a tiny knot across the road from the Abortion Rights Rally. A perfect storm was beginning to brew between the two politically-charged groups.

The teenager was still having a tough time accepting evil in the world, as personified at the moment by these spiteful protesters, who wanted to control women's bodies to such an extent that their mere presence was spoiling the rally. With her damp tank-top clinging lightly to her back and her mother following anxiously behind, she crossed the street to confront these hateful people on the curb.

Steel barricades had been erected to separate the anti-choicers from the pro-rights marchers. The girl carefully chose a spot that was a few yards away from a line of park policeman, not noticing that a photographer was taking an interest in the developing situation. She looked across the metal barrier and saw the angriest, most ignorant group of people she had ever seen. They were holding posters with pictures of fetuses reading "If she isn't a human being, than was sort of being is she?" and "If she isn't alive, then why is she growing?"

The girl could take it no more. She grabbed her mother by the arm and shouted to the hateful group. "Look at her! Look at this woman! She had no choice in life, thanks to people like you, who want to control women's bodies and subjugate them.

"My mother got pregnant at an early age before she was ready to have a child. She didn't need a baby and couldn't afford to take care of one, but thanks to people like you, she had no choice. My mother had to postpone her plans for college. She had to work two jobs – menial labor – for three years just to scratch out a living."

The girl spoke with wisdom beyond her years. Her mother beamed. The angry crowd looked stunned. The photographer carefully positioned himself.

"People like you are disgraceful! You want to take away women's freedom. You want to kill them in back alleys. You want to strip my generation of rights that women like my mother worked so hard for, because they never had that freedom themselves. You want to force me to have a child, just like you forced my mother. Shame on you hicks… you backwoods throwbacks! Keep your hands off my uterus!"

Her antagonists were speechless. Mouths hung agape. The girl turned to see pride shining in her mother's watery eyes. The woman swallowed, smiled, and with a swelling heart drew her daughter into an embrace.

As the photographer froze the climactic moment for history, the woman could be seen whispering something into her daughter's ear.

2001

Tuesday, September 11ᵗʰ, 2001
Sarasota, Florida

President Al Gore sat in front of a classroom full of young children, teachers and news reporters at Emma E. Booker Elementary School in Sarasota on the morning of September 11ᵗʰ, 2001. Everyone was seated in identically sized blue plastic chairs, which were quite sufficient for the children, but not so for the President, who perched delicately, as if on a short stool. Gore, dressed in a brown suit, focused his movements on the children, appearing enamored as he studied each of their faces with mock seriousness.

As with most public figures, the lighthearted expression on his face wasn't telling of the dark thoughts swirling through his mind, although he wasn't terribly bothered by the news that his Chief of Staff, Andy Harrelson, whispered in his ear a few minutes earlier – about a small plane hitting the World Trade Center's North Tower, probably due to some sort of mishap.

Rather, he was preoccupied with how his first two and a half years in office had been going. Since taking the reins, the unemployment rate had risen noticeably, over a million jobs had been lost, and the GDP had actually gone negative. The country was in a recession – and it was not the former Vice President's fault. No President has control over the economy he inherits, and Gore had been given one that was perched far higher than it should have been, as he found out after the tech bubble burst in the spring of 1999, just two months after he assumed office in the wake of his predecessor's resignation.

It was his choice, however, to downplay the dismal economic numbers during the election year, to convince the voters that growth was actually strong (thank goodness for James Carville, who could make a recovery look like a recession and a recession look like a recovery, irrespective of the facts). Now, with the Governor of Texas a distant memory, he was stuck with the reality of lost jobs and negative growth, which contrasted badly with his optimism the previous year. Pundits were grumbling about downsizing and the growing gap between rich and poor, two trends that were in full force under Clinton, but largely obscured by a booming stock market and the willingness of fellow Democrats to acquiesce their Reagan Era values.

It wasn't Gore's fault that the NASDAQ lost about seventy-five percent of its value nearly overnight in the late 90's, but that didn't stop the pressure on him, which was even coming from within his own party, where members were largely unimpressed with the tone of a "kinder, gentler America," taken in speeches that subtly implied that the dot.com years were about greed, leaving the country with "bills needing to be paid." "Greed is good," confidentially insisted one Democrat, "if it keeps us in office."

But the bad economy was not enough to prevent the Democrats from taking back control of both houses of Congress for the first time since Clinton's disastrous first term, since the voters were more impressed with the integrity shown by Al Gore and his party in 1999. That year their popular President faced impeachment for obstruction of justice, leaving them with a decision to make. It was obvious that Bill Clinton had lied to a Federal grand jury (a felony in and of itself) and tampered with evidence and witnesses to deny a young woman her day in court under a sexual harassment law that he had signed. He had blatantly lied to the American people as well.

But, after maintaining during the Watergate Era that public leaders should be held to the highest standards of truthfulness, the Democrats were not about to hold pep rallies for Bill Clinton, or tell Americans that integrity and character were incidental qualities for public leadership. They approached their Party leader, as their opponents had done twenty-five years earlier, and explained that a President was not above the law. Democrats would not be sticking their finger in the wind to see what could be gotten away with, or selling out their principles for political convenience.

After the fuss they raised in 1991 over a Supreme Court nominee, feminists were not about to look the other way either, knowing full well that failing to call for the President's head in far more egregious circumstances would expose the grandest hypocrisy ever seen in American politics – and compromise their credibility for a generation. Faced with this reality, Bill Clinton uncharacteristically put his party and his nation above personal ambition and stepped aside, making Al Gore the 43rd President of the United States. The voters rewarded the Democrats at the polls, including the 2000 Presidential race, which might have gone to the Governor of Texas had his opponents been seduced into betraying core principles.

So preoccupied was President Gore with his own thoughts that he was not aware of having ceased alternating his gaze from each of the small faces in front of him, and now sat staring intently, with a plastered grin, at one young boy. The boy began to look troubled, but Gore sat frozen while the wheels spun in his head. The boy began to cry, but it took whispering from the press corps in the back of the room to break the President out of his trance. He turned back toward the classroom teacher, who was in the process of introducing him.

"And so, boys and girls, we are so fortunate to have with us today, a very special guest. Do any of you know who this is?"

Gore smiled and gave a sly wink to the cameras in the back of the room as the children stumbled over each other, trying to be the first to blurt out the answer. He glanced back down at the kids with his eyes open wide, as if genuinely impressed with their power of observation.

The scene was spoiled by Andy Harrelson, who nearly tripped over a chair in his haste to reach the President. Gore looked up with mild distaste as his Chief of Staff came scurrying up to him. Harrelson bent down and whispered that another plane had hit the second World Trade Center tower. The aide stood there for a few seconds while Gore tried to digest the news. Except for a setting of his jaw, he did not move. Eventually Harrelson backed away, but the President continued to stare blankly for a few more seconds as the classroom teacher continued.

"Does anyone know where the President lives? That's right. Washington D.C. He's come all the way down here to Florida to visit with you all and read you a story. President Gore… President Gore?"

Gore forced himself to smile and picked up a book from the pile sitting on a table beside him. It was something about a goat, but it could have been a police report on a triple homicide and he wouldn't have noticed at that moment. Without any introduction, he began reading aloud to the children. His voice droned on for two full minutes, completely passionless, until he was interrupted again by the Chief of Staff, whose voice held unmistakable stress.

"There are other planes in the air, Mr. President. America is under attack!"

"Oh dear God!" exclaimed Gore, in a volume far above a whisper. The teacher to his left frowned and the children could be heard drawing in sharp breaths. Cameras captured the moment.

Oh damn, he thought (to himself, fortunately). He shouldn't have reacted that way, but now it was too late. There was compete silence. Jaws hung open as everyone stared. The situation begged for an explanation.

He knew what the others didn't. America was under attack! Terrorists were flying planes into buildings. More planes were in the air. Some of them could be over his head now, looking to take out the President of the United States – and there wasn't anything his Secret Service could do about it.

He rose slowly to his feet, not sure of what he would say, but desperately searching for words. He had to convey the urgency of the situation, while appearing dignified. How should he respond? Gore quickly took note of his audience. The teacher and most of the students were African-American. On the campaign trail, Gore had taught himself to adjust to the crowd. Normally he would talk in a rather wooden, rehearsed sort of way, unless he was speaking to a black audience, in which case he would become animated, sounding like a country preacher. Is that how he should act now?

He thought the better of it and spoke calmly, speaking to the cameras on the opposite end of the room. "I've just received word that two airplanes have been flown into the World Trade Center. Hundreds of people have been killed, thousands more may die." The children, sensing the tension, began to squeal, but he didn't notice.

"America is under attack. We are under attack at this very moment, because there are hijacked planes in the air ready to rain down on us. We must respond and take cover immediately!" Gore wasn't aware of his hand gestures, but the fingers on one hand were perfectly rigid as they motioned back and forth sharply into his forearm, simulating the anticipated collision of aircraft and building.

The wailing of the children was building to a crescendo, attracting even the President's attention. The teacher had risen out of her chair and was reaching toward a 7-year-old girl, who was thoroughly in the grip of a major emotional meltdown. Tears were appearing on the faces of others as well. Some were sliding to the floor and attempting to hide under the plastic chairs. Others were running toward the door. One lad even bolted behind the teacher and into the recess under the wooden desk, where small white knuckles could be seen clutching the modesty panel underneath. The press corps was buzzing in the back of the room, as Secret Service agents descended on the President like flies on a carcass.

"The children…!" Gore shouted, with a quick glance to the press cameras. "Think of the children!" The mass of second-graders swirled around him. He pawed unsuccessfully at the arm of the closest one, before managing to snag the shirt of another. He lifted the bawling young girl into his arms, pausing dramatically before the cameras to strike a pose that would appear on magazine covers the following week. An agent quickly knocked the girl out of his arms and, with the help of a second, hauled the President roughly to the door and down the hall.

Other classrooms in the school had been locked down with the President's visit, so he remained at the forefront of the wave of bodies that cascaded out of the library, washing through corridors, around corners, and finally spilling out of the building and directly into the perfectly positioned flag-studded limousine that always traveled with him.

Air Force One (Over Texas)

It took nearly an hour to coordinate the teleconference with the full security team and the Vice President. The President's nerves had steadied somewhat during that time. Air Force One could potentially stay aloft for a period of days, and all other air traffic was being grounded, with the exception of military fighters and transport planes. Images of smoke rising from the Pentagon were unsettling and he did not object when his Secret Service team suggested that he spend the next several days away from Washington.

Engine noise was muffled considerably by the deep blue carpet and soundproof walls in the President's private compartment. Except for the occasional light bounce, it was easy to forget that one was 30,000 feet in the air. Against the wall, was a bank of monitors showing the faces of the security team and those members of the Cabinet able to supply video stream. Others were participating via audio.

Gore spoke in his slow characteristic drawl to David Encino, the newly appointed National Security Advisor. "David, do you know who's behind these hijackings? Could it be a right-wing paramilitary group?"

Encino, who was also in the air, traveling to meet the President in Colorado, looked taken aback by the question. "I don't think that domestic terrorists are responsible for this, Mr. President."

"Are you sure?" asked Gore. "We lost nearly two-hundred people in Oklahoma City six years ago to a guy that was as American as apple pie. What if a few of these skinheads managed to buy tickets and … I mean isn't that possible?"

"Yes… I mean no… I… we're not sure exactly, but it would certainly appear that this is an overseas group."

"Overseas? What country would attack the United States?"

"I doubt that there is a country behind this, Mr. President, it's probably an Islamic terrorist organization."

"*Islamic* terrorists?" said Gore slowly. "I know several…"

"They are simply terrorists!" broke in Aziz Sahil, the Housing and Urban Development Secretary, who was a Muslim himself. "I'm sorry to interrupt, Mr. President."

"No, no that's quite all right, Aziz. David, maybe you shouldn't describe them as Islamic, after all that implies religion and…" he paused. "Whoever did this was clearly not religious. I mean, I've seen the devastation. People are jumping out of office windows to escape the flames and there's no telling how many people have been killed. I don't think that Muslims could be behind this any more than Methodists could be."

The monitor that Joe Lieberman was teleconferenced on was set far in the corner, but a sudden movement caught Gore's eye. It almost appeared that the Vice President rolled his eyes, but there was nothing said. Encino spoke again, "These are terrorists that belong to an international terror group, Mr. President."

"What sort of terrorist group?"

"Well, uh, one in which the members don't like America."

"No kidding!" snapped Gore. "But for what reason?"

"Their beliefs… religious beliefs…"

"We're going to leave religion out of this, David, remember?"

"I'm sorry, Sir. Perhaps they disagree with our foreign policy. Our support of the Hebrew… of Israel isn't popular in the Muslim… in the Middle East."

"Well, what do they want then? Have they made demands?"

"We have no communication from them, Sir," said Encino. "However, we believe that they're the same people responsible for the Embassy bombings and last year's attack on the U.S.S. Cole. This would be Osama Bin Laden's al-Qaeda network."

Gore put his head down and massaged his eyelids for a few seconds. His predecessor had been offered Osama Bin Laden on a silver platter by the Sudanese five year ago and turned them down three straight times before they gave up and shipped him off to Afghanistan. He looked up. "We aren't one-hundred percent on this yet, are we?"

"All signs are pointing in that direction, but no, we aren't fully certain yet."

"Ok, let's hold off on making public assumptions. There may be a silver lining to this if we play it right."

Lieberman spoke up. "Mr. President? Might I suggest…"

"Just a minute, Joe…" Gore cut off his VP and turned to his Chief of Staff. "Andy, get a hold of Mayor Giuliani and find out what he needs from FEMA. In fact, get him on the phone with the director. I want him to know that he has the full support of the Federal… Good God!" The TV screen behind Harrelson showed the collapse of the second tower. "Is that in slow motion?" Gore asked. "Can you guys see that? How can that happen?"

There was dead silence.

Conner Ranch, West Texas

Everything appeared normal to the ranch hands and to his father, who were only a few hours into the workday, but the 6-year-old boy could tell that something wasn't right that morning. The more experienced one gets in life, the less rigid are their expectations of the world around them in certain ways. An older person knows that sometimes the trains don't run on time, but a youth might expect them to conform precisely to the printed schedule, and would be more likely to note when they are off by even a few seconds.

In this case, the boy was particularly struck by the absence of planes in the air. The ranch, which was located on the dusty plains near the Pecos River, was near the route for several carriers. The boy was fascinated by the glistening machines that were barely visible on the many bright, cloudless days in West Texas. It amazed him that there were people in the sky that high up. The planes seemed to move so slowly that he marveled that they stayed aloft. His father told him that they were made out of heavy metal, but had engines that propelled them forward so fast that their wings glided on the air, just like the birds.

At the age of six, the boy already knew that he wanted to fly airplanes when he grew up. It seemed a lot more exciting than ranch work. He hadn't told his dad about that yet, but all of the questions and interest in airplanes had prompted a suggestion that they visit the airport in El Paso the next time they were down to see his aunt. The boy could hardly wait.

But now, squinting against the sun and searching the sky, he wondered if there were any airplanes left anymore. He should have counted six by that time of the morning, but he had not seen a single one. He already ran down to the spot near the corner of the ranch, where his dad was examining the fence with one of his hands, to ask about it. He'd been rebuffed and told to keep close to the house by the grownups, who were more concerned about running out of fence wire, than they were about aviation.

Now, almost back to the house, he thought he might have seen something low on the east horizon. He lost track of it for a few seconds and then it was back again, an unmistakable glitter – not just one but perhaps three or four – accompanied by a light roar. As the distance closed, he could see more of the planes as they were passing to the north. Three looked like fighter jets, painted a dull green, but the center one, by far the largest, was painted blue and had a curious bubble over the front section, almost like a camel's hump.

The boy watched them disappear over a distant mountain range. No other planes appeared. After waiting a few minutes in dead silence, he turned back toward the ranch house and continued his slow walk with a strange feeling in the pit of his stomach.

GNN Studios

"Welcome back to GNN. We're lucky to have film director Michael Moore join us in the studio to provide us with his insight into this tragedy. What are your thoughts this evening?"

"Well, I think it's important for us to remember that as Americans, we created this. We always abhor terror, unless it's us doing the terrorizing. The real tragedy here is that New York is a Democratic state. Most of those people that were killed today voted for Al Gore. This sort of stuff is going to keep happening until Congress ratifies the Kyoto agreement on the environment…"

"Pardon us, Mr. Moore, but it appears that the President is addressing the nation in a live radio broadcast, let's bring the audio to our viewers."

My fellow Americans, we have suffered a tragedy today that has struck deep into the soul of our great nation and left us searching for answers amid our grief. Who would do such a thing, and why?

As I stood today in a second-grade classroom, sheltering a young girl against the panic slowly rippling across our country and trying to offer some comfort to such an innocent mind, I found myself asking these same questions.

Some have suggested that these evil acts were perpetrated by right-wing extremists or paramilitary groups within our own borders, spurred on by the hateful rhetoric coming across our talk radio stations. Such groups exist... such people exist. They are dangerous. They weaken our spirit and war against our national consciousness.

According to our best sources, however, today's tragedy may have been engineered from abroad. Should this be the case, we would do well to remember the one-hundred and sixty-eight good citizens that were lost in 1995 to one of our own, lest we feel that we are somehow above such action ourselves.

There is no denying that the world has changed, and that we have done a poor job of changing with it. Americans have lived as an island for too long, isolated by wealth and privilege from the grievances of the international community. Though we don't know exactly who is behind today's attacks, we can say that they have our attention. We will do our best to find out who they are and why they did this...

Saturday, September 15, 2001
NORAD Cheyenne Mountain Complex (Colorado Springs, Colorado)

The stock market had been closed for four straight days. There was speculation that a financial collapse was imminent. Although his poll numbers were up, pressure was mounting for the President to speak at length to the nation. For four days he stayed largely out of the public eye, shielded by 1750 feet of solid granite in the four and a half acre complex that was carved out of Cheyenne Mountain. Built to sustain a nuclear attack, no one doubted that a barrage of hijacked 747s posed little, if any, risk to those inside.

Gore had issued a radio address each of the last four nights. His advisors felt that a video message, even a taped one, might be unwise. Even though there was sure to be broad agreement on the issue of the President's safety, there was a risk of creating resentment on the part of those without such advantage. This did not include the members of Congress, who had access to the White Sulphur Springs site in West Virginia, though only the Vice President remained there (on the orders of the President). Most in Washington were back at their desks, although succumbing somewhat to the "bunker-mentality" that was gripping much of the country.

The White House team was in the process of debating whether the President should travel back to D.C. for the live address or issue it from within the fortified facility in Colorado. As they gathered in the glass conference room, dubbed "Fishbowl II" for the resemblance to its White House counterpart, a monitor hung from the ceiling above the table, displaying live scenes from Ground Zero, where crews were working to recover bodies from the rubble. It was known that the Governor of Texas, President Gore's campaign opponent would be touring the site that day – not that anyone in the room cared about that.

There was a knock at the door and the team looked up to see the President open it a crack and provide some badly needed relief by good-naturedly asking, "Mind if I join you?" The last four days, though stressful, had been exciting. The heart of the mountain afforded a casual atmosphere that reduced the formality between the staff and the President. It reminded those who had worked on his campaign of some of the more relaxed times from the trail, particularly in 1992, before he became Vice President. Al Gore assumed a noticeable stiffness shortly after that election, measuring his words carefully and treating even his friends with curious formality. Some said that he was merely trying to scrupulously avoid giving the media any fodder for ridicule, hoping not to repeat the mistakes of his predecessor. Others noted that his public manner had always been mechanical.

The President was scheduled for a rolling Cabinet meeting, with members staying on-call as needed to go over the plan of action that would be detailed in his speech to the nation that evening. Most of his team would remain in the room with him for the conference. After some pleasantries, Gore opened the meeting.

"I understand that we are now certain that Osama Bin Laden and his terror network are behind these attacks. All of the hijackers have been identified, is that correct, David?"

The ever-patient NSA Chief nodded, "Yes, Mr. President."

"And how have we identified them? I've been told that there were hundreds of passengers on those planes."

"Well, these were Arab men, mostly of Saudi descent. Most had ties back to…"

"I guess I should have asked this question sooner. Are you literally just picking out Arab names?" Irritation in the President's voice belied the tension between the two, which had risen in the last four days.

"Well, no. There are other variables involved. None of the men are citizens. Most have ties to al-Qaeda. A few left suicide notes... things of that sort."

"How would it look if it turns out that one of the planes was taken over by someone named Jones or Smith and we've been sitting here profiling Arabs? I chaired a commission on airline safety back in '96, and one of our primary concerns was making sure that profiling did not occur at airport checkpoints so that no one would be offended. This is America after all."

Encino paled a bit, but did not immediately respond. After an uncomfortable pause he replied. "We know that this was an al-Qaeda plot. Al-Qaeda is an Islamic terrorist group..."

"Excuse me, excuse me, Sir!" It was the HUD Secretary, whose face could be seen turning an angry shade of red, even over the low-bandwidth video feed. He spoke with a slight accent. "Do not say 'Islamic!' These groups have nothing to do with Islam! You are simply advertising your ignorance, when you speak like that!"

"I'm sorry, Mr. Secretary," stammered Encino. "The truth is, however, that these terrorists are waging a religious war – a Jihad – against the United States. There simply isn't..."

"No Sir! No Sir! You do not know what Jihad is! Jihad is a personal struggle against sin. It is never used in the context of religious war. That is a lie!"

"Well," answered the National Security Advisor dryly. "I would bet that the terrorists themselves, such as those belonging to the Palestinian group Islamic *Jihad* would disagree with you, but..."

"Ok, kids," said the President, waving his arms like a referee, "back to the matter at hand. Americans are wondering how something this extensive could be planned right under our noses. Bin Laden is in Afghanistan. Assuming the attack was planned there, shouldn't the CIA have known about it?" Gore directed the question to the CIA director, who was fidgeting slightly.

"Well, Mr. President, it seems that the hijackers had been in the United States for several years prior to this attack. Although we did determine that some were worth keeping an eye on, it becomes the responsibility of the FBI at that point."

"But you never told us about them," broke in the FBI director. "How were we supposed to know that they were dangerous?"

"Why wasn't the information shared?" asked Gore pointedly.

"We were explicitly prohibited from doing this. The directive came from your Administration... well, from the Clinton Administration."

"Why?"

"That's not really a question that I can answer," said the CIA director. "We just follow orders."

"Well, good God!" shouted the President, looking around the room. "Does anyone know why this insane directive was issued... anyone?"

One of the aides, a holdover from the previous Administration, spoke up shyly. "It was determined that one of the ways to hinder the Special Prosecutor's investigation into President Clinton was to define a 'wall of separation' between the law enforcement and intelligence communities. At the time…"

"Is this true?" Gore asked incredulously of his Attorney General, who simply nodded in agreement. "Is there anything else I should know about… anything our political opponents might try and use against us… to divide the nation at this critical time?"

Phil Hudson, the Senate Majority Leader from New York, and one of only two legislators participating in the conference, gave a nervous cough, then spoke up. "Well, the truth is that we Democrats have traditionally been in favor of reducing military and intelligence funding. There didn't seem to be much use for maintaining the Cold War levels after the Soviet Union crumbled, and, uh, quite honestly we weren't too keen about the intelligence community prior to that, either. I would bet that there'll be some who bring up the Frank Church hearings in the days to come. We had a number of restrictions placed on intelligence gathering methods…"

"Well," broke in the President, "we'll just let those bastards bring that up themselves if they want. If they do, then we can accuse them of playing politics… trying to exploit a human tragedy." He paused. "Is there something we could say in advance to blunt that line of attack?"

Harrelson took the challenge, "As you said, Mr. President, this is a time for coming together. We simply take the high ground, extend the hand of bipartisanship. I don't think they'll try and bite it at a time like this."

"With all due respect, Mr. President," Vice President Lieberman interjected. "We should probably be discussing security, rather than how to save the Democratic Party. I think that the mind of most…"

"Point taken, Joe, and we have discussed that topic vigorously in the past four days. You were even a part of some of those meetings. As you know, though, there's more at stake here than the physical security of the nation. There's nothing we can do for Tuesday's victims, but we do have the power to make America a better place for their families." As Gore talked, he held his fist out in front of him and looked around the room. Someone passing by the Fishbowl might have thought that he was challenging another there to "rock-paper-scissors," but his staff cast knowing glances at each other. The President was speaking from his heart, and any notes they managed to take down would become the framework of that night's televised speech.

"This is not about the Democratic Party. This is about America. This is about opportunity… the opportunity to improve lives and change this country for the better. Isn't that why we're all here… in public service?"

Gore turned his head. "As I look around this room, I don't see the face of anyone who hasn't chosen to make sacrifices to pursue a career of devotion to the people of America. We're not here to protect the status quo, but rather to effect positive change. Change is inevitable now, whether we like it or not, whether they..." his palm flattened as he gestured to a monitor a few feet down from him that displayed a map of the United States, "whether they like it or not either.

"The world has changed, and we've been pulled kicking and screaming along with it. Now we have to accept it. Life will never be the same for anyone in this country again. We've been forced to confront the fact that we aren't well-liked beyond our borders. We've basically had our head in the sand up until now, thumbing our nose at the rest of the globe, protected both by oceans and our oceans of wealth. Now we've been given a small taste of what it feels like to be vulnerable to the machinations of foreign power. This is the new reality.

"But this is also opportunity! Not just for the people in this room or for any political party. But for all of America to wake up and recognize that the old paradigms don't work. What's healthy about competition and greed? Don't we attach more virtue to cooperation and sacrifice? The price of our wealth, in a global economy, is the poverty of other nations. We..." The President stopped abruptly as his gaze fell on the monitor above him. "Can you turn up the sound?" he asked an aide.

Everyone else looked up to see a dramatic scene unfolding at Ground Zero. There was the Governor of Texas, standing on top of twisted wreckage and debris, gripping a bullhorn. He was wearing a light jacket and jeans against a mild breeze. A weary fireman stood next to him, with smoke rising behind them. Even the White House staff couldn't help but be moved by the picture. As the sound was coming up, the word that rose to the minds of most was 'leadership.'

It didn't stay there long.

"USA, USA. USA..." the crowd was chanting. Others shouted "We can't hear you!"

"Well I can hear *you*," the Governor spoke back through the crackle of the bullhorn. "The whole world can hear you!" The crowd cheered. The Governor held up his finger and leaned toward the people slightly, in a determined, yet natural manner. His voice had a firm, gritty edge. "And the people who knocked these buildings down will hear *all* of us soon!"

The response from the New Yorkers at Ground Zero was overwhelming, but no one buried inside Cheyenne Mountain heard it. Groans and sighs cascaded off the walls of the Fishbowl. "Good God!" said the President, voicing one of the milder expressions in the room at that moment.

The scene played itself out in the room for nearly thirty seconds, with ample profanity in particular from the veteran staffers. "Who the hell does that guy think he is?" grumbled the President rhetorically over the commotion. The monitor was immediately switched off, the picture dying on the screen as quickly as the mood around the table.

"Unbelievable!" exclaimed Andy Harrelson, slamming his fist on the table. "No one gave him the right to do that! And to think – that asshole could have been President."

"We'd be looking at a nuclear winter right about now," one of the staffers called out. "Yeah, and anyone who isn't a WASP would be hiding under their bed," said another. Vice President Lieberman simply looked bemused.

The muttering continued for a few more minutes. President Gore sat in the middle of it all, staring at the table, deep in thought. Eventually, muted hushes circulated around the room, quickly quieting the voices. After another moment or two of quiet pondering, Gore slowly raised his head.

His dispirited staff was stunned to see the optimism in his eyes, and it was enough to brighten most of their faces again. They didn't know exactly what would happen there that afternoon, but they knew that it would make history.

New York City, New York

Having spent more time in his top corner office on the Eastside of Manhattan in the past four days than he had in the past four months, Bernard Greenly Jr. was a tired man. He counted himself fortunate that the attacks had happened when he was in the city, rather than on his ranch in Montana or, God forbid, his beach house on Oahu. With air travel grounded, there would have been no chance of making it back to New York this week. As it was, he still had to walk twenty-eight blocks to the office after traffic stalled his limo. He hadn't left since.

There were times, in fact, when he went months without seeing the inside of the Greenly News Tower. Such is the effect of second-generation wealth. Bernard's father wasn't a newsman, but rather a very shrewd business executive who managed to make several remarkable acquisitions in the broadcast and printed news industry, including GNN, the largest cable news channel. The old man was driven by success, still spending more than 80 hours a week in the office in his 71st year.

His son never understood the sense in that. Life was short and there was no point to wealth if you weren't going to enjoy it. He planned to retire right after his father died. He couldn't before, of course, or the old man would disinherit him. Their relationship was rocky. Bernard Sr. had no tolerance for his son's dearth of ambition, exhibited from an early age. Estranged from the boy's mother, he had tried to instill initiative the only way he knew how – financial incentive. He was pleased that Bernard seemed to take a genuine interest in college journalism, particularly since his business holdings were quite suitable to that career path.

Bernard did, in fact, nurture a passion for news. He didn't care much for reporting and he tired quickly of the day-to-day responsibilities of running a newspaper or news channel, but nothing excited him like breaking news. He wanted to be there when it happened, although he often wasn't. The next best thing was discussing it with his editorial staff, framing the layout, tweaking the spin and, most particularly, *controlling* the reaction of ordinary people to the events of the day. The ability to influence the thoughts of millions was an intoxicating power, something that he never tired of, despite his gradual disengagement from operations.

He did have a knack for showing up at the right time, and what was happening that week was the story of the century. His office looked as if it had been rummaged. Coke cans and copy spilled over the trashcan by the door and piled up on the floor. Heavily stained coffee cups, both ceramic and Styrofoam were scattered throughout. Drawers hung open. Folders were everywhere, along with stacks and stacks of paper. The only thing in its place was the folding sofa bed, since he was self-conscious about it. None of the other employees had such a luxury.

His secretary buzzed to tell him that Andrew Harrelson was on the phone. Before taking the call, he walked over to the four large TV screens built into the wall and turned down the sound. It would have taken him too long to find the remote. He picked up the line.

"Mr. Harrelson!" Greenly wasn't sure what to call the President's Chief of Staff, since he rarely spoke to him. Normally the White House dealt directly with the reporters or editors of his news enterprise. This was sure to be an off-the-record conversation.

"Hello, Bernard," said Harrelson cordially. "How's it going up there?"

"Other than a few thousand people missing, can't complain."

"I'll make this quick. Did you see the Governor's address?"

"I saw his remarks at Ground Zero." Greenly suddenly understood what this was about. "I thought it was inspiring... in a bellicose sort of way."

"I agree, but do you think this is a time for vigilante justice?"

"Vigilante? I've got to be honest..."

"You know, calling for revenge against 'the people who knocked these buildings down'?"

"Well," said Greenly, "I guess not..."

"Exactly," said Harrelson quickly. "This is a time for coming together. The nation is angry right now and the Governor is out there like some sort of firebrand, playing to people's prejudices. I'm sure that the

Arab-American community is in fear. Do you think that people will take him seriously?

"I don't know…"

"The President feels strongly that this is a critical time for America and its relationship with the Arab world. If we react to this tragedy by taking vengeance on people, either here or elsewhere, just because they're Muslim or Arab, then it will work against us in the long run."

"Well, of course it would work against us," stammered Greenly. "It would be disastrous…"

"Exactly. I'm glad that we see eye to eye on this, Bernie. I just hope that the President can get this across to the American people when he speaks later tonight. There's so much hatred in this country right now. The Governor really fanned the flames with his remarks. The President's got his work cut out for him." Harrelson spoke flatly, not even bothering to animate his words. It was as if he were following some careful script that had been committed to memory.

Bernard knew with certainty that this was not a spontaneous conversation, but he played along anyway. "Vigilante justice you say?"

"Well, you didn't hear it from me, but that's certainly how it could be interpreted. It's a cynical thing to do, at the very least. I'm just glad that we have a President who's trying to preach responsibility and tolerance at such a pivotal moment in our nation's history."

Finally, there was a pause in the conversation. Greenly didn't reply.

"Thanks for taking the call, Bernie. The President's speaking tonight at eight. He's already on his way back to Washington."

"It would be nice if he found the time to sit down with our anchorman… say next week sometime."

"I'll try and arrange it. Thanks, Bernie."

GNN Counterforce Program

"Welcome to GNN Counterforce! I'm your host on the right…"

"And I'm on the left. Tonight's topic: Vigilantism – Right or Wrong for America? Were the Governor's off-the-cuff remarks, in Manhattan this morning, out of line?"

"Lucy, I think we both agree that this is no time for Americans to be taking out their anger on members of the community who have had nothing to do with these attacks. That's not what the Governor's message was about."

"Not so fast Randy, of course I agree that vigilantism is wrong, but just the fact that we're having this debate tonight at GNN, proves that many Americans are concerned about the Governor's belligerent call to arms. This is a pivotal moment in our history and we need a leader who has the courage to take the right path at a time like…"

Washington, D.C.

Sherry Danforth, six months pregnant with Robert Jr., sat in the balcony of the chamber, looking down on President Al Gore as he addressed the world. He used the first part of his speech to extend sympathy to the victims and report on the recovery operation, but now he was speaking to the critical task that faced the nation.

"…and as that frightened seven-year-old girl in my arms looked up at me, I wondered what we could have done to bring this horror on ourselves. Why would others hate us so?

"America has always enjoyed a standard of living that is unparalleled in history. It has been easy for us to forget that much of the world does not live this way. Indeed, there are billions of souls on this planet mired in poverty, without hope for a better future. They confront disease and hunger on a daily basis in a struggle that we simply cannot comprehend. They are losers in a race in which they did not choose to compete.

"Although we see nothing wrong with advancing capitalism across the world, Globalism works to the disadvantage of nations which are simply not ready for international competition. Single-commodity economies, for example, can easily be devastated on the international market, leading to the misery of a million poor souls.

"And, while we enjoy political freedom, there are many in our world that do not. I am speaking, of course, of the Palestinian people and their struggle against occupation. Many among us have been skeptical of their pleas. Some have even gone so far as to claim that the Palestinians have brought their suffering upon themselves by refusing to recognize Israel's right to exist. Yet, how can they recognize the rights of others, if they have no rights themselves?

"So many in the world are demanding basic human rights that we take for granted in this country, yet, we ignore them. Is it because they are of a different religion, a different culture or a different race? Perhaps we forget the lessons of our own shameful history of bigotry and oppression, particularly against ethnic and religious minorities. Had our ancestors chosen to learn from the Arabs and Africans, rather than enslave them, we could have adopted earlier the same respect for political freedom and human rights that is a tradition of Africa and the Middle East.

"Perhaps we have remained deaf to the supplications of the downtrodden simply because we thought we could. Our oceans protected us, we thought. Our wealth protected us, we thought. Our military protected us. But, as we've seen this week, we cannot ultimately protect ourselves from the consequences of the injustices we may cause others. We know now that we must pay the utmost attention to the actions of our country, and how these are perceived overseas.

"Certainly it puzzles and perplexes us to learn that each of the identified hijackers was Arab. Arab-Americans are among our hardest working citizenry and Muslim-Americans among our most virtuous. I have listened to the concerns from leaders in these communities, who fear that there will be violence against them. All Americans should know that Islam is the religion of peace. It is safe to say that these were not religious men. One does not follow the way of the Prophet Muhammad by killing others.

"I realize that it isn't popular or easy to ask for reflection on the part of Americans at this time. Some would prefer that I stand on top of a bulldozer and call for vengeance against those who hurt us... that I call for more violence and death. But doesn't this just continue the cycle? Allah is judging the men who took our loved ones from us, and we gain nothing by becoming like them and taking revenge. Continuing the same policies that brought about this tragedy will not make us safer. We must heed the wake-up call.

"My fellow citizens, this country stands at her most critical juncture since the Civil War. There are two very different paths ahead of us. One is vengeful hate, the other is discernment. One repeats the mistakes of the past, the other uses insight to adapt to the reality of the present. One leads us to conflict, the other to peace.

"I love America. I am sworn to protect her people. It isn't easy to call for moderation and restraint in a time of hurt and anger. I hear the demagogues, playing to the masses and calling for war. War with whom, we might ask? It really doesn't matter. There is no country whose people deserve to have bombs dropped on their children. To do this, is to stoop to the level of those who have hurt us. Indeed, it simply plays directly into their hands and merely justifies their actions.

"On the other hand, if we work with other governments and seek what's best for them, then they will naturally want what's best for us.

"Now that we realize that we aren't an island, we should replace arrogance with sensitivity, condescension with social consciousness, and the foreign policies that worked against the world's development to those that cultivate its potential.

"We stand at the brink of a brave, new world, with an opportunity beyond our wildest hopes! 'We are all Americans,' read the headline from Paris three days ago. Along with the French, the rest of the world stands graciously before us with arms extended, ready to forgive past mistakes, ready to accept us back into the Commonwealth of Equals.

"My Fellow Americans, the greatness of our tragedy is surpassed only by the greatness of our nation. We can rise to meet the challenge at hand with grace and courage. I have faith that a new Age of Tolerance is dawning, not only for us, but for the rest of the world as well.

"Thank you and good night."

Sherry started to applaud with the rest, but dropped her hand to her stomach as the baby began kicking again.

Monday, October 15, 2001
GNN Nightly News

"Welcome back to GNN. It's been almost a month since Wall Street opened in the wake of the attacks on September 11th, and the markets have seen a steady decline since, with the Dow sitting well below 6000 after sliding further today. Of course, this was foretold by the Gore Administration a month ago. We're joined now by Senator Phil Hudson, who was appointed by his peers as Senate Majority Leader following the Democratic victories last year. Thank you for joining us, Senator."

"Thank you Ted, it's good to be here."

"Let's start with the obvious question. How long will the decline continue?"

"Well Ted, as you know, no one can predict the markets, least of all a young politician from Westchester, New York, but I would expect it to level off soon. President Gore said that the market was due for a correction, and I agree, I think it was highly overvalued and, perhaps, still is. I guess we'll find out in the days to come."

"Are we going to see a snowball effect, with a slowdown in GDP followed by a surge in unemployment?"

"I'm sure we will. The numbers are still coming in, but the economy took a severe hit on 9/11, probably upwards of a trillion dollars. This will certainly spill over into the areas you mentioned. It's inevitable, as the Administration predicted shortly after the attacks."

"Senator, critics are starting to be heard…"

"I'm glad you mentioned that, Ted, because I've unfortunately been hearing some of them myself. It is absolutely astonishing that anyone – certainly someone passing him or herself off as an 'expert' – would not understand the basic economics involved here. Three thousand people were killed. Two massive office buildings in the heart of our financial district were destroyed. Americans are frightened. Of course there's going to be uncertainty and pessimism, and it will be reflected in consumer spending and industry outlook. This is inevitable, and anyone who pretends like it isn't is just trying to take advantage of a tragic opportunity."

"Do you expect your political opponents to exploit the economy in the '02 and '04 elections if things don't improve?"

"That would speak very poorly of them if they were to try and do that. It's certainly not something that you would ever see Democrats do to win an election. I like the word you used, 'exploit.' That's what they would be doing; trying to exploit the economic fallout from a national tragedy to their own advantage… appalling, to say the least!"

"Senator, let's turn now to the response from the Administration to the attacks. The poll numbers are looking good for the President, but there is some criticism that he isn't moving fast enough against al-Qaeda overseas. Do you agree with the critics?"

"Absolutely not, Ted. First of all, President Gore showed tremendous courage in the wake of 9/11, in pressing for a diplomatic solution to bring these terrorists to justice. The American people realize that they have the right man at the right time in the White House, someone who understands that being accepted back into the Commonwealth of Equals is much more important than relieving short-term diplomatic impatience. As Jimmy Carter put it, 'Go to the negotiating table, not the battlefield.' Remember after the first World Trade Center bombing, when President Clinton warned us against overreacting? There were critics then as well."

"But Senator, the Clinton Administration was quite passive in response to additional terror attacks against American targets overseas. Critics have suggested that we were ignoring a war that had been openly declared on us for some time."

"There's that word again, Ted, 'War.' We keep hearing that word being thrown around recklessly by these chicken hawks inside the Beltway. It's tough enough for the President to implement prudent foreign policy in a complicated world these days without a bunch of paintball warriors running around, playing to people's prejudices and stirring up anger. They don't seem to realize that mainstream America is on board with the President's effort to secure our country by improving our standing in the world. I… just a minute, Ted, let me finish, because this is quite important.

"War is a very serious condition, both for us and for whomever we would decide to go to war against. It would be costly. It would hurt our standing in the international community. It would inevitably kill innocent people. And it would also be fantastically ineffective at breaking the cycle of violence. I don't think that these war advocates have thought much of this through."

"Senator, we're out of time tonight. Thank you for joining us."

Tuesday, October 16, 2001
Washington, D.C.

"Oh, for the love of God, Joe… not you too?"

Al Gore was being intentionally naïve, of course. He knew that his Vice President was tepid to the path taken by the Administration since 9/11. He had managed to put off a private meeting with Lieberman for more than four weeks, shrewdly inviting him into conferences that were already in progress, knowing that the man would be less likely to express himself candidly. Gore had to act carefully, because he would be relying on the loyalty of his former running mate in the days and months to come.

"Well, Joe, if we could just bring in the Secretary of…"

"No, please, Mr. President. This is a matter that we can discuss between the two of us. You've already got enough critics out there…"

The President raised one eyebrow.

"Oh, what I mean, Sir, is that I would prefer that we work out our differences behind closed doors," said Lieberman quickly. "I agree that we need to show unity, for the sake of the country and I hope you will agree that I've worked hard on your behalf."

Gore nodded. It was true. Lieberman had been out front, faithfully pressing the President's position on most of the issues. His calm demeanor helped balance the fallout from Gore's own unfortunate reaction in the Florida classroom last month – a bootleg video of which was slowly making its way across the Internet, much to his embarrassment.

"But, Sir," the Vice President continued. "Our strategy should be to secure the nation through an aggressive effort to obliterate these terrorists and the governments that shelter them."

"I understand, Joe, but we aren't going to become a rogue State. That would be self-destructive. We're going to work with the United Nations on this matter…"

"With all due respect, Sir, the UN doesn't have America's interests at heart. I would never say this publicly, but it's a corrupt, bloated organization where a dictator counts as much as a democracy."

Gore looked away. "I agree that the UN isn't a perfect organization. I don't think it's possible to have that at the international level, but it's all we've got to work with right now. If we disrespect international law by acting unilaterally, we're simply asking for the cycle of violence to continue. As it…"

"What cycle?" asked Lieberman. "We never retaliated for previous attacks, or deliberately targeted civilians. These folks started…"

Gore firmly cut him off, "As it is, the UN is sympathetic to imposing sanctions on Afghanistan, which is a good start. We've also added charges to the indictment that President Clinton imposed on Bin Laden, after he declared war on us in the mid-1990s. There's no debate here, Joe. What's your next topic?"

Lieberman swallowed hard, but relented. "Israel, Mr. President. Israel is not a terrorist nation, and I have to take exception to your bringing her into this issue."

"I know you have, Joe" said Gore softly, trying to sound as sagacious as possible. He got up and walked over to the window of the Oval Office, where he stood looking out over the South Lawn silently for a few seconds, as if to gather his thoughts.

"You know, more than a few pundits said it was unwise to choose a Jewish running mate... more than a few. After all, it had never been done before." The President turned back quickly, but not in time to see the other man roll his eyes. "Do you understand that, Joe?"

"Yes." Lieberman looked straight ahead, evidently choosing to stay quiet and let the President talk himself out.

Gore turned back to the window. "People said that voters would reject a Jew on the ticket... that it was a liability. America isn't that far removed from the anti-Semitic backwater that we were before our Democratic Party managed to triumph in its struggle for civil rights over those racists and their fire hoses back in the 1960s."

Lieberman narrowed his eyes somewhat quizzically and as he gave a sideways glance. "Actually, I think the people manning the fire hoses back then were Democrats, Mr. President."

"Well, anyway," continued Gore, "...ancient history. What's important, right now, is that we have a chance to bring about peace in the Middle East, which is more urgent than ever in light of the attacks. Israel is an issue because Palestine is a priority. Do you want to see another disaster take place on our soil?

"Of course not, Mr. President, but the fact is that the Israelis have been experiencing these sorts of attacks many times over since Arafat started the *Intifada*. We can't dictate their security policy to them."

Gore walked back to his desk and sat down. He hunched over for a moment with his hands together, as if deep in thought. "We aren't dictating to them anymore than they're dictating to the Palestinians. Our security is at stake right now as well." He looked up. "Don't you think a people deserve autonomy, Joe... even if they are... Arabs?"

Lieberman drew in his breath. "What about the *dhimmis* in Arab countries who are horribly oppressed by Muslim governments... those that manage to survive?"

Gore looked up with a sharp look of disapprobation over the Vice President's use of a term that had been banned from the Administration's vernacular. Lieberman looked away and Gore's features softened a bit. "Yeah Joe, I'm familiar with the story there, but this is a bad time to be criticizing Muslim governments, especially when we need their help with the mess that we're in right now. If Israel leads by example, then perhaps things may improve for others in the Islamic world, but..."

"But Sir!" interrupted Lieberman, clearly frustrated. "Israel does lead by example. There aren't any Arabs in the entire Middle East that have the social freedom and political rights that Israeli Arabs enjoy! By contrast, Jews can't live anywhere else in that region without extraordinary protection. Nearly a million were expelled by Muslim countries in just the five years after Israeli independence, and there aren't any left to speak of."

"I know, I know," said the President, who actually didn't, but tried to sound reassuring anyway. "I understand how you feel, Joe. We aren't talking about the end of Israel here, just the end of the occupation. If the Israelis show good faith to the Palestinians, then I'm sure it will be returned."

Lieberman looked like a man struggling to maintain self-control. Gore, as a former VP himself, had observed similar disagreements in the past, and knew that he held an advantage according to the ground rules. The office of President had to be respected at all times, and each visitor knew it. "What are your other concerns?"

"Homeland security."

Gore drew a slow smile. "That sounds like something out of 1930's Germany. Didn't they refer to the 'Homeland' or the 'Motherland' or something like that? Well, anyway," he quickly continued, "we're making progress with our security taskforce. Wouldn't you agree?"

"What progress has been made?"

Gore looked offended. "We're deciding on what measures to institute at airports to prevent another hijacking, of course. It's a delicate situation, Joe. We've got to balance security concerns with civil rights. We can't just go profiling every Middle Easterner that takes a flight."

"Why not?" asked the Vice President. "Are there Scandinavians or African-Americans looking to fly airplanes full of people into buildings yelling 'Allahu Akbar'?"

The President narrowed his eyes. "Now I hope you don't mean that, Joe. I hope that you're just speaking out of frustration. We're all frustrated. We're all angry about what happened. But this is America. I don't know about you, but there was some good news that came out of 9/11 that made me proud. Not a single one of the nineteen Arab hijackers had been racially profiled at the airport. Now that's something to feel good about!"

"Please don't use that in a speech, Sir." Lieberman was sinking lower in his chair.

"Look, if we had the ability to operate retroactively, then we would have instituted profiling at just those locations at just those times that morning to prevent the disaster…" Though looking away, he could feel the Vice President's eyes boring into him. "I understand that it doesn't appear to make much sense to shake down Japanese grandmothers at the gate, while more, uh… uh, interesting subjects might be walking by, but this is America. America is where we treat everyone equally, and our Muslim population will appreciate that."

"The Muslim hijackers were certainly aware of this, Mr. President, more than anyone else that morning. How appreciative were they?"

"Are you seriously recommending that we profile airline passengers?" Gore snapped.

Lieberman was quiet for a few seconds then spoke carefully. "I believe that we need to put common sense over political correctness at a time like this. Sometimes the mere impression of profiling is enough to discourage the terrorists. El Al, the Israeli airline, hasn't had a hijacking or bombing in over thirty years…"

"And Israel is hated for the way they do things… connect the dots, Joe!" thundered Gore. "Do we want to live like they do… with bombings, constant fear, and teenagers sucked into military drafts? For God's sake, any compromise would be better than that. Israel's made her own enemies. We don't need to travel down that same path. It's one of the reasons that we're trying to work with the international community in this time of crisis and adapt to the world around us."

Lieberman started to respond, but the President's secretary buzzed just then to say that his next appointment was ready. At Gore's nod, he gathered up his folders to go. "With all due respect, Sir, we should be considering more aggressive action."

The President did not respond. On his way out of the office, the Vice President passed Aziz Sahil in the waiting area. Both men quickly looked away without speaking.

Sunday, October 28, 2001
Bangor, Maine

The meeting between the local Imam and the Episcopalians had been rescheduled from Friday to Sunday when it was learned that someone had been careless in not realizing that it was the Muslim Sabbath. The people looked apologetic over the slight and surprisingly submissive when the Imam entered the conference room in the building's basement, which doubled as a dining hall for the small Episcopal Church there in Bangor. A place was set for him on a raised platform and he sat down quickly with a somber look after shaking just a few hands. He wanted to use the slight to his advantage for just a little longer.

This was not an ordinary interfaith meeting. White news vans were brazenly parked on the front lawn of the church, with satellite dishes positioned on top. Some of them were local stations from Bangor and Portland, but one was from GNN, whose reporters had interviewed him in his home office earlier that day.

The Imam had undergone a range of emotions since the attacks six week earlier. At first, he felt genuine fear that he and most other Muslims in the country might suffer physical harm or be killed in revenge. He did not get much rest at all that first Tuesday night, and it had taken about a week for his sleep habits to return to normal. Within a couple weeks of the attacks, however, he had fully realized that Americans were far less prone to identify themselves and others in categorical terms according to ethnicity or religious beliefs – in stark contrast to the country of his birth, with its sectarian violence.

In time, the Imam was amazed to find that 9/11 actually worked to his advantage. People were more interested in the Muslim faith. They seemed deferential to him when he went about town dressed in his religious garb, and acted as if it were important that he take a liking to them. Exaggerated grins were sometimes followed with self-deprecating humor about American ignorance and, if he implied any agreement, grave facial expressions along with a slow, penitent shaking of the head. The Imam wasn't sure if they sought his approval for reasons of fear, guilt or ego. All he knew was that Allah worked in mysterious ways.

The GNN interview was an example of this. He spent the entire thirty minutes talking about the need for Americans to gain an understanding of Islam. The upcoming interfaith meeting, he assured the reporter, would present the perfect opportunity for Christians to learn more about what Muslims really belief. The reporter began to look a bit exasperated as the interview drew to a close. She seemed to be dancing around something that she could not simply come out and say. Her questions sounded alike, as if she were trying to get him to respond in a certain way.

"What will be learned at the interfaith meeting?" Islam, of course.

"What sort of dialogue will there be?" Questions will be asked about Islam and I will answer them.

"Do you see both sides gaining from this exchange?" Yes, I will be happy to explain Islam and they will be happy to learn from me.

"Do you know what 'interfaith dialogue' means?"

This last question had been more of a statement, thrown out after the interview, as the cameraman was packing his equipment. The reporter didn't bother to wait for an answer, but shook the befuddled Imam's hand and walked out the front door. It wasn't until later that he realized what she had been trying to get him to say.

The Imam reflected on this as he waited for the local Bishop's opening remarks in the church basement. Except for what they thought of Islam, he had no interest in what these people believed. Anyone who expected him to have any desire to understand other religions simply had no understanding of Islam, the true faith and one that was impossible to renounce – under penalty of death. What sort of nonsense would suggest that a person learn deceptive falsehoods after finding truth itself? The reporter had spoken out of a deep sense of ignorance, one that seemed to run deep in America and was reflected on the faces in front of him. They wanted to be taught. Why else would they have invited him?

"Thank you for coming tonight," the Bishop opened, directing a quick glance toward the cameras in the back of the room, where technicians in blue jeans silently panned their equipment across the room. "I see that our little meeting has attracted a lot of attention and I suspect that some of you may be from out of town. Well, we're so happy to have all of you here for our interfaith dialogue tonight as we discuss recent events and how we can rise above them."

The Bishop introduced the Imam, taking care to mention the earlier scheduling faux pas and asking once again for forgiveness. The congregation appeared visibly relieved by the Imam's gracious nod. The Imam took the first question, from a young man with oily, black hair and a University of Maine sweatshirt. "What do you want us to know about Islam?"

"Well," began the Imam. "Islam is the religion of peace…"

Collectively almost, the audience turned their attentive gazes downward and began scratching notes.

Bahawalpur, Pakistan

For twenty years, Catholic and Protestant Christians alternated Sunday prayer services at St. Dominic's Catholic Church in the small Pakistani community. Cooperation was the key to survival for religious minorities in the overwhelmingly Muslim nation of over 150 million people. The last hymn of the morning rang out from the small group of about fifty Protestants as children squirmed in their seats, ready to break free and play after the service. The pastor was making his way toward the back of the congregation when a gunshot was heard from outside.

Three Islamists entered the building, carrying rifles and locking the door behind them. They calmly walked toward the pastor and shot him to death on the spot. People screamed. The Islamists turned their guns on the congregation, spraying the small group of people with bullets. They then exited the carnage, making their way out of the church to where several motorcycles were parked in the street under the watch of two other armed companions.

Seventeen people, including five children were left dead. Many others sustained debilitating injuries.

Monday, October 29, 2001
GNN Evening News

"...and finally tonight, there are signs of hope and bridge-building in America, just six weeks after the greatest attack this country ever suffered on her own soil. Our cameras were in Bangor, Maine this weekend, where lessons are being learned, as Americans continue the healing process."

The video segment begins with bucolic scenes of rural Maine, as the voice of the narrator speaks slowly, with dramatic pauses. "It is over 400 miles from Ground Zero. Bangor, Maine is a beautiful place... undisturbed by the terrorist attacks, except in the aching hearts of the people." Worshippers at a church service are shown singing as the narrator continues, "Hardened faces tell a story that most of these hardy New Englanders would rather not talk about." Now there is a shot of children playing in a yard, which fades ominously into the forest behind them.

The scene switches to a downtown street, as the Imam walks into the picture, wearing his religious garb. The camera begins to follow him, past parking meters and doorways. "He is the only Imam in Bangor... a man who must walk a balancing act these days between the practice of his faith and his concern over reaction from the community." The camera shot focuses from the Imam to a gawking man in a cap, standing several yards in the background. "The Imam knows the suspicions and fears that challenge him these days, whether they're expressed or not."

The Imam speaks, as he is sitting in his office. "I know that not everyone hates Muslims. There are still some good people in America who know that religious persons could never do the sort of things that were done on September, 11th. Those men were not Muslim."

The scene switches to the Imam at the podium in the basement. The voice of the narrator says, "The Imam brings his message of peace and reconciliation to this Episcopal church, where some from the community have gathered, both to ask questions... and to learn."

A church member is interviewed prior to the event. She is an older woman with glasses. "Well, I just hope that we can all come together and learn from each other tonight. It's so important that we move beyond the terrible things that happened and realize that we are really all the same."

A clip from the meeting is shown. A young man is asking a question. "There is talk that the United States may bomb Afghanistan if Osama Bin Laden is not turned over to stand trial. How do you feel about that?"

The Imam solemnly responds, "We Muslims are a peaceful people. We stand with America at this time of healing. For Americans to drop bombs on Muslims would be confusing to us. Is the American government no different than the insane people who hijacked the planes? Some perhaps would understand, but some would not."

The young man is shown nodding his head, as if absorbing a great truth. The narrator continues, "And there is much that is learned tonight. Many of the members of the congregation did not know of the struggles that Muslims endure on a daily basis here in America. The Imam himself was the target of several threatening stares and hand gestures in the days after the attacks. He tells of an event that happened to a fellow Muslim living in Arizona…"

The Imam is shown speaking from the platform, animating his words with hand gestures, "So my friend he says 'Yes, I am Muslim.' Then the men push him down and kick him. They say 'We are Episcopalians. We don't like Muslims. We will kill you'." There are audible gasps from the audience, as the camera finds the horror reflected in the eyes of those listening, including the elderly woman interviewed prior to the meeting.

The voice of the narrator: "Yes, it was truly a learning experience for both sides as they found out just how far they have to go to heal the divide and overcome suspicion in America."

An older man at the meeting asks, "What can we do to make Muslims feel welcome here?"

The scene immediately cuts away to an interview with the Imam, who is speaking as the crowd mills behind after the meeting. "I just hope that maybe I've made a difference tonight," he says. "If I can change the heart of one person here, then I will consider it all worth while."

The older woman, who was interviewed before the meeting, now has tears in her eyes as she is leaving. "That brave man! The things that he and other Muslims have had to put up with in this country… I'm just so glad that I came tonight. If only we could be more tolerant of other people… if only we could learn to treat Muslims with the respect and dignity they show others…"

The final scene is of the Imam walking down the same city street. The gawking man in the background has been replaced by one who smiles and tips his hat. The narrator slowly says, "He is just one man… on a mission to make a difference… to teach us how to live together… to make us all better people."

2004

Friday, August 27th, 2004
GNN Studios

"Welcome back. We're pleased to have Sherry Danforth with us tonight, the widow of Robert Danforth, who was killed in the World Trade Center on September 11th. Mrs. Danforth, welcome."

"Thank you, Ted."

"You had the opportunity to attend the release of the 9/11 Commission Report at the Capital this afternoon. As you know, the Commission was established to determine why the attacks of that day occurred and how the next one can be prevented. First, tell us how you're feeling this evening."

"Well, I'm just exhausted. It's been a very emotional day. I've thought a lot about my husband, obviously. I'm glad that the Commission took their task seriously, and I'm encouraged that my son, Robert Jr., will have a bright future."

"Do you feel that the Commission adequately answered the questions that it was tasked with? What's your perspective?"

"Well Ted, as to the main issue of why 9/11 could occur; it seems that the rest of the world sees a much different United States than what we do. They have a broader, more objective view of our country, and what they see and experience angers them. The U.S. acts very arrogantly in foreign policy matters. We attempt to manipulate the internal affairs of other countries and have, in the past, propped up dictators and despots, particularly in the Cold War. Then there is the issue of Israel. It's a brutal country that regularly stomps on the rights and dignity of the Palestinian people."

"You believe that our foreign policy choices are to blame for 9/11?"

"Absolutely. This is the finding of the Commission as well, which, as you know, included many experts from our universities, particularly the Middle Eastern Studies programs, along with prominent Muslim-American civil rights groups, which the President was very eager to include. There's no question that our government is no less culpable than the desperate men who hijacked those planes."

"That's an amazing statement, Mrs. Danforth. Are you able to forgive the men who did this?"

"I can forgive the poor men who mistakenly sacrificed their lives for the cause of others much easier than the ruthless figures in our government that devastated entire populations overseas fighting a Cold War that was supposedly meant to defeat an enemy no worse than us. A large part of the Commission's report is devoted to the 1973 coup in Chile that killed a democratically elected leader. This is worse than anything Pol Pot ever did…"

"If I may, Mrs. Danforth, do you agree with the Commission's recommendations?"

"Absolutely, Ted. I had the opportunity to review a draft of the report over the weekend, before it was released. There are many excellent suggestions, most of which tend toward the direction that President Gore has been leading us in the last three years."

"Mrs. Danforth, the President has been under fire from conservatives and, it's rumored, from some in his own Administration for not responding to the 9/11 attacks with military force. You, of course, have stood solidly behind the President during the last three years. Do you feel that he is vindicated by the report?"

"President Gore is vindicated by the good will that other countries are beginning to show us, in response to our respect for them. They appreciate our restraint and respect for international law. We are ceasing to dictate to other nations, as was the case in the past. There are still some problems with extremist elements in the Arab world, but forcing Israel to agree to withdrawal from Palestine has earned us the cooperation of these governments in winning the hearts and minds of the people. We can't expect to win if we don't change. Acting militarily would simply be self-defeating."

"Well put. Whether we wanted it or not, the world changed on 9/11. How should we adapt to that change as individuals and as a country?"

"Well Ted, the Commission has several good recommendations. On a personal level, for example, we can all try to learn another language. There are many people joining our nation each year that don't speak English, and it would certainly be practical to be able to communicate with each other, both for their sake and ours. This will bring us all closer together. I'm taking Arabic classes and learning more about Middle Eastern culture and history. It's helping me understand the tragedy of American foreign policy better, and I would certainly suggest that anyone searching for answers with regard to 9/11 consider the same."

"And what should we be asking of our communities and government?"

"Communities should be opening their arms to the refugees that cross our borders, be they Latino, Arab, African, or Haitian. If we show kindness to them, then it will be returned to us. Communities should sponsor educational programs that teach us about other cultures and how to show respect. We should pressure our government to adopt measures that provide basic benefits, such as food stamps, healthcare and education to these families, and resist the sort of reactionary, racist elements that make them feel unwelcome. Finally Ted, we need to reach out to the rest of the world, as Al Gore is doing, rather than disenfranchise the UN and its members."

"That seems to be just what the Commission's report suggests. Do you agree with the Pillar project?"

"Absolutely! If America better resembles the world community, then we will be less likely to make decisions that anger the other citizens of our planet. Diversity makes us stronger and safer."

"Mrs. Sherry Danforth, thank you for your time."

Wednesday, September 1ˢᵗ, 2004
Hartford, Connecticut

Joe Lieberman walked out of the theater, still shaking his head and glad that the press corps wasn't there to notice him on his day off from the campaign trail. The movie had been based on a very good Tom Clancy book in which Islamic terrorists threaten the United States and even manage to detonate a nuclear bomb within a major city. The realism that made the novel so entertaining however, had given way to the cause of protecting the sensibilities of Muslims, which seemed to be of paramount concern to Americans after 9/11. The movie had been changed so that the villains were racist Americans, betraying their own country.

No matter what Muslims may do to America, Americans will always think the best of Muslims. It was a very strange country that he was a heartbeat away from leading, he thought. As a Jewish man, he appreciated the people's ability to refrain from taking revenge on innocent individuals simply because of their religious affiliation, but he could not imagine a movie being released shortly after Pearl Harbor that changed the Japanese attackers into rogue Americans bent on their own country's destruction. It was a sort of self-loathing that he could not understand in a nation that had every reason to hold its head high.

The President had publicly praised the film's producers for their "sensitivity and courage" – sentiments that Lieberman did not share, although he kept his opinions to himself, as was his habit these days.

The closest that he had come to open protest was hanging an American flag from his beach house on the fourth of July, in full view of the press – this, after Al Gore cautioned Americans in a television address prior to the holiday to use "discretion" in expressing patriotism, being mindful that some in the community do not share their appreciation for America and might find the flag offensive.

The Muslim-American lobby and civil liberties groups hailed the "tolerance and respect" shown by the President while, at the same time, customarily professing their own patriotism. Lieberman responded by taking the elevator down to the garage and enlisting the help of a Secret

Service agent to align four American flag stickers rather conspicuously on the back of the VP limo for the trip out of town.

Tuesday November 2, 2004
GNN Studios

"Welcome back to GNN's coverage of "America Votes 2004." We're fortunate to have Gore campaign manager, Andrew Harrelson, with us from Memphis, formerly the President's Chief of Staff, who stepped down last year to take over the job of getting the President reelected. Andy thanks for taking the time to talk with us. I guess the mood there at the campaign headquarters is pretty jubilant."

"Oh you bet, Ted. Just listen to this celebration behind me. It's a great night for America!"

"What do you credit the victory to, Andy?"

"Well, you know, Ted, the President has done all he could to bring the country together over the last four years. The attacks on 9/11 helped us realize our common interests over our differences and this laid the groundwork for resolving many of the major areas of contention that had been sapping our strength and morale. Al Gore deserves the credit. The people know that."

"Gun control did not turn out to be the issue that some of us in the media thought it would this year, did it?"

"On the contrary," said Harrelson. "Gun control was made an issue by the gun lobby, and these extremists were soundly defeated. They gambled and lost. All the pompous rhetoric this year from the Right about 'cleaning the President's clock' over the 2003 Firearms Act only proved the extent to which their agenda clashes with that of ordinary Americans. After 9/11, the people in this country want to feel safe, and they appreciate a law that limits each household to just one registered firearm that must be kept only in the home. They won't have to worry about encountering someone carrying a gun on the street anymore, because it is now illegal to do so."

"What will be the President's top priority in the new term?"

"Without a doubt, he'll be pressing ahead with his plan for providing basic health care to every citizen of this country. As you know, his opponent ran against the plan and you can see who the voters sided with."

"Will the President see this victory as a mandate?"

"Well," chuckled Harrelson, "we're not using that word. The victory speaks for itself. The people clearly approve of how the President has handled himself. He's moving ahead with other domestic issues, such as the Pillar project, which makes America more secure through diversity and inclusion, and he also plans to create the Department of Cultural Affairs. This win represents a decisive affirmation by the people of the policies that the President's critics have been trying to cast as controversial."

"What about those who say that the Administration is moving too slowly against the Taliban and the Iranian nuclear program? There are some who believe that we should be applying military pressure, as you know. Is there any truth to the rumor that the Vice President is among those critics, or that he is contemplating resigning?"

"Vice President Lieberman is among the President's strongest supporters, Ted. He's been 100% behind Al Gore and campaigned strong on his behalf. Like most Americans, he appreciates how the President has strengthened the military by opening up combat positions to women, fully integrating them within our armed forces. Our defense capabilities have also been reinforced by openly including gays and lesbians, which means a larger pool from which to draw our best fighting men and women. The Vice President knows that Al Gore can be credited with making America more secure through education and tolerance. As for foreign policy, just look at what's happening in the Middle East."

"Yes, we have seen impressive progress on that front. Israel has pulled out of the Gaza strip entirely now and reportedly has a timetable to do the same in the West Bank."

"Again, Ted, *this is Al Gore*. He had the courage to use America's influence in the region to bring about a resolution to the conflict. The Palestinians will respond kindly to Israel's unilateral efforts as mandated by the President. Peace is at hand, Ted, make no mistake about it…"

Friday, December 17th, 2004
Hoboken, New Jersey

Sherry Danforth wrestled with her girdle, while kicking shoes on and off and managing to keep an eye on the 3-year-old in the next room with the help of a carefully positioned mirror. She knew that her figure would never recover from what she'd put it through over the last three years. For many women, pregnancy can be the point of demarcation between a hot body and one that has clearly seen better days. Sherry had the added stress of losing her husband, Robert Sr., in the World Trade Center when she was three months due. She told friends that she almost suffered a miscarriage and was very fortunate to have Robert Jr.

The truth was a bit different, however. Losing her husband was almost a relief. She was sure that his girlfriend was a lot less happy about it than she had been, and the two million dollars came in handy as well. Needless to say, the baby was delivered without complications.

In fact, the stress came more from the pace that she had put herself through after she was back on her feet. Sherry became known as one of the "Jersey Girls" in the aftermath of 9/11. This was a group of Democratic loyalists who happened to be World Trade Center widows, and used their newfound status to defend Al Gore against anyone foolish enough to try and criticize him or his predecessor for the attacks. The women would get together with party advisors in low-profile meetings to synchronize their agenda and talking points. This was before critics noticed, and began pointing out, that they were parroting similar expressions and phrases. They had gotten wiser as of late and rarely appeared together, except at memorials.

It was debatable as to just how much of his victory Gore owed to the Jersey Girls, although they did make it highly unfashionable to point out the obvious, that the Democrats had let the country down during the Clinton years, for which it was now paying the price. After all, if a 9/11 widow didn't care how terrorists gained access to the country and assembled an elaborate plan years before putting it into action, what business was it of anyone else's?

The women praised the President's leadership in the wake of the disaster and vocalized full support for every move he made, making it nearly impossible for a critic to gain a foothold. "I wasn't a Democrat before September 11th," Sherry was fond of telling the media (quite untruthfully) "but thanks to Al Gore, I am now."

She was sincerely proud of the President, and he was certainly grateful of her support as well. They had met on several occasions after the State of the Union address, including fundraisers and campaign appearances. She and the other "Jersey Girls" stood behind him at every 9/11 memorial event at Ground Zero, and were invited guests that evening at the annual Holiday Celebration in Washington.

Sherry decided on a pair of shoes and checked the clock before turning her attention to the dress laid out on her bed. She had about thirty minutes before the limo to the airport was due. Hopefully her mother would be there by then to take care of Robbie. From the corner of her eye she could see him sitting on the floor and playing with something or other. Even though she didn't work, she still insisted on dropping him by daycare each morning, and waiting as long as possible before picking him up. She appreciated the freedom to do as she wanted and wasn't about to let a 3-year-old slow her down.

The doorbell rang, followed by the sound of the front door opening and her mother's familiar voice.

Washington D.C.

Everyone was careful not to call it a Christmas event, so as not to offend the sensibilities of non-Christian Americans, as the White House requested following 9/11. The 'Winter Holiday Celebration,' as it was now known, was still held at the National Building Museum, but with a strong Muslim presence, as was the habit during the last four occasions. About a third of the observances were Islamic, and many of the children serving as background props for the cameras wore headscarves and even *keffiyahs*. Gore himself insisted that first year on reading to the children from the Hadiths about "Allah" and the Prophet.

This occasion was marked by the conspicuous absence of the Vice President, who usually read from the Torah at the chosen time in years past. Washington was abuzz with rumor that Lieberman's differences with the President were much sharper than either one was publicly indicating. There was even speculation of a possible split some time in the second term. No one expected it any earlier because of the splendid work that Lieberman had done on behalf of the President's campaign.

Sitting next to Al and Tipper Gore on the floor of the makeshift theater, were the HUD Secretary, Aziz Sahil, and his wife. They read from the Hadiths this year and the Gores read from the Bible. A prominent rabbi had been summoned for the Torah reading.

Gore was happy. The events three years earlier had left an indelible impact on the economy, which was something of a relief to the President. The markets had plunged after 9/11 and hovered at levels around 40% of their respective averages prior to this. The cost of the attacks was being measured in trillions... but no one blamed Gore. How could they? Nothing like this had ever happened before.

His opponents were too timid to accuse him of being opportunistic about the attacks, even though his campaign used the images from that day in nearly every advertisement. Democrats insisted that it was the most important event to occur on U.S. soil since Pearl Harbor and the President's leadership was a legitimate factor for the American people to consider in the November election.

Of course, there was more at issue than post-9/11 leadership or the economy. America was changing, from her role in international affairs down to the average elementary school curriculum. The people were realizing Gore's multicultural vision for a land that had so much to offer the world. Other countries, particularly in Europe, were impressed with the patience that the President exercised in the months following the attacks. Negotiations with the Taliban had not gone well, but there was recent progress, particularly after the State Department agreed to permit the direct handover of Bin Laden to the International Crimes Court, rather than facing justice in the United States. This was fitting, since more than sixty nationalities were victimized by the attacks. Gore was optimistic about bringing the matter to a close within the upcoming year.

The Kyoto treaty had been signed. The United States had also taken the significant step of apologizing to the world for the greenhouse emissions that its citizens generated disproportionately, and promised to commission studies to determine the nation's responsibility for natural disasters that might be caused by global warming.

So absorbed was the President in his musings, that he almost missed the cue to approach the platform and give the closing remarks for the evening. Tipper's soft elbow against his arm spurred him to the task, as the rabbi at the podium made way for him. He realized once he assumed the position in front of the microphone that his notes were left back at his chair. The cameras were rolling. He looked back at his wife, who gave him a blank stare, and he knew that he would just have to wing it.

With a script, Al Gore was like a wind-up doll. Just point him in a particular direction and watch him go. He could get worked up about either side of any issue, and indeed had experienced several fascinating, yet curious changes of heart over the years, as he sought election from such diverse groups as the "Middle America" voters of Tennessee during his Senate runs, to the delegation at the Democratic National Convention in 1992, replete with "Lesbian Power" signs. The man who once told his constituency that he was pro-life, for example, was now in the process of constructing a government health care plan that provided abortion services. His opponent had tried to make an issue of this during the campaign, but America was changing and Gore felt safe discarding the values that he once claimed to hold dear earlier in his career.

Now, without a piece of paper to follow, the President felt naked before the cameras. It wasn't that hard, really, he just needed make a few light remarks about the children's costumes, thank everyone for coming, and then exit stage left.

"Well," he said, looking around, "I see that some lovely *hijabs* are being worn in celebration of Christmas this year…"

The White House would issue an apology the next day.

Muslim-American groups would make a show of graciously accepting it.

2005

Tuesday, January 4th, 2005
Ila, South Carolina

Walid al-Rahahti (dubbed "Alrighty" by his Ila classmates) hid behind a dilapidated garage, waiting for the faded red Ford pickup to pass. He could hear the rumble of the truck's lower gears echoing off the faded and cracked walls of the old wood-framed houses that lined the quiet residential street near the main part of town.

There wasn't much to Ila these days. Most of the local businesses had closed shop, defeated by the large Coop-Mart complex on the northeast side of town, which was run by the giant Cooper-Redmond Corporation. Boarded-up storefronts and abandoned buildings were more common now than the mom and pop shops that used to dot the city center. Many former business owners had reluctantly become clerks or managers at Coop-Mart in order to keep food on the table. They were sought out for technical advice over the younger clerks by familiar customers, who had defected to cheaper prices years ago, but felt entitled to the same level of expertise from the very people depleted by the unfaithful relationship. Coop-Mart did not mind the arrangement, provided the advice was accurate. Such skill could merit a 50-cents-per-hour wage increase each year, provided that the former business owner did exactly what the assigned 19-year-old manager told him to do.

At fourteen years of age, Walid wasn't old enough to have known the town's once-vibrant business district, even if his family had lived there at the time, rather than relocating just four years earlier from Maine. He had been born in Jordan to parents fortunate enough to have acquired their education in the United States years earlier. This facilitated an application for asylum after the Hashemite government began a new round of crackdowns on pro-democracy activists. Walid had done a good job of adjusting to life in the United States, although his two older brothers weren't that fortunate. He was the only one in the family to have completely lost his accent.

Regrettably, this wasn't enough for Leeman Arnold, the school bully and owner of the red pickup truck slowly cruising down the street looking for him – at least that's what Walid assumed. The truck had passed by him earlier, with Leeman hanging out the window calling him an "Arabian towel-head" and making a crude gesture. Walid took evasive action on seeing the truck make a U-turn at the end of the street.

The terror attacks had only exacerbated an already tense situation at school. Leeman was two years older and sixty pounds heavier than Walid, with close-cropped hair and a face that was anything but kind. He was popular with his friends, having been the first to drive his own vehicle to school, but not so much with the younger or smaller students, and certainly not to those born outside the U.S. Walid qualified on all three counts and spent much of his time in the hallway walking quickly between classes and keeping an eye over his shoulder.

Leeman wasn't the one to give Walid his nickname, but he made sure everyone else picked up on it by caroling "alrighty, alrighty, alrighty…" in a loud, goofy chant whenever he spied the younger student. Most everyone else called him that in a friendly, casual sort of way, as one would expect in place of a name difficult to pronounce, but Walid bristled every time he heard it in Leeman's voice. He tried not to let his humiliation show, and would often eyeball the other when it happened, though it invariably resulted in nothing more than a louder chant.

There were a few other rednecks at the high school, but the tide was turning. An influx of Muslim refugees and Hispanics into the area was changing the face of the community from the bottom up. Most of the white kids seemed fairly indifferent to race. Cliques were far more common among the ethnic minority groups, which were rapidly dominating and Balkanizing the high school. As a matter of fact, Walid's two best friends were white, and seemed about as angry at Leeman Arnold as Walid himself. Unfortunately, neither was around that day, as he huddled against the rotted siding of the garage, waiting for the truck to pass.

"Alrighty, alrighty, alrighty…" The ridiculous chant bounced through the bleak alleys and driveways of the desolate neighborhood, sounding for a few seconds as if it could be coming from anywhere. Gradually, it faded along with the sound of the truck's engine, melting into the general roar from a distant highway. Walid waited a few minutes and then crept cautiously around the side of the garage until he was in a position to slowly lean around the corner and check the street.

It was empty.

Wednesday January 5th, 2005
Washington D.C.

"I think it's time."

These were the words that Al Gore had been waiting more than three years to utter, knowing very well that a question would be asked to which he could provide that answer — if the circumstances were right and he were standing at a press conference, with Aziz Sahil at his side, to announce that a new Vice President would be taking the Oath at the inauguration in three weeks. Gore had gotten the idea from seeing Lyndon Johnson use the same phrase in the 1960's as he answered questions after announcing the first African-American to sit on the Supreme Court. He was hoping that no one else's memory ran that far back.

To Al Gore, Joe Lieberman was an outlived convenience. Hardly anyone in America was truly anti-Semitic when the Senator from Connecticut was hand-picked to fill the open VP slot after Clinton's resignation, but it had the façade of being a bold move at the time, simply because a Jew had never held the office. The decision served another purpose as well. The Democratic Party had done the right thing six years earlier, in putting principle ahead of partisanship by asking for a leadership change once it became clear that laws had been broken, but the disrespect that their former President demonstrated to his position still bothered many Americans – after all, Ronald Reagan refused to remove his coat out of respect for the Oval Office, yet Clinton toyed around with his intern at that same desk one evening, while on the phone with a Senator, discussing sending U.S. troops overseas. The choice of Joe Lieberman, who was respected as an honest man, was an attempt to further erase the stain of bad behavior from the Democratic Party.

In retrospect, it was probably unnecessary. Because of the integrity shown by the Democrats in the late 1990's, the nation rewarded them with three straight national elections, increasing their lead in Congress each time, as the political opposition slowly faded.

Joe Lieberman, on the other hand, had become a major thorn in Gore's side, particularly following 9/11. The two did not see eye-to-eye on national security policy or the Middle East. The Vice President had pressed hard for immediate military action against Afghanistan and anywhere else that al-Qaeda existed. He wanted to declare a "War on Terror," and privately ridiculed the efforts of the Administration to keep terrorism a legal matter.

"What's the point of having the FBI involved in preventing terrorist attacks?" he once demanded, as it became apparent that Gore would be following Clinton's lead. "Their specialty is investigating crimes *after* they happen. They don't have the intelligence resources, particularly overseas, for effective preemption." Staffers would attempt to explain that there was no compelling reason to change strategy from the Clinton years, since terror attacks had been occurring throughout, including the first World Trade Center bombing. The Vice President refused to be mollified. "That's the sort of mentality that got us into this mess!" he arrogantly stated, "al-Qaeda declared war on us a long time ago. It's time we rose to the challenge!"

But there had been no major terrorist attacks on American soil since 9/11, beyond a few sniper shootings. Clearly the strategy of the Gore Administration – a healthy respect for international consensus, along with fostering multiculturalism – was working, but Lieberman was far from satisfied. He was convinced that the country was still being targeted by shadowy terrorists, despite the sympathy and growing esteem from a world that held the greatest appreciation for Gore's efforts to negotiate rather than bomb.

Gore put off dealing with Lieberman as long as he could, even as he relied on his running mate's defense-friendly reputation during the campaign. Many in America were not on board with the course that the President had courageously charted in response to the attacks, but the forces of tolerance and common sense were winning out against the deep-rooted foes of hatred and ignorance, despite having been disadvantaged by several centuries of American history.

Things changed quickly after the election. Although, it would have been awkward for the President to ask for his subordinate's resignation, subtle hints were strategically seeded to suggest that a sharply reduced role awaited the Vice President in the second term. The implied humiliation was insulting to the man who had exhibited remarkable loyalty in difficult circumstances, prompting an angry phone call on Christmas Eve while the President was vacationing in the Smoky Mountains.

Gore tried to appear nonchalant, guessing that his casual manner would probably be confusing to Lieberman, who initially harbored expectations of compromise. He certainly didn't say that he had secretly been hoping for this moment or that he had already picked out a replacement, but it became obvious that he would be not be taking any constructive steps to keep Lieberman on board.

"I'm sorry to hear that," Gore had said.

"Excuse me…?"

"Your service, both to your country and to your President, has been appreciated, Joe. I want you to know that."

"Yes. Thank you." There was a long pause. Gore knew that Lieberman had not necessarily intended to offer a resignation, but rather an ultimatum, under the impression that it would be answered much differently than it had.

"I'm serious, Joe. You stood by a lot of decisions that you disagreed with. We both know that. Neither one of us had any idea of the challenges we would face. I'm glad that you were by my side… even as the world was changing."

"Yes, the world is changing…" Lieberman said softly, almost wistfully as if grasping the words for the first time. "Mr. President?"

"Yes, Joe?"

"If we hadn't made it in 2000… if we had lost the election and I decided to run on my own in '04… would you have supported me all the way through the primaries?"

"Of course I would have, Joe, of course! That's why I chose you – because I knew you were the best man to succeed me. Who do you think I am… some sort of shallow bandwagon-jumper?"

"I'm sorry to question your fidelity, Sir. It had been something that I'd wondered about for a while. It seemed like a good time to ask. It's been an honor to serve you."

The Vice President was not at the press conference. He also refused interviews as a last measure of loyalty to Al Gore, declining to provide even the slightest fuel for the raging inferno of speculation that gripped the beltway. The focus was now on the man standing to the left and slightly behind the President as Gore took questions from the eager journalists gathered in the Brady Press Briefing Room of the White House.

Aziz Sahil was articulate, politically savvy, and a true believer in both the Qur'an and the platform of the Democratic Party. He had one large problem, however, something that threatened to put the nation in a state of Constitutional crisis, should Al Gore have an untimely misstep and float off to meet the Party's wonderfully ambiguous yet morally vague god. Aziz was delivered in a Tehran hospital to Iranian parents, thus making him ineligible to succeed the office of President according to the Constitution.

Gore was disappointed that this was the first question that he faced. "Well, obviously we've thought about that," he said. "Our Founding Fathers provided for a process whereby the Constitution can be amended. The requirement of native birth may have been practical at the time of the Revolution, but it makes no sense now to deny a great patriot and highly qualified individual the opportunity to serve. Obviously the Secretary had no control over where he was born, and he should not be penalized for it."

Gore deliberately set his gaze to the back of the room and pointed to the reporter from a reactionary publication, which was usually ignored at Democratic press conferences.

The young man in horn-rimmed glasses may have been the best dressed and possibly the most surprised at having been chosen over the major networks on the front row. He scrambled quickly to his feet, dropping his notes in the process, but choosing not to reach back for them. Such rare serendipity calls for immediate action and he had evidently formed the question similar to what Gore was hoping would be asked anyway. "Mr. President, are you trying to send a message with your choice?"

This wasn't exactly what Gore was expecting, but he decided to act on it anyway. He recalled the way Lyndon Johnson had looked down at the podium, seemingly embarrassed to have to defend the choice of a black Justice. There would be no such dropping of the eyes for this President, who looked past the reporter and directly into the cameras with a determined expression. "I think it's time."

Some of the journalists appeared a bit bemused, since the answer didn't seem to follow the question, but there was a ripple of excitement as they sensed that the President was intent on making this a historic occasion. Gore did look down at that moment, to sneak a peek at his carefully prepared notes, but then returned his gaze straight in front of him.

"The question has to do with the fact that the Secretary is a Muslim-American. Perhaps there are indeed people who are unable to see past this man's religion." (The young reporter at the back of the room quickly sat down). "But just as the television show 'Ellen' caused many Americans to look at sexual orientation in a more open light, so we hope that many more will be inspired now to challenge the religious bigotry that is an unfortunate presence in many of our churches and synagogues. It will take the courage and commitment of a nation to fight the prejudices that have had so many years... uh..."

Gore threw another quick glance down to his notes, "...to ingrain themselves in our consciousness, but America is a great country that has shown a willingness to correct the mistakes of the past and adapt to a changing world. People who give the Secretary a fair consideration will find that he is no different than any other human being. In fact," Gore glanced behind him with a slight smile, hoping that he didn't appear too rehearsed. "He is a proud new grandfather."

The press corps gave an appreciative murmur and Aziz Sahil smiled shyly. Gore turned back and pointed to a representative of a major news network on the first row.

"Thank you, Mr. President. Do you expect this nomination to enhance our international standing?"

"Well, my first responsibility is to America and her citizens. Aziz Sahil is a remarkable man with an extraordinary career in public service. He's done much for this country already and I know that he looks to serve with honor and distinction as Vice President. He wasn't chosen for this purpose, but I do think that many overseas will appreciate the fact that America is an open society where anyone can succeed. As you know, we've been working hard to win over many people, particularly in the Muslim world, who might have reason to resent us. I want to make it clear, however, that the Secretary was chosen for his qualifications."

"Mr. President," inquired another front row occupant. "There is a petition circulating the Internet..."

"Oh no, the Internet!" Gore raised his hands to his cheeks in mock horror, a rare moment of spontaneity that amused nearly everyone.

"Well, Sir, what I mean is that there are parts of your proposed Health Care Act that are controversial – capping medical costs without limiting civil liability, for example. This on-line petition has been signed by ten million citizens so far who say they'll refuse to pay taxes if the new government health care system provides abortion."

"Well, we live in a democracy," declared Gore, "and the majority of people in this country want total health care. They expressed this with their vote on November 2nd. We can't have legislation be held hostage to the demands of a small minority. Listen, the other day I heard from a woman named Ellie May Thomas from Enid, Oklahoma. She's 108-years-old and suffers from a degenerative bone condition that requires expensive treatment that she would *not* be able to afford without this legislation. I'm not going to tell her and others like her, that they have to live in pain everyday because we have to accommodate a bunch of backwards bozos who want to strip women of their right to choice. Next question."

"Concerning the Pillar project, Mr. President, as you know, many Americans are somewhat wary of immigration following 9/11. Are there any new timetables or targets; and will the Vice President assume any immigration responsibilities?"

Gore paused, gave a nervous cough then spoke slowly. "Xenophobia is not a new phenomenon. I think you'll find that the same people having a problem with immigration now are also the same folks that had a problem with it prior to 9/11. The events of that day provide a convenient cover for the sort of prejudices that we've been working so hard against these last three years. As I've said, Muslims make up about one-fourth of all people in the world, yet only about seven percent of America, which, I'm proud to say, is two points higher than when we started a few years back. We are, in a sense, missing one of the great pillars of the world's populations, and this is part of what makes our great country out of step with other nations. Many here have forgotten that we owe our success to diversity, multiculturalism, and, yes, the immigration policies of the past that enriched our society."

The President looked down for a second and then continued. "Each group of people that came to our shores was greeted with the same derision that we see today in some unfortunate quarters. The Irish are a good example of this. Yet, each group has been woven into our society's fabric, making us stronger." Gore meshed his fingers together in front of him in a brief gesture. "It doesn't surprise me that there is opposition to the Pillar project, after all, we're up against four hundred years of racism. This irrational fear of Muslims, however…" Gore turned and extended an arm to Aziz Sahil. "This irrational fear of someone like him, a fine public servant who is a strong believer in civil rights… well, let's just say that it steals from all of us. Mr. Secretary, would you like to add to this?"

Flashbulbs popped furiously as Gore stepped aside and Sahil came forward. His voice betrayed a hint of nervousness, at first, but rapidly assumed a level of comfort. "I would just like to thank the President for his kind words. Like many of you watching right now, I am a proud American. This is a country that is trying to make an effort to learn from its mistakes. I am proud of what the President has done in reaching out to the Muslim community here in America and in the world over the last three years. The fight against bigotry is never easy, but I have faith that intolerance will join slavery and segregation on the ash heap of history…"

Friday, January 7th, 2005
Aceh Region, Indonesia

Rothermel might not otherwise have drawn attention in a region where others of his age are starting families, were it not for the dreadlocks bouncing across his head to the rhythm of his steps along a busy, filthy street in northern Indonesia. There were plenty of other white people around, not the usual tourists, but mostly employees of relief organizations that were coordinating the effort to assist recovery operations in the wake of the Tsunami. Unlike 16-year-old Rothermel, they were all very busy with their work. It wasn't that he didn't want to help out, which was his purpose in being there, but rather that he didn't know how to fit in – which was typical for the older teen.

Rothermel was the son of two university professors. His mother taught Women's Studies and his father History. He grew up in Berkeley, reading the footnote-free works of Howard Zinn and other like-minded populists that helped galvanize the worldview of his parents, which always revolved around the tragedy of American aggression and transgression. He attended an exclusive private school along with others whose parents were a mix of progressives and social elites. Sometimes it was hard to tell the difference. Academia paid very well, as did the other high-status jobs filled by the culturally sensitive. They all had at least one thing in common, however. None trusted their kids to the same public school system that they advocated strongly for others.

With some exceptions, his classmates were not as serious as Rothermel, whose sense of activism had been drummed into him at an early age by his parents, intent as they were that his young and malleable opinions be brought into strict compliance with their own. There was a school of thought in America, rarely practiced, that a child could be inculcated with core values, and then be taught to think critically on more specific issues from examining both sides of the argument. This was not a priority of Rothermel's parents. Although the bumper sticker on the back of their hybrid electric vehicle read, *"Minds are like parachutes: They only function when they're open,"* they had no intention of risking their child to opposing ideas any more than were interested in challenging their own progressive assumptions of people and politics.

The Winter Holiday this year was called Kwanzaa around the house, not because his parents believed in the tradition (they were among the tiny few who knew of the founder's true history, having personally known one of the women that he imprisoned and assaulted) but rather because their son was going through an "African-American" phase. Hence the dread-locks, grown over the previous summer after Rothermel found inspiration from an author invited to speak at his school. The man had grown up in the streets of Richmond and had written a book called "Makes Me Want to Screech" in which he detailed the violent things that he had done to white people from an early age and into adulthood because of his anger at being black. The book had a picture of the author on the back cover, as-suming a pensive pose and presumably reflecting on his misdeeds. Rothermel devoured it, and then decided that he could identify with the "Black Man."

The dreadlocks looked positively dreadful on the boy, whose body was already taking on the short, dumpy characteristics that would promi-nently identify his appearance as he grew older. His head had sunburned at the end of last summer and the exposed areas between the hair bunches were still more pinkish than white, with occasional shavings of dried skin flaking off every so often. Though continuing to endure the taunts of his schoolmates, which he considered appropriate penance for having been born white, he had thankfully dropped the most ridiculous piece to the ensemble – a contrived and ludicrous ghetto accent that his parents begged him not to use when they were in public together.

The Tsunami occurred the day after Christmas. Rothermel initially did not have the same interest as his parents, until learning that Somalis living on the extreme eastern coast of Africa were marginally affected as well. Those were "his people," he believed, and he had an obligation to help. He immediately petitioned his parents for a plane ticket, but they were not about to send their only son into the dangerous no-man's land that masqueraded as the country of Somalia, and offered to send him to Indonesia instead, at a cost of $2200 – enough to feed a family of six there for about a decade.

So it was that the young white man with dreadlocks found himself walking down a debris-strewn road, dodging vehicles and donkey carts while blissfully unaware of the humor that his appearance was inspiring in the open-mouthed natives fortunate enough to look up at the right time.

A powerful stench hung over the entire area, an amalgamation of rot and decay. Shockwaves generated by the undersea earthquake had rocked the water to generate a huge wave more than a week earlier. The ocean swelled over the land, surging deep into the island before receding with a 15-minute titanic pull that sucked an enormous amount of human life out with it. Most of the bodies that floated back in were buried by the time Rothermel arrived, but mud was everywhere and concrete buildings stood gutted and stark amidst the rubble that had once been structures of far less superior construction.

There was a palpable sense of self-importance in the teenager's mind. He felt as if he were at the center of the world, knowing that all of the globe's attention was on the natural disaster. He wondered if there were any news cameras pointed in his direction at that moment, capturing this image of compassion... a California student giving up part of his Winter Holiday break to help the neediest of people.

He hunched over a bit and assumed what he thought to be a more rugged and wary pose, occasionally lifting small pieces of debris on the side of the road, as if checking for victims that may have been missed by all of the thousands of others traveling the same road. He ceased doing this after a few minutes, becoming dimly aware of the fact that he was arousing the suspicions of onlookers, who may have been concerned that he was looking for something to steal. He noticed a group of people working on a shack a few yards away from the road and went to investigate. It seemed to be a family in the process of rebuilding a partially damaged structure. There were some scraps of building materials lying in the mud not far from them and Rothermel went to pick one up, thinking that he had finally found some work.

Just as he got his hands around a piece of plywood, a loud stream of words that he didn't understand gushed from one of the women, who saw what he was doing. Rothermel continued to lift the plywood from out of the mud and turned toward the building site, where he was stunned to see that the attention of the entire group was now focused on him. He took a few hesitant steps toward them, but was met by couple of angry men who knocked the piece out of his hand and began verbally assailing him.

Raising his hands, almost above his head, he gave a weak smile and hoped that it would translate his good intentions, but it seemed to have the opposite effect. They pressed around him, blocking his way back to the street. The children began jeering at him from around the edges of the growing crowd. One of the men gestured to another standing back at the shack. The second man nodded and reached down to pick up a machete. Rothermel's smile vanished and he swallowed hard.

"But... I'm an American... an American!" pleaded Rothermel, oblivious to the shrillness in his voice.

The world began to slow down at that moment. The man wielding the machete began a slow walk over – a little too slow as a matter of fact, but Rothermel wasn't catching on. Nor did he notice that the people behind him were no longer blocking his way. He spun around quickly and pushed hard against thin air, losing his balance and tumbling headfirst into the mud. Crawling forward with impressive speed, he eventually stumbled to his feet and raced down the road, mistaking the fading laughter behind him for cries of disappointment over a lost headhunting trophy.

"Relax, they wouldn't have killed you." Rothermel was so busy looking back over his shoulder for brown-skinned machete-wielders, that he hadn't noticed the weary looking white man with a blue baseball cap walking next to him.

His presence and casual manner were an instant relief. Rothermel had shunned the offers of assistance from the counter clerks and fellow Americans at the airport in Java and on Sumatra after the charter flight earlier that day. He preferred to wade out into the disaster and get his hands dirty right away.

The encounter with the angry builders was humbling, if only for a moment. He was under the illusion that these people would reciprocate the solidarity that he had with their cause, the cause of the Third World against capitalist oppression.

"Not in front of their children like that anyway," the other man continued, in a soft British accent. "They were just trying to scare you... and have a little fun in the process."

"Some fun," snorted Rothermel, visibly relaxed both by what was said and the mere fact of finally having some company. He was beginning to regain a bit of his bravado. "Can't say that I'd blame them if they had, of course. People like us have been trying to dominate these poor souls for centuries. Coming here on our wooden ships, exploiting them, enslaving them... it's just terrible!"

The other man didn't say anything. Rothermel continued. "I can see them being suspicious of someone with white skin, after what they've endured. I guess they're showing restraint by not butchering every last one of us. We owe these people so much..."

"You really are an American, aren't you?" said the man.

Rothermel looked down at the ground. He had planned to tell anyone who asked that he was Canadian, but the previous series of events had unwittingly forced his hand. His companion had apparently heard his high-pitched protestations. "Yes," he said, still looking down. "But I'm not a criminal."

The other man laughed in such a way that Rothermel figured must have been his first such laugh in some time, which was not unreasonable given the circumstances. "Well! Thanks for setting the record straight." He laughed again.

The boy looked up. "People shouldn't have to live this way. Not when others have so much wealth."

They walked on for another mile, before finally breaking out into an open area with a mass of people milling around several grounded fishing boats. It looked like an effort was underway to pull the boats back into the water, where a rickety wooden dock remained stretching out into the sea.

The sun was beginning to drift downward and Rothermel knew that he only had a few hours left that day to make a difference in these people's lives. He studied the situation carefully. Some of the men were digging ditches in the sand that led out from the front of the boats and extended to the water. One such nearby trough seemed to be complete and full of water. There were several men on either side of the boat, pulling on ropes that wrapped around the hull and over the deck. Rothermel walked over, trying to see if there were any ropes free that he could grab to assist with the effort. He didn't see any, but one of the men closest to him was short enough to where Rothermel was able to reach the line behind him. He clutched the rope in his hands and began straining with all the force he could muster.

There was a man standing in front of the boat directing the others, who did not notice Rothermel's insertion until another man, standing to the side began gesturing and yelling. The first man held his hand up for the other to stop his antics and walked over with a quizzical expression on his face. The men around the boat gradually ceased what they were doing. Everyone was looking at Rothermel, who tumbled yet again into the mud as the rope went slack. No one helped him to his feet, but at least no one was pumping a machete this time.

Rothermel was abruptly shooed away as an argument commenced behind him in the local language. He walked back up toward the road with his head hanging, feeling about as dejected as he had ever been in his life. His companion was waiting back at the road again to bail him out of the gloom.

"Looks like tough luck again, eh? Don't worry about it. You see, the men that are digging those boats out are being paid by the owners, like that fellow over there." He pointed to the man that had been supervising the operation from which Rothermel was just chased away. "Now the other guy, the one that threw the fit back there, was waiting for a job to become available, and he got upset because he thought you were taking his place."

"I was just trying to help out," sniffed Rothermel. "Don't they understand that? What's wrong with these people?"

The other man turned away quickly, perhaps to hide a smile, and led the way back to the road. "Your intentions are good my friend, but as you can see, there's no shortage of manpower."

"But I paid... my parents paid a lot of money to send me to help out."

"Didn't you really come for yourself?"

The boy didn't have a chance to answer as they had to split quickly to allow a large truck to pass. It was loaded down with bags marked with the USAID logo.

"You see there," the man said, meeting Rothermel around back and pointing to the bags. "Those are aid supplies sent by the U.S. government. Did you know that the United States provides more international assistance than any other country?"

"The United States provides more poverty, racism and death than any other country," replied Rothermel haughtily. "The world would be a much better place without a superpower, particularly one that is dedicated to the destruction of the poor and colored."

"Are you from California?"

Before Rothermel could answer, his companion pointed to a GNN camera crew that was about to pass. He turned back to shake the boy's hand. "I've got to get back to my job site, but it was a pleasure meeting you. Follow these folks here… they're headed back to town." Then, just like that, he was off. Rothermel watched the blue baseball cap gradually bob and float away along with the stream of people.

The news crew was slowing down on sighting the haggard young American, with clothes muddied, it was assumed, from a hard day's work.

Rothermel jumped at the opportunity for the interview. He didn't mind waiting the twenty minutes or so that it took to get the camera set up and positioned correctly against the fading afternoon light. When the time came, he looked straight into the lens with as solemn an expression as he could manage.

"Well, it just feels good to make a difference in these people's lives. They need all the help they can get right about now. So much of the world is turning their back on the victims of this disaster, particularly the United States. The devastation isn't pretty, I know, but sometimes you just have to do the right thing. No, I don't mind the work. It is tough, as you can see by all this." He reached down to knock some of the caked mud off of his shirt. "But it's worth it. It feels good to help out."

For the rest of his life, Rothermel never failed to let it be known to anyone who had so much as a casual friendship with him of the time that he had flown to Indonesia as a teenager to lend a much-needed hand to tsunami victims.

Sunday May 1st, 2005
Berkeley, California

"I don't give a rat's ass about God," said the sympathetic young man, whose wonderful ambitions and dreams were about to be cut short by the murderous Christian fanatic, blocking his way on the subway platform.

Rothermel sat on the floor of his bedroom, glued in anticipation to the television. It was one of his favorite shows and one of his favorite themes coming together. This episode of Cold Case was about a serial killer who claimed that God picked out his victims for him. His dementia was a product of a strict religious upbringing, under parents that were maniacal about instilling the rules of their faith into their child, thus creating a murderous madman.

"You must die then – the Lord commands it!" said the pietistic lunatic, lurching forward to strangle the energetic and resourceful victim, cutting short a promising entrepreneurial career.

The young Rothermel felt a rage bubbling up inside him. Although this was just a TV program, he was sure that it was based on a real-life situation somewhere and that such people did indeed exist. The smart, young detectives on the show shared his disdain for religion, believing also that it was an irrational system that warped the mind. He just hoped the message was being heard and that these dangerous people and their primitive myths would continue to be exposed.

Thursday June 30th, 2005
Ila, South Carolina

Walid al-Rahahti picked up the phone nervously. It felt heavy against his sweaty palm. He held it in front of him for a few seconds and tapped it absent-mindedly with his other hand before giving up and smacking the receiver back down on the hook in one quick move. He had lost his nerve again.

Monday July 4th, 2005
Ila, South Carolina

This time he was doing it. Walid was actually dialing the toll-free FBI hotline number that was advertised in the Muslim community. His heart was pounding in his ears and his hands were trembling. The line on the other end began to ring. Hypnotically almost, Walid laid the receiver back down slowly, disconnecting the call. He still couldn't bring himself to go through with it, but he was getting closer.

He had been to the mosque once since he had last tried to make the call. The bearded cleric had repeated the same firebrand sermon, calling the United States a "whore" controlled by "filthy Jews, the children of farm animals." "It is the duty of every true Muslim to wage Jihad," he declared, as Walid's older brothers nodded in agreement. "The Qur'an demands the purification of the infidels by the faithful!" The cleric ended the sermon with the same call: "Death to Israel, Death to America!" They were then ushered out the door, squinting in the bright sunlight and smiling courteously to the people passing by, as if nothing insidious were occurring inside the house of worship.

Walid was horrified by what was being said at the mosque each week. It was like a secret club, plotting to overthrow the broader society, very much out of place with the America that had taken in his family and so many other Muslims. His parents didn't go to mosque anymore, except for occasional *salat*, but his two brothers were devout, attending several times a week. The mosque had been changing with the recent influx of Jordanians, Palestinians and other Arabs into the community over the last couple of years. The sermons became louder and bolder, stopping just short of laying out specific plans for insurrection, it seemed.

He wondered what effect this had on his two brothers, who didn't talk much about their religious views when he was around, except to affirm their faith that "there is no God but Allah" and "Muhammad is his Prophet." He knew that they believed there was no point to science, literature, music or other cultural traditions outside of Islam. Occasionally, he would overhear them speaking with each other about the oppression "their people" were suffering, usually assigning the blame to Israel, but sometimes to America as well. They would grow quiet if he approached. They treated him differently than they did their friends, other young Muslims who were having the same problems adjusting to a new culture and language. Walid felt like an outsider in his own family.

He dared broach his concerns to his parents only once. Questioning authority was a step to be taken with great caution in the al-Rahahti household. Walid suspected that his parents' sympathies for America were similar to his own, but they did nothing to discourage the militant drift of his brothers, at least that he knew of, and appeared displeased when he asked them one day about the contradiction.

"Your brothers are simply going though a phase," said his mother. "It isn't unusual for a young person to have zeal and idealism that fade with age. I would far rather them be drawn to Islam, than to the decadence that this country is so determined to instill in young minds. Most parents here have to worry about their children seeing filth on TV or sordid images on the computer. These are not things that we had to worry about in our homeland. Nor do I have to worry when my boys want to spend time at the mosque."

"But there is such hatred for the United States expressed there. The Imam said…"

"Can you not understand that, Walid? Don't you see the moral decay? What other country goes to such great effort to inspire lewd thoughts? Yet the pushers of this debauchery are protected by the government. Their disease spreads to other parts of the world and contaminates culture and family. Certainly there is anger in the mosque, but Muslims believe in peaceful change from within…"

The phone rang directly in front of Walid's face, startling him out of his thoughts. No one else was home and he preferred not to answer it, but picked it up anyway after a few rings, just before the answering machine was triggered. The man on the other end introduced himself as an FBI agent, following up on a call placed to their hotline from that number. Walid felt lightheaded, but his hand had been forced and he carefully explained what he had heard in the mosque, including the call to Jihad.

The response was not as he expected.

"Did you hear about specific plans to commit a crime?" asked the agent.

"No."

"Well," said the agent, who sounded as if he were rustling through some notes. "Jihad is… can be interpreted in a number of ways, but it almost always means a spiritual struggle against sin. It is a personal battle within the soul of a Muslim believer. Would you like for us to send you some information about this or about Islam?"

"No. That won't be necessary," mumbled Walid. "I am Muslim."

"Oh," said the agent. "That's OK, you see this hotline was established on Executive Order last year by the President for the Muslim community to report any hate crimes that may occur. Are there any incidents that you're aware of… where someone has harmed or insulted your person or property?"

It took Walid a few seconds to adjust to a conversation that he had not anticipated having. Thoughts of Leeman Arnold flashed across his mind. "I don't know. I'm fifteen. There are always a few people who give me a hard time, but it's…"

"A few people?" repeated the agent, who sounded excited. "In your neighborhood… in your school… has anyone been hurt?"

"No, no, of course not." Walid was having regrets. "It's just a person or two at the school who taunts a lot and gives me the finger."

"They have a problem with your religion?" The agent could now be heard typing as he was talking.

"Well, I guess so. It's really not a big deal. It wasn't what I was calling about."

"Is this at Ila High School?" asked the agent, apparently getting the information from the telephone number. "Can I get your name?"

Walid's hands were feeling numb. "Listen, I can't talk anymore. This isn't what I was calling about. Do you understand?"

"Yes," said the agent who continued to type for another twenty seconds. "We'll treat it anonymously, as we do most of our tips. You have nothing to worry about. Is there anything else we can do for you?"

"No." Walid hung up the phone weakly and sat on his bed for a few minutes, thinking about what a strange country this was.

Monday, September 12th, 2005
Ila, South Carolina

On the first anniversary of the terrorist attacks there was a candlelight vigil planned for the students in the school auditorium, in defiance of a national directive from the Department of Education. A local Muslim-American activist, emboldened perhaps by the directive, complained to the school board that the vigil could turn into a hate rally, and asked that it be cancelled. The school decided to proceed with the vigil, perhaps fearing that more harm would be done if word got out that Muslims were attempting to block it. The vigil appeared to conclude without incident. A local Imam was even invited to give an invocation.

By the next anniversary, however, the school board had gotten the message. Instead of one activist, there were now several groups, some with national affiliations. All insisted that the vigil from the year before had created anxiety among Muslims in the community, and that dozens of incidents had occurred in which these religious minorities were intimidated or had property vandalized. The school board decided to forego any memorial service.

That was two years ago. This September, the Gore Administration recommended that local schools use the anniversary as an opportunity to teach religious tolerance. Though he was not yet fifteen, even Walid knew what this was supposed to mean. At the noon assembly, the only speaker introduced was the Imam, who had been invited to speak three years earlier, the same person who called for Jihad in his brothers' mosque.

The Imam sang a different tune that afternoon, speaking of how Islam is the religion of peace, and that Muslim-Americans are very peaceful people who want nothing more than to be free to practice their faith in the country they love, free from persecution. He gave examples of instances in which Muslims in the community had been victimized by "Baptists and Christians," who threatened them or damaged their property, including burning down a house.

The assembly was mostly quiet, but the Imam was interrupted at that point by an older student with blonde hair and ragged jeans who shouted "Where is that? What is the address of that house?"

Murmuring began. The Imam hesitated then tried to go on, but the student interjected again. "My father's a firefighter! There's been no arson!"

Several teachers, who had been creeping slowly up the bleachers toward the boy, immediately kicked into gear and converged on him like a gang of piranhas. The assembly buzzed as the student was hauled away. The principal quickly made his way up to the podium and leaned in front of the Imam to address the students. "Let me make this perfectly clear.

Any more outbursts like that will result in suspension. The Imam has been kind enough to join us and since the theme of the day is tolerance, we would all do well to practice it right now."

He turned away and gave the podium back to the Imam, who was sweating profusely. Clearing his throat and speaking with a much thicker accent than he had been using before, he said, "Well, I apologize for the misunderstanding. It seems I meant to say that Muslim-Americans have been threatened with arson, not that it has happened yet. Of course, I now wonder what your friend has in mind." It was meant to be a joke, but it didn't go over well.

Hours after the assembly, Walid was walking down the hall when he heard the chant start up behind him. "Alrighty, alrighty, alrighty…"

Usually it kept up until Leeman lost sight of him, although sometimes not even then, as he could hear the older boy's voice echo around hallway corners. This time something different happened. Leeman's voice stopped in mid-taunt with a crashing sound. Walid whipped around to see the larger boy with his face mashed against a row of lockers, where he was being held by an older black student. A crowd began gathering around them.

"What is your problem?" the older kid demanded loudly.

Leeman didn't say anything, he just looked very embarrassed.

"Every day, about this time, you go into some kind of crazy spasm and start spouting gibberish. What is your problem?"

"That towel-head… that's his name," mumbled Leeman, pointing rather weakly at Walid, who was somewhat frozen by the turn of events.

The other student looked down at Walid, then back at Leeman. "And that's what makes you act like an imbecile? You got problems, buddy. If I hear you mouthing off again, I'll pop you good. Pick on someone your own size or you'll answer to this." At that, he raised his fist and Leeman ducked his head, quickly squirming out of the other's grip to run off in the opposite direction.

It would have been an awkward moment if the older student had said anything to Walid, but perhaps knowing that, he turned immediately and walked the other way. Walid turned as well and headed back down the hall toward his last class of the day, but not before finding out that the person he suddenly wanted to get to know well was named Pat Ridley.

2006

Monday, March 20th, 2006
Ila, South Carolina

Walid flipped on the television to see a GNN correspondent reporting from a massive rally called "Americans United against Hate" at the Mall in Washington D.C. Although the rally was supposed to be a protest against the climate of "fear and intimidation" that Muslim-Americans were said to be under, according to the reporter, only about 20% of the demonstrators were Muslim. The rest were "sympathetic supporters."

"Ted, as you can hear from what's going on behind me, this demonstration is certainly loud enough to make itself heard. They're just hoping that the right people are listening. The crowd really peaked about two hours ago when the Vice President spoke. He exhorted Americans to 'put aside the hate' and 'open hearts for those who are different.'

"The speech was briefly disrupted by a group of radicals chanting in Arabic. We aren't sure what they said, but it was enough to cause a twenty minute delay as Vice President Sahil was moved to a safe area while the demonstrators were being cleared. It's possible that they were upset over the perceived failure of the government to protect the al-Raz mosque in New Jersey."

"Steve, if I may break in. We're getting word from our on-staff translator that the men were chanting 'Death to Sahil, traitor to Islam'."

"I understand. The other protestors here were calling the police, 'brownshirts' and 'Gestapo'. As you can see from these pictures, they weren't happy about the sight of Middle-Eastern men being hauled away by uniformed police officers at a rally for tolerance."

"Is the al-Raz mosque burning the most prominent issue?"

"Without a doubt, Ted. This rally was timed to coincide with the one month anniversary of the morning that the nation awoke to the horrible news that a New Jersey house of worship had fallen victim to an arsonist. This, of course, has been front-page news for the last several weeks and the Justice Department has worked diligently on the case."

"Steve, as we've been reporting here, the suspect whom the FBI has been holding apparently confessed to the crime. Has this been of any consolation to the people that you've been talking with there on the Mall?"

"Not a bit, Ted. There is deep skepticism over both the bombing and the investigation. Many down here are insisting that the CIA was involved in the bombing and that the FBI is merely covering it up. Above all, there seems to be a strong conviction that a larger conspiracy exists, and that one individual could not possibly have acted alone."

"Well, as you know, Steve, the man in custody insists that he did, and that he acted out of frustration over the 'lack of action,' as he puts it, on the part of the Administration toward pursuing global terrorists."

"Yes, they're aware of that down here, Ted, but this only fuels skepticism. It's just too convenient, they say, that the suspect attributes this hate crime to the government's choice of negotiation over aggression. The demonstrators here believe that this is simply a ploy to justify going forward with a war plan. One man, wearing a pro-Palestinian t-shirt, put it rather bluntly when he said that 'Gore is looking for an excuse to destroy the Muslim nations.' They also blame the government for the five church arsons that followed the mosque burning. Those cases are still open, of course, and the FBI has declined to get involved.

"Many in the crowd are still enraged by the FBI's conclusions following the burning of the Bangor mosque last year. The agency determined that the local Imam was in fact responsible for the fire. As you know, the President asked the Justice Department not to press charges in the case, but there's still a lot of bitterness among many Muslim-Americans, who feel that the FBI was simply trying to make a scapegoat out of the Imam, despite the evidence and eyewitnesses..."

Walid turned the sound down as the network went to commercial, which he had no desire to hear. They were all usually the same anyway. Typically a male character would be doing something comically stupid until a woman would correct his folly by employing the product or service that was being advertised. White men were the dumbest, unless they were correcting other white men.

He stretched out in bed, puzzling over what he had seen.

The GNN translator was half right. The men were chanting "Death to Sahil" and proclaiming him a "traitor to Islam," but the bulk of their diatribe was directed at the United States, as they declared that the great nation would be humbled and broken by the forces of Jihad. They were quoting verses from the Qur'an that condemned Muslims who would not join the fight.

He wondered about the long-haired, mangy whites, some in tie-dyed shirts and sandals, who were screaming and throwing objects at the Mall police that were working to subdue the chanters and take them into custody. Did they not understand what the men were saying, or was it that they felt the same way about their own country? Certainly this would appear to be the case, from the signs they were beating over the heads of the cops; and Walid was sure that there were plenty of Arabic speakers in the crowd to translate for the rest, if they so desired.

Perhaps there was an odd marriage of convenience between the two groups of radicals.

2007

Friday, September 7th, 2007

Atlanta, Georgia

Pat Ridley forgot all about the white card shortly after putting it on the hotel room nightstand along with his change and anything else that happened to be in the pockets of the stiff military uniform before turning in for the evening. He noticed it again in the morning. It had been passed to him by a man on the street and was blank except for a website address printed on the front and a handwritten password on the back. The password would identify him to the site, where he could view a software demo, and then choose to accept a job that would pay him more for three days of work than he made in six months with the Army.

The software company needed models who were willing to have electronic devices strapped to various parts of their body so that optical motion systems could capture and record the 3-D images for simulation programs. Basically, Ridley would be strapped up, and then told to go assume certain movements or poses that would generate data used to construct the characters in video games. The man had assured Ridley that he had just the sort of physique that the producers were seeking. There was something about him, though, that didn't seem right. He had been well-dressed, but his eyes were oddly expressionless.

Ridley picked up the card. From the Web address, it looked as if the video game was something called 'Grand Larceny III', which he had never heard of before. After dressing, he plugged his laptop computer into the hotel's network and booted the operating system. On logging into the website, he found that he could download the "trailer" for the game, which was a sort of commercial. Once it downloaded, the trailer started playing in the browser.

He made himself watch the entire sixty seconds, although Ridley knew it was unnecessary from the first scene, which showed a gang robbing a liquor store. Subsequent scenes showed African-American characters in a variety of street situations, from selling drugs to shooting down a police helicopter with a rocket launcher. The characters acted stereotypically, using macho slang and displaying psychotic tendencies while gangsta' rap music thundered in the background.

When it was over, Ridley closed the laptop in disgust and tore the card twice before throwing it in the trash can.

Monday, September 10th, 2007
Conner Ranch, West Texas

The old ranch manager stood at a respectful distance from the two figures sitting close together on the grassy hill, beneath the tall oak. He could still see the 12-year-old boy holding his father's hand as they gazed out over the flat valley. The sun had dipped behind the dark mountains on the other side, leaving a spectacular trail of color scattered across the clouds that rippled across the big West Texas sky. A light breeze fed into the valley from the same direction, blowing softly in their face. It was a peaceful scene.

The old man wasn't sure if the boy's father had died yet. He was propped against the trunk of the tree, and very well could have passed by now. If so, the boy didn't seem to be aware of it. They had been talking quietly to each other for most of the last hour, but not loud enough for Diego to hear the words.

The ranch manager had done all he could, rushing off to the house to call for help upon seeing his boss collapse as they were working the western side of the land. He left explicit instructions with the operator and hurried back to see if there was anything that could be done. He knew that there wasn't, except help the boy get his father to the top of the hill so the two could sit quietly and enjoy their last moments together. They had been sitting there for a long time, but there was still no ambulance.

The old Mexican had fought back the urge to join them. He loved them both and didn't mind the tears that came to his eyes. He had only been a lowly ranch hand some twenty-five years earlier, just a few months removed the hard-scrabble existence of Guadalajara, when the man who had hired him, the boy's grandfather, fell victim to a heart attack at an early age as well. The son had worked hard to save the ranch then, twice having to let go of the workers, only to hire them back within months. Diego had also been on the ranch the day that his boss got married, on the very same hill on which he now lay dying.

Those were the happiest times for everyone. The beautiful bride brought a certain contagious joy that livened up the ranch and the surrounding community. It was the only time that large parties were thrown. The daughter of a politician who grew up in Washington D.C., she was more than eager to learn a great many of the things that were unique to life on a remote ranch west of the Pecos.

Unfortunately she let go of the one thing that she should have kept – a distrust of strangers.

The couple lived happily for nearly a dozen years before having their only child, Kerry. The boy was almost six the day his mother's body was found partially nude in a neighbor's field a day after she went missing. She had fought like a demon against the illegal Mexican drifter, who wasn't hard to identify from the claw marks, broken hand, and mangled ear meted out in the struggle. He had not been able to get the woman's clothes off, while she was alive. He subsequently received only twelve years from a sympathetic Hispanic judge – a rising political star who was more concerned with respect for international sovereignty than the pleas of the Mexican ranch hands, who stood in court to urgently press for the death sentence in broken English and less than eloquent Spanish.

The boy's father spoke less and seemed to age faster, but he was determined that nothing else would change on the ranch. His bride would have wanted it that way. The hands offered to work a year without wages, to help the ranch recover from debt, but the boss would have none of it. The old ranch manager quietly took on some of the duties left vacant in the wake of the murder. Young Kerry was raised as normally as possible, as fluent in Spanish as any of the hands, and without a hint of ill will despite the circumstances of his mother's death. He was graced with his mother's optimism and his father's work ethic.

He would need both more than ever now, the old Mexican knew. Losing both parents before reaching one's teens was tough enough, but having nothing else in life was even worse. The entire ranch would go to the bank, other than a few pictures and personal effects. Diego expected the boy to be taken in by his aunt in El Paso, an austere woman who obviously had to force herself to be polite when interacting with the brown-skinned ranch hands. In spite of this, the old Mexican intended to tell her quite bluntly that he wanted to remain in the boy's life. He had a nephew in El Paso who was in the process of bringing his family up from Guadalajara, including a boy about Kerry's age.

Darkness was falling by the time the siren was heard in the distance behind him. Diego slowly ascended the hill toward the boy, who was now standing straight and tall over the crumpled figure of his father, with his silhouette framed against the faint glow… all that was left of the magnificent sunset.

It was a beautiful way to die.

Saturday, September 15th, 2007
Ila, South Carolina

Walid was excited to see Pat Ridley again, even if it was just for an hour or two at a farewell party. His friend had recently finished training at Fort Benning, Georgia and was on a two-day leave before heading out again for his first active duty assignment in California. The get-together was at his mother's small house, which was out on the edge of town in a working-class neighborhood, where the only things that distinguished one house from another at first glance was the interesting assortment of cars parked at the curb, in driveways, and even up on blocks in some of the yards.

After getting to know him, he realized quickly that his first impression of Pat, as a sort of bully of bullies, wasn't right. In fact he was a sensitive person and a good student. The two did not share similar backgrounds, but a bond naturally formed between them as it does instinctively between any two people with common values. They did not spend a great deal of time together over the last two years, but became good friends nonetheless.

Pat was not quite the bookworm that Walid was, but he enjoyed learning. He could have gone straight to college, but enlisted in the Army out of a sense of patriotism following the abbreviated Afghanistan bombing campaign in March, which was a last resort effort by the President to force the Taliban into extraditing Bin Laden. Public patience with the unsuccessful diplomatic efforts had grown thin and, after five years, the United Nations finally offered a clear resolution that authorized the American President to act militarily.

It quickly became evident, however, that the lives of ordinary Afghans were of no concern to the Taliban. International criticism of the U.S. mounted right along with the bombing casualties. Overseas demonstrations indicated that Gore was in danger of squandering the goodwill built up through years of impressive restraint following 9/11. After members of his own party began to lose their nerve, the President relented to pressure and brought the military operation to a halt after just a few weeks.

The controversy raged on, however.

The Imam at the local mosque was incensed. "Oh Muslims, the enemies of Islam are fighting us, our morality, our faith, our religion, our economy, our holy places, and our rights. Their tyranny does not prevent them from declaring their hostility towards us and our faith." Other fiery sermons accused the United States of waging a "crusade" against Islam in order to kill or subjugate followers of the Prophet.

Even Walid was a bit unnerved by the claims, but it seemed odd that an allegedly nefarious government was unconcerned with the presence of mosques on its own shores, which would surely have been easier to destroy than anyplace half-way around the world – if this was indeed a war on Islam. He also wondered why his brothers weren't bothered by the sight of Muslim women in Afghanistan reduced to begging in *burkas*.

Hollywood did its part as well, generating a flood of movies and documentaries over the summer that lampooned the military and depicted past campaigns, from the Indian wars to the Persian Gulf operation, waged in amoral fashion with little regard for humanity. Americans had no stomach for this sort of brutality, even on foreign soil.

In spite of this general drift, there were still some who argued that the country's honor was at stake and called for the President Gore to intensify the pressure on the Taliban, even to the point of sending in ground troops. Reports were leaked to the media by malcontents in the intelligence community, which indicated that al-Qaeda was organizing more attacks inside the country. No one was sure how Gore would respond.

In spite of the uncertainty, Pat had faith that the President would step up, and he enlisted in the Infantry believing that he would soon see action on the ground. Although Walid was more inclined to believe that the influential media critics of the truncated bombing campaign would carry the day instead, he was nonetheless inspired by his friend's example.

Seeing Pat for the first time, standing in the kitchen doorway, was something of a shock. It was evident that the past five months had been quite physical, as he must have added about thirty pounds of muscle. There was still that same hearty smile though.

"Hey there my friend!" he shouted, coming over to shake the teenager's hand with a firm, solid grip.

"Look at you," said Walid. "You've really bulked up!"

The new soldier gave a modest shrug of the shoulders. "Well, you know, we do nothing but eat and exercise, so it's bound to happen."

He had a mature look about him that was only just beginning to bud when he left for the service after graduation in June. His facial features were more chiseled and he seemed to stand straighter, with clothes hanging somewhat conspicuously over a hardened frame. This, perhaps, is what people meant by having a 'military bearing,' Walid thought. The two walked out to the backyard where many of the others were to do some catching up.

"Leeman still around?" asked Pat.

"He's got a job down at the chicken processing plant. That's probably about as good as it's going to get for him.

Pat laughed, "I agree. Say, I hear that you've got ambitions of becoming a lawyer. Is that right?"

"Yes it is, although we prefer the term 'attorney'. I've got a long way to go, but if my grades stay like they are, then I've got a shot at getting a full scholarship."

"How's your family doing?"

"They're fine. My brothers aren't in school anymore. One of them works at a garage and the other stays home. They're both spending a lot of time at the mosque. How's yours?"

Pat looked away for a second, over at his younger sister, Letitia. "Not that great, really, my sister's been getting into trouble, driving Mama crazy."

"She's probably just going through a phase."

Pat seemed to bite down on his jaw a bit as he looked down to meet Walid's gaze. "She's pregnant." He looked back. "She's not getting married either, which – although I hate to admit it – is probably a good thing given that the man she was fooling around with is a loser. I think he's got another pregnant girlfriend somewhere in another high school."

Pat turned away and took a few swallows of his soft drink. "I don't know, Walid, doing something like this at that age can really mess your life up. It's pretty dumb to bring a child into the world when you can't even take care of your own self. It's really giving Mama fits. She had a lot of hope for Letitia."

Walid knew that Pat's mother, like Pat himself, was a church-going woman (as Americans would put it). His sister, on the other hand, was in Walid's class at school and had a reputation of living for the moment. He hadn't known that she was pregnant, but he figured that he knew a few other things about Letitia that Pat probably didn't want to know. He wasn't about to add to his friend's misery at the moment.

"She was kind of young when our dad died," continued Pat. "Mama's great, but she doesn't lay down the rules the way that Pop did with me."

They talked for several more minutes, before Pat had to excuse himself and mingle with some new arrivals, being the guest of honor.

Walid stayed mostly in the shadows for the rest of the evening. Being a 16-year old Jordanian, he felt somewhat out of place in the group of mostly Southern black adults, although no one was the least bit unfriendly. When the time was right, he exchanged e-mail addresses with Pat, shook his hand and called it an evening.

Friday, December 21st, 2007
Ila, South Carolina

The teacher's name was Wyland. She was not only new to Ila High School, but was, from what Walid gathered, in her first assignment since graduating from a Northeastern university in June, being just four or five years older than the students. The first semester had gone much better for her than anyone would have expected.

There were incidents along the way that tested her control of the classroom, but she handled them in unusual fashion, rarely yelling, and always projecting a sincere dedication to see every student succeed. She acted as if education were critically important to each individual, appearing to assume that even the most obstinate troublemaker shared her interest in their own success. The students thought her naïve, but played along in the game, occasionally punctuating her lectures with ridiculous and obviously comedic questions, but leaving a relatively conducive learning environment for the other students.

Another control technique that Ms. Wyland adeptly employed was a subtle appeal to each student's ethnicity or race. This obviously didn't do much for the white kids, but they didn't merit much consideration anyway, being a dying breed in the county's public school system. Bringing up Islam to recent Muslim immigrants who might otherwise have tuned her out, however, or making mention of an African-American student's heritage in a positive context seemed to inspire each individual to raise their own standards. There was a subconscious sense of obligation toward ensuring that one's conduct did not have broader implications in the minds of others.

Reinforcing identity and distinction was also perfectly in keeping with the historical themes in the curriculum. No matter what era of American history they went over, Ms. Wyland always found a way to criticize the tradition of an American "melting pot" and explain that it was just an excuse to impose "Anglo conformity" on immigrants and undermine diversity. The others in the classroom seemed to enjoy this frequent topic of discussion and were not shy about venting the pride and hostility that Ms. Wyland encouraged – in rampant disregard for the small cluster of whites in the back corner of the classroom.

Walid did not share the enthusiasm of his Muslim peers, although he wasn't sure why. He was one of the best students in the entire school, which may have been the reason that the teacher frequently called on him, although he was becoming somewhat resentful of it. At first he'd been blindsided by her questions, after all, what did Islam have to do with American History? Yet, somehow Ms. Wyland invariably found a way to weave his family's religion into the curriculum.

She taught, as fact, the contributions that she believed Muslims had made to early America, beginning with the Arab navigator that supposedly guided Columbus, to the presumed Islamic identity of certain African slaves brought to the New World. Walid wanted to comment that any Africans who followed Islam would have learned it from their Arab slave masters, but he did not want to raise the ire of the black students. There was no mention of the Muslim slave trade or the fact that it had been ended by the Europeans. No statistics were given, but from the way it was taught, Walid assumed that at least half of all Americans in history had owned slaves, with the wholehearted approval, perhaps, of the other half. *Why was there a war to end slavery*, he wondered to himself.

There were others in the class who enjoyed talking about the Crusades or how the Jews were responsible for the planet's misery. Yet, for whatever reason, Ms. Wyland seemed to enjoy trying to get the reluctant Walid to participate in class discussion when the topic bordered on Islam. Unfortunately for him, this seemed to happen quite a bit as Muslims (or

Africans) were credited in some form or fashion with every European invention that made its way to the American continent.

"Did you know that we wouldn't have mathematics," asked the teacher one day "without the Arab invention of zero?" Some of the students snickered, but the teacher continued. "Without the number zero, there would be no algebra or calculus. Our understanding of physics would not be possible, nor would the engineering products that we take for granted, such as bridges, buildings and automobiles. And so, we are very grateful to Walid's ancestors for their ingenuity…"

"Thanks Walid, for your mighty ancestors!" The sarcastic comment came from a student in the back, wearing a football jersey over a sizable midsection. Laughter ensued.

Walid sunk a bit in his chair, self-conscious of his classmates' stares. The teacher did not immediately respond, perhaps finally realizing that her indulgence was a bit embroidered. There was a long unbearable pause, which Walid finally broke by mumbling, "It was from India."

"Pardon?" asked Ms. Wyland.

"The Hindus invented the concept of zero. The Muslim armies that conquered the region simply borrowed the knowledge and then introduced it to Europeans. This was the case with most of the other inventions that you're crediting 'my ancestors' with – they were simply introduced from one culture to another by Arab traders who were geographically located to bridge the Eastern and Western cultures. Islam does not encourage knowledge outside of the Qur'an."

Walid's voice had lowered steadily almost to a whimper by the time he was done, and his gaze focused on the tile pattern at his feet. Every ear in class was tuned to what he was saying. Although the teacher was frequently challenged by smartasses looking for laughs, no one had actually corrected her before now. Glancing up, he saw the astonished look in her eyes.

The incident marked a slight change in Ms. Wyland's habits. Although she continued to praise Islam, the teacher no longer called on Walid, but instead referred to other Muslims in the class during the course of her lectures. These others, some of whom wore *hijabs* and traditional Middle Eastern apparel, were quite pleased with the opportunity to explain their faith in long evangelical discourses. The other students were sometimes impatient with this, but the teacher always insisted that the greatest tolerance be shown. "Open your minds, class," she would say, to pacify the murmuring. "You owe it to yourselves to find out about other cultures. America is changing and the more you know, the better you'll be able to adapt."

Walid thought it odd that the rule of tolerance did not apply to the few remaining rednecks in the classroom, trying to bring up the Bible or

Christianity. The teacher would roll her eyes a bit whenever this would happen, and usually cut the student off abruptly with a comment along the lines that anyone so interested could attend a church of their choice on Sunday to find out more.

On this Friday, the last day before the Winter Holiday break, a student had the temerity to ask why they had to learn about Eid al-Adha but not Christmas. Walid thought it an honest question, but other Muslim students seemed visibly offended, which did not go unnoticed by Ms. Wyland. "An attitude like that is one of the reasons why Americans find themselves disliked by the rest of the world," she said with a mildly annoyed look toward the unfortunate girl posing the question. "I'm sure that everyone here, including you, knows what Christmas is. What you really have a problem with is the fact that we're learning about someone else's culture and beliefs. You don't think this merits the same respect that you feel entitled to yourself. This is called Ethnocentrism – the belief that one's own culture is superior to others. Class, is this a good thing?"

Everyone shook their head and there was a long pause. The girl at the back of the room began to tear up and Walid felt embarrassed for her. He wasn't sure if the teacher was waiting for her to apologize or burst out crying, or perhaps both. Slowly he raised his hand. Ms. Wyland's face brightened as he caught her attention, since he had not spoken much at all in class since the incident a few months back. "Yes Walid?"

"You believe that one culture is as good as another?"

"Yes," she said quickly, "because there is no way to make a judgment between cultures. The individual making the evaluation is subjective and therefore biased. What may seem wrong to one people might be practical to another in different circumstances. There is no basis for making a judgment, and anyone who tries to do so is simply being bigoted." She said this last part with an obvious glance toward the girl at the back of the class.

Walid cleared his throat, trying hard to raise his gaze from off the floor. He was starting to regret opening this line of discussion, but it was too late to stop now. "Do you feel that a culture which makes an effort to discourage value comparisons between cultures is superior to those that see others as beneath them?"

There was dead silence. A flash of anger flickered on the young teacher's face before she turned to walk back to the front of the room, evidently gathering her thoughts in the process. When she turned back around, Walid could see that the smile had returned to her face, although it was not reflected in her eyes. "No, I don't think that one society can be superior to another, although there can be elements in some that are to be encouraged…"

She seemed to falter at that point and Walid wasn't sure if she were finished or just waiting for the words to come.

He asked, "Is the society which provides this encouragement superior to one that does not?"

Now it was Ms. Wyland's turn to study the tiles on the floor for a few moments, as a slow buzz started up in the classroom. She held up her hand and raised her voice to calm the whispers. "Perhaps we can't be completely objective, but we can know enough to know the faults of our own society and then seek to remedy them. For those of us in the United States, for example, there is very little in our nation's history in which we can take pride. Our nation, as we are finding out in this class, is built on genocide, slavery, and subjugation. We have the worst record on the planet when it comes to any of the elements by which we might judge another society. Perhaps it is this inferiority of ours in so many categories that gives us the ability to appreciate cultural relativity and that this balances our culture with others. Who's to say? This simply proves my point that…"

The bell rang. Without missing a stride, Ms. Wyland exhorted the class to have a safe holiday and to enjoy their break.

She did not look up as Walid walked past, nor did he look at her.

2008

Monday, February 11, 2008
Manchester, New Hampshire

"Damn."

It was all that Al Gore could say because it was the only thing that came to his mind. *Damn. Damn. Damn.* He didn't moan "dear God" or blurt out "oh, holy crap" this time, although "Damn" wasn't much better, but at least the cameras weren't around again to capture another inglorious moment.

His National Security Advisor, David Encino, sat across the table in front of him, with an expectant look on his face. Other advisors crowded around him as well, in the plush conference room on Air Force One, which was sitting at that moment on the ground at the Manchester International Airport. Slowly the wheels began turning in Gore's head.

He had almost made it through his second term without a major terrorist attack, but now word was coming in that morning of a plane hijacking and downing in the Blue Ridge Mountains, just east of Washington D.C., with over a hundred people thought to be on board.

It could hardly come at a worse time. He was in New Hampshire to campaign for his Vice President, Aziz Sahil, who was in a very tough race against Senator Hillary Rodham-Clinton for the Democratic nomination. It was all but assumed that whoever got the party's nod would win handily in November, given that the opposition was in disarray, but Gore felt that a large part of his legacy depended on his Vice President's victory.

"It was a hijacking, confirmed. One hundred and two, including the crew," reported an aide to Encino, who then nodded at Gore, given that there was no point in repeating the information. Gore lowered his head and tapped his fingers against it. After a few seconds he looked up at Encino with an unusually dark look in his eyes.

"How did this happen, David?"

Encino looked surprised by the question. An aide spoke up for him. "One of the passengers reported that there were four hijackers with weapons of some sort. Apparently they were quite brutal."

Encino looked down at the notes handed to him by another aide and picked up the story from there. "They wanted to prevent another Flight 93 situation, Mr. President, where the plane was brought down by the passengers over Pennsylvania back on 9/11. It looks like these hijackers began trying to kill everyone right away in a real blood bath. We're not sure what the weapons were. The passengers still managed to down the plane though, just a few minutes after the whole mess started over Virginia." He looked up. "This is what we're piecing together from cell phone calls. There are no reports of other hijackings at this time."

"So David, how does this happen," repeated Gore impatiently, with irritation in his voice.

"Sir?"

"You know what I mean. How is that these guys weren't caught at the terminal back at Dulles?"

The tension between the two men had only gotten worse over the years. Encino had been nearly the headache to Al Gore that Lieberman was at one time, but the option of engineering his resignation was never on the table. After decades of voting down defense budgets and pressing for intelligence restrictions prior to 9/11, the Democratic Party didn't have many of their own to choose from when it came to filling high-profile positions that required security expertise and unquestionable patriotism. Encino had both; and he was a loyal Democrat as well, with bi-partisan respect, but he fought others in the Administration tooth and nail over the contents of each security mandate – or more importantly, what he felt was missing. He lost every time.

"I can't answer that until we've conducted an investigation, Mr. President, but I assure you that we'll find out if security procedures weren't followed on the ground."

Gore decided to drop the argument for the moment. He was angry, but right now he didn't have what was necessary to make a scapegoat out of anyone, yet.

He decided to make a few calls and left the meeting briefly to head down the plane's narrow corridor to his private office. Bending over, he could see the press corps through the windows, massing in anticipation on the tarmac. Gore knew he was in for a tough day.

At his desk, he immediately began taking calls from Senate and House leaders, a political formality that needed to be done. Each pledged their support and tried to sound optimistic. He was as brief as he could be, but nearly a full hour passed before he noticed the time. As he was getting up, an aide burst through the door and rushed in with a videotape in his hand.

"Mr. President, you've got to see this!" he exclaimed, with an enthusiasm that seemed out of character with the events of that morning.

Gore gave a puzzled look. The aide ran over to a monitor that was turned to GNN, as it had been all morning, with a live shot of the wooded area where the plane went down, taken from a helicopter camera several miles away. The picture alternated between a very shaky close-up that was nearly impossible to watch, and a long range view that was steadier, but too far to make out any detail.

As the aide rewound the tape, Gore could see that it was an interview with the Vice President, which was odd, he thought, given that his own staff had been unable to reach him. He recognized the reporter from a couple of his news conferences. She was Penny Zahn, one of the young up-and-comers that GNN called "sexy" in their commercials. The aide hit the play button right as the interview started. Gore reached over to turn on the volume.

"...of you to take a few minutes from what is turning out to be a very tragic morning to talk with us. Do you know any more than what we've been reporting thus far?"

"Well," said the Vice President tersely, with his usual slight accent. "I don't know what you are reporting, since I haven't had time to watch, but obviously we know that a plane has been hijacked and was brought down near West Virginia. This appears to be an isolated attack and there is no need for anyone to panic."

"Sir, if these hijackers turn out to be Islamic terrorists, do you think this could have an adverse effect on your campaign?"

Gore's eyes widened and his jaw dropped open. He stared at his aide, whose gleeful look confirmed that he had not misheard the question. He hadn't heard the phrase "Islamic terror" used in years. Certainly it was never uttered at the White House, where a directive to the entire Executive branch had been issued almost immediately after 9/11, instructing staffers to dissociate the Islamic religion from any mention of terrorism, a lead that seemed to be followed by reputable news organizations as well, until now. He wasn't sure whether to feel elated or depressed, but he was intensely curious to see the Vice President's reaction to this insensitive question.

Aziz Sahil didn't disappoint. At first, he looked absolutely stunned to the point of speechlessness, and then he lit into the young woman with a verbal fury. "Ma'am!" he thundered. "I don't know what to do with a question like that! Is this 2008 or 1908? What do you mean, asking me how it would affect my campaign? Is this what we've come to in America? A Muslim can't run for office without his religion being made an issue of, or having to answer for deranged individuals who have nothing to do with Islam? What sort of bigotry is this?"

The GNN reporter began stammering. The Vice President wasn't finished and angrily cut her off. "Your question reflects a deep ignorance; one that is surprising for a person in your position. There are no Islamic terrorist groups because terror is against Islam. Islam is the religion of peace. It is completely incompatible with anything like what we're seeing in those mountains this morning. I can't stop you from thinking the way you do about those of us who are Muslim, but you do yourself a disservice by opening your mouth and revealing your ignorance."

Gore was almost feeling sorry for her as the reporter managed to get out her next question. "I'm sorry, Sir," she said in a weak voice. "I didn't mean to offend you. Do you have any idea who these terrorists are?"

"No. No I don't," snapped the Vice President. "I just know that they are not Muslim. Despite what people like you would think. A Muslim would not do this, so perhaps you should be talking to a rabbi or a priest right now, instead of me. We have been under suspicion too many times over the last eight years, and this hateful way of talking and acting needs to stop. We are tired of being discriminated against. We are tired of having our mosques burned down. It isn't the American way."

Gore pumped his fist when he heard that last part, as the aide switched off the monitor and pulled out the tape. As long as more planes didn't rain down out of the sky between now and the end of the day, it was possible that they might just survive this after all.

Now he knew what to feel... pure elation!

Ila, South Carolina

Walid had never been in so much of a rush to get to the mosque, as he had been on hearing of the hijacking. His brothers would have been proud of his fervor, but it wasn't religious piety that drove him on that day. In fact, he had become quite cynical over the last couple of years, which did not go unnoticed by his family, although he didn't talk about it with them anymore. It wasn't that he was losing his faith in God, but rather in the Imam, who seemed to operate with a sort of shameless duplicity.

When he was speaking at the mosque, the Imam would talk about Jihad and rail against the "Christians and Jews," warning that their day of judgment was coming and that there would soon be neither a rock nor a tree for them to hide behind. He quoted liberally from the Qur'an to support his violent exhortations: "fight and slay the unbelievers wherever you find them; seize them, beleaguer them, and lie in wait for them in every stratagem of war." Other itinerant speakers at the mosque were no less extreme in their sermons either.

Yet, when speaking to these very infidels, the same speakers played to Western sensibilities by using only the language of peace and tolerance. "War is deceit, according to the Prophet," the Imam frequently reminded his followers.

When Walid arrived at the mosque that afternoon, he was surprised to hear a much gentler tone than usual in the Imam's voice, which he didn't understand until he rounded the corner and saw his teacher, Ms. Wyland, sitting in the back of the room behind the others. She immediately caught his eye and waved, although he was too stunned to wave back. He took an open chair and sat down.

Was she really Muslim, he wondered? He hadn't thought so. After all, she seemed to be a strong supporter of women's rights. Then again, he remembered bringing up the treatment of women under the Taliban regime a few months ago, thinking that she would appreciate the injustice of their plight. Instead, she had nodded politely then quickly continued railing against America's rejection of the Equal Rights Amendment and the economic disparity between men and women.

There were other areas as well, in which she was completely unwilling to lend the same sympathies and excuses to Christianity that she did to Islam. These included slavery, war and many other human rights issues that Christian societies had almost universally resolved. Certainly she was an excellent propagandist for Islam, but he never suspected that she was Muslim.

Neither did the Imam apparently, since he was tripping over himself to serve up an ample helping of manure, as he had during the student assembly a few years ago. Now he was explaining how similar Islam and Christianity really were. How they all worshipped the same God and followed the same teachings. Walid had to cover his mouth to hide a smile when the Imam ended by stressing the "brotherhood" of man.

"Ah, I see we have a visitor today," he said softly with a gentle smile to the woman in the back. "Welcome to our worship. Are you a part of the *Ummah*?

Ms. Wyland seemed to blush and stood up, "No Sir. I just came to offer your people my support in this difficult time and to let you know that that there are many of us who know that you stand shoulder to shoulder with us in the fight against hatred and bigotry. I wanted to let you know that we are with you as well. If you encounter any sort of backlash because of what happened today, please let the authorities and the newspapers know."

"Thank you, Miss," said the Imam beaming. "We appreciate your gracious words. It's not easy being a religious minority in America, but we know that there are good people, in addition to the bad ones that struggle against us."

He turned back to the others and called them to s*alat*. As they stood up and began clearing the chairs for prayer, Walid noticed Ms. Wyland slip out of the room, but not before giving his older brother a strange look that he had never seen in the classroom.

Thursday, February 14th, 2008
Washington D.C.

Gore returned the favor to his Vice President by returning directly to Washington, where he huddled in the fortified bunker beneath the White House for a few days, downplaying the threat of further attacks and trying to exude confidence. Polls indicated that he had made the right choice, as his approval rating rose slightly in the wake of the Monday morning incident.

He didn't have to worry about being skewered on the airwaves either, the way that his predecessor would have been. New legislation enabled the FCC to crack down on talk radio stations that did not provide a "balance of opinion." This forced many into a change of format, given that there were no profitable liberal talk shows. People who were smart, educated and socially conscious preferred a more eloquent medium because, as a leading Democrat once put it, conservatives communicate with crayons and liberals with quill pens.

Another break for the Administration was that, by sheer chance, one of the passengers in the doomed plane had been none other than Orenthal James Simpson, better known simply as O.J. At one time, he was America's most famous football player and a well-known media celebrity, yet he managed to accomplish the task of eclipsing this with notoriety of a different sort, as a murder trial defendant a dozen years earlier. Now, the media was engrossed by credible reports that he was one of the first to be knifed horribly to death by members of al-Qaeda while trying to hide under his first class seat, as other passengers rushed past to storm the cockpit.

Al Gore's mood improved so remarkably from that dark hour on the Manchester tarmac that it undoubtedly buoyed those around him and even had a positive effect on the nation's reaction to the attack, as reflected in the polls. Americans may have been willing to forgive the Administration for the loss of a single plane after six years of relative safety, but they had no tolerance for Islamophobia, and the "Penny Zahn" episode (as it was now known as) underlined a more troubling undercurrent that presumably existed even as the face of America was changing.

In a bold move, reminiscent of Johnson & Johnson's masterful handling of the "Tylenol crisis" twenty-five years earlier, Bernard Greenly and GNN decided to confront the problem head on. Anticipating the outcry, they immediately released the reporter, whose only previous brush with controversy had been when anti-immigration extremists criticized her allegedly "soft" coverage of the Pillar project. The network gave not the slightest hint of a defense or justification for the reporter's embarrassing actions, even as al-Qaeda released a claim of responsibility for the hijacking and promised that their next attack would "horrify the world into accepting Allah."

GNN broadcast a statement at half-hour intervals for the next several days, in which it apologized for the "unfortunate" remarks made by the *former* staff member and repudiated any implication that Muslim-Americans did not "stand shoulder to shoulder with Americans fighting terror." The network made a public commitment to hiring Muslim news writers, editors and broadcasters. It was also in the process of producing several public service spots in which prominent community leaders assured Americans that Islam is "the religion of peace."

This didn't stop massive protests in major cities, in which Muslims carried banners alleging that the "climate of suspicion" was just the latest chapter of "1500 years of genocide" against their people.

The coverage of the actual plane crash, precipitated by the unsuccessful hijacking attempt, was being treated more like an ordinary air disaster. There was some mention of the passengers' heroism in forcing the plane down, but the tragedy was not reported much differently than if mechanical failure had been responsible. Terrorists, like faulty rudders, were innate risks that the airlines and government were burdened with mitigating, just as with the physical integrity of the aircraft themselves.

Like GNN, the Gore Administration promised to find which of their own was responsible for the lapse of security that was squarely to blame for the downing in the mountains of western Virginia. The poll numbers were holding steady, benefiting in part from the "sympathy factor" that played to the Vice President's advantage. Even his political opponents were forced to focus on the issue of Islamophobia and openly pledge support for the Pillar project. No one was about to sound like a bigot by criticizing a program that enriched America with cultural diversity at a time when tolerance was of such critical concern to the national consciousness.

Friday, February 15*th* 2008
GNN Public Service Spot

It isn't a close-up, but the picture is tight on Sherry Danforth, holding six-year-old Robert in her lap as the camera pulls back slowly. A park forms the background behind her.

"Hi. My name is Sherry Danforth. On September 11*th*, 2001 my husband, Robert, was among the victims in the World Trade Center. Like thousands of other families, it was a dark day." She pauses to look down at young Robbie then slowly back up, with a somber expression. "For those of us who lost loved ones, our hearts will always be heavy. We still wonder what could have been done to prevent that day from happening… to prevent the hate."

The camera pulls back further to reveal a young woman sitting next to her in traditional Middle-Eastern garb. She is holding a baby. Sherry continues. "Though we can't bring back the victims of that day, we can honor their memory by fighting hate in our community."

A diverse group of actors, including one dressed like a priest, appear and gather in behind the two women as the picture widens. Each has a solemn, determined expression on their face. A person in a wheelchair is now on the other side of Sherry, who concludes by asking, "After all, isn't that what they would have wanted?"

She smiles and reaches over to caress the baby, whose mother recip-
rocates with a smile of her own from under the headscarf. Those around
them nod lightly in dignified approval. The picture fades to a GNN logo
on a black background as words "GNN Cares" appear gradually underneath.

Saturday, February 16th, 2008
Los Angeles, California

"What's wrong with what I said?" snapped Gore to the unfortunate
aide sitting across from him, as Air Force One lifted from the ground to
begin the trip back to Washington, following the memorial service to O.J.
Simpson.

The aide, who was black, simply squirmed in his seat, clearly unable
to form his frustrated thoughts into words.

"I was told that African-Americans believe that O.J. Simpson was
framed on account of his race," continued Gore, clearly exasperated.
"Why would they get so upset then, when I compare his situation to others? What's wrong with saying that the Scottsboro Boys were innocent
like O.J.?"

Again the aide couldn't speak. His eyes begin to bug out slightly and
he loosened his shirt collar while taking several deep breaths.

Friday, March 7th, 2008
Berkeley, California

"Little Eichmanns!"

The phrase bolted out of the speaker's mouth, striking Rothermel
with brilliant clarity. The professor from Colorado followed others in the
symposium that expounded on the theme of America's sin and shame
through the centuries, a motif with which the young college student was
well acquainted.

History was no longer told from the winner's point of view, but rather
from that of the oppressed and the poor. These were the people who built
America, not the White Man controlling them with whips and wealth.
Rothermel doubted that anyone would be willing to fight for this country
if they knew the true story of exploitation and struggle, from the earliest
days of European subjugation of Native Americans to last year's effort to
grind the Afghan people under the nation's mighty heel.

The United States existed only to oppress "inferior" classes. Indians
were nearly wiped out with disease and massacre, Africans were worked
to death under the lash, and women were objectified and disrespected in
every possible way.

Today the country resembled a great feudal machine, oiled with the
blood of the workers and existing merely to serve the greedy interests of

ravenous corporations, too powerful even for the government to challenge. Capitalism was the greatest sham in human history, a terrific con
job whereby the masses toiled and died in factories or battlefronts for sly
puppet masters, who counted their cash with each defense contract secured and each toxic waste dump concealed in the drinking water of the
poor.

Democracy was an illusion, a true opiate of the masses that deludes
average citizens into thinking that they have some control over a system
that is, in fact, crushing them. The true power in America wasn't held by
servile politicians, but rather the large corporations and wealthy white
men over whom they fawned. These are the wizards behind the curtain,
pulling levers to make the voters see what they want them to see, with no
idea of how they are being manipulated. The proof was in the money
trail. Wealth in America always went in one direction: from the pockets
of those needing it most, and into the pockets of those needing it least.
The rich always got richer over time, and the poor poorer. That was the
reality of the American Dream – itself a fantasy invented by the power
brokers to keep their minions laboring, ignorantly striving toward an unreachable goal with effort that worked only to their master's advantage.

There was nothing in American history, from slavery to the 'war on
drugs' that could not be explained in terms of class and greed. It was a
system expertly designed to maximize profit and protect privilege for
those with wealth and status at the expense of those with neither. And
America could not resist exporting this brutal system of economic and
human oppression across the globe, wherever the potential for exploitation of resources and people exist.

There was no misery in the world for which imperial America could
not be held ultimately responsible, as speaker upon speaker assured the
large audience of several thousand at Berkeley that afternoon in the auditorium. The program was building to a crescendo, with the man from
Colorado poised to deliver the final blow to Western civilization.

"Islam wasn't responsible for the attacks of 9/11 anymore than they
were responsible for the Crusades," he said flamboyantly from the podium. "America's greed, America's foreign policy, America's people
who feed off the rest of the world and leave starvation in their wake, these
are the people responsible. These office workers, these 'Wall Street'
types in the buildings that day, were merely part of a technocratic corps at
the very heart of America's global financial empire. They were little
Eichmanns, serving the engine of profit. The men who hijacked those
planes were their desperate victims, whose gallant sacrifice reflected the
courage of their convictions." The speaker concluded. "I don't want to
see America brought to her knees, in fact, I don't want to see America at

all. I want this country pushed off the planet and out of existence altogether!"

The applause was deafening. Rothermel was on his feet with the rest,
not caring where his notes wound up on the floor as he expressed his enthusiasm.

It was a brilliant end to the symposium. The attendees spilled out of
the theatre and into the harsh California sunlight like energized Pentecos-
tals leaving a tent revival. The symposium was timed to coincide with a
massive anti-war demonstration across the bay in Golden Gate Park, protesting the U.S. for its threat to resume the bombing campaign against the
people of Afghanistan. The student contingent would be well-represented
at the rally, and events on campus were designed to spur participation.

Rothermel boarded a University bus that was running the circuit between Berkeley and the park. He rode by himself across the Bay Bridge,
pleased to see banners strung across trusses and dangling from cables, all
hung by the activists. A prominent one, just past Treasure Island, had the
words "Fight Eco-Terrorism" drawn across the top with pictures of well-
known corporate CEOs below, each under an overlay of a red bull's-eye.

It was an exciting time. He wished that he had friends to share it
with, but his second year was turning out to be about as lonely as the first.
There were a few people that he knew, all children of professors as he
was, but he still felt out of place. He always assumed that he would be a
big fish in the Berkeley pond, having practically grown up there. He had
gotten to know many of his parent's academic peers, and felt that he had
been able to speak on their level for some time in matters social and political. In the back of his mind, he expected to impress the other first-year
students with his passion for social justice and rapport with the professors.

In fact, it wasn't much different for him than high school had been,
with a curious twist. Whereas he was an outsider at his prep school, here
he was an insider while everyone else it seemed, other than the professors,
were outsiders. This was quite puzzling to him, because the comments
that he made in class, though offered with greater passion, were in basic
agreement with what nearly everyone else believed as well.

Once, he had interrupted a class lecture to reinforce, with his own
opinion, the speaker's point that the patriarchal nature of Western society
was too deeply embedded to expect that it could be repaired. The only
solution was to tear down the social structure – beginning with traditional
marriage – and start over. Without citing the source, Rothermel repeated
a story his mother had told him about a friend of hers who had been asked
by her company to work beyond eight hours a day "like the men did."

After making the comment, Rothermel expected his esteem to rise
somewhat among the most dedicated feminists in the class, who were distinguished by the scissors hung around their necks (signifying the sup-

posed desire to castrate men) but no sooner were the words out of his mouth than a an angry young woman with a crew-cut began shouting at him, telling him to shut up and stop pretending as if he could understand what it was like to live under rape and oppression. For once, the professor did not take Rothermel's side, but quickly genuflected to the bobbing heads of the feminists, attempting to smooth over the situation while staying in complete agreement with them that any man, by his very nature, is absolutely unable to empathize with the plight of women in this, the most hostile and misogynist of cultures.

Oddly enough, nearly the same thing had happened in a different class, "Sociology of Body Size," in which Rothermel saw an opportunity to relay an example of racial discrimination that he happened upon in his readings. As he was talking, he noticed that the white professor seemed uncomfortable and was casting an occasional furtive glance toward the African-American students, who were in turn looking at Rothermel with expressions of utter disgust.

"You don't know what the hell you're talking about," exclaimed one of them, when Rothermel was finished. "You don't know what it's like to be a Black man in America! You don't know nothing... so don't even pretend to know."

Rothermel was stunned. He had not been around African-Americans much, other than friends of his parents, who were always cordial to him – although somewhat cooler during his "dreadlocks" phase.

The other student continued. "This is part of the problem. A white man thinks that he can atone for what he's done to Africans, by pretending to understand. 'Hey Black man, Hey Negro, Hey brother man... I'm right with you. I feel you.' You don't feel nothing, Man. You just want to try and fool me into thinking that you believe I'm better than you, while all you really want is to find a way to steal what's mine in the name of capitalism. You're no different than any of the rest, just waiting to steal from the Black man... steal our music... our labor... even our speech. I'd rather be sitting with a skinhead, because at least they're up front about it."

The other black students nodded and muttered approval. The white students, including the professor, nodded slightly as well, while biting their lower lips with grave expressions, as if digesting weighty philosophical truth. Rothermel was speechless. For the duration of the class, he was unable to recover from the shock and embarrassment that the other had so casually forced on him simply for trying to empathize. He did not speak out again for the remainder of the term. As time went by, however, he came to the firm belief that racism must be so deeply embedded in his own white genes that it precluded him from even knowing when he was being offensive. Although he was not aware of any racist thoughts,

Rothermel knew that, like all white people, deprogramming himself of the vestiges of racial superiority would be a lifetime journey of apology and guilt.

Of course none of this was on his mind at the moment. The bus was caught in traffic around the Presidio, which was a fitting place for Rothermel to mull over the dark thoughts inspired by the symposium concerning the U.S. Government and its military. The former Army base was now a National Park, but it had an awful history, having been wrested from the Mexicans in the illegal war to confiscate Western territory. Afterwards, it had served as a launching point for genocide against Native Americans as well as the imperialist wars in the Philippines and Pacific. The Presidio had even been the site from which General "Black Jack" Pershing instigated his outrageous incursion into Mexico to pursue the Mexican freedom fighter, Pancho Villa.

Needless to say, the young student was quite keyed up by the time the bus doors opened. As he disembarked with the rest of the students, a serious looking young man wearing a grimy T-shirt with profanity written in large letters handed him a pamphlet. "We're marching to the Golden Gate tonight after the rally," he said then repeated it to the person behind Rothermel, who was pushed ahead with the crowd down the sidewalk, up the steps and out into an open field.

It was a splendid picture. People and banners were everywhere. Tie-dyed shirts and other colorful clothes made for an iridescent scene. A stage was set at the end of the field, where the crowd was thickest. Loudspeakers blared music from the Vietnam era between speakers, as people with untamed hair waved their arms in front of them in wild dances that continued even after the music stopped. Rothermel's attention was drawn to a banner near the platform that read "We Support Our Troops When They Kill Their Officers." It was a reference to the incident a few weeks back when a Muslim Marine tossed a hand grenade into a tent where his chain of command was meeting, killing two officers and injuring another dozen. Berkeley was naming a street in his honor.

Only three speakers remained on the schedule, two of whom Rothermel had already heard earlier in the day at the symposium, including the professor from Colorado. The speech given was nearly verbatim of what had been said back at Berkeley, but Rothermel's passions were rekindled.

The previous speaker told the crowd that America's martial aggression was the result of "frustrated sexuality" and that the key to stopping it was to encourage unrestrained physical gratification, much to the approval of the crowd. Of course, the same people cheered just as loudly when the final speaker called for a "million Mogadishus" to halt the U.S. military machine overseas. The sunlight was fading fast as the loudspeakers blared a song about revolution, and the mass movement toward the park's exits began amidst an excited buzz over plans to march on the Golden Gate Bridge. Some of the crowd split off at the street to go home, but a sizeable contingent moved in the direction of the bridge, carrying banners and shouting. Rothermel moved with them.

As they spilled out onto the main thoroughfare leading to the bridge, he could see that the traffic had already been stopped. Ahead of them, at the bridge entrance was a contingent of Army soldiers, dressed in battle fatigues and holding M-16s behind flimsy barricades in an effort to seal off the massive burnt-orange structure rising behind them. Rothermel's heart beat faster and he began maneuvering past the others, toward the front of the column, which wasn't hard given that many ahead of him slowed down upon catching sight of the uniforms. He could not understand their reluctance.

Here was the personification of evil in the eyes of the young student. The very military that had been vilified over a long day by a glut of angry activists was now clearly trying to block their peaceful effort to protest a war. He detested everything about them, from their boots up to their hands, which dripped the blood spilled by their predecessors.

Upon approaching, he could see those in his column stopping just shy of the small group of about twenty soldiers, standing as best they could behind a few construction sawhorses with flashing yellow lights. About half were female and most were as young as Rothermel. They looked quite frightened against the angry crowd that threatened to swallow them. A notable exception was a confident looking black officer, apparently the leader of the group, standing tall in front. It was obvious that he was the sole reason the others were not backing down, and the only person that truly stood between the crowd and the bridge.

The radicals in the crowd were filtering forward, knocking over sawhorses and screaming at the soldiers. It was a tense moment, but the young officer stood unflinching in the middle of it, even as some of his companions were backing away. Someone yelled "Kent State!" which aroused the crowd's rage all the more, even as an uneasy divide of several feet was settling in between the two groups.

It was at that moment that young Rothermel made a bold decision, one that would literally power his career. Being quite certain that the young troops would not fire on the students (and guessing that the rifles they carried did not even have live ammo) he jumped ahead, breaking in front of the crowd in full view of everyone. He knocked over a barrier and ripped the weapon out of the hands of the surprised soldier directly to the officer's left. A photographer captured the moment, perfectly preserving the shock in the young soldier's eyes and the look of righteous indignation in Rothermel's. He had never held a gun before. As he turned to throw it over the side of the bridge, however, a hand quickly snapped out and snatched the weapon back, spoiling the possibility of a second dramatic picture.

Rothermel turned to see that the officer had been the one to seize back the weapon, even though its original owner had turned tail and was running back down the bridge along with most of the other soldiers. The officer was now standing virtually alone, with two rifles in his hand but no authority to use either – and everyone knew it. In the split second before the young soldier was knocked down and dragged under, Rothermel, acting very much in the heat of the moment, managed to spit twice, once catching his antagonist in the face and then again on the hated uniform – right over the name tag reading "Ridley."

Friday, March 14th 2008
Kabul, Afghanistan

The trip to Afghanistan was a gamble, but Aziz Sahil, Vice President of the United States, was a desperate man after having fallen behind in the delegate count to Senator Rodham-Clinton for the August nomination, only a month after the bounce in the wake of the Penny Zahn interview.

He was getting so much contradictory advice from his campaign staff that it was almost worthless. At least he had done the right thing and stayed quiet for the first few days after the interview, as the fallout consumed the nation. His nature was to be more aggressive than his managers would let him, but a timely call from the President convinced him that it was better to let others do the talking for him.

"The country's still not where it needs to be, Aziz," Gore explained. "There is some truth behind the noise that we're making about Islamophobia, you know. It's not all spin."

"Of course, Mr. President."

"We're up against several centuries of entrenched hatred. America was a homogenous land for too long. There have always been religious and ethnic minorities, of course, but they were denied a voice during that time. We can't expect to undo in sixteen years, what our political opponents have had two centuries to reinforce. Do you understand?"

"Yes Sir."

"Things are changing in America though, Aziz. These hate-mongers can't just come out and say what they really think anymore. They have to couch it in innuendo and code words. Look at all the resistance to the Pillar project, for example. On the surface they'll say that they're concerned about bringing in people who may not accept our way of life, our commitment to freedom of belief and expression, but we know that this is merely a disguise for racism and bigotry. They don't want to share this country with people that are different from them. They think that since

America was founded by white Christians it should exist only for white Christians."

Gore continued. "It isn't wise though, to come out swinging on this, Aziz. You need to stay above it. You had the perfect reaction to Penny Zahn at the time, but right now it's best to let public outrage run its course without giving the appearance of manipulation."

"I am thinking simply of wearing the *kufi*," said the Vice President, "at the next interview."

There was a pregnant pause on the line. The President gave a nervous cough. "Well Aziz, I don't think you should, at least not right now. Let me explain it like this, and I'll speak bluntly since it's just between us. At the moment you have a tremendous advantage. The Islamophobes are on the defensive and the country's sympathies are with you. If you play your hand too strongly though, you risk undermining your own position."

"I'm not sure I follow you," said the Vice President.

There was another nervous cough. The President was obviously quite uncomfortable talking like this. "If our argument is that America hates Muslims, then why dress like a Muslim to protest? The strategy is obviously contradictory in that it is plainly designed to appeal to the very tolerance that you're complaining doesn't exist."

The President made sense, of course, but it was standard fare for Muslim-Americans to do exactly what he was talking about, particularly since 9/11. He recalled the September 2002 incident, in which three Muslim-Americans were detained after someone overheard them joking in a restaurant about blowing up a Florida bridge. Their families immediately changed into *hijabs* and *galabiyyas* to go before the news cameras and allege discrimination.

But that conversation with the President was a month old, a political lifetime during the early stage of a campaign primary. It had since come out that not only were the hijackers al-Qaeda, but they were assisted by an American convert to Islam inside the Transit Security Authority who had previously sued for religious discrimination in order to keep his job. Though Americans still claimed to be concerned about Islamophobia, the media had to work to keep the public from drawing conclusions about the only common bond between the terrorists.

This was never more evident than when two experts on terrorism appeared on a talk show to sadly shake their heads and declare that "the true motives of the hijackers would remain a mystery." Several consecutive callers seemed to feel otherwise, although they were quickly disconnected before they could offer their own theory.

The Sahil campaign was running out of options, particularly after the President himself unwittingly proved the very principle that he had been preaching for the last seven years through the failed Afghan operation, namely that bombing terrorists is not a solution because it only creates more terrorists. Democrats were smart enough not to explicitly tie the hijacking to last year's sorties, but they shrewdly implied to the nation that military action was obviously not the answer.

With this in mind, the Vice President knew that it was time to let his flagging campaign ride on a bold spin of the wheel. He would personally travel to Kabul itself to meet with the Taliban and press for the extradition of Osama Bin Laden. He would descend to the tarmac in the *galabiyya* and play the last card that he had left to play with a theocratic government that could not be moved even by the death of its own people.

And so it was that the Vice President of the United States of America became the honored guest of the Islamic Republic of Afghanistan, even as Afghan training camps were in the process of turning out Mujahideen fighters to destroy his country.

2011

Friday, November 11, 2011
El Paso, TX

   "*Permisa luchar... permisa luchar!*" was the cry that echoed off the walls of the brick buildings on both sides of the alley behind the high school, presently congested with teenage school kids, mostly Mexican or Mexican-American. Let them fight. At the center of the commotion was a 15-year-old white boy in jeans and boots with blood running from his mouth and an older Latino with skin peeling from his knuckles and an uncertain look.

   "You hit like a girl!" spit the white kid in Spanish. He wiped the blood onto his wrist in a futile effort to prevent it from seeping down into his shirt. The other started for him again, but was driven back this time by an onslaught of punches. Now it was the Mexican who was bleeding. Spurred on by his peers, however, he rushed toward the white kid and tackled him. The two rolled together for a few minutes, kicking and clawing, until someone in the crowd began yelling that the principal was coming. Others caught on and the knot of students quickly dissipated.

   The older antagonist ran off as well, leaving Kerry Conner lying in the dust. He rolled over slowly onto his back and stretched one of his arms behind his head to cushion it from the hard pavement, assuming a relaxed pose while counting his teeth with his other hand. An airplane moving across the sky caught his attention. He looked comfortable.

   After a while he said, "I recognized your voice, Felipe."

   A tall, brown-skinned kid moved shyly out of the shadows between the buildings and approached the prone figure from behind. "I assume you preferred that to either getting your ass kicked or having me jump in to help?"

   "I could have taken him, you know." Kerry sat up then got slowly to his feet, brushing off the dust. His shirt was beyond repair, but the rest of him, including his faded blue jeans and oversized belt buckle, would live to see another day. He had the air of a rodeo bull-rider, picking himself up after getting bucked off. All that was missing was a Stetson.

   Felipe laughed, "Just like you took care of the last *turba*, what was his name? You know... the one that nearly put you in the hospital?"

   "That's been a while," said Kerry, sucking his lip and turning away to spit out some blood. "I heard that he went back to Juarez and got into some real trouble."

   The two walked down the alley together and out onto the main road that ran adjacent to the school. An old Ford F-100 pickup truck was waiting near the end of the road on the corner. It would soon be Kerry's, but right now it belonged to his aunt, a tough-looking lady in her late-fifties, who always wore pants and had never married. She was waiting for them on the driver's side, wearing the same grim expression on her face that was always there when she had to drive into town.

Her face turned even darker as they got closer and she could see the blood on Kerry's shirt. She got out anxiously and slammed the door. "Who was it? Which one of them damn wetbacks did it to you this time... no offense, Felipe."

"None taken, Ms. Conner" smiled the Mexican teenager, whose English had improved a great deal in the last five years thanks to Kerry's patient tutoring.

"It doesn't matter, Aunt Sarah. It looks worse than it is. Fact is that it's just a cut lip, so don't worry about it. Let's go."

Kerry got in the truck and Felipe began to walk off until Aunt Sarah ordered him to get in. It was a routine they repeated almost every day after school, minus the bloody shirt. Felipe knew the woman didn't like Mexicans as a rule, but she had always made an exception for him and his family.

What Kerry had told his aunt was true. Felipe had seen him suffer much worse in the past. The Mexican kids who stayed at the school from year to year had gotten used to him, one of the few white kids left, but newcomers occasionally made trouble for the "tough as nails" kid when he stuck up for the other *yanquis*. Like his aunt, he refused to accept second-class status.

Nearly all of the white families that were still living in the rural part of the badly gerrymandered district sent their kids to private schools, but there was a palpable hatred on the part of the Mexican gangs for any of them who remained. The last white girl fled the previous year after being threatened with rape. Her family attempted to sue the school district for the annual cost of tuition, but a Hispanic judge threw out the suit. "You have your school," he told the parents. "We have ours. *La escuela nuestra*." He was the same judge who later ordered foreclosure on the family's house when they refused to pay a portion of their property taxes out of principle.

Most of the gang members were not American citizens and could have easily been deported under the laws still on the books, but these weren't enforced anymore. In fact, all of the local towns along the border had "Sanctuary" ordinances that prohibited law enforcement from even inquiring about citizenship status. These "hate-free zones" were common in municipalities throughout the Southwest and as far north as Minnesota, with civil liberties groups there to monitor enforcement. Several police departments had been forced to settle expensive lawsuits filed on behalf of Mexican citizens and Mexican-Americans, alleging they had been victims of discrimination.

The schools now provided education to anyone under the age of eighteen, no questions asked. State driver's licenses could be obtained merely by showing a Mexican license. A driving test still had to be passed and the licenses carried a special designation, but the ACLU was fighting both of these, calling them 'Jim Crow' measures. Even welfare benefits could be obtained in some places by simply claiming a street address as proof of residency.

People like Kerry's aunt were fighting a Second Mexican-American war that they couldn't bring themselves to concede had already been lost. Their last stand was when a group of military veterans calling themselves 'Minutemen' attempted to patrol the border years earlier, in a symbolic show of protecting the country against illegal immigration. They wanted to draw attention to the fact that more than a million people were crossing into America each year, finding it easier and easier to blend into the vibrant Hispanic communities.

The Gore Administration moved quickly to neutralize the Minutemen, with the President, himself, declaring that they were emblematic of "a shameful time" in America's past when such activities were conducted "in the dark by men wearing hoods." The media picked up on the racial overtones, which, in turn, encouraged lawsuits by civil liberties groups as well as the Mexican government. Flag-waving supporters of the project were assaulted by angry counter-protesters, who threw food and seized the flags only to trample and burn them while yelling "No to Fascism." Under public pressure and heavy scrutiny by the Justice Department, the project folded and the border was all but officially declared free and open.

Felipe Posada watched the anti-America demonstrations with a sense of bewilderment. His father was desperate to bring them north four years ago to escape a corrupt political system that threatened their lives. He was a Roman Catholic police officer in Guadalajara, who had risen slowly through the ranks to a position where he could take on the organized crime that kept the local population impoverished and in fear. His successes met with the disapproval of both his superiors and the town's elected officials. He was told that he would not be protected if he persisted. He did anyway – up until the night Felipe's older brother didn't come home.

Felipe had been twelve and living in hiding with his family when they secured permission to permanently cross the Rio Grande. His father had provided the U.S. government with valuable information on drug trafficking over the years as part of his assigned job duties, which were apparently not meant to be taken seriously by his superiors, but fully appreciated by the DEA. He was rewarded with citizenship for his family, which he made sure they valued.

The 12-year-old's English was weak when he first arrived in El Paso to meet his cousins for the first time. He needn't have worried about it. English was a dying language in the Southwest. Everything from road-sides to public school classrooms had long since been ordered bilingual, although no one complained when it was all in *Español*, which was gradu-ally becoming the case. His father had other ideas, however, and believed that immigrants who required their host country to adapt to them were ingrates. This was an old-fashioned attitude that was not popular in the community, but he didn't care. He demanded that the children learn Eng-lish, although this was difficult in a social system that didn't require it. Two things helped Felipe make the transition, television and Kerry Con-ner.

His favorite show was a new one called 'Jenna's Army.' It featured a 21-year-old actress named Starr Sterling, who played the role of an Army officer, sent to investigate problems in various hotspots around the globe. Usually the problems encountered in each week's episode were caused by the arrogance or ignorance of her fellow soldiers toward the native popu-lation, whoever that might be. She was always able to engender a solu-tion by teaching cultural sensitivity to the initially skeptical troops. Occa-sionally, the bad guys would stage a militant attack on a friendly base or facility, during which Jenna would fight bravely while her male comrades, particularly the more sexist ones, would hide under their desks moaning for the shooting to stop.

His friend Kerry would laugh at shows like that. He wasn't much of a television fan. He arrived in El Paso shortly before Felipe, having grown up on a West Texas ranch before being orphaned. Felipe's great-uncle Diego treated Kerry like a grandson. The boys would go to the former ranch manager's house on most weekends to help with chores or hang out. Sometimes they would meet at Aunt Sarah's, if there were chores to be done there instead. The old man was the only Mexican that the spinster seemed to have an obvious amount of respect for, although she was unusually patient with Felipe's father when he attempted to strike up a conversation with her, despite his limited English. Felipe or Kerry would intervene after a time to translate as tactfully as possible, but still to the man's mild embarrassment. Felipe also knew that the older woman had a soft spot in her heart for him as well, despite her outward crustiness.

Kerry and Felipe quickly became the best of friends. It helped that Kerry spoke the language, of course, and he didn't mind helping the new-comer out in his effort to adapt to a new country, although, in truth, it was Kerry and his kind who were gradually becoming the outsiders in the new America. Felipe's dad, who ironically commuted to a factory job back across the border each morning, insisted that the boys only speak English with each other, which they tried to do when he was around. It became easier as time went by. They never spoke in Spanish around his aunt, of course, whose boundaries were better left untested.

One of their latest projects had been to put up a security fence around her house following a burglary that had occurred, thankfully, when no one was home. The house that she and Kerry lived in was just six miles outside of town at the foot of a dry, dusty mountain, but there were no close neighbors.

"What's your Papa up to these days, Felipe?" asked Aunt Sarah, as they bounced along down the dirt road that led out to his house.

"Oh you know, Ms. Conner, he's always working."

"Is he still working down in Mexico?"

"Just across the line at the plant there in *La Ciudad Juarez*."

"What for?"

"No jobs here."

"The politicians don't give a damn either that American wages are being depressed by all the cheap labor flooding across the border, just as long as they get their votes."

The boys didn't say anything. The older woman leaned her head out the window to spit tobacco juice.

"Felipe, do you know that the Mexicans are suing our government over the deaths of those illegals that die out there in the desert trying to break into our country?"

Felipe knew that, of course, because she had mentioned it before several times. Immigration and change were the only things the woman ever seemed to talk about. He did take note of the way she referred to the United States as 'ours' and wondered if she had meant it inclusively of him, as it appeared. It was best not to ask.

"They're going after the ranchers also," she continued. "They're claiming that we're negligent in not providing these illegals with water and food. They want more medical supply stations set up in these remote areas so those bastards will have an easier time breaking our laws. Hell, they're even willing to pay for it!"

She gave a sarcastic cackle then paused to wipe off a bit of tobacco juice from her lip. "Now why do you think the Mexican government cares about flooding our country with their own people?"

Felipe knew to respond automatically with the answer she was looking for. "Because they send American money back to Mexico."

"That's right! I'm telling you, boy, it's a cash cow for that government down there – the biggest part of their economy. They also don't have to worry about their own folks calling for reform or getting too upset at the government for not improving the Mexican economy. The ones that complain are just sent right out of the country and the government gets to keep feathering its own bed with the money that's sent back down."

Felipe agreed that she made a good case. He thought about the predicament that his own family was in when his father became a threat to the system in Guadalajara. Maybe his older brother would still be with them if they'd gotten the message sooner.

Aunt Sarah continued, with a scathing review of the Pillar project, which she said only encouraged Arab governments to dump its troublemakers off on America's shores for the much same reasons. Eventually, the truck pulled up to the front yard of the modest, but neatly-kept manufactured home. Kerry and his aunt swapped positions as Felipe got out, so that his friend could practice his driving. Felipe waved to them both from the driveway and went into the house to turn on the TV.

Jenna's Army wasn't on, of course, but there was an old rerun of CSI (a show that his mother would not approve of if she understood the dialogue) from 2004. Each week featured the discovery of semen in bizarre locations. This particular episode was about a group of cross-dressing transgenders with lines like "I perform fellatio on my wife... we're normal people!" At the end of the episode, the lead investigator, in what was meant to be a profound response to a transsexual's personal angst, pointed to an oyster and said "It can change genders. Maybe we were originally programmed with the ability to change genders as well, and being limited to one sex is just a mutation."

Felipe had to laugh. Maybe his friend was right about TV.

2015

Tuesday March 10th, 2015

Highway 455, West Bank, Palestine

With the radio squawking angrily behind him and the dull thumping of mortar rounds progressing ever closer to his position, Captain Pat Ridley stepped out of his lead Humvee and marched quickly down the line to count the vehicles and what was left of his battalion and the evacuees. The tan boots that complemented his light brown camouflaged uniform made very little noise on the dusty pavement of the open highway.

Eleven of the twelve Light Armored Vehicles (LAV) that originally hit the Green Line that morning were operational, as was the only Medical Evacuation Vehicle (MedEvac) left after the other had made off with the lieutenant colonel. The mission had started with two dozen Humvees, but only seventeen remained, and two of these might need to be abandoned since one would not start and the other had dark smoke pouring out from under the hood. Amazingly, one of the two cargo trucks was still moving, riddled as it was with tight bullet patterns, the telltale sign of automatic weapons fire. Close to half of the passenger cars had been abandoned or disabled. Some were riding on beat up rims, the tires having been lost to shrapnel several miles back. Everyone looked terrified.

The captain was concerned about the human cost as well, but their lives at the moment were entirely contingent on the state of the vehicles. He knew that he was on the brink of a decision that would cost him his rank, a court-martial and the probable lives of several hundred people. At least the court-martial wasn't bothering him, since he knew he wouldn't be alive to face it.

It was less than a month ago, in February, that the first-year Northwestern MBA graduate student arrived home from a long day and a late night at the library to find a summons taped to his door. He was given 48-hours to make arrangements and then report to the Rock Island Army Facility to join his Reserve unit for possible deployment.

Ridley had begun his Army career as an enlisted man, straight out of high school. He was quickly recommended for OCS by perceptive superiors, and received his commission well before finishing his college degree. He had not seen much active duty as an officer, other than the mandatory six months spent on light assignment at Fort Benning, where he conducted Infantry training classes at the end of his hitch. The last couple of years in the Active Reserve had required nothing more than one weekend a month and two weeks in the summer. He felt that he had developed a good physical presence with the enlisted men and women, although the high turnover rate made it hard to assess with any certainty. He might give the Army another year or two, but he knew that his career would not be in the military.

He learned quickly after arriving at Rock Island that he was going overseas, as he suspected. It wasn't until he got to a base in Italy though, that he learned he was being assigned to participate on the ground in Palestine with the evacuation of West Bank settlements.

Although his hectic pace left little time for outside interests, Ridley did keep up with current events. He knew that the United States had pressured Israel some years ago to agree to a unilateral withdraw from the West Bank, as they had from Gaza under the Gore Administration. An independent Palestinian State was assumed to be the last step in the road-map to Middle East peace. The last fifteen years had been brutal for the Israelis. The concession of the Gaza strip in 2004 had not quelled the *Intifada* as it was hoped at the time. The Palestinians had demanded the full withdrawal of Israeli forces from the West Bank as well. Qassam rocket attacks from Gaza occurred with near regularity, but any military response by the Israelis was met with global outrage. The tiny nation was deeply divided over its commitment to cede the West Bank.

200,000 Israelis lived in about 150 settlements in the entire region. There was no survival for them if the military withdrew. The United States, under President Hillary Rodham, offered to pay the full cost of relocation and reconstruction in the Negev Desert. A complete cutoff of U.S. aid and intelligence support would be Israel's price for failing to sign an agreement, and there was even the hint of economic sanctions. Although it is doubtful that Arial Sharon would have relented, as he did in Gaza, the current prime minister, a popular Labor party leader, did not need much arm-twisting. The accord was historic. All three parties shared the Nobel Peace Prize the next year for their efforts. The Palestinian Authority even took steps to discourage the "resistance" groups, who normally intensified their bombings and Fedayeen attacks whenever peace seemed eminent. These groups preferred war with Israel, and they had always been able to control the debate with well-timed violence. Not this time. There was a noticeable decline in attacks as the withdrawal drew close, and everyone held their breath.

In late 2014, the first settlements were emptied in model fashion. Tractor trailers pulled up to street curbs, contents were loaded, and the convoys then proceeded under military escort across the Green Line and on to temporary housing in the Negev. The neatly manicured neighborhoods were subsequently looted, vandalized and (in some cases) burned to the ground by the mobs that converged immediately as the last trucks left the gates. The next phase of evacuations was far more chaotic, with clashes between the Israeli Defense Forces (IDF) and Palestinians eager to "reclaim their land" (as the newspapers put it). Even the Palestinian police force, mandated with preventing the destruction of property that was earmarked for political cronies, was unable to deter the crowds, who surged over the fences and provoked the IDF into defending themselves with deadly force.

The political fallout was spectacular. The evacuations were put on hold, and entire West Bank communities lived under siege as international parties attempted to negotiate a solution. The Palestinian Authority would not accept an incursion by the IDF into their territory, even for the purpose of evacuating persons and property. It was strongly suspected, however, that the real interest of the PA was in the property itself, even as several thousand settlers were effectively being held hostage by the mobs outside the gates.

The United States military was forced to step in and coordinate evacuations from the remaining settlements. The IDF was ordered to stand down. In fact, the Americans insisted on the abandonment of Israeli Air Bases and military installations until the operation was complete, as a guarantee of their own safety. In February, the first convoy of Humvees, APCs and cargo trucks with U.S. insignias rumbled through the abandoned highways in the West Bank that were originally intended as sheltered expressways for settlers to commute back and forth into Israel. The first several evacuations had reasonable success. The Jews were loaded onto the cargo trucks carrying suitcases to be whisked away. Some wore yellow "Star of David" displays on their clothing as a protest. There was a great deal of anger among the settlers, who did not want to lose their possessions or be displaced. Some had to be physically subdued.

The Palestinian terrorist groups soon began to catch on to the modus operandi of the Americans. Sniper fire into the settlements became more effective, as were the landmines that somehow materialized on roads that appeared quite safe as the military vehicles were passing over them on their way into the settlements. Humvees began going up in flames, but the Americans limited their response to simply extracting the bodies and then fleeing with abandon. The military was under strict orders from the Rodham Administration to maintain as low a profile as possible.

One week earlier, and the day before Captain Pat Ridley arrived in Israel, a most embarrassing situation for the United States occurred in a medium-sized settlement not far from Jerusalem. It was being called the "Menora incident" after the name of the community where things went so horribly. In this case, the soldiers attempting to clear the community of all residents had wilted somewhat under brazen Palestinian fire from the surrounding buildings. Strict procedures were not followed to the letter and a certain contingent of well-armed settlers eluded their detection. It was determined afterwards that there had been a bomb shelter beneath the streets that was unknown to military planners, in which the group of about two dozen men hid with a veritable arsenal of weaponry and ammunition.

The soldiers who participated in the evacuation later reported that there was nothing out of the ordinary that day. Women and children were crying, as usual, and there was the ubiquitous horde of Palestinians, many in black masks, clamoring at the security fences, waiting for the Americans to leave. Two settlers, a man and a woman were killed at different ends of the complex by sniper fire, and six people, including a child and two soldiers, were injured during the course of evacuation. A grenade was hurled at one of the vehicles on the way out of the gates, but it caused more damage to the crowd that it fell back into, than to the occupants. All of the Humvees had been stripped of their .50 caliber machine guns, as ordered by the Rodham Administration (so as to appear less menacing to the Palestinians) with the exception of the designated lead and trailing vehicles. The gunner on the rear Humvee was ordered down, however, as the mob closed in behind with a barrage of rocks and bullets, then began to descend on the presumably deserted settlement like ants on candy. No one in the convoy saw what was happening behind them.

The Israelis who chose to martyr themselves had quickly taken positions at the east and central areas of the complex as the convoy was departing. They knew the neighborhood well and had the advantage of choosing the most strategic points from which to stage their defense. The victorious throngs swelling into the community had no idea what awaited them.

No one, including the masked men shooting their AK-47s in the air in celebration, noticed the bearded snipers lying prone just over the peaks of rooftops with skull caps and rifle barrels barely visible, or those that crouched inside of houses feeling the blood of *Haganah* forefathers rushing through their veins. Arab teenagers tore through the complex, spray-painting slogans urging death to the 'Jewish pigs' on formerly spotless walls, and racing to be the first to break windows and urinate on living room carpets. As the mass of people descended on the rows of houses, police officers took up guard outside the best residences, as a warning to vandals. The rest of the community might be demolished by the mob, but these houses now belonged to the *Fatah* party, and they would stay unblemished.

The melee was in full swing when the first sniper shots rang out. At first they did not cause much notice, since most assumed it was coming from their own Kalashnikov-brandishing gunmen. Then people began to notice that the masked gunmen were not firing, but rather falling over dead, having been picked off like fish in a barrel by mysterious snipers. Panic ensued, as reality set in, and people scattered. Those that stayed in the streets ripped off their masks and threw off their *keffiyahs*, in order to get a better look at what was happening. They were cut down where they stood. Others, who ran into houses to take cover, were met with booby-trapped explosives that mangled torsos and sheared off limbs.

Those who could still run fled in sheer terror. Arabs that, only minutes earlier, were cheering their own snipers' clever efforts to put bullets in the backs of Israeli children, were now watching their neighbors writhing on the pavement or laying silent in the fields. It was estimated that the well prepared attack cost the lives of an estimated eighty Palestinians in the first twenty minutes that afternoon; although the damage could have been far worse had the Israeli snipers not limited their primary targets to those carrying weapons.

As word got around, Fedayeen gunmen rushed to the scene, drawn from Hamas, al-Fatah, Islamic Jihad and even the PFLP. Several dozen were cut down as they attempted to breach the bare expanse between the fence and the streets, which had been constructed for just that purpose. Many more waited till after dark, but they were not any more successful. The barrage of bullets and shrapnel from the Palestinian community, concentrated as it was into the center of the encircled enclave probably resulted in little more than the death of their own via stray bullets and misplaced salvos. By dawn, another eighty bodies of the most rash and ambitious laid strewn across the field and street on all sides of Menora. There were even a few hanging from the fence, with their belts having snagged the heavy mesh wiring as they fell back from the force of the bullet, creating a grotesque and humiliating spectacle for the Arabs.

Over the course of the day, mortars and rockets fell within the complex, although few dared to brave another charge over the fence just yet. As darkness fell again, bulldozers were brought in to clear the fences, and mobile barriers were erected to slowly encroach the open distance that had worked so effectively to the Israeli advantage. At dawn the rockets began again. Sidewalks and streets slowly disintegrated into rubble. Green, weed-controlled yards became muddy craters, and the houses that provided shelter to the hated *Yehud* defenders caved into piles of splinters, sheetrock and glass. A fire started at the west end of the complex. Palestinian snipers began to score their first hits against the enemy, and the crowds, who materialized again toward the end of that afternoon, cheered as the first hated Jew was relentlessly cut down while crawling out of a house that had taken a direct shelling. Children boldly threw rocks toward Menora, though they all fell harmlessly short.

Finally, after darkness fell for a third night, a flood of Fedayeen poured into what was left of the settlement across the narrowed gap, yelling "Allah Akbar" at the top of their lungs and "Death to the Jew." Grenade blasts took down some, but they were determined. They overran houses around the edge of Menora and gradually pressed inward. Ironi-

cally, dozens were killed by friendly fire that night as tightly stretched
nerves snapped much too quickly. Occasionally there would be a cry of
victory as the body of an infidel was discovered, but more often than that,
there would be a violent explosion followed by horrendous moans, as the
defenders refused to be taken alive – with the exception of one badly injured young man, bleeding to death from stumps that used to be limbs,
and quickly stomped to death by the mob.

As the night went on, there were random shootings across Menora,
with the Fedayeen prowling the devastated streets among distorted shadows cast among the mangled buildings. There were still Jews roaming
among them, picking off the Arab invaders who weren't mistakenly shot
by their own.

The next morning, there were another 136 Arab corpses mixed in
among sixteen dead Jews. No sign of anyone else was immediately visible beneath the rubble. Efforts were undertaken to clear the debris, lasting
the rest of the day. Cautious gunmen peered warily into each nook and
cranny as it was exposed by the heavy machinery. Only one other Israeli
was discovered (half of him, anyway) before the sun set.

That night all was quiet, and the next day the lieutenants of the resistance, the ones who direct the violence from afar, giving bombs to children, along with religious admonishment, began to appear at the site, their
faces covered and under heavy guard as they stood on top of the largest
heaps of rubble with Palestinian flags. Cheered by the people, they
claimed victory over the Jew and assured the crowd that the Americans
were behind the fiasco.

Two months before, the same people had celebrated the Hamas gunmen that infiltrated the same Jewish settlement and slaughtered the better
part of two families. Only the previous week, they cheered a suicide
bombing that left twenty-eight dead commuters on the number 9 Egged
passenger bus in Tel Aviv. Now they wondered aloud how it was that the
"dirty" Jews could be as soulless as to inflict such suffering on others.

Yet, there were two Jewish infidels still alive beneath the demolished
community, quite intact and hiding in the very same bunker from which
they had staged their defense, undiscovered by those swaggering above
their heads. They spent their time praying and reading from the Torah,
waiting for the right time to act.

Their hand was forced, however, when the bunker was discovered by
workmen as the sun was beginning to set late in the afternoon. The workers, who called for guns, were dead by the time the masked gunmen arrived. These too were dispatched by a couple of grenades and automatic-
weapons blasts. The last two settlers crawled out of the stairway and into
adjoining houses, armed to the teeth. Another two dozen Arabs were
killed and many more wounded by the time the last settler went up in a

ball of flame after a lucky shot triggered the belt of explosives around his waist.

Outrage at the Americans reached a fever pitch in a world unmoved by the Islamic terror that claimed tens of thousands of innocents each year. The United Nations held a special session to universally condemn what had happened at Menora and to hold the United States entirely responsible for the events that left over three hundred Palestinians dead. The pleas from the Ambassador, who protested that his military could not adequately search a community when it was under sniper fire, fell on deaf ears. It was the job of the Americans to oversee the settlement evacuations and, as was the custom, the world was only interested in the matter in as much as blame could be assigned to the United States. President Hillary Rodham issued a strong apology, and several commanding officers were relieved of their duties, including the captain in charge of the company that was last out of the gates that fateful afternoon.

So it was that Captain Pat Ridley found himself in command of a company of soldiers, forty men and twenty women, in the same light infantry battalion that attempted to liberate Menora for the Palestinian cause. He knew absolutely no one in the entire battalion, not even the lieutenant colonel, who had also been hastily inserted in place of her deposed predecessor. He was in a strange land with a group of strangers, whose lives were in his hands. Other than a few lieutenants, the only officer who wasn't new to the battalion was a major, in command of the other company. Ridley was third in the line of succession, with no premonition of what that would soon mean to the lives of so many.

The bitter resentment of the Palestinians fueled a mood of desperation over the few remaining evacuations. Rumors of vengeance were running high, and no one in the region was talking about the wonderful peace that was sure to follow the Israeli withdrawal from the newly established State of Palestine. The Army was racing against the terrorists, hoping to finish their job before an effective insurgent attack could be organized against one of their operations. At the same time, however, the politicians in Washington were scrambling for spin control, and there was intense pressure on the military to avoid aggressive maneuvering in the field. Heavily armed fighting vehicles were banned from the convoys. The few remaining .50 caliber machine guns were stripped from the MedEvacs, Humvees and even some of the armored personnel carriers (APCs) as well, since they were so visible on top of the vehicles. The disgruntled troops took the guns down, but many simply hid them, along with adequate ammunition, inside the carriers. There was a near mutiny when it was suggested that M-16 rifles be left back at the base as well, but fortunately the brass knew where to draw the line, for once.

This was Ridley's third evacuation in the week since he had arrived. Despite the concern in Washington over each settlement being swept completely clean by the evacuating force, the soldiers were not able to implement the full policy without placing their lives at extreme risk. There quickly developed on the ground the same disconnect between theory and practice so common on the part of America's political leaders and intelligentsia. The intensity of the Palestinian mobs outside the gates ensured that operations were hasty affairs, whereby the armored APCs would attempt to shield the cargo trucks and other vehicles as they rumbled down the interior streets of the settlements, picking up anyone who remained. The local security forces were usually the happiest to see them. They were not prepared to hold back the sort of assault that beset Menora, and there was a great deal of anxiety that they might be overrun before the Americans arrived.

Despite the snipers and suicide runners, Ridley had not lost a single soldier in the first two operations. He studied maps of each settlement in the days prior to the evacuations and planned strategy accordingly, skillfully using the vehicles and buildings to block off entire areas from hostile fire while they were being loaded. It was the job of the battalion commander, however, to map out the best route across hostile territory and coordinate security along the way. Although knowing that he was pushing the envelope, Ridley lobbied hard for mounting the machine guns back onto the roofs of the Humvees, and for the presence of heavy armored fighting vehicles. The lieutenant colonel had smiled at him, as if he were a child, and told him to improve his attitude. "We're not at war, you know, Captain."

Their mission that day was to make a last sweep through the Benjamin region, to the north and west of Jerusalem. This was further away than Menora, which had been only a few kilometers outside the Green Line. Originally, there had been 20,000 optimistic Israelis living in about thirty settlements that were scattered like islands in a sea of Islamic hatred. The Army estimated that about 1,000 people were left, mostly security staff and their families.

The light infantry battalion hit the Green Line early in the morning with two companies of sixty soldiers apiece, about a third of whom were female. The slimmed down unit (a product of tenacious defense cuts) also consisted of twelve LAV APCs, two MedEvacs, two large cargo trucks and twenty-four Humvees. The lead APC was also a mine sweeper and had heavier armor than the others. The lieutenant colonel traveled in the vehicle right behind that one. The cargo trucks were the least protected, but Ridley had required that two armed soldiers ride with the driver for protection. He allowed them to draw straws for the duty that no one wanted.

The convoy roared unopposed across the abandoned highways for about forty-five minutes before pulling into the small Ofra settlement, which was their easternmost destination. About a hundred frightened people were huddled into just four of the houses at the nearest edge of the community, and they insisted that there was no one else left, although the captain sent a few Humvees around to make sure. As they were loading, Ridley noticed that several cars had pulled up on the main road that they had just come down, which was fairly devoid of buildings along the long empty stretch. The cars turned back in the direction that the convoy was now heading in, just as it left. Ridley saw them again each time the battalion stopped to load settlers, as the morning progressed. The occupants were keeping their distance.

Things began to go badly when they got to Bet El, just north of Ramallah. Smoke was rising from the far end of the complex as they pulled through the gates. The lieutenant colonel immediately ordered a platoon of Ridley's down to the area to check it out, as the rest began to execute the evacuation plan. Unlike the other settlements that morning, there were large numbers of angry Palestinians in dark garb outside the security fence that ringed the community. They were wailing, shaking their fists, throwing rocks, and encouraging their children to do the same.

About 250 badly shaken people were left in the settlement. They had their cars loaded and ready to go. The soldiers explained that the policy discouraged civilian vehicles. If problems occurred during the ride out, their safety could not be guaranteed. The few remaining children were parceled out to the APCs, but not many of the drivers elected to leave their packed cars. The officers didn't mind, because they were taking on more passengers than they had anticipated. There were about 1,500 so far and they still had to clean out the Talmon settlements to the west.

Ridley's platoon reported back from reconnaissance at about the same time that the snipers started shooting. Two Humvees came screeching around the corner. Three had been sent, but the third wasn't with them. He could see that the sergeant in the lead vehicle was yelling, and he ran over to it while keeping his head low. Just as he approached, there was a huge explosion from around the corner.

Ridley looked up to see an awful sight. The third Humvee came coasting slowly down the street, completely engulfed in flames. Even the tires were on fire. It wobbled, jumped a curb and careened into a house, as the crowd outside the gates cheered. Ridley knew that he had just lost his first four soldiers to an anti-tank rocket. He dropped his head, but managed to hold down the sickening urges in his stomach.

His sergeant was completely pale and gripped the officer's arm. "They're overrunning the yard, Captain! They've got enough firepower to take us all out!"

There was sheer terror in the man's voice. Ridley was having trouble digesting everything that was happening. He felt like he might be about to pass out. He straightened up and began walking over to the burning vehicle as if to collect his thoughts, while taking deep breaths. The fire extinguisher was still intact below the door. Ridley detached it and sprayed down the inside of the cabin. Charred bodies and body parts littered the interior with an awful stench. Nothing was alive.

Reality hit the captain hard as he reached in to collect the only two dog tags that he could find, yanking them from the smoking flesh of their owners. He put them in the front pocket of his uniform and turned around with a crispness that contrasted well with the slightly dazed manner in which he had approached the vehicle. It was a defining moment for the captain, and the confidence and control that he now exuded was not lost on those watching him.

He directed the rest of the maneuvers with an impressive coolness, ordering several of his soldiers out of their vehicles and placing them in supporting positions behind the convoy to provide cover against the unanticipated front. Minutes felt like hours. Soon, he heard the sound of M-16's behind him and radioed the lieutenant colonel that they were out of time. Needless to say, there would be no house-to-house search for anyone looking to do harm to the militants that were presently threatening them with annihilation – or the mob of people outside the gate, livid with bloodlust and cheering every volley of sniper fire.

All of the troops were back in the vehicles and all of the vehicles were in single-file position, with the exception of the lost Humvee. Ridley was in the front seat of the last vehicle in the convoy and in radio contact with the commanding officer, as they barreled over the gate and through the gauntlet of bottles, rocks and small-arms fire. The soldiers had been told to stand down by the lieutenant colonel, so the bullet-resistant glass windows were raised, making the temperature inside the cabins even worse. Ridley happened to be in the only Humvee with a .50 caliber still mounted to the top, but he directed that no one take the gunner's position, since they were under orders not to fire.

Three civilian cars were ahead of Ridley's vehicle, so he had a good view of what happened next, as they were forced to slow down to make a hard turn. A masked man emerged from a doorway and calmly sprayed the inside of the passenger car in front of them with automatic weapons fire, as if he were cleaning it out with a hose. As the Humvee had done earlier, the vehicle continued coasting, gliding slowly past the turn and onto a sidewalk.

"Good God!" said the sergeant sitting next to him.

"Run that animal over and keep driving," the Captain growled through his teeth.

The sergeant readily obliged and the Humvee made a speed bump out of the gunman. As they took the turn, Ridley could see that no one was moving in the car. "Just keep driving... there's nothing we can do."

Once they were on the highway, the colonel radioed to say that they were going to be taking the bypass around Ramallah and heading straight for Jerusalem, rather than continuing northwest to the Talmon settlements. They had picked up more civilians than was anticipated to that point, and did not have the capacity for anymore evacuations. Ridley could tell by her voice that she was also shaken by what had happened and wanted to regroup back inside the Green Line. She was also in no mood to listen to the major's protests that the new route had not been secured.

The road south was built specifically to bypass the Palestinian areas of Ramallah and Betunia, which were quite hostile to Jewish commuters trying to get down into Jerusalem. The four lanes were built with barbed wire, concrete barriers and buffer zones on either side, although it was not entirely impermeable, as several unfortunate drivers found out over the years. As it turned out, however, the most vulnerable piece of the highway (at least to this convoy) was a section that ran as an overpass to another main road that was used by the Palestinians.

The force of the explosion rattled the vehicles, some of which came to a controlled stop, but with the others barreling into them. The pavement was still shaking even as Ridley managed to get his boots onto it after pushing his sergeant out ahead of him. He ran towards the front of the column, calling to no avail over the radio for the colonel. As he got closer, he could see that a huge section of the road had collapsed, taking the lead APC and the colonel's APC down with it. Another Humvee was teetering on the brink, with one wheel hanging over the side.

Looking down, he could see that it was no accident, of course. Three of the supporting pillars were gone, but a charge on the fourth had failed and was clearly visible wrapped around the base. There was movement below. The armored vehicle was on its side like a beached whale and a Humvee was completely upside down next to it, with the wheels still spinning. It looked as if it had landed on its nose and toppled over. Ridley could see people trying to crawl out of each.

The vehicles were roughly twenty feet below, but there was no clear path down. The broken side that Ridley was on had been cleanly sheared. Obviously no one was across the gap, where the rubble was more layered due to the failed explosive charge. Ridley stood in silence for a few seconds, pondering various recovery scenarios, until the major came up beside him.

"I'm thinking that we can hoist them up with winches," suggested the captain.

"Yeah, that's about all we've got."

As the men pulled the teetering Humvee back onto the bridge, the officers ordered others into position where the cables on the front could be dropped. Ridley went back to secure the rear of the convoy while the major handled the recovery. There was no way to leave the highway at that point, or go forward, of course. Ridley began organizing the vehicles into the proper sequence for traveling back the way they came when he heard rifle fire coming from the head of the column. Leaving a small contingent to hold the rear, he made his way back toward the front, ordering his people to mount any .50 calibers they might be carrying.

There was a firefight going on where the recovery operation was taking place. Nine of the injured had been brought up so far, including the lieutenant colonel, who was screaming hysterically. The only dead body hoisted was that of a child, which was placed in the back of Ridley's Humvee. The captain learned that twelve soldiers remained below, including the major who had gone down to assist, but all were relatively healthy (Ridley calculated that five others must have died on impact, along with several civilians). They were trying to take cover behind the vehicles, but were exposed to incoming fire, as snipers could be seen further down each side of the road. The soldiers at the top had the advantage of position, with the concrete barriers providing excellent cover for them to keep the gunmen at bay for the moment as the cables were lowered again.

A mortar shell landed from out of nowhere onto the highway behind Ridley, lifting a civilian vehicle six feet in the air and blowing apart the two civilians standing next to it. At about the same time, two groups of Fedayeen came bursting out of adjacent buildings to the right of those down below, obviously trying to stage a suicide attack. There were about a dozen in all. Ridley lay prone with his head over the side of the gap, looking down on the scene below, but helpless to intervene. Four of the Fedayeen were cut down by M-16 fire, but the others were still charging and closing the gap rapidly.

A female soldier below, with the best vantage, lost her nerve and dropped her weapon. She then ran behind an overturned LAV with the rest, where she pulled a grenade pin and attempted to toss it over the vehicle toward the murderous fanatics. Ridley was vaguely reminded of Carol Mosley Braun's notorious attempt to throw out the first pitch at a baseball game some years back, only this was no laughing matter. The grenade never cleared the top of the LAV. It bounced back into the middle of the unit, where it was oblivious to everyone except the thrower, who responded by curling up in a ball. Ridley scooted back so fast that he nearly lost his helmet over the side.

After the explosion, he looked down on a much different scene. The entire squad had been reduced to a bloody mass of body parts, achieving the sort of military integration that only a feminist could appreciate. What the grenade hadn't done, the Fedayeen would surely finish. Ridley could see that the major was the only one still moving. He was looking up, yelling and gesturing for the captain to abandon what was left and "get the hell out of here." A burst of automatic weapons fire from the Palestinians made the matter academic and the major's body went slack. As the Fedayeen overran the area, Ridley dropped a grenade below and slid back. He was on his feet and walking away as the blast sounded.

He assessed the convoy, where another mortar round had taken out two additional vehicles. They were being decimated in place. The colonel was shuffled into a MedEvac with a dozen other victims. She wasn't coherent enough to be helpful and Ridley was relieved when they finally took off, along with a Humvee escort, as it eliminated any ambiguity over who was in command.

The highway was specifically built to block access to and from the surrounding areas. This was particularly true for the bypass, which ran through a dangerous urban district. Clearly their only option was to go back the way they had come. It was not a graceful retreat however, as a few more mortar shells hit the column before it could leave. Ridley ordered the victims pulled from the vehicles and everything else abandoned, including at least two passenger cars with blown tires from shrapnel. It was not a pretty sight, and it got uglier as they moved slowly back up the road to the split with highway 455, where they intended to turn west toward the Talmon settlements along their original course.

In some places, the walls were high enough to block visibility, but others were no more than mesh fencing and razor wire, which did a poor job of blocking bullets. Unlike the Israelis, the Americans did not have experience with sealing off these throughways and it was apparent that the Palestinians had taken advantage of that and compromised the route. Small-arms fire and a couple of roadside blasts began steadily knocking out the vehicles, except for the LAVs, which were holding up rather well. One of the cargo trucks had to be abandoned when a roadside mine scored a direct hit underneath the cab, destroying it along with the crew. The occupants of the other vehicles were extracted as best as could be managed under the withering fire along with any weapons or salvageable ammunition.

From his position near the rear of the column, Ridley ordered that all .50 caliber gunners fire at will from vehicle roofs and that M-16's be hung out open windows to provide additional support for the convoy. Sharp bursts of fire were directed toward the buildings that flew past, not very effective at killing, but discouraging return fire nonetheless. The gun at the top of Ridley's vehicle pounded out a staccato rhythm and the empty shells casings made pinging sounds as they bounced off the roof. The sound stopped abruptly, at one point, and the gunner slumped back down into the vehicle with a hole through his helmet and head. Ridley nodded to the corporal sitting next to the dead man and she immediately pushed the body out of the way and stood up to fill the breach.

The battered convoy made the turn onto highway 455, finding that the ambush tapered considerably as they left the urban landscape of Ramallah. The open rural area on the road to Talmon was deemed safe enough by the captain to stop and assess the situation after a few miles. He also sent a couple of Humvees up the road to scout out their egress. A few more cars had to be abandoned, with the occupants consolidated into the other vehicles at the expense of any cargo. Ridley also took advantage of the lull to rearrange the convoy, trying to maximize the effectiveness of what was left. He gave the order to proceed and radioed his situation back to base.

The first thing requested back to him was a report on the condition of the colonel. Ridley relayed the frequency for the MedEvac unit. After a minute or so, the call came back that there was no contact. The captain switched the channel and tried as well, but was unable to reach either the colonel's vehicle or the Humvee that was sent as an escort. Ridley was perplexed. He had assumed that they were both safe inside the Green Line by that time.

"Look up Captain!" His sergeant was pointing in a rather anxious manner to an approaching Humvee that looked to be in bad shape. It was one of the two that had been sent ahead to scout out the settlements. There was no sign of the other. It came to a stop about thirty feet away and Ridley could see that there were no soldiers inside. He began to get that same sick feeling in the pit of his stomach. There had been ten soldiers and two civilians in those vehicles.

He got out of the Humvee and drew his sidearm, pointing it straight in front of him at the driver. Approaching, he could see that there were three occupants, two of whom wore masks. The third, sitting in back, was an elderly Jewish man, white as a sheet and visibly trembling. At his head was an AK-47.

"Where are my men?" asked Ridley, pointing his weapon right into the chest of the driver.

The terrorist in back shook the old man, who blubbered something in Arabic. Ridley realized that he was meant to be the interpreter. The terrorist said something back, looking directly at the captain as he spoke.

"They were taken prisoner," said the hostage, whose eyes were telling a different story. Ridley noted that he was not one of the civilians originally in either vehicle that left the convoy.

"Have they?" asked the captain, eyeballing the large amount of blood inside the vehicle. The terrorist shook the old man, who repeated the question. Nothing was said back.

"They've got an ambush up ahead. There's no getting through. They want you to surrender your weapons." The old man quickly repeated what he had said to the masked man, who nodded in agreement.

"What is the situation at the Talmon settlements?"

The old man winced. "I'm the last one left. They came and butchered everyone else. My family…" He hung his head sobbing.

Ridley's heartbeat was thundering in his ears, as the gravity of the situation pressed down on him. So absorbed was he that he barely noticed the shooting and yelling behind him. When he did, he backed away slowly from the vehicle and did not turn his head until he was well away. Three of his soldiers came along the side of the convoy next to a ditch, unceremoniously dragging a fourth who was wounded in the leg and shouting in Arabic.

"What the hell happened?" asked one of the sergeants who had been covering Ridley.

"This guy just unloaded a full magazine into a civilian vehicle!" shouted one of the men. "He wiped out a whole family! We took him down before he could do more damage."

The injured man wore a private's insignia and he looked up and leered at Ridley with dark, glistening eyes. The name on his tag said "Akbar." He was obviously a trusted Muslim-American translator for the unit, perhaps a Pillar immigrant showing less than anticipated gratitude for the country that welcomed him, Ridley speculated wryly. "You have a choice to make, Captain" said Akbar with a thick accent.

"It was you who gave away our position, wasn't it?" Ridley demanded, not bothering to hide his disgust. Something had seemed very wrong about the whole series of events. They were not supposed to be on the Ramallah bypass, yet there was a neat little trap laid there.

"You are being asked to lay down your arms. If so, you and your men will live. This is not your country. These are not your people. This is not your war. This…"

"…is not your day," finished the captain, jamming his boot hard into the man's wound. The traitor fell to the ground howling in pain. The other soldiers laughed nervously, but the terrorists in the Humvee started yelling and beating the old man. Ridley whipped around and held up his hand. "Stay here," he ordered the men around him. He walked back to the Humvee, stepped inside and picked up the radio.

"This is Captain Pat Ridley with Blue Unit Nine in the green zone."

The reply came back after a few seconds. "Go ahead, Captain."

"We need air support in…" Ridley paused while he spread his map out beside him on the seat. "Three clicks off tango four delta four. We've got a situation."

"Switch to channel yankee one-nine-six please, Captain."

Ridley hit a button and turned the knob on the radio. He knew that he could speak more freely on the secure channel. "Right, the situation is not good. We're stuck on a highway that goes nowhere in one direction and into some sort of ambush in the other. We've lost several vehicles so far, thanks to a broken arrow. The bridge behind us is completely blown. We either need air support or a heavy combat unit to clear the path ahead."

"Negative, Captain. We've gotten word of what you're looking at up ahead. You won't be able to go through. They've got rockets and barriers set up. How long can you stay in your present position?"

"Not long." Ridley was becoming aware of the muffled thumping of mortar rounds behind the convoy, and knew it was just a matter of minutes before the enemy had its range. "We need air support. I think they slaughtered the settlers and probably our own reconnaissance."

"Copy that. Hold please."

Washington D.C.

The President was just finishing a late-night staff meeting when the Secretary of Defense got through to her. She had him wait a few minutes longer while she went over final details of the following day's agenda, which included a visit to the White House by a famed antiwar bomber, who had killed a graduate student and injured several others on a college campus in Wisconsin in 1970, before turning himself in a few years earlier for a slap on the wrist and immediate offers to teach at several renowned universities.

The Secretary explained the situation on the ground to Hillary. A battalion was trapped behind the lines in Palestine with about 1500 Israeli evacuees. The officer in charge was just a captain (and a Reservist at that). The original commanding officer had been killed or captured after her MedEvac unit was ambushed in the Talmon area. The Palestinians had apparently breached the perimeters of the Talmon settlements and overran them, killing around one-hundred Israeli residents, although some had been able to escape by car. The Fedayeen were waiting for the convoy and expected to turn it into pulp if it attempted to pass through.

"We can't let that happen," said Hillary.

"No, no we can't," said the Secretary, who sounded quite relieved. "I've got several Apache gunships that can level that area and clear the way, and there's also some heavy armor that we can…"

"No! Absolutely not!" shrieked the President. "You'll do no such thing! This is a diplomatic matter, not a war zone. We aren't going to have anymore embarrassing international incidents right now… and we're certainly not going to start a war! Do you understand?"

"Yes ma'am… sir…"

"I didn't nominate you for your job so that you could start acting all gung ho and macho, Mr. Secretary. Please remember that you're a civilian."

"Yes sir… ma'am…"

"When you say 'level that area' you're talking about killing a lot of innocent people, including children. You may not mind having that on your conscience, but I do! What are our other options?"

After a pause, the Secretary continued, with the tension now back in his voice. "One of the men in the unit was working for the other side, an Arab. He's offered up an ultimatum of surrender."

"Don't call him an Arab, Mr. Secretary. You don't know who he is."

"With all due respect, I don't think this is the time for political correctness, Madame President. My point is that we have only three options: put up a fight, surrender as requested, or die in place." The irritation was beginning to come through and Hillary didn't press the issue. She massaged her forehead with her fingers for a few seconds, while trying to reach a decision.

"Will they be killed if they surrender?"

After a pause, the Secretary answered. "I don't think so, but there is the matter of the 1,500 or so civilians…"

"Well, they aren't American are they?"

"Some may have American citizenship, I really…"

"You know what I mean, Sir. We aren't going to start a war, and we can't afford to have American blood spilled for non-Americans – it just wouldn't be wise, politically – so our only option is to tell them to… uh… what is called?"

"Stand down?"

"Yes, that's it. We'll start negotiations for their release immediately. Tell them that they'll get a hero's welcome back in the States!"

Negev Airbase, Israel

Tensions were running high at the Israeli base. Word had gotten out about the plight of the evacuees and the American battalion that was originally charged with their protection – so much for secure radio channels. The Army guard detail had to be beefed up at all points as several Israeli pilots were trying to get back onto the base to reclaim their aircraft. The American commander on base was shorthanded. Even so, he had to make sure that his own crews were ready as well, in case the call came back to provide the requested air support to the lost battalion. Several rotary craft including the AH-1 Cobras and BlackHawks were sitting on the field with pilots and crew in place, as were several fighters at the end of the runway. B-1 bombers were a phone call away, as well, if needed.

The commander, who was looking out the window of his temporary office near the top of the tower, heard the conversation start up again on the radio behind him, and bent down to hold his ear close to the speaker.

Highway 455, West Bank, Palestine

Five minutes had gone by. That was Pat Ridley's estimate anyway, based on the fact that it felt like five hours. The mortaring behind him went through several cycles during that time. A minute or so of silence would be followed by two or three rounds, always closer than the last. He was sweating to such an extent that the windows were fogging, even in the dry desert air, but he didn't want to open the door. The men outside the truck were staring at him, not sure of what was happening in there. He knew their nerves were on edge. Occasionally, one of the convoy's civilians would come up to his vehicle at the head of the column and scratch at the window. Ridley would respond by frowning and shaking his head until they went away.

Finally the radio came back to life. "Blue Unit Nine, do you copy?" "Yes."

"Request for air support denied. It's all over, Captain. You did the best you could."

"Are you ordering us to turn ourselves over?" asked Ridley incredulously.

"It appears to be your only option."

Ridley snapped. "I've got more than a thousand people here who are going to be massacred if you don't get someone down here now!" The mortars had started falling again.

Ridley didn't need to wait for an answer. Out of frustration, he kicked the radio, then the dashboard. He got out of the truck, slamming the door behind him. Without saying a word, he marched down the line, for the ostensible purpose of counting the vehicles yet again. He knew that no matter how old he lived, he would never face a decision of this magnitude, on which the lives of more than a thousand others turned. Would they all be dying together, or it would it just be the civilians? He looked at the people as he passed. There were men in shirtsleeves looking back at him, sheltering their wives in their arms. The women were holding their children's heads against sweat-soaked blouses. Everyone was terrified.

Near the end of the column was the car that the rogue Army private targeted. Some of its windows were shattered, others were spattered with blood. The smell of smoke still hung vaguely in the air. Four bodies were in the car. In the front seat, a man was stretched across his wife, where he had obviously thrown himself in an attempt to protect her. The woman's eyes were wide open in death. Their murdered children sat in the back, still in their seatbelts.

Captain Pat Ridley had his mind made up before reaching this point in the convoy, but what he saw stiffened his resolve all the more. He gave a crisp turn on the heel of his boot and jogged quickly back to the front of convoy, where he couldn't help but notice the anxiety on the faces of his men, as well as Private Akbar's smirk. The man was standing up by the side of a Humvee again, using it for support. A bandage was tied around his leg. He knew that he was in the catbird's seat, despite the painful wound, and turned his head to give a grin to those in the commandeered vehicle a few yards ahead. "So, what's it going to be, Captain, life or death?" he asked confidently, but turning slightly nonetheless to shield his injured leg from the captain's boot.

Ridley grabbed the man roughly by the collar and hauled him over to the back of his own Humvee, where he pulled open the door so that the other could see the body of the Israeli child pulled from the wreck under the highway bridge. "What do you think of this?"

"*Dar al-Haarb*," Akbar sneered, with no detectable shame. "This is an infidel in the house of Islam, *Dar al-Islam*. Your people will suffer the same fate if you do not submit."

Ridley didn't respond. He shut the back of the truck and then dragged the injured man back over to the other Humvee, where the two terrorists sat disagreeably with their hostage. They went right up to the side of the vehicle.

"What is that?" he asked, pointing to the old man.

"It is the *Intifada*, the great 'shaking off'." Akbar laughed nervously.

"Well then, shake off this!" In one swift move, Ridley calmly pulled his sidearm and put a bullet neatly between Akbar's eyes which were just beginning to widen in astonishment.

All hell broke loose. The driver screamed, while his companion hesitated for a split second then fired a quick burst into the hostage, but not before Ridley saw the look of admiration in the old man's eyes. He might have been the only one to die that day with a smile on his face. The three soldiers standing nearby immediately opened up on the Humvee with automatic weapons fire, killing the occupants and pulverizing the vehicle. Ridley held his hand up to stop them as he tried jumping away from the flying glass fragments and metal splinters.

He sent the men back to their positions then called for his two lieutenants and the two enlisted men with the highest seniority. Under their uniforms they were two Hispanics and two whites being led by one black man. It was a diverse group of Americans that spread a map over the hood of the captain's Humvee that afternoon in the dry heat of a hostile

Arab country with the simple goal of making it out alive. They conducted business out of earshot from the rest of the convoy. The option of surrendering their arms to the enemy was not discussed, although Ridley knew that it was probably on the minds of all.

"We've got no choice, Gentlemen" he said matter-of-factly and without regard for proper deference to the female lieutenant. "We're going straight ahead. I want everything staggered in three different columns where possible, so that a mine won't stop the others. I will take the truck by myself to draw the fire, with three Humvees following. The APCs will be behind these, crammed with as many people as possible, then the rest of the Humvees. All cars should be wedged in the middle, although no one needs to be in a car if there's room in an armored vehicle."

The female lieutenant was trembling. Ridley wasn't sure if it was from his order to shoot the line, or rather from the hell they had already gone through. The periodic mortaring wasn't helping anyone's nerves.

"Are you sure, Captain?" asked a sergeant major, an older veteran with two stars over his combat infantryman badge and a look about him that would have brought to mind, in those old enough to remember, a different sort of American fighting man, motivated by honor and sustained by grit – symbolic of what had been left behind on the other side of the 'bridge to the 21st century.'

Ridley knew that this was not a man who made a habit of questioning an officer's orders. He looked directly in the sergeant major's eyes. "The men and women in those two Humvees that we sent out are dead. The people that we are carrying are dead as well, if we turn them over. Is there a chance that we'll be spared if we agree to castration? Yes... but is that how a man is supposed to live?"

The sergeant major held his glance and nodded slowly, as did the others, including the lieutenant, who seemed to be in the process of collecting herself. They would be standing up and marching down the cannon's throat together. The worst that could happen is that they would die with dignity, as fighting men should.

"It's time to stand and deliver."

Ridley straightened up and they shook hands all around under the graying sky, with the captain stepping back from each and saluting. He knew of no other way to convey the respect he felt for each of the others. They finished just as the mortaring began again, this time with a renewed precision and vigor that confirmed the suspicion that they had been under observation for some time. There was truly no turning back now.

Negev Airbase, Israel

The base commander dropped his head for a moment after hearing the news. Was this the United States military? Were these soldiers anymore or had they all transformed into blue-helmeted bull's-eyes that the UN calls 'peacekeepers?' Armies were supposed to fight, not roll over at the first sign of trouble. He looked forward to his retirement, now just eighteen months away.

Reluctantly he got up and made his way to the window. He knew that the pilots and crew were probably listening to the same channel, but he slid the sash open anyway, stuck his head out and drew his hand across his throat to signal that the all engines should be cut and crews disassembled.

Highway 455, West Bank, Palestine

Captain Pat Ridley of Ila, South Carolina sat in the driver's seat of a U.S. Army heavy cargo truck at the head of a doomed military column stretching behind him, knowing that he would soon be dead. He was completely at peace and ready to meet his Maker, proud of the opportunity to stand like a man and die for a righteous cause, as God would want it.

The only thing that gave him a bit of chagrin was that the soldier sitting next to him would not be dying as a man along with him, although he suspected that she would probably go down fighting like one, from what he had seen so far.

Like most military men, Ridley wasn't a fan of having women in combat, even volunteers. His opinion was in no way mitigated by watching a dozen soldiers lose their lives because one of their girls "threw like a girl." Being a life and death situation, combat was not the place for social engineering, such as including women simply for the sake of including women. Having a weaker team member, be it one who cannot carry as much equipment into battle or is not as coordinated, places an inordinate burden or risk on the other members. Since the early days of gender integration in the armed forces, the politicians always lowered the physical requirements in order to make their experiments work. This may not have mattered when it came to peeling a potato, but it had lethal consequences in the field.

He had to admire the guts inside of this corporal, however, the same one that had immediately replaced the fallen gunner in the back of his vehicle as they fled Ramallah He thought he might have to force his lead platoon to draw straws for the most dangerous position in the convoy, but she immediately volunteered and acted as if it were a privilege to ride in a lightly protected behemoth with a an officer hell-bent on a suicide run. Ridley noticed that she was holding rosary beads and a crucifix in hands that were shaking only slightly. The barrel of her M-16 hung out the window and she had an extra magazine clenched between her knees. The other clips were attached to her vest, in case she survived the near certainty of being blown out of the vehicle.

"Can you pull me out of this wreckage if you have to?" growled the captain, casting a disapproving eye at the corporal's light build.

"Probably not, Sir" she said, with a glance of her own. "Looks like you Reservists don't miss too many meals."

The captain turned his head to hide a grin, while revving the engine to pick up speed. He kept an eye in the mirror and on the line of smoke-belching machines that stretched out behind them, arranged three columns across, with the armored transports mostly on the outside to provide spotty protection for the smaller vehicles. Gunners with goggles and brown helmets were perched behind .50 caliber machine-guns on top of the LAVs and some of the Humvees. Everything was moving as planned.

After making the decision that he had, Ridley had ordered everyone to advance about a mile up the road to buy some time. There, he had his platoon leaders arrange the transports while he talked to some of the Israeli settlers. It was obvious that the enemy knew their every move and fully expected them to head due west on highway 455, right into Ayn Qiniya, the Palestinian community straddling the road ahead, and then on to al-Janiyah, outside of Talmon – if they even made it that far. These two areas were where the ambush was certain to be, given that there were buildings from which the terrorists could stage their assault. The Israelis knew, however, of a road that turned off right before Ayn Qiniya and bypassed the heart of the town before meeting the highway again on the other side. There was also the possibility that they could avoid al-Janiyah as well by detouring through the three Talmon settlements, which were arranged like beads on a string with their own private network of roads. One of the Israelis volunteered to ride in the jump seat behind Ridley to provide navigation, but the captain deemed it too dangerous and had him ride in the accompanying Humvee instead, where a signal could be given as a turn approached.

They made the first turnoff just as they were coming up to the outskirts of the first town. The burned out shell of the other lost Humvee was smoldering about seventy yards past the turnoff, with no visible survivors. There was no sign of an imminent ambush, but the town's streets looked empty, which was certainly unnatural in the middle of the day. The convoy took no chances and turned down the dusty side road.

They were halfway around the loop when the first cracks of bullets began echoing around them. Ridley saw a small stream of people moving in their direction from the center of town, where they had expected the convoy. He knew that the Palestinians had been outwitted and had no time to set up effectively from their distant positions, but he was hoping that they did not have the presence to try and cut them off where they were to meet up with the main road again past the other side of town. At the very least, Ridley knew that they would now have hostiles on their tail as they made their way west toward al-Janiyah, confirming that they had passed the point of no return.

The cargo truck finally rumbled to the end of the dusty road, where the Humvee ran out ahead of it and made the right turn, which wasn't hard to guess, given that the other direction ran back into town. There were a few buildings there, but no barriers or rockets. They had certainly dodged a bullet for the time being. It took just under a minute for the final car to fall in line on the highway behind the rest, with nothing but small-arms fire behind them, but there was a report a few minutes later that they were being pursued.

Ridley sent back orders that one of the Humvees, armed with a .50 caliber, was to fall back to the rear and take out anything within range. "Go easy on the ammo," he cautioned, "we don't have much to waste." Periodically over the next several minutes, short and contained bursts of fire could be heard, indicating that they were keeping the wolves at bay for the moment.

The turnoff for the Talmon settlements came well before al-Janiyah and much earlier than Ridley was expecting. The convoy left the highway again and traveled down a long road that wound through dry, dusty fields. There were no buildings to be seen, except remote farms in the distance. They had to make another turn after a few miles, and the gates to the first community loomed ahead.

Talmon looked like something out of a horror movie. The security checkpoint was in shambles. One gate was hanging open and the other was broken off. The bodies of Jewish settlers were swaying from the arch above. They had obviously been bludgeoned to death before being strung up. Ridley was glad that the APCs didn't have windows, but he knew that there were civilians riding in the other vehicles that would be in for a hard time.

The community wasn't deserted altogether, just devoid of its Jewish residents, except for the rows of blood-soaked bodies that lined the curbs. Arab looters, mostly women, were milling about, fighting over suitcase contents and pieces of furniture. They scattered upon seeing the convoy. Ridley guessed that the unfortunate settlers had concentrated themselves in the first few houses closest to the entrance, as was the habit of those in the other communities awaiting evacuation. He expected that the sight of bodies would taper off after a few blocks, which it did. Nor did he see many more Palestinians either, as they were probably a bit shy about penetrating the community too deeply just yet, with fresh memories of Menora.

He noticed in his mirror that one of the cars near the end of the convoy had pulled over and stopped, with a woman running out to embrace the corpse of another young woman. He gritted his teeth. *Get back in the car... get back in the car...* Her husband finally dragged the grieving woman back. Ridley heard the corporal next to him whispering a prayer. They were truly in the belly of the beast, particularly if there was no way out of the back of the last settlement. The women they had passed were no doubt racing back to al-Janiyah to relay word of the convoy's whereabouts to the men there, although they would probably be beaten to the punch by the terrorists trailing from Ayn Qiniya. The enemy would recognize it for what it was – a desperate move by those who knew that additional military support would not be coming.

They rolled on slowly into the second settlement, deserted as well, except for the occasional Arab looter. The houses were empty, but had not yet been vandalized. It reminded Ridley of some movie he once saw where a virus had wiped out all the people. The only other sign of life in the suburban landscape was a few sprinklers – obviously on timers – that sputtered surreally as the trucks went past. He had hoped that there would at least be a few people left alive, but no one rushed out of the buildings to meet them, as they surely would have done. He began to pick up speed as they left the second settlement and entered the final one.

Ridley could see the Palestinian town off in the distance to his right. A lieutenant with binoculars riding in the cab of an APC reported that he could see a few cement barriers set up on the main street, along with piles of tires that were probably soaked with gasoline, ready to be set aflame. It would be a very grim scene indeed if they had to turn around and go back through, particularly with the gunmen from Ayn Qiniya now lurking behind them.

They lost sight of the town again as they penetrated the third community. As with the last, there was no sign of life. Everyone held their breath to see whether or not the promised egress waited at the other end. Ridley got his first clue when they broke out into the open again and he could clearly see fighters and vehicles swelling out of al-Janiyah and rushing west. This meant that there was a road of some sort ahead, which the Palestinians were racing to cut off.

In fact, it was an old construction trail, raised over gullies and running through the open expanse toward the main highway to the west of the Palestinian community. There were two rows of concrete barriers wrapped in razor wire set about ten yards down the trail. Ridley expected that there would probably be the same or worse at the other end, but that couldn't be seen from where they were at the moment. He quickly directed the removal of the obstacles, knowing that every second worked to their enemy's advantage. Most of the concrete sections had thick iron shackles embedded, which provided excellent loops from which to attach winch cables. Since there were no cutters, the razor wire also had to be moved with winches, which was time-consuming.

Finally, the cargo truck was able to pull ahead and flatten what was left. The road was too narrow for three columns, so Ridley ordered that the armored vehicles form behind one another on the side facing the town. They moved forward just as the first rockets came in.

Ridley clinched his teeth. The clock was about to strike midnight for the battered convoy. He could see the Palestinians swarming out of their buildings, moving down the main road toward the point at which the trail intersected it. The head of the trail was still too far to be seen when the first rocket slammed into the side of the cargo truck, instantly kicking up splinters and showering Ridley with shattered glass. The main hold had taken the brunt of the impact, but no one was inside, as the captain knew that the largest truck would be the most popular target.

The original goal was to hit the barriers as hard as possible in a suicidal impact that would hopefully force them out of the way for the vehicles that followed behind. Being the lead vehicle and largest, the big truck would also take on the burden of the ambush. Ridley knew, however, that a hit on any part of the truck other than the cargo hold had an excellent chance of disabling it, either by snapping the driveshaft, knocking out the engine, or killing the driver. He had to pick up as much speed as possible before that happened so that the momentum still had a chance of carrying the truck into whatever was at the end of the trail. If all went well, the obstacles would be cleared enough so that the vehicles behind him might have a chance, assuming they could get past the wreck.

The captain gunned the engine. This was it. He would be heading out in a blaze of glory – with a blonde-haired Catholic by his side no less. Bullets knocked small holes through the tempered glass of the windshield, causing him to flinch and duck his head. The corporal put her knee on the seat and knocked out the cracked windshield with the butt of her M-16 and her foot, as Ridley dodged the glass shards. She then leaned forward, with her elbows on the dash and her weapon hanging out over the hood, and proceeded to hammer out a few rounds with impressive effectiveness.

With the mirrors out, Ridley could no longer see what was happening behind him without turning his head and leaning out the window, which was impractical under the circumstances. He had a very good head of speed built up when he felt the left front wheel go out. He had already lost the rear wheel on that side, so it was a struggle to keep the big truck straight. They were nearing the end of the road – in more ways than one.

From her place on the hood, the corporal threw an empty magazine back into the cab and inserted the one that she had been clutching in her teeth. She locked and loaded the clip just in time to direct a blast of automatic weapons fire into the chest of a Fedayeen, who burst out from behind a roadside scrub brush firing a pistol of some sort, like an Indian attacking a stagecoach in an old Western. The only round he managed to get out slammed into the metal right behind Ridley's head, ringing his ears.

Straining through the distance, Ridley finally caught sight of a double row of concrete barriers that looked similar to what they had cleared behind them. An armed crowd was congregating behind it and around the edges of the area. The corporal was able to drop a few and scatter several others before neatly flipping onto her back and popping in a new magazine, all the while keeping her legs locked inside the cab.

The raised trail dropped to meet the road ahead and Ridley could see that there was room to go around the barriers, but the Palestinians had pulled cars up in places, in an effort to seal off the edges. Houses stood across the highway and stretched off in either direction. It was the perfect trap.

Ridley couldn't resist leaning out of the window to take a last look back at the convoy. Only two of the smaller vehicles lay smoking in the distance, both completely overturned, as they had obviously run off the road after getting hit. He turned back and made a final decision. The parked cars were heavier than the concrete, but they had a much better chance of moving upon impact. Ridley was tempted to run the truck into the mass of gunmen that were gathered on the left, taking as many out with him as he could, but he knew that the remaining vehicles would stand a better chance if he went to the right instead. He turned the wheel.

In some ways the impact was more successful than he had hoped, given that they were not going quite as fast as he would have liked. The two cars on the other side of the fence were not enough to stop the weight of the truck, and careened backwards, flattening the gunmen. The corporal was shot out of the truck like a human cannonball, completely disappearing somewhere in the tangle of buildings and ditches on the other side of the road. Ridley survived the collision thanks to a seatbelt and helmet, but the helmet was knocked down by the steering wheel, breaking his nose and leaving his face numb. At least two fingers on his right hand were grotesquely caught and broken. The truck carried past the ditch and flipped over on top of a crushed car.

Overall, however, the gamble appeared lost. With blood streaming down his face and his right hand all but useless, Ridley left his helmet behind and managed to crawl out of where the truck's windshield had been, just in time to see the smoke rise from an array of Palestinian firepower being brought to bear on the rest of the convoy as it came within range. Gunmen were opening up from a well-situated corner building with automatic weapons, supported by others with shoulder-launched missiles. There was nothing that the captain could do. He didn't even have a rifle, though he would have considered putting a bullet through his own head had he been able to draw his sidearm, rather than watch the terrible devastation of human life.

The sound of the rocket from above was hardly audible over the din of weapons fire, the trial of smoke barely visible, but there was no mistaking the sight of the earth violently lifting up under the Arab fighters as the first Hellfire missile exploded beneath their building. Dirt and body parts flew up in the air then rained down as the ground shook. Stunned, Ridley looked back to see a single Cobra attack helicopter sweeping down with its 20mm gun chewing up the buildings around him. Another missile came slamming in, erupting under another mass of Jihad warriors and scattering the rest. The hostile fire dropped off immediately.

It took a moment for Ridley to gain his bearing. His ears were ringing and the earth was rocking. A bullet round zipped into his protective vest with a thud, bringing him back into focus. He put his head down and raced to the other side of the overturned truck. As he had guessed, it was blocking part of the path that was supposed to be cleared for the other vehicles. The lead Humvee had been attempting to clear the car on the far side of the gap by slamming into it. Ridley could see that the driver had apparently been killed by enemy fire, along with at least one other soldier on the front seat. The civilian who had provided navigation to the team was hunched under the bodies on the floorboard. Several others were crouched down in the back seat as well. Bright red splatter and human tissue coated the inside of the windows on the passenger side.

Ridley opened the door and pulled out the driver's body. He didn't like the idea of leaving a soldier behind on the battlefield, but the concern at the moment was for the living. Oddly enough, the truck was still running, and he slid into the bloody seat, attempting to work the gears with his mangled hand. He finally succeeded in backing up past the next vehicle, which immediately rushed past him and slammed headfirst into the wreck, in an effort to clear it. The obstacle remained, but the civilian car behind it pulled up too quickly, blocking the Humvee from making another run. They were now under fire again, Ridley got out and attempted to direct traffic, telling the Israeli driver to pull over to the other side and holding up his hand to stop the car behind it from filling the gap. This gave the lead Humvee the space to back up and try again.

This time it managed to clear the gap, and the column proceeded to shoot through it. Ridley waited until the first APC rumbled up before raising his hand to allow the car behind him to get back in line. At that moment, some sort of explosive hit the ground behind him, shattering ear drums and spewing an array of shrapnel into Ridley's left arm and through the two-inch crack in the side of his flak vest.

When he regained his senses, he noticed that the tires of the passenger car that he was about to wave in were blown on the driver's side. He could not allow the vehicle to try and shoot the gap now for fear that it wouldn't clear the ditch and wind up blocking the others. He motioned out the three passengers and ordered them into the Humvee. They barely fit in amongst the rest of the traumatized occupants, but pulling out the second body helped matters. There were now ten people crammed into the seats and back cargo area.

The APCs rumbled past, along with rest of the Humvees and passenger cars. The lone Cobra was periodically spraying the Palestinians with its 20mm guns, providing cover for the convoy. Ridley also noticed that the helicopter was drawing a lot of the fire away from them as it swayed back and forth overhead. There were no other choppers visible. He leaned into the Humvee and snatched the radio as best he could with his bad hand, and then ordered the convoy to pull down the road as far as possible before regrouping and then continuing.

An APC was smoking badly on the trail behind him, the only vehicle that wasn't advancing, other than a few empty passenger cars. The captain was hoping that the survivors had been able to find another transport, but he stopped the last moving LAV and had the driver hold while he ran back to check. He would not have gone back for a passenger car, but the APCs, overloaded with around 35 people apiece, were worth checking.

He reached the disabled vehicle just as a rocket flew over his head and into the distance. It was apparent that a missile of some sort had clipped the back end of the vehicle, doing damage both to it and the occupants. Ridley wondered whether the charge had detonated or not. White powder was spread all around, indicating that an extinguisher had been used to put out a fire. At least fifteen people were lying injured among the dead in the back. Anyone else seemed to have found another ride. Ridley turned to motion for the other APC to fall back, but it appeared that the driver had lost her nerve and shot the gap anyway. The vehicles that had made the road were long gone as well, as Ridley had directed.

The captain surveyed the APC to access its drivability. One of the tires was blown off, and the rear axle was mangled. Since the damage appeared localized to the back of the vehicle, Ridley theorized that it might still be drivable, and put it to the test by climbing up into the cab and turning the ignition. It was then that he noticed a female private, hunched down on the floorboards and trembling like a leaf. "Get up!" he snapped. Cautiously she pulled herself up onto the seat, though keeping her head well below the dash. Ridley turned his attention back to the engine.

As he suspected, it was still working. Ridley worked the gears and the vehicle lurched forward a foot or two before stopping with a sudden crunch. The driveshaft was jamming against the rear axle underneath. Ahead of him, he could see the Fedayeen attempting to advance on the lone Humvee, with its civilian occupants faithfully waiting on the captain. He turned to the private, grabbed her by the shirt front and pulled her fully back up into the seat. "Do you see that Humvee up there?" he screamed in her ear.

She nodded meekly, looking like she might burst out crying at any second. Ridley did not adjust the volume. "You will go up to it and drive it out of here! Do you hear me? You will drive those people out of here!"

"Yes, Sir!" The crack of bullets was sounding around them as she jumped down from the truck and ran like hell in the direction of the Humvee. Either she was discovering a bit of fortitude, or she just wanted to get away from him. Most likely it was a little of both. Ridley didn't have time to watch. He reached under the seat for the tool box then jumped down from the cab, still protecting his right hand, which hurt worse then his arm or side.

There was an older man in the back, an Israeli civilian with a polyester shirt, who looked to be in the best shape, despite a blood-soaked scalp. The captain called him out and explained that they needed to go under the truck and try to disconnect the drive shaft from the rear axle. They both slid under the vehicle, where Ridley, unable to work with the wrenches, attempted to direct the other into pulling off bolts and applying pressure as needed. They finally managed to kick the U-joint loose in coordinated fashion, just as another rocket screamed past and into the sparse grove of trees on the other side of the trail.

The vehicle was four-wheel drive and Ridley hoped that freeing the driveshaft from the rear axle would enable it to turn the front axle via the transfer case. Before getting back in the cab, the two men attempted to close the back hatch, which was blown open from the missile's impact. It was too mangled, however, so the men pulled the pins from the side and left it in the desert to keep it from dragging like an anchor, although the back compartment of the carrier was now completely exposed.

Audibly mumbling a sincere prayer, Ridley started the engine again and attempted to move the vehicle forward. It lurched and hesitated then rolled a foot or two before catching again. The rear of the vehicle wasn't cooperating, but Ridley hoped the front wheels could still move them down the road. The cycle of jolts and drags repeated itself in steady fashion as they attempted to close the fifty yards remaining to the highway. Ridley noted with some satisfaction that the Humvee near the exit was gone, meaning that the private had survived the run and then managed to pilot the vehicle – hopefully having the presence of mind to turn right onto the highway, rather than back into the town.

The battered LAV would not do much better than ten miles an hour as it limped along, dragging its rear wheels but closing the gap nonetheless. Ridley clenched his teeth. The cracked tempered glass in front of him began to give way as bullets beat against it. Glass shards were starting to be kicked back into the cab. The radio underneath the dash crackled as a voice came through it. "Blue Unit Nine in the last APC. Do you copy?"

Ridley reached over for the microphone with his bad hand and held it up to his mouth. "Copy."

"I've been trying different frequencies. Who is this?"

"Captain Pat Ridley… trying to ride the last batch of civilians out of this disaster. My situation…"

"I see your situation. I'm right above you."

Ridley looked up. There was still only the one Cobra in the air, darting back and forth and drawing ground fire in heroic fashion. It would not survive at that pace, but just knowing that he wasn't alone was a great comfort to the captain at the moment. "Thank you… very much. Where are the rest?"

A hellfire missile shot out of the bird just then and slammed with pinpoint precision into a building forty yards off Ridley's position. From the bodies and weaponry kicked up with the rubble, it was a good guess that that this had been a primary source for the stream of rockets. They would have had point blank range in just a few seconds.

"It's just me, Partner. Are you that crazy bastard that's been running around down there?"

"Probably so," answered Ridley. "Do you know the status of the rest of the convoy?"

"They're free and clear. The last vehicle's already scampered down the road. How many are with you?"

It was a delicate question. The attack helicopter was taking a lot of fire and would not last much longer hovering in its present position. Based on the extraordinary valor that the pilot had exhibited thus far, Ridley guessed that the man would continue to risk his life if told that the LAV was carrying a full load of healthy people, although this was not the case. "What's your name?" he asked, with the gap looming ahead of him.

"Aaron Bernstein. Lieutenant Aaron Bernstein… for now anyway."

As Ridley neared the fence, he could see a Palestinian vehicle approaching rapidly from up the street, perhaps in order to seal the gap. A second later, the car was blown thirty feet in the air, causing notable damage to the surrounding structures, many or which were already in flames. "Wow!" he exclaimed.

"That wasn't all me," answered Bernstein. "I think that car was loaded down with explosives. Probably a Fedayeen trying to chase down the convoy and do some damage."

"Hang on a second," said Ridley. He dropped the mike and put both hands on the steering wheel to maneuver what was left of the vehicle through the broken fence, over the ditch and up onto the road. The truck groaned and shuddered, but made the transfer. Withering fire was coming from the two-story buildings that lined the first fifty yards of the road. The enemy had apparently gotten a chance to form a nice little ambush, as the last truck struggled to make it past.

Ridley hunched as low as he possibly could, just as the bird came swooping in sideways with 20mm guns blazing. Chips of wood and brick were blasted off the buildings and rained down amidst brass shell casings on the street below in flakes and chunks, as the structures virtually disintegrated along with the lives of the Jihad warriors at the windows.

When he broke out of the cloud of smoke and haze, Ridley reached back down for the mike, knowing that the man above them had earned the right to hear the honest truth. "We are carrying about a dozen people, mostly injured civilians. Our back hatch is open and they are exposed, but I can't get this wreck moving any faster than it already is. The rear wheels are locked and dragging."

Ridley figured that they were about eight kilometers out from the Green Line. He didn't expect that there would be another ambush along the way, but there was no possibility of outrunning the pursuit from al-Janiyah. A single well-placed missile would annihilate the crippled transport and everyone in it. The pilot in the air above them was now aware of that as well.

After about fifteen seconds of silence, the answer came back on the radio. "Just keep driving," he said calmly. "I've got your back."

At their present pace, it would take over thirty minutes to make it. The Cobra acting on its own would not be able to hold out for that long. Ridley guessed that at least half of its eight Hellfire missiles were spent and probably the better part of the 750 20mm rounds in the ammo container underneath the gun.

Two more missiles rained down behind them, shaking the earth, thirty seconds apart. The Cobra was trying its best to discourage the pursuit until the APC was out of range. A few sparse 20mm rounds sounded as the transport finally cleared the community. Then there was nothing heard at all for the next ten minutes.

Ridley was beginning to wonder if the pilot had abandoned them, but his voice soon came back over the radio to explain that traffic was bottled up behind them due to the failed suicide car bomber. Soon an explosion was heard, followed by another a few minutes later that sounded much closer. Sweat began a slow trickle down Ridley's brow again, mingling with the dried blood on his face and washing into his uniform. He knew that he could literally get out and run faster than the APC was moving, particularly with the incentive from behind. At the very least, he would certainly make less noise, as the racket from under the vehicle seemed to be getting louder each time he managed to push the needle up to fifteen miles an hour.

He wanted to get out and make a stand, but he had to think about the injured lying in the back. He knew that dying for the cause he had chosen was no less honorable than facing the enemy to fight, but his instinct was to take out as many of them as possible before going under. Certainly no one would accuse him of cowardice, even if he were killed from behind in a fleeing vehicle.

There were a few more 20mm rounds heard from the Cobra, followed by silence. Ridley saw the bird hover past him in the same direction that he was heading. Bernstein's voice broke in on the radio. "Still there? Good. I'm out of things to throw at them. There are still some cars on the road behind you, but I've got an idea. There's a place up ahead on the highway where the walls rise up on either side. When you get to that, take a look behind you and act appropriately."

Ridley wasn't sure what that meant, but he could see the place on the road that the pilot had mentioned creeping up a few hundred yards away. The chopper flew back behind the convoy again. Ridley could hear small arms fire coming from the road behind, but it didn't seem to be directed at him. He reached down into the floorboard and found a jagged piece of broken mirror that he held out the window to try and see what was happening.

There were several pursuing vehicles, and it appeared that the Cobra was attempting to hold them back with nothing but its hull and blades to offer as deterrents. Wild-eyed fanatics were hanging out the side of the car, firing up against the armored cabin. Ridley turned his attention back to what was in front of him. The road was empty. It narrowed at the point where the walls rose up on either side. The big truck finally lumbered through them and the captain looked back to see one of the pursuing vehicles completely flipped over. He figured that the Cobra had managed to hook a leg under the roof and pull it up and over.

The attack helicopter, which now had a trail of black smoke coming out of its tail section, appeared to be trying to land in the same narrow gap he had just passed. Ridley understood that the pilot intended to land the craft there and use it as a makeshift roadblock. He grabbed the mike again, wincing as his broken fingers accidentally knocked against the stick shift. "Come on, Lieutenant. We've got room for you."

There was no reply, but as the bird set down, a helmet was jettisoned from the cockpit and a thin young man in a flight suit jumped out and raced toward the mangled carrier. Ridley was tempted to slow down for him, but he didn't think it was necessary. Eventually the pilot caught up and then disappeared into the back. The Cobra quickly went up in flames behind them and Ridley knew that they were living on borrowed time, still two kilometers away from the Israeli checkpoint.

Bernstein's idea worked as brilliantly as could be expected, but it wasn't enough to hold back the determined Palestinians. After a few minutes, they had worked their way around the burnt-out hull and were back on the chase. Sweat poured down Ridley's face.

They weren't going to make it.

Washington D.C.

President Hillary Rodham took the call from the Palestinian Prime Minister himself, whose voice was quivering in anger. "Are you invading us?"

"We are trying to evacuate the Israelis from the settlements," she replied, somewhat befuddled. "There were reports of an ambush. Perhaps you know something about that?"

"I know that there is an air attack on Palestine from the American Army!"

"An attack from the air?"

"Yes," the Prime Minister spoke in a thick accent, "from the air!"

"You're mistaken. We have a convoy that was ambushed and requested air support, but their request was denied. We assume that you will treat the prisoners with the full measures accorded by the Geneva Convention until they are released. We are not at war with you. There is no need to even hold…"

"Listen to me!" shouted the Prime Minister. "There are attack aircraft in the air over the sovereign nation of Palestine. They are killing thousands of innocent civilians!"

The President paused. The Palestinians always had a penchant for exaggeration, but why would the Prime Minister be so insistent unless something really was going wrong? Perhaps the Israelis had gotten involved in the matter and messed up the operation. "We have authorized no action against Palestine, Mr. Prime Minister. Let me look into this and I'll call you back when I know more."

The next call was to the beleaguered Secretary of Defense. "Yes," he said wearily, "there was an isolated incident in which an aircraft took off from the airbase there in Israel and attempted to intervene in the situation on the ground in the West Bank."

"What do you mean 'intervene'?" Hillary snapped. "Didn't the convoy surrender their arms?"

"Well, as a matter of fact, no they didn't, Madame President. Apparently the officer on the ground decided to complete the mission."

"Mr. Secretary, may I remind you that I am the Commander in Chief! It's my call to make; and I ordered your officer to lie down... or stand down, or whatever it's called. Why didn't this happen?"

"We can't order our officers to surrender. We can only suggest that they do so in certain situations. They aren't under UN command..."

"What a silly rule," snarled the President. "How do you expect to maintain an effective Army if you can't even get your troops to surrender?"

The Secretary of Defense muttered something, but made no effort to clarify.

"What was the intention of this aircraft? What did they do?"

"It was just the one, a single attack AH-1 attack helicopter. Normally it carries two crewmen... make that crewmembers, but this was piloted by just one... uh, officer. We believe that it fired on Palestinian fighters that were in the process of attacking the convoy."

"Why didn't you shoot it down?"

"It seemed to be limiting its attack only to those who were engaging our troops in hostile action. No different really than the troops themselves shooting back."

"No different!" shrilled the President. "You've got someone out there trying to start World War III! Do you have any idea how much trouble this is causing? The international community will never accept that this was an accident!"

The Secretary of Defense did not respond.

Highway 455, West Bank, Palestine

It had been a good fight. Ridley had done the best he could. Dying didn't bother him as much as failure, or not having the opportunity to meet the man in the back of the transport, whose uncommon valor had saved the lives of over a thousand people. He expected a rocket to slam into the truck at any second. He heard small-arms fire from the rear and reluctantly stuck out his ad-hoc mirror again to get an idea of what was going on.

The pursuing vehicles were still about thirty yards back. They were being held at bay by conservative bursts of fire coming from the back of the carrier. Ridley knew that it was probably the pilot with his sidearm, making a last ditch attempt to keep the Palestinians from getting their balance and launching a rocket. It was only a temporary measure of course.

The 9mm held a 17-round clip and the pilots never took more than that with them.

The firing stopped after a few minutes. Ridley couldn't be sure, but he thought he saw the spent handgun fly out of the back and bounce off the windshield of the car behind them. He gave a wry smile. At least they would be going down swinging.

They crawled around a small curve, with the car behind easily speeding up to catch them. Ridley could see the excitement on the faces of the Jihadis. One of them stuck a rocket launcher out of the car then leaned out with it, barely keeping his balance. Here it comes, thought Ridley. He began talking to God out loud. The man next to him was earnestly muttering in Hebrew.

A tremendous volley of automatic weapons fire rushed past him, startling him and causing the mirror to be abruptly dropped, although not before he caught a split-second glimpse of the windshield on the car behind him disintegrate and the vehicle began to flip. He snapped his head up just in time to avoid colliding with a light-armored vehicle heading in the opposite direction, with its heavy machine gun blazing on top, which, along with the appearance of the lone Cobra earlier, were the two most beautiful sights Ridley knew that he would ever see in his lifetime!

The sergeant major behind the wheel gave a quick wave as he went past. Ridley's eyes misted over then began spilling tears. The man next to him was yelling uncontrollably and slapping the captain on the back. He could hear the people in the compartment behind him making noise and celebrating as well.

They were still at least three minutes away from rolling into the checkpoint, but Ridley knew that they had made it. Life was beautiful and he didn't care about anything else at that moment.

The other transport took up a defensive position behind them. Ahead, he could see the other pieces of the convoy, just beyond the checkpoint. A crowd was milling about. As they got closer he could hear them cheering as well. He drove the carrier through the gates and pulled off to the side where the people parted for him. The trailing LAV pulled up alongside.

The sergeant major got out and stood in front of the vehicle at full attention, saluting the young captain. That meant more to Ridley at that moment than any medal that any general could have pinned on his chest. He returned the salute and opened the door to step down. As he put his boots on the ground, his knees began to weaken and he fell on his hands, put his face to the dirt and thanked his God.

138

AGE OF TOLERANCE

Wednesday March 11th, 2015
Washington D.C.

It was seven o'clock in the morning and President Hillary Rodham was cranky from not having gotten more than a few hours of sleep. She was also livid. The Secretary of Defense was in the Oval Office with her, along with a few of her aides. Light was beginning to creep through the windows on the east side of the room.

"Aaron Bernstein?" she asked. The Secretary nodded meekly.

"Aaron Bernstein! AARON BERNSTEIN!" she shrieked. "There was a pilot put in control of a U.S. attack helicopter, in Israel, with the last name of Bernstein, the first name of Aaron, and this didn't set off any warning bells in anyone's head?"

The Secretary shook his head. "We don't profile by religion in the military."

"Well maybe it's time we started," snapped the President. "No, I'm not talking about Muslims," she said to a wide-eyed aide in front of her, who was wearing a *hijab*. "We all know that Muslim-Americans fully support their country. Would it be too much to ask, however," she said with a dark eye back toward the Secretary, "that we not put a Jew, even one who is born and raised in America, in control of a machine capable of leveling a small town when we are performing maneuvers in an Arab country? The Jews hate the Arabs, you know. They started a war to rob them of their land and, then spent the last seven decades oppressing them. Put a Jew behind the controls of a war machine and it doesn't take a genius to figure out what he'll try to do with it."

The Secretary was staring straight down at the floor, looking as a man does when he is wrestling over whether to say what's really on his mind. Without looking up he spoke quietly. "Madame President, Israel has had the capability to destroy every Arab nation on the planet for many decades now, and they've never threatened…"

"Well, I'd say they made a damn good start of it!" interjected the President.

"We've been looking into this. Despite the Palestinian claims, the rogue pilot made every effort to limit his attack to those elements that were a threat to the convoy."

"Oh for God's sake, Mr. Secretary, I've seen the pictures on GNN with my own eyes. There were women and children among the dead."

The aide in the head-scarf nodded intently.

"Did you see one of those 'dead bodies' jump out of the coffin and run away when a surveillance plane got too close?" asked the Secretary of Defense. "I did. The Palestinians have been playing this game for years. They send suicide bombers into cafes and hotels without the slightest remorse, and then shout to high heaven when Israel kills one of the leaders responsible for the terrorism."

"That is because the Israelis kill civilians as well," interjected the aide.

"Not intentionally. There's an effort made to minimize collateral damage. Why not blame the terrorists for hiding behind women and children?"

"Because there are other ways to seek peace, if peace is what the Israelis truly want," said the aide again with an eye toward the President.

"Yes, that's true," said Hillary. "What is it with you men and your testosterone? I thought we'd made more progress in eliminating this masculine aggressiveness from our armed forces. This is very disturbing." She lowered her head for a few quiet seconds then looked up. "Let's get back on subject. The issue right now is that a... as you call him, a rogue pilot acted against orders and launched several missiles into a sovereign country, killing many people. It doesn't matter what those people were doing at the time, because it's their country."

"They were trying to kill American soldiers and Israeli civilians," said the Secretary. "So, yes it is our business."

"That's just what I'm talking about!" Hillary's face darkened again. "The Palestinians have a right to defend themselves if they think they're under attack, and I'd say that an attack helicopter shooting missiles at them could certainly make them think so. The Israelis are none of our concern, either. This is an internal matter, and we're simply there to carry out a UN mandate to turn Palestine over to the Palestinians. As for our soldiers... they brought this on themselves by refusing a gracious offer of safe passage. Who is this officer on the ground that was responsible for the fiasco?"

"I guess you mean the captain, Pat Ridley?"

"Yes, is he some sort of head case? Why would a reasonable person go so far out of his way to avoid a common sense solution, particularly when it's handed to him on a silver platter? What does it say about the quality of our troops in uniform when they would rather fight than negotiate a peaceful compromise? It's scary."

"Indeed," agreed the Secretary, but perhaps for a different reason.

"Can we court-martial this individual? I think it would be a good start toward repairing relations with the Palestinians."

"Based on our preliminary investigation, it appears he did nothing wrong... except..."

"Except?"

"Well," the Secretary returned his gaze to the floor. "He may have executed a soldier in uniform. This would be the, uh, person who *happened* to be Arab."

The eyes of the Muslim aide grew very wide. Hillary cast a quick glance at her then looked back to the Secretary. "Oh really? It sounds like he got upset and did a little religious profiling of his own there in the heat of the moment!"

"No ma'am... sir... it wasn't like that, we think. The individual killed was the person that had betrayed them into the ambush. Military justice allows..."

"How do you know?" said the President smugly. "We're you there? Is that what the individual said before he was murdered?"

"I... I'm not sure. I mean, no I wasn't there, but I... there is good reason to believe that the individual was a traitor."

"I guess it helps that he was Muslim, eh, Mr. Secretary," said the President with another quick, knowing glance to her aide, whose expression hovered somewhere between feigned shock and self-righteous indignation. "You don't have to ask too many questions when dealing with someone who worships a different god, isn't that right."

The Secretary looked up and gave her a level stare. "You have my resignation."

"Good! I'm going to need it!"

Wednesday April 8th[th], 2015
Bethesda Air Force Base, Maryland

Pat Ridley sat in a chair to the side of his hospital bed, fully dressed with bags packed, waiting to go home. The four weeks since he arrived at the hospital just a few days after the harrowing trip across that distant highway had been one of the most depressing periods of his life.

The lawyers had gotten to him early as he was passed into medical care almost immediately at the checkpoint. They kept him sedated and barely conscious for nearly forty-eight hours as he was transported back to the States and underwent surgery. The captain was then "debriefed" in a windowless room for about a week under the rigorous measures imposed by the lawyers to restrict access. There was no television or clock. The nurses were forbidden to speak with him. Only a doctor under close supervision and the lawyers were allowed to ask questions.

Ridley lost track of time, not knowing whether it was day or night. He felt isolated and helpless, without even a set of clothes, beyond the flimsy hospital gown. He had to answer questions in his bare feet, which put him at a natural disadvantage to the interrogating lawyers in wing-tipped shoes and sharp suits with vague scents that subtly reminded him of a life he might never have again. He slept a lot when he wasn't being interviewed, usually being roused to groggily answer questions, wondering all the while what was happening to him. He learned quickly that his own questions would not be answered, so he began to harbor suspicion and fear. Not being able to see the sun or have contact with the outside world wore on his nerves, leaving him cranky and paranoid, which was just what they wanted.

On the last day, before he was moved to a new room with eased conditions, a government lawyer that he had not seen before walked into his room and began asking questions that had already been asked by others. It was as if the whole process was starting over from the beginning, except that this conversation was controlled and guided based on information he had previously provided.

"Did you order your men to fire on Palestinian civilians?"

"Define a civilian."

"Someone who is not in uniform," answered the lawyer.

"Could this mean someone who is attempting to kill troops under my command?"

"Citizens have a right to protect themselves."

"Then, technically, I suppose the answer is yes."

"Did the men resist your orders or attempt to reason with you that this was against the rules for combat?"

"No," answered Ridley.

"Do you hold yourself completely responsible for what happened?"

"No."

"No?"

"I was not in command when we were ambushed."

"You mean on the bridge?"

"What was left of the bridge after it was blown up under us," said Ridley.

"But you ordered your men to fire on civilians who were not necessarily responsible for the unfortunate incident on the bridge, particularly on the way out of Ramallah and on the highway home."

"Yes."

"Even after this, however, you were given an offer of peace, were you not?"

"We were told that if we laid down our guns that we would be allowed to live. The same guarantee could not be made for the…"

"Did you give your men the opportunity to consider this offer?"

"No."

"Why?"

"The Army is not a democracy."

The lawyer made a scratching motion on his legal pad. "So you hold yourself responsible?"

"Yes."

"Fully responsible for what happened afterwards?"

"For what I had control over, yes."

"Did you execute an unarmed person?"

"Yes."

"Did you do so because of his religion or ethnicity?"

"No."

The lawyer looked up. "Are you sure, Captain?"

Ridley hesitated. He recalled the arrogance of that man, who had looked at the body of a Jewish child and expressed no remorse, but rather a sort of smugness. *"Dar al Harb."*

"Pardon me?" asked the lawyer.

"Dar al Harb. Do you know what it means?"

"No."

"What about *Dar al Islam*?"

"It sounds related to the Muslim faith. Is that what this man said to you?"

"Yes."

"So you knew he was Muslim?"

"Yes," answered Ridley.

"Did that make you angry?"

"At that moment? I guess…"

"Did you shoot him because you were angry?"

"Yes."

The lawyer wrote a few notes in a frenzied manner on his legal pad then continued the interview in much the same manner, asking carefully crafted questions to gain a new series of concessions from Ridley. He left for about an hour then returned and asked a smaller subset of the questions asked before. These were the ones that seemed most damning out of context, yet Ridley felt compelled to provide the same answers that he had just given, for the sake of consistency. The lawyer then left again and returned a few hours later with a piece of paper that Ridley was asked to sign. It was a statement that read:

I, Captain Pat Ridley, was assigned to the 51ˢᵗ Light Infantry Battalion, where I found myself placed in command on March 10ᵗʰ, 2015, after the Battalion's Lieutenant Colonel had fallen wounded in gallant service. Following this event, I gave a series of orders that instructed my troops to fire on civilians. Furthermore, I rejected an offer that promised my troops safe passage from the contended areas. Furthermore, I executed an unarmed prisoner, who happened to be a member of my own company, but who expressed religious statements to me that I took offense toward. I take full and complete responsibility for these actions, of which I agree not to discuss outside of a military tribunal, without first securing the explicit permission of….

Ridley knew that his military career was over, whether he signed or not. They had spun a brilliant web around him, using narrow language to gain small concessions, and then using these advantageously to secure further concessions. As he wearied and wore down, they were able to guile him into taking shortcuts by answering questions that had been asked before, but without the qualifications or arguments previously given; gradually boiling everything down to the words on the piece of paper that he held in his hand.

Ridley picked up the pen. "I'm holding my own court-martial here aren't I?"

The lawyer didn't say anything.

"I would be kind of foolish to sign this, given that it would put me in Leavenworth?"

"The Army doesn't send anyone to Leavenworth anymore. It's a civilian facility."

"What would happen to me?" asked Ridley, who put the pen down.

The lawyer's body language registered disappointment. He dropped his head for a second then asked in a low voice, "Do you know the difference between a summary court-martial and a general court-martial?"

"Yes."

"You will be given a summary court-martial. You won't serve any time, because you aren't the one we want."

It took several seconds to fully absorb, but Ridley began to understand that the lawyer had just said more than he should have. Like sunlight burning away the fog, the words suddenly began to eat through the drug-induced lethargy and artificial paranoia that had enveloped Pat Ridley's brain like a hazy cloud over the last seven days. It was all making sense to him now. They were using him to get to someone else…. and he knew exactly who it was.

He picked up the pen again, bringing a slight smile to the lawyer's face, and wrote three words on the signature line of the document with resolute flourish.

Now, a little over two weeks later, the captain sat writing quietly on his notebook computer. His left arm and side would always bear scars, but they were largely healed. He no longer had to wear the mask at night to protect his nose while sleeping, but it still felt tender, as did his fingers, which remained in splints. The physical injuries weren't going to last, but there was permanent damage of a different sort. Pat Ridley was a changed man. He had used the solitude of the last couple of weeks to think deeply about himself and his country. He had no regrets about Highway 455. His conscious was clear, so were his thoughts.

There is an implicit bargain between a country and its soldier, one that is tacitly required in order to make the arrangement work collectively. For his part, the fighting man will risk everything, including the very real possibility of death. He will do this because the country that sends him into battle will be worth such sacrifice.

Ridley thought about what he had been taught growing up, and how that had changed over the years. When he started at the elementary school in Ila, in the mid-1990's, his class began each day with the Pledge of Allegiance. The flag still hung in the classroom and they were taught that America was a great nation that had conquered slavery, Nazism and Communism to bring freedom and democracy to the world. Pat's father was proud of how his own father, whom Pat had not known, fought bravely in an integrated unit in Korea and was even decorated on the battlefield after holding the line with his comrades during an intensive assault by the enemy on their positions that lasted from dusk to dawn. It was the longest night of his life, but when reinforcements broke through the next morning, the battalion commander made the fresh troops line up next to the pile of Chinese bodies and said "See, this is what happens when you hold your ground and don't panic." Ridley's family was poor, but they believed in their country and the opportunity for their children to succeed.

Ten years later, it had all changed at school. The new textbooks spoke only of America's crimes. They emphasized sexism, racism, genocide and slavery. The black kids that Ridley grew up with began to identify themselves by race and fostered resentment of "the White Man's World," an insidious institution which would always make their best efforts futile while conveniently justifying their failures.

They seemed to interpret every past injustice in present terms and projected their anger towards others who simply had the misfortune to be white. Proof of guilt was in the textbooks after all; why else would there be so much emphasis placed on the sins of the past if it wasn't meant to shape present attitude? Then there was the seduction of moral superiority. Making others feel confused or apologetic for crimes they never committed was quite addictive. A new generation of teachers assisted, by establishing the rules of grievance and sensitivity within the new class hierarchy, reinforced as well by a plethora of television shows and movies that traced America's institutional evil from the savage pilgrims of Plymouth Rock to the trials of modern-day Muslim immigrants that struggled against prejudice and profiling.

Clearly a country that loathed itself to such an extent was not worth dying for, but Ridley had been prepared to do so anyway. His grandfather would have been proud of what he had done on that desolate Palestinian highway. Yet, the country to which he pledged his life would have betrayed his sacrifice. How then could he continue to serve? How could anyone?

The armed forces were in a spiral, after decades of hemorrhaging quality soldiers, like the sergeant major, and disillusioning the best recruits, who signed out of a sense of duty, but became disenchanted with the social experiment that passed for the modern military. The politicians wanted to treat it as if it was just another occupation, installing workplace rules that contrasted with the nature of a ready defense force. Under Al Gore, for example, unmarried or expectant mothers had a right to stay on their home base with their children, even in time of war. The pregnancy rate climbed each time there was a threat of hostilities, and the government was there to ensure that military women enjoyed all of the same amenities as their civilian counterparts, including reduced work hours and family leave.

Failure to conform the armed forces to the prevailing vision of socialist utopia immediately drew the ire of powerful voices on the airwaves and in Washington. The military was used for inner-city restoration projects, building cheap housing for Mexican immigrants and even constructing alternative energy systems in the desert. It resembled more of a Peace Corps on steroids than a fighting institution.

Yet, opposition to the military was never higher in the United States, particularly on college campuses, where recruiting had long since been banned by Executive Order. Pat rarely revealed his military background or status as a Reservist to fellow students at Northwestern, where professors openly railed against the armed forces and encouraged their classes to picket recruiting facilities. He had seen men in uniform harassed, not on campus (where none would appear in dress) but simply while walking down the street or eating lunch. On one occasion, a young Army officer had fries dumped on his head at a table right next to Ridley's by a wild-eyed man screaming "land of the free!" The rest of the patrons chanted "Hey, hey, hey, goodbye…" as the officer, who would have given his life for them in the line of duty, stormed out in abject humiliation.

Patriots, according to Hollywood, were either rubes or racist kooks.

From what he had been able to gather since being moved to a new room, Ridley could tell that the nation was embarrassed by what happened on Highway 455, although he never heard his own name mentioned. The bulk of the attention focused on the consequences of Lieutenant Aaron Bernstein's unauthorized action. He was being called a "misguided young man" by some and a "homicidal Zionist" by others. Only a few were suggesting that he may have heroically saved the lives of people in the convoy.

President Rodham had issued an apology to the Palestinian people and there was serious talk of massive financial compensation. International outrage prompted the UN to unanimously pass a resolution condemning the action and demanding that those responsible be handed over to the International Criminal Court, under the treaty agreed to by the Gore Administration many years earlier.

"There really isn't anything you can do now," one of the lawyers told him. "This is the most diplomatic way of handling the matter and you shouldn't try to interfere or you'll only wind up making trouble for yourself… and the United States."

The United States be damned, thought Ridley. A nation that betrays its own soldiers should hardly expect loyalty in return, to say nothing of the sort of sacrifice required on the battlefield. What kind of country goes out of its way to denigrate itself and the men who built it? The death of patriotism is indeed the death of a nation.

America once had a way of life that made it more successful than any other, yet it no longer had the courage even to ask those knocking on its doors to adapt to it as a condition of entry. How long would it be before the nation was consumed from within by a class of people that wanted merely to enjoy the rewards of past sacrifice, but without any obligation toward preserving the way of life that made such privilege possible?

There was a soft knock at the door and he closed the laptop monitor and grabbed his bags, knowing that it was time to leave for good. He also knew that he owed nothing more to his country. He was no longer Captain Pat Ridley of the United States Army. From now on he would live for God, family, and himself.

He walked out of the hospital with his head held high.

Thursday, October 1st, 2015
Bozeman, Montana

The dusty trail out behind the airfield wound its way through spruce trees and eventually to the banks of a rolling creek, nestled in the shadow of the Rocky Mountains. This was a route that Fillmore and the young pilot had walked several times in the past, as they discussed business. He liked this young Texan, who seemed to appear out of nowhere two years earlier, with a lean frame, chiseled features, and aspirations of being a pilot. There was something about the confident look in the eyes that reminded Fillmore of another young man without any flying experience whom he had seen in the mirror fifty years ago. He made a place for him at his company and watched him for a few months before deciding to make the investment in training.

Airtana Airlines was originally an intrastate carrier with only one plane to its name. It mainly ran the local circuit for Montanans, before Fillmore realized that there was a lot more money to be made in bringing tourists in from the West Coast for hunting and fishing trips; so he expanded operations to Seattle and Portland. The company slowly grew into a regionally recognized name with five small, but solid aircraft. There were twelve pilots on retainer and about the same number of mechanics. For the last twenty years, Fillmore had insisted on having a pilot and copi-lot on every flight, no matter how small. This also made it easy to transition the ambitious young man beside him into his desired role.

Kerry Conner wasn't just a good pilot; he was a good businessman as well. He had made several suggestions that reduced operating expenses and improved the company's visibility on the West Coast. The owner felt confident with the decision that he was about to share with the young man.

Fillmore reminisced on the short hike about the good times and bad, as the company progressed over the last forty years. Kerry, who was not particularly loquacious anyway, listened attentively and stayed quiet. Finally, they reached the site of the creek, which bubbled over rocks as it exited the National Forest land a few miles ahead of them. It was a beautiful scene and one that was repeated in nooks and crannies all across the western part of the Big Sky state. The two men, dressed for a day at the office in blue jeans and boots, stood watching the water for a few minutes then found a log to sit on, beneath a tree. The old man continued slowly.

"This company is my life, Kerry."

The younger man nodded.

"It's not just a business. It's a part of me. When you put so much effort into something, it almost becomes your identity. I'm proud of what was built here. I'm also proud of you and the work that you've done for us."

The younger man looked down.

"And I'll tell you what," continued Fillmore. "I know that it isn't easy sometimes. I don't regret my decision in March to put you in charge while I was out sick, even though my son didn't like it. I love my boy, but I'm afraid that we gave him too much too soon in life – his mother and I, that is. He hasn't learned how to earn. He doesn't know what it is to suffer."

The old man looked away for a few seconds then turned his gaze back to the gaunt, hardened twenty-one-year-old sitting next to him. "You've been like a son to me, Kerry, like the son I never... like the son I wish I'd had. I made a decision, one that I didn't want to have to make." He shuffled his feet and looked down. "An old cowboy like me wants to die with his boots on, riding this business out to the end and going out on top."

He drew in a deep breath. "The truth is, though, that I can't support what our government is doing. I can't support it with my tax dollars." He saw the younger man look up suddenly with a quizzical expression. "That's right, Kerry, I'm one of them. I don't know what they're called really... what we're called. Conscientious objectors, I guess."

The younger man finally spoke. "I never knew. You didn't seem..."

"Religious? A right-wing political kook?" The old man laughed. "They've got us all nice and stereotyped in the newspapers and TV shows. I guess for a while, I even denied it myself. I didn't seem to resemble those ridiculous caricatures, so I thought maybe I wasn't really one of them, just a man that goes to church on Sunday and believes what he hears. My wife never bought it for a minute, though. She's been pretty firm about standing up for what's right from the very beginning."

He reached over to knock an advancing bug of some sort off the log then spit out a stream of tobacco juice at another. "Well, I guess it takes a while for it to dawn on a man that the world has changed. If you're raised like I was, to love your country, even to the extent that you go over to some jungle and fight for it when you're barely eighteen, it isn't easy to come around to thinking that it could be doing something so wrong. The fact is though, that this thing crept up on us, a little at a time. Now, I wake up to find that my money is being used to fund a practice that I think is killing the innocent. You don't have to be particularly religious to see what's wrong with that."

Kerry looked up at the creek, but didn't say anything for a while, before finally asking, "What are you going to do?"

"Well, I'm going to sell the business to you for one dollar and then stop paying taxes," Fillmore said bluntly.

The younger man seemed far more interested in the fate of his boss than in the business. He looked over, "They've been putting people in camps, but I guess you know that."

Fillmore didn't have to answer. Airtana had started a very lucrative Miles City run three years ago, when the first detention facilities were opened there on the Montana prairie by the government to accommodate the massive number of tax objectors. True to its word, the Gore and Rodham Administrations had punished them as ordinary evaders, either confiscating their property or imprisoning them as the case warranted. Legal challenges posed by conservative interest groups to the health care program faced no chance in a Supreme Court packed with over two decades of Clinton-Gore-Rodham appointees. Influential sources in the media were able to sway public opinion by billing the confrontation as one between responsible taxpayers and the radical fringe, shirking their patriotic duty. Support for the government held steady and the most vocal opponents were soon lost in the penal system anyway.

The trickle of tax evasion convictions turned into a stream and then a river that threatened to overflow its banks, as the sacrifices of early objectors served to inspire others. The momentum seemed to wash through every town in America, either carrying people with it or leaving them deeply ambivalent. New facilities were being built to accommodate the new criminal class, which consisted of some of the most upright members of society. People who had never even received a speeding ticket suddenly found themselves convicted of a felony and serving out a prison sentence in tents that had been hastily erected on open expanses of land in the western states. By 2015, four million families had either filed zero returns or declined to file altogether.

The country scratched its head over the strange sight of these oddballs sacrificing jobs, businesses and liberty to live in the camps. Hollywood had a field day with these "Bible wavers," enjoying the upper moral hand after decades of pillory from these same people. Starr Sterling, of "Jenna's Army," played the lead role in an acclaimed movie with a fictitious plot that portrayed a young woman raped by a man who also refused to pay taxes for "religious reasons". Her character had to make a difficult decision as to whether her attacker should serve time for rape or for tax evasion. She chose the later, since it was "a crime against society" rather than just one person.

The tax objectors were vilified in nearly every quarter for refusing to contribute to the common good while placing an unnecessary burden on the rest. Economists calculated the broader cost as enormous, far more than could be recouped from property confiscation. Government revenue declined as wage earners left the workforce and businesses had to increase expenses in order to replace them. Productivity declined as well, though no one could say exactly why. Some speculated that the people accepting imprisonment had been more reliable than their replacements. Others pointed out that many of those who left were small business owners, betraying their employees and spreading the misery by closing their shops.

The economic decline and the skyrocketing cost of incarceration only fueled public anger toward the rising number of objectors from a public that appreciated free health care. There was little pressure on President Hillary Rodham (who changed her name after the election) to drop publicly-funded abortion. It also didn't hurt that her opponents, as felons, were losing their right to vote, along with their money and freedom. She stayed the course and boldly pledged to uphold the law regardless of resistance.

The old man had made a practice of not discussing either religion or politics with his employees, except as it related to the business. There had been a new Federal law passed a few years back that allowed union representatives to come and talk to his employees about organizing and, at the same time, restricted him from mounting a counter argument, on the grounds that it constituted unfair pressure. He wouldn't hear anything of it and kicked the union men out of the building. They tried, but couldn't find an employee who would lend his name to a lawsuit, and the matter quietly died. Fillmore made no secret of his belief that he could run his

business however he wanted, including selling it for a dollar. All he had
to do was convince the buyer.

"You know I can't do that," protested the younger man. "I'd rather
pay your taxes for you."

"You would be doing me a favor. I don't trust the company to anyone else."

"Can't I just hold it for you until you get out?"

"No," said the older man. "I thought about that, but the fact is that
I'm through with this country. I'm going do my time and then head up to
Alberta. I transferred just enough up there already so that I can live out
my years. It's not the way I would have wanted it, but sometimes you just
have to play the hand you're dealt."

"I've never been to college or business school…" started Kerry.

"Neither have I," responded the old man quickly, knowing where
Kerry was going with it. "You can run this business better than I can.
You've already helped reduce red ink on the books by better than a third
just in the last two years. If you'd been with me from the beginning we'd
probably be one of the largest carriers in America right now, and I'd have
to ask for two dollars instead."

The younger man smiled softly then asked, "You know he's going to
leave don't you?"

Fillmore knew who he meant. "My son's got some growing up to do.
He'll throw a fit then stomp off then, hopefully, find out how life really
works. Maybe he'll go fly for someone else. He's got plenty of hours. I
think he'll come around eventually. He's got good genes." He looked
over at Kerry again. "There is someone that I want you to hire in his
place, though."

"Who?"

"That helicopter pilot that they're trying to court-martial."

"Bernstein?" asked Kerry. "Do you know him?"

"No, but I like what I've heard." The old man stood up to begin the
walk back. "Kerry, did I ever tell you how I got that Silver Star in Vietnam? If I did the same thing today, they'd have me sitting right next to
that Jewish kid…"

PART TWO

THE INHERITANCE

2023

Tuesday, July 4th 2023
El Paso, TX

The call came in around 6:00 that evening. Felipe rolled his eyes a bit after turning down the volume on his shoulder radio. He was standing over the Rio Grande, in a desolate area sheltered by brown mountains just outside of the city, where two bodies had been found the day before. They were related to a long string of murders that had plagued him since he first started on the force about eight years earlier. Over two-hundred murders, mostly of prostitutes and others affiliated with drug smuggling – and those were just the ones they knew about. There was no telling how many more bodies were buried or decomposing to dust out in the desert on either side of the border.

This was not a serial killer. Even if it were, it wouldn't have gotten much attention relative to, say, the killing of any two students on a Boston college campus. No one cared much about drug dealers and prostitutes, even in El Paso where most of the bodies were being dumped.

Felipe knew that the Mexican mafia was behind the slayings. They were quite active in Texas and throughout much of the Southwest, though they operated with relative impunity from Mexico. There were chapters in every major American city, controlling nearly all of the drug traffic through street gangs and front operations. It was a violent business that had only gotten worse as the border between Mexico and the U.S. blurred to near irrelevancy. The Mexican government was highly uncooperative, due to both the power of the drug lords and the boost to the economy that the trafficking provided.

The police were getting nowhere with the investigation. People that knew something didn't want to talk, and there were obviously a lot of them given the number of victims. They were now finding an average of one per week. The frustration sickened Felipe. How could these criminals operate with such license? He suspected that they were getting help from within the system. There was a higher tolerance for corruption now than there had been twenty years earlier. The community and government, even down to the police departments, were gradually beginning to resemble their counterparts across the border, as immigration went virtually unchecked between the two countries. Even a significant number of Arabs were coming across each day, since they could pay more to the smugglers than the poorer *Mexicanos*.

Against these dark thoughts, the prospect of breaking up the annual 4th of July melee at Arroya Park was actually a relief. He turned the cruiser back down the dirt road, which was littered with trash, and made his way toward I-10.

Each year, a small band of mostly white Texans held a patriotic rally in the park, originally for the purpose of waving flags and enjoying a cookout. Their numbers were shrinking dramatically each year however, and the only food to be found at the rallies now was what was thrown on them by protesters.

As he entered the park gates, which were slightly elevated above the meadow where the confrontation was occurring, Felipe could see a small knot of people, identifiable only by their red, white and blue colors, dwarfed and completely surrounded by a much larger crowd of angry protestors. He parked the car, after sounding the siren a few times, and waded into the melee.

To say that this was a conflict between Mexicans and whites wouldn't be exactly accurate. There were several Mexican-Americans proudly holding the Stars and Stripes among the group of mostly elderly whites. The real diversity was among the protesters around them, however. They were largely Latino, but it seemed that the loudest and angriest were young white college students, pushing their way into the tenuous space that divided the groups and screaming at the pale and shaken flag-wavers. Felipe guessed that these Anglo hotheads felt they had something to prove to their Hispanic peers. It never ceased to amaze him how some people think they can prove their tolerance by the most vivid displays of intolerance.

To his dismay, he saw that one of the young women doing a great deal of shouting near the divide was Felipe's own little sister, Maria. So absorbed was she in her harangue that she didn't notice her brother approaching. The target of her wrath appeared to be holding her own rather well, which wasn't surprising to him, given that it was Sarah Conner. The grumpy woman was now over seventy and recovering from hip replacement surgery, but she was standing toe to toe with Maria, with fire in her eyes.

"Pepita!" he said sternly, using the nickname for his sister that caused her to stop in mid-sentence and turn red. The buzz around them softened as well.

"Officer," said Aunt Sarah, addressing Felipe, but glaring intently into the girl's eyes as she pronounced each word deliberately, "if you don't get this girl out of my face, my boot is going to shoved so far up her ass that it will take her a month to pass it!"

Felipe realized at that moment that the two women didn't recognize each other. Although Aunt Sarah knew him well, she had not seen Maria since she was a little girl, long before Kerry left. Maria had been away at college in California the year before when great-uncle Diego died, and she wasn't at the funeral. The old man was buried out on the old Conner ranch, per his request. It was the only time Felipe had ever seen Aunt Sarah cry.

Of course, no one was crying at the moment, as the old woman's comment had riled up the protesters, who began ranting anew with accusations of racism and fascism. His sister screamed something he had heard the others shouting as well, "This is not your country anymore!"

As if to accentuate the point, someone threw a beer bottle at the old lady, missing her, but smacking squarely off the forehead of the person standing next to her. He fell backward with blood starting down his face.

Felipe lost his temper. For a moment he was tempted to draw his gun and fire it in the air, but he began bellowing instead, in a way that caught everyone's attention. While roaring threats to disperse the crowd, he reached out and grabbed his sister by the arm, then unceremoniously dragged her back to the police car. It was enough to send the rest of the protesters packing, but he didn't care at that moment. After radioing for an ambulance and checking on the injured man, he turned his attention back to Maria.

Barely able to keep his voice below a yell, he began barking at the girl in Spanish. "What are you doing here? Why are you acting this way... using such ugly language? What would your parents think? Are you trying to dishonor them? Is this how you repay us?"

The girl wasn't used to this sort of anger from him and struggled not to cry. He didn't know what to think of her anymore. Maria was the last member of the family born in Mexico, less than two years before the family emigrated. She was the youngest of his siblings, now eighteen and about to start her sophomore year at Berkeley. The family had sacrificed for her education and had high hopes for her, the most beautiful of their children.

Yet, here she was making an ass out of herself, yelling at a group of old people that came down to the park simply to fly the flag and celebrate a country that had been very good to the Posadas. If Felipe were not in uniform, he might have been tempted to cross the line and stand with that small group. He certainly had more in common with those proud *gringos* than he did with the self-righteous herd around them.

His sister was different, though. She had never known the hardships of life in Guadalajara, even though she had heard the stories. To his knowledge, she had never even crossed over into Juarez. In fact, she had a kind of romantic view of old *Mexico*, fueled by the new textbooks and educators who emphasized Latino pride and heritage. She was always an independent sort that her parents were never able to tame, but she drifted away even further in high school, running with a crowd that abhorred Anglo-America and the English tradition. She liked to say that she was more Mexican than anyone else in her family, although her parents would not tolerate that sort of foolish talk in their home. She was embarrassed by them anyway. Their philosophy of assimilation into American culture was at odds with the social system around them, which treated *El Norte* as if it were simply an extension of Mexico.

As Felipe got older, he appreciated his parents' dedication to the process of adapting to their new country. The three siblings between him and Maria all worked their way through public colleges and easily graduated with honors. Each was successful in their young careers, though none still lived in El Paso. Thanks to their father's insistence, they all spoke perfect English. Of the five children, only Felipe, the oldest, retained a mild accent. Not that it mattered a bit in the country's southwest. Spanish was dominant, even at the police department and courthouse.

His little sister, however, purposefully used a pronounced accent when speaking English in high school (something she since dropped). Her parents would not have approved, of course, but their own language skills had not developed to the point that they were able to notice. There was no hiding her style of dress however, and it resulted in enormous arguments that raised the roof of their small house. The other girls at school may have been able to get away with the *barrio* fashion in their homes, but Maria had to duck in the school bathroom each morning to change into clothes that were smuggled in her book bag.

Still, she was a bright and very attractive girl with a good head on her shoulders. Or so Felipe thought before seeing what he had seen. His rage began to subside and his composure returned. He noticed that his sister's hand was trembling a bit, even as she tried defiantly to hide it from him. He realized that he had used profanity in the heat of the moment when pulling her away from the group, which she had probably never heard come out of his mouth. It was a bad habit of nearly every officer on the force. After a few years of lapse, he resolved to keep his language under control, even under the worst of circumstances. Usually he succeeded, but staring two-hundred corpses in the face can sometimes distract a man from his personal goals.

Clearly he had made his point. With a softened tone he said, "I don't want to see you waste your life, Pepita. You know that it's costing our family a lot of money to send you to California, even with the scholarships. What are they teaching you there that you would come back here and shout down a bunch of old people waving the American flag?"

Anger flashed in her dark eyes. "That flag stands for a lot of things, Felipe, but none of them are good. The very land we're standing on right now used to be ours."

"Ours? What do you…?"

"You know what I mean. The Y*anquis* killed us for it and stole it.

"Pepita…"

"Stop calling me that! You know I don't like it."

"Maybe I'll have it carved on your gravestone, since you believe that you were killed two hundred years ago."

She ignored him. "The American flag stands for slavery, war and genocide. There is no reason to take pride in it."

"Even if I agreed with you, which I don't, it doesn't explain why you would come out here and make life so miserable for people who don't feel as you do? Don't they teach you to tolerate a difference of opinion at Berkeley? Why be like the rest of these clowns?"

The question took her aback for a moment. She looked away and said, "Well, if we don't challenge them where we can, then maybe they'll repeat the awful things they did."

"Awful things? Do you know that our Papa used to stand with them before his surgery – holding the same flag?" He ignored her obvious embarrassment, as she glanced quickly around to make sure that none of her cohorts were listening. "Do you know any of the rest, Pepita, and the 'awful things' you accuse them of? Those are ranchers and business owners. Together they probably employ about half the private workforce in this city, including a great many Latinos. You know that woman that you were screaming at? She's the aunt of one of my best friends growing up, the guy that taught me how to speak English, which wasn't easy for a 12-year-old. Hell, I realize that she's not the most politically correct..."

"How convenient," she coldly interrupted. "A white man teaches you how to talk like a white man. Did he also teach you how to think like one as well?"

Her bold sarcasm shocked him. If she'd said something like that eight years ago he might have slapped the back of her head. As it was, he struggled not to let his anger rise up again. There was no reasoning with her, he knew. It was a waste of effort just standing here.

"I know it wasn't your parents who taught you to think like a racist," he said quietly. "We're through here, Pepita. Go back to California."

He turned away and walked abruptly back to the group of people tending to the injured man on the ground, chasing away the last two shaggy protesters. The ambulances soon arrived and Felipe offered to give Sarah Conner a ride home, knowing that she was recuperating from hip surgery and hadn't driven her own car to the event. He had her ride in the front seat, as he traced the familiar route back to her isolated ranch house.

Aunt Sarah was like a crusty old bird from the Jurassic period. She had never made the slightest effort to change with the times. She refused to learn Spanish and had little patience for anyone who didn't speak English. Of course, there were times when encounters with service providers, such as cashiers, were unavoidable. Her precept seemed to be that anyone could understand English so long as it was spoken slow and loud.

Other than himself and his late grandfather, she had no Mexican friends. The older white generation that she grew up with had nearly all moved away, being unable to compete with the militancy of the younger activists, who now dominated the local government. Policies that once seemed controversial, such as requiring street and business signs to be posted in Spanish, were now so entrenched that the government was actually considering a rule to require that Spanish lettering be twice the size of English lettering on any public sign (in the decades-long manner of the Quebecois). Critics were sardonically suggesting the council also require that Spanish be spoken twice as loud.

The business community had changed as well. Despite Felipe's claim to his sister, white businesses were becoming rare in the Southwest. He heard the complaints from owners, who were cheated and discriminated against by the system, but there was nothing that could be done about it.

White business owners were unable to get the courts to rule in their favor against Mexican-American plaintiffs or defendants, no matter how clear-cut the evidence. Some judges were worse than others. The younger appointees were true activists, and proud of it. They believed that the wealth of the community was concentrated in the hands of the whites, and needed to be redistributed. They used the same rationale that his sister just had, although they weren't quite as blunt about it in their rulings.

In Felipe's opinion, the methodology was self-destructive, despite its short-term appeal. White businesses relocated or their owners retired, costing the community jobs and tax revenue. Of course, the declining economy was then used as justification for new measures against businesses, such as higher minimum-wage laws or restrictions on employment decisions that simply accelerated the cycle.

He remembered a couple of years ago when the white landlord of an apartment complex wanted to evict a family that had never paid rent beyond the deposit. The Hispanic tenants showed up in court, carrying their children and arguing to the judge that they were simply unable to pay based on the fact that they couldn't find work. The welfare benefits they were receiving from the state didn't afford much beyond household expenses. The landlord, who made the mistake of wearing a suit to court, pointed out that they were eight months behind on their payments and that his own creditors couldn't wait. Felipe never forgot the look of frustration on the man's red face as the judge lectured him on his heartlessness, and ruled that the tenants did not have to pay rent until they found the means to do so. On top of that, he was required to pay their court costs.

The same judge later ordered the landlord to make costly repairs and improvements to his complex when the same tenants, who were still not working, solicited him again six months later – this time with a new baby in their arms. He also required the landlord to absolve their past obligations, since the living conditions were retroactively deemed sub-standard. Rather than comply with the new expense, the owner simply relinquished his holdings and left town. He had once been a respected member of the community, but now the judge declared him a fugitive and ordered his arrest on the grounds that he had to face a civil suit from the same tenants, who were filing for punitive damages. The apartment building became the property of the county and was turned into low-income housing while the taxpayers and creditors absorbed the loss.

The judge was reelected in a landslide.

Felipe went out at least once a week to check on Aunt Sarah. Kerry flew down every couple of months as well, but it was becoming harder for him, now that he was getting so busy with his airline business. His aunt was proud of her nephew, although she had never ridden in one of his planes, being afraid of flying. It was kind of ironic, Felipe thought as he sat next to her on the drive home, because she wasn't afraid of much else.

"I'm sorry that I didn't catch the guy that threw that bottle," he said as they pulled out of the park and onto the highway for the drive north. "I didn't see who it was."

"You shouldn't have any problem pulling him out of a line-up," she said plainly. "He'll be the one with tobacco juice all over him."

Felipe knew she was serious. "How's Kerry doing?" he asked

"Very well, as a matter of fact, Airtana's got the whole Northwest now, all the way over to Chicago, and he's expanding as far as San Diego in the Southwest. He's got a presence in Dallas, as you probably know, and there's even talk of adding an El Paso leg."

"Why don't you consider moving up there," he asked. "You know that he worries about you."

"My home is here. Always has been. How's your family doing?"

Felipe hedged a bit, but he decided to come out and tell her. "That was my little sister out there today."

"Pepita?"

Felipe was surprised. He never imagined that she would remember the names of family members she had barely met twenty years earlier. "Well yes, but she doesn't like to be called Pepita anymore. Given that she's all grown up now... but still acting like a child," he added with a glum mutter.

"Diego used to talk about her. Said she was going to be the most trouble your parents ever had."

"I guess he was right."

"That girl's got quite a way of expressing herself," growled the old woman. "I bet she makes a terrific wife to some lucky man one day."

Felipe had to chuckle at that one. He couldn't imagine his little sister with a man. Her first year away at school had changed her into a radical feminist, although she was not exactly known as a raging heterosexual before then, either.

They pulled off the highway and traveled down a side road for a couple of miles, then off onto the unpaved driveway that wound around to the back of the mountain to the familiar house at the base of it.

The fence that he helped put up a dozen years earlier was still standing, but rusty. It was encompassed by another fence with razor wire across the top. This was meant to be a buffer zone, in which the dogs could run free to protect the isolated property. There were no dogs here anymore, however. Burglars had learned to feed them food mixed with shards of glass, which killed the dogs as they bled out from within. Aunt Sarah couldn't bear to see more dogs die that way, so she stopped using them and tried various other methods to protect her property. She'd been broken into more times that he could remember.

It was hard to believe that this could be happening in the United States, he thought, yet he had known that there were folks who lived this way even as far back as the 1980's. The difference now was that it spread far beyond just the border towns, and well up into other parts of the country.

As was his habit, he got out and checked the area and house before leaving her alone.

2026

Wednesday, April 1, 2026
New York, New York

Beads of sweat rolled down the gray hair plastered to Michael Moore's forehead beneath his trademark ball cap, sliding down to his pasty white jowls that wiggled back and forth as he strained against the pedals of his bike to propel it down Fifth Avenue. His anti-NRA t-shirt was stretched tight across an ample torso, but the damp stains weren't yet visible from under the open shirt worn over it.

At seventy-one, the filmmaker knew that he was fortunate to be alive given the morbid obesity that dogged him for most of his life. After his doctor bluntly informed him that his fourth heart attack would be his last, he began exercising, eating less and gradually losing some of the massive fat that ringed his midsection and thighs. The bicycling helped. Down to 300 pounds now, he figured that he was hardly recognizable to the people he passed, or to those zipping by him on Segways.

He was wrong.

A well-dressed, but angry young man was waiting with clenched fists several blocks away, knowing that the portly filmmaker would be pedaling past as he always did that time of the morning. He was an immigrant, but unaware of the director's lifelong enthusiasm for the "browning of America" as a means of keeping conservatives out of power. Not that it would have made any difference.

The filmmaker was preoccupied that early spring morning, as shops and office buildings passed by in a blur. He was actually excited, in a way that seemed unlikely nearly a year and a half earlier when President Hawking was elected, breaking the Democrats 32-year stranglehold on the White House.

There was a lot of anger in the nation, and many held Moore's beloved Progressive Party responsible, even though it had garnered nearly as many popular votes as the other two. By electing not to cast ballots in the Electoral College, the Progressives threw the election to Hawking and the Nationalists (who won despite having the smallest share of the popular vote since John Quincy Adams, in the 1824 election exactly 200 years earlier). This was done as a protest against the Democratic Party, which was not changing fast enough to keep up with the rest of the country. Such were the complications of a three-party system.

Moore hated that Hawking had won, particularly with the prospect of war looming. The archconservative had run on a national security platform that played well to paranoia. He even threatened to wipe out the terrorist training camps across the Middle East. It was an insane sort of bravado that hadn't been seen in America since the 1980s. Michael Moore, however, was seeing dollar signs.

The man who had gotten rich by telling others that it wasn't possible had fallen on some hard times over the years. Nothing to threaten his life-style, of course, but the money wasn't rolling in the way that it had back in the glory days. He had lost the support of many of his Hollywood backers after his production company dropped him over "Subjugation," a bold documentary that publicized the mistreatment of Muslim women by members of their own families. He knew that there would be a backlash in the Muslim community, which was approaching 20% of the overall population in the U.S., but he was taken aback by the reactions of long-time associates and supporters.

One by one, they had denounced him and impugned his film as offen-sive and dangerous. Hollywood celebrities even appeared at televised candlelight vigils (along with hastily veiled Muslim women) to criticize "Subjugation" and claim it to be "full of lies." The irony is that the film was perhaps the only honest piece of work that Michael Moore had ever done. It was iconoclastic, but hardly bigoted; and the women whose sto-ries he presented were certainly real, as was the abuse they suffered. No one in Hollywood seemed to care about that. Their only concern was to appear as broad-minded as possible, irrespective of the underlying facts.

He wasn't worried about the death threats either. He had been foster-ing antagonism with conservatives for more than four decades now, and if those right-wing whackos hadn't made good on their threats, then what reason did he have to fear anyone else?

Moore chuckled to himself as he turned the corner to head down an unclogged side street. He knew that the same fair-weather detractors would soon be right back in his corner again, provided that he found someone to produce his latest project. The idea for the documentary was a comprehensive ridiculing of the Hawking Administration for everything from an occasional verbal stutter to the drumbeat for Iraqi war. Moore knew how easy it was to make others look foolish. Just a few minutes, or even seconds of an ambush-style interview on some unprepared, but trust-ing subject could be edited to the point that they could appear to be saying almost anything. Extracting comments from context and divorcing ques-tions from answers only to marry them to unrelated partners were part of the overall splicing and dicing techniques that Moore perfected for the purpose of leading audiences to preferred conclusions. He relished that power.

Various ideas for titles and marketing crossed his mind as he went over a curb, the bike straining under his weight. He was especially inter-ested in visualizing what the movie poster might look like. His image was sure to figure prominently on it, as was his tradition. Perhaps he would appear as waking up in bed with a sleeping cap on, wide-eyed to find Hawking lying next to him with the title "What Have I Done?."

A sharp horn blast jolted Moore from his musings. He looked back quickly to see if he were about to be run over and was somewhat relieved to see that it was just some fool, activating their car alarm in the most annoying, but fairly common manner of scaring the hell out of anyone walking past. What was the point of that, he wondered to himself. Are you trying to send a message to anyone nearby that the car has an alarm? Everyone knows that you have to have an alarm anyway these days, with things the way they are.

He rarely left the city anymore, except on occasional air jaunts out to his beach home in southern California. At 30,000 feet he didn't have to deal with the so-called "transipolitan" urban areas of most major cities, which were beginning to encroach against suburbia as well. These were the residential and commercial districts being swallowed up in a seemingly irreversible spiral of poverty, crime, and economic decay under the burden of supporting millions of immigrants and "undocumented" aliens. Nor did Moore have to worry much about his own safety, though many others in the country were plagued by the steady rise in the rate of crime across all categories in the last two decades. His beach home in Malibu, like all of the others there, was watched over by a private security firm.

Normally, the filmmaker was accompanied by a personal bodyguard on his way about Manhattan, but this had not been the case for the last couple of days. His employees had organized a union several years ago and were currently in the midst of one of their inopportune "work stoppages." The greedy bastards were demanding more money and less work (in the form of an increase in paid leave). He would have loved to fire them all and start over. With unemployment around 12%, there were plenty of talented people who wouldn't mind putting in the 35 hours a week for what he was paying.

Since the Gore years however, the country had adopted strict worker's rights legislation to deal with the problem of unemployment. The Labor Relations board would never let him fire his entire staff at one time, unless he went completely out of business. Moore knew that his employees would get what they wanted eventually, but he was happy to let them twist in the wind for a while on 40% wages, which, by law, he had to pay while they were on strike.

From the corner of his eye, he thought he caught sight of one of his editors sitting in the window of a coffee house and smugly downing a cappuccino on his dime. Moore turned and raised his right arm in a statuesque, one-fingered salute. The figure in the window was not anyone he knew however, and he turned back in disappointment.

Right then, he felt a sharp pain suddenly in his chest, like he had run into a wire strung across the sidewalk. His pedaling went slack and he grabbed his chest with his right hand while steering with his left, keeping his eyes ahead of him to avoid hitting anything as he coasted. After a second or two, he became aware that his hand felt sticky, and he looked down to see a red stain spreading across his t-shirt.

The front tire of his bike rammed into the side of a concrete stoop, violently upending the bike and smacking his massive body into the hard sidewalk on the other side of the steps. His head opened on impact, sprinkling drops in a bright red pattern away from him. He landed on his back, shattering his left arm and trapping it underneath. Weak and groggy, but still conscious, he noticed the blood forming into a pool at his side and the sound of shouting and screaming. People were running past him, in the same direction that he had been heading.

Two people, evidently a couple, stopped next to him. The woman bent over. "He needs help," she said. "He's been stabbed in the chest."

"That's the guy who did it!" stammered her companion, trying to grab her arm. "He's coming this way... let's go!"

"We should stay and help him. He won't be able to defend himself."

"No, no!" The man was shouting. "This is an internal matter. This doesn't involve us."

"But you've got a gun. You should use it. You can stop this!"

"Quiet, quiet, not so loud! We shouldn't intervene. What business do we have sacrificing on behalf of others? Let this guy rise up and defend himself... it's not our concern." He pulled his companion up and hustled her down the street.

Moore watched them recede into a dull haze, and then turned his head slowly to watch his attacker approaching from the other direction through the thinning crowd. He had never seen the man before, but he knew who he was and in which God he believed. The man smiled as he walked methodically, with a knife in his hand that was dripping a bright color that matched the long line of splatter on a carefully buttoned white oxford – the same color as the pool spreading rapidly from Moore's own twisted body.

He walked up to the deposed filmmaker and pulled a folded sheet of paper from his pocket. After unfolding it, he carefully placed it on top of Moore, then raised his arm and nonchalantly drove the knife through the paper and into the director's chest. The pain was sharp, but quick, as the filmmaker began to fade. "Can we not talk about this?" Moore mumbled.

The attacker had come prepared with an additional weapon, another knife, which he then proceeded to plunge repeatedly into the poor filmmaker's bloated belly, as casually as gutting a fish. The dying man groaned. "Don't you have a gun that you could just get it over with?"

The other paused for a second and spoke his only words with a thick accent. "Do you have any idea how hard it is for a law-abiding person to buy a handgun in this country?"

Friday, May 15th, 2026
Berkeley, California

"D or P?" asked the Professor. He knew by the way the student cocked his head that Danforth wasn't prepared for the question.

"D or P?" repeated the Professor. "Are you a Democrat or a Progressive?"

"I am a... a... Progressive," answered Robert Danforth Jr. hesitantly.

"That's interesting. Your mother is a Democrat, you know."

"Yes sir."

"So, on what do you take issue with the Democrats?"

"I don't know..." Danforth paused. "I guess I really like porn!"

The rest of the students in Professor Rothermel's graduate studies class did not react with the bawdy laughter that may have been the case thirty or forty years ago when pornography was the pariah that it no longer was.

"Well," said the Professor, with a nervous glance to the four female students, who traditionally sat as a group on whatever side of the room the nude Darnell Massey was not, "I don't think that the Democrats have any intention of taking away your freedom of choice, wherever your personal interests may lie. They aren't the Nationalists, you know, who support freedom of choice only if it is to enslave minorities or oppress women."

Each of the eight students in the small Berkeley classroom nodded slightly at the short, bearded man with horn-rimmed glasses and disheveled hair, pacing nervously at the front of the classroom in a wrinkled set of khakis and a t-shirt with light food stains that read "Whitey Will Pay."

They were a diverse group of intellectuals, hand-picked by the little man for his two-year Cultural Studies program, which was offered as an exclusive Master's degree that also counted toward the post-graduate work each of them was pursuing in other areas. He was pleased at having managed to bring together students who represented a broad spectrum of interests, from theology to law, with minimal overlap.

Yet, they had several things in common. Aside from being among Berkeley's best and brightest – in Rothermel's partial opinion – they were idealistic, morally ambiguous and socially conscious. Collectively, they could have formed a movie cast, as they were the young, smart and attractive people about whom most movies were made. Despite the question to Danforth, Rothermel knew that everyone in the room had been active in the Progressive cause, because that was how he encountered each of them.

"Of course, Robert is older than the rest of you," the Professor continued. "Perhaps he can remember a time when this country was a greater threat to the rest of the world than it is now, if you can imagine that. When this century began, we almost had a genuine, born-again, backwater snake-handler sitting in the White House, a man every bit as evil as Hawking, but intent on making this nation a religious State as well. Back then, we had more reason to be pessimistic about the planet's survival. This country's arrogance in the previous years caught up with it, as those who suffered under our oppressive global policies managed to strike back in one stunning masterpiece – the resistance strike of 9/11! Yet, even so, we were fortunate to have a man like Al Gore in the White House at that critical hour, someone smart enough to learn from the country's mistakes, rather than repeat them."

There were some snickers in the classroom.

The professor gave a sly smile. "Yes, I know what you're thinking. At the time, however, it was necessary to act the patriot, if simply for the purpose of redefining patriotism. You can't judge Al Gore against our present standards, but rather against the opposition that he faced at the time. The political winds were different twenty-five years ago, particularly in the wake of 9/11.

"People were angry. Half the country wanted revenge overseas. The other half wanted immediate revenge against their neighbor. Gore thought he had no choice but to wave the flag and eventually drop the bombs. Thanks to the efforts of university volunteers across the country, who traveled to Afghanistan in the years following the imperialistic attack, we know the names of all 252 civilians killed by the American war machine. They appear on plaques in most campuses in the country (including Berkeley, of course) as a reminder that nothing is worth war.

"Still, matters could have been worse for the Afghan people. Gore could have waged a broader war against them instead of finally sending Aziz Sahil to work with the Taliban and bring Osama Bin Laden to justice in the International Crimes Court – setting the precedent that has successfully guided American foreign policy ever since. Diplomacy is the only humane solution to any crisis and nothing is worth war, because nothing could be logically worse than war. In this case, millions of Afghans would have died horrible deaths under a military assault and the slow famine that would have consumed the country in the years following. It would have been worse for them then than it is now, even as Iran and Pakistan wrestle back and forth across their land.

"In keeping with its long history of genocide, the United States could also have inflicted a terrible toll on the innocent and impoverished people of the Arab world by using force to kill the terrorists living among them, instead of having the patience to hear out their grievances. Gore helped

America to understand that we are no better than the enemy that attacks us, something that is taken for granted now in a way that it wasn't twenty-five years ago.

"There were reactionaries living in this country at the time, who mocked President Gore for daring to wage a sensitive war on our enemies. These genuine flag-waving bigots demanded a warrior, someone who would take the battle to the 'enemy' and destroy it with the same aggressive policies used during the Cold War – policies that put America on the same level as those who attack us. They forgot the words of Abraham Lincoln, who said that the best way of destroying an enemy is to make him a friend."

The professor smiled, knowing that he had just spoken eloquently. "It's hard to say where this nation would have been without President Gore. He helped us understand that *our* policies were responsible for the disaster. People today hardly notice that in the aftermath of losing 3,000 Americans, a most amazing thing happened – not one Muslim-American was killed in revenge attacks in the years that followed. Not one! How unimaginable was that, only a decade removed from Ronald Reagan's nearly successful effort to turn this country into a Nazi State? That's a tribute to Al Gore!

"What would it have been like if we hadn't had this man in office, to remind us that Islam is the religion of peace? What if that right-wing religious whacko had won instead? It would have been holy war in the streets of New York, with Muslims dying by the thousands at the hands of American bigots! Hell, Rahim, tell us what it would be like in your country if someone had taken down one of your office buildings."

Rothermel had spoken quickly, without thinking. The question was directed to Rahim Sahil, the grandson of the former Vice President, whose mother opted to raise him in Palestine in order to draw attention to the people's cause. There was an immediate change in the room, almost a collective sucking in of breath. Rothermel knew he had just made a faux pas and tried to keep his face from showing it. His question presupposed a cultural distinction and, worst of all, one that indicated a value bias in favor of his own. Fortunately Rahim seemed to be the only person in the room not to notice.

"For every life the Jews take from us, it will be returned one-hundred fold on their streets, their cafés, their shopping malls, their synagogues, their…"

"Thank you, Rahim," said the Professor quickly, with a nervous smile. "I think you will find that Muslims and progressives have the same enemies – Zionism, imperial expansion, capitalism, globalization, and many other pathologies unique to Western culture. And please forgive me for implying any difference in value between our cultures… other than what I just mentioned, that is. You and your people have so much to teach the rest of America, but we are too blinded by our arrogance at times to learn. Thank you for putting up with us."

Rahim smiled back; in an odd sort of way that Rothermel took as an invitation to dispel any lingering anxiety. The Professor walked behind his desk, looking down for a few seconds while pacing back and forth in an effort to gather his thoughts. Finally, he looked up.

"I realize that many of you are offended by what seems to be a defense of Al Gore, even if you're too polite to say so. But he came along at a critical time. Thanks to his effort, a country as racist, sexist, xenophobic, and Islamophobic as we are, was able to exercise restraint in response to the resistance attacks. He warned the people against overreacting, just as Bill Clinton warned against the very same after the first World Trade Center bombing eight years earlier. The precedent was set, and our pursuit of terrorists remains a legal matter rather than a military one... for the moment, anyway."

The little man's tone softened. "Certainly there were many problems that Gore appeared to ignore in his ten years. For example, the unemployment rate among minorities was still higher than that of whites, even with the passing of the Non-Discrimination Act (NDA) of 2006 that required employers to interview candidates in exact proportion to the racial composite or sexual orientation of the community. But the provisions of this act, which was expanded to protect religious minorities, as you know, allowed protected candidates not receiving job offers to sue, and those who lost their jobs could also petition the government to investigate their dismissal. Over time, employers were forced to hire minorities simply to avoid costly legal challenges, and the numbers improved.

"Likewise, the NDA in Lending, passed that same year, placed the same burden on banks to make loans to applicants in exact proportion to community demographics. This was in an effort to increase home ownership among minorities and provide the same financial opportunities that whites enjoyed. Unfortunately, many banks used this new mandate as an excuse to raise interest rates across the board, which forced many minorities to default on their loans in greater proportion to other borrowers, but," he said with a wink, "we know what really happened, don't we? Good old-fashioned greed. Fortunately the government was able to step in and put a stop to it. These banks began to realize that the world was changing and they weren't prepared to change with it, so many chose instead to go out of business."

The professor brought his hands together in front of his chest, as if to emphasize the point. "Equity in employment and lending occurs slowly, but it progresses because of the groundwork that Gore was able to put down. In the last two decades, we've seen the resurgence of unions, to the point that it's nearly impossible to work for a Fortune 500 company without joining a union, and this bodes well for workers and progressives alike. Power is shifting from the wealthy to the proletariat, and we're seeing these corporations respond to the pressure for increased benefits and shorter workdays.

"Understand that America had much different priorities before 9/11. There was this strong sense of individualism and unrestrained capitalism. Americans were heady about having 'won' the Cold War, a war that was a product of their own imagination of course, but a destructive one for the planet in places like Vietnam nonetheless. There was unwarranted pride and a national spirit among some that coldly suggested that the poor and needy are responsible for their predicament, while the wealthy deserve what they have."

Though they had heard it before, several students couldn't help shaking their heads in disbelief.

The professor continued. "The leadership of Al Gore in a time of crisis brought together what was left of this nation and presented unique opportunities for internal change. After realizing the courage to ask forgiveness from the rest of the world, the country's new-found humility enabled us to recognize internal priorities that had been ignored. The proper role of government, you see, is to provide for the citizens, particularly those who have been on the losing end of this brutal capitalist economic and social system. Many of the more compassionate acts of Congress in the last two decades would not have occurred in absence of the example set during the Gore years, and much of that progress would have been rolled back by our current 'leader' were it not for Gore's key judicial appointments at a critical hour. We…"

"That's easy for someone like you to say," broke in Darnell Massey. "You don't have to worry about some lynch mob showing up at your door under the President's orders. As a black man, I do!"

Darnell was one of two minorities in the class. Though he didn't know it, he was the reason that Parker Whitehead, the theology student, was included in the group. Rothermel's first choice had been a young woman who had written a published thesis on Liberation Theology, thoroughly reducing Christianity to naked irrelevancy. She balked at the Professor's invitation however, after learning that Darnell Massey would be sitting in as well.

Massey was certainly no dummy, but he made a good subject for the clandestine betting pool that certain faculty members held to place wagers on the SAT scores of certain students. Under pressure from the Gore Administration, the California courts had finally declared unconstitutional the Proposition from the late 1990's that prevented the Board of Regents from using an applicant's race as a criterion for acceptance. Undoing the damage of the prior years had taken some time, however. It was not until the system was adjusted to the extent that an applicant's status as a minority counted twice as heavily as their secondary grade point average that the University was able to achieve the desired composite in their freshmen class.

But even so, for some strange reason that no one had yet been able to say, the dropout and failure rates were far greater for minorities – to the extent, even, that ethnic graduation rates remained remarkably similar to the Proposition years.

Clearly, something had to be done and, as a last resort, the University adopted a pass/fail grading system and also began aggressively counseling the faculty, to root out any racist subtleties that might have evaded the original screening process. Minority students were interviewed as well, and, in keeping with the University's commitment to progress, their opinions were used as input into the annual faculty review process. Amazingly, the disparities vanished overnight.

Darnell pushed the envelope of academic immunity a bit further than the rest, putting little effort into his school work. He had even stopped wearing clothes on campus during his graduating year, as a protest against the oppression under which his people had suffered ("I refuse to facilitate the White power structure with my conformity"). Many of the feminists found that offensive, although others students were quietly respectful. Most agreed that non-minorities were prohibited from commenting on the matter, since they could not truly understand the African-American struggle.

In response to Massey's remark, Rothermel nodded quickly and agreeably, as most whites had learned to do whenever an African-American brings up the issue of race. This was a way of figuratively elevating oneself above the white herd through an implicit display of empathy. "We all know that President Hawking is a racist, of course, and that his agenda represents a grave threat to anyone in this country who wasn't born a wealthy white man, but…" the Professor looked down to collect his thoughts. "But, I can't help feeling optimistic about the eventual destruction of these institutions of… of class and greed.

"Most people in this country are angry," he continued. "They know they didn't elect a Nationalist to the White House. They know what's going on. They recognize the attempt to steal the people's hard-won gains away from them. Unfortunately the Soviet Union is no longer around to keep America in check. Still, there are more Progressives than Nationalists in Congress…"

"Amen to that!" The enthusiastic interruption was from Parker Whitehead and the rest of the class chuckled softly in agreement.

Rothermel wasn't sure about Parker Whitehead. He was certainly solidly on the Left, in fact he was fond of telling people that "Jesus was a Communist," but there was something about him that made Rothermel uneasy, and it wasn't a mystery. The Professor had always been suspicious of religious people, and Parker seemed to take such superstition to heart. Most of the theology majors whom the Professor knew at Berkeley were deeply cynical of absolute truth and lived not much differently from anyone else. Although he was no less passionate than others in the class, Whitehead was not an amoral radical. He used religious doctrine to justify his socially-conscious actions.

Rothermel had gradually gotten used to this. After all, why complain if they both reached the same end, even if by different means.

The Professor himself might have seemed an angry zealot to those who disagreed with him, but that didn't apply to anyone in the classroom, including the four young women.

Bernice Greenly was the daughter of GNN news mogul Bernard Greenly, who also owned many of the larger newspapers in the country. She was already picking up her father's nickname of "Bernie."

Phyllis Hughes studied media communications and had aspirations of becoming a television producer. Like most of the others in the classroom, she was a child of privilege and had the connections necessary to realize her ambitions.

This was not the case with Maria Posada, the youngest of the group. Her family was poor (certainly by the standards of her Berkeley peers) having emigrated from Mexico shortly after she was born. She was well-respected, however, both for her intelligence and passion for the Latino cause. She was head of the Atzlan chapter on campus, a group dedicated to returning most of the Western United States to Mexico by any means necessary. Like Bernice and Phyllis, she wore scissors around her neck in the familiar style of feminists on campus. She may have turned heads, but the guys knew to keep their distance.

The most promising student was Jill Hudson, a dynamo and natural leader in campus politics and in the classroom. She was a beautiful young woman from an established New York family with a long and storied political history. In fact, her father, Senate Majority Leader Phil Hudson, was rumored to be the inside favorite for the Democratic nomination in 2028. Her mother had first attained fame as a 16-year-old girl in a famous photograph taken at an abortion-rights rally, after she had just finished telling off a group of archaic anti-choicers.

Jill was extremely popular and well-spoken. Men wanted to please her, and the female students would often try to imitate her. If Jill led a protest rally wearing a beret and preaching the "reinvention of democracy" (one of her favorite subjects) one could expect to see beret-clad,

pseudo-intellectuals in Berkeley cafés the next day pretending to understand and discuss the issue. Rothermel noticed that she was also the first
among the group to temper her populist leanings with political pragma-
tism, perhaps due to the influence of her Democratic father.

She did not wear scissors around her neck or the popular shirts that
blended the President's name with various profanities, nor was she to be
seen at the most radical protest rallies, such as those advocating social
nihilism. There was a rumor, however, that she was suspected to be heavily involved in the dynamiting of the old campus World War I memorial,
on the grounds that the obelisk resembled a phallic, and was thus a repressive symbol.

Still, she was the brightest of the bunch, he thought, and probably had
the most potential.

"Even so, I agree that we face the gravest threat to our future in thirty
years," concluded the Professor. "We must fear for our freedom. There
are elements in the government that want absolute control over our lives,
over our bodies. They want to roll the clock back to a time when women
had no freedom and minorities had no rights. Our fragile environment is
in jeopardy, as is public education, health care, and our hard won civil
liberties. President Hawking is waging an international crusade that can
only squander our credibility and respect among nations.

"Now," he said sitting back on his desk and crossing his arms with a
smile. "What are we doing this summer?"

Wednesday, June 24th, 2026
Baghdad, Iraq

Two of the most exciting weeks of their lives were coming to a close
as Robert Danforth gathered with the other three students, in the basement
bar of their Baghdad hotel on their last night. The sun was well below the
horizon and the plan was that they would get thoroughly wasted before
carrying additional drinks out onto the roof to sit and enjoy the night.

Parker Whitehead was the last to come down, which didn't matter
since he wasn't a drinker anyway. Of the four, he had spent the least
amount of time with the group. Though he attended most of the major
functions with the rest, he usually stole away to visit the Christian en-
claves in the city, and meet leaders and groups that he had been corresponding with prior to the trip. Danforth did not approve of this, and Rahim could hardly keep from sneering at him, but Jill had actually gone
with him a few times, even though she had no stomach for religion. This
upset Danforth, although he stayed quiet. He did tell Parker in front of the
whole group, however, that he thought his "church" activities were a danger to the rest of them, with which Rahim readily agreed.

The dark-haired grandson of the former Vice President was their guide and translator. He looked the part of the Arab, even though he was technically of Persian descent. Few in America could tell the difference, but that was certainly not the case in Iraq where Sunnis ruled and Shias, particularly those with Iranian ties, were viewed with suspicion. Rahim, of course, was in no such danger. The grandfather to whom he bore a mild physical likeness was still the most respected Muslim in America, even with plenty of other public Islamic figures to compete with. It was because of him that Osama Bin Laden was serving a twenty years to life sentence in a Swiss prison for the 9/11 attacks.

Jill Hudson, of course, was the center of attention wherever they went. Blondes weren't too common in Iraq; in fact you were more likely to meet a redhead (descended from the Assyrians, who were conquered by the Arabs centuries earlier). Even Uday Hussein was visibly enamored with her when they met with him to discuss the devastation that Iraqis would have to endure in the event of war. He made every excuse to touch Jill on the elbows, arms and shoulders as much as possible during their interview – not in a crude way, but visibly annoying to the independent and proud young woman. Though he had often fantasized about rescuing her from some sort of imagined danger and being her "hero," Danforth only watched the Iraqi leader's not-so-subtle advances. So petrified was he to be in the actual presence of Uday Hussein, that he truly believed that he would not have done anything more than clear his throat had the leader decided to force himself on Jill right then and there – and probably not even that.

He doubted that it bothered Jill anyway, as he told himself afterwards. He was sure that she wasn't the sort of woman who would have appreciated a man standing up for her. Perhaps she wasn't a "scissors-wearer," but she was a strong feminist nevertheless. Despite his efforts, he felt that the distance between them had grown wider, both during the trip and ever since he had first entered their circle of friends some years earlier.

Impressing others was an avocation for Robert Danforth. When he was 13, his junior high class was divided into two groups for track and field events based on their performance in a massive race, with some one-hundred and fifty students huffing their way around the circumference of the playground. Although he had decent running ability, the boy threw the trial by holding himself back so that he would finish in the bottom half. For the rest of the term, he came in first at every event within the weaker group, even impressing those in the top half of the class who often watched the races and cheered him on.

He was the son of political socialite Sherry Danforth and a father he never knew, killed when the north tower of the World Trade Center collapsed 102 minutes after being hit by a hijacked passenger jet. Although the events of that day were still treated reverently in the small New Jersey community, which was hard hit by the tragedy, his Berkeley classmates referred to the attacks as "resistance" – after first clearing it with him in an informal way, so as not to appear insensitive. This surprised him at first, but he harbored no real animosity over the loss of his father. He gathered that his mother had far less personal attachment than one might guess from her public appearances, given that there were no pictures of his father around the house, and the only mementos were saved in a small box in the attic of the garage.

It wasn't hard for him to agree to a magazine's request a few years earlier for a joint interview and photo-op session with the son of one of the hijackers. It was billed as "finding closure," or "children of peace," or something like that. The magazine cover had a picture of the two boys solemnly shaking hands, with small insets of their fathers appearing in the background.

At the meeting, Robert had made the usual conciliatory statements that he knew would play well in the story, but he thought it odd that the other boy had made no attempt to offer an apology for what his father had done – not that Robert held it against him, although he was sure that he would have at least felt compelled to apologize, had the shoe been on the other foot. Instead, the interview focused mostly on the conditions of the Palestinian people that were said to have precipitated the attacks. Robert actually found himself offering an apology for the presumed complicity of the United States in the matter, which the other graciously accepted.

Fortunately, this played well at Berkeley where Danforth was a brief celebrity in just about any group. Professors like Rothermel would recognize his surname and ask if he were "Sherry's son." Occasionally, some in the class would approach him afterwards, though Robert realized that his status as a curiosity faded quickly if there was nothing else to keep the interest going. As such, he began to get involved in the more visible political and social causes on campus, to which he had no real attachment other than gaining favor with other students for his effort. He learned the language quickly, and could sound as earnest as anyone else when it came to the need to protest arctic oil drilling and nuclear power, for example, while paradoxically blaming the Hawking Administration for the high cost of energy.

It wasn't difficult for him. His mother had championed such issues for as long as he could remember, advocating government health care, the Pillar project, environmental policy or anything else asked of her by successive Democratic Administrations, all the while somehow managing to tie each concern in with her own personal loss on 9/11. Not having known his father, Robert's appeal to tragedy was somewhat limited, but his name did offer some opportunities, although his political passions were always superficial and generally no more than a means to an end. What he really sought, as he would admit only to himself, was popularity. He envied those who were respected and admired on campus, but no matter how hard he tried, he was never quite able to scale the final summit, and always found himself playing second-fiddle or less to someone else, without understanding why.

Right now he felt like he was basking in Parker Whitehead's glow, which didn't make much sense. The guy wouldn't even share a drink with the rest of them. He drank coke instead. Robert sometimes tried to embarrass him in situations like these by loudly asking if he wanted a "Shirley Temple" or whether that would be pushing it with "the Big Guy upstairs." Parker always came up with some sort of smooth response that was entirely self-deprecating, yet usually managed to make whatever Robert said sound personally insulting. This in turn made him feel like an ass, which only heightened his social insecurity.

The more time that he spent with Parker, the more he hated him. It always seemed to come easy to guys like him, without even trying. He was barely around during the day, playing with his church buddies while the rest were touring devastated neighborhoods and meeting with high-level officials (who warned of the humanitarian crisis that would surely develop in the event of a war). Then he would meet the others at the end of the day, grimy and sunburned, to modestly touch base and share a few squeaky-clean jokes.

No matter how much dirt he was covered in, or how freshly-scrubbed the rest of them were, he would become the reluctant center of attention, with Jill usually trying to sit next to him. Even Rahim got along with him fairly well, although he had no patience for hearing about his Christian activities and would sternly lecture him on the role of *dhimmis* in an Islamic society. These dire lectures, which became more candid in proportion to consumed alcohol, were always shrugged off by Parker, who seemed to have an irrepressible faith in mankind and would say things like "Oh Rahim, you know you don't mean that," as it would go in one ear and out the other. Robert wished to hell that something nasty would happen to him, anything from a stomach bug to a Jihad hit. But of course nothing ever did, and he would be there with them at the end of every day to share his stories nonchalantly.

There was added tension that night, facilitated as it was by a comment that Danforth made about the fact that Whitehead was turning prematurely grey. "You're turning into a whitehead, Whitehead," he said through the haze of four and a half beers.

Rahim laughed and Parker started to respond in sort of a good-natured way, but Jill cut him off with an angry look. "Robbie, don't you have anything good to say about anyone?"

She was serious and Danforth was taken aback by her display of irritation, which had never been that direct before. Perhaps his observation that she had been drinking more than usual that night was correct. Everyone at the table was looking at him now, and he was beginning to feel quite embarrassed. Unable to maintain eye contact, he looked down at his bottle and started stammering.

He wasn't sure what he said, but fortunately Parker rescued him by "assuring" Jill that he hadn't meant it in a bad way. Danforth's thoughts turned dark, and he hated him all the more. It didn't help matters that the most coveted woman on campus was practically throwing herself at him and he didn't even seem to care.

"What are you going to do after the trip, Parker?" Danforth finally asked.

"Rahim and I are going to be at the Edina demonstration in D.C. on the first. There were five more cases of the virus reported this year and two additional deaths."

"Of course," interjected Rahim, "all new cases are in the Bonan community, so the government and newspapers don't care."

Danforth wasn't so sure of that. He had noticed a great deal of media attention on the Edina virus in the last year or so, although apparently the disease had been around for years in relative obscurity. The government seemed to be under pressure as well.

The Bonans were a Chinese ethnic group that had emigrated in the 1990's to escape persecution for their Muslim faith. Their tiny community of about 2,000 was located mainly around the Minneapolis area. The virus was named after the suburb where it was first discovered, although it was originally called the 'Bonan Virus' up until Muslim activist groups complained of insensitivity.

"I thought the BIR was making a big deal about it," he said, referring to the Bureau of Islamic Relations, the Federal agency that Rahim's grandfather led.

"They're trying," said Sahil, "but America is controlled by a class of people that will not use their power or influence unless it is in their best interest. Since there have been no cases reported outside of the Muslim community, then it's not a concern, and they choose to ignore it. Thirty-six people are dead, but they aren't white Christians, so who cares?"

Danforth thought he might have an opening to stir up a little tension. He turned to Parker. "Well, why don't we ask the only white Christian that we know about it, since he happens to be sitting with us. Reverend Whitehead, why don't you Jesus freaks care about anyone but yourselves?"

He was satisfied by the visible discomfort on Parker's face as he struggled with his words. "I, uh… I don't know that Christians are less concerned about the virus than anyone else. On the contrary, as I mentioned, I'll be demonstrating in Washington with…"

"What is it you really want from Muslims?" asked Danforth boldly. "You want them to convert to your religion, don't you?"

"Yes!" Rahim answered for Parker, who simply looked flustered as he could only shake his head.

"Of course they want us to convert, and if we won't convert, then they kill us!" continued Rahim. "Remember the Crusades? They were a military incursion into peaceful Muslim lands…"

"I'm not looking to convert anyone," said Parker. "I believe that God calls people to live according to the law that he writes in their heart. I'm sure that all great religions are essentially alike, because I believe that there is only one God."

Rather than appear placated, Rahim seemed all the more disgusted. He'd been drinking longer than the rest of them, having been the first to the bar that afternoon. He set down his beer and said slowly, "Islam is truth. What is not Islam is heresy. You Christians are realizing this, and that is why you are turning from your false religion and seeking truth from those of us who believe in their faith enough to die for it. Did you know that there was an upsurge of conversions to Islam in New York City following the resistance attacks on 9/11?"

No one answered. Rahim picked up his beer again, but before taking another swallow he stated, "By your democracy we will invade you. By our religion we will dominate you."

Parker's mouth hung open.

Danforth could hardly suppress a smile.

Jill was unfazed. She gave them a mocking look, as a mother might to a child caught in the act of sneaking a cookie. "Maybe the problem, boys, is religion itself. It only provides false hope and a reason to hate one's fellow man. If society was completely cleansed of…"

"Religious cleansing?" asked Parker.

"Well, yes. I mean… you make it sound as if it's as bad as ethnic cleansing. I'm not talking about…"

"Cleanse away!" commanded Rahim, raising his mug. "Do your best to destroy religion. You will only succeed in destroying your own. Islam cannot be stopped any more than truth can be hidden."

"I'm not talking about destroying Islam, Rahim," responded Jill, who was somewhere over her alcohol limit as well. "As you know, I'm a strong supporter of diversity through immigration. America needs more Muslims, if for no other reason than to counter the Religious Right – the people that elected Hawking. I believe though, that if Americans have a culture with multiple religious choices, each on equal standing and exposure, they will come to realize the relativity of religion. Once they get beyond making value judgments between the major faiths, they will eventually come to realize their irrelevance altogether."

Rahim laughed. Parker looked uncomfortable. Danforth was secretly congratulating himself on completely turning the focus of the conversation.

Jill ruined the moment by giving Parker a good-natured punch in the arm and suggesting that they move the "party" up to the roof. Everyone grabbed their drinks and headed toward the elevator, with Danforth making a pit stop along the way in the hope that it would sober him up a bit.

The night was breezy and mild, with more stars visible above them than would be typical for a North American city of that size. Wide boulevards with softly swaying palm trees spread out below. They seemed to originate from directly underneath them and extended outward, in a star pattern, to an abrupt end at the edge of darkness. The Euphrates glistened in the distance, looking somewhat enchanting from their vantage point, although they each knew from daylight inspection, how badly polluted the water actually was.

They talked quietly with each other late into the night, as the darkness seemed to obscure the earlier tension and draw out their common interests. The purpose of their trip was to travel as citizen-diplomats to Iraq and promote a message of peace, love and harmony. They were children of prominent American figures and their trip to show solidarity with the Iraqi people was not going unnoticed back in the States.

In the calm darkness, Parker painted a visual picture for the rest of what would happen if the bombs started falling out of the sky and into the neighborhoods below. He vividly described the toll on property and human life, drawing from their experiences with victims of the Gulf War, now living with amputated limbs and disabilities suffered as children in that conflict thirty-five years earlier. The group of victims had been gathered for the students by the government of Iraq as part of the highly-scripted visit.

The conversation lulled after a time, and they each sat back in their chairs with their heads tilted up, pondering the stars above and enjoying the placid setting. Danforth's plan had been to stay until at least Jill called it a night, but he left along with Rahim when he noticed her sitting very close to Parker. They were lightly playing with each other's hands, although he couldn't tell if it was in a friendly or more serious manner.

The next morning, as Robert stumbled out of his room, thoroughly in the grip of a hangover, he saw Jill leaving Parker's room wearing the same clothes from the night before. They did not make eye contact.

Thursday, July 30th, 2026
Sweetgrass, Montana

Their vantage point, on a hillside overlooking the highway, afforded Rothermel an unparalleled view of one of the most beautiful sights in America these days. It wasn't the distant mountains, which hid Glacier National Park behind them, or the gently rolling grass plains leading up to those mountains, but rather the line of cars, trucks, campers and masses of people that clogged the northbound lanes of the road below. It literally stretched back as far as the eye could see, and had for the entire two weeks that he and his students had volunteered to assist with the emigration.

Though many in America lamented the loss of these "conscientious objectors," as some called them or "tax-evading crooks" and "right-wing extremists" as others did, Rothermel gloried in the moment. He shared none of the ambivalence expressed by any of his peers, even the occasional Progressive dissenter, and firmly argued that this was about evolution. "Imagine the progress toward economic equality and elimination of class structure that could be made in this country," he would rhetorically ask his students, "if our worst elements, the racists, homophobes, and utter sexists who called themselves 'Religious Conservatives', voluntarily removed themselves." Social reformers would be unhindered in their quest to mold America into a refined, multicultural civilization – in stark contrast to the backwater that this abominable, intolerant herd below them would be building across the border.

It wasn't as if the United States didn't have enough people wanting to take their place. The flow of immigrants from Muslim countries had risen dramatically, even after the Pillar project was officially ramped down. The original plan had been to bring the superpower into balance with the rest of the world, which was now one-quarter Muslim and growing. Though limited to those fleeing persecution, the immigrants had the right to bring over family members, and their numbers were climbing. Between these and the strong flow of people across the Mexican border, the country was changing dramatically and it was a very exciting time, even if Rothermel rarely left the confines of Berkeley.

The story of modern Alberta really began with the secession of Quebec eleven years earlier. This, in turn, was due to the rise of the Palestinian State, made possible by the pressure that the Gore and Rodham Administrations brought to bear on Israel. Since Canada was a strong champion of the Palestinian cause, it had to accord logical respect to the Quebecois independence bid, even though it meant the literal dissolution of the country. The former French Canadians celebrated, even as the "English" provinces glumly pondered the dim prospects of holding themselves together over the new reality that their country was entirely bisected by a foreign government.

Ottawa began the process of spinning off its regions, largely to the Americans. The Atlantic Provinces were the first go, as their isolation and poor economies were a drag on the Western governments. The fishing industry had been in decline for a half century and the area had little more to offer other than picturesque real estate, which the Americans rushed in to buy up even before the ink was dry on their formal declaration as a U.S Protectorate. This fueled a mild economic boom (at least by Canadian standards) and had many believing that there might soon be a 51st State added to the Union.

The experience in the East influenced the trend toward independence in the West, particularly in the strange case of Alberta. The province had always been Canada's political "red-headed stepchild," highly resistant to Ottawa's progressive polices, which, although serving as a model to the United States, were not popular in the business-friendly, Rocky Mountain province. Albertans had consistently elected Conservative Party candidates as far back as the 1970's, in defiance of national trends. Clashes with the national government became even more bitter however, as the province began to fall under the control of the American "objectors."

When one looked at an electoral map of America these days, it was a peaceful sea of Progressive green and Democratic blue save for one offensive streak of harsh red directly below Alberta. Montana, Idaho, Utah and Wyoming were sometimes joined by North Dakota, Kansas and even Colorado on rare occasions, as the last holdouts for the Nationalist Party. Although the population had been growing rapidly since the tax-evasion camps were set up in the region, they still constituted less than 15% of the country. Now, many of these people were heading across the northern border as liberals in Washington goaded the Federal government into cracking down on the underground economy and old-fashioned moral values that were burgeoning with the concentration of religious conservatives in the Red States.

Alberta became the absolute dominion of these yahoos and even declared complete independence, going so far as to form an independent government and "militia," a term that unnerved Rothermel, particularly since he was standing only yards away from several of these armed men, patrolling the international line in battle dress uniforms. The border ran across the knoll, not far down the hill from where the 38-year-old professor had organized a protest demonstration with his students.

The soldiers were an ominous presence to what was otherwise being treated as a festive occasion. Rothermel had arrived along with Phyllis Hughes and Darnell Massey, to offer volunteer assistance to the Federal government by processing the hopeful emigrants. During the long days, they dutifully interviewed candidates and entered data into computer applications that fed into databases back in Washington. There were probably close to a hundred-thousand people trying to get through just that one border crossing at that particular time. More than nine million others had legally left the country to start their new lives, and it was thought that perhaps several million more had simply crossed over on their own without giving notice. The new government of Alberta was working up an elaborate method of controlling its population, with identification cards that were difficult to counterfeit. They were well on their way to becoming a police state.

Dealing with these sorts of people day after day was exhausting to the young students and even to Rothermel, who knew what to expect from his dealings with the occasional campus conservative. These were narrow-minded, antiquated dinosaurs that may seem harmless on the surface, but harbored deep hatred for the policies that were finally beginning to bring about a progressive America.

Rothermel wished that his friends in Washington, some of whom seemed to genuinely lament the loss of this detestable segment of the country's population, could spend some time in his shoes, finding out just how offensive these extremists really were. He knew all of the arguments, particularly the one about entrepreneurs or business owners taking jobs with them, but from what he was seeing, the U.S. would never miss the loss of a few religious or conservative nuts. America was changing, and they were not prepared to change with it, so they might as well pack up and let the rest of the country move forward.

The lines of those waiting to exit the country wrapped around tents, down highway roadsides, and even out into the neighboring prairie. Men and women stood holding babies, or trying to keep their snotty kids out from underfoot while volunteers processed them, trying to make sure that their applications to Alberta had been accepted and that there were no criminal charges pending against them in the States. The jubilant mood of the applicants failed to carry over to the volunteers, who angrily warned them against singing hymns or trying to evangelize.

Sometimes, the smart young volunteers around him would take a few liberties at the expense of these religious rubes. A question commonly asked the first few days, but one that wasn't on the questionnaire was, "Are you a patriotic American?"

Usually the applicant would reply in the affirmative, in which case the volunteer would pretend to cease the processing and say something like "Well, I guess you won't be leaving us then."

The befuddled applicants would then try to explain themselves, which in most cases was even more boring than simply sticking to the routine.

After a while the practice was dropped, although volunteers did amuse themselves by handing out American flags on the 4th of July.

One of Rothermel's favorite pastimes to break up the monotony was to adopt an exaggerated Southern drawl as he asked questions. This provided sheer entertainment to the other volunteers within earshot, who played along as best they could without giving him away. The applicants, of course, usually didn't know what he was up to, and would smile kindly at him as if trying to be polite to someone considered an intellectual inferior, which is exactly what Rothermel actually considered each of them. He was, after all, a university professor at a most prestigious institution, while they were merely business owners, computer technicians and plumbers.

Most were also ex-felons, having broken the law by refusing to pay taxes after the Gore Health Plan was enacted nearly twenty years ago. They were sent to the low-security camps to serve 12-month prison sentences that escalated to 24 and 36 months terms in a largely unsuccessful effort to deter recidivists. Their families usually followed them and put down roots in the area.

The character of these Red States became even more distinct from that of the rest of the country, resembling (in the minds of many) 1950's America, where "family values" were of high concern. Often the National Guard was called up to protect the handful of abortion clinics, although none of them seemed to do very much business. Occasionally "freedom riders," usually college kids on break, would stage convoys through the various states to call attention to the erosion of free speech or other civil liberties that were rumored to suffer as the areas became concentrated with conservatives.

Tensions mounted, particularly after Congress passed legislation requiring that every Red State tax return be audited to assure compliance, despite the added bureaucratic expense. There was deep suspicion among those in the rest of the nation that the former tax-evaders were finding other ways (such as bartering) to avoid paying their fair share for the rising cost of the nation's social programs. Academics like Rothermel welcomed their voluntary ouster to Alberta. At least it relieved the cost of running the camps, and freed up badly needed funds for the government-run transitory communities elsewhere that provided temporary living facilities to Hispanic and Muslim immigrants (those that *want* to be a part of America).

The people who passed in front of him in the tents that week were in no position to negotiate with the society they had so flagrantly betrayed; and their loss from the voting rolls and political process simply moved the nation's center well to the left of where it had been. Rothermel knew that this could only be of benefit to the cause of progress and social justice.

What troubled him at the moment though, as he stood there on the hillside with Phyllis and Darnell, looking down on the mass of people waiting to get out of the country, was that many of them did not fit the stereotype that he had drawn up for his students in the classroom. Mixed in among the white Christians were people who were not white, and even some who may not have been Christian. What was of urgent concern to him, in fact, was a rather large black man climbing the hill toward them from the Alberta side, behind the group of soldiers. He seemed to be taking offense to their antics.

At the end of each workday, they would take off their ID badges and stage a demonstration on the hill for the news cameras, donning costumes to mock the émigrés below them. Phyllis was dressed like a nun and Rothermel like a Nazi. They were both giving the "white power" salute (and shouting out the slogan at the same time, for anyone not familiar with the gesture). This was much to the obvious chagrin of the people below. Darnell had really outdone himself and was dressed like a black Colonel Sanders, the Kentucky Fried Chicken icon, complete with a white goatee and a large sign that read "Uncle Tom Alberta."

Rothermel guessed that it was this last part that seemed to offend the man slowly making his way toward them. As he got closer, the smaller professor stepped instinctively behind Darnell, who did not see the malcontent approaching. This was an unfortunate decision as it were, because Darnell was knocked rather decisively into Rothermel, who fell to the ground underneath him as both men went down in a heap. He looked up to see the soldiers laughing as the black man turned and made his way back down the hill. Two of them actually slapped his back as went by.

Darnell was either unconscious, or pretending to be. Rothermel didn't have time to evaluate his condition. He scrambled to his feet in a rage and approached the soldiers, who stopped laughing and immediately tensed up a bit, as Rothermel came screamed at them. "What do you mean standing there like that? Did you see what that man did? Who the hell do you think you are? I am an American citizen. You can't treat me that way. I'm an American!"

None of them responded, which angered Rothermel all the more. He gathered that one of them was the team leader and the little professor walked up and spit on his uniform. It was only the second time in his life that he had done that. The first time propelled him to minor fame when a photograph was snapped, but this time he would be propelled somewhere else, as the squad leader looked down at Rothermel's saliva then turned to ask his corporal to hold his weapon. The Professor's eyebrows rose as he took note of the look of mild humor in the corporal's eyes.

"Well," said the leader, quickly gathering up Rothermel in his hands then hoisting him over his head. "Let me help you get back to America, because you're standing on Albertan soil right now."

With that, he threw the little man as hard as he could toward his stunned students, thus completing the process of international extradition in the most unceremonious way.

Wednesday, August 5th, 2026
Washington, DC

On the day that Parker arrived back in the States, he opened the paper to find that the National Cathedral had been firebombed. The arson was thought to be in revenge for the al-Raz mosque burning in New Jersey, although it did not fall on the anniversary of February 20th, which is when most of the dozens of church burnings took place.

The paper contained two editorials on the incident. One was written by Aziz Sahil, which theorized that no Muslim could have been responsible for such an act of vandalism and that right-wing hate groups were probably to blame. The other took a bold position that the arsonists were indeed Muslim, as they were in all of the other fire-bombings. To temper this, however, the remainder of the article argued that the incident underscored the disenfranchisement that Muslim-Americans were feeling, as well as the need for social programs to remedy their situation.

Friday, September 11th, 2026
New York City, NY

A cool breeze whipped through what was left of Al Gore's gray head of hair, as it did with the other dignitaries seated with him on the raised platform. A crowd of fifteen thousand carefully-screened attendees stretched out in front of them. Secret Service officers in sunglasses paced the twenty-five foot buffer zone between the stage and the audience like big game hunters, sometimes putting their hands to the side of their heads occasionally, to hold tiny earpieces in place. Every now and then, their lips would move as they searched the crowd intently trying to keep their eye on some target of interest.

The wind was feeding across the water, where the Statue of Liberty could be seen in the distance, as well as Staten Island. Coast Guard and police vessels patrolled the shores, and there were no commercial or private boats visible at all.

The ceremony marking the twenty-fifth anniversary of the attacks on September 11th, 2001 was marred by protests, despite the Herculean efforts by area law enforcement groups to contain the demonstrators. President Hawking was determined to speak at the event despite the strong resistance from some of the more vocal 9/11 family groups, led by the Jersey Girls, who, though aging, were as outspoken as ever.

Sherry Danforth even fell on her sword by standing up to disrupt Hawking's speech, knowing that security would have to take her away. The spectacle of a 9/11 widow hauled from a memorial service for her husband, while an embarrassed Hawking stood gaping in the background, was a photogenic moment, albeit one that was carefully engineered. Even Al Gore almost felt sorry for the Nationalist, who had said nothing offensive, but was made the goat of nonetheless.

The President spoke first, emphasizing the great loss that the country suffered on that day, and repeating the old myth that America did nothing to bring it upon herself. Though his speech was punctuated by disruption, it was at that moment that a coordinated group of protesters, dispersed throughout the audience, began yelling in unison and continued to do so until the last of them was inconveniently removed, after about twenty minutes of complete distraction.

Though Gore did not like Hawking, he didn't feel completely comfortable with the interruptions, because he knew that he might be in for similar treatment himself, as there were people still angry about his decision to bomb Afghanistan nearly twenty years earlier. No one cared about counting or naming the 3,000 civilians estimated to have been killed by his predecessor's aerial bombardment of Serbia, but Gore never seemed to hear the end of the 252 people who died from his poor decision to bomb a government that refused to hand over the terrorist, Bin Laden, for six years. As acts of terrorism were becoming more common in America, he was forced to reduce and eventually eliminate public speaking engagements. Now seventy-seven, the former President sat and listened to the accolades and mild rebuke from others, who openly discussed America's responsibility for 9/11, and complimented Al Gore's leadership in the wake of the disaster.

Directly after Hawking was Robert Danforth, Sherry's son, who was not even born when his father was killed. "I wonder what kind of world I would have grown up in," said the young man, with an unmistakable look of contempt toward the seat occupied by President Hawking, "had we a lesser man in office in the months and years following my father's death. If instead of a man of peace, vision and courage, we had elected a vigilante, some sort of cowboy that responded with a terrible aggression that only would have made our enemy stronger.

"Perhaps this is the sort of disastrous foreign policy that we have to worry about today," he continued, while turning to Gore, "but such was not the case twenty-five years ago. President Al Gore had the courage to ask serious questions about America's role in the world, and what we may have contributed to the circumstances that impelled nineteen men to martyr themselves. Not to have asked those questions would have been a be-trayal to the victims, including my father."

Danforth was followed by an actress named Starr Sterling, someone whom Gore had met before at events for various social and environmental causes. She was presently the star of the hit TV show, The Advocate, in which she played a kind-hearted government worker, fighting each week to qualify the needy for subsistence programs. Her adversaries rotated between callous corporations that refused to hire willing workers, fire-brand citizen activists that wanted to cut social programs, and unsympa-thetic Federal bureaucrats (boldly identified as Nationalists) that pressured her to discontinue her charitable efforts. The latter category had become the preferred antagonist since the election of President Hawking two years earlier, particularly since the recurring villain in the series had been a Na-tionalist Senator bearing a strong physical resemblance to the former mi-nority leader. It was even more suspicious perhaps, that this character's ascension to the White House coincided with Hawking's, but the show's ratings rose as the President's declined.

Sterling stood at the platform in an attractive, low-cut dress with an Edina ribbon pinned to the shoulder – a token of her concern to the (mostly Bonan) victims of the epidemic. Her speech was similar to the young man that preceded her, but with a harsher edge toward the Nation-alist President. "Today as the country finds itself on the brink of a possi-ble illegal, unethical and brutal military campaign against the peaceful people of Iraq, we would do well to remember the patience and conviction of a leader who refused to give in to the demagoguery of the day by fight-ing a unilateral 'war against terrorism' with guns and bombs, as many in America were urging him to do. President Gore understood that it was more important to rejoin the international community as an equal mem-ber, rather than a dictatorial bully that arrogantly wills its way..."

And so it went on, until it was the former President's time to speak. He ambled down the line of dignitaries toward the podium. It brought him satisfaction to see that many were prominent Muslim leaders, includ-ing his own Vice President, Aziz Sahil, who had served humbly as head of the Bureau of Islamic Relations since his failed run at the Presidency in 2008. Gore briefly clasped his elbow and gave him a wink as he passed by and took the podium. When the applause died down, he cleared his throat and began to speak.

"Thank you very much for those kind words on this sad occasion as we remember the three thousand victims..."

Gore got no further than that, because at that moment about fifty peo-ple rose as one and began chanting the familiar refrain that had dogged him over the last twenty years: "TWO FIFTY-TWO, TWO FIFTY-TWO, TWO FIFTY-TWO..."

The ex-President didn't have the patience or fortitude for standing his ground and waiting out the demonstrators the way his contemporary had less than an hour before, despite the fact that he was only ten years older than Hawking. He carefully gathered up his notes and walked past the same line of Muslim dignitaries – at least two of whom were now chanting softly along with the protesters, though trying not to make eye contact with him. His Secret Service detail followed him down the steps at the end of the platform and around back to a waiting limousine.

It would be Al Gore's last public appearance.

Tuesday, November 3rd, 2026
Tucson, Arizona

Danforth didn't know much Spanish, but it really wasn't a problem at the moment, since his assigned task was to keep his eyes on Maria Posada, which wasn't hard. In fact, he welcomed the opportunity to drink up as much of her as he possibly could, no longer having to sneak peeks from the corners of his eyes as he ordinarily did. This held true for most of his female classmates, with the exception, perhaps, of Phyllis, who was nothing much to look at and had made no secret of having sworn off men anyway.

There were rumors about Maria as well, which was a shame if they were true. She was a gorgeous Latina, but had never been known to have a romantic interest in anyone of the male persuasion at Berkeley, least of all Danforth. It didn't stop him from fantasizing however, and right now he was soaking up a lot of material for his imagination to dwell on, as it was his job to follow her hand signals from where she had stationed herself inside the library that served as a polling station.

Their trip to Tucson was being sponsored by a Chicano Civil Rights organization that was trying to protect the rights of Mexican-American voters during the mid-term election, officially at least. Implicitly their goal was to see that anyone was able to vote, regardless of registration status or even citizenship. The Mexicans who lived in the area had as much right to influence the government they lived under as anyone else and, as Rothermel taught them, the resistance was coming from whites unwilling to give up power. The immigrants (whom Hawking and his ilk still referred to as 'illegals') were simply trying to better themselves economically. Were they any different than the ancestors of other Americans?

What it really boiled down to, of course, was race and power. The Nationalists played to the prejudices of the old guard, couching their racism in deceptive language that sounded acceptable on the surface, while hiding darker intentions. The argument that Mexican and Muslim immigrants were refusing to assimilate, thus Balkanizing the country, was really meant to protect the deeply ingrained notion of cultural superiority on the part of those with European heritage.

The Nationalists played this cynical game because they knew that every new voter would count for the opposition – although which party could lay claim to them wasn't clear. The Democrats and Progressives fought for the Hispanic bloc just as hard as they did the African-American and Muslim blocs. Democrats generally held an advantage within the major ethnic groups, by virtue of being more experienced in appealing to group identification. But the Progressives were making significant inroads into the core Democratic base. Their open support for reparations, for example, was pulling over black voters; and the newer economic immigrants from Mexico and Islamic countries were attracted by the opportunity to shortcut the American Dream via wealth redistribution.

Thirty-two years of tolerant policy had gradually loosened voter registration requirements to the point that one merely had to show proof of residence on Election Day to obtain a ballot in most states. Hawking's election two years earlier, although an acknowledged fluke, still made the task of getting new immigrants into the voting booths all the more urgent.

Right now the embodiment of obstruction was a gray-haired, grandmotherly type, who sat behind a folding table with an enormous list of names spread neatly in front of her. It was her job to confirm each person in line, before they could get their ballot. The volunteer wore her hair in a tight bun and peered over her glasses as each person gave her their name and address, usually in broken English. She would then flip the pages over until she found a name to compare with the ID that she also required. If everything matched to her satisfaction, she would send the person on their way with a numbered card, which would then be exchanged for a ballot, but if not (and frequently this was the case) no amount of argument could prevent her from casually dismissing them and dealing with the next in line.

Maria stood watching her like a hawk from about twenty-five feet away. Danforth wasn't sure if the woman knew she was being observed, but there wasn't anything the poll worker could have done, since the Chicanos had a legal right to observe the process.

Of course, they were engaged in more than simple observation. As Danforth stood with his eyes glued on Maria, he would occasionally see her make a hand signal to him. Usually it was an open hand, but sometimes it was a closed fist, which meant that he was to make a signal of his own to another volunteer behind him, who would then make sure that a potential voter from a special pool was inserted in the line leading up to the poll worker.

Prior to Election Day, the Chicano organization illegally obtained copies of the voter registration rolls on computer disks from a sympathetic electoral insider. They compared the Hispanic names on the lists to the actual addresses, to see if the party still lived there. The community was highly transient, so about half the time the names didn't match, in which case the volunteers would either register the existing resident or find a stand-in. The stand-ins were given on-the-spot credentials that usually allowed them to pass through the voter confirmation process after they were trucked to the polls by the activists.

If a stand-in were challenged by a poll worker, they were instructed to simply step out of line and exit the facility. Even though voting fraud was a felony, there was no fear of prosecution for two reasons. First, the community did not want the legal system tied up with victimless crime, as it surely would have been, given how common the practice was; secondly it was politically imprudent. Most of the establishment benefited from the fraud, and those who didn't could easily be marginalized by accusations of racism (the unpardonable sin) if they were foolish enough to press for enforcement.

The civil rights group that sponsored them was particularly concerned with poll workers such as the gray-haired woman, who were easy to spot as they were nearly always older and white. The other poll workers were far more likely to simply take the word of the person standing in front of them and send them down the line, although there would be occasional "hardasses of color" that would hold the confirmation procedure to the strict letter of the law, and even attempt to have violators arrested.

The Chicano group was trying a new strategy this year. It had seeded some of the van pools it brought in with "ringers." These were people specially trained to appear fraudulent, when they really weren't. The civil rights workers would dress them like bums while instructing them to mumble incoherently and act suspicious. The goal was to draw one of the "hardasses" into denying them a ballot, which would then give them grounds to protest, leading to further relaxation of standards.

The woman that they were dealing with that morning was proving a challenge for them. Several ringers had already been sent through on hand signals, but each one was given a ballot after being confirmed by the poll worker. Morning had turned into afternoon, and they were literally down to their last try. In this case, it was an older Mexican who not only looked like a bum, but smelled the part as well. Danforth wasn't sure where they found him, but he hoped he wasn't the one tagged with driving him back home.

The old man sauntered past him, with what looked to be developing stains on both sides of his pants. Danforth stepped back in search of fresh air. As he did, the man turned and winked at him. Perhaps this was all part of the act, he thought. Maria was absolutely unfazed by the man's appearance or odor. She was quite focused on her task, and her face registered a slight desperation, as she knew that this was their last shot.

The old man stood in front of the poll worker, who looked up with a rather startled expression, which was quickly replaced with a wrinkling of the nose. "Name or *Nombre*," she winced.

The man didn't say anything, but just looked at her with a blank expression. She repeated the question, and he still didn't say anything, nor did he move. A sense of excitement began to grip Danforth, who tried to follow what was happening without seeming conspicuous. If the poll worker suspected a trap, then it was probably all for naught.

The lady bent her head and said "Ok, that's enough. Go on." But as the man turned to leave, she immediately looked up with a sly smile. "I see that you do understand me, then. If you want to vote, you'll need to give me your name. How 'bout it, Amigo"

The old man froze. It was a moment of truth. Danforth wasn't sure what would happen. Even Maria was leaning forward expectantly with a quizzical expression.

The man, as it turned out, was well-chosen. There was only a slight hesitation before he turned and spoke slowly, with a dignity that seemed remarkably out of character with his manner of dress. "We do not know each other. My name is not 'Amigo.' Perhaps you are confused because we *Mexicanos* all look alike to you. In fact, I am a human being and an American citizen, entitled to the basic civic freedoms that you enjoy yourself! I may be just another brown-skinned 'spic,' as you just put it, but…"

"Sir!" said the lady angrily, "I did not call you a 'spic' and you know it. I didn't mean to offend you, but neither do I appreciate your playing games with me and not identifying yourself when asked. Now, if you give me your name, I can…"

The man exploded in a surprising fit of rage. He began pounding the table with his fist, thoroughly rattling the elderly poll worker, who held her ground nonetheless. Other workers immediately rushed over, as did Maria, who pulled the man back from the table.

One of the others was clearly a supervisor, and as the older woman attempted to explain what happened, the angry man shouted over her, claiming to have been called a racial slur and denied his right to vote. The woman protested and the supervisor simply looked exasperated. "I didn't hear what happened," she said. "Did anybody hear what happened?"

No one responded, not even Maria, who had heard the conversation perfectly, but seemed to be struggling to put words together.

"I did," said Danforth, stepping forward and looking the supervisor in the eye. He gestured to the unfortunate poll worker, whose look of relief quickly disappeared as Danforth stated, "She called him a 'spic' and said he had no business standing in a line to vote with white people."

Two things he would never forget. The look of utter betrayal on the face of the woman was expected, and even enjoyable in a snide sort of way. The look of disappointment on Maria's face however, was neither.

Saturday, November 28th, 2026
Denton, North Carolina

As they predicted, there was no one working the weekend after Thanksgiving at the Denton Medical Research Center, save a few security guards gathered around a television set, watching a football game at one end of the set of long buildings. The target of the group was a particular lab on the far end, which was not well secured, since it only contained live animals, rather than expensive equipment or records.

Officially, Jill was in Washington D.C., spending the holiday with her family. In reality she was doing something far more exciting; a last fling of sorts before retiring from the clandestine life of an animal rights activist and settling in to a public role with her father's Presidential campaign.

She was not entirely comfortable sneaking around at night with a ski mask over her face and breaking into government facilities to sabotage research projects, even if they were being performed inhumanely on innocent pigs, given that both she and her father had a lot to lose if she got caught. She reasoned that a great many students participate in various pranks around college graduation, so perhaps it could be written off as something like that if it came down to it. Freeing a group of animals from cruel experiments was certainly nobler than getting drunk or streaking through the quad.

They moved swiftly, once the guard passed on his circuit. They had inside floor plans and knew exactly where to go and what to do. Windows were broken, locks cut off, and alarms were disconnected – all with perfect precision.

Once inside, the pigs began squealing in their cages. Jill had never been around farm animals in her life and was surprised by the volume of noise. As some of her companions smashed what little equipment there was in the adjoining rooms, she worked with the others to form a line and transfer the cages with pigs out to where the trucks were parked.

They were in and out in less than twenty minutes.

2027

Tuesday, January 5th, 2027
GNN Special Report

"Welcome back. Even if you're just joining us on this extraordinary news day, you've no doubt heard that late last night, at about eleven o'clock Iraqi time, the night skies over Baghdad were lit up by anti-aircraft guns and other weaponry, as U.S. forces commenced a massive bombing campaign designed, as the President says, to topple the government of Iraq.

"All through the night, GNN has been covering the event, with reporters on the ground there in Baghdad broadcasting live pictures and sound to those of you watching at home. As day broke over the city this morning, the devastation from last night's campaign became apparent, particularly on the military facilities, but the city's power grid was hit as well.

"We were told late last night that President Hawking would address the country at exactly this time, but we're still waiting for him to enter the briefing room. We are joined in our studio by the…. Excuse me, I'm just being told that the President has entered the briefing room. Let's go live there now."

White House Briefing Room

The President looked haggard as he took the podium. Although there was the characteristic confidence in his demeanor, the smile that usually graced his features wasn't present, and the weariness of a long night was evident. "Thank you for being here this morning," he opened to those gathered in the room, before looking directly in the camera.

"My fellow Americans, late last night I ordered our military forces to begin bombing military targets within Iraq. For the last two years, this Administration has been warning our great nation of the threat that the Hussein regime poses to the rest of the world. We have also explained how Uday has been brutalizing the unfortunate people of Iraq, as his father did for decades.

"Intelligence reports tell us that Uday had been stockpiling the same weapons of mass destruction that Saddam used against the Kurds and Iranians. Terrorist training camps operate within the borders of Iraq. Some have existed for thirty years, and others were shifted from Afghanistan after the Taliban were overthrown in the Iran-Pakistani war.

"It's been nearly thirty years since the Hussein regime allowed the international community to conduct weapons inspections, despite the passing of no less than two-hundred and six UN resolutions requiring their compliance with the terms agreed to in the 1991 treaty that ended the Gulf

War. Though we have tried and failed to obtain approval from the United Nations to enforce its own mandates, we cannot sit crossing our fingers any longer. We must act in our own defense and in the interest of the Iraqi people, with a clear objective of removing the illegitimate Iraqi government from power and installing democratic rule. Once the situation is stable and secure, we will leave.

"I realize that most Americans are opposed to war. I also know that military intervention is contrary to the policy of my predecessors, who have been content to watch totalitarian revolutionaries topple a succession of Western-friendly governments like dominos in the Middle East and central Asia, as was the case in Iran many years before. Civil liberties were the first victims of these Islamists, and they were quickly followed by the executions of the best and brightest, including human rights advocates. The flow of refugees and asylum seekers to our own shores has been constant, and it has severely overtaxed our ability to accommodate them.

"My opponents say that America is a big country and that we can certainly afford to absorb these people. Surprisingly, they hold Europe up as an example, despite the tensions and obvious decline of quality of life there, as the clash of cultures turns violent. Even if the European experiment were a success, it would not justify our having to do the same, for this is not Europe.

"I realize that this is not a popular thing to say in this day and age, but it's time that we stop taking in the populations of other countries and instead require them to demand freedom and economic opportunity in their own land. The isolationist policies that we've been following have enabled dictatorships, autocracies, and religious tyrants to triumph. Much of the Third World now lives under despotism, including oil-producing nations that virtually control the global economy. While my progressive colleagues laud these "people's revolutions" and decry any Western influence, they ignore the reality of death and despair that is taking place in these countries. Basic political and civil freedoms do not exist, nor do the people have any means of ending their own suffering. Their brutal governments jail, torture and execute dissidents.

"'Let them rise up,' say my colleagues, 'they aren't worth the sacrifice of American life, just look at what happened in Eastern Europe.' Yes, I believe in keeping our military from harm's way, but it is foolish to believe that countries without the industrial and communications infrastructure to facilitate revolution can be compared to those that overthrew Communism in the last century. Eastern Europe, whose literate masses never forgot what it was to be free, benefited from a free World that proactively challenged the Soviets, breaking them economically, and shaming them into relinquishing control. This has never been successful in the Third World, and it never will be.

"It is naïve as well, to believe that if the rest of the planet collapses into totalitarianism, the United States will be unaffected. We can't afford to let this foolish experiment proceed or it will have irreversible catastrophic effects. Already, we see that most of the planet's people and an alarming amount of its resources are controlled by a handful of evil men, many of whom are bent on our destruction. We must make our stand and challenge them here and now, to reverse the tide. Our survival, and the survival of many others, depends on it.

"I am confident that this will be our finest hour."

GNN Studios

"And so, that was the President, presenting a live address to explain his rationale for ordering the bombing campaign in Iraq. This was anticipated for quite some time; in fact he made certain references on the campaign trail over two years ago to the need for America to act proactively, in his opinion, to protect herself.

"We're joined now by two Senators who may have a different interpretation, I think it's safe to say, of this remarkable series of events. Senator Phil Hudson, a Democrat from New York and Senator Fish, who is serving his first term as a Progressive from Washington. Senator Hudson, let's start with your reaction to what the President just said."

"Well thank you, Steve. I'm very alarmed by both the action in Iraq and the bellicose language being used by the President. In the first place, this is an end-run around Congress, which he knows would never approve of military action overseas. Secondly, it undermines twenty-five years of very admirable effort to win the respect of other nations. The President's policies are backwards and self-defeating."

"Senator Fish?"

"I guess I feel pretty much like the Germans did when they woke up one morning and found Hitler in charge. This bombing is an outrage. Innocent people are dying. If the last twenty-five years have taught us anything it's that peace works and war doesn't. It's also difficult to believe that such xenophobic language can still come out of a prominent politician's mouth in the 21st century, particularly when Muslim and Hispanic immigrants make up such a large portion of our population. His staff might consider sticking a swastika armband on him the next time they push him in front of the cameras, especially if he's going to rail against ethnics invading our motherland."

"Is there anything about the speech that stands out for you?"

"Other than our most visible public figure clearly trying to incite violence against immigrants? Well, where to start? I think... well, let me say that the President using the word 'evil' to describe leaders who are not in the process of bombing other nations into the Stone Age, as he is, is particularly ironic. It will poison diplomatic relations at the very least."

"Senator Hudson, do you think it was a wise choice of words for the President to use?"

"Personally, if I could, I'd like to retract every word he's ever said in the last two years, beginning with the Oath of Office. At a time when we're trying to convince the Iranians to allow inspections of their nuclear facilities, it makes no sense to call them 'evil' or to use threatening language."

"Senator Fish, if you…"

"Pardon me for a second, Steve, but I want to build on what Senator Hudson just said, because it's important. Whether we like it or not, the Iranians have nuclear weapons. It makes no sense to make them angry. There is no good that can come from this sort of insulting rhetoric from the President, but there can be a catastrophic amount of harm. I hope he's not foolishly suggesting that our next Imperial target is going to be Iran."

"How do you feel, Senator Hudson, about President Hawking's argument that we need to stop, as he put it, the fall of 'dominos' and work on pressing for internal change within other countries as an alternative to taking in their refugees?"

"Well Steve, dropping bombs is not an acceptable way to bring about change. And, speaking of a poor choice of words, the Domino Theory was what right-wingers called the Soviet threat back in the last century. As you know, it led to war and a lot of needless suffering, but not much else. The corporate fat cats loved it, of course, since war boosts their bottom-line, but I hope that we, as a nation, have moved beyond such casual barbarism. I suspect other motives are at play here, in the President's mind."

"Senator Fish?"

"Yes, clearly there are other motives and they have to do with this ongoing war on diversity. Multiculturalism is under assault in America today and, as a skillful politician, the President knows just how to appeal to the prejudices of the dominant group in society without being overly candid. But, although what he says may appeal to the Neanderthals up in Montana or the billionaires on Wall Street, there are a lot more of us than there are of them. The anger in the Hispanic, Muslim, African-American and other working-class communities is palpable and I'm fully confident that we'll run the Nationalists out of power next year… even if we have to join forces to do it!"

"Well, that would be something to see. Thank you both for joining us."

JFK Airport; New York, NY

The mid-winter sun had already set by the time his plane landed in New York. Robert Danforth was very tired from the different legs of the trip that began the day before with a nine hour drive from Baghdad. It would have taken longer had people really believed the Americans would bomb.

He had his first look at the assault on a Paris airport monitor, in the company of a virulently anti-American audience. They had actually attacked a waiting passenger just for wearing an American flag pin on his lapel. The police arrived, but made no real effort to find the one's responsible. The frustrated victim, a middle-aged man gripping paper towels to his head in a vain effort to stem the bleeding, was escorted to a private area as a hail of paper cups and cans were brazenly thrown at him by the others. Danforth didn't blame the crowd at all. The man should have known not to wear the flag.

It weakened him a bit to see the devastating bombing campaign, and knowing that he probably would have been dead had he remained behind for the original purpose of the trip, which was to serve as "human shields" for the Iraqi people against the crushing military might of the United States.

The mission statement of the group that recruited him promised to protect the "schools, hospitals and mosques" of Iraq. Privately, he was assured that he would be perfectly safe, because of the pinpoint precision capabilities of the American "smart-bombs." The implication, of course, was that the American military was going to deliberately avoid the very places that the group was publicly accusing them of targeting, but no one actually came out and said it.

Of the twelve that set out with him a week ago, six were Christian clergy. There were no Muslims among them, which he thought odd. Once on the ground, they were rushed to meet Uday, whom, Danforth was disappointed to find, did not recognize him at all from his trip just six months earlier. He spent a few minutes listening to the earnest apologies from each member of the group for their diabolical President and their earnest commitment to defend the people of Iraq, nodded his head every few seconds, then left abruptly.

Danforth was taken with the rest to a building in the middle of a military base just outside the city, where they stayed for a few days while waiting to be dispersed to schools and hospitals as soon as arrangements could be made. As the days passed, Danforth grew quite anxious. The others were uncomfortable as well, knowing that if the war started, they would most certainly not survive, since they were locked in a room that was right next to an anti-aircraft battery. No one except Danforth made much noise about it, even after four days of killing time and worrying.

No one wanted to talk about it with him either. His anger manifested it-self with the translators, whose responses were always noncommittal. It didn't take a genius to see that they were being played.

One afternoon, he found himself screaming at them, much to the em-barrassment of his more docile companions, who pretended to ignore the commotion. The next morning, he was on his way to Amman in an NGO vehicle.

It all seemed surreal to him now, as he made his way slowly through JFK, stopping at each TV screen and hoping to catch a shot of the after-math at the military base, although he knew that the Iraqis would never allow the media to film it, since they strictly limited the press coverage to damage done on residences and presumed civilian facilities. They would probably move the bodies of his former companions to a school, even if they had to destroy one just to create the scene.

As he passed a bagel shop, Danforth heard the unmistakable voice of his mother echoing down the corridors of the airport. Anyone else would have been unnerved, but he was used to seeing her on television. The woman loved attention. He knew it was the main reason that she never remarried. It would have taken the edge off her status as a professional victim.

At the moment, though, she seemed genuinely upset.

"It disgusts me, Sir. It just disgusts me that the President would use the image of September 11th to justify this illegal little war that he's started. He's exploiting the memory of the victims. He's using their families for his own political ends."

"But Mrs. Danforth, we just had two family members of a man who was killed…"

"Yes I know that and I'm very disappointed that GNN would choose to have someone like that on. They're either under the influence of the Administration or they're just being opportunistic about their loss on 9/11."

"Mrs. Danforth…"

"I want your viewers to know, Steve, that I intend on working with other concerned citizens of this country to give voice to the victims of this conflict. We will require that the military count every civilian who loses their life as a consequence of this illegal act of aggression, and then force the government to compensate their family. We intend on holding Amer-ica accountable…"

"There are those however, who say that more than a million Iraqis have already disappeared under the regime and that…"

"And we will also count every young American in uniform that loses their life overseas, as well. We will make sure that there is a running tally kept…"

"Please, Mrs. Danforth…"

"And another thing, Sir. I want you and your audience to know that my son, Robert Jr., is in Iraq right now, serving as a human shield against Hawking's war machine. His body is the only thing standing in the way of the obliteration of schoolchildren and hospital patients. The images that you're showing on the screen from Baghdad are making me very nervous; as I'm sure you can understand. It would be a shame to lose both my husband and my son to American foreign policy!"

Robert Danforth immediately turned back down the corridor, glad that he heard that last part before catching a taxi and showing up at his mother's doorstep, as he had been planning. He made his way in the direction of the very last gate in the terminal, confident that he could avoid detection for a few days while thinking up a miraculous tale of survival.

Wednesday, February 3rd, 2027
Quantico, Virginia

As Walid suspected, he would not be lunching alone that afternoon in the cafeteria, there in the basement of the FBI building. It was for precisely this reason that he usually he ate at his desk or went for a jog on the grounds of the former Marine Corps base.

He had no intention of meeting anyone, of course, but he saw a small group of analysts from the Arabic group watching him as he walked past to a table located well away from them, and knew that he would be joined before too long. He barely had time to sit down and wrestle open a bottle of juice before a large bearded man plunked himself down rudely across from him.

"Walid, Walid," he said in a sort of mockingly sympathetic way.

"Hello, Fasil," replied Walid, glancing at the man's ample girth. "No aerobics today?"

Fasil's face tightened a bit. "I'm worried about you, little man. What others are saying about you, you know."

"Your concern enriches me," Walid replied dryly. He had pretty much had it with the other interpreters in the department, but he wasn't going to let them get under his skin anymore.

"They say that you are really an Arab Jew, Walid," said the other, leaning close. "Is that true?"

Walid took a long sip of juice then set down the bottle. "Why don't you pull up your pants a bit, Fasil? The man sitting behind you is not a proctologist and I believe that your butt-crack is scaring his wife."

Fasil's face went deep red. "*Yehud!*" he hissed. He rose and walked back over to where the others sat staring menacingly at Walid – being careful, Walid noticed, to first pull his belt up a bit. They all sat whispering together and glaring back at him, as Walid carefully ate his lunch and pretended to read the paper. It had been like that with the other Arabic translators on staff at the FBI even before he was assigned last August to the investigation of the National Cathedral firebombing, though it only served to make him an even bigger target.

The Bureau was desperate for Arabic translators when he joined directly out of law school nearly twelve years ago. It was his friend, Pat Ridley, who had inspired him to join, merely by his own service in uniform, although the two had not spoken since Ridley left the Army right before Walid graduated, despite the younger man's best efforts to renew contact. The last e-mail exchange between the two concerned a violent terrorist video that Ridley had sent to him, asking him to interpret the Arabic in it for him, which Walid had been willing to do, despite the sadistic murder being recorded. The banner and the language on the video were verses from the Qur'an and, of course, the ubiquitous chorus of "Allahu Akbar" as the victim's throat was being cut. Walid never received a reply after that.

He threw himself into his work at the Bureau, gaining quite a reputation among the other translators in the Arabic department. At first, he naively assumed that everyone had the same primary loyalty, but he soon picked up on resentment from the others. It wasn't so much directed at him at first, but rather at the Bureau and America in general.

Political opinions were expressed in a cautious yet deliberate way around him, as if gauging his reaction. When he did not respond (feeling that it was out of place to share such things in a government office) he was asked directly about his thoughts on U.S. foreign policy, then domestic policy, then Islam. He revealed nothing other than his support for the mandate to which they had been tasked, namely the investigation of crimes against the United States, preemption of future crimes by means of intelligence, and the analysis of foreign threats. What could be controversial about that?

Plenty, as it turned out. There were not many in the department who thought as he did, and most were quite radical in their beliefs. Though they stopped short of declaring their support for the terrorists, they nonetheless were not shy about insisting that the government was unfairly targeting the Muslim community, both at home and abroad. Their attitude expressed itself in the quality of their work, which was sloppy, erroneous, and largely unreliable, as Walid found in his proof-checking duties, which involved reanalyzing translated documents or dialogue to ensure integrity.

His Muslim co-workers were suspicious of anyone without a beard. They even went so far as to demand their own restroom, so they would not be "defiled" by "infidels." Many acted as if they were subversives in an enemy organization that targeted the Islamic faith with mosque surveillance and infiltration. One of the disgruntled agents even had a photograph of a plane flying into the World Trade Center with a Qur'anic quote underneath.

Still, the Bureau was afraid of disciplinary action. If any of the men were fired, they could easily sue for religious discrimination, and it might ruin the career of anyone bold enough to take action – no matter how sensible it seemed. Walid was one of the few agents who stood fearlessly on principle.

He had at one time noticed blatant irregularities in the work of one man, and had proceeded to let him get bolder and bolder with his mistranslations, until finally they went beyond simple disinformation and into clear sedition. He approached his superiors with the information, but instead of being fired, the man was reassigned to a job where he could presumably do no further harm to national security. Walid was immediately *persona non grata* with the others, who tried to convince agency management that he was a troublemaker. The FBI was under enormous pressure from the Muslim Intelligence Workers Union to reduce discrimination complaints from their agents.

He had been called on more than once to infiltrate domestic terror cells in mosques around the country. Generally the tips came from Muslims in the community who had concerns about the word on the street. Walid found them to be different from the radicals, in that they were decent, hard-working and hardly fanatical about their faith, except as it pertained to treating others fairly.

He was very good at this work, having learned the language of Jihad from attending his brothers' mosque in Ila, and he enjoyed a sense of purpose in his occupation. Every time a Jihadi was taken off the streets, it reduced both the chance of a terror attack and a negative reflection on the Muslim community.

There were others in America who felt as he did and supported his work, but they were in the distinct minority. Certainly not everyone who disagreed was a terrorist, but it disappointed Walid that apathy ran so deep in the community. Islam had a dark side to it that can seduce a person to violence or make them quite indifferent to it. His own brothers were proof of that.

They were both married, one of them to Walid's high school teacher, the former Ms. Wyland. Of course, anyone who knew her before probably wouldn't recognize the quiet woman in the *hijab* as the talented, vivacious young teacher with such a potentially bright future.

The change was not sudden, of course. She met Walid's brother twenty years earlier and was drawn by the allure that a foreign man sometimes has with an American woman. She became interested in his religion as well, although this was after Walid graduated. She wasn't raised with a religion of her own, at least not one that she was expected to take seriously, so Islam filled a spiritual void, as she told him. It disappointed her that her husband did not permit her to work outside the home, but she submitted to his will as the Qur'an instructed.

She enjoyed Walid's visits immensely, far more than he, in fact. They would sit on the couch and talk quietly late into the night, as his brother watched TV in the next room or fell asleep. He doubted that the married couple had much in common. Occasionally, he would see a light bruise on her cheek, similar to what he sometimes saw in the mirror as a kid after a tussle with his brother, but she never let on that she was un-happy.

Both his brothers attended the same mosque, which had gone through several clerics over the years – all firebrands preaching Jihad. Time had not mellowed their views, but rather embittered them. Walid wondered if it were only a matter of time before his brothers put words into action. He would be the last to know, of course, as they disrespected his occupation so much that they made it clear that he was not welcome in their mosque.

His brothers would probably be surprised to learn that Walid actually attended mosque in Virginia, a Sufi group that did not mind a Sunni join-ing them. He appreciated the fact that the people there did not have to hide what went on, but were instead quite transparent about a reformed Islamic faith that rejected the harsher elements of the religion and em-braced the call to character building through introspection and the estab-lishment of healthy relationships with others.

There was no doubt that the firebombing of the Cathedral last year was in response to the al-Raz mosque arson twenty years earlier. There were no injuries in either case, but the man who burned the mosque in New Jersey was still being held in Federal custody under a hate crimes statute. The al-Raz burning had prompted national outrage, and the par-tially damaged building was restored in four weeks by an outpouring of donations. The same thing could not be said for the many dozens of churches that were casually burned to the ground each February 20th, even though several resulted in serious injuries and death. Each year, however, a memorial service was staged at al-Raz, where celebrities and leaders appeared in solidarity against anti-Muslim bigotry.

He was uncomfortable working a firebombing that had happened so close to home. Investigation meant speaking with the local community in the capacity of a despised Federal agent. He was treated like a traitor. "Why don't you tell your Jewish masters to stop harassing the *ummah*?" was a familiar phrase thrown back at him in one form or another. The odd thing was that he didn't think he had ever met a single Jew at the FBI, although he knew it would make no difference to these people, who be-lieved what they wanted to in a community rife with outrageous conspir-acy theories. Most thought that the Jews or the CIA were behind all of the terror attacks, from 9/11 to the church burnings – in spite of videotaped confessions from dedicated and well-known Islamists.

Even more frustrating than the misinformation and paranoia of the Muslim community was the timid approach to investigation and prosecution by law enforcement, including the FBI. Muslim activists were extremely petulant about police activities in their community. They successfully petitioned previous Administrations to put draconian restrictions on surveillance efforts to protect the right to privacy – requiring in most cases that the suspect first be notified that they were being monitored.

So successful were they in using the nation's laws against itself, that the mere hint of a challenge was enough to deter prosecution, as was the case when he finally produced a suspect for the firebombing, who turned out to be an unemployed young man spending too much time at a radical mosque.

"It's better that we save our ammo for bigger game," his superiors hedged, apparently preferring to wait until the young man actually killed someone, rather than fight the civil rights activists.

The bearded translators were no longer there to glare at him as he gathered up his newspaper and tray, but he knew they would be waiting upstairs, as they always were, casting angry looks and whispering among themselves. The less it bothered him, the more frustrated they became.

All he really cared about was getting the job done.

Saturday, March 27th, 2027
Berkeley, California

The poster on the wall of Rothermel's small University office always caught the attention of anyone who came to see him there. It depicted a well-dressed black man in a business suit putting a coin into the cup of a white beggar, an older vagrant sitting on a city street and looking quite desolate. The race of the two men featured prominently in the implied message, with the punch line summed up underneath in bold letters: "Now that's progress!" Rothermel had been told that the photo was taken in downtown Johannesburg. He later learned that the bum had been an engineer of some sort in the Apartheid era, while the black man was a high-ranking member of the ruling ANC party.

This morning, it was Bernice Greenly sitting across from him in the cluttered little room that seemed unfitting for his reputation, but quite in keeping with his ruffled appearance. She was the editor-in-chief of the campus newspaper, which was unsurprising given that she was expected to someday assume the reins of her father's news empire – an assumption hardly muted by the energy that she applied to her duties at the campus news office.

At the moment, Rothermel was studying a photograph in the previous day's edition that showed Darnell Massey being wrestled to the ground by two white men at a debate. It looked like a classic racial attack, although the professor knew that, in fact, the large man had been in the process of charging a conservative speaker with a pie in his hand, when he had been taken down from behind by her security staff. The image of a tall, 250-pound man bearing down on an obviously terrified 110-pound woman would never have made it into the paper, and Bernice deserved credit for finding a photo that completely transfigured the episode for those who weren't present. Already there was talk on campus of mounting protests against racism the following week, combined with demands that the University president take action against those responsible for these "Gestapo" tactics.

Bernice broke his thoughts. "I'm sure you heard about the Passover bombing this morning in Israel?"

Indeed he had. Twenty-nine Israelis were killed by a Palestinian suicide bomber as they were celebrating Passover at a hotel. Over one-hundred others were injured in the attack. The Professor understood the problem this posed to the newspaper.

"I know your dilemma," he replied. "This is a resistance attack to protest the historical injustices inflicted upon the Palestinians, of course, but it might appear to be unjustified to your readers. I would suggest waiting at least a day or two to report it, since it's a Saturday. By that time, I'm sure the Israelis will respond in kind and you can frame the two actions together. This may actually be a good thing, because sympathy for the victims of the bombing can be channeled into anger against the Israelis for forcing the Palestinians to such desperate acts."

Bernice's response was somewhat hesitant. "It's getting harder to justify the violence given that the Palestinians have been getting what they originally asked for."

The Professor hedged a bit. He knew that Bernice was Jewish, and wondered if there was some sort of identity crisis brewing beneath the surface. "Wherever there is violence against power, then there must be legitimate grievance, Bernice. Don't be confused by apparent facts. Yes, there is a lot of land in the Middle East, and Israel sits on less than one percent of it, but they still have the power

"Think of the Palestinians as heroes. It would be easier for them to get on with their lives and build their economy the way the Jews did after the Holocaust, but they choose instead to be martyrs against colonial oppression." To bolster his argument, the Professor ran down a list of mostly Islamic countries founded in the last twenty years. "Without the Palestinian sacrifice there would be no Quebecois; Kashmir would still be a part of India, Moroland of the Philippines, and there would be no independence for the southern Thai provinces either."

"What if there is no military response from Israel? They've been far more…"

"Rothermel cut her off with a laugh. "Oh, I think there will be, but even if there isn't, you can still arrange this with past Israeli atrocities to project equivalence at the very least. There is certainly a wealth of historical information from which to choose. And, of course, if all else fails… well, no one is to say just where in the paper this news item should appear – or the amount of ink wasted on it."

The Professor gave her a wink and Bernice responded with a grateful nod.

Friday, June 11th 2027
San Francisco, California

Rothermel didn't remember the name, but he was pretty sure that it was the same speaker from the rally twenty years earlier with the same message: America's war was the result of sexual frustration, with the solution, according to the aging speaker, being a channeling and release of these repressed emotions into erotic freedom. This time the speaker was joined on stage by two women dressed as cheerleaders (the hair on their legs was visible even from Rothermel's remote vantage point) who jumped up and down and yelled things like, *"Two, Four, Six, Eight; Masturbate, don't detonate; Orgasms are really great!"*

The crowd in the park enjoyed the presentation for the most part, lending cheers, laughter or boos, as the remarks warranted. The same stale odor emanated from the mass of bodies; a mixture of marijuana, rank flesh, and clothes that appeared to have missed the last several laundry cycles.

There were subtle differences however, that did not escape his attention. One was a far greater proportion of Muslims at the event, perhaps about 25%. Those that weren't readily identifiable from traditional garb could be assumed as such from the way they took offense at the current speaker and did not laugh at the crude humor. As the "cheerleaders" were bouncing up and down, several dark-eyed men in khaki-colored *galabiyyas* were waiting a few yards away for their turn to speak. They stood with arms crossed, glowering at the girls with expressions of disgust. A few gazed out over the twenty thousand demonstrators, eying the crowd with a look of ownership, almost like a rancher proudly counting cattle that he knows will soon be his.

The next speaker in line was a thin, pale-skinned Literature professor from a rival Bay area university, who lamented that the "million Mogadishus" didn't happen, but that there was always hope that the burgeoning insurgency in Iraq would gain momentum. This was the anticipation of many in the crowd, particularly the Muslims, who were disappointed that the United States military had not sustained heavy casualties in their relatively easy triumph over Uday Hussein's forces. Mass graves were being uncovered in Iraq, which further dampened the mood of those present, not out of any grief for the victims, but rather that they bolstered the justification for overthrowing the regime.

Yet, many were excited by the prospect of elements of the old regime creating havoc in the country with the help of radical Muslim groups. Hawking had waited too long to invade. While he was vainly appealing to the international community for support, as his political opponents required, insurgency cells were being organized in Iraq.

The media was already beginning to call the transitional period following the ground victory an "occupation," which lent credibility to the insurgency. If the planned elections could be postponed, even by violence, then it would further legitimize the uprising and perhaps lead to the withdrawal of American forces… another Vietnam! America had to lose in Iraq because America had to be stopped, otherwise there could be more war.

The Muslim speakers had their turn, speaking eloquently about America's intolerance for religious minorities and referring to the Iraq war as "Hawking's crusade to force Christianity onto the Arab people." One of the speakers wanted to offer a prayer to Allah, which many in the crowd respected, with the exception of several unruly protesters, who began screaming during the invocation. A number of fistfights broke out as a result of this, as angry Muslims left quite a few secularists with blood running down into their profanity-printed shirts.

Sherry Danforth, head of CTV^2 (Count the Victims/Compensate the Victims) spoke next. Her group was pressing the government to pay reparations to the families of those killed inadvertently by American bombs and bullets. The crowd shared her outrage when she gave her estimate of the number of civilians killed, but she also got the biggest cheer of the day when mentioning the number of U.S. soldiers killed thus far, since larger numbers could presumably turn public opinion against the war.

Two more speakers followed and the crowd began to disperse by five o'clock, so that everyone could get home before dark. There would be no nighttime march this evening, as the streets of San Francisco were no safer now than those of Oakland three decades ago.

Thursday, September 9th, 2027
Tucson, Arizona

Hours earlier, Robert Danforth had been sitting in an Indian casino watching a shabbily-dressed man named Villegas pour about $300 into slot machines and blackjack tables, as he had every day for the last two weeks. The money was given to him as a "retainer fee" by Danforth, and Villegas was always excited to see it. Usually a day's worth of begging only brought in about $50, which hardly lasted a full hour in the gambling parlor. The casinos ran "shuttles" to the poorest sections of town at $5 per ride and kept a close eye on those who made the trip, ready to escort them quickly back onto the vans after the money ran out, lest their odor or mannerisms offend the other clientele.

Danforth shook his head to the pleading look in Villegas's eyes after the last $20 was lost on the wrong number of a roulette roll. He had no idea whether the man would be eating anything that day, after they drove back into Tucson, although it was his job to keep partial tabs on him while the lawsuit was being finalized.

Danforth was the first member of Rothermel's class to leave the university. Two others, Darnell Massey and Maria Posada, were law students as well, but only Danforth had completed all requirements for graduation prior to attending Rothermel's special program. He went to work for the ACLU just as the summer began, with his first assignment being the Villegas case, which was appropriate, given that he had been the one to bring the issue to the attention of the organization nearly a year earlier.

It was during the election-monitoring trip to Tucson last November that Danforth found himself in the right place at the right time. He and Maria were waiting for a shuttle to the airport outside their hotel when a poorly-dressed woman threw up on the sidewalk a few yards down from them. Robert's inclination had been to move further away from the sick woman, but he acted against his natural habit out of a desire to score some badly needed points with Maria. She had not said a word to him since the incident at the polling station the day before.

Robert moved closer to the sick woman, but hesitated slightly, letting Maria overtake him. She soothed the woman in her native tongue, holding her oily hair as she puked a foul concoction directly out onto the sidewalk. *Couldn't she have just made it to the curb*, Danforth wondered as he edged slowly backward.

Maria encouraged the woman to go to the emergency room, but, as it turned out, she had already tried to gain admittance earlier at Paterski General, the only operating hospital left in Tucson, but had been turned away. Maria called for an ambulance anyway and relayed the woman's jumbled story to an impatient Danforth while they waited. She was an immigrant from Mexico, who had crossed the border with her "husband" two years earlier to find work. He didn't pay much attention to the rest of what was said, as he was more interested in shifting positions periodically as the breeze changed, to stay upwind of the stench

The woman began to slip away as the sirens sounded in the distance. Danforth celebrated the fact that he would no longer have to feign interest in her useless story. The EMTs arrived and, undaunted by the disgusting odor, immediately began CPR with a plastic bag that was designed to force air into the subject's lungs without the technician having to put their mouth on a complete stranger.

Maria chose to ride in the ambulance and asked Danforth to take the luggage to the airport on the shuttle and see that it got on the plane. He gave her a pensive, concerned look, biting his lower lip and looking as if he were reluctant to leave the two of them. In fact, he was simply irritated that she wouldn't be accompanying him and deeply annoyed over the prospect of missing the flight.

He didn't give any more thought to the woman until Maria showed up at the airport three hours later trying to hold back tears, distraught because the woman had died right next to her on the way to the emergency clinic. As he found out later, the cause of death was extreme alcohol poisoning, which explained the woman's incoherence on the sidewalk. As they waited for their bags at the conveyor in San Francisco, Maria wished aloud that she could complete her law degree and "go after Paterski."

This piqued Danforth's interest and he contacted the ACLU the next day to see if they would investigate the matter. He already had a rapport with the organization, and was considering going to work for them after graduation.

He learned that the woman went by the name of Villegas, the sur-name of her common-law husband. She was turned away from Paterski General because she had not paid her bills from previous visits. This was quite common in many metropolitan areas, even outside of the Southwest, where immigrants simply showed up at the emergency room to receive treatment, with no intention of paying. Most hospitals complied, and made the difference up elsewhere, but Paterski was different.

The company was a sole proprietorship, started by a former Montana real estate investor named Dennis Paterski, who decided for whatever reason to move into the health care field a few years ago. The company's policy of requiring insurance or other means of payment prior to treatment was repulsive both within the industry and to the public at large. Working for Paterski was like working for the Hawking White House. It wasn't a career ender, necessarily, but you'd better have a good story prepared if you hoped to be hired elsewhere later in life.

There were some two dozen Paterski medical centers across the country, and many of them had on-going demonstrations outside their gates; small groups of earnest young people with picket signs, screaming profanity at the cars passing through. The company was vilified in the news media, which never lacked for stories of indigent Muslim or Hispanic immigrants turned away, either because they couldn't afford service, or had substantial past due balances outstanding. These 'human interest' segments never failed to evoke sympathy for the victims and scorn against the hospital.

The national health care plan compensated private hospitals for most of the charges related to the medical care of citizens, although complaints regarding bureaucratic hurdles persisted. Illegal aliens, of course, weren't covered by the plan, and usually couldn't afford the out-of-pocket costs. The city of Tucson passed a local ordinance several years before that required emergency rooms to provide service to "any resident in need." Other municipalities had either done the same or were trying to come up with creative ways of preventing hospital agencies from using local law enforcement to collect on patient debts.

Yet, through it all, Paterski had remained profitable, the only one in its field to do so in fact, despite the controversy. It aggravated the socially conscious; including Danforth, particularly as he began paying closer attention to the issue during his final year at Berkeley.

As it turned out, the ACLU had been interested in filing civil charges against Paterski for some time. They were having as much difficulty trying to find a "Rosa Parks" to carry the standard for them as their civil rights counterparts of the 1950's had (before eventually using their own secretary for the purpose). The ACLU needed an immigrant, of course, but it had to be someone who would evoke sympathy both from a jury and the American public. At one time, they thought they had the right person, but the prospect turned out to be an Arab, who had used a Hispanic surname to cross the border and was actually involved in a terror cell. The ACLU had unwittingly blown his cover, but they did manage to pressure the government into releasing the poor fellow from custody.

Danforth was able to convince the organization that Mr. Villegas had suffered in a way that no one with a heart could help but feel sympathy towards. They agreed, and Danforth went to work for them, which is how he came to find himself in casinos on the eve of the civil trial, watching his client throw away every dollar that was given to him for the ostensible purpose of supplementing his daily necessities while his lawyers maneuvered on his behalf against the hospital defense team.

Each of the last fourteen days that he had been in Tucson followed the same routine. Danforth would withdraw $300 from the bank and give it to Villegas. The only condition was that it not be spent for alcohol, as it was assumed that public drunkenness would erode public sympathy for a man who was suing, ultimately, because his wife drank herself to death.

Sometimes Villegas would buy a late breakfast, but most of the time they would go straight to the casino in Danforth's rental, since the lawyer couldn't tolerate the smell from the other shuttle passengers for the length of the drive – not that Villegas was all that pleasant either, but at least the windows allowed some control over the flow of fresh air into the vehicle.

At the casino, Danforth would act the babysitter and idly watch the older man blow through the money. Usually it was over with by about two or three in the afternoon, and Danforth would drive back into town while listening to his passenger lament over his bad luck and make vows to "never do that again." Villegas would then beg Danforth for more money. Danforth would refuse, and they would go their separate ways – Villegas to the ratty motel that was prepaid by the ACLU at the beginning of every week, and Danforth to the office for legal preparations.

His assignment this afternoon, he decided, was to give Maria Posada a call and make sure that she was still planning to appear as a material witness for them. He was very much looking forward to seeing her again.

Friday, November 12th, 2027
Tucson, Arizona

It was strange to hear Maria talk proudly about her family's journey from Mexico to start a better life in America, particularly when she privately referred to them as *Ladinos* and deeply resented their conservative values, but at least the story was relating well to the jury. By their body language, they also reacted positively to her testimony regarding the morning in front of the hotel, when she held the dying "Mrs. Villegas" (as they were calling her) in her arms, lamenting the cruel-hearted corporation that refused to recognize "universal rights."

His team had been able to pick an all-Hispanic panel of jurors by first leaking to the media that the defense team wanted to keep Hispanics out of the pool. They didn't know whether this was actually true or not, but felt that it might pressure their frustrated opponents into making concessions as the two sides were trying to agree on the jury, which was exactly what happened

The young Danforth would have liked to be the one directing questions to Maria, but he wasn't complaining about the more high-profile assignment of helping to cross-examine the plain-spoken Dennis Paterski. In fact, he relished the opportunity to draw out the business owner's blunt opinions, which had the potential to nail the case for them.

He only hoped that Maria would be there to see it.

Thursday, November 18th, 2027
Tucson, Arizona

From the minute that Dennis Paterski walked into the courtroom that morning, Danforth had to struggle to keep his nerves under control, even though he was confident that the case had been won the minute the jury was finalized. It was a critical point in the trial, even the jurors knew that, as he could tell from the way they set aside the needlepoint and doodling projects that normally consumed their attention.

Paterski was in his mid-30s, only about seven years older than Danforth, but with an enormous head start on the freshman attorney in terms of career accomplishments. A receding hairline, slight paunch, heavily-rimmed glasses and a perpetually dour, irritable expression contributed favorably to Danforth's intended tactic of playing him up to the jury as a hackneyed "angry, white male." Knowing how smart Paterski was, he had been meticulous in his preparations for cross-examination.

He started by asking questions related to the man's success in business, strategically working his way into the personal lifestyle that such wealth affords. Even the judge was starting to agree with the defense team's objections by the time he finished this portion, but he wanted to lay the groundwork with the jury, whose members were poor and either unemployed or working for the government, and thus highly susceptible to resenting the wealthy and successful.

From there, Danforth slowly wound through the process by which the hospitals made money, with careful emphasis on the point that it was from the misery of others. If a person came into the emergency room in great pain, would the staff immediately assist or simply begin demanding insurance information? If a former patient was unemployed and could not pay their bills, would the hospital still harass the individual for payment, even while he or she was in recovery?

Paterski's answers began to show a terseness that belied a growing tension between the two men. Of course the hospital had to be paid, he asserted, otherwise they would not have the ability to pay their own bills. He was running a business. Every business is supposed to make money, isn't it?

"If your own mother needed emergency treatment, would you turn her away if she didn't have the money?" asked the young attorney.

"No. I would pay for the treatment myself, of course."

"I congratulate you on your ability to pay for your family's needs," replied Danforth, turning his head so that the jury could see the slight look of contempt on his face. "Not everyone is as privileged. Suppose, however, that she were living in another country, as Mrs. Villegas was, and needed the same sort of treatment. Would you not expect her to receive this from a medical center, even one that is so… uh… devoted to profit?"

"My mother does not drink. She's the wife of a retired businessman who started with nothing in life, but worked to ensure that his wife has the means to pay for whatever expenses she may accrue."

"Yes, yes," replied Danforth, with another turn to the jury. "It's nice to hear that you are *unburdened* with the responsibilities that so many of the rest of us have. Please answer the question though. If your mother could not afford medical treatment, should she still have a right to it?"

"Of course not," answered Paterski.

Danforth had been waiting for this moment and seized it with exaggerated incredulity. "Your own mother?" he practically shouted.

Paterski hesitated for a second, with a puzzled expression on his face. "No... not my mother. As we've established, my mother made choices in life that would preclude her from being dependent. The hypothetical woman that you are calling my mother in this discourse is someone who apparently spends her spare money on liquor instead of paying her bills. Is this person then entitled to further services from the same company that she has chosen not to reimburse as she finds herself in a drunken condition entirely of her own device? Not if it's my company."

Danforth figured that it was time to draw a few deep breaths and collect himself while under the pretense of ruffling through his notes. There had been several audible sighs in the gallery over what Paterski had shamelessly said, and as the young attorney stood looking down at the papers in his hands, he heard someone behind him stand up and start shouting at the witness in a thick accent. Everyone except for Danforth turned to look. The judge banged the gavel against his desk and ordered his bailiffs to escort the offending parties out of the courtroom.

Danforth coolly continued. "Mr. Paterski, did you know that Mrs. Villegas was a mother of five children?"

Before his lawyer could object, the witness blurted out, "I don't care."

The courtroom buzzed again.

"The jury will disregard the question and answer," stated the judge solemnly, upholding the objection but no doubt knowing that absolutely no one would be forgetting what they just heard.

Danforth was feeling his confidence surge, and he moved in for the kill. "Do you have a picture of Adolf Hitler on the wall of your office?"

Paterski was caught completely off guard. "I have a... there's a cartoon that has a caricature of Hitler," he sputtered.

Danforth raised the level of his voice and asked forcefully, "Is it true that you have made statements complimentary of Adolf Hitler?"

There was a pregnant silence in the courtroom as everyone waited for the response. Everyone except Danforth of course, since he had just made up the accusation on the spot. This was to be the crowning finale. Paterski would lose his cool, angrily deny the assertion and the attorney would then quickly say "No further questions" and leave the witness extremely agitated and the jury with fuel for the imagination over the course of the evening.

Instead, Paterski hesitated for a second then looked visibly relaxed. "Paterski is a Polish name. I'm Polish, you idiot. Why would I have anything good to say about Hitler?"

"No further questions," blurted out Danforth instinctively, even though it was the wrong thing to say at that point. His face was flushed as he sat down, and he didn't bother looking at the confused people around him, either on the jury or his own bench.

2028

Wednesday, February 16th, 2028
Malawi, Africa

It was turning into one of the best days of Malika's young life when her grandfather came home from the factory to tell her that he had managed to find a job for her there. The money that the 12-year-old would bring home from six hours of work each day wouldn't be much, but it would help the small family pay for food, clothing, and perhaps even contribute toward her future education.

She was the oldest of the four children living with her aunt and grandparents in a dirt floor shack made of plywood scraps on the edge of a large town with other shanties, where open sewage ran in trails down littered streets. Even if they didn't have much, it was still more than some around them, since her grandfather was quite diligent in pursuing work of any sort.

The reopening of a local factory, in a previously abandoned warehouse, brought some excitement to the community. Job seekers stood in long lines for days, including her grandfather, who slept with the rest of the applicants by the side of the road, as the family brought food to him periodically. He was rewarded with his first steady job in years.

The pay was average, but it was solid work – all twelve hours a day of it. He told his family that the computer manufacturer that opened the factory was selling the components assembled there to America, where the demand was high enough to prompt the business to expand operations. He said that the company was using Africans to do the work because they could be paid much lower than American workers.

Her grandfather didn't have very kind words for the local nurse, even though she was volunteering her services to the community that year. She was from America, but was very critical of her country and insisted that the most dangerous threat to the world was "American consumerism."

"That consumerism creates my job," insisted her grandfather, when they went to have an open sore on her grandmother's foot treated. The American, however, had arguments in support of her position that sounded more sophisticated, so Malika privately believed that the educated nurse must have known something that her grandfather did not.

The old man warned her against telling the nurse that he was seeking work for her at the factory. "She wouldn't understand," he said, "and she might cause trouble. The nurse had been relocated to a different community anyway by the time Malika learned she would be going to work. All she could think about now were the things her grandfather taught her about hard work and a good attitude.

Wednesday, May 3rd, 2028
Eugene, Oregon

Even Phyllis Hughes had to begrudgingly admire the President's gall in making a campaign appearance in a Green state in which he would place no higher than third in November. Perhaps he believed that since he ordered troops into Iraq, then he should at least travel to Oregon. What annoyed her was that so many supporters showed up for him, although this helped her co-conspirators blend into different parts of the auditorium.

She expected this to be her last act of protest for a long while, since she had just accepted a job with a television network in New York, which began two weeks following her upcoming graduation. She was looking forward to working as an assistant producer, at least while paying her dues. Even the daughter of an influential network executive had to start somewhere.

Hawking was introduced by a local official, perhaps the only elected Nationalist in the state of Oregon, and the President took the stage. Phyllis's heart beat a little faster and she checked her watch, which was pointless, since there was no planned synchronization to their scheme. She noted that there were some boos mixed in with the cheers for the President, which was odd, given that it was a carefully-screened crowd.

She and the others gained access to the event through press passes secured by Bernice Greenly, although that was the extent of her contribution, as she had her reputation to consider – in an industry that demands objectivity. Phyllis and the others shredded and disposed of their IDs to cover the trail.

"Thank you for welcoming me to Oregon," Hawking said, after some opening pleasantries. "There were a lot of folks who warned me against coming, saying that there are too many people here who are too 'open-minded' to consider a difference of opinion."

Phyllis and the other self-described "Warriors of Tolerance" carried oversized fanny packs with a variety of food items and colored syrup in squeeze bottles. They had actually considered carrying water pistols to shoot dark red liquid onto the President as he spoke, but then someone raised the issue of whether it was wise to point something that resembled a gun at a man protected by armed Secret Service agents.

"Well, I respect anyone who thinks differently from me," the President continued, "and I want to listen to them so that I can learn from them and find out why one of us is wrong. In my life, I've gone through various adjustments and conversions, as I've grown and learned from others. As you know, I've been on both sides of many issues since beginning life as the son of devoted Communists just up the road in Washington State.

They were so far to the left that it deeply disappointed them when I became a Democrat."

The crowd laughed as expected and Phyllis edged closer to the floor in front of the President, noticing out of the corner of her eye that others were doing the same.

"One thing that I've always believed in, however, is that it's necessary to maintain a sense of humility, because no one is ever right about everything. It pays to keep an open mind and to respect the opinion of others. Listening to others and examining my own beliefs against theirs has made me a richer man."

He looked up and smiled, "I'm sure that Oregonians realize the same value in dialogue, even though we may have a difference of opinion on issues such as the future of Iraq…"

That was the signal, quickly confirmed by a tossed egg. With the squeeze bottle clutched firmly in her hands, Phyllis burst past the last few people in the way, to where the President was standing with a look of resolve on his face under the barrage of food, as his security team closed in. Screaming tolerance and anti-war slogans, her hands pressed down on the bottle, shooting a long stream of ugly, red liquid onto Hawking. The bottle was quickly knocked out of her hands by a man standing next to her.

"What are you doing?" she shrieked, as if acting legitimately.

Rather than answer, he calmly asked. "What's wrong with allowing free speech? What's the worst that could happen?"

"We… we would lose our rights," she stammered, as the crowd closed between them and she was taken into the custody of a large agent, kicking and screaming.

GNN Studios

"Welcome back to our conversation with Senator Phil Hudson, who is expected to receive his party's nomination for President this July in New Orleans.

"Senator, as you know, there was a disruption during the President's speech in Eugene, Oregon this morning, which seems to happen quite a bit these days. Members of the audience shouted him down and threw food at him. His speech was nearly cancelled at that point by the Secret Service, but he insisted on returning to finish. What do you make of this?"

"Well Steve, there's a war going on and people are upset. I guess it's a little like the beating of Reginald Denny, following the first Rodney King verdict. It's not something that you necessarily want to see happen, but, in the words of Maxine Waters at the time, 'it's a righteous anger'…"

Friday, June 30th, 2028
El Paso, Texas

Felipe stared into the open eyes of the dead man lying next to another murder victim about ten years older in the middle of a street that literally ran nowhere, petering out after a hundred yards into gravel and brush out on the edge of town. It was built with the intention of residential development, but the gang graffiti and broken glass that littered the houses of the adjoining neighborhood meant that such expectations were misplaced.

The police detective felt much older than thirty-three years of age. He had lasted thirteen years on a force with an average lifespan of eighteen months. Since joining as a young recruit, he'd seen enough to push most past the breaking point. There was a string of prostitute murders during his first year on the force, and, of course, the never-ending stream of mafia killings that surfaced bodies at regular intervals every few weeks.

The worst thing he had witnessed so far was a mass grave of about two dozen young Indians from Central Mexico. They were from a remote tribe that was renowned for its gentleness and lack of aggression – in short, perfect targets for the Mexican drug lords. All two dozen men had been abducted and brought to dig an elaborate tunnel for drug smuggling that actually ran under the Rio Grande. It was two years of hard work and after the docile Indians finished, they were executed where they stood and then dumped.

It was the most brutal thing that Felipe had ever been forced to confront, and it affected him deeply. He went through a serious bout of depression, which was treated with medication. He stayed on the pills for over a year, finally getting though the episode in one piece with the help of the people in his family's church.

Two days earlier, he was sitting in his office when an older woman was shown in to speak with him about her son, who had been missing for two days. Through trembling tears, she insisted that he was a good hardworking boy – which his employer later confirmed. He wasn't the type to get into trouble. They had come up from Mexico last year to make a better life for themselves.

She held his picture in her hands; an oversized portrait that showed a normal young man, smiling broadly. He was her only son.

Now he stood looking directly into those same eyes, tainted dully by death, and felt like he was losing it again. Here was a boy loved by a mother, who had the highest hopes for him. He would never grow older or marry his fiancé. He would never have a future. His mother would never have grandchildren and might have no one to look after her in old age.

There was a deep wrenching in Felipe's stomach and he realized that he wasn't doing himself any favors by standing over the body and letting his thoughts roam.

He had to get a grip.

Walking back to his car in a mild daze, he was oblivious to the things that were said to him by the passing medics and police staff. He reached into his cruiser for a bottle of water then sat down, turning the ignition so that he could get some cool air on his face.

It looked for all the world like he was sitting in a stupor, but in fact his mind was in overdrive.

How could he do this any longer?

Who killed the boy?

What would he do if he quit?

How would he tell the boy's mother?

Where would he live if he left El Paso?

Would the killer be convicted?

"Oh God," he said, putting his forehead down against the steering wheel. It was part prayer and part groan.

He got no further than that, as he had to raise his head, quickly toss aside the plastic bottle, and open the car door to vomit.

September, 30ᵗʰ, 2028
Road to Mosul, Iraq

Suicidal religious extremists with a soft spot for the days of torture chambers and rape rooms made the drive from Baghdad up to Mosul unpleasant enough without having to endure the company of the woman who demanded the unnecessary trip. Fortunately, she didn't care for the young lieutenant either and had positioned herself as far from him as possible, where she sat glaring out the window of the Humvee.

He was a rarity in the American military, a true believer – part of a small wave of recruits that entered the service out of a sense of patriotism following the election of President Hawking four years earlier. Pledges to increase defense funding, toughen physical requirements, and restore military pride were a morale boost for the few real fighting men that managed to hang on through the series of executive orders issued by President Rodham, which were designed to make the armed forces less aggressive and less masculine.

Up until the Iraq war, there had been no repercussions from these demoralizing feats of social engineering, because there had been no military action to speak of. Democratic Presidents since the time of Carter stood idly by while Middle Eastern and Asian nations fell, one-by-one, to Islamist regimes, nor did they intervene during the raging bouts of genocide that periodically left millions of Africans dead. In the meantime, military budgets and personnel rolls were steadily reduced, with the liberated funds helping to offset the soaring cost of ambitious social programs. National defense was the only section of government where downsizing was not just acceptable, but actually encouraged, as the military was cut to the bone.

The lieutenant was proud to serve in the Army under the current Commander in Chief, but he wished that he could have been a Marine, like his father and grandfather before. The Corps however, was a casualty of its refusal to allow women in combat, which gave President Rodham the excuse to eliminate it in the lame duck period at the end of her second term.

Hawking had put off the Iraqi action for a couple of years while he worked to build up the armed forces. Although he was largely unsuccessful in getting a hostile Congress to agree with his requests, the perception of having a leader in the breach, fighting to preserve the disintegrating core of what had been the most powerful military ever seen was enough to rally the old guard and attract a trickle of new blood, although the pregnancy rate among active duty women reached a record high as war approached.

Even with its ancient equipment and crippled ranks, the ground forces routed the enemy, perhaps more on the strength of reputation than actual ability. The mission was swiftly accomplished in three months, and President Hawking formally declared an end to major combat operations.

From his vantage point on the front lines, the young lieutenant agreed with what was happening in Iraq. A brutal dictatorship was overthrown, mass graves were opened, elections were held and people were experiencing freedom. Murderous elements of the former dictatorship, intent on reclaiming autocratic rule, made it tough on ordinary Iraqis, but the battle was being won.

But not at home, however, where Democrats and Progressives saw opportunity in the media's tilted coverage, and were skillfully engineering anti-war sentiment. Each stumble in Iraq, each terror attack by the "insurgents" was eagerly exploited by these political charlatans, and their rhetoric merely encouraged the enemy and left the Iraqis one step closer to abandonment.

His passenger was an older, cantankerous woman; a special guest of a New Jersey Senator on whose authority she justified every personal demand, such as the dangerous trip to Mosul, where there had just been a surgical air strike against an al-Qaeda cell. Her purpose, apparently, was to talk with local hospital staff to verify the official version of civilian casualties. She wanted to interview survivors as well, but the lieutenant would probably draw the line at that point, even though he would catch hell for it when they got back.

"Stop staring at me, you pig," snapped the woman.

"I'm not, Ma'am," he replied, not sure if he were being called a pig because she held the delusion that he found her attractive, or simply because he was in uniform. Back at the base, she had literally beaten her hands against the chest of his commanding officer, demanding that she be allowed to sit against the vehicle's window, where it was cooler. She called him a pig as well.

"You macho swine are all alike," she asserted. "I'll bet you're a Nationalist, aren't you boy?"

The lieutenant started to answer, but thought the better of it. "So you're here to count bodies?" he asked.

The woman turned away, choosing to respond with her back to him. "My group is trying to keep a record of the devastation that this illegal war is imposing on the people of Iraq. Yes, we count bodies, but we also talk to the survivors and their children to try and account for the psychological damage of bombs and military occupation."

"You were the ones that went into Fallujah last year, after we took the city and drove out the terrorists?" he didn't wait for an answer. "We had that city locked down, and then you guys came with your clipboards and threats of lawsuits. You even counted the bodies of the Fedayeen and called them civilians; went to their families and tried to enlist them in suing your own country."

"Perhaps."

"We went door-to-door in that operation specifically to minimize civilian casualties, even though it put us at greater risk. I lost two good friends because of it."

"Maybe you shouldn't have been there in the first place," replied the woman coldly.

"You'll be happy to know that we're not there anymore. We were pulled out of Fallujah because of political pressure and…"

"Good! I'll bet the residents were able to get a good night's sleep."

"Don't you know how many people have been killed there since?" asked the officer incredulously. "The citizens are brutalized by these Islamists and thugs, who've killed far more than the offensive that liberated them, yet you're blaming us for the very violence that we're trying to end. You're merely encouraging the enemy to keep killing…"

"Liberation?" snapped the woman again. "You call it liberating when an army comes through town with guns and grenades? Is that how you want to live back in East Pigsty, Mississippi?"

"The people of Iraq are better off now, under self-rule, than they were under a dictatorship," continued the lieutenant. "Have you asked anyone outside of the Sunni Triangle what it was like for these people under Saddam and Uday? Over a million Iraqis disappeared during that time and their circumstances were…"

"Don't give me that crap!" the woman cut him off. "There wasn't a war happening then. Nothing is worth war and nothing is worse than war, particularly when it's a superpower attacking a tiny country."

"But, the people lived in terror then."

"They live in terror now, Mister… whatever your name is. All we've done is taken the place of the last dictator."

"What do you think will happen if we leave now? Do you really expect them to be able to maintain democracy?" asked the lieutenant, who was slightly distracted by the image of a small Fiat darting around the Humvee behind him, visible on the passenger-side mirror. The vehicle was accelerating rapidly, as if to pass the convoy on the right.

"I don't give a damn about that! It's not our business what happens in Iraq. I only care about what our country is doing to these people now. Islam is a religion of peace and I expect that…"

The fireball swept through the front of the Humvee, literally incinerating the woman in mid-sentence. The force of the explosion lifted the vehicle in the air slightly and drove the officer's body through the door on his side, along with a few of the woman's body parts. He came to rest two lanes over, with window glass wrapped over his chest and his right arm mangled beneath the twisted door. The right side of his face was burned and he couldn't hear anything except a high-pitched ringing from the concussion of the blast.

He lay there completely stunned for a minute or two before lifting his head. Others from his unit were using extinguishers against the blaze, while trying to lift what was left of the woman out of the vehicle. Although one other soldier had blood on him, no one else appeared to be critically injured. Two of his men stood over him, with black smoke drifting up behind them, quickly lifting the debris from his body and bringing him to his feet. Once up, he noticed the woman's left arm laying just a couple of yards away, with all five fingers intact. He began to reach for it absent-mindedly, but his men held him back and firmly directed him to the undamaged vehicle, where they dumped the contents of a canteen over his head to soothe the burning.

Cars were stopped in each direction, and many of the drivers were now trying to turn around, with the horror of the scene reflected in their eyes. He noticed that a house about ten yards from the road had sustained damage and that several passersby lay dead on the roadside. The smell of the explosive was still thick in the air.

After a few minutes of medical attention, he lay back in the truck bed with water still dripping from his hair and a bandage on the side of his face, listening to the sirens wail in the distance. He turned to look at the charred and still-smoldering corpse of his former passenger, which his men had placed beside him for the time being. The arm and part of a leg were tossed on top before the tarp was pulled over.

"I'm sorry, my dear," asked the lieutenant, "but did you say religion of peace or religion of pieces?"

Sunday October 8th, 2028
Hoboken, New Jersey

Jill Hudson sat next to Parker Whitehead, trying hard to focus on the funeral, but her mind was consumed by preparations for the upcoming Presidential debate on Tuesday, which would be a formal three-way session between her father, Senator Fish and President Hawking. Democrats and Progressives were billing the upcoming election as "the most important" that we are likely to see in "our lifetime." T-shirts reading 'Vote or Die' were hitting the streets and a whisper campaign was quietly launched that alleged an upcoming military draft in the event of Hawking's reelection.

"...and so, I have suffered the loss of both my parents to the foreign policy mistakes of my country." Robert Danforth's voice finally began to vie for her attention.

"Like my father twenty-seven years ago, my mother was taken from me; a victim of America's negligence and aggression. Let us pray that their deaths will not be in vain." The brown-haired young man solemnly bit his lower lip as he concluded his remarks, in a mannerism that may have seemed profound for the news cameras in the back of the room, but mildly overplayed to the people gathered together in the community center there in Hoboken to say goodbye to Sherry Danforth. He was the last to speak, and the music began as the ceremony ended. The attendees rose to mingle and offer condolences.

Jill stood together with Parker, her arm on his elbow. They made a handsome couple. Parker was tall and distinguished, with a head of graying hair that made him look older than he actually was. Her blonde hair and soft beauty provided the perfect complement, and their intimate manner of interaction fooled many, including their close friends at times, into believing that they were involved.

The small crowd included older women in print dresses, young men with earrings and boots, and many who were attired somewhere in between. Darnell Massey was the only other member of Rothermel's class to show; although he probably would not have come had he not lived right across the river in Manhattan. Thankfully, he was in the habit of wearing clothes these days, which suited his career as a rising star at one of the city's most prestigious law firms.

Jill had made her peace with Darnell. Their relationship had gotten off to a rocky start in college, when she approached him that first day in class and bluntly informed him that his nudity offended her. He simply replied, "I'm offended by your offense," which left them at an impasse. It was only within the last couple of months that they had begun speaking with each other again, when she asked him to support her father's Presidential campaign.

The African-American vote was hotly contested between her father's party and the Progressives. The Democratic promise of aggressive Affirmative Action policies was losing out to Progressive support for reparations. Darnell was one of the few black persons that Jill knew from Berkeley, since, like most other campuses across the country, the African-American students insisted on their own dorms, fraternities, and eating facilities as a buffer against the racial intolerance said to be ingrained in the rest of the student body. Most were in Black Studies programs, which were heavily segregated as well.

She was hoping that Darnell could be of use to her father in wooing young black voters, progressively more radical than their elders. Such was not to be, however. The young lawyer was a huge proponent of reparations and his expressed paranoia about "White" America had not mellowed with age. "You just don't know how hard it is for a black man in America," he told Jill, when she went to see him at his upscale apartment near the top floor of a coveted Upper West Side building. Neither were his political views in danger of shifting to the pragmatic center, which itself had shifted to what was once thought of as hard Left.

Nor, of course, was she under any illusions that the man standing at the front of the room, in the direction that Parker was slowly guiding her, would be voting Democratic this year either. Robert Danforth looked up at them, frowning as he saw them both together. He was neither the apolitical player they knew six years ago, nor the lip-biting deliverer of the thought-provoking invocation, but rather just an impetuous activist-lawyer with pale skin and a thin, colorless face. Parker quickly removed his arm from the small of Jill's back, while sticking out his other hand to offer his sympathies for Robert's loss. Robert took it in a brief mechanical grasp that was nearly as chilly as his frown had been.

"Well, if it isn't the Baghdad bed buddies," he said dryly.

Jill could feel Parker tense up and knew that he was clenching his jaw. She rolled her eyes and began forming a sentence around a particularly nasty word, while trying to remember that it was entirely inappropriate for the circumstances. Robert quickly gave a weak – if insincere – smile and said apologetically, "Oh, I'm sorry. I guess that's rude of me, isn't it. Please forgive me. I'm under a lot of stress as you can see."

"How's the Paterski case coming along?" asked Parker, abruptly changing the subject.

"It's finally over. His last appeal went down in flames before the Texas Supreme Court. This kind of surprised me, frankly, since he was technically in compliance with Texas law. Thank God for judges who follow their hearts! I think the state legislature may be changing the law anyway to mandate medical treatment for any person needing it."

"That's good," said Parker. "I'm glad to hear that."

Jill gave a slight nod and Danforth turned his head and looked at her with a sly smile. "Of course, it would be nice to see this sort of humane measure become federal law as well."

He said it almost as a question and Jill realized that her face was warming a bit. She could not maintain eye contact and looked down while saying, "I hope so. Right now we don't want to give the unions an excuse to vote against us. We'll just have to see how things go after November."

Danforth continued. "I'm going to be leaving the ACLU in a few weeks and starting my own company called Corporate Social Responsibility, Inc. We're going to try and hold other companies accountable for what they do to the environment, their employees, consumers, and the community as a whole."

Jill looked back up again. Parker had his arms folded across his chest and was nodding repetitively while maintaining an intense expression. All he said was, "Really?"

"Yes. You see, after Dennis Paterski lost his last appeal, he closed down the hospital in Tucson before we could file an injunction to prevent it. He literally just closed the doors one night and relocated most of his staff."

"You're kidding," said Jill incredulously. "I knew the guy was a jerk, but I never thought he'd take it that far."

"Well, even having dealt with him personally, I have to say that it was still a surprise to me as well, although he had threatened to do it during the deposition." Danforth drew a hand through the front of his hair and gave a quick smile at a passerby as he spoke. "He just left the people of that city high and dry. The poor folks there barely have health care; just a few overloaded city clinics. It's going to get real bad for them until someone else steps in. Paterski's also threatening to close his other hospital in Dallas if the state law gets passed, but it shouldn't have as much of an impact. There are plenty of other hospitals, even in the transipolitan areas."

Danforth quickly gripped the hand of another well-wisher, though not missing a beat in the conversation. "So, anyway... I believe that it might be possible to get the upper hand on these corporate crooks by hitting them where it counts."

"In the wallet, eh?" said Parker.

"Right. Bad publicity is a powerful weapon. If the public were made aware of a company's bad practices, it's likely that they would choose to do business elsewhere, and might pressure other clients or vendors to do the same. My vision for CSR is a true 'better business bureau.' I want it to be a company that aggressively promotes socially responsible business practices on the part of U.S. corporations."

"Can't argue with that," said Jill. Parker seemed to concur.

"Well," said Danforth brusquely, with a smile that nearly bordered on genuine, "I've got a burial to attend to. It was a pleasure seeing you."

Jill and Parker smiled politely and watched their former classmate brush off the line of people waiting to offer him condolences with a wave, as he rushed down the opposite aisle away from them and out the door.

Tuesday October 10th, 2028
GNN Broadcast of the Presidential Debate

Moderator: Welcome back to the municipal auditorium in Oak Park, Illinois for our final Presidential debate. We apologize for the delay. As you can see, the live audience is no longer with us, as we were unable to control the demonstrations and outbursts. On the panel, however, we still have our three candidates for the general election in November: Senator Fish of Washington, the Progressive; Senator Hudson of New York, the Democrat; and President Hawking, the incumbent, who is a former Senator representing Montana.

In the last segment we discussed the war in Iraq. Now, we raise a series of other topics that will give you the opportunity to explain your position to the American people. First, as you all know, the former Canadian Province of Alberta declared independence two years ago, which Canada agreed to recognize under the condition that it become a U.S. Protectorate. Each of you has gone on record to express your support for the proposal, but the people of Alberta are firmly opposed to this and believe that their territory exists as a separate country. They've gone so far as to form an organized military, which many Americans find alarming. How do you intend on addressing this?

Hawking: Well, being from Montana, I can tell you that no one there shares the same alarm that the folks in Manhattan or West Palm Beach claim to have, which makes me a bit suspicious. I'd like to bring Alberta into the nation as a protectorate and then try and convince the good people there to rejoin our great union. We can use people of that caliber.

Hudson: I disagree with the President. It concerns me that we don't know what's happening in Alberta. It's almost like a black hole – and that should worry all of us.

Fish: Alberta is full of racists, bigots and religious fanatics; former Americans that could not bring themselves to live with people of other color or religious faith here in our multicultural nation. They are our reactionary rejects, and we're far better off without them. If this is what the President calls 'people of caliber' then we would be better off without him as well.

Moderator: Next, along the same lines, there is the issue of Maine and Alaska, which are both experiencing independence movements as well, although in very different ways. What is your opinion of these situations?

Hawking: No states will be leaving the union under my watch. This has always been my policy.

Hudson: I would like to echo the President's desire, but I don't share his confidence that the Alaskan independence movement is illegitimate. There are serious questions about the legality of their statehood in the late 1950s, and their patient bid for independence now has United Nations sponsorship through the Republic of Iran. I would not arbitrarily rule out international law, as it appears the incumbent unfortunately has. The situation concerning Maine is different, however. While I respect that there are a large number of Muslims in the state that wish to live under *Sharia*, the Islamic law, I feel that there are positive measures to accomplish this that are far less radical than outright secession.

Fish: I agree with my colleague from New York.

Moderator: First on the domestic agenda is health care. President Hawking, you've been trying unsuccessfully to get Congress to amend the Gore-Rodham Plan and exclude coverage for abortion, even though this has diminishing support among a public that is more likely now to identify itself as "pro-choice."

Hawking: It would be hypocritical for someone to call themselves "pro-choice," yet favor a system that forced people to subsidize what they believe to be murder. I fully sympathize with those who feel compelled to leave our country rather than see their tax dollars go toward the arguable extermination of human life. How would you feel if you were a Jew forced to pay taxes to Nazi Germany?

Hudson: There he goes again; using extremist rhetoric and providing justification to the nuts that bomb abortion clinics and kill doctors. The majority of Americans will reject this dangerous attempt to roll back our entitlement to universal health care. He's simply pandering to a base that's rapidly eroding anyway.

Fish: The President should be ashamed of himself. He wants to return to the days when women had no freedom over their bodies and no political rights. Frankly, it amazes me that any woman in this country would vote Nationalist. They would betray themselves by the very act.

Moderator: I want to ask you about the on-going battle to raise the minimum wage. Even though it would affect less that 1% of the workforce, the unions are pushing quite hard for a significant increase. Do you all agree that the minimum wage should be raised?

Fish: Frankly, the minimum wage should be two or three times higher than it is currently – which is right at the poverty line. This will improve the standard of living for our poorest workers. When I'm elected next month, you can bet that I'll do everything in my power to see that this happens.

Hudson: The working poor have a right to higher wages. Raising the minimum wage will put more money in the pockets of those who need it most.

Hawking: It amazes me to hear this kind of talk. You can't create wealth by raising the minimum wage. No legislation can create wealth.

Moderator: Similar to this, perhaps, is the topic of taxation. President Hawking was able to persuade Congress to pass several successive tax cuts for the wealthy that have been highly controversial. Senator Fish, your opinion?

Fish: Well, there's no mystery there. I've always opposed tax cuts, as has Senator Hudson. Unfortunately other Democrats were seduced by their big money donors into joining the Nationalists. The disastrous effect on lower and middle class Americans may take a generation to correct.

Hudson: I agree with Senator Fish. Cutting the taxes of our richest citizens places an undue burden on the lower classes and it is blatantly unfair to ordinary Americans.

Hawking: Well look, my populist opponents are certainly playing to the masses on this one, but they're purposefully leaving out several critical details. First, tax revenue from the wealthy has increased steadily as the tax cuts have taken effect, just as they did under John F. Kennedy and Ronald Reagan. More importantly, they've stimulated business investment and job creation. We've enjoyed lower unemployment and ten straight quarters of economic expansion for the first time in thirty years.

Hudson: We've also seen an alarming decline in budgetary funding for social programs for the first time, as well. Less money spent on housing the poor, feeding the hungry and helping those in need.

Fish: This Administration has been criminal in its disregard for the Federal government's responsibilities in the life of the average American. It's not simple negligence; it is a determined, consistent effort to crush those on the lower rungs of the social ladder.

Moderator: Well, it would appear that positions are well-defined on this...

Hawking: Excuse me, because I'm sick of hearing this. Your programs only foster dependency and reward bad behavior. You Democrats and Progressives cynically play groups against one another and use the taxes of one to buy the votes of the other, all the while cultivating a reliance on government that borders on psychological enslavement. You bring to fulfillment the very prophecy you predict, by reducing incentives for people to accomplish, to build, to create...

Fish: I know it doesn't matter to you Mr. President, but in America right now a 10-year-old girl is going to bed hungry. She...

Hawking: What's her name?

Fish: Excuse me?

Hawking: What's her name?

Fish: I... uh... Well, it doesn't matter, because she's representative of the millions of...

Hawking: It matters to me… if a citizen is going to bed hungry that is, or if a Presidential candidate is attempting to manipulate the…

Fish: I don't remember her name exactly. She was someone that I met on the campaign trail. She represents…

Hawking: And she's still going to bed hungry? Why, Senator Fish, you're one of the wealthiest men in America; an heir to the Cooper fortune, I believe. You didn't take this starving girl down to Winn-Dixie and buy her some food? In too much of a rush to get back to your 50-acre lake estate in Redmond, I presume… or was it the beach house in Santa Cruz?

Fish: You are out of line Sir! You know that I can't feed every person in America, no matter how much I want to. Only the government can do that.

Hawking: Yes, Heaven forbid that people should take responsibility for their own condition.

Hudson: I'm glad you said that Sir, because this illustrates just the sort of mean-spiritedness that we've had to put with from you Nationalist Nazis that want to starve the hungry, roll back the clock on human rights and take away our freedoms! Mean-spirited!

Fish: They're coming for our children! They're coming for the poor! They're coming for the sick, the elderly, and the disabled! They're mean-spirited! They're…

Moderator: Gentlemen, Mr. President, Senators, I'm sorry to have to cut you off, but we are out of time.

November 7th, 2028
GNN Election Night Coverage (Commercial Break)

Someone in the control room pressed the wrong button as the Election Night special went to commercial break late in the evening, well after the polls were closed and the results already known. Instead of a public service spot regarding the Edina virus and an ad for Coop-Mart, the Presidential campaign commercials were broadcast instead.

Senator Hudson's spot ran first. It shows him sitting in a school playground, surrounded by children of all races and ethnicities. Several of the children wear *hijabs, kufis,* and other Muslim garb. The camera pans down from the swirling fall color of the leaves in the trees above.

"The autumn leaves are beautiful, aren't they?" says the Senator with a wistful pause, before turning his full attention to the camera. "We shouldn't forget though, that the diversity of color makes them so." He pauses to look reflectively at a young African-American boy sitting on his lap.

"It's that way with people too, you know. Diversity makes us beautiful... richer. Not just our race and skin color," he says, turning to a Muslim girl standing next to him, "but our religion as well." She smiles reverently at him and he gives a dignified nod in return. He sets aside the boy on his lap, stands up and walks toward the camera and away from the children, as if wanting to say something he fears would be disturbing to them.

"Of course, not everyone in our country feels that way. Like you, I am disturbed by those who want to return our country to a darker time; a time of hate."

The picture changes from the playground to images from the Segregation era. Scenes of well-known hate crimes flash across the screen, as well as Confederate flags and people carrying signs with racist or Islamophobic slurs. "They want an America that looks like them, talks like them... and even thinks like they do."

The scene then cuts back to the Senator. The children are huddled together in the background just over his shoulder. Their mildly fearful expressions turn expectant as the camera pulls back to reveal more of their Protector. The picture cuts away to each of their faces as they take turns asking questions.

"Who will take care of me when I'm sick?" asks one.

"I will," answers the Senator.

"Who will keep my older brother from dying in Iraq", asks another.

"I will," answers the Senator.

"Who will take care of my parents when they're old?" asks another.

"I will," answers the Senator.

"Who will take care of me when I'm old", asks another.

"I will," answers the Senator.

"Who will make sure I have a job when I grow up?" asks another.

"I will," answers the Senator.

"Who will protect me from large corporations?" asks another.

"I will," answers the Senator.

"Who will help me when I need help?" asks another.

"I will," answers the Senator.

"Who will tie my shoe for me?" asks another.

The Senator gives a compassionate smile and the scene switches to him on his knees, in the dirt, kindly working out a knot for the young lad.

The camera pulls back and then up to the swirl of color in the trees.

The Progressive commercial begins with a view of Senator Fish, walking through a housing project in blue jeans and leading a column of poorly-clad families with children.

"Some say that the American economy has been doing better over the last four years, according to their fancy formulas and statistics." He turns and looks at the people behind him. "But don't tell that to these people."

He stops in an open area as the line files into a group behind him. "Like you, they've been on the losing end of this so-called 'economic resurgence' – these games that big business and the rich play with government at the expense of people like you. You have less, because they have more... and it's not right."

The camera angle rises to reveal a community of upper-class homes located some distance in the background, outside of the housing projects.

"There's no reason why some should live in luxury while others live in squalor. There's no reason why wealth should be concentrated in the hands of a few, when there are so many in need."

The picture cuts back to Senator Fish.

"There was a time when America was ruled by the people, not by the rich; a time when America was about workers, not corporate honchos, and when votes counted more than dollars. Now the rich are even sending the poor off to die in an overseas war to line their own pockets. It's time that we put power back in the hands of the people. This is what I'll do when you elect me President."

Another camera angle show the Senator bending to his knee, as a beautiful little girl in a shabby dress walks over and stands beside him. The Senator smiles warmly, grasps her in a light hug then turns back to the camera.

"Oh, and by the way, President Hawking. Her name is Joanna. She won't be going hungry anymore, thanks to a...," here he gives a wink, "well, an anonymous benefactor. But unfortunately the same cannot be said for the millions of Americans living in grinding poverty."

He stood up. "The American dream has become a nightmare for most people living within our borders, as the alliance between government and big business works unfairly to the advantage of the powerful and wealthy. It's time to take America back."

President Hawking chose a construction site as the background for his final campaign advertisement, which appeared to have been produced after those of the other candidates. Blue-collared men in heavy work clothes and helmets manage tools with thick, gloved hands behind and above him, as sparks periodically shower down from welders. An American flag hangs from one of the girders, catching dramatically in the breeze.

"When I came into office four years ago, there were many in this country who said that our best days were behind us and that America was dying under her own weight. Now we know they were wrong."

His salt and pepper hair ripples a bit with the wind, as he smiles confidently. "I'm proud to call myself an American. I'm a conservative. I believe in our country, our economy and the resourcefulness of our people. I believe that you, as an American, hold your destiny in your own hands, and that opportunity exists for anyone willing to work in this system of free enterprise to realize their ambitions.

The camera angle starts to rise, showing more of the activity on the construction project behind him.

"I believe in holding educators accountable for our children's progress; and that schools should be in the business of teaching basic skills rather than excuses for failure.

"I believe in protecting our borders and rigorously enforcing our immigration laws.

"I believe in letting Americans keep as much as possible of what they earn, because they're better stewards of their own money than is the government.

"I believe in confronting and standing up to terrorists, rather than allowing them to dictate terms to us. Neither should our foreign policy be subject to the United Nations.

"I believe that we exist as individuals and not members of identity groups, and that recognizing this fact will bring us together and unify us for the future, as we put our country back on track.

The picture switches to a close up of his face for the final line.

"Oh, and by the way. Teach your child to tie his own shoe. He'll thank you later."

When the GNN studios returned, the anchors apologized for the slip and posted the latest projections showing that Hudson would beat Fish in the popular vote, 41% to 37%, with Hawking trailing at 15%.

2029

Monday, March 5th, 2029
Malawi, Africa

Malika had been told to stay home that day, rather than report to work for her usual six-hour shift of sweeping and cleaning, but she had nothing else to do and volunteered to take lunch down to her grandfather, which she usually brought anyway on the days they worked together. Her job wasn't difficult and it paid $1.50 a day. She enjoyed contributing to the family's bottom line, which helped especially after her aunt died of AIDS the year before – the same disease that struck down her mother before Malika was old enough to remember.

She entered the back door of the factory as usual, carrying the bread and meat wrapped carefully in newspaper out onto the floor where her grandfather worked. Things seemed to be different that day. Workers weren't smiling, and there was tension in the air. The usual buzz of voices on the floor was missing and the only thing heard were sounds of working hands and the steady drone of machines.

Instead of the usual smile when her grandfather caught sight of her, he frowned as if she had done something wrong. He glanced nervously at a small group of people that were walking back and forth, talking quietly and writing on clipboards. She recognized three of them as the factory managers, but two others were unfamiliar, including a thin, pale man with sharp eyes that darted quickly from side to side, as if trying to catch everything.

Her grandfather left his station and approached her with a smooth, rapid gait, subtly motioning her back the way that she came. As she turned, she noticed that the white man was now watching her as well. She scurried back into the mud room, where workers changed clothes before entering the floor. Her grandfather came in quickly behind her and snatched the food out of her hands.

"Go!" he commanded. "You're not supposed to be here. Go home!"

Her feelings were hurt, but she pushed open the door and stepped out onto the dirt track that buffered the building from the forest. As she came around the side of the building, she was surprised to see the same white man standing in the bright sunlight at the end of the building, near the front door that he had apparently come through for the purpose of crossing her path. She wondered how he had known to be there, since she assumed that a stranger would be unfamiliar with the premises.

Following the advice of her grandmother to avoid strangers, she crossed to the other side of the track. The other man waited until she was almost parallel with him then quickly crossed over and blocked her path. No one else was around and she was very uncomfortable.

"Don't be afraid," the man said with a smile that seemed out of keeping with his harsh stare. "My name is Mr. Danforth. I only want to ask you some questions because I saw you inside. Do you work at this factory?"

She nodded.

"How old are you?"

"Thirteen."

He asked what she did, how long she worked, and for how much money. She hesitated over the last part, because her grandfather told her not to talk about what she made with neighbors and friends. She told the man anyway, because she believed that he worked for the factory and could easily find out.

When he was through asking questions, the man pulled out a camera and took her picture.

Thursday, May 3rd, 2029
GNN Studios

Jill barely had time to sit down before the broadcast returned from commercial and the anchorwoman introduced her to the viewers as both a Special Advisor to the President and his daughter. She knew to expect a tough interview. Bahira al-Zubayi was only a few years older than her, but had several years under her belt at al-Jazeera, where she developed a hard-hitting reputation that caught the attention of GNN executives looking for Arab anchors.

"As you know, Ms. Hudson, the Administration is being evaluated on its performance during its first 100 days. What do you feel are some of the accomplishments that the President can claim?"

This was an easy question. "As you know, Bahira, we came into office after four of the most disastrous years in American history. We inherited a country that is far more angry and divided now than it was before the Hawking Administration reversed hard-won gains from the previous three decades. We are addressing the grievances of each group, and setting the country back on the path that it belongs.

"First, minorities can be assured that the President will enforce the Non-Discrimination Act, which places the burden of proof onto employers to ensure that they have interviewed candidates for open positions in proportion to the racial and cultural composite of the community and provide justification for any anomalies between the employee base and the broader demographics. This will facilitate discrimination lawsuits and ultimately reduce the employment disparity among groups that complain of bias.

"Secondly, we are reversing the regressive tax code and shifting the burden away from ordinary Americans and back onto businesses and the wealthy.

"Third, we are restoring the funds for social programs that so many poor and hungry Americans have counted on to help with needs that are taken for granted by many of us. We are also pushing for the last stages of nationalization within the healthcare industry, although we know that it will be too late for some, such as the Villegas family in Tucson. Through continued reform, we hope to erase the harsh climate of the last four years."

"You would not agree then," asked the anchorwoman, "that the Nationalists are correct when they say that the largest health problems suffered by our poorest citizens are from the effects of obesity?"

"Technically, this has been the case since the 1970's," answered Jill, carefully, "but look at how the statement is qualified. They use the word 'citizens' as a means of excluding the neediest among us, who are the refugees from Mexico and other parts of Latin America. Our responsibilities should extend to anyone living within our borders. We need to provide these people with more than just tents in the desert, as some of the transitory centers have become, but rather with holistic programs. We're working with the Mexican government, which, as you know, felt completely alienated by the Hawking Administration, to come up with educated solutions."

"Critics are charging that the Mexican government will be put back in a position of control over U.S. immigration and other policies. Do you…"

"Completely false," interjected Jill. "These are racist charges. Clearly the real issue is that there are some Americans who, regrettably, are still uncomfortable sharing their country with those who don't look like them."

"As you know," said Bahira, smoothly switching gears, "the Muslim Coalition Party sided with the Democrats last November. It is widely believed that had the MCP thrown its support to the Progressives, there would be a President Fish in office now. What concerns of American Muslims do you intend on addressing, and when?"

Jill anticipated the question. "We intend on pushing for the extension of non-discriminatory legislation to cover religious affiliation. No one will be denied a job, loan, tenancy, or other opportunity because of their religion and, since the burden will be on the employer or provider to prove non-discriminatory intent, we believe that they'll be making every effort to categorically include Muslim-Americans in proper proportion to the community.

"We will also bring an end to the regrettable act of spying on private citizens without their knowledge and will require that intelligence agencies be called to account for any disproportionate targeting of a particular religious group. Any approved surveillance operation at a mosque, for example, will not be justified unless it can be shown that an equal number of operations have been conducted at churches, temples and synagogues. Muslims will no longer feel as if they're under the microscope."

"As you know, Ms. Hudson, many Americans are concerned about the Edina virus. Muslim-Americans are also worried that there are some in the community suggesting that this disease is endemic only to certain segments of the population. A nurse, who happens to be Bonan, has sued the HHS because she believes that she was unfairly targeted for testing. Does the President share the concern of Muslims?"

"Absolutely the President shares their concern. There will be no profiling or singling out of anyone, as we take the steps necessary to deal with this terrible virus that has claimed the lives of over forty people. We understand that the marrow tests being required of health care workers are quite painful, but this will be required of everyone in the industry with no regard for ethnicity. We regret the horrifying ordeal that this Bonan... this nurse, who happens to be Bonan, had to endure upon learning that not all of her peers were being tested along with her."

Jill hoped she sounded sincere. The Edina testing was controversial in the medical community and there was mounting resistance to the mandated bone marrow exams. The rumor that all infections were limited to the tiny Bonan community was true, in fact, although only a handful of people knew it. Muslim rights activists in Washington picked up on the issue and publicized it as yet another grievance against a government that was neglectful at best and nefarious at worst.

The news media had to tread carefully as it capitalized on the minority discrimination dimension of the issue, which played well to a socially conscious public, while taking care not to convey the impression that the problem was limited to the Bonan community, lest interest wane or bigotry mount. The disease desperately needed a 'Ryan White'; an infected individual outside of the stereotype, who could skillfully evoke public empathy and concern.

In truth, forty deaths over twenty years hardly justified putting millions of medical workers through the grueling (and expensive) marrow tests, but the disease had captured the public consciousness and the government needed to step forward with a plan – one that did not anger the Muslim community, even if it did face stiff opposition from hospitals and clinics.

"We hope that this poor woman can recover from the trauma of disenfranchisement to..."

"Let me interrupt you for a moment, Ms. Hudson, because we're short on time. Everyone seems to be wondering what the Administration's plans are for Iraq. As you know, the Progressives are calling for full withdrawal and are critical of President Hudson for not providing a timetable."

"Yes, my fa... the President is quite focused on Iraq and committed to finalizing a timetable for the withdrawal of U.S. troops. There is a balancing act between the democratically elected government there, which is asking us to stay, and world opinion, which is unanimous in wanting us to leave."

"It's been over three months now and so far there has been no change," said the anchorwoman, adjusting her headscarf.

"Well, there has been. You just don't see it. We're negotiating with the Iraqi government behind the scenes. As you know, they're under tremendous pressure from the insurgents. There are complexities to deal with and, as I'm sure you would agree, we can't just abandon the people there until they can defend themselves."

By the cold glitter in al-Zubayi's eyes, it appeared that she did not agree. Although Jill may have sounded like an apologist for the previous administration, the situation in Iraq was a lot more complicated than they realized during the campaign. The criminals there were staging attacks on the Iraqi security infrastructure and doing everything they could to raise enough instability to make it nearly impossible to create a timetable for withdrawal. Policy is much easier to criticize than it is to create and implement, but at least they still had a scapegoat in those who acted before.

Naturally, this didn't mean much to her interrogator. "You understand that Americans, along with others in the world, are beginning to wonder whether the President intends on keeping his campaign promise to bring 'peace with honor'."

"Let me assure you that peace is at hand in Iraq," said Jill, hoping she sounded more confident than she felt.

Monday, September 24th, 2029
Washington, DC

Robert Danforth was playing to his biggest audience yet, as he sat at the long table in front of the panel of Senators at the hearings into SplintCo Computers. He knew that this was a defining moment for Corporate Social Responsibility, Inc. His young company was making a name for itself by publicizing the findings that prompted the Senate investigation. Since his trip to Malawi in March, on the tip from a former girlfriend who had done volunteer nursing work there, he had thrown everything he could into bringing the computer giant to account for its labor practices there.

He had found sub-par working conditions for employees at the warehouse, and unacceptable twelve-hour days in some cases. The average pay was less than a third of what the minimum wage was in the United States, even before the recent hikes by the Hudson Administration.

His ace-in-the-hole, however, was evidence of child labor. The little girl he had cornered on the road outside the factory wasn't the only underage employee there, but she was turning out to be the most photogenic. His focus groups seemed to respond well to her picture, and he hoped the broader public would also, as he had it framed in poster size and prominently set on an easel right behind his shoulder, where it was being captured by the array of cameramen and photographers that kneeled in front of him, in the narrow void between his table and members of the Senate panel.

His only day of scheduled testimony was winding down. He spent most of the morning talking about the conditions at the factory, and most of the afternoon detailing his effort to lobby SplintCo, either to force its supplier to bring the conditions at the Malawi plant into line with American standards or to close the doors. Since March, he had organized a boycott against the computer giant, which put pressure on the company's vendors and clients as well.

The Democrats and Progressives on the panel lent questions that provided ample opportunity for him to express his outrage. He was afraid that the lone Nationalist might give him some problems, but, in fact, the Senator had been effectively neutralized by a pre-hearing press conference the day before in which Danforth had expressed "fear" that he would be maligned by the only member of the panel to receive campaign funds from SplintCo. No doubt the Senator now felt that he would be doing the company more harm than good by speaking out, although he did force Danforth to acknowledge that there was no proof that SplintCo knew about the factory working conditions, since it was owned by a separate company and not a direct subsidiary.

"Any corporation that does business in America has an obligation to carefully examine its trading partners to determine if they share the same values," countered Danforth to the frustrated legislator. "This is the choice that retailers, corporate clients, and ordinary Americans will now have to make when they decide whether to put SplintCo computers on their store shelves or in their homes."

When asked whether he had any concluding remarks for the panel, Danforth paused, to ensure that the cameramen on the floor had time to shift in his direction, and then turned to point at the picture behind him.

"Gentlemen, I just hope that when you make your final recommendations to the Justice Department, you keep in mind this little girl. Her name is Malika. She's 13-years old, and when I found her six months ago, she was working up to six hours a day doing menial labor at this same horrible sweatshop for about 25-cents an hour.

"Like all children, this little girl deserves a childhood – a chance to enjoy life and relish the simple innocence that we Americans are so captivated by in our own children. There's no reason why her opportunity for youth and innocence should be stolen from her by a greedy American corporation."

He turned back to face the panel and cameras, and bit his lower lip.

"Do it for Malika… do it for the children."

Burlington, Vermont

Dr. Sanjay Guptapara turned off the television and stood by the oversized window of his living room, where the view of Lake Champlain was especially captivating in the fall. The leaves on the trees between his house and the lakeshore were in the process of turning into a gorgeous tapestry of brilliant color. Boats floated lazily across the water in the distance. None of it cheered him.

He came home early to watch the testimony before Congress just as his wife was leaving to pick up the children. He knew that he would feel better when they pulled back up the long driveway and came bouncing in the house, but right now he was alone with his somber thoughts.

He had taken an interest in the small organization run by the man giving testimony that afternoon, after the research company that he worked for was contacted by CSR back in July. At the time, no one paid much attention, since they were always being harassed by activist groups of some sort that were concerned about their genetically-modified food products. Although the food was usually accepted by consumers in the United States, and had been for years, there was serious international controversy, despite the absence of any shred of evidence that it was dangerous.

As a leading geneticist, Sanjay knew very well that GM food was safe, particularly after clinical trials, but there was this insane resistance to it, as if it could turn people into monkeys. He was worried about his own project, to which he was emotionally attached.

Growing up in an impoverished region of India, Sanjay had seen many children die from a particular parasite that found its way into local wheat crops. The government had been making progress with pesticides, but in recent years there was pressure from environmental groups to cease using these substances.

Although Sanjay had done quite well for himself, transcending the disadvantages of his background with ambition and perseverance, he had not forgotten the problems still suffered by those with whom he had grown up. He appreciated that he was able to use part of his time at the lab to develop a new type of wheat – one that was resistant to the parasite that killed thousands of poor Indians each year.

Somehow word of his success was leaked to CSR (Sanjay suspected a younger disgruntled worker that left in bad circumstances after arguing over the program). The organization had called to express their concern over Sanjay's work, even though his employer had previously suggested that his research might win the Nobel Prize in biology. Now, however, the company wanted to tread cautiously on the project, due to CSR's maturing reputation, despite the fact that lives were hanging in the balance.

It also didn't help matters that the sympathies of the new Hudson Administration seemed remarkably susceptible to CSR's influence.

Hawking wouldn't have given those radicals the time of day.

The crunch of tires on gravel and leaves, along with the distant rumble of his wife's Land Cruiser interrupted his thoughts for the time being.

Thusday, September 27th, 2029
Juneau, Alaska

President Hudson had sent his Vice President to Juneau for the independence ceremony. The poor woman had to stand in the rain with a dour expression on her face, looking every bit as depressed as Prince Charles when he stood in a similar downpour during the handover of Hong Kong to the Chinese. Alaska's future, particularly with local control of its oil reserves and drilling operations, was probably brighter than those of the former British colony, however, who saw their political and human rights crushed, eventually, by their new masters.

It was because of the oil that the President wanted to maintain good relations with Alaska, although the Administration presently faced a decision on whether to institute a boycott in response to the ANWR drilling, which began even as independence was imminent. Jill suspected that this wouldn't happen, since gas was already between $8 and $10 a gallon, due mostly to the toppling of the Saudi regime by the Islamic fundamentalists at a time when the influx of immigrants into America was skyrocketing energy demands.

At the time, the Rodham Administration felt it best not to intervene in the Islamic revolutions that were steadily placing most of the world's oil resources in the hands of those hostile to Western interests, even though the subsequent religious courts cranked out body counts that ran into the millions. Nothing was worth war, particularly oil. The solution to the oil crisis lay in establishing good international relations, which would persuade the Middle Eastern countries to lower prices and convince the countries with the highest energy demands and pollution rates over the last forty years, such as China, to sign the international environmental treaties that would reciprocate the good faith shown by the Americans.

It was for this reason that President Hudson careful not to appear belligerent toward the global community, particularly the Middle Eastern countries pressing for Alaskan independence under international protocol. Combined with Iraqi withdrawal and an indefinite suspension of support for Israel, it was only a matter of time before their good will would dissipate suspicion and win over the Arab street.

2030

Thursday February, 21ˢᵗ, 2030
Washington D.C.

"What are we doing to our children!" moaned Starr Sterling, to the group of grim-faced Senators, sitting as still as statues across from her on their raised platform. Each had a hand located somewhere near their mouth, striking a pose that was carefully designed to convey empathy to the viewers at home. Their only movement was an occasional rotation of hands as the cameras periodically shifted angles in front of them.

The actress had been building to this climactic point in her testimony before the committee, which was charged with determining how much of the budget should be allocated to Edina viral research. She had been presented as an "expert witness" by a special interest group that made her their "spokesperson" only a few days before, but she was carrying the script well. The message was that the future of the nation rested with the Senator's decision to fund Edina research.

She repeated her final line once more, this time banging the table with her fist, then clutching the cloth covering and raising it slightly so that the cameras could catch her trembling fingers.

"What are we doing to our children!" she shrieked.

Monday, March 11ᵗʰ, 2030
Washington D.C.

There were supposed to be thirteen detonations that morning, but three of the backpack bombs were found intact. The other ten were set off simultaneously with cell phones, doing significant damage to the three Metro stations and hundreds of D.C. commuters.

The bombers had apparently cased the Yellow line, from Huntington to Silver Spring, since all of the targeted stations were along this route. Dozens were killed in the Crystal City and the Archives stations, but the hardest hit was the hub at L'Enfant Plaza, which was still packed at nine o'clock, although the bulk of the rush hour had passed.

Four lines converged on the underground station. As the bombs tore through the platform and trains in quick succession, panic ensued and people began rushing up the stairs, bumping into each other, stepping on top of each other and pouring up out of the street entrances like ants from a mound. The shaken but intact were followed by the bloody, as people began staggering out with progressively serious injuries over the next fifteen minutes. By the time rescue workers arrived, the remaining injured had to be carried by others.

Emergency workers descended into the smoky chaos, through the gates, and onto a terrible scene. At least seventy bodies lay on the platform, along with hundreds of the maimed and bleeding. The train that had borne the brunt of the explosion was stripped to the frame in some places. Corpses were entangled in the shredded metal wreckage. Arms and legs were strewn about, with limbless torsos scattered in between. A sickening stench of seared bodies and death hung in the air.

At least one body was blown into the station's ceiling. Rescue workers only noticed it by the cell phone that was ringing in the victim's pocket.

Four hours after the blast, as Muslim-American activist groups were still warning against a rush to judgment and suggesting that Israeli groups were probably behind the attack, al-Qaeda posted proof positive of its culpability on the Web, saying that the attacks would continue until the "occupation" ended.

The White House was deluged with phone calls and e-mail begging the President to immediately pull the last of the troops out of Iraq, but he gave no indication of this when addressing the nation that evening to assure the Muslim-American community that every effort would be made to protect them against any retaliation by "patriotic vigilantes."

On the floor of the house, a member of the Progressive Party from Georgia insisted that the President had foreknowledge of the attack, and allowed it to happen in order to benefit his "buddies" in the defense industry. Back in Atlanta, her father said that Jews were behind the attack. He even spelled it out for the reporters.

"J-E-W-S!"

Tuesday, March 12ᵗʰ 2030
Washington, DC

The numbers were finalized by the time Jill left at three o'clock in the morning. Two-hundred and one people had been killed and about fourteen hundred other commuters injured. Despite getting less than two hours of sleep, she was back at her desk at six and took the call from Rahim a few hours later. Her former classmate was working for his retired grandfather, who was rumored to be in bad health.

"I have heard ordinary citizens expressing their anger over the resistance attacks of this morning," he told her, somewhat mechanically. "I am concerned about this climate of fear and intimidation that Muslims are now under in this country. I'm sure that it will only get worse."

"Didn't you hear the President's speech last night?" she asked. "He specifically addressed that issue and warned Americans against reacting. He's committed to making sure that no one is disenfranchised by this catastrophe. We're learning, for example, that several of the bombers are American, so the President is planning to appoint a task force to look into the problems that Muslims are facing in this country that might cause them to turn to violence. You can bet that most of the appointees will be Muslim…"

"I know it's very hard for me, as a Muslim, to feel like a loyal American, when there are soldiers with guns in a Muslim country, looking to kill others that look like me," snapped Rahim bitterly.

"There haven't been any major Iraqi offensives, since we took office," insisted Jill, "and we have reduced deployment by 50%."

"It's not good enough! You sound like a damn Nationalist. When will the infidel invaders leave Iraq?"

"Infidels?"

"Well, *I* don't think that," said Rahim, dropping his voice a few decibels, "but it's hard to convince others of that, when a Christian army patrols an Islamic nation."

"It's not a Christian army, for God's sake, Rahim. Why don't you use your influence to correct these misperceptions, instead of perpetuating them?"

Jill wasn't sure what to make of her friend. After her father assumed office a year ago, she began to realize that her relationship with Rahim over the years had been distinctly one-sided. In college, she supported every issue that was important to him and his fellow Muslims, from Palestine to religious tolerance in America, yet there was not the slightest reciprocation. Religious tolerance was not so important to him, she noticed, when they tried to enlist him for rallies in support of the rights of Tibetan monks, and he was completely absent on any other cause in which Muslims had no personal stake.

After her father was elected, Jill thought that her Palestinian friend would be more sympathetic to the complexities of the situation in Iraq. Although the Democrats had ripped the Nationalists at every opportunity, the Iraqis were able to elect their own government and enjoy freedoms that obviously didn't exist when the college students enjoyed their carefully scripted visit there four years earlier. Just the fact that so many bodies were being unearthed from mass graves, seemed to belie what they had been told by the Hussein regime. Then there were the videos of torture and execution…

"I'm only looking out for my fellow Americans," said Rahim. "Iraq is not our country, and what is happening there is not our business. It's certainly not worth the shedding of American blood… either in Baghdad or L'Enfant. Iraq is an internal matter. Let the people decide what they want."

He had a point, Jill had to admit. She had said exactly those things herself in front of large anti-war rallies not long ago. What changed with her? Was she being corrupted by the very system that she had accused others of being done in by? Was she being seduced by power? After all, what right did her father have ordering men to their death overseas? Was it any better than Johnson sending troops to Vietnam?

"What do you think will happen if American forces are withdrawn from Iraq?" she asked.

Rahim paused. "There will be some strife at first, no doubt, as the country settles down. Without occupation, of course, there will be nothing to resist. In fact, I would suggest that the influx of committed religious fundamentalists will mean a revival of Jihad, which will mean peace."

"Jihad?"

Rahim laughed. "No, no. Jihad doesn't mean war, at least not the sort of war that you paranoid Westerners have been brainwashed into thinking it means. Jihad is the spiritual war that a Muslim fights against personal sin and corruption. It's a struggle to build character through confession and atonement. Honestly Jill, I never thought you were one to be smitten by Islamophobia."

Jill was glad that Rahim couldn't see her blush over the phone. She was embarrassed for herself. "I'm sorry Rahim. Of course you're right. I… Well, I'm sure that my father will make the right decision on Iraq. I'm sure we all want the same thing at heart."

This time, Rahim did not say anything back.

Saturday, November 2nd, 2030
New York, New York

It had taken only two short years for Bernice to move permanently into her father's former office, after he formally relinquished his duties and made her president of the cable news giant, with the expectation of inheriting the entire news empire within a few years. He had never put much of himself into the position, preferring instead to lie on remote beaches or enjoy other pleasures that semiannual four-month vacations offered.

Bernice, however, shared her grandfather's passion for work with a drive and enthusiasm that won the respect of those around her, greatly facilitating the move to power at such a young age. Her work hours were legendary. She loved the business of news, seeing it as a means to influence the public for the greater good of society.

Now, as she sat in the same corner office that her father called home in the days and weeks following 9/11, her thoughts were occupied by a more inconsequential matter, but one that still needed to be treated delicately considering its explosive potential.

Nearly a week earlier a short, but powerful research paper on the Edina virus was posted anonymously to the Internet. It offered incontrovertible proof that what was rumored about, both in the medical community and general public, was absolutely true. The virus only affected members of the tiny Bonan ethnic group. It was not a threat to the general populace because its sequence of nucleotides required a complementary sequence in human DNA in order to replicate, and this was found only in a mutation unique to Bonans. No one outside the community could be infected.

One problem posed by the findings was that the government had spent a great deal of public effort forcing medical workers to submit to painful and expensive testing for the virus, despite tremendous opposition. Another was the obvious racial implications of the research and the support that it might lend to bigotry in America.

The news network could not afford any more big mistakes. Three years ago they had erroneously reported that a black man in handcuffs was beaten by a white police officer in Detroit. The next six hours were filled with interviews of outraged African-American leaders and coverage of the impromptu, yet heavily attended demonstrations by civil rights organizations against police brutality. Politicians, local and national, jumped on the bandwagon as well, pledging their support for investigation and prosecution, as rioting broke out in Detroit and people died.

It was extremely embarrassing for the network when it came to light that the beaten man was actually white and the officer black. After reporting the retraction, GNN anchors took their lumps from the angry people they had previously interviewed, who accused the network of setting them up with a news item that "wasn't worthy of interest." The network apologized, and the story quickly died by the next morning, although the bitter taste remained.

Bernice knew they had to tread carefully on this one. After giving a prime-time interview to the Bonan nurse who successfully sued to force her coworkers into unnecessary testing (a victory against racial profiling) the news giant gave ample airtime to other Muslim activists expressing their fear that this "eugenics" report would be used to persecute and further alienate them from mainstream society. They claimed that it was all part of a plot that many in their community believed started earlier in the year with the Metro bombings – a government conspiracy to discredit and destroy Muslims.

The big break for the news media, however, came that morning in tragic circumstances, when a contact at the Bureau of Islamic Relations (BIR) called to announce that Aziz Sahil had passed away peacefully in a Baltimore hospital surrounded by family. Although the respected leader would probably have been among those whipping the Muslim community into a paranoid frenzy in his prime, she hoped that his death would provide the distraction needed to drown out and put to rest the series of events surrounding a virus that killed forty-two people in twenty-five years.

Sunday, November 22nd, 2030
New York, New York

The death of Aziz Sahil, did not come as a surprise to Phyllis Hughes, who had been working on her first project as a full-fledged producer when the call came to drop everything and crank out a made-for-TV movie about the former Vice President.

The new assignment was more interesting than what she had been doing, which was a series about a renegade cop who plays by his own rules, much to the chagrin of his hot-tempered, heavyset chief (who had to answer to the mayor for the unorthodox, yet surprisingly successful style of the cop). Over the next two weeks Phyllis applied herself almost maniacally to the writing, casting and frenzied production of the television movie. Commercials aired even before taping was finished and the movie debuted the Sunday before Thanksgiving.

"A Man Called Aziz" began with a young couple in Iran under persecution by the American-supported Shah. To drive the point home, Phyllis had an American flag posted prominently in the background as the man is being tortured in a prison office by the secret police. After giving birth to Aziz, the young couple escaped to America (although even the magic of television couldn't explain this anomaly).

The young boy grew up with awful slurs and projectiles raining down on him from his Islamophobic classmates and neighbors. He rose above it all and was elected to the U.S. House, before being nominated to Gore's cabinet. Although the record showed otherwise, Phyllis took the liberty of portraying the political opposition as deeply prejudiced against Sahil during the confirmation hearings. She had the disgruntled Senators yell in the chamber, and even strip off their clothes and shoes before the cameras in anger, as they protested the ascension of a Muslim to such a high office. Through it all, Aziz remained calm and dignified.

The same was true when the character playing Al Gore asked him to step into the Vice Presidency – after Joe Lieberman was shown having a nervous breakdown, deliriously demanding that the President "exterminate every last towel-head on the planet" before being dragged away by the Secret Service. Again, Phyllis appreciated the disclaimer of dramatization.

Aziz performed magnificently in office, as the Gore Administration sought to keep the war-hawks at bay and resolve the 9/11 crisis via peaceful means. He was portrayed offering principled opposition to the President's plans for bombing Afghanistan, then cringing as he watches coverage of the war on television, alone in his office. At one point, he stands up and leaves the room, only to return wearing a *galabiyya*, then gripping the robe in his hands and kneeling before the screen as he cries in anguish.

Later, after the bombing, he was shown traveling to Afghanistan, where he is put to moral shame by the Taliban, who hold the lives of the bombing victims over his head and ask, "How can you say that you are any better than us?" as Aziz solemnly nods. Although no one really knew what he said to the Taliban that prompted them to hand over Osama Bin Laden to the ICC, Phyllis wrote a fifteen-minute speech that ran the gamut of every crime America had ever committed, from the Indian wars to Japanese internment camps and ended with Aziz asking, "Do you really want to be as bad as we are?"

Rather than follow Sahil's post-political career in the BIR, which was rather uneventful, save the constant moralizing against institutionalized intolerance for Muslims, Phyllis chose to end the movie with the famous photograph taken during the 2008 campaign, of a man standing by the side of a rural road holding a sign that read "No Towel Heads in the White House."

Though the picture had been well-publicized in the twenty-two years since it was taken, particularly in the Arab world, Phyllis wanted to leave the audience with the image in their minds, as a tribute to Aziz Sahil and what he stood against.

Monday, December 23rd, 2030
Westchester, NY

Jill Hudson wasn't sure of what to expect when told that Maria Posada was on the phone. She had slept in that morning after taking a late flight home the night before, following a very long weekend in Washington so that she could afford three days off with her family in New York.

"Happy Holidays," she yawned.

"Merry Christmas," was the reply, which surprised Jill. Christmas was never even referred to in retail advertising anymore for fear of offending non-Christians, and certainly not by anyone in their Berkeley group. Even Parker realized the insensitivity of projecting one's religious observances onto others, and never greeted anyone that way himself.

"Well," Jill said, setting down her beloved late-morning cappuccino, "are you getting caught up in *La Vida Nueva*?" This was the troubling new religious revival that was sweeping through many Hispanic communities in the Southwest. According to the ACLU and other civil rights watch groups, the 'revival' had started in the evangelical Protestant churches, but was spilling over into the Catholic community as well. Jill knew it was a potentially dangerous trend that could threaten First Amendment freedoms if left unchecked.

"Don't worry. Just thinking of my father," said Maria.

Jill remembered that Maria's father passed earlier in the year. She had heard about it through Phyllis, but not in time to place a call before the funeral. She sent a card instead. It puzzled her that Maria seemed affected by her father's death. She seemed ashamed of her family in college and had never talked much about them. From what Jill understood, Maria's father was old-fashioned, and tried to instill certain values in his children. Her relationship with him was principally strained.

"I was sorry to hear about his passing."

"Thank you, Jill. I appreciate your card. I also appreciate you taking this call, and I'm sorry to bother you at home, especially for matters of business. I wanted to ask you about the Administration's support for extending anti-discrimination law into management, particularly for Latinos."

Maria was referring to the proposed legislation that would amend the NDA (Non-discrimination Act) to require that employers not only hire in proportion to community demographics, but also ensure that management and executive positions within the company reflect this composite as well. If successful, it would correct the income gap by putting minorities into higher paying positions.

Jill assumed a diplomatic tone with her young friend, who was a rising star in the Department of Labor. "As you know, Maria, the President appreciates the support from the Latino community, and wants nothing more to ensure that Latinos are represented in proportion at all levels of the corporate hierarchy. One of the arguments posed by business leaders is that there are language and educational barriers that need to be resolved."

"So resolve them." Maria's voice was resuming the hard edge that Jill remembered from their college days. "White people don't mind us 'wetbacks' mowing their lawns or cleaning their homes, but when it comes to actually working for one of us, then that's out of bounds. I thought this sort of bigotry was supposed to be behind us."

"Well, I think it is for the most part," stammered Jill. "As for education, we're spending more per pupil to educate children in the Hispanic communities than any other minority group. Bilingual school programs are mandated even in places like Montana, where there aren't too many Spanish speakers. We've also placed bilingual requirements on employers as well, but you can't expect overnight change.

"There are many other areas in which we're making progress for both labor and the Hispanic community. For example, we doubled the minimum wage – and just in time too, since businesses raised prices shortly after that! Undocumented aliens also have access to health care, which wasn't easy to do since taxpayers are now responsible for what used to be absorbed by private medical institutions."

"Yes, yes, I know…"

"We've had to offset the cost by pushing a special employment tax onto businesses, based on the number of employees. Although we say that it's because they no longer have to pay medical insurance premiums, now that the industry is nationalized, in truth it's about twice what they were paying before, since the workers are no longer sharing the cost."

Maria cut to the chase. "How well would the Democratic Party do in two years without the Latino bloc?"

Not well, in fact, was the real answer, although Jill would never admit it to Maria. Competition between the Democrats and Progressives over the minority blocs was fierce. Many blacks, Hispanics and Muslims had already crossed lines and defected to the Progressives. The President was barely hanging on to pluralities in Congress, despite being credited with a complete rollback of the Hawking policies.

"Shouldn't Latinos appreciate what the President has done by aggressively enforcing the NDA on employers and lending institutions after four lax years? How about his vocal support for Sanctuary?" she asked, referring to the official practice of certain municipalities to resist cooperation with Federal immigration authorities. "What does he have to do, return California to Mexico?"

It would have been an impolite question in most circumstances, but Maria had been a vocal member of the campus group that championed the cause of placing most of the American Southwest under the Mexican government. Jill wasn't sure whether she was still of that frame of mind.

"Well, I guess that would be a start," answered her friend, although Jill could tell that she was not as serious about it as she had once been – or she was speaking carefully now that she worked in the Labor Department.

"You know, Maria, the Latino bloc is not as tight as the others. In fact, it appears that one out of five Latinos actually vote Nationalist, which I'm sure you're aware of?"

She could hear her friend sigh on the other end of the line then say, with disappointment in her voice, "Yes, you're right. I don't know what's wrong with those people. The Nationalists don't make special promises to them, yet they still get their support. It doesn't make sense."

Their conversation then proceeded to more personal matters, as they dropped some of their pretensions and began catching up on what was happening with each other and their group of friends. They ended on a good note.

Afterwards, Jill stood up and finished her cappuccino by the large window of her bedroom office, enjoying the early sprinkling of snow that covered the park behind her family's estate. She switched on GNN and watched a segment on a family's Winter Holiday spent with a member who had returned from military duty in Iraq after the troops were pulled out following the Metro bombings. Stories like that helped balance some of the horrible news coming out of Iraq lately.

Allowing foreign affairs to take their course enabled the Administration to focus on domestic problems, such as the inexplicable surge in unemployment and wage depression since her father took office. Greedy businesses seemed to be punishing their own employees for progressive government measures, such as non-discrimination and benefits mandates. Small business owners were especially resistant to the new Benefits Act that required them to offer their employees four weeks of annual paid vacation, daycare compensation, and up to twelve months of family leave with 50% pay.

The popular measures were hardly in jeopardy, however, since workers had more votes than employers, but Jill hoped that the business community would eventually recognize the virtue of civic duty over profit, and fully accept its social responsibilities. But, if it came down to it (and as Rothermel had taught them) there is no problem for which government cannot provide a solution.

Tuesday, December 24th, 2030
Hollywood, California

The top movie at the box office for the second straight weekend was a holiday story about a driven corporate executive who worked long hours and was demanding of those working for him. As the movie progressed, the man learned that the key to true happiness was to give all of one's money away to beggars, and to work far fewer hours.

None of the theater patrons had any illusions about a wealthy man appearing in their lives to make them rich, but they could certainly agree that less work meant more happiness.

2031

Friday January 3rd, 2031

Malawi, Africa

The Belgian drove by for the second time, as Malika hugged the shadows near the lighted intersection and watched the taillights disappear around the corner. She was sure that he was doubling back around again and would pick her up this time. She hoped so, because it had been a slow night – for a Friday.

It was a stroke of luck for the prostitutes when the United Nations peacekeeping force set up base a few blocks from the center of town. Other women were also seduced into selling themselves for the relatively large sums of money that could be had from the UN workers. The workers seemed to enjoy being with the younger girls and even took pictures of them in various poses. This made it easier for Malika to make money that was desperately needed, since she was responsible for her family after her grandfather died working in a dangerous South African mine for half the wages that he was making from the factory.

As she stood waiting for the car to come around again, Malika thought about the pale, white photographer with the brown hair and clipboard that had taken her picture at the factory. That was the last time she had been allowed through the door. Her grandfather lost his job a few weeks later and the plant closed suddenly about eight months after that, when more white people showed up to ask questions. Over one hundred people lost their jobs, devastating the local community.

Spots of light began narrowing on the building opposite her and she knew that it was the Belgian again. After confirming it with a quick glance, she stepped out into the street light, lifting up the front of her skirt to expose her vagina.

She wondered what that white man with the clipboard was doing now.

Newark, New Jersey

"Relax, now. Deeper and deeper," droned the low voice of the group leader to the room full of about a dozen men and women sitting cross-legged on the floor with eyes closed in meditation. "Now, let's try to get in touch with that inner child; that little boy or little girl that lives inside us… the one forced to grow up too soon, who still wants to be with their mother… still pampered… still coddled."

Robert Danforth sat with the rest, slowly rotating his head and trying to focus on finding his inner child. He had been attending the $300 an hour sessions for over a year now, and was enjoying them as a means of finding out more about himself. Along the way, he discovered that he was codependent as a result of the distance that his mother imposed on their relationship when he was young. It was an emotional and behavioral defense mechanism that he adopted to compensate for his dysfunctional relationship with himself.

Now he was learning self-nurturing and other techniques that helped him focus inwardly and connect with that inner child to heal the wounds caused by the irrational guilt and shame in a world free of moral absolutes. He wanted to experience true freedom in his life in whatever form – unrestrained sexuality, self-indulgence, or simply the power to dictate personal relationships. He would not be a victim to compunction or society's pre-determined moral constraints.

As he was slipping into deep meditation there on the floor, with a proscribed barrier of space against the people around him (so as not to allow their "auras to interfere") the pager went off in his shirt pocket, startling him and thoroughly extinguishing the pleasant visions he had conjured. It was the office, reminding him that he needed to be back for the celebration.

"All cell phones and pagers need to be turned off." insisted the leader, in the same low voice, as Danforth rose in a huff, deliberately ignoring the dark looks from the others.

"Go to hell," he replied evenly.

After gathering his things up, he walked down the hall and out into the street, pausing to pull a parking ticket off his windshield and tear it into small pieces before throwing it into the trash bag that he kept behind the seat in his electric car. The holidays were always a tough time for him, but they were over. On the brief trip back to the office, he reflected on how well things were going for both him and Corporate Social Responsibility Inc.

It had been a little over two years since he quit his job with the ACLU and formed the small company with money from his mother's estate. The staff had grown from three to twelve. How many other companies could brag of a four-fold increase during that time? Not many, since unemployment had been rising dramatically. Corporations claimed that downsizing was necessary to accommodate the tax increases, but Danforth knew it was a lie. His own success was proof of that.

His small organization was raking in plenty of cash from its operations, some in the form of corporate donations, others in consulting fees. They had just made a lot of money from offering their services during a telecommunications merger. Danforth didn't know much about telecommunications, but he knew how to get in touch with the CEO, who listened to his stated concerns over the impact that the merger might have for small minority-owned firms. The board of directors gladly accepted the CSR offer to be on retainer for the corporate giant and facilitate the inclusion of minority-owned businesses. This was pretty easy work, since CSR maintained a list of such companies – drawn from its own pool of donors. The donors, in turn, were likely to be even more generous as they benefited from the new business – particularly if they wanted to continue showing up on future CSR lists.

CSR was doing so well, in fact, that they planned to move from their New Jersey offices and across the river to Manhattan by the end of the year.

Things were definitely going well for him and his inner child.

Malawi, Africa

The five dollars that Malika got from the Belgian was as much as she would be making for a full day's work at the old factory.

Still, she thought somewhat ruefully as she pocketed the cash and stepped out onto the dark sidewalk, she would trade the work in a heartbeat. She had adapted in some ways, such as developing the ability to mentally detach herself from her surroundings when with a man, by pretending that she was not a child, but a grown woman, driving down the road in a car of her own. In other ways though, she knew that she would never feel right about this.

She decided to go home for the evening.

Newark, New Jersey

"Like all children, this little girl deserves a childhood – a chance to enjoy life and relish the simple innocence that we Americans are so captivated by in our own children."

The words brought a smile to Danforth's face as he entered the conference room, after rushing back from his therapy session. He could see the image of himself on the large LCD screen at the other end, giving testimony to Congress two years earlier. His technical team was putting together a promotional video for CSR, a highlight reel of the firm's accomplishments over the last two years, along with their vision for the future. It would be going out to businesses, large and small, as well as to lawmakers and other elected officials in all forty-nine states. The purpose was to increase CSR's influence.

The video began with the campaign against SplintCo, which was billed as a "David versus Goliath" victory. They not only forced the closure of the overseas plants that exploited local populations, but had secured a one-million dollar donation from the corporation, as a public show of its "commitment to civic values." It was all part of the price that SplintCo had to pay to rebuild its image. Other corporations took note, and slowly the "insurance" donations began trickling into the CSR coffers.

They successfully shut down a research program into genetically modified (GM) wheat at a Vermont company that was about to receive approval from the FDA, since it had passed the clinical trials. Other video highlights included the blocking of the power plant constructions in Ghana and Zimbabwe, legislation mandating that auto manufacturers sell two electric vehicles for every gasoline engine by 2037 (and at the same price) and the close call over the fight to keep African countries from using DDT to combat malaria.

This last accomplishment was particularly satisfying as it was a very hard-fought battle. Millions of Africans in tropical climates died from malaria each year. Their governments wanted to use DDT to combat the mosquito-borne virus, as they had in the 1960s when the disease was nearly eradicated. In fact, the science that had originally been used to justify the ban of DDT was debunked not long after that, and it was known that DDT was relatively harmless, but it was still a sensitive issue for environmentalists, who felt that any retreat would only embolden their opponents.

Of course, DDT was still used regularly to control mosquitoes in the U.S. and other European countries, whose populations were far less tolerant of malaria outbreaks than corrupt Third World governments, which could be bought off fairly easily with large sums of foreign aid.

They had not been successful at everything, however. Uganda was on the verge of building a dam and power plant to supply electricity to 11 million people, which CSR had bitterly opposed, even to the point of blocking $50 million in foreign aid to the African nation, although Uganda would not be moved.

CSR was able to prevent the state of Georgia from building a nuclear plant to handle the strain of accommodating the soaring immigrant population around Atlanta. They were also partially responsible for a 12-month boycott of Alaskan oil over the issue of arctic drilling.

The promotional video ended with an idyllic scene of a multi-racial group of children playing in a park which, as the picture pulled back to reveal, was surrounded by a sparsely-populated neighborhood of earth-tone homes that blended into the heavily-treed environment. Snow-capped mountains framed the background and there was not a car to be seen. It was all courtesy of special effects.

Danforth smiled and he could see the corresponding relief on his technicians' faces. "Let's go with it."

Friday February 7th, 2031
Quantico, Virginia

So Walid's career had come down to investigating an Internet posting on the Edina virus that had absolutely nothing to do with national security. It wasn't even a crime, as far as he knew, unless political incorrectness was now against the law... which it may well have been, were it not for the fact that there were not enough prisons to hold alleged offenders.

The peevishness of American society was pandemic. Newspapers refused to print the race of non-white convicted criminals or even those that roamed free, terrorizing citizens. "The suspect is described as tall, muscular and about twenty-five," said a local news anchor the other day, to an audience that surely could have used more detail on the brazen serial killer. For a time, adaptive methods of interpretation were used. Since white suspects were always identified as such, the public knew that the omission of race meant a minority. The trick then became to listen for a surname. If it was not Hispanic or Muslim, then the subject was probably an African-American.

Walid recalled seeing an interview of a businessman visiting from Alberta. The journalist asked him about how it was that an African-American could find success there. The man replied that he was not an American. Embarrassed, the reporter apologized and asked if he referred to himself as "African-Albertan." The man laughed, said that he had never heard the word, and declared that Alberta was not the sort of place where people "had time for hyphens."

Such was not the case in the U.S., where the country was caught up in a frenzy of labels and sensitivity measures. Streets, schools, and even whole cities were being renamed to reflect "respect for ethnic and racial sensibilities." There were no schools with names like Washington or Jefferson anymore, since both men were slave-owners; instead one was more likely to find schools honoring African dictators, such as Mugabe Elementary or Mengistu High.

The loudest civil rights groups were Muslim-American, whose constituents swelled well beyond the levels intended by the Pillar project. As the Middle East, Central Asia and parts of Africa fell to Islamic theocracy, and Europe to pressure from refugees and home-grown Islamists, asylum seekers clogged American shores. The nation opened its doors to these "huddled masses" that then contributed to the growing contingent of activists advocating still more immigration. America was drowning according to the laws of physics.

Assisting the transformation was the fact that Islam is a one-way street. It was perfectly acceptable for anyone to become Muslim, but the religion proscribed a death sentence for anyone wanting to convert out of it. The population swelled as well from the simple Qur'anic principle that only a Muslim man could marry outside his faith, and that all children from such a union were to be raised Muslim. Naturally these practices meant that enormous inroads were being made into the general population, as was the case in Europe. Nervous politicians, vying for the support of the powerful Muslim bloc, praised "the changing face of American society" and denounced any restrictive measures as "racially motivated."

This explained the inordinate attention brought to bear on both a disease that affected so few and the research paper that explained why. He felt that his resources could be better used to help break the terror cell behind last year's Metro bombings. There were other Muslims assigned to the case whose enthusiasm for solving it was certainly less than Walid's, but Americans were feeling confident that there would be no further danger to them now that they conceded the terrorists' demands.

It really wasn't that hard to find the party that posted the paper. The research was solid, and there weren't many laboratories left in the country that could have done that sort of analysis. No one posts anonymously to the Internet anyway, since there is always a trail of addresses and logs that lead back to the source.

The man behind the commotion readily confessed, when interviewed by Walid. He was a brilliant geneticist, who had developed a type of wheat that was resistant to a parasite responsible for the deaths of many in his native India. Activist groups successfully prevented his product from receiving FDA approval, and he reacted rashly by releasing information that purportedly could have been used to induce malice against the Bonan community.

All it really induced, of course, was a flood of sympathy and further research funding for the victims. Naturally there was anger among medical workers, who were vindicated by the report, but it was directed at the government and not the Bonans. Some were calling Sanjay Guptapara a hero, although not the media, of course, which vilified him as a modern-day Joseph Mengele, the Nazi doctor of Auschwitz.

The man would be losing his job, no doubt, and perhaps his entire career, even if there were no charges filed against him. He had already been tried and found guilty in the court of public opinion, which was far more punitive than any legal system.

Thursday, March 6th, 2031
Burlington, Vermont

It had been two weeks since the firing and the Guptaparas had already found a buyer for the house. The real estate market was hot, particularly for property with the sort of majestic lake views that theirs commanded. There was no point in staying, of course. Burlington was a small town and there were not many opportunities for geneticists, and certainly none for any who were as reviled in the community as Sanjay was.

A small knot of protesters stood down by the end of the drive, barely visible, even through the leafless winter trees. Sanjay guessed that they wanted to savor their victory to the bitter end. It wasn't enough to run him out of his job and his family out of their home; they had to be there to relish his final humiliation. With the moving trucks gone and his being the only car left in the drive, the excitement was probably building below, and he would soon have to run through their gauntlet.

He walked through the magnificent log home one last time, letting his thoughts wander. All of his children had been born in Burlington and grew up in this house. Every part of it had memories. He appreciated his family all the more through this tough time, especially his wife, who remained his biggest fan.

He would have liked to spend more time reminiscing, but it was winter and the light was already waning in the short afternoon. He took a last look out the broad living room window, at the snow covered ground with bare trees stretching down to the lake, and then left through the front door. Locking it behind him, he walked out toward the car, with the snow crunching under his feet.

Hearing a commotion down below, he looked up in time to see an old Hummer making its way up the main road that ran past the dirt driveway. He hadn't seen one of those in years. The universally reviled vehicles did not exist in Vermont, where they would surely be vandalized by tree-huggers as quickly as an owner turned his back. The gas guzzlers were symbolic of greed and waste.

Whoever's driving that must have some stones, he thought to himself.

The demonstrators below spotted the Hummer and responded with a chorus of boos and anguished groans. Sanjay had a better view of them now, than from inside the house. They were a mangy bunch, even under their winter clothes; an amalgamation of goatees and goat-roper's caps, clutching signs that disparaged Sanjay, GM food, and technology in general. They'd been out there for months, jeering him and throwing things at his family's car, even when he wasn't with them. Now their wrath was vented on the Hummer.

Sanjay was surprised to see the big vehicle make an abrupt turn into his driveway, hitting a muddy puddle right next to the protesters and showering them with a tsunami of filthy water. For the first time in months, the geneticist threw back his head and laughed.

The shiny black vehicle had no trouble with the slippery drive and soon pulled up neatly beside where Sanjay stood. The driver's mirrored window lowered and a slightly balding man stuck out his hand.

"Dr. Sanjay Guptapara?"

Sanjay nodded and shook the hand extended to him.

"Hi, I'm Dennis Paterski. Looking for a job?"

Sanjay's head was spinning a few minutes later as he sat in the heated leather seat next to Mr. Paterski, rumbling back down the drive in the behemoth SUV.

The protestors caught sight of him through the windshield and began to converge in an angry mass around the front of the drive again... right next to the puddle.

Paterski grinned at Sanjay. "Watch this," he said.

Nearly a full a minute passed before they were able to stop laughing and talk about a future that suddenly seemed much brighter to the geneticist.

Thursday, May 22nd, 2031
Ila, South Carolina

At the time, it seemed like an insignificant event, but when Algerian-born Kamel Rahmouni applied for and received a job processing drivers' licenses for the State of South Carolina, it set in motion a series of events that threatened one of the most sacred institutions in 21st century America: racial preferences.

Not at first, of course, but only after it was found out that he intentionally used a color-coded form in the application process that identified him as an African-American seeking a job reserved for African-Americans.

Monday, September 15th, 2031
Plumas National Forest

Chief Manasas of the Kiwok Tribe of Northern California stood on the summit peak, high above the Plumas National Forest with his Indian bride by his side. The highest point of the mountain was a jut of granite with a flat top that made a natural dais, as it sat about two feet higher than the surrounding rock. It was on this perch that the Chief stood, dressed in a mantle of animal hide, colored beads and feathers looking out over the expanse of the valley laid out before them. His woman stood just as dignified, with her arm resting slightly on his back. Both were about sixty years of age, with long gray hair and thick glasses. There was only the sound of nature around them.

The Chief raised a cow's horn to his lips and blew into it.

A group of about sixty people, mostly college students, sat scattered behind the raised natural platform and facing the same direction. Some had their eyes closed and hands raised, with palms extended to the heavens. All were respectfully silent except for a muted sigh that followed the dull, almost comical burst from the horn. A few more raised their hands toward the back of the Indian couple, as if to bask in some mystical aura carried by the ridiculous echo.

Professor Rothermel stood near the back of the crowd, shifting his weight from one foot to the other. The surface was hard and he had not brought the most appropriate footwear for the climb. At the moment, he was more concerned about emerging blisters than catching good vibes from the ceremony. He was never one to denigrate the value of cultural sensitivity, in fact he played a role in bringing about the event, but there was something disagreeable about the attitude of the students there that irritated him.

These were kids who wouldn't be caught dead at a church service. They didn't just mock conventional religion; they were personally dedicated to eradicating such drivel from the public consciousness. Most had nothing but contempt for superstitious hayseeds, and enjoyed ridiculing their devotion to myth. Yet, here they were, moaning and softly rocking back and forth as if there were some reality beyond this archaic tradition of "blessing" the mountain.

What sort of human impulse requires this sort of solace, he wondered. His students were trained to evaluate reality in humanistic terms, yet, here they were, enraptured by this nonsense as if it were Nietzsche. There must be some sort of "religion" gene, the Professor thought, some DNA sequence that persisted through history against all known rationalism. What else would explain this sad proclivity to abandon the existential and chase primitive traditions of spirituality, simply because they're outside the domain of Western religion?

The old Chief that half his students seemed to be worshipping at the moment was really just a scruffy guy named Joe, who owned a rundown body shop a few miles back down the highway that ran through the valley spread out behind them. His "Indian bride," Eunice, worked the counter at the truck stop next door. He'd been smart enough to claim his Kiwok heritage through the years, and lucky enough to stumble across a classified ad placed by the Cooper foundation some time back that solicited the help of local Indians with a project to return their land, the brainchild of the Professor. Although he wasn't exactly what the Professor had in mind when he articulated the program to the foundation five years earlier, Joe was still the first to respond, so he got to be Chief. He immediately began growing his hair long and wearing buckskin and beads for the long string of public appearances, as the Cooper lawyers battled their way through the courts.

"The white man stole our land," he proclaimed for the cameras and courtrooms, in an acquired accent that his garage customers wouldn't recognize. "This much is beyond dispute. We seek justice. We seek our land back."

The case received national attention, well before reaching the Supreme Court not quite a year earlier. Public opinion was overwhelmingly with the Indians – once it became known that they were not seeking private property, but rather about 6000 acres of the Plumas National Forest, including the mountain where the day's ceremony was being held. The Supreme Court upheld a lower court's ruling and the land was theirs. In the week following the verdict, more than three dozen claims were launched by other Indian groups across the nation. Their chances of success were enormous given the established precedent.

Opposition to the process of turning land back over to the Indians, oddly enough (in the Professor's opinion) came mostly from environmentalists, who feared that the integrity of the preserves might be damaged were they to leave Federal protection. These challenges were effectively turned back with insinuations and outright charges of racism. The Professor himself, in lectures and interviews, explained how pristine North America was before the arrival of the White Man, who had plowed under forests to build parking lots and strip malls. Anyone who couldn't see that the Indians would take far better care of the land was simply paying homage to unfortunate stereotyping. It also helped that none of the mainstream environmental activist groups would take a stand, since many received significant funding from the Cooper Foundation.

Not as well-known, however, and certainly not the least bit controversial, was the Professor's "Community" project, the culmination of a life-long ambition to establish a model residential sanctuary for people of all ethnicities and income backgrounds. His dream was a 'city on a hill'; a village rich in education, the arts, and culture that would serve to inspire the nation at a time of unprecedented opportunity, when the country was changing to embrace progressivism.

The Professor had worked tirelessly to secure a sizable grant from the Cooper Foundation for the project, as well as several low-interest bank loans. He purchased a tract of land about five square miles, located almost in the shadow of the Plumas forest just a mile or so outside the gates. Development had already begun on the 1000 home sites that would house the most diverse community of people ever established. It would be a sociological Sistine Chapel, far more important than the original painting, which had been destroyed by the Mujahideen four years ago, and enduring forever in the hearts of the people, who would follow the example of America's "new frontier" beyond the borders of labels and bigotry.

A sharp jab of pain through his left heel brought back Rothermel's wandering thoughts just as the ceremony was concluding. He reached down to pull the shoe off his foot as Chief Manasas and his wife turned to face the small group of young people, most of whom were passing radiant smiles back and forth as if they were Baptists who had just witnessed a faith healing.

"This concludes our ceremony," stated the Chief. "Now, we would ask you to leave our land."

A nervous titter swept through the gathering, but no was getting to their feet, yet.

"Seriously," said the Chief again. "You white people are cordially invited to get the hell off our land. Now move it!"

Any remaining smiles faded quickly and the Professor knew not to bother removing his shoe. As he hustled down the mountain with the rest, he heard one woman exclaim, "Well, I can't say that I blame them... after what those Native Americans have been put through..."

Everyone else murmured in agreement, except the Professor, who yelped as the blister on his heel popped open.

Sunday, October 12ᵗʰ, 2031
Berkeley, California

A month after the ceremony, Rothermel was set to relish a moment of a different kind, as he walked down the long, empty hallway on the second floor of the Biology building and toward the office of Dr. Greg Dijkstra, one of the more popular professors in the Science department and perhaps the most reviled as well.

Things were going well for Rothermel. He was receiving enough money from the Cooper Foundation to leave his job at the end of the next term and focus his efforts full-time on the community, where student volunteers labored on weekends under the oversight of professional construction workers. The project was receiving national attention and his star was rising. He had even received a call from a Hollywood agent about the possibility of a movie deal.

By contrast, it was turning out to be a tough year for his colleague, Dr. Dijkstra, whom everyone called Greg – his supporters because of the colloquial connotations, and his detractors because they didn't feel that he deserved to be teaching anyway, certainly not at Berkeley. And now, he wouldn't be. The board had made its final decision that afternoon to release him, doing so on a Sunday, when it was less likely to stir student protests.

Rothermel had to admit that Greg's popularity was impressive, especially at a university like Berkeley. By all reports, he was an excellent lecturer with a knack for drawing the interests of a diverse group of students into the material. Several doctoral candidates testified on his behalf, claiming that they owed their success to his encouragement and tutoring.

He had nearly won the Nobel Prize in biology a few years back for his stunning research in the specialized field of epidemiology. This was unusual for a man barely into his thirties, but each year he published highly acclaimed articles in science journals, and it was rumored that he might be on the verge of a stunning breakthrough in an AIDS vaccine… which made the task of dispatching him all the more urgent for Rothermel.

For all of the biology professor's brilliance, he was completely lacking in political sense, perfectly fitting the stereotype of the absent-minded professor. When he published a short article two years earlier, criticizing the Darwinian hypothesis of cellular evolution, it came as a huge shock to everyone but himself. The slight, sandy-haired man with thick eyebrows and perpetually smudged glasses did not understand the uproar, and probably remained oblivious to this very day.

Rothermel thought he recognized an opportunity to make a fool of the little man and challenged him to a much-publicized campus debate on Evolution. He felt that it would be about as easy for him to win as arguing that the earth was round.

It was a mistake… and an embarrassing one at that. Rothermel should have taken notice of the fact that professional evolutionists do not debate details with their critics face to face; they drop stones from 30,000 feet. As it was, the point of contention that Greg had with the Darwinian paradigm was localized to the narrow area in which he happened to be one of the world's foremost experts. Rothermel may have had the rest of the biology department behind the scenes on his side of the debate, supporting and educating him as best they could, but when the curtain rose on stage that evening, it was obvious why he was standing there alone.

Although he knew the crowd was on his side during most of the debate, he was made a fool of nonetheless. The worst part of it was that it was done without intention. Greg wasn't nasty or impolite by any means, despite Rothermel's best attempts to goad him, and this only made the situation that much worse. He graciously explained his position as best he could, as if educating Rothermel, while showing genuine befuddlement over Rothermel's desperate insults.

By the time it was over, the biology professor received a standing ovation from half the crowd, while the red-faced Rothermel sat stewing and sputtering, barely hearing the polite clapping from those of his supporters still left. He could not even shake the other's hand afterwards.

Time was on his side, however, and Rothermel was far more success-ful in pressing to have his colleague removed from his position than he had been challenging him in open debate. The majority of staff in the science departments supported his effort to get the board of regents to review Dr. Greg Dijkstra and recommend dismissal, although hundreds of student supporters and doctoral candidates came to his defense.

The biology professor did himself no favors by honestly answering the board's questions about his religious faith, not realizing how easy it would be for his critics to make the logical argument that he was critical of evolution because of his theistic beliefs. He apparently assumed that it would not be an issue, since he plainly said that religion affected neither his scientific methodology nor the conclusions reached.

After calling him a "creationist" and insisting that his very presence was damaging to the University's reputation, Rothermel eventually suc-ceeded in forcing the board to dismiss Dijkstra that very morning. Now he could see the light on in the office and heard the sound of packing. He rounded the corner with a triumphant smile on his face and knocked on the open door.

Greg looked up as he entered. He was wearing jeans and a sweat-shirt. The smile on his face remained, even when he saw who it was, al-though it was a bit strained. "Well, hello," was all he said, before turning back to placing items from his desk drawer into a box.

"Hello Greg. Gee, sorry about your tough luck."

"That's all right. It happens you know."

"Yes," said Rothermel, with mock sympathy. "I guess the university just didn't want to take the risk of having a creationist on staff... makes it tough getting grants and all. It might also be difficult for you to find an-other position. Do you have any options?"

"As of about twenty minutes ago," smiled the other. "How about yourself?"

Rothermel was taken aback by his enthusiasm. As clueless as Greg was, he doubted that he had the presence of mind to think that far ahead and have something lined up so easily. Rothermel was sure that he would have been blacklisted anyway. It was very strange.

"Why, uh... well, I've got the community project happening. It's really picking up steam, you know... generating a lot of interest out there."

"Oh, yes," Greg smiled warmly – genuinely in fact, which took some of the fun out of it for Rothermel. "I'm glad that's working out. I did some volunteer work up there with a few of my students last semester. We dug a few ditches and laid sewage pipe."

"You did?"

"Yes, it was a good experience," said Greg, closing the last empty box and putting the lid on top. "I like getting outdoors and working when I can. I've always supported your project, so it felt good to contribute."

Rothermel was speechless. He knew Greg was telling the truth. He searched vainly for something to say as the other brushed past him and out into the hallway, wishing him a good day.

After he heard the last of Greg's steps echoing down the stairwell, Rothermel went over to the window that looked out over a narrow parking lot that was empty, save for the space right beneath him. There sat a large black Hummer – an obnoxious status symbol that would have been torn apart by the students had this been a school day, whether the driver was in it or not.

He was sure that it wasn't Greg's, but there was his former colleague, walking down the sidewalk toward it with a box in his hand, and then opening the back door to put it in the rear of the truck.

Greg then sat in the passenger seat, but before the black truck pulled back, the driver's window came sliding down and a slightly balding man stuck his head out and waved up at him there in the window.

Without thinking, Rothermel started to wave back automatically, then backed quickly away from the window, trying to pretend as if he hadn't seen them.

2032

Tuesday, August 31st, 2032

Interstate 87, Irvington, NY

Even the holy warriors of Islam had their standards, though it varied between terror cells. Some avoided killing Muslims; others were unconcerned – reasoning that paradise waited those where were true to Allah, and those who weren't deserved to die anyway. Some refrained from killing in a mosque; others showed no hesitation about blowing the mosque itself to bits along with anyone in it.

Fortunately for Walid al-Rahahti, the cell that he agreed to infiltrate was a little queasy about killing a fellow Muslim in a house of worship. Unfortunately it was just a temporary reprieve.

The boredom of a desk job investigating the politically incorrect was looking pretty good from his current vantage point, in the trunk of car heading north out of the city. His mouth was bound with duct tape and his hands and ankles were tied with plastic restraints. The blood on his face was mixing with sweat in the sweltering darkness, as the car shuddered over bumps and into potholes. He knew that he would not have long to live once the car left the tollway.

The men who were about to kill him were quite confident in this as well. So much so, in fact, that they told him exactly which agent had betrayed him, perhaps hoping to instill additional fear or despair. The joke was on them, Walid thought grimly, because he was already as scared as he could possibly get.

He had the presence of mind to feign unconsciousness during the beating, which gave him a few extra minutes to try and work out a plan in the trunk of the car. He also kept his wrists tight and parallel as they were putting the restraints on, because he knew it would give him extra leverage when attempting to snap the plastic.

The plastic cuffs were tested to resist a subject's attempt to break them, but they were not tested against the will of a man whose life hung on such success. Walid finally heard the snap about the time his aching back muscles felt as if they had reached their breaking point as well. The plastic was so deeply embedded in his flesh by then that it did not fall away.

Not bothering to remove the duct tape from his face, he began working at the cuffs on his legs. There was no natural leverage there, and he stopped after a short time to fumble for the lever on the inside of the trunk that would pop the lid. He thought he had his fingers around it about the time he felt the car slow down.

He guessed that they were coming to a stop at a toll gate, and he could soon hear other cars around him. Leg cuffs or not, it was time to make his move. He yanked at the lever and was elated when the trunk swung open. Without hesitating, he raised his upper body up into the twilight and slid over the back of the car, using the bumper to pull his legs out after him.

The car was indeed in the middle of idle traffic, waiting at a tollgate. Drivers and passengers in the cars around him gaped at the sight of a gagged, battered man emerging from the trunk of a car. He got to his knees then his feet, and began hopping madly away from the car behind him.

Walid heard one of his abductors open the car door as he scooted away, using his bloody hands to pull himself around the tiny electric car that had pulled to a stop behind them and onto the hood of a Mercedes, where the female driver was trying desperately to lock the doors and roll up the windows.

The one that he knew as al-Yala came around the side of the car, as if to drag Walid back into the trunk. He most certainly would have been able to do so had he tried, but he underestimated the impressive American instincts of self-preservation and apathy honed by decades of ease and freedom from sacrifice. No one would be opening their doors to help the agent, even if they had known that the native Jordanian's life hung in the balance only because of his commitment to protecting them.

The terrified woman in the Mercedes was sinking into her seat, desperately trying to avoid making eye contact with the man leaving bloody hand prints on her window, along with all of the other lily-white drivers exiting the Upper West Side. Would it have mattered to her that she was about to cross the very bridge that the terrorists had been plotting to destroy? Walid suspected that she would simply take a different bridge or perhaps the tunnel, cursing the inconvenience of it.

al-Yala gave a nervous glance at the cars around them, deciding (inaccurately) that he would not be able to get away with a shooting or abduction in front of so many witnesses. He turned and closed the trunk then got back into the car.

Walid collapsed on the pavement and took a deep breath as he heard the screeching of tires, knowing that his abductors were on the run. He rolled over just in time to avoid being crushed by the Mercedes, and to catch the "Visualize World Peace" bumper sticker on the back, as it pulled up to the gate to pay the toll.

Wednesday, December 1ˢᵗ, 2032
Malawi, Africa

The stomach pains were starting again and her baby was crying. Its hair was turning orange and the belly was distended. Malika suspected that her younger brother was eating the food that was meant for the infant. She didn't blame him, because she knew that he was starving as well, by the way he was eating his own mucus.

At sixteen, Malika was now the head of the family. Her grandmother had passed the year before. The girl tried as best she could to find food for her brother and baby, as well as her two younger cousins. The men at the United Nations camp had left over a year ago, but she had become pregnant just as her primary source of income dried up. There were rumors that food aid might be on the way.

Malika remembered her grandfather's stories of working in Zimbabwe, on the white-owned farms. He said that it was a time when the crops were good and food was plenty. He could work for four months and have enough saved to feed his family back in Malawi for the entire year.

A man named Robert Mugabe changed that for the people, not just in Zimbabwe, but in much of southern Africa. He took the farms away from the whites and gave them to his friends and political supporters. Armed groups of men would force the farmers off their land, sometimes killing them as the people cheered.

They weren't cheering anymore. The loss of the farms affected not only jobs, but the food supply as well. Famine was persistent in the region, but it didn't stop the politics of race from spilling into Malawi, Botswana and South Africa, where property was confiscated from whites and doled out to cronies until finally there was nothing left to steal – and nothing left to do except wait for the White Man to send more food.

Albuquerque, New Mexico

Danforth sat on the toilet with his elbows on his knees and his head resting miserably in his hands. He had made the mistake of chasing a bean dinner with a large order of ice cream and it was turning into an evening to remember.

The meager dinner failed to fill him, which was the point of it. It was part of a fundraiser for raising awareness of the plight of those in the refugee camps. The insufficient portion of food was meant to impress the attendees with the hunger that newly arrived immigrants were said to be suffering there in the planned communities that were meant to provide temporary housing until they were absorbed into the mainstream.

Danforth didn't think it was necessary to starve the very people who were paying $500 a plate to attend the fundraiser, as it was pretty obvious that they already knew about the hunger and were sympathetic to the victims. Still, it was an attempt by the organizers to forge solidarity between Americans and the Mexican immigrants that were waiting to find jobs.

Point taken, he had noted, when pulling into the drive-through of the nearest ice cream shop on the route back to the hotel.

Now he was paying for his unwise dietary choices with an agonizing session in the bathroom of his hotel room when the cell phone rang. He was grateful that he had thought to bring it in with him.

The call was from an associate at the office, informing him of something they suspected, but didn't have confirmation of until now. The enormous shipment of corn and grain that the U.S. sent to Malawi the week before had indeed included genetically-modified (GM) food.

Robert hung up and considered his predicament. Should he place a call to Jill Hudson from where he was sitting?

His anger drove him to dial the number. The worst of the mini-explosions were probably over with anyhow.

Washington D.C.

The call from Robert Danforth came at an inopportune time for Jill as well. She had been looking at several economic reports and was quite puzzled over the rate of inflation.

During her father's first term, the Democrats and Progressives had successfully rolled back the regressive tax system put in place by the Hawking Administration. The tax burden was shifted back to those who could afford it: big business and the wealthy. Funding for social programs was restored to pre-Hawking levels and even a little higher as the Administration cut military spending significantly.

There was no point in maintaining a standing Army anyway, now that the March 11th bombings precluded the possibility that the American public would ever tolerate an overseas military campaign, no matter the cause. Although Baghdad may have fallen back into the hands of a genocidal regime, she believed the example that the United States was setting in the world, by avoiding war at all costs and pursuing patient diplomacy, would inspire other countries to do the same.

Nor was it likely that a foreign power would cross the ocean and invade the United States. Even if the improbable did occur, there would certainly be enough time to muster the nation's defenses, as was the case following Pearl Harbor.

Continuing to waste a large part of the nation's budget on unnecessary martial capabilities robbed the people of badly needed government programs that provided a whole range of social security at a time when the Democrats were facing strong opposition from the Progressives. The cost of humanely absorbing the tens of millions of immigrants escaping foreign dictatorships and bad economies, for example, was placing a strain on the economy.

Now Jill sat in her tiny office in the West Wing of the White House, puzzling over a very strange set of numbers that an aide brought to her attention a few minutes before. It concerned an odd correlation between corporate tax increases and the rate of inflation.

Each of the last four years, the Administration had raised taxes on businesses, only to see the rate of inflation rise by the same amount shortly afterwards. Now Jill was looking at new data which confirmed an 11% rate of inflation that year, following an 11% increase in the corporate tax rate. It was almost as if corporate America was one step behind the government, raising their prices to pay for each tax increase.

Suddenly it made sense to Jill! Greedy businesses were cheating by passing the cost of taxes to consumers in the form of higher prices, rather than absorbing them as intended. Either they didn't understand the point of corporate taxes or they were refusing to accept their civic duty.

Jill sat pondering ways of resolving the dilemma. A price freeze might work in the short term, but businesses might also use this as an excuse to release workers. Perhaps they could discourage this by also passing an act that linked the freeze to a mandate forcing employers into paying 50% of an employee's salary for the first 12 months following a layoff...

Life would be much simpler if these corporate swine would simply agree to pay their fair share.

An aide interrupted her thoughts to say that Robert Danforth was on the phone. *What now*, she wondered. The last time she'd heard from him, he was still upset about Alaska. He had no appreciation for the delicacy of international diplomacy.

"We can't afford to disrespect the United Nations anymore," she had told him. "If we make a habit of flouting the resolutions we don't like, then we not only undermine the global community, but we set a bad example for the rest of the world."

Robert simply couldn't see past single minded obsessions to the broader picture. She wondered what he was upset about now.

"Hey guy!" she said cheerily.

He got right to the point. "Jill, what's this I hear about GM food being sent overseas?"

"Why are you calling me? I didn't authorize it."

"So it's true?"

"I think so. We're scraping the bottom of the barrel right now on famine relief. Charitable donations always seem to decline when the economy slows and..."

"My God, Jill, we can't afford this risk to the environment... to say nothing of human health!"

Jill didn't say anything.

"We can't monitor this stuff once it leaves our borders," Danforth continued. "What if it gets into the food chain? What if it's fatal to some rare butterfly over there? We could be talking about killing off an entire species!"

Jill continued to let him ramble for several minutes, until she thought she heard the sound of a toilet flushing.

"What's going on over there?" she asked.

"Don't worry about it." He sounded like he was having stomach pains. "Look, just see what you can do about it."

"Maybe we can get the State Department to apply some pressure to Malawi," she suggested.

"Ok," Danforth groaned. "Look, I have to go now."

Jill made a note to herself after she got off the phone then turned back to the economic reports.

2033

Wednesday January 5th, 2033
Jackson Springs, North Carolina

The new pigs weren't hard to pick out from the rest. They were the skinny ones. About six of them had appeared over the last couple of days and were blending in with the rest of the herd.

The farmer figured that they had come out of the Uwharrie National Forest, where a few wild pigs were known to live. They were escapees from other farms in the area, but pigs weren't branded like cattle, so there was no telling who the original owners were.

He was an honest man and would have returned them if he knew how, but he counted his luck instead. The hard winter had driven them out of the forest and onto his farm. By the middle of the year, the new pigs would be as fat as the rest and ready for selling.

The economy was not good and he needed the money.

Thursday, January 27th, 2033
El Paso, Texas

Felipe Posada was shaking with sobs in the sturdy arms of his old friend inside the dimly-lit funeral home on the outskirts of town. In a way, he was glad that there weren't many others there to see him like that. He had been holding back tears all the way from Charleston, but the sight of Kerry's aunt in the casket finally broke the dam, and the emotion washed over him.

It wasn't just the passing of Aunt Sarah under such circumstances that was tearing him apart, but everything that it seemed to symbolize from his days on the police force in El Paso – murder and corruption.

Five years earlier he had to tell a woman that her only son had been murdered – not because he'd done anything wrong, but simply because he happened to be working late with someone who had. The other man had stolen drugs and the woman's son was kidnapped along with him, simply because the drug dealers didn't want any witnesses.

When Felipe sat down with the associate of the person who he knew had committed the crime, the man's lawyer warned him against saying anything. Felipe knew the lawyer to be an idealistic Hispanic, who thought his mission in life was to assist other Hispanics by "correcting society's power imbalance" and prevent his clients from serving jail time. His passion reflected in the quality of his work. He was very good at using every legal measure to keep his clients from self-incrimination, even if it meant completely shutting down cooperation with investigators – which it nearly always did.

The lawyer had gained quite a reputation and did not lack for business, as word of mouth spread throughout the El Paso underworld that here was a man who had the know-how and willingness to work the system – as long as the client was Latino. Felipe wondered why it did not seem to matter to this young idealist that the criminals he released back into the community almost always victimized other Latinos. When did the predators become more deserving than their prey?

In this case, Felipe's patience wore too thin. He knew that the man sitting in front of him had witnessed the murder and could turn state's evidence. They had taken a necessary risk in bringing him in, because if he refused to cooperate, then he would certainly walk out of the station and inform the murder suspect that they were on to him. The suspect would then cross over into Mexico and never be caught.

It was imperative that they get the witness to talk, and it's likely that they could have, had the lawyer not encouraged him to keep quiet. Whenever they reached a critical point in the interview, the lawyer would hold up his hand, turn to his client and explain that it was in his best interest not to say anything.

Felipe's frustration was building to the point that he could hardly keep his voice down. Eventually he snapped and grabbed the lawyer by the tie while holding up the photograph of the dead boy to his face.

"We're through here," said the lawyer, calmly and cordially. He picked up his notes and escorted his shaken client out of the room, looking back at Felipe and saying "You're finished too, Detective."

He was right, of course. It was the beginning of the end for Felipe's law enforcement career in El Paso. He watched helplessly as the killer fled the country, after a warning from his accomplice. The conversation was even wiretapped, but a judge threw out the evidence based on a "violation of privacy" and the "threat it posed to the broader [law-abiding] community." Felipe finished out the year and then resigned to do some soul searching.

Eventually he decided to go back into law enforcement, which was all he knew, but in a different part of the country. He wound up in Ila, South Carolina, a small, southern town that was also busting at the seams with an influx of immigrants, although mostly Muslim. The police chief, who was Muslim as well, said that he was "looking for a good Mexican" to put on the force. Apparently the roots of political correctness did not go very deep in the Arab world.

That was three years ago.

When he heard the news about Kerry's aunt, he made arrangements to fly down for the funeral a day or so earlier than necessary. He wanted to talk with the investigating officers and try to use what little influence he may have had left to ensure that the murder was handled correctly.

She had been found on the living room sofa in her isolated ranch house, surrounded as it was by two layers of security fence. Holes had been cut in several places, indicating that it had been a long while since the fences had sufficiently served their purpose. Twice in the past, the police were called to cart away the bodies of those burglars who made the mistake of crossing her threshold while she was home. This was no exception.

Two unknown Mexicans were found dead on the floor, but a blood trail ran out of the house before collecting near tire tracks. Aunt Sarah was found sitting up with a gun in her hand. Apparently she had died almost instantly, as there was not much blood found on the cushions beneath her. The crime scene photos made Felipe sick, as he stood looking at them under cold fluorescent lights in the file room. He felt responsible.

He did not know the detectives assigned to the case, but talking with them brought back the same sickening frustration that he knew so well from back in the day. They thought they knew the killer. A man checked himself into the hospital with a gunshot wound the night of the murder, but no bullet was recovered. There was none at the scene, either, which meant that he had managed to dig it out prior to seeing the doctor. He insisted that he had been the victim of a drive-by. By the time they matched the blood, he had long since disappeared back into Mexico.

At least Felipe was convinced that they were doing all they could. He had been fearful that the murder of "another *gringo*" would be treated with the apathy that it usually was. There were few white judges left in the border towns anymore. Many of the new Latino bench-sitters were steeped in the philosophy of "dispossession," and believed crime to be an inevitable product of an unjust society. They had little concern for those outside their identity group, and focused on correcting the "institutional injustice" that was said to cause crime. Likewise, multi-racial juries had difficulty reaching decisions in cases involving white victims, and all-Hispanic pools become the favorite tactic of defense attorneys seeking acquittals, even in cases this serious.

Kerry Conner appeared to be handling the situation far better then Felipe. Of course, he only had one murder to deal with and not a string of thirteen years worth. He held his friend stoically in his arms, listening to his sobs and apologies while shaking his head and insisting that it wasn't anyone's fault.

The visitation hours were about over, and Kerry insisted that they leave for a bite to eat. Felipe collected himself and they went out to the lot where Kerry had parked his aunt's truck. It was the same old pickup that both boys learned to drive on twenty years ago. Despite his pain, Felipe had to laugh when he saw it.

"I never could get her to get rid of that old thing for something better."

"Neither could I," said Kerry, climbing into the cab, "but it always
ran good, so maybe she knew something we didn't."

They drove in silence for a while before Kerry spoke again, "It was
like that with the house, Felipe. She insisted on living there. Don't think
I didn't try to get her to move up to Bozeman. I begged her to, every time
I saw her."

"I should have stayed," responded Felipe.

"Of course not. It wasn't your responsibility," his friend contended.
"She was almost eighty when you left and it wasn't like you were living
with her anyway. It would have happened regardless. I'm just glad she
took a couple of the bastards with her. You know that's how she would
have wanted it."

They stopped off at a fast food joint and ordered takeout, then drove
out into the desert, pulling off the road in a place familiar to both of them.
They sat on the hood of the truck, leaning back against the windshield and
looking up at the stars shining brightly in the dark sky.

Felipe had not seen much of Kerry since his friend left for Montana
right after graduation. He'd been busy building a major airline carrier
over that time, the success of which still amazed Felipe. He was sitting
there in the middle of nowhere, sipping beer on the hood of a 44-year old
truck with one of the most powerful men in business, and the owner of the
only private company in the Fortune 500.

Airtana was the most profitable airline in the country, although it
didn't always make it into the black each quarter. Kerry Conner had built
his company against the odds, at a time when the industry was hammered
by hijackings and bombings, not to mention soaring fuel costs and a re-
cessionary economy. He had made careful decisions over the years,
which was possible, he told Felipe, because he owned the company himself and was unaccountable to a board of directors or shareholders. He
was able to take strategic losses in one quarter for long-term gain, and had
the freedom to take risks that corporations could never have considered.

The result was an airline that dominated its market. Other carriers
simply couldn't compete in the carefully chosen areas serviced by Airtana. Having been founded in Montana, the company's core business was
in the West, particularly in the so-called Red States, where the economy
was much better. They also had some cross-country runs which did well,
although the company usually declined a presence in the larger, well-
known airports, where there would have been political resistance anyway.

By choice, Airtana did not operate under the same social constraints
as other large businesses in America. They also flew under the radar, in a
manner of speaking, and did not make noise. Kerry confided certain

things to Felipe about his business over the years that made sense to him, but would probably not sit well with anyone in government. They both agreed that it was only a matter of time before some bureaucrat decided to make the company into their personal vendetta.

Felipe could see that Kerry had somehow inherited his aunt's independent streak. He just hoped it wouldn't be the death of him as well.

They finished their beer, talked a little more, and then reluctantly drove back into town.

Friday January 28th, 2033
El Paso, Texas

The funeral service was depressing enough without the gray weather. Very few people were at the burial. Aunt Sarah didn't have many younger friends, so the casket was carried by the employees of the funeral home.

A knot of older, white people stood huddled in the open field under the cloudy sky, trying to keep warm in their Sunday best, as the minister read a few words that were barely audible over the wind.

After the casket was lowered, Kerry scooped up a handful of dirt and dropped it down on top. He thanked his aunt's friends for coming and watched them hobble off before saying goodbye to Felipe as well. Rather than stay in a hotel, he wanted to stay at his aunt's house for a few days, to fix it up and work out some of his grief.

Felipe would have preferred to stay with him and help out, like old times, but the flight to Atlanta was scheduled shortly after the end of the service, and he had to make it or he would miss the connection to Charleston.

Kerry laughed and said, "What you need to do is buy your own airline, Felipe. Then they'll have to wait on you."

Sunday, February 20th, 2033
Washington, D.C.

He was an older man, a long-time resident of Washington, and a Presbyterian, although he rarely thought much about his denomination. He had worked for thirty years in the service of a well-known D.C. lobby group that described itself as an "ecumenical cooperation" of most of the Christian denominations in the country. Their mission was to promote legislation that was "consistent with the message of Christ" in an increasing pluralistic and multi-ethnic nation.

This meant advocating a number of issues that seemed suspiciously similar to the Progressive Party platform, from wealth redistribution to immigration. They championed the rights of religious minorities as well, particularly Muslims; and they were on the compassionate side of many other social justice matters.

Right now, however, the Presbyterian was standing at a church pew and looking forward to hearing a young man named Parker Whitehead, who sat in a chair on the platform at the front, waiting to be introduced. Whitehead was generating a lot of excitement in liberal religious circles, as he was a dynamic personality with an enthusiastic drive for interfaith dialogue and social justice.

This was his first visit to the National Cathedral, although there was speculation that he might be offered a permanent staff position in the near future. His sort of religious passion was rare for anyone outside of Evangelicalism, and it was a good time to be injecting new blood into the church, as Christianity was steadily dying in America. There were already more mosques than churches and perhaps even more mosque-goers than church attendees.

The Cathedral, however, had no problem packing the pews that morning. Parker rose to address the congregation as they prepared to be seated.

Just then, the Presbyterian's vision was distracted by movement in the aisle. He looked to see a dark-haired Arab man walking slowly down the aisle, who appeared to be sweating profusely under a bulky trench coat.

The Presbyterian gave him a broad smile and moved to make room for him. "Welcome friend!" But the man looked right through him and walked past him, with wide eyes blinking back sweat. The Presbyterian saw that he was trembling as well. Perhaps he was sick.

Others also noticed him, and began leaning toward him to offer their assistance. It was unclear how many might have caught sight of the explosives in the split-second before the blast.

Arlington, Virginia

Jill was watching Parker on a local station when the video feed cut out. By the time the news team appeared with talk of an explosion, she could hear the sirens wailing in the distance. She scrambled for her things and shot out the door of her Crystal City apartment and into the stairwell, not bothering with the elevator.

Fortunately, traffic was light that morning and she made good time to the Cathedral, although she had to park several blocks away, as the police had already set up barricades. Just as she was getting out of her car, the phone rang. Instinctively she picked it up, hoping it might be Parker.

It was Danforth, thanking her for the Administration's public pressure against the Malawi government to keep them from distributing the GM food.

"Not now, Robert. I think that Parker might be hurt. There was an explosion of some sort at the church where he was speaking. I'm there now."

For once, he didn't hassle her at the mention of Parker's name. "Fine," he said, "but I want to talk to you about the drug patent issue when you get a chance. Reducing the patent to four years means that the pharmaceuticals might skimp on testing, which would mean danger-ous…"

"Reducing the patent life means a shorter wait period until the price of a drug falls, making it affordable to people who need it sooner. Good-bye Robert."

She hung up abruptly, never taking her gaze off of the chaotic scene in front of her. Her credentials got her through the perimeter, but only to the point of being within eyesight of the front of the building, where emergency workers were pulling out the dead and injured, as black smoke poured out the doors and windows of the Cathedral.

There was so much blood; so much crying.

Jill's phone rang again. Again she answered.

"Jill, did you hear about what happened?" Rahim asked.

"Yes I'm there now," she said, almost in a whisper. A woman came out of the church, screaming and holding a mass of bloody clothes in her arms.

"I'm concerned, Jill. I'm worried about a backlash against the Mus-lim community."

"Are you?" she asked.

"Of course. Every time someone commits an act of terror in the name of Islam…"

"Is this a bombing, Rahim? Is there a Muslim terror group behind it? What do you know about this?"

Rahim hesitated. "I know nothing more than you."

"Well, I just got here and no one is talking about Islam."

Again, her friend paused before answering. "Well, if it does turn out to be the work of someone who mistakenly attributes this to his faith, what guarantees will you give us that there will be no retribution against Muslim-Americans?"

Jill watched as the lifeless body of a child was carried down the steps. Another woman, this one with bandages covering half her head and the empty area where an arm used to be, was following behind the dead child and crying hysterically.

Jill spoke mechanically, with her full attention focused on trying to find Parker. "I don't know, Rahim. What are your concerns?"

"My people suffered tremendously in the aftermath of the Metro re-sistance attacks," he stated matter-of-factly. "There were four cases of assault in the twelve months that followed and several people had their cars vandalized with anti-Muslim slurs."

"Anti-Muslim slurs?" said Jill, watching a bloody man helping his badly burned wife down the steps.

"Yes," said Rahim, with more enthusiasm, "there were over one-hundred hate crimes against Muslims reported to BIR last year. We are clearly living in a climate of fear and intimidation."

Jill caught site of Parker. He was walking under his own power, with a bandage on his hand that appeared to be soaked with blood.

"I'll have to call you back, Rahim," she said, clicking the phone shut.

Friday April 8th, 2033
Rothberg, California

Pat Ridley really enjoyed the view of the mountains from where he stood in the open field at the center of the brand new community, nestled just outside of the Plumas National Park. Some of the distant peaks were still snow-capped. The only thing marring the view was a strip of commercial construction that looked terribly out of place on the side of one of the hills, located well inside the park. He had been told that it was related to a Native American tribe that now owned the land.

This was a long way from the flatlands of South Carolina, although it wasn't his first trip to California. He had been stationed near the Bay area twenty-five years ago as a young soldier and thoroughly enjoyed spending his free weekends camping and hiking in remote areas of the Sierras. Even as a busy executive in Manhattan, he still found time to get away to the Catskills or Adirondacks with his 12-year-old son, Matthew.

He was glad that the boy could make the trip out to California with him. It was a good bonding time and they were having a lot of fun. Even now, he noticed his son hanging from the playground bars, laughing and hamming it up with his cousins at the community's 'Children's Park' not far from where the ceremony was being held.

Although he wasn't too bothered by it, he thought it quite ironic that he would find himself unemployed at a time when things seemed to be going so well for his sister. Letitia was working her first job (at age forty) and thankfully past her baby-making days, but the damage had already been done.

She may have had a tougher set of circumstances to deal with earlier in her life, but much of it was of her own making, particularly in her choice of friends. Letitia could have been successful in school, but good students were ridiculed by her clique, and she wanted to belong. The desire to be popular among people who pulled others down with them (lest they be outperformed) carried more weight than the simple obligation that every person has to do their best and realize their potential.

Popularity is a temptation powerful enough to induce drinking, drug use, promiscuity and many other self-destructive habits from those who would ordinarily avoid them. But when avoiding ridicule also means traveling the path of least resistance, the lure can be overwhelming. It is much easier, for example, not to put the energy into writing a term paper. When those who turn in term papers are made fun of by those who don't, the incentive to accomplish the arduous chore becomes all the more elusive. It frustrated Pat to think of the potential that this self-inflicted despondency robbed of the lives of so many others in inner-city schools around the country.

After getting caught up in a group of friends that wanted to enjoy the moment, without regard for long-term consequences, Letitia gradually adopted this myopic tack and drifted further from the values that Pat's father made sure to instill in him. She was a mother of five, dropping out of school after the first baby, and then going on welfare after the second. The payments were larger if she stayed unmarried, so she did exactly that, even though she it meant living with a string of idle (and sometimes abusive) boyfriends. One of her children was killed on the street at age seventeen. Another made it to age twenty, before dying from an overdose.

At one point, she was in danger of being forced off welfare and into work, but the law was changed to waive work requirements for women with more than two children. She managed to pump out two more babies just in time to qualify. Welfare advocates had campaigned for the waiver with testimony from criminals who claimed that their actions resulted from parental neglect. The younger kids were about Matthew's age. As far as Pat knew, none of the children had relationships with their fathers.

As luck would have it, it was her status as a long-standing welfare recipient that brought about her current arrangement with the new community, which included a job and a brand new house that was lavish and three times larger than her old apartment in the projects.

Rothberg was a planned community in the truest sense of the word. It was a utopian ideal of what a progressive society should look like, down to the apparently random nature in which the residents were drawn. Every effort was made to provide equal standing among each household, regardless of economic class, education, occupation or any other sort of distinction in normal society. The community's theme was "No Labels."

Of course, as Ridley noted with no small sense of irony, a great deal of attention had apparently been paid to the very class and racial distinctions that the planners claimed to disdain. The organizers took pains to ensure that the race and economic class of the residents would be in exact proportion to American demographics. He read that exactly 21% of the community was Muslim, 19% Black, 30% Hispanic, 42% low income and so on, as cultural characteristics were relentlessly mixed and matched to provide the perfect microcosm of the broader society.

Despite the care taken, however, several groups found cause for complaint. There was an enormous uproar four months earlier when it came to light that the planners had (inadvertently) overlooked the physically challenged. Two busloads of ill-tempered activists in wheelchairs were brought in one afternoon, along with national news cameras, to chain themselves to the main gate, as dump trucks and heavy machinery backed up behind them waiting to leave the construction site. "We are tired of being discriminated against and excluded merely because we don't have the same physical abilities as others," charged their spokesman.

The police were tasked with clearing the protesters, of course, and the ensuing chaos was somewhat comical, as those in wheelchairs punched the vexed officers from behind at each opportunity, then feigned bewilderment and theatrical distress as they were eventually pulled from the chairs and relocated.

To accommodate the handicapped, it was necessary to draw from other groups, which cascaded the affront, as each affected cultural set publicly accused the community organizers of blatant discrimination against their constituency. In the end, the planners worked through a frenzy of mathematical formulas that factored physical disadvantages into the other ethnic and cultural categories to arrive at a new composite. Wanting to leave no stone unturned, the programmers even included transsexuals and cross-dressers. Not surprisingly, the sponsors were in the habit of referring to the community as "the most diverse on earth."

Although he did not agree with the concept, Ridley had to admire the management effort that was put into making a project of that scale successful. He had been reading up on the development, after learning that his sister was chosen, and it had helped fill some of his free time as he looked for a new job. He welcomed the opportunity to attend the community's inaugural ceremony and actually see the ambitious undertaking with his own eyes.

He wasn't disappointed. The community looked like a movie set. Most of the 1,000 homes were completed and stood brightly painted, with gleaming solar panels on natural-composite roofs that were to provide 10% of the residential energy needs. Tasteful turbines stood arrayed in the distance to provide yet more energy from the winds that rushed past on their way up the mountains (Pat thought it interesting that the community could not achieve energy self-sufficiency and actually depended on the very industry that its organizers enjoyed denigrating).

There were clean streets and lush green yards, with carefully arranged shrubbery and flower beds outside each house. The community had its own store, theatre and recreation facilities. There was everything one might expect to see in an average town, with the notable exception of industrial smokestacks and church steeples.

The invitation his sister secured for him was actually quite coveted. He guessed that there were about 8,000 others standing with him in the center of the field, facing a stage that had been ostentatiously decorated with banners and streamers. Several dignitaries, including the Governor, were present. There were even a few Hollywood figures, including Starr Sterling, the actress from 'Jenna's Army' and 'The Advocate.' She was sitting on stage right next to Ridley's sister, as a matter of fact, which must have been a big thrill for Letitia.

Letitia loved 'The Advocate' and watched it religiously during its nine-year run. At the end of each show, the producers would list actual government subsistence programs and contact information for each, as well as tips on the qualification process. His sister would write down as many as she could then act on the leads that were promising. It wasn't hard for her to find the time, since she was already on public support and thus did not have a job to distract her from the repetitive task of filling out applications, which she referred to as 'lottery tickets.' Pat often wondered why she did not put the same diligence into education and employment, but she was as equally perplexed by his opposition to an easier lifestyle that was presumably there for the taking.

One thing that he could at least be grateful for was that she would be off the public dole in her new situation – and working for the first time in her life. He would no longer have to send money to her, as he sometimes did, worrying about where it wound up, while also supplementing her lifestyle with his tax dollars.

Not that he was currently paying taxes, although at least he wasn't collecting unemployment. Ridley was proud of never having taken subsistence in his life. He had made the right choices on top of that; entering the military at a young age then paying his own way through college. Rather than a court-martial, as he had been told to expect at one time, he had received an uncharacterized discharge that was later upgraded to honorable. Not that it mattered much by the time he finished his MBA and entered corporate America.

He had worked for only three companies in the last fifteen years, but most of it was at one firm. He left his first job after six months upon finding out that he had been hired because of his race, which explained why his co-workers seemed to expect less of him. This was unacceptable to him, even though he sympathized with the strain that the organization was under to comply with NDA regulations. After growing up with the stories about what life had been like for his grandfather under Segregation, he had absolutely no tolerance for any system that distinguished by skin color.

After careful examination, he accepted a position at a second company that worked out well for him. It was a small family business with about forty employees, nearly all of whom were laid-back and hardworking. The money was less at first than what he could have been making at a larger shop, but there was no substitute for enjoying one's job and working with good people. He managed to build up a decent nest egg over the years, as the owners made sure that bottom-line contributions were appropriately rewarded.

It was a family business, and the company held its collective breath when the owner's son went to Iraq as an Army officer, and stayed there for two full years, dodging bombs and bullets. He was a good kid, about twenty years younger than Ridley, but with more stories to tell – such as the time that he was nearly blown apart by a suicidal Islamic extremist that only managed to kill a very disagreeable, but mildly famous woman sitting next to him, who insisted on the dangerous trip out of a compulsive desire to denigrate and demoralize the very soldiers trying to protect her.

Ridley trusted them enough to share his own experience on Highway 455 with both the young veteran and his father, something that he had never talked about. The older man's eyes were moist as he shook his hand and said with deep sincerity, "I knew there was something special about you, Pat."

Most of the employees, including the owner, made no secret of supporting the Nationalist Party, which caused Ridley a bit of anxiety at first. He had been apolitical since his recuperation following the injuries received in Palestine and did not even care to vote anymore, since he could not, in good conscience, support the Democrats after the experience, but felt the other parties to be too extreme. His co-workers realized his discomfort and avoided buttonholing him on political topics.

Three years ago, the company hired an accountant who happened to be Muslim, the only one other than their resident handyman/janitor (who was a far more affable fellow). The accountant was let go after it was discovered that he was not doing his job and that his habits appeared incorrigible. Not surprisingly, he filed a lawsuit alleging discrimination and took the company to the DCA (which by then had expanded their name to the Department of Cultural Affairs and Minority Rights) over an alleged failure to comply with the NDA. According to the government, approximately 20% of the company needed to be Muslim for it to avoid assumption of guilt. Word of this apparently leaked through the office, because when the DCA conducted private surveys it turned out that over 80% of the staff had evidently converted to Islam. The Department had no choice but to throw the case out.

The owners knew that their days were numbered. It would be only too easy for a disgruntled employee or ambitious government regulator to bankrupt the firm. Compliance with the exact letter of the NDA was nearly impossible, but particularly so for a company that simply wanted to hire the best employees without regard for irrelevant characteristics, such as race. The law was passed so that everyone would be under the same constraints, and it was strictly enforced to catch the cheaters who gained an unfair edge by hiring on merit.

Rather than waiting for the other shoe to fall, the owners made plans to immigrate to Alberta, even though it meant starting over from scratch. Many of the employees also went with them, but Ridley never considered it for a minute. The people he worked with may have been nice and normal, but he had heard rumors that minorities were not welcome in Alberta. No amount of pleading could persuade him, and he helped his good friends sell what they could and went back to looking for work.

The lag this time was longer than it had been fifteen years earlier. He wound up in a temporary position with an even smaller company; a services firm that was minority-owned. Most of the employees were African-American, but that wasn't what made it a strange experience.

The company was qualified to handle what were called "set-aside" contracts – business that was reserved for minority-owned firms. Most of this was to the government, but they had relationships with large corporations as well. Ridley was initially unfamiliar with the way the process worked, but learned quickly that the world of set-asides existed in a very different business climate from what he had come to know.

His previous company competed for contracts with pricing and service. They knew that they would not win business if adequate value was not provided for the services for which their clients were paying. The focus was on quality and keeping their pricing competitive.

This new company however, did not seem to have the slightest regard for market value. Each potential deal was analyzed in terms of the maximum amount of money that was allocated by the agreement. There was no core specialty for the firm, and they bid on everything from computer support to pipe-fitting. Neither did they keep employees on staff that could service this wide variety of work. Once a contract was signed, the firm would go through the process of subbing out the actual work for about half the price while pocketing the enormous margin. The subcontractors that performed the work were usually white, which amazed Ridley, who was sure that this did not go unnoticed by their clients.

Six weeks earlier he approached the owner of the company with a solid business plan that would gradually wean the organization "off the plantation" and into the competitive marketplace. It would take determination and commitment, but he was confident that they could make it work.

"We've got our system, Mr. Ridley," said the tall, distinguished gentleman with graying hair and a slightly patrician accent. "There are no laws being broken. We're simply providing a service that the government requires. It's difficult to do business in America these days without some means of including disadvantaged firms."

Ridley tried not to sound too incredulous. "Disadvantaged? If anything the law gives us an obvious *advantage,* which we exploit by failing to provide the same value that could be gotten elsewhere."

"The law protects us," said the other, with a trace of displeasure. "If the law weren't on our side, then you would see that we could not stay in business."

"We wouldn't stay in business because we aren't competitive," insisted Ridley. "There's no reason for Cooper-Redmond to pay us $200 an hour for a programmer that they could get just as easily for $60 across the street. That's why we need to change our business plan and go after this the right way."

"Well," said the other, with a condescending smile, "in the case of Cooper-Redmond, I think you would find it to be a very progressive company. I doubt that we would lose that business. Unfortunately this is not the case with most other corporations, who would not care to do business with a firm that is black. Every person of our color in America knows that they live under additional scrutiny and suspicion. It's twice as difficult for us to succeed as it is for the White Man – who lives in a world of his own construction, where he chooses the rules. Our opinions are disregarded and our ambitions are unreachable in a nation that is so hostile to people of color."

This was starting to seem surreal to Ridley, as he sat there in the posh office listening to this aristocratic, wealthy individual speak of grievances and injustices with the fervor of a South Central street thug, but with the eloquent and measured rhetoric of an Oxford professor. Did he really think that he was "keeping it real with his 'brother'?" Would they now break open a couple of 40-ounce cans of malt liquor and further complain about how Whitey was keeping them down? Would they drive home that evening in their high-priced luxury sedans while keeping a nervous eye out for 'the Man'?

Perhaps sensing the contradiction between his articulated role of victim and his defense of the very system that he claimed as the source of oppression, the older man tried a different tack. "I won't deny that we're making a lot of money right now, Mr. Ridley. It's all part of the compensation package to Black America for centuries of exploitation. Wouldn't you agree?"

Ridley didn't reply. The other man leaned forward and gave a sly smirk. "It also puts money in our pockets... and that's nothing to complain about, eh? You do like getting paid, don't you Mr. Ridley? Good then. Let's get back to work and make more money!"

Ridley gave notice the next day. He was asked to leave immediately, which he understood. It was a cardinal rule that one should never question the successful philosophy of an organization, even if it is ultimately self-destructive to the interests of all concerned. The set-asides that were meant to help minority businesses simply encouraged the very dependency they claimed to mitigate, by insulating them from the reality of the corporate world. A handful of opportunists were getting rich at the expense of the ordinary Americans forced to subsidize the higher costs associated with these artificial business arrangements.

Of course, he knew that he was solidly in the minority. The country was becoming nearly as identity-obsessed as the planners of the new community in which he was now standing. His frustration had eased over the last several weeks, particularly on the trip with his son. They had stayed for a few days in the Black Hills, home of Mount Rushmore and the Crazy Horse Memorial (his son informed him that the Indian warrior was a "Native American Rights Activist," according to his teachers). Ridley marveled at how the temperature had dropped thirty degrees as they left the prairie and climbed the mountains inside the park boundaries.

He had chosen to go down through Wyoming and hit Highway 70 at Denver for the rest of the trip, rather than risk the drive through Montana and Idaho. What he had heard about the backward attitudes of the Red States made him nervous, since they purportedly wanted to return to the days of Segregation. Although Ridley would have risked a visit by himself to see whether this were really true, he didn't want to chance exposing his son to the sort of discrimination that his own grandfather experienced.

It was with a sense of reluctance that he turned his gaze away from where the boy was playing, to the raised platform where the grandiose inauguration was taking place. The master of ceremonies was the former professor that had engineered the project, and for whom the community was named. He was a short, rumpled-looking man with wire-rimmed glasses and street clothes that seemed out of character for the event. Ridley thought he looked vaguely familiar. Perhaps he had seen his picture somewhere.

A woman who communicated only in song was wrapping up her remarks. The lyrics seemed spontaneous and when they happened to rhyme, the people around Ridley bubbled with pleasure. He was merely glad that he didn't have to live with such an annoying neighbor. She was followed by a representative from Cooper-Redmond's charitable foundation, the main financier of the project, and then Professor Rothermel himself. The little man rose and moved the podium to the side of the stage after removing the microphone.

"We are so grateful to the many people who have chosen to join us on our journey. It isn't often in America that we can come together to celebrate the human spirit, the way that we have here today. We're on the verge of building not just a residential enclave, not just a neighborhood, but a true community, where everyone participates as an equal, and is respected for their unique contributions to humankind. Without each member of our diverse group, we would be all the poorer, and I would like to offer my thanks."

The little man fumbled with some cards that he held in his hand as about two hundred future residents filed in to take the small bleachers set up behind where his sister and the other dignitaries were sitting. Ridley quickly noticed that every black person in the group was wearing traditional African garb, which made him chuckle a bit. He had been to Africa twice on business, and the people there dressed almost exclusively in Western clothes.

Every identifiably distinct group of people under the sun seemed to be sitting behind the stage now, which the Professor turned to face as he continued. Slowly, he went through a carefully-scripted formal eulogy, as groups from the bleachers stood in turn to receive their homage.

"Oh woman and man of Africa," said the Professor, as the African-American contingent rose, "thou hast taught us humility with thy patient suffering under our lash, and grace by thy unwavering forgiveness for our horrible sins. Though you were brought here in chains, you showed us that it is we who are really in chains, as our hearts are bound by evil and greed. Thank you for blessing us with your presence..."

To those of Asian descent: "Oh woman and man of the East, thou hast also taught us the evil in our hearts as we made war on you. We crushed you with nuclear bombs and killed your children...

To Native Americans (most of who were wearing colored beads and even a few feathers): "Oh people of this land, people to whom this land belongs, may we worship it and the creatures who live on it as you have tried to teach us. Like so many others on this small planet, you too suffered our efforts to eliminate your people from this world..."

And so it went on at length, as the little man echoed the prevailing racial and social orthodoxy that extols diversity while paradoxically denying the existence of differences. The people around Ridley stood with sanguine expressions, some with their arms raised, as if in worship of something that eluded his comprehension. Tributes were read to those of every sexual preference save heterosexuality, every religion save Christianity, every race save Caucasian, and every gender (all seven of them, in fact, with an apology to anyone feeling omitted) except male.

Ridley couldn't help a sardonic laugh when the "the people of Muhammad" were praised for "spreading thy Religion of Peace" to "fortunate lands," though he instantly drew surprisingly hostile looks from the nearest devotees. He didn't care. He had seen the "peace" of Islam reflected in the eyes of an old man with a gun pointed to his head, and in the screams of a young woman as her throat was being cut by "holy warriors" singing the praises of their God and capturing the moment on video. He wasn't ashamed of his opinion and would have argued openly with any of these aging hippies, had they not turned quickly away and back to their placid state of adulation.

"Oh Woman," concluded the Professor, as the better part of the people behind him, including Letitia, rose, "oh Mother of the earth and goddess of humanity. You are the source of all things good and the patient sufferer of every evil that men have produced…"

Pat turned his attention back to where a 12-year-old boy was merrily chasing around a playground with a group of kids in rapt tow, and began to think about the long drive home.

Sunday July 14th, 2033
New York, New York

Phyllis Hughes understood that sympathy for famine victims in southern Africa was running high and clouding the public's judgment over GM food. CSR was facing an uphill battle to keep the government of Malawi from releasing GM food to the people there, and she decided that her friend, Danforth, could use a boost.

The television producer scheduled the network debut of an older movie called "GM Zombies" on the Sunday evening before Danforth was to testify before a House subcommittee on famine relief. The premise of the movie is that the ingestion of genetically-modified food can have serious health consequences. In this case, a group of organic food enthusiasts in Los Angeles wake up to find that the rest of the country is turned into zombies by a virus originating in GM food.

The network established a toll-free number for counseling viewers needing help dealing with the personal anxiety that the broadcast was sure to induce, and the show ended with the address for sending donations to CSR.

Monday November 21st, 2033
Denver, Colorado

The bad morning was about to get worse for Maria Posada, as she made her way down the narrow aisle of the plane and toward her seat in the third row of the coach section. The bags strung over her shoulder caught each seat as she went by, pulling her off balance briefly then swinging violently into her back as they released.

This sort of early morning travel routine was standard fare for the young career-climber in her fifth year at the Department of Labor, where she was hoping to be appointed Assistant Secretary by the end of Hudson's term. That would reduce some of the travel demands, presumably, although it would mean even longer hours.

A man sitting a few rows back on the other side of the plane was watching her come down the aisle, with an odd expression on his face. His eyes never left her as she lifted the bags into the overhead and sat down. She felt violated by his look. If this had been Berkeley, she would have filed a complaint of sexual harassment or even waved her scissors at him, hoping to chase him away with the threat of castration.

From the looks of this guy though, he probably would have laughed at either one of those threats. He was a rugged-looking man in a mechanics jacket with a hint of grease on it. The denim shirt, blue jeans and boots seemed to work rather well for him, she had to admit.

She quickly set her mind to something else. Technically, she was on the clock, although for her the job never really stopped. She had not flown this particular airline before, which was ironic, since it was the very subject of the case that she was hoping to build with her visit to Bozeman. She had paid close attention to the check-in process, keeping her eyes open for any irregularities that could be used in her report.

One thing that stood out right away was the extra attention that she and her fellow passengers received from the airline's security staff. The company enforced an additional layer of security, which was rare among the other airlines, which simply trusted the general TSA screening process at the terminal. She noticed that a Middle Eastern man ahead of her in line was submitted to scrutiny that the rest of them weren't. If she could find out who that person was, then she might be able to add it to her report and perhaps encourage him to file a claim with DCA.

Of course, she might be able stir up a little more heat with an old trick that she often employed when first dealing with employees who were unaware of her identity. The law required any business that serves the public to have at least one Spanish speaker on staff at all times. Ostensibly this was for public safety reasons, but, as most people well knew, it was really designed to facilitate the upward mobility of Latinos in the workplace. Often however, Maria would find that a company did not meet this requirement, which would give her a quick upper hand with management during initial negotiations.

Her ruse was to pretend that she didn't understand English, and it looked as if it would work for her this time, since the stewardess looked entirely embarrassed, as Maria gave her an earful of Spanish.

"I'm sorry, I don't understand," she stammered. "I don't know if any of us speak Spanish." She looked around nervously before turning back to Maria and asking some very rudimentary Spanish phrases, evidently expecting a simple *si* or *no*.

"Are you in pain?"

"Are you in labor?"

"Do you need a doctor?"

Maria responded by acting even more indignant. Searching for something to say, she began lecturing the stewardess (in Spanish) on the particular Civil Rights act in which the airline was in violation. Just before she broke it off to sit down in a scripted huff, however, the same man who watched her board and was sitting calmly observing the heated dialogue rose out of his seat and told the stewardess, "It's alright, Ma'am. I'll look after the little lady."

It was a drawl that she recognized from growing up in South Texas, and it made her cringe. She looked up to see the man take his bag from the overhead above his seat then transfer it to the one over hers. Her nightmare was confirmed as he plopped down next to her and said in flawless Spanish, "That's quite a little mouth you've got there, but seeing as how you're so concerned about your personal safety, I'll be glad to accompany you up to Bozeman."

Maria knew it would be a long time before she tried this trick again. The man's accent was nearly perfect, she noticed, as he gave a not-so-subtle wink to the stewardess and settled in. She wasn't sure, but she thought she caught a hint of humor in the woman's eyes, as she turned and disappeared toward the front of the cabin.

Up close, the man's rugged facial features were more attractive and refined than one would have guessed from his rumpled clothes. His sandy hair was complemented by piercing gray eyes and a light tan. She noticed that he had tucked a bag of tools under the seat in front of him, and that his hands were calloused and lightly scarred.

"Do you work for Airtana?" she asked.

"Yes."

"As a mechanic?"

"Sometimes."

"Has the airline treated you fairly?" she asked.

"Can't complain."

"Do you know of any rules violations within the corporation?" She hoped that he wasn't bright enough to pick up on the subtle implication of her question.

"Airtana's not a corporation," responded the other. "It's a company that's owned by one man, Kerry Conner."

At first she was taken aback by this. Airtana may not have been the largest in its industry, but it was large enough to be a Fortune 500 company.

"Well… what do you think of Mr. Conner?" she asked.

"Oh that's easy," the man laughed, "the guy's a class-A bastard! His employees hate him. They'd probably string him up like Mussolini, if given half a chance."

"Really," responded Maria, unable to contain a smile. Perhaps having to sit next to this chauvinist might have its advantages after all. It was sounding as if Airtana could be a career-maker for her.

Not much was known about the airline in Washington. The company did not make political noise, nor was it a campaign contributor to either the Democrats or Progressives. As she realized now, the fact that it had no shareholder accountability meant that it was not subject to the same rules of disclosure that opened bare the inner workings of other large businesses and forced every facet of operation into line with public morals.

The airline had come to her attention in the wake of several complaints by job applicants in El Paso, who alleged that they were discriminated against because they did not speak English. Maria wondered if perhaps the man next to her had any inside information.

"Have you noticed any irregularities with how the airline treats Spanish-speakers?" she asked slyly.

"Irregularities?"

"Yes, something that seems a little different…. unusual," she condescended, breaking down the large word into smaller chunks that she felt a working man could better digest.

"Well, there was this one thing I noticed," he said, putting his fingers to his chin, as if deep in thought.

"What?" she asked eagerly.

"One time I was on a plane and this very attractive woman got on behind me."

"Yes?" said Maria, wondering if perhaps there might be grounds for sexual harassment involved in the story.

"Yes. It was the oddest thing. She indicated to the stewardess – a wonderful woman who has nearly fifteen years with the company, by the way – that she couldn't speak a word of English. She only understood Spanish."

He turned and looked directly at her. "Well, the airline found a dupe to come sit next to her to, you know, to calm her down… make sure she felt comfortable."

Maria began sinking a bit in her seat, but the man continued. "Well, this old cowboy didn't need much coaxing to sit next to such a beautiful woman – and an intelligent one at that – but during the course of their conversation, it seems that she forgot all about not knowing any English, because that's what they wound up speaking just a few minutes later."

He was right, of course. She'd been so intent on getting information out of him that she didn't notice that he had neatly switched languages on her. She felt played for a fool… probably the way she had been making the stewardess feel before he intervened. Now it was the very same woman coming to her rescue, by approaching her seatmate and telling him that there was a problem at the gate and that they needed his assistance.

"Looks like she speaks English after all," he said to the woman, jerking a thumb in Maria's direction as he got up, "but I'll have my seat changed anyway."

Maria was extremely embarrassed and could not look either of them in the eye, but fortunately they showed more grace than she would have expected, letting the matter drop immediately and carefully making their way toward the front of the plane. She watched him put an arm on the stewardess's shoulder and say something in her ear, which must have really been funny from the way she reacted. Neither of them looked back at Maria.

She turned to look out the window with her thoughts not much brighter than the gray weather outside. What had made her play that stupid game with the stewardess? She used to do things like that for the first couple of years in the Department, but not much since her father passed away.

That experience changed her in ways that she didn't want to admit, even to herself.

When she got the call that the old man was dying three years ago and didn't have much time left, she was surprised at how she was able to drop everything immediately and catch the next flight to El Paso. She didn't know why she was fighting back tears on the way there, either.

She wasn't close to anyone in the family. She rebelled at an early age and never reciprocated the least bit of appreciation for the sacrifices made for her education. They did not approve of her college friends or her lifestyle, which made for a mutual case of disrespect, since she was embarrassed by their conservative values.

In the middle of a long corridor in the cancer ward, she came upon her family outside the hospital room and was surprised by how they immediately reached out to her. She was told that her father wanted to spend some time with her alone. She entered the room and closed the door behind her, with tears streaming down her face.

Her father was pale and gray, hooked to monitors and IVs, obviously too weak to rise out of bed. He smiled at her.

"Pepita, my little Pepita."

Crying like a little girl, she went to him and put her arms around him, like she used to do when she was six.

"Hello, Papa."

They embraced each other for a long while and it seemed that the years melted away, along with the bitterness. She pulled a chair close by his bed and they talked quietly for hours. For the first time in her life, she asked about what it had been like for him growing up in Mexico. He told her about the rough existence and how he prayed that his children would not have to live like that. He talked about his struggle to be true to God in a corrupt police system and the way his faith was tested when his oldest son was killed.

She asked about what he went through to bring them to America and what it was like raising a family to succeed in life where he had not. With quiet dignity, he said that his success was his children. A new round of tears was set off when he told her that he was proud of how she got her law degree and worked hard in her job.

The last thing he told her before the doctor entered and brought an end to her visit was that he was dying happy because he knew he was going to a better place.

The words stayed with her that night, as she tossed and turned in a hotel bed. She didn't think that she was an atheist, but neither did she have much respect for those Alberta types – the objectors, as they were sometimes called.

In the morning, she woke to the news that her father had passed away peacefully. Three days later, she was back in Washington, far more confused than when she left.

The first casualty of this muddled introspection was her relationship with Jean. The two women had been partners for a year and a half, and it was not the first such relationship for either of them, although Maria always had doubts about whether she belonged.

The boys in her high school were overly macho, insensitive, crude and shallow. They acted as if the single pursuit in life was sex, a tenet that was reinforced by what she saw on television. Since she did not share the enthusiasm for intercourse that the girls around her and on the screen did, she wondered if she were different.

At Berkeley the men weren't like those she had known growing up, but this failed to impress her as well. They were docile, effeminate and highly deferential to the women on campus, never ceasing to argue what they thought was the female point of view in a sexist society, while railing against the patriarchy. They hated masculinity as much as any of her feminist friends and their example was hardly inspiring, as she reluctantly made decisions concerning sexual orientation.

Of course, just because she didn't like men did not necessarily mean that she was a lesbian. She never shared the certainty that Jean had, who was older by a few years, but she found the relationship convenient, nonetheless. It was a difficult breakup. The worst part about it was that neither knew why Maria was doing it.

She had gone to church a few times in the years since, but it seemed hollow and empty. The sermons extolled the shrinking congregations to act unselfishly by feeding the hungry, giving to the poor and welcoming the immigrant, but there was no hope offered beyond the contentment of personal moral superiority. With no God and no heaven, what relevance did the church have? She could just as easily have heard the same civil homily from any speaker at a Progressive fundraiser.

Her thoughts were interrupted by the sound of the voice of the man sitting next to her, although it was now coming of the intercom over her head. He informed the passengers that the tower was ordering them to get out on the tarmac with the others, since it looked like there might be a break in the weather.

Maria poked her head around the seats in front of her and saw that the man was indeed standing in the cockpit of the MD-88, joking with the pilots and other crew. They seemed very respectful of him, far more than what one would assume for a mere mechanic.

"Is there something I can help you with, Miss?" The stewardess was standing behind her, waiting to pass.

"Oh, uh… no thanks," Maria said shyly. She watched the other woman go past her then spoke up. "There is something…"

The stewardess turned around. "Yes?"

Maria swallowed. "I apologize for what happened earlier. It wasn't personal. You see I work for the Department of Labor and…"

"Oh, we know that now," smiled the stewardess.

Maria was stunned. "You do?"

"Yes, Mr. Conner looked it up just a few minutes ago. Don't worry about it. It's all part of my job. I remember one time there was this passenger who…"

"Mr. Conner? Kerry Conner?"

"Yes, the man sitting next to you. Whoops! It looks like someone's having some trouble in the back. I've got to run."

She dashed off, leaving Maria to ponder the situation. The man that she had just made an ass out of herself to was the owner of the company that she was charged with investigating. Her prank was really backfiring now.

She poked her head out again and looked back at the same scene in the front of the plane, which made more sense to her now. Just as she did, however, Conner looked up and saw her. Embarrassed again, she quickly sat back in her seat. It was not more than a minute later that he came to sit back down next to her. After a few seconds of silence, she realized that she would have a very awkward three days ahead of her if she didn't set the record straight immediately.

She looked up. "I'm sorry that you didn't see me at my best, Mr. Conner. I assure you that I will represent the Department of Labor in a professional…"

"Well, I wasn't exactly honest with you either," said Conner, looking her straight in the eyes. She noted that the home-spun drawl was considerably reined, and that he better resembled the shrewd businessman she now knew him to be. "We try to make our customers comfortable," he continued, "and it looked like you could use a cowboy. I was a cowboy at one time in my life, in fact. Let's just forget about the whole thing and start over."

The plane lurched softly and began pulling back from the gate.

Presumably, they were both being honest with each other now, but Maria felt strangely intimidated. The other man was only about ten years older, but he was clearly in his element – there on a plane that he owned, surrounded by servile employees.

"I guess you know that my name is Maria Posada. I'm from Washington D.C. and will be investigating Airtana through Wednesday over complaints made by minorities against the company. Is now a good time to discuss the allegations, or would you prefer to have an attorney present?"

The man laughed. "What are the complaints? I'll tell you if they're true or not and save you some time."

"The main ones are charges of discrimination. Does your company discriminate?"

"Of course."

Maria had never in her life expected to hear someone in business answer that question in the affirmative. She thought that perhaps he had misheard her. "You're saying that your company does discriminate?"

"Absolutely we do. So does every other business and every person on the planet, including you. You discriminate every time you change the channel on a television set."

"I see your point, but we're talking about something more serious than television," said Maria. "I don't discriminate when it comes to people."

"Sure you do."

"I do not."

"Do you ride the Metro?" asked Conner.

"Yes."

"When you get on the train and see that there are only two seats available, one next to a man wearing dirty clothes and the other next to a well-dressed woman, do you flip a coin to determine which seat you'll take?"

Maria hesitated, "I suppose that given these narrow premises, I would make the obvious choice, although I doubt... I doubt..."

"It's that way with a business," continued Conner. "I have to use discrimination in determining who I hire to work for me, which vendors I do business with, and even the customers that I serve. If a person is drunk or acting suspiciously, then they won't be allowed to board the plane, even if it means refunding their money. If they did board, then they might bother or harm the other passengers, and that would cost me money in the long run."

"Perhaps we aren't talking about the same thing here. Most of the complaints concern several people in El Paso who allege that they were not hired for positions at ticket counters because they spoke Spanish. However, given that you seem to speak the language remarkably well, I would assume that this is either a misunderstanding or something with which you are unaware?"

"Those people are lying about why they weren't hired. It wasn't because they spoke Spanish. It was because they didn't speak English. In fact we welcome bi-lingual employees..."

"Hold on a minute." Maria's eyes were wide. "You're basically confirming their claim that they weren't hired because they were Spanish-speakers."

"Non-English speakers," corrected Conner again.

"It doesn't matter. The law requires that no one can be denied employment because of..."

"Everyone can be denied employment," Conner broke in, "because no one is owed a job. If a potential employee can't show me that I'm better off with him or her in my company, then they won't be hired. In this case, the position being applied for was a service position that required interfacing with English-speaking customers."

"But there are measures that your company can take to accommodate such people. Surely it would be possible to maintain a backup staff member who speaks..."

"All of these measures cost money," interrupted Conner, "...my money."

Maria was flabbergasted. She was used to dealing with executives who would stumble over themselves to assure her of their eagerness to comply with regulations. Here was a man who seemed to be flaunting some sort of right that he thought he had to act as he pleased.

"Other companies have found ways to meet the requirements of non-English speaking employees, Mr. Conner."

"That's their choice," he replied. "This is my company. I will hire who I want, and run it as I see fit."

"Mr. Conner, a business has an obligation to society. We..."

"Mine doesn't. It has an obligation to my bottom line – and nothing else that I don't deem a priority."

His voice had a certain edge to it. Maria felt as if she were in the presence of a real-life Ebenezer Scrooge.

"You don't feel that the public welfare of the community should be a concern of business?" she asked incredulously.

"No."

"What about the welfare of your employees? Are they just minions that serve your own interests? Do you treat them as if they're beneath you, and then discard them when they've outlived their usefulness to you?"

"That wouldn't make good business sense, would it?" he posed. "Do you think treating someone that way would inspire them to do their best for me? Would it attract the most qualified people to my staff, or would they choose a competitor that's smart enough not to treat their employees that way?"

He continued, with his voice a little softer. "This airline has one of the lowest turnover rates of any comparably-sized business in the country, regardless of industry. Everyone on this plane, as a matter of fact, has been with me for over ten years. Do they seem unhappy to you?"

Maria thought for a second. "They don't speak Spanish," she offered weakly, instantly regretting bringing the embarrassing episode back to mind.

"I've flown a long time," said the other, "and met an awful lot of travelers from many other countries, some who didn't speak English," he cast a sideways glance at her, "*at all*. Up until this morning I never met anyone who expected the world to cater to her. They all seem to realize their own responsibility for the choices they make."

The plane was sitting on the runway now, with snow swirling outside the window. Violent gusts rocked against it, but the mood around them was cheerful. People were starting to break free of the early-morning stupor.

Maria would have been happy if they were stuck there for several hours. She had never enjoyed this sort of access to the mind of someone that her old professor, Rothermel, would have called a Robber Baron. She was realizing a sort of strange fascination with this man, who seemed entirely oblivious to the rules of business in America. Yet, he was obviously highly successful, in spite of going entirely against the grain.

She chose her words carefully. "There are laws... we have laws in this country, concerning who a company must hire and what rights they have in the workplace. Your competitors follow these laws..."

"And they're hemorrhaging money," he interrupted again. "No, I'm sorry for cutting you off. Please go on."

"Well," she said thoughtfully, "perhaps that's why they're losing money – because of you. If you're cheating by not following the rules, then it means that you're hiring who you want to, which means that you have a better chance of getting the best employees... which means better service, and more money!"

The last part was being worked out even as she was speaking and it came out in rather triumphant fashion.

"And how do you spend your money," he asked crisply.

"Pardon?"

"You heard me. Do you want the freedom to make your own financial decisions, or do you want them to be predetermined by an outside agency?"

"We aren't talking about how I spend my money," said Maria. "We're talking about... about how... how..."

"How I spend mine," finished Conner for her. "Who do you think the business belongs to? It's as much mine as what's in your wallet right now is yours. The issue is financial freedom."

This was true. Maria had never thought about it that way before. She turned her head, letting her eyes rest on the seat in front of her for a minute. Had he cast some sort of charm on her that was making this right-wing sophistry sound legitimate?

Conner set his hands down on the armrests and said something that she would never forget.

"There are only two kinds of power in this country, Ms. Posada. There is the power to make and the power to take."

Outside, the engines began rumbling. The plane eased forward.

Maria sat with her eyes glued ahead of her; not wanting to hear what he was saying, but as powerless to stop the words from sinking into her brain as she would have been using her bare hands to try and stop the plane from picking up speed.

No matter how often a person has flown, they are always aware of that moment during takeoff when the plane reaches a certain ground speed that is at the edge of one's comfort level. Objects whip past the window at an unnatural rate, and the passenger knows that they've reached the point of no return. The craft will either leap into the sky within a few seconds or disintegrate against the slightest obstacle. Maria was very cognizant of that moment just then, because she knew that her life was entirely within the hands of the man sitting next to her.

These were his engines. This was his plane.

This was his company.

As they lifted from the ground he said, over the roar of the turbines, "Those who produce wealth and innovation are battling against those seeking to squeeze it from them with their rules."

The plane shuddered as it shot into the teeth of the blizzard, the battle between the product of Man and the forces of nature that sought to crush it. She realized an implicit faith in the ingenuity of the designers and the diligence of the builders.

"Which side will you be on, Maria… the makers, or the takers?"

Wednesday, November 23rd, 2033
Malawi, Africa

Malika said goodbye to her younger brother and cousin, sitting on filthy blankets on the dirt floor of their rank shack, to join the crowd of people down the road that were organizing a march on a nearby government warehouse that stored grain sent by the United States. The three of them were all that was left of the family of eight. The famine had taken her baby and one of her cousins. Her brother was not well and would probably die soon without food.

There was a lot of anger toward the government in the cluster of shanties. It had food, but was unwilling to distribute it because it was supposed to be bad. For Malika and the people around her, it was far worse watching their families slowly starve.

She left the plastic and plywood scrap hut, and made her way down a dirt road, caked with raw sewage, and out to the end of the street where the people were organizing. There was something different about them this time – a sort of excitement and anticipation in the crowd that was infectious.

Malika began to harbor hope that perhaps they would not be coming away empty-handed this time.

Thursday, November 24th, 2033
Hoboken, New Jersey

Danforth gave a loud belch and pushed back a bit from the restaurant table, with the remnants of his Thanksgiving dinner spread in front of him. He was so full that he thought he might hurl, but there was still that large piece of pie waiting there. He didn't know if he was going to be able to get to it, but he sat back to take a breather, hoping that his stomach would make room.

He had plenty of time. No one was going to be at the office on Thanksgiving, or any of the next four days for that matter. He had nothing to do until Monday morning except either work alone at the office or try and kill time at the movies or shopping mall.

He hated the holidays with a passion. They simply reminded him that he was alone in life, despite having fathered a baby by a woman who worked for him for a short time. He didn't see his daughter much, although he faithfully sent the support check each month, which he could easily afford.

Beyond that, he had no family and few friends, in spite of his growing wealth and modest claim to fame as the head of Corporate Social Responsibility, Inc. Next year, he planned on accepting the standing invitation from the Landau Group, which was composed of socially-conscious Manhattanites that met each month in the large Upper West Side apartment of Beth Landau, a well-known heiress and socialite, to discuss issues and concerns over wine and cheese.

The ringing of his cell phone startled him out of the post-feast lethargy. It was a co-worker calling to tell him about the riots in Malawi. Apparently a group of people had tried to storm a warehouse where GM food was being housed. The situation was desperate enough to force government troops to fire on the demonstration. Several people had been killed.

"You might be contacted by the media, Robert," said his co-worker, "because one of the persons killed was Malika."

Danforth held the phone away as he burped, then brought it back and asked, "Who?"

"The African girl in that picture from a few years back that you used in the Senate hearings. Remember... against SplintCo?"

"Oh yes. Tell me though, did any of the grain get taken, or is it still secured?"

"I... think it's all still there in the warehouse."

"Well, thank God! I wish the government would destroy it all before it causes more problems."

Danforth hung up and got to his feet, glad that he had something to do that afternoon – an excuse to get back in the office. He would not be eating the pie after all, so he made sure to turn it upside down on top of a plate with a half-eaten turkey leg before leaving.

Friday November 25th, 2033

Bozeman, Montana

Maria trudged deep in thought through the Bozeman airport, which was bustling even at this early hour. She suspected that it was not usually this busy, even on the day after Thanksgiving, but air travel had been shutdown since Wednesday evening due to the snowstorm that swept through the mountains and down into the long valley. This exacerbated swollen travel schedules that were already under pressure from the ranks of holiday travelers.

It also meant that Maria wasn't able to leave on Wednesday as planned. She did not have much to show for her time in Bozeman anyway. Airtana's lawyers weren't nearly as candid as its owner, and getting dirt on Airtana in Bozeman was like trying to find someone at the Vatican with a bad word about the Pope. Still, she had a come across a few things that might interest her superiors in Washington.

Through the first three days, Kerry Conner stayed out of her way, quietly running his company from behind the scenes. Occasionally, she would catch sight of him in a meeting with executives or walking through hangers with engineers. He always wore faded jeans, a casual shirt and boots. Sometimes he would have on a sheepskin coat; other times a mechanic's jacket.

She thought it odd when she actually found herself looking forward to the times that they might bump into each other. He was always cordial, though not in the folksy, condescending way that he had been with her initially on the plane. Nor was he as blunt or as brusque as he had been later in that same conversation. Rather, she was seeing him in his element – running a company that he enjoyed, with people who enjoyed working for him. This was unusual to her. She had been taught in college that a constant struggle existed between the workers and those in power. It was the government's job to side with the proletariat, and help them realize their demands against those motivated only by profit.

After her conversation with Conner on the plane, Maria had expected to find employee grievances hanging like fruit from a tree, just waiting to be plucked. Instead, there was a collective spirit among those at Airtana, which came across as a common desire to see the airline succeed. Despite what she expected, the employees she talked with seemed to feel that the owner genuinely cared for them. They cited merit bonuses and profit-sharing plans, along with a strange program that Maria was unfamiliar with, whereby employees were rewarded for ideas that made money for the company. It was even rumored that at least four low-level employees (including a gate agent) were retired on the proceeds from innovations they suggested.

When Maria asked why the employees didn't organize a union, nearly each one would laugh and ask her why they should. Indeed, the benefits were comparable to other companies, better in some ways, though not in others. There were no allowances for domestic partners, and family leave was provided at a level that was actually lower than Federal mandates.

Montana was different from the United States that she knew. It was part of the "other America" that was denigrated by the politicians she supported, as well as her friends. It was a part of the country that was demeaned and ridiculed by the rest in every reference from political speeches to television shows that were not shy about judging the people to be "culturally inferior," uneducated and "easily manipulated" by demagoguery.

This was how the South was thought of at one time, before immigration and shame eventually raised the caliber of the population to the point that Progressives were far more likely to be elected than Nationalists. There were still a few pockets of backwardness in the region, but they held little power and were gradually succumbing to attrition, as their own children were reeducated in a public school system designed to promote multicultural values.

There had been a great demographic shift over the last thirty years, which began even before the camps were started in the early part of the Rodham Administration to accommodate the objectors. Red State America was shrinking into highly concentrated pockets in the middle belt of the country. These were the rural areas in the Rocky Mountain West that were chosen by Washington to host the camps for those who refused to pay their taxes over the issue of government-funded abortion.

Whole communities of the families of these objectors sprang up around the camps, as members tried to stay in proximity to each other. The recently released chose to put down roots there as well, with the result being that the Red States became even more conservative and highly resistant to Federal pressure. These were the only areas of the country that sent Nationalist politicians to Washington, and nearly all of the states had laws on the books that were in blatant contradiction to standing rulings by the Supreme Court.

Maria had only been to the region a few times, and never to Bozeman, although it was a main hub for the largest airline that serviced the region. Each visit seemed to contradict the prevailing orthodoxy of what life was supposed to be like there. It was certainly true that there was a large emphasis on "family values" and religion, but there was none of the open racism or slack-jawed illiteracy that she had expected. The people were conservative on issues like crime (which she thought ironic) and welfare. They made it hard for pornographers to operate, while proudly pointing to a much lower sex crime rate.

There was an entrepreneurial spirit that intrigued her as well, particularly after her original conversation with Kerry Conner. It was a primitive sort of individualism, holding that one was the result of their own choices, rather than societal forces over which they had no control. Unlike some of her friends, Maria believed that individual responsibility did have its place, as long as it was strictly applied to certain personal choices, such as the decision not to commit crime. A broader interpretation caused her to shudder and remember the poor citizens of Tucson, who were left without decent medical care for a time, after Dennis Paterski closed his hospital.

Maria found the line at the ticket counter and waited her turn. It was at about that time the previous morning that she stood at that very counter, trying to keep from berating the agent informing her that all flights would be cancelled that day due to weather, when a door that clearly led to the outside opened and Conner entered, brushing snow off of his jacket and stomping his boots on the mat. He then walked boldly up to Maria, as if knowing she was there all along, and told her that she would be having Thanksgiving dinner at his home with him and the "others" as was their tradition.

"No one at Airtana has Thanksgiving alone," he insisted.

Before she could protest, he said that he would send a car to pick her up at 11:00.

It was certainly pretentious of him to assume that she would show up at his house while she was in the process of investigating him, no matter who else would be there. She felt that she should decline the opportunity, but found herself dressed for the occasion when the knock on her door came at the precise time.

The woman in the hotel hallway was the stewardess from the flight, looking quite different in jeans and a sweatshirt with her hair tied in a ponytail and a man Maria didn't recognize by her side. "*Buenas Dias*," she said with a loaded smile.

Maria knew she was blushing, and the two people outside the door burst out laughing. "Oh don't worry. I just couldn't resist! I'm Angela, by the way, and this is my husband, Hank."

Maria shook hands, realizing that there was no point in protesting the invitation, since she was obviously dressed for it. She got her purse and they went downstairs, where an older Toyota SUV was waiting with two children and Angela's mother. They all apologized for the mess, although the interior looked perfectly fine.

The drive through the snowy mountains was gorgeous. Angela and Hank talked non-stop about their wonderful life in Montana and how great they thought Airtana was for the community. They mentioned, as well, that they raised their own turkeys for Thanksgiving, although Montana had never been affected by the supermarket poisonings that animal

rights radicals conducted each year to bring an end to the traditional Holiday dinner.

After a time, they left the main road and started up an unpaved driveway that seemed to wind up the side of a mountain. Hank had the truck in
four-wheel-drive for the climb. Eventually they came out near the summit
on a large log home that looked out on a breathtaking panorama of the
valley.

There were several dozen cars parked there, scattered among the trees
on various parts of the property. Maria noticed a few snowmobiles as
well. They knocked on the door and it was opened by Kerry Conner himself, who smiled broadly when he saw who it was.

"Well, *Buenas...*"

Angela held up a hand to stop him. "She's already been through that
this morning, Kerry. Leave her alone."

Her boss immediately looked embarrassed and motioned them in.
The inside of the home was like something out of a magazine, with spruce
walls soaring up to dramatic beams. Windows were abundant and there
were several lofts as well. Two crackling fires at either end of the great
room made for a cozy atmosphere.

Guests were everywhere, some sinking deep into the oversized leather
furniture, others standing by the fire or by the windows, appreciating the
snowy view. There was a lot of chatter coming out of the kitchen. Maria
recognized some of the people from the office, but most were strangers.

"We get together like this every year for three days during Thanksgiving, so that everyone has a chance to be here," Conner told her, as he
took her coat. "A lot of our employees work on the holiday, but we make
sure that they have at least one of these days off so that they can join us, if
they wish."

She had a wonderful time. There was a sort of simplicity and genu-
ineness about the occasion that was in pleasant contrast to the parties she
occasionally attended in Washington, where it was necessary to impress
others with contrived, formal decorum. Here, people seemed free to be
themselves.

There was no alcohol visible, although she occasionally caught a
whiff of beer on someone's breath and figured that there must be something going on in some part of the house that was outside the domain of
the children, who otherwise seemed to have the run of the place.

A simple prayer was offered by one of the baggage handlers before
they ate, appreciated by all with a certain sincerity that reminded Maria of
something from her childhood that she couldn't quite recall. The atmosphere around her, of God and family, was not something that she was
used to, and she felt out of place.

Perhaps sensing that, Angela and the others made an effort to draw her into the conversation. Conner amused all of them by playing with the children, many of who called him "Uncle Kerry." She was amazed at the businessman that she had, only days earlier, likened to a cold-hearted Ebenezer Scrooge.

She asked Angela about Conner during a quiet moment together near the end of the afternoon, when long shadows were reaching across the valley outside the window and darkness loomed. She told her about their conversation on the plane, when she had asked Conner about where non-English speakers in El Paso would work if they could not be hired.

"We'll be glad to take on anyone who wants to work hard in a lower position, while they improve their language skills for future considera-tion," Conner had said bluntly at the time. "Anyone who doesn't like that is free to start their own airline."

When Angela heard about that she smiled. "Yep, that's Kerry. He built his own company, so why couldn't others build theirs?"

"But surely he had advantages in life… money and privileges that others…"

Angela laughed. "He had nothing, honey. He was an orphan grow-ing up in El Paso. He couldn't afford to go to college, so he followed his dream and came to Montana to build his life. He owes everything he has to his own ambition, so he doesn't have much patience for people who say that it isn't possible for a man to stand on his own two feet."

"That's the mentality that makes losers." Kerry had come up behind them and caught the tail end of the conversation. "Mind if I join you?"

"Please do," said Angela, rising from the couch. "Do you know where my little girl is, Kerry? It's time I started gathering them up."

"I think they're all outside throwing snowballs at each other," said Kerry. He gave Maria a look before sitting down, and told Angela, "You and Hank take off whenever you feel like it. I'll drive our VIP back later."

Maria did not object. She felt quite comfortable in the large house, even if it was just the two of them.

Kerry sat back and put his drink down on the end table. They both turned instinctively to watch the last of the sunlight fade against the land-scape. She asked about what life had been like for him growing up, and mentioned that she was from El Paso as well. It was a bit surreal, talking of a dry, hot land that was so different from where they were at the mo-ment.

The house had emptied and they were completely alone on the top of a Montana mountain, with pitch black outside. The wind roared against the windows, sometimes making its way down the chimneys far enough to shake the flames in the fireplaces. Kerry would get up every now and then to stoke the fire and put on another log. Eventually they were both curled up near it in separate chairs, talking softly and enjoying the glowing embers and the shadows cast around the dark room.

He seemed unusually interested in her family, raising his eyebrows a bit when she described various members. She almost felt comfortable enough to talk about her father's death, but realized that it was inappropriate to be sharing so intimately with a man she had only met days before and would probably be bringing charges against as soon as she got back home.

Rather than talk about his company, Kerry told her about how he had built the house that they were sitting in with his own hands. It wasn't in a bragging sort of way, and he did admit that he needed help in places, such as putting up the roof and pouring the foundation, but his pride was evident.

Maria was fascinated with this man, who was unlike others that she had known. He was not the juvenile that many men aspired to be, as if that is what impresses a woman, or the 'Alan Alda' clone that others thought was all the rage. He was a man who believed in himself and accomplished his goals. He was masculine, but not vulgar; sensitive, but not weak. From watching him at work, she noticed that he seemed to bring out the best in others merely by expecting it. At his home, she saw that he was comfortable with himself, which made those around him comfortable.

It was well after midnight when he got her coat and went out to bring the truck around for her, as she waited for him on the porch, shivering in the cold with snowflakes swirling into the light, around her body and out back out into the darkness.

They didn't say much on the ride back down the slippery mountain drive and along the remote highway that led back into town, with the headlights of the old pickup battling against the black night and the falling snow. She realized how much she enjoyed the ride, with only the glow from the dashboard and the gentle rumble of the engine and heater to entertain the senses.

It was peaceful in the truck there with him. She felt like she belonged.

She was sharply disappointed when the lights of the town appeared around a bend.

Now, as Maria trudged through the airport the next morning, still half asleep, she wondered if perhaps Kerry had driven a little slower than he needed to on the drive. She hoped that he had.

The night was still on her mind, as she passed through security and made her way down the long corridor to the terminal. The hallway was framed with large glass windows that offered stunning views of the jagged mountain ranges that rose above the bustling Montana town. Maria found herself standing in front of one near her gate and taking in the panorama, when she looked down and saw Kerry standing on the icy tarmac.

He was with a group of pilots, and in shirtsleeves against a bitter wind that was whipping his sandy hair. It looked as if he was giving a lecture of some sort about the plane, which he would gesture to occasionally with his arms while the others listened intently. At one point he went over and put his hand up against the hull, as if trying to dramatize a point. The others nodded.

Eventually he said something that caused them all to laugh, and the meeting broke up, with the others heading back up the metal steps to the gate. Kerry stood looking at the plane for a moment, then turned suddenly and looked up in the window, where Maria stood watching.

They immediately caught each other's eye.

Although startled, Maria held her ground. Five days earlier she would have turned in embarrassment without acknowledging him. Now she returned his wink with a bold wave, before walking down the ramp to board the plane.

Over the weekend she wrote the most damning report against Airtana that she could possibly compose within the bounds of truth, knowing that it had the potential to bring the carrier to its knees.

On Monday she filed it.

2034

Sunday, February 19th, 2034
Washington, DC

Jill realized that she might have to get used to attending church, if her campaign to win her father's old Senate seat in November was successful. Americans may have become increasingly agnostic, but it seemed to be oddly comforting to them when their leaders attended religious services, even if the politicians assured them that they would not be influenced in the slightest by spiritual conviction.

Such attendance wasn't a burden for her this morning, thanks to the national news cameras that were covering the rededication of the National Cathedral following last year's bombing, and the fact that Parker was there as well. She enjoyed seeing him in his element, even if she didn't share his faith.

The scars on his hands, and the reduced mobility of one of them, would always be there, but he had gotten off lucky compared to the more serious injuries suffered by dozens of others, as well as the seventeen who were killed. He had even become quite a celebrity in the months following the blast, as he called for unity, and resolutely urged the nation to reflect on how to improve relations with religious minorities.

The bomber had been upset over the fact that there was a National Cathedral, but no National Mosque. Parker took up the cause as well, after he was released from the hospital, and the groundbreaking began shortly thereafter a few blocks down the street. It was scheduled for completion in about two years, which would certainly beat the eighty years that it took to complete the Cathedral.

The Imam for the new mosque was to be the man seated next to Parker on the platform, who spoke perfect English with a British accent. It was his job to introduce Parker and, as the hymn was finishing, he rose to speak. "We were all horrified by what happened here a year ago," said the Imam pensively. "For me personally, it was astonishing to find out that the person who perpetrated such violence claimed to be a member of my own faith, the Religion of Peace."

Those in the pews shook their heads softly, as if sharing his disbelief.

"Of course, I know that this isn't so, but it concerned me that others might think this to be the case. We live in a time when there is unprecedented hatred toward Muslims in America. Just two weeks ago, a man in Seattle ordered a Qur'an from an online bookseller and it arrived with slurs written on the inside of the holy book that said "Death to Muslims.""

There was a low murmur, as the people present expressed amazement and discontent that such things could happen.

"Fortunately we have a man like Parker Whitehead, who is big enough to see beyond the borders of his own religion and understand that all Americans have a right to worship as they choose. It was Parker who realized the inequity suffered by Muslims in America. He took up our cause for a National Mosque and, I'm proud to say, will be standing next to me when it is dedicated."

The Imam stepped back and motioned Parker up and toward the podium. Jill thought he looked absolutely splendid in a dark blue suit that complemented his graying hair and handsome features. The congregation gave him a warm round of applause and the Imam sat down.

"Thank you. Thank you for those kind words, Imam Rastaban." Parker gave a nervous cough and went through some light-hearted comments before getting down to the heart of his message in a slow, dignified manner.

"We know well the scars that hate can cause. It would be easy for me to stand here and hold up my own hands to show you my scars, but this would not be honest of me, because it isn't the full story of what happened a year ago.

"The fact is that a man in our society felt disenfranchised, and we must assume that he represented many others, who did not choose his method of protest. As with all such acts of violence, this too brings us to a fork in the road and begs us to make a choice.

"On the one hand, we can react with fear and loathing. We can put our faith in police and government agencies to protect us against that which we do not understand. I know that it was disquieting to me this morning, as it may have been to others here, to walk past the barricades and through the security checkpoints just to be able to enter a house of worship. Let us hope that these are temporary measures that will soon be removed.

"For in the other hand lies our glorious alternative, which Christ teaches us. We can choose to listen to those around us and understand their grievances, as well as their needs. If we do this, then we will find that they are exactly like us, with the same desire for peace and tolerance, along with the same frustration when those desires are unsatisfied..."

Thursday April 13th, 2034
Ila, South Carolina

The phone rang around eight that night. Walid had just finished watching an old episode of "Law and Order" from the 1990's that he had seen before. Two Muslim women are killed by a white racist while on their way to an interfaith dialogue conference. The racist was an American patriotic type; the sort that usually plays the villain on television.

Walid wondered sometimes what Americans would be doing if they didn't have themselves to kick around. Evil TV characters were rarely foreign, although sometimes a Serb or a member of some other select group of white Europeans would be portrayed. South African villains recurred occasionally, but they were not as realistic, since there were very few whites left in Africa. Corporate crooks were the preferred target of wrath, followed by conservative politicians, Nazis, and skinheads respectively.

It puzzled him that corporations were always depicted as evil, with the exception of an occasional "Mom and Pop" that was invariably marked for destruction in the plot by a larger business. It was these larger companies, after all, that underwrote the programming with their advertising dollars, yet they were strangely willing to appease and feed the popular prejudices against corporate America.

He thought at first that the voice on the other end of the line was someone angry at him for his latest and most famous lawsuit. "What are you doing to my people?" was the angry question. He pictured himself talking to a large, irate black man.

He received harassing calls like this every so often, though not usually at home. He understood the anger. It was something he knew would be part of the package when he agreed to represent Kamel Rouhmani shortly after leaving the Federal Bureau of Investigations the year before last.

Walid thought it rather ironic that a Patriot (yes, he didn't mind being called that) ready to sacrifice his life for the government one year would be suing it the next, but being hung out to dry the way he was can breed a quick measure of cynicism. If the Bureau had taken decisive action in the wake of what happened last year, against the agent that had betrayed and nearly got him killed, Walid would not have been bitter, although he doubted that he would have gone undercover again. Instead, the Bureau played the whole thing off as a "he said, he said." They suspended the other agent to a less sensitive position, but let Walid know that it would not be easy to resolve the "issue," since the BIR had prohibited them from requiring that Muslim agents submit to polygraphs.

Even under the circumstances, Walid understood the pressure that the Bureau was under from civil rights organizations and Islamic special-interest groups. The government set the tone long before by forbidding employees from using phrases like "Islamic terrorist" that would in any way imply the religious affiliation of groups looking to kill Americans. Now, the roots of political correctness ran so deep that any disagreement between a Muslim and non-Muslim agent would usually result in the Muslim being promoted (so as to prevent him from suing) and the other being reassigned or released.

Walid knew of cases, other than his own, where fellow members of the Arabic translation group had tipped off targets of investigations and blatantly conducted other acts of sabotage to disrupt operations. In each case, the Bureau wanted to avoid bad publicity, and acted as best it could to neutralize the situation without angering the Muslim Intelligence Workers Union or other special-interests.

Walid left and went back home to practice law in his hometown, which had changed for the worse since he left. Needless to say, there were plenty of opportunities for a lawyer with Arabic language skills to make a decent living for himself.

Kamel Rahmouni was someone whose case he was familiar with prior to getting his call last October. It was not often that Ila received national attention, but there was a simmering legal problem in that corner of the country that threatened to boil over, with far-reaching political implications.

The Algerian-born Kamel, who received U.S. citizenship as a boy in Maine, had applied for and received a state job three years ago. He was a fine worker, but after a time, someone in human resources noticed that he was in a slot reserved for African-Americans. When asked, he insisted that he was African-American. The government disagreed and promptly fired him. Now Walid was helping him sue for $10 million over unlawful termination.

Walid presented the succinct argument that Kamel, a naturalized U.S. citizen born in Africa, was eminently qualified. As expected, there was uproar in the community, as black leaders demanded that the courts reject this reasoning, while local Muslims feigned outrage and made demands of their own for "equal treatment under the law." A Federal court ruled in Kamel's favor and awarded him half of what he was asking for in damages. An appellate court upheld the ruling just a few weeks later and it was now on its way to the Supreme Court in D.C., where Walid was confident of his chances.

So was the opposition. There was a grassroots movement among African-Americans and their progressive impresarios to raise enough money to settle the case before the Court could hand down an adverse ruling, as they had done sometimes in the past when white people sued on the grounds of reverse discrimination.

Now Walid was sure that he was dealing with a call from another angry member of the black community, but he always tried to give such people a chance to have their say before excusing himself. He didn't want to have to live looking over his shoulder all the time and he felt that allowing another to vent might reduce the chance of violence.

"Your people?" he asked, playing dumb.

"Well sure," was the reply, "didn't I dial the right number? Aren't you the one trying to stick it to the Black Man?"

The voice sounded very familiar. Walid suddenly thought he recognized it. "Is this who I think it is?" he asked?

"That's right my friend. How have you been?"

Walid hadn't talked to Pat Ridley in eighteen years. Not since…

"Damn, it's good to hear from you, Pat! Obviously you know that I'm about to be knee-deep in money, but how are things going with you?"

Pat talked about his new job at the Hope Tower in New York City, and the men caught up on the missing years. The Jordanian learned that his friend was the very proud father of a 13-year-old boy. As Walid talked about his own career, they both laughed about the fact that each had nearly lost their life to radical Islamists. It turned out also that Pat fully supported the spirit of the lawsuit and hoped that the Algerian client would go forward and resist settling.

Two hours went by before they knew it. As they were about to say goodbye, Pat apologized for cutting off contact. "It wasn't personal," he said, "there were just some things that I was dealing with at the time."

"I understand," said Walid. "I'm really sorry about… about her. Were you close?"

"I only knew her for a few hours," replied his friend, "but she didn't deserve to die like that."

"I agree, Pat. It's haunted me for a long time too. I'm glad you can finally let go of the bitterness."

Walid hung up with a sense of elation, despite the down note at the end of the conversation. He had more in common with a man that he had not talked to in nearly twenty years than he did with his former Islamic "brothers" at the FBI. After sitting quietly for about twenty minutes, he decided that if Pat could put the past behind him, then he should as well.

He went over to his computer and drilled down into an old folder that had been copied from hard drive to hard drive with each upgrade over the years. In it was a video attachment that Pat had sent to him eighteen years ago with a request for language interpretation – the last time they had corresponded.

Walid decided to watch it one last time before deleting it.

The video was one that was like hundreds of others that he had seen over the span of his career at the Bureau. It showed the killing of an "infidel" by Islam's "holy warriors." They wore black masks and stood in front of a banner that praised Allah. Kneeling before them was a young woman in an Army uniform, who had been badly beaten and was barely conscious.

As the camera moved closer to record the movement of the dull knife against her throat, a corporal's insignia came into focus beneath her blonde hair and terrified eyes.

Saturday, August 26th, 2034
New York, New York

"And what is it that you have against African-Americans?"

It was not a question so much, as an angry statement. The thin, diminutive white man who posed it to Jill Hudson stood in the center of the large open area of the luxury apartment near the top of one of Manhattan's most prestige buildings. His voice was trembling with rage, as were his extremities, including a thin, gray mustache, as he stood there on the plush rug.

Jill was as startled as much by the look of utter self-righteous indignation in the man's eyes as she was by the question itself. Any conversation that had been buzzing around them immediately stopped and Jill, who was too stunned to think clearly, began scrambling for something to say.

"Oh Lucian," said the host, coming to her rescue, "be nice to our guest!"

The little man backed down a bit, taking a seat in the chair behind him, while those around him reached out with reassuring gestures.

Jill had been invited to the monthly Landau group meeting by her friend from Berkeley, Phyllis Hughes. She thought it might be an opportunity to raise campaign contributions for her Senate race, which was about two months away from concluding at the November polls. These were Manhattan's most wealthy and progressive citizens.

There was almost a bizarre game of one-upmanship at play in the room, where each person would attempt to impress and outdo the others with their open-mindedness or commitment to social justice. One person would mention an obscure environmental issue, another would do the same with animal rights; still another with an al-Qaeda detainee in Kuwait or the arrest of a serial killer in San Francisco that may have involved an illegal wire tap. The rest would gently rock their wineglasses and nod in an urbane sort of way, as if they were a step or two ahead of the speaker and had already reached the same wise and charitable conclusion regarding the seriousness of the issue.

Most of them clearly supported the Progressive candidate, her only real opposition in the 'blue-green' state. As the group gathered in a circle for introductions and the traditional purpose of discussing the issues of the day, Jill found herself buttonholed on several topics. Why didn't she favor raising income taxes as much as her opponent? Why was it taking so long to downsize the military? Why didn't she want to pledge as much to welfare and other social programs? Jill tried as best she could to explain budgetary limitations, but she was met for the most part with blank looks. Any restraint on social spending, no matter how sensible, was interpreted as an insidious and heartless attempt to undermine either the poor or the affected identity group.

These were not people who had experience in government administration, or even practical business experience for that matter. They inherited their wealth or built up their estates through lucrative positions in civic foundations that had been assured for them before they were even born. The closest thing to a businessperson in the room was Robert Danforth, and he wasn't about to jump in and help her try to explain the complications involved with balancing a budget.

By far, however, the most hostile part of the discussion revolved around the issue of slavery reparations, the issue that was gradually eroding African-American support for Democrats and handing political momentum to the Progressive Party. Everyone else in the room professed their strong allegiance to the idea of compensation for the descendents of America's slaves. Jill found herself in the uncomfortable position of having to explain the impracticality of such an undertaking, something that never would have occurred to her eight years ago, when she blindly championed the cause as well.

The little man who had all but accused her of being a racist, sat staring straight at her, still quivering with anger even as he was consoled by his friends. He had probably spoken for many others in the room. Jill was shocked by the apparent hysterics over the issue. How do you combat raw emotion with fact, or smear with logic? This was no way for a Democrat to be treated.

"Surely there are ways for African-Americans to rise above our country's shameful history and realize the opportunities that now exist," she said hesitantly. "Particularly since we've enhanced Affirmative Action programs and…"

"Then why haven't they?" snapped an angry woman sitting a few chairs down from her, who, like everyone else in the room, was as white as Jill herself. "Why do people of color still lag behind in education, income and occupational status?"

"Well, we hope… I hope to remedy that by expanding Affirmative Action requirements into the corporate structure to ensure that minorities are well-represented at all levels of the management hierarchy. Democrats have also pushed hard for non-discrimination enforcement in lending…"

"Why can't we pay back the debt we owe to African-Americans, without demanding that they adapt to the ways of the White Man?" asked the woman again. "Like the reparations to Japanese-American internees in the 1980s."

"Well," began Jill, clearly uncomfortable having to defend the unpopular side of such a sensitive issue, "the reparations were paid directly
to the survivors of the... these American concentration camps. In the case
of slavery, however, we would be asking people who never owned slaves
to pay money to people who never were slaves and..."

There was a collective gasp from those in the room and Jill knew that
she was not doing herself any favors. "We are open to working with community leaders and fellow legislators to find a solution to the problems
that keep those on the lower rungs of the ladder from attaining the economic security that the rest of us enjoy," she quickly finished. Thankfully, the conversation moved on to other topics.

It was a strange group. Phyllis Hughes was a regular. By the TV
producer's side was a mysterious bald man known as "the Artist" who
was so pale that he looked as if he might be an albino. He sat wearing
dark glasses and nibbling on a small cracker, which he had been working
on for the better part of five minutes.

Then there was the host, Beth Landau, the editor of "Vagina Now"
Magazine, a radical feminist publication that fiercely advocated issues
extending well beyond women's rights. In a country that was increasingly
comfortable with taxpayer-funded abortion, there weren't many frontiers
left to champion.

She was wearing a "Free Willie" t-shirt that looked somewhat out of
place among the polished crowd – the fashion choice, not the opinion.
Beth was the wife of the lawyer representing Willie Powell, a black man
serving a life sentence for killing a police officer. His cause had been
taken up by a broad section of America, from the solid support that he
enjoyed among poorer blacks, to the trendy upper-crust represented by
those around her.

The group was virulently opposed to the police, which they accused
of "creating criminals, by protecting the social order that produces them."
They certainly did not like the idea of Secret Service agents in the same
room with them, or even in the hallway outside ("we aren't living under
martial law, dear") so Jill had to ask her security detail to wait downstairs.
She did not understand what the fuss was, but perhaps it was because she
was used to having the agents around her and knew them to be decent
people.

Before they gathered in a circle for the meeting, Beth told her about
how she had almost been "carjacked" by a Federal agent on the Tappan
Zee Bridge a couple of years back. Apparently the man had popped out
of the trunk of the car in front of her and demanded to use her phone.

"He got blood all over my Grid," she said with a pained expression,
referring to her electric Mercedes. "It was like I was living in some sort

of totalitarian country where the government can just order you to give up your phone or your car whenever they want."

Her husband put his arm around her reassuringly. "Naturally we thought about suing," he said. "A person should feel safe in their own car without something like this happening."

Jill had never heard of the incident.

The group concluded that day with a progress report on the "home-land" movement, which was the bid by Muslims to make Maine into an independent country. Jill could tell that the idea was exciting to many of those present. There was a consensus that since Alaska had been granted independence, then Maine should be as well.

Washington D.C. was not quite as monolithic in its opinion of Maine. Although the state was majority Muslim, and had been for some time, there was a fear on the part of non-Muslims living there that *Sharia* would be adopted and that they would become second-class citizens. Socially conscious intellectuals scoffed at that. Jill thought it was sad that Islamo-phobia persisted in America, despite monumental efforts to eradicate it through education. She supported her father's efforts to promote a sort of dual legal system in Maine, in which Islamic courts would be allowed some authority within the voluntary community, similar to what Old Canada had adopted several decades earlier.

"I heard a caller to a radio station claim that we would be having the same problems as the Europeans," said Beth, referring to the civil crises in France and the Netherlands. "I wanted to tell her, 'Hey, this is America, don't be an idiot'."

"I thought all the knuckle-draggers left for Alberta!" chimed the woman sitting next to Jill.

"That's just the sort of attitude that causes the fear and injustice be-hind the violence," agreed another.

Jill thought about the bombing of the National Cathedral last year, when she almost lost her dear friend. Though she might not be able to count on the votes of those around her, she certainly had to agree with what they were saying. Criticism only provokes. The key to peace be-tween Americans and Muslims was found in dialogue and understanding. She was glad that Muslim-American leaders were willing to forgive America her sins, and extend a hand of reconciliation.

She just hoped that she would be there in the Senate to extend a hand of her own next year.

Thursday, March 6th, 2036
Ila, South Carolina

Walid was wrong about Leeman Arnold. The former bully was still a bigot, but he had made more of his life than plucking chickens on an assembly line. Thirteen years earlier, he opened a small convenience store, and had been making a decent living up until the trouble started.

The interesting thing about bigots is that they never think of themselves that way. Whether it's a white person hating blacks, a black person hating whites, or anyone hating anyone, they'll all say the same thing. They aren't bigots (or racists) just straightforward commentators of what they observe.

What Leeman had observed since the days that he used to terrorize little Arab kids at school, was that they all grew up to return the favor. Not just to him, of course, but to the entire community. The once sleepy southern town was becoming a ghetto, where row after row of subsidized housing stretched into outlying areas. Arabic graffiti coated buildings and the stately old mansions in the city center, which had long since been abandoned to drug users and vagrants.

His children couldn't walk to school anymore because they were likely to be assaulted along the way. If they rode bikes, the bikes would be stolen and they would still be assaulted. His wife even had things yelled and thrown at her when she tried driving them to school. Eventually, they pulled the kids out and took their chances with home schooling. It pained Leeman to know that his children would not be going to college or rising above the level of their parents, which was the dream of most Americans.

It's possible that there was a time in his life, shortly after the birth of his children, perhaps, that Leeman would have changed more dramatically than he did. Watching his kids grow up caused him to reflect on how he treated the others around him when he was younger, and the headaches that he must have caused other parents, to say nothing of the pain and fear he inflicted. If, during these times of reflection, he had been fortunate enough to meet and grow close to the right people – good people of other races – then it's possible that there would have been more to Leeman's evolution than the subtle mellowing and maturity that usually accompanies age.

He got along fine with several people who were not white, either customers or those with whom he regularly did business. He had to grudgingly accept their presence in his neighborhood, as there were no more places he could move to around Ila that were not integrated in some form or fashion. His only real friends remained the few whites with whom he had grown up, and who had not left.

It was only to his like-minded friends that he expressed his candid beliefs about minorities; namely that they had too many children, didn't work, went on welfare, and contributed disproportionately to the soaring rate of crime. The opinion of a progressively-minded intellectual, that these beliefs were primitive and insensitive, would matter as little to Leeman as their statistical correctness would to the progressive (exaggeration and extrapolation being to blame for Leeman's erroneous conclusions). Up until that year, the two never had to worry about crossing paths, but that all changed thanks to a 19-year-old kid named Nidal Phad.

Like most unemployed Arab men in Ila, Nidal had too much time on his hands. The others his age usually turned to the mosque or to crime. He did more of the latter, but unlike the others, he had a new purpose as well, and that was to make life miserable for Leeman Arnold and his family.

Ironically, the situation never would have happened had the big man not hired him at his store to replace a murdered night clerk. Nidal happened along at the right time and was hired on his ability to speak English and count money. Although there was no problem with Nidal's punctuality, Leeman noticed after a few months that the register activity was significantly lower when the young man was working. After analyzing video footage, he found out why and called the sheriff.

Leeman preferred to deal directly with the sheriff when he had to report problems, rather than the underlings. He certainly didn't trust the Arab officers, since most of his problems had to do with Arabs, and he couldn't understand the Mexicans that well. The officers were usually new anyway, as the police force had a hard time retaining honest and capable cops in a justice system that increasingly favored the criminals.

The Mexican sheriff was different. He had started his career working a border town in Texas, and claimed that this was a "cakewalk" compared to what he had to deal with down there. He was dedicated to his position and respected in the community, although he had only been there for six years.

He used to come into Leeman's store occasionally, and share a cup of coffee with him. There were times like that, when they would be talking, that Leeman would start to feel ashamed of his attitudes toward Mexicans and would privately wonder whether it was wise to judge others by their race. The sheriff was one of the most decent people he knew.

Nidal Phad was arrested for embezzlement. His day in court came not long after that, and with the videotape evidence Leeman thought it was a slam-dunk.

It wasn't.

The judge was a younger white woman, new to the bench. She asked more questions of Nidal, about his background, than she did of the crime, paying particular attention to his tales of having been disrespected by his employer. There was not the slightest interest expressed in Leeman's background or finances. It seemed to be assumed that he had all of the money and power.

When rendering her verdict, the judge reprimanded Nidal for taking the money, but commended him on accepting a job and trying to rise above the circumstances of poverty and discrimination. Nidal hung his head contritely, looking for all the world as if he were making a better man of himself right on the spot – up until the moment he caught Leeman's eye and gave a sly wink that went undetected by the judge.

The woman then turned her attention to Leeman, lecturing him on the obligation that those in power had to realize the grievances of those around them and act compassionately. She suggested that he hire Nidal back, but regretted that she could not "force" him to do so. She then knocked her gavel against the desk and proclaimed the case resolved.

Leeman was astonished. There was no verdict of guilt? No sentence rendered? He tried to protest, which angered the judge, who warned him that the case was over and that if he persisted, she would hold him in contempt. He did persist, to the point of yelling in fact, and wound up spending the night in jail.

The frustration ate at him, but it still would have ended there if not for the young Nidal. The 19-year-old seemed to appreciate the aggravation he could cause the man who once had power over him, so he made regular visits to Leeman's store, usually when Leeman's 17-year-old daughter was working the register by herself.

Nidal never bought anything, of course, but he would walk around, sometimes for a full hour, distracting the clerk's attention and occasionally harassing customers. Leeman would call the cops, but there was nothing anyone could do, as a crime had not been committed.

One day, Leeman walked in while Nidal was leaning on the counter and commenting loudly to his daughter about her genitalia. This was enough for the big man and he grabbed the 19-year-old from behind and carted him outside where he informed him that he was not allowed back into the store.

The very next day, Nidal showed up again, this time with friends. Undaunted, Leeman told him to get out, and then hauled him roughly toward the door when he refused. The owner told the other youths that they were not welcome either.

Three more days went by quietly, until Leeman looked out through the glass doors one morning to see local news cameras in the parking lot. A television reporter stood outside, interviewing Nidal as he was surrounded by family and friends, all wearing *hijabs* and other sorts of Muslim apparel that were almost never seen in Ila. Leeman watched it all, with a frown on his face. The journalist asked him afterwards if he would answer questions about his "ban on Muslims."

He declined.

Friday, April 4th, 2036
Washington, D.C.

"Have no mercy on the Jews. No matter where they are, fight them.... Wherever you are, kill the Jews, the Americans... and those who stand by them. Don't love them or enter into agreement with them. They should be slaughtered. They should be murdered."

Thus spoke Imam Rastaban on the thirtieth anniversary of 9/11 at his mosque in Los Angeles. But that was five years ago and he had come to regret those words and many others like them, which defined Jews and Christians as descendents of "apes and pigs" and blasphemers deserving of death. Not because it wasn't true, after all the Qur'an and Sunnah were quite specific about this, but rather because it almost cost him the position of a lifetime at the new National Mosque in Washington.

The statements that he made years earlier were unearthed by the "apes and pigs" following his appearance at the rededication event at the National Cathedral two years ago. Very intense pressure from Muslim-rights groups, along with the cooperation of the media kept his ambitions on track. He also owed his survival to the man now introducing him to the crowd at the dedication ceremony.

Parker Whitehead was an interesting person. Publicly he disparaged Rastaban's detractors and claimed that the accusations were the result of an "aggressive strain of right-wing, religious zealotry." Privately, however, he approached the Imam and expressed his concerns over the remarks.

Although Rastaban respected the young Christian, he had no qualms about using the man's gullibility to dispel apprehension. He began by implying that perhaps the Reverand was battling his own religious prejudices. This immediately put the man on the defensive and all the more eager to accept the Imam's explanation in order to confirm his personal tolerance.

Although Rastaban didn't quite understand why, he found that these sorts of people were even more anxious than Muslims to package Islam for intellectual acceptance by their fellow Americans. This meant secularizing the harsher elements, such as the Imam's remarks regarding 'blasphemers,' and interpreting them as a metaphorical response to political and social injustice. Meanwhile, it was assumed that the core of Islam is no different than that of Western religion, merely because it is a religion and therefore entitled to the same respect.

Of course, the Imam knew differently. Islam was different, because it was truth. This explained why people like Parker Whitehead, who followed a false god, were so eager to extend sympathy to Islam that they would never allow their fellow Christians. Even if the Reverand didn't yet recognize the truth of Islam, it was already working on his heart and making him submissive to the will of Allah.

Rastaban watched as the dignified, young man made his introductory remarks to the people and cameras. Just as the Imam hoped, Whitehead spoke out against the mishandling of the Qur'an, "intolerant speech," and other provocative acts that merely precipitated violence. Those in the large hall nodded solemnly, and Rastaban prepared to take the podium.

It was a diverse audience. There would be no mention of apes and pigs from the Imam on this occasion.

Wednesday, June 11ᵗʰ, 2036
Billings, Montana

It was an odd feeling for Maria, knowing that she had seen the genitalia of the judge presiding over *U.S. Department of Labor versus Airtana Airlines*, swinging freely in the breeze each time he entered Rothermel's classroom ten years ago. If she and her friends had used their scissors back then, it might be Darnella Massey to whom the case was now being presented, there at the U.S. District Court House for the Ninth Circuit in Billings.

Maria's career had taken off in the years since she had first submitted her report. She was now the Assistant Secretary for Labor and rumored to be in the running for the top slot if the Democrats retained the White House in November.

Some around her thought it odd that she stayed attached to the case against Airtana, when she could have easily turned it over to one of her staff, allowing herself extra time for other duties, of which there were many. She hung on to the suit anyway, even traveling to Bozeman on occasion, to meet with Airtana officials, which was highly irregular for someone in her position. Those that knew her felt that she was taking the case too personally and was determined to bring down the airline. Even the Secretary warned her against allowing a grudge to become an obsession.

In the years since, she rarely talked with Kerry Conner. She had not been out to his house again. He did not call during the few times that he visited Washington. He invited her out to dinner once, when she was in Bozeman for the first time after filing her report, but she refused, hoping that he would understand the circumstances. It was very important that she maintain both her objectivity and the integrity of her office. He did not ask her again, but neither was unkind to her in any way. It was as if he accepted the misfortune that befell the company as an inevitable circumstance that had nothing to do with her.

Airtana's lawyers dragged the case out for two years before both sides came together to pick a jury. Maria worked closely with the legal team and tried to be present during the six-week trial as much as possible. It was not going well for Airtana, as the company had clearly broken Federal law in a number of ways. But, the company's lawyers were very good at muddying the waters by appealing to "founding principles" and "property rights."

Maria informed the team that their best chance of contrasting Airtana's practices with government mandates was to get Kerry Conner to testify under cross-examination. She even fed them certain questions which she felt would draw out the distinctions between the maker of wealth and the maker of rules to the satisfaction of both sides.

She would have moved heaven and earth to be in the courtroom on the day that he was scheduled to testify, and it practically required both, since it was right in the middle of the last week of the trial. He wore his usual blue jeans and boots, and even winked at Maria as he was being sworn in by the bailiff. The jury members were all familiar with the owner's name, since it was impossible to find people in that part of the country who weren't. Though fighting obvious boredom through much of the trial, they seemed to take a visible interest in the proceedings when Kerry was on the stand. Maria leaned forward as well, from where she was sitting with the other attorneys directly in front of the witness. Kerry looked at her as he spoke, as if knowing that she was behind many of the questions that were asked.

For nearly two hours, the prosecutor went through formal procedures with nothing particularly distinguishing about the exchange with the 41-year-old businessman. Things changed after they returned from adjournment in the afternoon.

The prosecutor asked whether Kerry felt like he was fair to his employees.

"Yes."

"But you don't give them the full twelve months of family leave required by law."

"That's federal law, Sir. I do comply with what is required of me by the State of Montana."

"Why don't you provide the full twelve months of leave?"

"Because it wouldn't be profitable to pay two individuals for the job of one."

"Why do you provide any leave at all then?"

"Primarily, because I compete against businesses that do."

"Are you not in favor of people spending time with their families?"

"They can spend all the time they want," replied Kerry, "just don't ask me to pay them for it, because it's not performing a service for my company."

The prosecutor chuckled. "It all boils down to profit at that business of yours, doesn't it, Mr. Conner."

"Yes."

The prosecutor raised his eyebrows and looked at the jury. "Well, your unexpected candor is appreciated."

"You're asking for honest answers, aren't you?" asked Kerry.

"Why of course."

"Well, let's be honest then. If people like me don't make a profit with our businesses, then we aren't able to pay the taxes that people like you need to make your mortgage payments. You live off of the work of others. There's nothing that government does to contribute to the GDP. You only exist to take from those who do."

The prosecutor couldn't help a look of genuine astonishment. "You have the nerve to accuse me of living off the work of others? You make millions of dollars every year by doing exactly that yourself. Surely you don't think that you're out there loading bags or fixing engines or flying planes, do you, Mr. Conner."

"I have at one time or another," replied Kerry, "but I hire people to do those things for me now. I enter into voluntary, honest agreements with them. They're free to accept what I offer, and they're also free to decline it and go to work for another carrier if they wish. I don't force anyone to…"

"You act as if people have a choice," interrupted the prosecutor.

"Of course they have a choice."

"No they don't, Mr. Conner," argued the prosecutor, as Judge Massey watched the exchange with interest. "If Airtana is the only company in town, then there's nowhere else for them to work."

"If there is a demand for air travel, then they're free to build their own airlines," said Kerry.

"Ah, yes… let them eat cake, eh?"

"No. Let them start their own business. What prevents them from doing this?"

"Perhaps they don't have the wealth and power that you have, Mr. Conner."

"I started with nothing but debt," said Kerry.

"You were very lucky then," replied the prosecutor.

"Yes, and the harder I worked, the luckier I got. Any theories… or is this just a strange coincidence to you?"

"Nevertheless," said the prosecutor, looking down at his notes and ignoring both the question posed and the stir in the courtroom, "the law says you have an obligation to the community and must hire in proportion to certain levels."

"I am no one's nursemaid," said Kerry, "and I'm not obligated to hire *anyone*. In fact, I have a constitutional right to hire who I want, for whatever terms we both agree to."

"Oh," said the Federal prosecutor, clicking his tongue, "this isn't true, although I'm glad that you aren't shy about giving the good people on this jury some insight into your ignorance of the law."

"This country wasn't founded on the principles of a 7-hour workday and twelve-months of paid family leave," responded Kerry. "It was founded and made great by the doctrine of free enterprise, and the freedom of a man to spend his money as he pleases, and the freedom of another to barter with his qualifications rather than a claim of entitlement or group identity."

The judge's interest was obviously piqued by this last part. Although technically questions could be directed from the bench, it was an option that was rarely exercised. Not so for the first year Circuit judge.

"Are you saying, Mr. Conner," he asked, "that your company doesn't seek to bring the racial characteristics of your employee base into harmony with the community to which you serve?"

Kerry turned to face the judge. "We seek to hire the most qualified people. Race is not a qualification."

"Do you mean," thundered the judge, "that if your company had no African-American employees, you would not be interested in hiring a person like me, a black man, to help correct the imbalance?"

"You would be considered on the basis of your qualifications, Sir. If I were considering you for a position that required the sort of impartiality that would normally be expected of a Federal judge, for example, then I would probably deny your application."

The courtroom erupted in laughter and Darnell Massey's face grew dark. He banged his gavel with unbridled violence, willing the court to come to order. After a few seconds of pretentious silence, he returned to the witness with a hard glint in his eye.

"Mr. Conner, do you see the black woman sitting in the second chair of the first row of the jury? Tell me, in the same scenario that I laid out, would you turn her down as well?"

"She would receive no special consideration because of her race," replied Conner evenly. "Neither would the white man sitting behind her."

Thursday, July 17th, 2036
GNN Studios

"Welcome back to GNN. We've been talking with Judge Darnell Massey, who presides over the Ninth Circuit courthouse in Billings, Montana, where a case that gained a modest amount of publicity was decided last month. This is Judge Massey's first interview since the verdict and, although judges do not normally give interviews, it turns out that Judge Massey is no ordinary judge.

"Thank you again for joining us, Sir. Before the break, you mentioned that this verdict is a set-back in the struggle for civil rights. Can you elaborate on that?"

"Yes, Bahira, that's what I firmly believe. Even as a black man growing up in racist America, it still would have been hard for me to believe that a jury of twelve people, in the middle of the 21st century, would choose to acquit a large company, simply because the owner makes a pledge not to hire African-Americans. It's like something out of 1930s Mississippi."

"Let me remind the viewers that we don't know exactly what their motives were, although you were much closer to the case than anyone outside of the jury box and are certainly qualified to provide insight."

"Yes, I sat there and watched in amazement as they seemed to be buying whatever the defense attorneys were selling, and I don't understand it. None of the jury members were rich. I don't think any of them owned businesses. They probably all worked for a company of some sort, just like the employees of Airtana.

"Here they had the power to literally take control of big business and demand more from it... more for themselves. Yet they chose to squander the opportunity, as if they didn't think they would need to be taken care of down the road. It's very frustrating when people are given the power to force the wealth out of the hands of the powerful and into their own pockets via the voting booth or the jury box, yet they elect not to do this."

"What do you think is the reason for this, Judge?"

"It's probably racism, since the defendant clearly played the race card in his testimony. It could just be stupidity, since this is Hawking country. This was a local jury pool and speaking as a black man I can tell you that..."

Wednesday, September 3rd, 2036
Ila, South Carolina

It was about midnight when the phone woke him. Felipe answered it groggily, expecting it to be a dispatcher from the office, or one of his officers. This usually didn't happen more than once a month, but it was always something big when it did. Instead of someone he knew, however, there was a girl's voice on the other end of the line. "Are you the sheriff? Daddy wants you to come quick. He shot a man that was breaking into the garage."

Felipe knew who it was now – one of Leeman Arnold's kids. He hung up and dialed the station to ask if there were any reports of shots fired in the area. There weren't, but he had another unit dispatched while he threw on his clothes and walked out his front door to where his patrol car was parked in the gravel driveway beside the old house.

On the way over, he thought about Leeman's plight over the last six months. An illegal boycott was instigated against his store by the Muslims in the community. Not all of them, of course, just the more vocal and ill-tempered ones. They had been receiving plenty of attention, thanks to a sympathetic local media that was hungry for drama.

The sheriff tried everything he could to disrupt the boycott, which included ordering the disassembly of sidewalk barricades and demonstrations. Even his own police department was divided, with some of the officers openly supporting the boycott and grumbling about following the orders.

Felipe's biggest problem was with the Muslim mayor, who refused to condemn the illegal boycott and made public statements that framed the issue in racial terms, which directly undermined the sheriff's attempts to assuage the tension.

The mayor was unprofessional in other ways, suggesting, for example, that the town had "too many Mexican policemen" and that perhaps funding should be cut until the department learned religious tolerance. Since Felipe only had one other Hispanic working for him, it wasn't hard for to figure out who was really having the tolerance problem.

It was all moot anyway after Leeman closed the doors of his small store following three months of declining business. No one wanted to walk past the angry protesters and have obscenities screamed at them. Felipe could not station anyone permanently at the store, and the demonstrators had a knack for materializing quickly.

Why not start your own business rather than tear down someone else's, he wondered. It wasn't as if they didn't have enough idle time on their hands to give it a try.

A Muslim gang burned down the store shortly afterwards, which meant a fat insurance check for Leeman. He'd been laying low in his house, considering his options, but apparently this wasn't enough for Nidal Phad, the young hooligan who had started the trouble. The kid would drive back and forth outside his house at night, honking his horn and disturbing the peace. He also made threats against the family, dumped trash on their lawn, and decorated the side of the house and garage with crude graffiti, mocking Leeman and making lewd comments about his daughters.

Felipe had the boy arrested a couple of times, but his family always made bail and he was never in for more than a matter of hours. The judge, who openly supported *Sharia*, was sympathetic and always had the charges dismissed. The sheriff suspected that he had been influenced by the boycott, particularly the way it was portrayed in the local newspaper, which were unambiguously biased against the storeowner.

Now, as he pulled into the heavily wooded subdivision with middle-class homes spread out on one-acre lots, he wondered just what was happening. As he neared the end of the street, he saw flashing lights in his rear-view mirror and knew that he had barely beaten the other squad car to the scene. There was a group of people standing by the Arnold garage, so he pulled his car into a position where his headlights illuminated the group. As he suspected, it wasn't good.

A man lay on the ground, with obvious gunshot wounds. Leeman's daughter sat over him, pumping his chest in a CPR maneuver. Felipe could see that a piece of clothing, perhaps a shirt, had been tied around the young man's torso in a vain attempt to stop the bleeding. He was glad to see the shotgun propped against the side of the garage, and went to secure it while calling for a medical unit over his shoulder radio.

Sure enough, the man on the ground was the apparently expired Nidal Phad. Leeman stood a distance away, pale as a ghost. The other car came up and Felipe directed the officer to take the big man into temporary custody in the back of their patrol car. He noted that Leeman went without argument.

After the med team arrived, Felipe talked with the family, who were the only witnesses to the shooting. They maintained that their father heard someone in the garage and went out with his gun to check on it. They heard two shots and came out to find Nidal dying on the driveway.

Before talking with Leeman, Felipe went into the garage with a flashlight (since there was no overhead light) and confirmed that there had been two shotgun blasts at different angles, with blood splatter consistent with witness testimony. The family car had been freshly spray-painted with graffiti that was identical to the walls of nearby buildings. Felipe scooped up and bagged a spray can and a .38-semi-automatic that were lying on the floor in two different places.

Leeman was still pale by the time Felipe got around to taking his statement.

"I saw someone out there and went out with my gun. I opened the door and saw an intruder with something shiny in his hand and I shot him twice as he moved toward me."

"I'm going to have to take you in and record your statement," the sheriff told him, "but I imagine that you'll be home by morning."

The big man nodded and Felipe went back to processing the scene.

Friday, September 5th, 2036
Washington, D.C.

Rahim stood at the window of a modest office just a few blocks from the White House, looking down on the busy street four stories below, where traffic was jammed with government workers, young and old, desperately fleeing the city for the weekend. Sandwich and clothing shops mixed with adult bookstores and other pornography outlets, no different than most other city streets in America. There was even an X-rated production put on in Ford's theatre a few years ago that managed to cause a slight stir.

It had been two years since Rahim followed his friend Danforth into the lucrative field of public interest activism. Unlike CSR, Rahim's own organization was non-profit, so as to facilitate donations. It was also focused exclusively on Muslim interests, although under the guise of "bettering America's understanding of Islam and building bridges."

At one time, Rahim was expected to follow in his grandfather's footsteps and head the BIR (Bureau of Islamic Relations) at the Department of Cultural Affairs. He chose instead to start BAIR – the Board on American Islamic Relations. He was smart enough to keep terror groups at arm's length, thus avoiding the primary pitfall that plagued similar organizations over the last forty years. BAIR was also fortunate enough to have missed out on the Edina Virus hysteria, which tainted the loudest groups, after the issue was neatly dispensed by science. Everyone was being a lot more careful about the issues they championed.

His first big payout came when a friend of his, and fellow activist, ordered a used Qur'an from a bookstore that sold online through the Internet book giant, Inetbooks.com. Rahim did not question why his Muslim friend, who had plenty of other Qur'ans on his shelf, would be ordering a used copy with no special significance, nor did he inquire about the authenticity of anti-Muslim slurs found written inside the front cover.

Inetbooks.com claimed that it was not responsible for a transaction involving two separate parties, and the owner of the used book shop pledged to inspect all used Qur'ans prior to shipment. This was insufficient, however, and BAIR applied pressure by contacting government officials, conducting press conferences, and carrying out demonstrations against the Internet giant. Eventually the larger company caved and disconnected its relationship with the smaller bookstore, effectively putting them out of business. Inetbooks.com also made a large donation to BAIR, along with pledges to hire Muslim workers and promote favorable Islamic works on their Web site, while discontinuing those that were critical of the religion.

Rahim tried to build on this momentum by lobbying various municipalities to extend the definition of hate crimes to the desecration of the Qur'an and other elements of the faith that were sacred to Muslims. He was having success with this, particularly along the East Coast, but it was a tedious process, and he realized that his efforts would be better spent lobbying for protection at the national level. With the balance of power evenly spent between Democrats and Progressives, it was easier for identity groups to exercise their muscle and play the two parties against one another.

At the moment, however, Rahim was chewing over a report from one of their chapters in Ila, South Carolina, about an overnight shooting involving a Muslim teen. Ila had been on BAIR's radar for the last several months, as there had been a boycott against a local store that had tried to institute some sort of ban. It was not a large chain, however, just a small proprietorship, so it was difficult getting the national media to take an interest, given that boycotts were so common.

Now it appeared that the storeowner was involved in killing one of the Muslim teens. Rahim nervously jingled the change in his pocket as he listened to the news, trying to control his excitement. The thirty-fifth anniversary of 9/11 was going to be the following week and, although the legitimacy of the attacks was now accepted by large segments of the American public, it was still an embarrassing occasion for many Muslims in America, particularly since the violence went unreciprocated.

In the wake of 3,000 American deaths, many Muslims in the U.S. at the time initially feared that they would be targeted in revenge, yet not a single such person lost their life to vigilantism on the nation's streets. At first this was welcomed by the community, although the stage of public gratification was summarily skipped and activists used their new platform as an opportunity for grievance, discovering that Westerners often rewarded Islamic violence with concession.

As time went by, and more attacks added to the mounting toll of dead Americans, it became somewhat of a burden for Muslim activists not to have a fatal hate crime of their own to exploit for neutralizing the moral argument against Islam. The bombing deaths in Afghanistan were obviously incidental to the campaign against the al-Qaeda camps, and the civilians killed in Iraq from military strikes against insurgents were always collateral. Their significance was greatly diminished as the Fedayeen quickly exceeded the casualty count with their own bombing campaigns against fellow Muslims, even while American troops were in Iraq trying to stop them, to say nothing of what happened after they left.

Groups like BAIR desperately needed a standard-bearer, a Muslim-American whose death at the hands of a bigot would galvanize the movement and provide them with a moral superiority that would shame America into further indulgence.

Rahim wanted to believe that Nidal Phad would be what they had been waiting thirty-five years for, but he needed to find out more before praising Allah just yet.

Saturday, September 6ᵗʰ, 2036
New York, New York

The only difference that a weekend day had from the weekly grind for Bernice Greenly was that she actually stopped for a cappuccino on the way to the office, rather than ordering it from her desk. She would usually be home by midnight as well, but that was a long way from where she sat that afternoon, evaluating various news stories on her desk for determining which were worthy of GNN's attention.

It wasn't a simple matter of discerning what the public wanted, of course, but rather what it needed. The news media had a responsibility not merely to entertain, but to educate; and not merely to educate, but to shape opinion. Certainly many would enjoy the salaciousness of a politician accused of rape by a woman he encountered twenty years earlier, but if the politician was a Democrat in a tight race with a Nationalist for the Senate seat of a "border" state, then it was deemed in bad taste to air.

Racist graffiti on the side of a barn in Montana would be national news, even if the local community vehemently disowned it. This would not be the case with economic figures that showed booming growth in these cultural backwaters (the so-called Red States) however, since it would appear to contradict the editorial consensus on what was best for America.

As her assistant buzzed to tell her that Rahim was on the phone, Bernice held pictures in her hands that her viewers would never see. They showed the aftermath of the latest café bombing in Paris, in which five French patrons were killed in mid-bite by an Islamist bomber. She set them down on top of a pile of other stories of violence from across Europe. With the end of the Pillar project under Hawking, GNN's editorial position was that Europeans should not be allowed into the United States either, no matter how many of them wanted to emigrate from countries they no longer felt safe in, which many were blaming on the effects of Islamic immigration. Bernice privately felt that the U.S. would be far better off without such xenophobes anyway.

"Rahim, how goes it?"

"Hello my friend. I hope you're doing well."

"Yes." She wondered what he was calling to complain about now. In the past, she had heard directly from him whenever GNN aired an item that hinted at Islamic violence, no matter how hard they tried to scrub their stories. Regardless of how blunt the terrorists themselves were about their religious motives, GNN always strove to present each bombing or shooting as if it were entirely independent of anything other than random pathology. They even took caution not to say the name of the terrorist, if it were Islamic or Arab, unless it was absolutely necessary.

"I'll get right to it, because I know this is your weekend. Have you heard about the hate crime in South Carolina against an innocent Muslim? A boy was killed, Bernice, by an angry, white male – a genuine Southern bigot. Do you think GNN might be interested in that?"

With her free hand, Bernice swept the non-newsworthy pile of photographs and news articles from the edge of her desk and into her office trash can. She replaced it with a fresh pad of paper, which she then began tapping anxiously with a pen.

"I'm listening."

Sunday September 7th, 2036
Ila, South Carolina

On the way back into town from a planned fishing trip over a long weekend, Felipe turned on the radio for the first time in days to find that Ila was the center of a national media circus over the shooting death of Nidal Phad four days earlier. He also learned that the police had arrested Leeman Arnold in his absence, which didn't sound right, given that he had personally cleared him to return home.

As he started to pass the subdivision where the Arnold family lived, he noticed a remarkable amount of activity for that time of the night. News vans were mixed with a lot of ordinary passenger cars, nearly all of which were parked illegally. *Where were his officers*, he wondered, easing his car down the street. He could see batteries of bright lights near the end, outside the Arnold home. Traffic was so bad that he eventually pulled his car into someone's front yard and got out to walk the hundred yards or so to the house.

It was a mad scene. Angry protesters were yelling obscenities and waving signs for the cameras. Cables and lights were everywhere. Felipe slipped through the crowd and made his way to the front door, past a phalanx of reporters, some of whom were conducting live newscasts. The house had been badly vandalized, with graffiti and broken windows. Shrubbery was torn up from the yard.

As he knocked on the door, a woman, standing behind him with a microphone in her hand, told him that they weren't answering.

Felipe knocked again. "This is the sheriff!" he yelled.

That was a mistake. Suddenly the news people converged on him, pressing him against the door. He had a hundred questions thrown at him, none of which he had any intention of answering.

Fortunately the door opened a crack. Felipe could see Leeman's wife peering through. She grabbed his elbow to pull him in and they both turned to press the door shut against the crush of reporters. The inside of the house was a mess. Broken glass was everywhere. Furniture was strewn about and cardboard covered the windows. He could see the family huddling fearfully in the hallway.

Leeman's wife told him that it had been like that since a squad car came by Friday night to take her husband away. The reporters and demonstrators started showing up the next day. They had called for the police several times, but no one came.

"We'll see about that," said Felipe. He went over to the phone and called the station, ordering that they send at least two cars over to disperse the crowd. His next call was to the mayor, after learning that he was the one who ordered Leeman's arrest.

"Well, I hope you had a good day off," said the man, as if Felipe was a child returning from Holiday break.

Felipe ignored him. "Why did you order Leeman Arnold arrested," he asked.

"Because he shot and killed a young boy."

"That 'boy' was a 20-year-old burglar on his property," responded the sheriff. "The story checked out. I checked it out."

"Well, the prosecutor looked into it and decided to press charges. We were only…"

"Why would he have done that without talking to me?" asked Felipe, knowing very well that it would have been on the mayor's personal order.

"Look Posada, I realize that you may have trouble understanding the anger that the Muslim community is feeling over…"

"Oh don't give me that crap," snapped Felipe. "I processed the crime scene myself. The forensic evidence from the garage is as plain as day. There are blast marks, blood stains, graffiti and even a handgun to prove that Leeman Arnold is telling the truth about what happened."

"Well the handgun wasn't registered to the victim," replied the mayor coolly, "and it had not been fired that night. On the other hand, Mr. Arnold has admitted that he owned his shotgun illegally."

"Everyone with a gun owns it illegally," shouted Felipe, "since they made it a Federal crime to possess one! This obviously explains why the handgun wasn't registered, since it would have meant confiscation. As for it not being fired, well, a man shouldn't have to take his chances by being shot at, before he's justified in defending himself on his own property. Besides, the garage…"

"Oh, haven't you heard, Sheriff? The garage doesn't exist anymore."

Felipe felt the hair rise on the back of his neck. He looked up and immediately saw the fear in Mrs. Arnold's eyes as she stood in front of her children, clutching the doorframe for support.

Carefully, he laid the phone down and went to the window; where he peeled back some of the cardboard from a corner. With all of the people milling about on the way in, he had missed seeing that there was nothing but a pile of charred wood at the end of the driveway where the garage once sat. Even now, there were several men with beards picking through the rubble.

There was a sick feeling in the pit of his stomach, as he went back over to the table, picked up the receiver and laid it back into the cradle, not caring whether the mayor was still on the line. He looked at the family.

"You need to get your most important things together, because I'm going to be back in a few hours to get you out of here. Now, where's the back door?"

He passed a couple of patrol cars on his way into town, responding to his call. At least he still had control of the department, or part of it anyway.

There were a few more news vans outside the station. He pulled around back and let himself in the side door. Without saying hello to anyone, he went straight down to the basement to look for the box of evidence related to the shooting incident. Surprisingly, it was still there, but it felt lighter than he knew it should have as he pulled it down from the shelf.

Opening it, he found that the gun was missing, although it might have been removed for testing purposes. What concerned him more than anything, however, was the binder with his notes and photographs. His heart was beating hard when he pulled it open.

The notes were still there. The photographs were not.

Thursday September 11th, 2036
New York, New York

The location for the thirty-fifth anniversary of the resistance attacks of 9/11 had to be moved at the last minute because of credible reports that al-Qaeda was planning a truck bomb attack against the lower Manhattan ceremony. The event took place instead on Ellis Island, where access was more controlled.

This year, there was even more emphasis on the suffering of Muslim-Americans following the attacks. This built on the working trend to shape the annual memorial into an event that gave equal tribute to the victims of Islamophobia.

Half of the speakers were Muslims old enough to remember the climate of "fear and intimidation" that followed the attacks. Some spoke of how they were verbally insulted or how their property was vandalized. This was in keeping with the memorial's theme: "America's Tragedy, America's Shame."

The biggest moment in the commemoration, however, came when Parker Whitehead climaxed his remarks with a reference to the events in South Carolina.

"Add one more name to the list of 3,000, America," the Reverand said dramatically. "Add one more name to the list of victims. Add my brother... our brother, Nidal Phad!"

The roar of the crowd carried across the water.

Friday September 12th, 2036
Ila, South Carolina

His footsteps echoed off the cinder-block walls around him, changing in tone as he moved further down the hallway and toward a room at the end that he knew well. No jail that he had ever visited had carpeting, not even in the offices or the reception areas. Neither were there any bright colors, other than the jumpsuits that the inmates wore. It was a depressing place even to visit. He could hardly imagine having to live there.

At the end of the hall was a heavy door that led into a private room, where a man was waiting for him at a table with shackles on his ankles. He was a big man, with close-cropped hair, a red face and a large pot-belly. He looked up with an air of expectation as Walid al-Rahahti entered, but didn't say anything.

Walid gave him a hard look, then set his briefcase on the table and opened it. He removed a few items, including a notepad, and set them on the table before sitting down.

He stared straight at Leeman Arnold. This was the first time that he could remember seeing him in twenty-five years, although his picture had been well-publicized as of late. Suffice it to say, the man looked like an older version of the bully that used to torment him thirty years ago, except that now he was the one fighting fear.

Walid understood this, and indulged himself just a few short seconds to relish the moment. The life of the man who made his own life miserable so long ago was now in his hands. Leeman was at rock bottom. He couldn't even leave the room they were in under his own volition, or use the bathroom without permission. Walid was free and entirely in control.

"I hear that you're the only one that would take my case," said the larger man, breaking the silence.

"I'm the only one who volunteered to take it," corrected Walid. "You have a Constitutional right to representation, so the court would have appointed someone, I'm sure."

"I'm not," said Leeman.

Walid looked down for a moment, at his blank pad, then raised his eyes and locked them onto Leeman's own. "My name is Walid al-Rahahti," he said.

There was no response. No flicker of recognition or any indication that Leeman remembered him at all.

"How's my family?" he asked.

Walid picked his words carefully. "Your home was burned to the ground two nights ago, as I'm sure you know. Your family is currently living under police protection."

"I know that," said Leeman, dropping his eyes down to the table. "I just want to know if they'll be all right."

"Oh, they should be OK… *'alrighty'* you might say, although your kids will more than likely be in for a pretty rough time at school."

Leeman looked up. Now there was that flicker of recognition that Walid was secretly hoping to see.

"What did you say? Alrighty?"

"Did I?"

"I knew you growing up, didn't I? You were that Arab kid that I used to pick on… weren't you?"

Walid didn't reply.

Leeman sat back, with a look of resignation on his face.

"I see now why you volunteered for this. I guess I'll be seeing if they do appoint me someone after all, won't I? Well listen to this."

He leaned forward and crossed his arms on the table in front of him. Walid stayed still.

"I did some stupid things when I was young. I didn't have to get religion to know that. You know what happened? I'll tell you. My kids have been run out of school by people like you… friends of yours maybe. My daughter's had her shirt and bra pulled off by a bunch of Arabs, who left bruises on her body after cornering her after school one day. My son came home so many times with blood seeping out of his head, that we finally stopped sending him out of the house."

Leeman's voice was trembling. "And what do you have to complain about? Some asshole kid used to follow you around and call you names. Well, I'm sorry that happened. I don't know why it happened. I wish I knew; then I could tell you why. Maybe it had something to do with having to watch my father get drunk every weekend and beat up my mother. Maybe it had to do with getting picked on myself back when…"

"Mr. Arnold," said Walid evenly, "we don't have much time. I would strongly advise you to reconsider your decision, and accept my counsel. You may not realize it, but right now I'm the best lawyer in the entire country willing to take your case, and your best hope. Together we can beat this charge, and I give you my word that I will do my best."

Leeman began to cry.

Monday, September 15th, 2036
Washington, D.C.

The weather turned cooler over the weekend, and the breeze that Monday morning was stronger than usual. The leaves in the trees outside Maria Posada's window were swaying gently when her assistant buzzed to say that Mr. Kerry Conner was on the phone for her.

Whatever had been on her mind quickly vanished, as she got up to close the door and then returned to her desk to pick up the phone. She watched slowly as her finger moved to press the button for the line, marveling that three years worth of fear and apprehension could be relieved by such a tiny motion of her hand.

"Hello."

"Hello Maria, would you like to have dinner with me?"

"Yes." She answered plainly. There was no point in playing games anymore. She figured that he would only be in Washington for a few days anyway.

"How does November 27th sound?" he asked.

Apparently he was in Montana, and in no hurry to see her. Maria took it in stride, not letting her disappointment show. "This year or next?"

"This Thanksgiving, in Bozeman. I'll fly you in and put you up at the same hotel. My secretary will make the arrangements. Do you mind flying out of Baltimore?"

"I don't think so."

"Good. As you may have heard, the city of Washington has banned my company from flying out of Ronald Reagan. I'll see you in November."

Maria hung up the phone and let her thoughts wander like the wind that rustled the leaves in the crisp morning sunlight outside her window. What kind of a fool instantly agrees to fly all the way across the country to spend the afternoon with a group of people who invariably felt betrayed by her?

Someone who feels that she deserves the humiliation perhaps?

Monday, September 15th, 2036
Ila, South Carolina

Felipe Posada was reading a short article on the back page of the newspaper about the spate of deadly bombings by Islamic separatists in Maine, when he looked up to see a very familiar face peering at him through the glass door of his office. The odd thing about it was that it wasn't someone whom he thought he'd ever met. He sat at his desk staring for several long seconds at the face staring back at him, before realizing that it was someone that he knew from television. There were a lot of national news personalities in town these days.

Out of curiosity, he got up to open the door without waiting for the receptionist to buzz him. Just as he mentally exhausted the list of news anchors, the receptionist announced on his speaker that "a Ms. Sterling is here to see you."

Starr Sterling the actress! Felipe remembered watching Jenna's Army as a kid, though he didn't care much for The Advocate. He opened the door and beckoned her to come in, noting how much older she looked in person, although, as he did the math in his head, she should only be about ten years older than himself.

"Thank you, Sheriff. Thank you for seeing me." She swept into his office and deposited herself into a chair in dramatic fashion, where she sat facing Felipe's empty chair with a grim expression.

Felipe went back around the desk and sat down. He decided to be gracious. "I used to watch Jenna's Army as a boy, shortly after arriving from Mexico. I used it to help myself learn English."

"Good, good, glad to hear that," said the woman casually. "I'll get right to the point. I can see that you are a man of color and an immigrant to boot, so I'm sure that you are under a tremendous amount of pressure."

"Pardon?"

The actress leaned forward and clasped her hands together. "I'm speaking of the crisis in this town. This is why I'm here, to offer my support to you – to all the authorities."

Felipe gathered that she was speaking about the death of Nidal Phad, which was had caused an enormous commotion over the last week.

"What do you feel that you can do for us, Ms. Sterling?"

The actress looked down and gave a modest smile in a way that seemed rehearsed to the sheriff, who had gotten quite good at reading people over the years. "Well," she said, "I admit that I'm no forensics expert or prosecutor, but I am good at generating publicity. I know that you can probably use the support."

"You want to attract publicity to a case that was initially ruled to be justifiable self-defense?" asked Felipe, wondering if they had been talking about different things this whole time.

"Yes, of course," smiled the actress. "You see, I understand how the death of a black or brown person, particularly if it's at the hands of a white man, is likely to be ignored by the general public, which…"

"Did you not see all of the cameras and news trucks outside this office and all over town?" asked Felipe, somewhat incredulously.

"Well yes, but I was thinking that perhaps the Muslim community in Ila could use some reassurance that they are not alone in their grief or their quest for justice. That there are others in the country…"

"Listen," said Felipe, trying to keep the impatience out of his voice, "two weeks ago, a 20-year-old white kid was in a bad section of town in a car driven by his friend, when the police pulled them over. Drugs were found in the car, so it was impounded and the driver arrested. The passenger, who did nothing wrong, was left to walk home by himself through the rough neighborhood at night. He was quickly surrounded by a gang of black kids, who doused him with gasoline and burned him to death right there on the sidewalk."

The passive expression on Starr's face did not change.

Felipe continued. "There was barely a mention of this in the local newspapers, and certainly nothing in the national news. No one outside of his family seemed to give a damn about it at all. Why do you suppose that was?"

Sterling blinked a few times, evidently gathering her thoughts as she stared straight at the sheriff.

"Well," she finally said, "I want you to know that I'm here, in town, through Wednesday. Please let me know I can help you in any way."

With that, she reached over to shake Felipe's hand and turned to go.

The sheriff did not even bother rising out of his chair. He just sat and watched, shaking his head slightly.

Tuesday, September 16th, 2036
GNN Studios

Felipe could not resist watching GNN the next evening, after learning that Starr Sterling would be one of the guests on a live one-hour interview segment, concerning Ila. He was just starting on his microwave dinner when the show came on.

The GNN anchor prefaced the interview with a news clip, introducing "the latest" in what was being called a "possible hate crime." Felipe had to laugh at how seriously they were reporting mundane proceedings, such as Leeman meeting with his attorney, as if these were breaking news events. Finally, Starr Sterling was introduced on a satellite feed from Ila. She was looking comically somber and sitting between two women in black *hijabs*.

"Thank you, Steve. I'm sitting here with the mother and sister of young Nidal Phad, who, as you would expect, are heartbroken over what's happened. I've spent the afternoon with the family, talking with them and trying to comfort them as best I can."

Felipe had met with both women himself, although neither had been dressed like that at the time.

"Starr, tell me what the town is going through right now. How are the people coping?"

"There is shock here, Steve, and I can also say that there is shock all across America. This sort of violence against Muslim-Americans has reached epidemic proportions. It is an entire segment of our population that is under siege, and it's been like this for thirty-five years."

"One of our affiliates is reporting that a young man was burned to death in the same town not long before the shooting. What can you tell us about that?"

Felipe leaned forward. Was he about to be proven wrong? Would there be interest in that horrific killing after all?

Starr looked embarrassed. Both of the women with her gave puzzled looks.

"Uh, I talked to the sheriff about that yesterday morning, Steve. It's not a cause for concern."

"How so? Wasn't the victim a Muslim in that case as well?"

Starr raised her eyebrows and looked surprised. "I'm not sure about that. The sheriff didn't have time to provide me with details. My understanding is that the youths responsible for the burning were motivated by a righteous anger over the historical disenfranchisement of minorities. If the victim was Muslim then it must have been a case of mistaken..."

"Yes, I'm sorry Starr. I've just gotten further details and it does appear that this was an unrelated incident. So tell me, Starr, where does the energy come from? You seem to be involved in so many things these days, from boycotting corporations to reaching out to a family in need there in South Carolina. How are you able to give so much of yourself to others?"

Starr looked down with the same modest smile that Felipe recognized from the day before. "Well Steve, it's hard not to give when I see so much need in the world, particularly among people of color and those who are different in other ways, such as the Phad family here. I think I've always been driven to try and draw publicity to causes and people that might otherwise fall though the cracks, even though doing so isn't exactly popular among..."

Felipe flipped the channel.

Thursday, November 27th, 2036
Bozeman, Montana

Maria had called Kerry's secretary three times in the last two months to say that she would not be joining them for Thanksgiving. Each time, she was put on hold for a few seconds, before the secretary picked back up to declare that "Mr. Conner says he will see you in Bozeman that day. Is there anything else I can do for you?"

When the limo arrived at her apartment that morning, Maria was waiting with bags packed. She didn't say a word to the driver at any point during the 50-minute trip up I-95. He knew exactly what airline to drop her off at, and insisted that the fare was "taken care of" when she tried to pay him.

She had a first-class seat to Bozeman, where another driver was waiting to take her to the hotel. The air was crisp, and banks of snow were already piled up by the side of the road, as were that Thanksgiving three years earlier. She had been back twice since then, but never in winter.

The driver gave her an hour to get ready; then they were off, down the same winding highway that led out of town and into the mountains. She had only been down that road once before during the day, and then, of course, on the return trip that night, but she relived the drive so often in her mind since that the route seemed familiar, as if she were returning home.

There was a familiar SUV waiting at the turnoff, where the long drive began its climb up the mountain. Maria had been wondering how the limo was going to make it up the hill. Instead of Angela and the kids, it was just Hank waiting for her there with a grin on his face, as she got out and stepped gingerly through the slush. He waved to the limo driver and opened the passenger door for her, then went back around to the driver's side.

After a few pleasantries, Maria finally gave in to her apprehension. Before Hank could start the truck, she grabbed his wrist. "Do they hate me?" she asked.

The man pulled his arm back and sat back in his seat. The time that it took him to chew over his answer told her more than he might have been willing to admit. He spoke carefully, "Some of us understood. Others didn't. Kerry tried not to let anyone speak badly about you. After a time, we all stopped taking it personally and began to realize that it's just a part of the larger battle taking place for the soul of the country."

A gust of wind carried suddenly into the side of the truck, violently whipping ice granules against it.

Hank smiled and reached for the keys again. "Besides, if Kerry never held it against you, then how could anyone else? Ultimately it's his company, you know."

Fifteen minutes later, Maria could tell that Hank had been honest with her, although she didn't have the nerve to enter the house by herself. She waited until he came back to the porch after parking the truck, so that she could shrink behind him as they walked through the door.

Angela was waiting to take her coat, acting as if the last three years hadn't happened. Indeed, it looked very much the same as it had on that Thanksgiving before, even down to the last detail of the furniture, which had been engraved in her memory. Even the view outside the window was exactly as she had remembered, although the mountains were a little greener, since the trees weren't holding as much as much snow.

She did not immediately see Kerry. As if reading her thoughts, Angela said, "He's downstairs playing with the kids, but he'll be up soon, since we're about to eat."

In a few minutes there was a clamoring in the stairwell, as a stream of children began pouring up out of it and onto the main floor. She was surprised that she recognized nearly all of them except the youngest ones. Three years can have a dramatic effect on a child's appearance.

Finally, the owner of Airtana Airways emerged, looking somewhat less dignified than his position engendered, with a bawling toddler hanging from his neck. He handed the sobbing child off to her mother, turned, and immediately locked eyes with Maria on the opposite side of the room.

They might have stared at each other longer, oblivious to the people swirling around them, had the call to prayer not interrupted them. They stood on opposite sides of the large circle of friends, bowing their heads and holding hands with those around them.

She waited in line to gather her food then went to sit on the end of one of the stone hearths. The atmosphere was no different than it had been three years earlier. She wondered if the evening would end the same way, with the two of them sitting by the fire in the otherwise empty house.

"Thank you for coming," he said. Somehow she had missed him as he came up beside her with a plate of food in his hand.

"Did you miss me?" she asked.

"Yes."

He answered with the same bluntness as she had when accepting his invitation in September.

The rest of the afternoon passed at an excruciatingly slow pace for Maria, as she and Kerry mingled with the others. She gradually got over her awkwardness, realizing that she wasn't going to be punished for what she had done, as she had expected when the invitation was first extended. In her heart, however, she knew that it would have been different if she had not lost the verdict.

Snow was falling briskly outside when they stood on the porch and waved goodbye, as the last of the guests disappeared through the trees and into the fading light. They stood for a moment, appreciating the peaceful-ness of the moment, with the soft flakes falling silently around them.

Back inside, Kerry went through the house, turning off lights just as the electricity went out. The gentle hum of a gas generator automatically started up outside. Kerry paused for a moment then went downstairs to cut it off, leaving just the heat and gentle noise of the fire. By the time he returned, Maria had two chairs pulled up to the hearth and was comforta-bly buried in an oversized throw.

They were deep in conversation for hours, barely giving the fire enough attention to keep it from dying. The flames cast shadows on the walls around them as the wind howled outside the windows. Not once did they talk about what had happened over the last three years.

Maria told him about her father's death and how it changed her. Kerry talked about the death of his own father when he was twelve and what had been said to him that afternoon on the soft knoll that overlooked the peaceful valley set against a west Texas mountain range. They knew that nothing was being held back now.

It was after three in the morning when he went out to get the truck. As before, she stood on the porch, shivering in the cold and watching the snow swirl around her coat and into the darkness.

As they were slowly inching down the mountain, toward the main road, Maria finally said, "Kerry, I'm sorry."

"You don't have to be," he replied.

"I just needed to know if…" Even after all they had shared with each other she still couldn't bring herself to say it. "I just needed to know…"

"Then it was all worth it," he said, understanding.

They reached the road and drove slowly along, with the soft glow from the dash in the warm cab exactly as she remembered, as well as the headlights cutting against the darkness and the snow that fell madly in and out of the beams. She had relived this experience a thousand times in her mind.

They rounded the last bend and he pulled down the main street, fi-nally passing the first vehicle of the drive, a snow plow that was vainly attempting to keep the road clear.

Kerry pulled up slowly to her hotel, where there were not many lights on. She undid the seatbelt and put her hand on the handle, pausing before slowly pushing open the door.

The harsh wind whipped into the cab, but she found that she couldn't move to get out. He didn't say anything either, as she sat there frozen for two or three minutes, with both of them oblivious to the icy air and snow-flakes rushing past her.

Without getting out, she pulled the door shut.

The truck was in gear before she could even reach for the seatbelt.

Thursday, December 4th, 2036
Washington, D.C.

Whoever had the bright idea for an outdoor ceremony should be shot, thought Senator Jill Hudson, as she fought to keep the smile on her face against a bitter wind. It was one of those rare days, when the temperature actually drops over the course of the afternoon. The morning had been balmy for that time of the year, but the sky had only gotten grayer and now they were huddled around the table, trying not to shiver in front of the press corps.

The Executive Order that her father was in the process of signing had been too controversial to consider before the November election. His Vice President had won a very close victory; too close, in fact, to exercise the sort of recklessness that previous Administrations habitually enjoyed during the "lame duck" months before leaving office.

The Order that was the subject of that afternoon's ceremony on the White House lawn extended hate crimes protection to religious minorities. No further specificity was provided, but everyone knew that it was meant to address the plight of Muslim-Americans against the desecration of the Qur'an and other clearly provocative offenses that tended to incite rioting and acts of violence. A special agency within the Bureau of Islamic Relations was being created to work in cooperation with the Justice Department to establish guidelines for defining such crimes.

The prosecution of hate crimes was always an uncertain area in which extenuating factors had to be considered. The mere use of the 'N-word,' for example did not necessarily denote racist intentions, since it was frequently used within the African-American community. Likewise, words such as "queer" and "fag" were acceptable among homosexuals, so long as it was one of their own employing such language.

The Department of Cultural Affairs (DCA) required a sophisticated system with a great number of employees arranged in hierarchical committees to analyze ambiguous statements against the circumstances and background of the speakers to determine if hate crimes were in fact committed. Generally at least three members of a specialized panel (consisting of members of the identity group in question) were required to agree that they were in a state of offense.

Standing with the Senator, was Rahim Sahil (whose group, BAIR, pressed hard for the Executive Order) along with a Muslim boy who had lost an eye in the rioting that followed a reported "mishandling" of the Qur'an by a Federal official during an interrogation session with a terrorist implicated in the Metro bombing.

If such mishandlings were enough to force the followers of the religion of peace into violence, then it only spoke to the dire situation that the government had put them in by failing to protect their sensibilities. Hopefully the expansion of Hate Crimes prosecution would quell the periodic unrest, by confirming to the Muslim community that the government was no less committed to religious tolerance and respect than were their own leaders.

"Muslim-Americans are among our most socially conscious citizens," said her father, in his scripted remarks to the press corps prior to signing the Order. "Members of this community played prominent roles in the peaceful efforts to end the war in Iraq. Muslims have also pressed undauntedly for religious plurality and taken the rest of us to task when we have shamefully neglected our duties in this area, as is the case in the matters that this legislation hopes to amend. There is no further proof needed of the promise of peace and tolerance that Islam offers to the world, than the commitment that Muslims have made to pursue these standards right here in America..."

Saturday, December 6th, 2036
Ila, South Carolina

The streets of Ila were finally beginning to clear. The news vans, with their antennas and satellite dishes, were fewer, now that the trial date was set eight months away. Felipe didn't expect to see them out in full force again until then. It was the same with all of the celebrities that showed up to have their picture taken in the demonstrations (preferably with their bodyguards out of the frame).

When the phone at his desk rang, he figured that it was another network wanting his opinion on the Hate Crimes order signed by the President a few days before. Although he didn't say it, he had enough real crime to worry about in South Carolina without having to discern what people were thinking while they were doing it. In addition to the rising ethnic violence, the state was beginning to see a number of honor killings within the Muslim community, in which women were murdered by their families for alleged impropriety. It was tough getting convictions, because the families and the community tended to close ranks.

"Hey Felipe!" It was his friend Kerry Conner, calling from Montana.

"Well, hey there *mi amigo*! How are you?"

"Doing better than you are, I suppose. I hear there's some excitement down in your neck of the woods."

"Yes," said Felipe. "Excitement I could do without."

"Well, it's about to get more exciting for you. I'm marrying your sister."

Felipe was glad that he was sitting down. He only had two sisters, and one was happily married in Dallas. He was so surprised that he was nearly speechless. "Maria... the lesbian?"

"She's not lesbian," said Kerry.

After a few seconds, Felipe asked suspiciously, "How would you know?"

"Aren't you going to ask how we met?"

"I know how you met. I was there... remember? You were twelve and she was two."

"You know what I mean."

"Does she know that you used to sit behind her in our living room and toss sunflower seeds in her hair while she tried to watch TV?" asked Felipe.

"She has no clue," replied Kerry.

"This is really good news, even if it is shocking. Tell me more." Felipe leaned back and sighed. This was the best news to come his way in a long time.

Sunday, December 28th, 2036
New York, New York

"The Leeman Arnold Story" beat the made-for-TV movies of rival networks by two days. It was qualified as being a "dramatization, based on actual events," and it took a fair measure of artistic latitude before Phyllis was satisfied with the script.

The movie begins with the young Nidal Phad growing up as a wise and loving child in South Carolina, where his parents immigrated before he was born. Despite the bigotry of the white community, the boy exhibits tremendous grace and saves the lives of both a bully who teases him, and a crippled homosexual who is threatened by a group of angry Southern homophobes.

Nidal's dream of attending a local college is crushed when school administrators candidly tell him that as a Muslim in America, his scores must be "twice as high as a Christian's" before he can be considered for admission. He resolves to work on his test scores, while taking a part-time job at a local grocery.

The store is run by Leeman Arnold, a respected community leader and head of the Ku Klux Klan. He tells Phad that he is only hiring him because of "them damn bleeding heart liberals in Washington."

"If you make one mistake, boy, then I'll kill you," drawls Leeman as he spits tobacco juice on the floor, before ordering the lad to clean it up.

In the movie, Nidal becomes a model employee, whose work ethic and friendly attitude save the business. Unfortunately, it also gives Leeman's daughter an opportunity to steal from the till. Nidal brings the matter to her father, who destroys the evidence and accuses the boy, himself, of stealing.

After firing him, Leeman is unable to let the incident go and harasses Nidal on the street. He follows the boy to both his home and to his mosque, vandalizing both, as peaceful Muslims stand by, refraining from intervention for fear that it might lead to violence, which is "not the way of Islam."

At the movie's dramatic conclusion, Leeman calls Nidal and tells him that he wants him to come by for a meeting in his garage. In the last scene, Nidal opens the door, sees the gun, and says "Please, Mr. Arnold, in the name of Allah…"

The screen fades to black, as two shots are heard.

Wednesday, December 31ˢᵗ, 2036
New York, New York

"Marvelous!" exclaimed the man in the tuxedo.

"Simply brilliant!" said another, standing next to him. "I love the way you seemed to personify Islamophobia in the character of Leeman Arnold."

"Yes, thank you," said Phyllis shyly. "I wanted to objectively capture the evil that would cause a person to kill someone else simply for being different."

Beth Landau came over to join them, dressed in a stunning New Year's Eve gown and swilling a glass of champagne. "I loved it, my dear. It takes courage to produce something like that in this day and age."

"Yes," said the first man, "that's the word I was looking for. It is truly a courageous film. It isn't easy to criticize racism and bigotry, but you've shown true grit in doing what you did."

He took a half step back and raised his glass. "To Phyllis."

"To Phyllis!" said the rest, as she modestly received their toast.

2038

Wednesday, January 13ᵗʰ, 2038
Rothberg, California

Professor Rothermel sat in his chair, staring up at the mountains on the edge of the community. They would have made a better backdrop for the televised interview, but those damned Indians had now shaved the nearest ones and were putting up large homes that looked out over the valley.

When their intentions became evident, the Professor had driven into the National Park to see Chief Manasas. Of course, it wasn't much of a park anymore. There were trailers everywhere, some of them with sanitation problems that contributed to a malodorous stench that varied according to the direction of the wind. On warm days, it drifted down into parts of the Rothberg community. The chief and other privileged members of the Kiwok tribe were building expensive homes for themselves on the mountain, high above the rest, with proceeds from the new casino. Hardly anyone up there except the chief was a true Kiwok. Most had bought their way into the tribe by purchasing honorary memberships, which gave them the rights to purchase land for personal use.

The chief and his wife, whom Rothermel simply called Eunice, having since forgotten her supposed Kiwok name, lived in an enormous log home, located on the very spot that the "blessing of the mountain" ceremony was held seven years ago. Rothermel would never have recognized it. Even the natural stone platform the two had stood on then was replaced by a four-car garage. The view was heartbreaking. Most of the valley behind the mountain had been clear-cut. The virgin forests were gone, including giant redwoods that had stood for over a thousand years.

The chief came out to meet him, having known that he was coming after Rothermel identified himself to the security station at the foot of the mountain. He was no longer wearing buckskin or beads anymore, and looked very much like the guy who used to run the body shop down the road before his fortunes changed. His beard was grown a little longer, but his hair was cut.

He transferred the beer bottle into his left hand and reached out with the other. "What do you think, Professor? Have you been up here since we put the house in?"

Rothermel told him what he thought of both it and the rest of the development, which was very nearly the end of their conversation. Chief Manasas straightened up as the professor lit into him. His face turned deep red around an imposing frown. After Rothermel had his say, the chief bluntly responded, "You and your kind have been telling my people

where and how we should live for centuries, since you first came and stole
our land from us. I see that nothing has changed."

The Professor stared open-mouthed. "Good God! Do you not remember that I'm the one who helped you get this land? The least you
could do is respect it, particularly when I have to look up at it everyday.
There should be zoning laws in…"

"Zoning laws are for white people," interrupted the chief. "Do I look
white to you?"

Actually he did, but Rothermel decided not to press it.

The chief went on. "This is our land, Professor. We earned it by surviving your massacres… your genocide. We are the rightful owners of all
of this land, which you white people call 'California'." He pronounced
the word as if it were foreign to him, which sounded ridiculous to Rothermel, who knew the man's background better than anyone. "There is nothing," continued the chief, "that gives you the right to tell us what we can
and can't do with our own land. Surely you know your own shameful
history? Isn't what you did to our mothers and fathers much worse than
what we could ever do to a tree?"

Now, nearly eight months later, the Professor was still fuming over
the situation. He had not been back to see the chief, nor did he even attempt to enlist the support of the state, since his lawyers had ensured the
complete autonomy of the Kiwok land seven years earlier.

He barely noticed the young woman applying make-up to his face.
He turned to look behind him, at the community buildings that would
serve as the backdrop for the interview. From a distance they wouldn't
look so bad. The visible sides had been freshly painted in the last few
days, as the residents prepared for the attention that was expected with the
release of the movie.

The Professor frowned a bit when he saw new graffiti on a wall that
had just been freshly painted. They were never able to stay more than a
few days ahead of the "urban artists," as some still preferred to call them.
It wasn't enough that the council had designated certain areas for such
expression, given that they didn't want to completely muzzle this non-
violent form of protest, but the graffiti artists simply saw these rules as
another form of repression, and rebelled by drawing their pictures and
slogans specifically in the places where they were most unwelcome.

Breaking the windmills and smashing solar panels must have been
another form of political expression, as well, not that either one of these
ever generated the wattage to justify the original cost or on-going maintenance. Rothermel turned back around, nearly having his eye poked by the
cosmetics prep, who was valiantly trying to adjust to his shifting position.

"We're on in fifteen," yelled an assistant. The make-up person gave a
last gingerly swipe and quickly scurried out of the way as the producer

began a countdown with his fingers, before giving the thumbs up sign. Rothermel's attention was drawn to a television screen next to the camera, where he could see the anchors from the morning show look up and address the audience.

"Welcome back. This Friday, America will at long last have the opportunity to see the much anticipated movie, "The Community," with Starr Sterling. Of course the movie is based on the real life California project that so captured the public's imagination several years ago. We're fortunate to have Professor Rothermel with us this morning, live on satellite from Rothberg itself. Good morning, Professor!"

Rothermel softly cleared his throat. "Good morning to you Katie."

"Tell us first of all, have you seen the movie?"

"I have not seen it yet, Katie, but I hope to this weekend. We're very excited about it."

"I assume that you'll be watching it there in the community, where I understand you have your own theater?"

"Uh… yes." Actually he had been planning to drive down to Sacramento on Saturday. There were usually a lot of noisy teenagers in the community's theatre that tended to ruin the experience for the others there. It was the same way with the shared recreation center, which was nearly always taken over with a full-court basketball game that left no room for anyone else to enjoy the gym.

This had been a source of controversy not long ago, when Rothermel and several others had approached both the kids and their parents about the behavior. The parents openly speculated that they were being targeted because of their ethnicity, which Rothermel failed to anticipate; and so this ended any further effort to control the atmosphere at the shared facilities, including the theatre. Rothermel did not attend shows there anymore, nor did most other members of the community, although the theatre was still a significant part of the entertainment budget.

"Professor, there was a lot of excitement when your community was first proposed, along with a lot of skepticism as well. People said that it would not work because…"

"Because they couldn't see people of all races living together," finished the Professor for her. "Well, it's typical of the bigotry that…"

"Actually I was going to say that it had more to do with the civic infrastructure that was being proposed," said the host, with a rather firm edge to her voice. Rothermel decided not to interrupt her again during the interview. "For example," she continued, "the community has no jails and not even a police force. That's hard for the rest of us to imagine. Tell us about that."

Rothermel chuckled. "Well Katie, we break a lot of the rules and traditions that are supposed to govern how people live together. We do this because they don't work. If you look at America today, you see that it is stratified by social order. Wealth and status create barriers between the layers of society, which in turn causes the friction that leads to social problems. All of the so-called pathologies that exist in the world are the result of inequities. If the inequities are eliminated, then harmony will follow."

"But to live without a police force…" interjected the host.

"The police exist merely to preserve the social order," insisted Rothermel. "But it is the social order itself that produces the disenfranchisement and unfulfilled desires that produce crime. Are people who commit crime worse than the rest of us? Of course not. Their only difference is that they have needs that the rest of us don't."

"What sort of a need causes a person to rape or murder?"

Rothermel swallowed. He had not anticipated such a hard question, and had to choose his words carefully. "Such crimes are the extreme manifestations of the catastrophic frustration that many on the edges of our society feel from being denied access to the mainstream."

He paused and looked down to collect his thoughts, trying to preempt the next question. "Certainly there are many with the same experiences of nonfulfillment, who manage to rise above their righteous anger in constructive ways, but…" he looked back up into the camera, "but surely this speaks to the true virtue in all of us. In our community, we eliminate the obstacles to egalitarianism, plain and simple."

He hoped that he would not be asked about Judi, the "singing resident" who sang her last note before the rape. The community had handled the matter internally. The rapist was not identified, since doing so might have caused ill feelings toward the minority group to which he belonged. The man fled anyway, and Judi left a few months later. It was a tragic, but isolated incident.

"Tell us about how the community finances work, because this is intriguing as well."

Rothermel gave a sly smile. "Well Katie, that seems to be the most difficult thing for those outside of our community to fully understand. Eliminating artificial social boundaries means abolishing economic ones as well. We operate collectively, with a system in which needs and abilities are determined independently of one another."

"Well, how does this actually work? Is there a common fund that everyone contributes to? How do you determine expenses?"

The Professor enjoyed speaking in theoretical terms a lot more than explaining the practical working of the community's finances. In fact, the system was a constant source of friction that had only gotten worse over the years. In theory, those who did not hold jobs outside the community to bring in common income, were expected to contribute by performing civic duties, such as cutting grass or painting over the damn graffiti that kept popping up.

The reality was somewhat different, as the initial enthusiasm of those who were not working, and who came from lower income backgrounds, seemed to be waning. The council was trying to come up with various solutions for the problem, but in the meantime, it was typical to see those who worked jobs during the week, out in their yards on the weekends, cutting their own grass, while the yards of those tasked as community caretakers grew unabated.

"Katie, what belongs to one of us belongs to all of us." He gave a nervous chuckle. "We all have jobs to do and I don't think anyone even remembers anymore which ones bring in 'money,' and which ones contribute directly to our social well-being by, for example, enhancing our cultural awareness with neighborhood plays and musical productions."

He cleared his throat. "But to answer your question, yes, there is a common pool of funds and it is divided equally among the households, depending on size."

The professor looked closely at his image in the monitor, where movement distracted his attention. It looked as if there were people standing behind him. Absent-mindedly, he turned to see what was happening.

Two of the older kids from the community were engaged in various antics for the cameras. One had both of his middle fingers extended. The other was simulating masturbation. They both laughed when they saw Rothermel's angry expression, but did not break their poses. He turned back to find the camera almost in his face as the operator was attempting to pull a tight close-up that would obscure the lewd foolishness going on behind him.

"Well," said the host, clearly embarrassed, "it looks like you've got your own fans there with you, Professor."

"Yes, we don't judge here at the community," said the red-faced man. "Rothberg is not a place for passing moral judgment on others…"

Saturday, February 20th, 2038
Bozeman, Montana

Kerry told him that some thought was given to El Paso, but Felipe knew from the way Maria talked about Montana, a few weeks after the engagement, that there was no question where the wedding would be held. Kerry had no roots in Texas anymore, and Maria had developed a strong emotional attachment to the rugged, beautiful land of her new home.

Much to Maria's surprise, Felipe had visited them there before the wedding. That was when she first found out the secret that her fiancé and brother had kept from her, about their close friendship. "I taught him to speak English, Maria," Kerry said modestly, "that's why he never lost his accent."

"And he already knew Spanish before we met," responded Felipe, "which is why he doesn't have one."

Maria took it better than they expected. She seemed embarrassed that Kerry had known her when she was a child, and wanted to know everything that he remembered about her, gradually accepting that none of it obviously mattered to him anymore. Finding out everything finally solved the mystery of how it was that Kerry happened to call her "Pepita" at times.

Felipe was surprised to see that she was still sleeping in the guest room six months after their engagement, although at some point between then and the wedding, she moved into her husband's bedroom. He knew it wasn't his business.

Felipe could barely believe the change in his sister. The spoiled brat that was in Aunt Sarah's face fifteen years ago (which he gracefully declined to remind her of) had more than matured during that time. Her opinions on freedom and success had changed nearly 180 degrees, as well as the consideration with which she treated others. There was a dignified confidence about her now, as there had been in her husband for as long as Felipe could remember.

She was happy; happy in Montana and happy with Kerry.

Felipe was best man at the ceremony. He couldn't stop grinning for the entire three days. Each time Maria or Kerry would see him, they would tell him to "shut up," even though he hadn't said anything. It was one of the happiest times in his life, and certainly the most unexpected.

Thursday, February 25th, 2038
Columbia, South Carolina

Walid stood beside Leeman Arnold, with his hand on the shoulder of his former bully as the jurors filed into the room. As with all defense attorneys, he had prepared his client for the guilty verdict by telling him that it was probable. This measure was designed to minimize the risk of outbursts in the event that the jury decided against his client. Privately, however, he harbored much higher hopes.

He had done his best to pick a neutral jury, without regard for ethnic or cultural characteristics. As a Muslim himself, he knew that his faith sometimes inspired the best in people, so he did not arbitrarily exclude members of what the media was calling 'the affected community' from the panel. In the end, he felt that he had done a good job of exploiting the prosecution's shallow 'skin-deep' methodology of picking only minorities, by carefully examining background and demeanor to find the most open-minded jurors.

He played up the wanton character traits of Nidal Phad during the trial, trying to dispel the prejudices that were bound to have risen in the minds of anyone even the least bit familiar with the media's version of the case. Fortunately, the Arnolds had thought to remove supporting videotape from their business and residence before both structures were burned to the ground. It plainly showed Nidal stealing from the store, as well as his harassing behavior since being fired.

At the end of the day, no one wanted to feel unsafe in their own home, or to be harassed on the street. That it was a member of one's own ethnic group or religion breaking into their home at night would hardly be of solace to the victims. Walid wanted the jury to transcend the inconsequential circumstances of the case and put themselves into Leeman Arnold's shoes that night.

Since much of the physical evidence was destroyed, most of the defense argument regarding the events of the shooting hung on the credibility of Sheriff Felipe Posada, who testified brilliantly in support of Leeman's version of events. His earnestness and humble bearing seemed to resonate with the jurors.

Of course, none of this made any difference with the atmosphere outside the courtroom, where massive demonstrations gathered on a daily basis in front of the battery of lights and cameras. It wasn't hard to guess where most unemployed South Carolinians stood on the issue – nor the vast majority of other Americans. No one wanted to speak out publicly on his client's behalf, although Walid knew that there were many who would have made the same decision, in a darkened garage, facing an armed intruder.

Through it all, Leeman remained composed, almost resigned to his fate. He once told Walid that regardless of what happened to him, he would be just as satisfied to know that his family was taken care of, even if he wasn't there to do it. The two men never spoke about their shared past again. It had been put behind them during that first visit.

The jury finished filing into the box.

"Madame Forewoman, have you reached a verdict?"

"We have your honor."

Walid could feel Leeman trembling through the thick jacket. Both men held their breath.

Friday, February 26th, 2038
Bozeman, Montana

Their honeymoon lasted all of a day and a half. By Monday morning, they heard the news that Airtana was banned from SFO, the San-Francisco airport, because it did not provide benefits to domestic partners.

Maria spent the next five days on the phone, in blue jeans and a pony-tail, working like mad to maintain a presence in the area for the airline. On Friday she finally got a confirmation from the San Jose city council, which saved the jobs of their Bay area employees. She went home early to celebrate.

Saturday, February 27th, 2038
GNN Studios

"Welcome back to GNN. It's been a very busy couple of days for us here in the studio, as well as for many law enforcement officials in so many cities across America, particularly along the East Coast, as rioting as has claimed the lives of nearly sixty people so far in the wake of the Leeman Arnold acquittal.

"You're looking at live scenes now of Boston, which has a large Muslim community that is quite sympathetic to the Maine independence movement and very upset over the events in South Carolina. As you can see, it's not a pretty picture.

"We're joined by Rahim Sahil, the founder of BAIR – the Board on American Islamic Relations – who is on the phone with us from Washing-ton. Rahim, what can you tell us about the outrage in the Muslim com-munity?"

"That it's very tangible, Steve. For decades now, we've seen our faith spit on by others. We've been taunted, humiliated…. A good friend of mine bought a used Qur'an that had been desecrated. A mosque down in Houston once had dead fish dumped in its parking lot. Clearly America is not committed to ensuring religious tolerance…"

"Excuse me for a second, Rahim, but we're getting footage right now of what appears to be a young man dragged from his truck and beaten in the head with bricks and what looks like a fire extinguisher. Are you see-ing what were seeing?"

"Absolutely, and I can tell you that this is a righteous anger…"

"My God, it looks like he's being beaten to death… I'm sorry, Ra-him, what was it you were saying?"

"It's a righteous anger, Steve. Muslims have lived like second-class citizens in America for so long now; and this case, of a jury acquitting a bigot who goes out and shoots a Muslim boy to death is simply confirma-tion of it."

"Rahim, what will it take to stop the violence? As you know, Federal charges are…"

"I'll tell you Steve, allowing all Muslims in America the option of civil *Sharia* courts would be a good start. The system has worked well in Maine. I know that it is being considered in South Carolina and Massa-chusetts. Muslims in America tend to become lost in the secular courts that do not understand our laws, with the result being that we don't feel free to practice our religion. What is happening today is a manifestation of this frustration."

Grandfather Mountain, North Carolina

Walid watched the coverage on GNN with utter disgust. Rahim Sahil was a race-merchant, feeding off manufactured grievances. A real leader would stand up and speak the truth, moderate the anger, and subdue the violence. Instead, this man was doing what he could to stoke the flames for his own personal benefit.

He went to the window of the hotel room and looked out on a very different scene, where the sun was bright against the dull mountains. Pine trees mixed in among the bare branches of deciduous trees in winter. From his room, he could see the peak of the highest mountain, towering above. He desperately wanted to get out of the room and scale the side of it – as high as he could climb in the cool crisp air, but he knew that the Marshals would never allow it.

He had been under Federal protection since the moment of the verdict, but this was something he could live with – for a time. What bothered him more than anything was what was happening to Leeman Arnold right now.

He felt a shudder of relief wash through his client when the verdict was read. The big man sat down immediately, with his knees too weak to support him. His family and friends openly cheered in the courtroom, despite stern warnings from the judge. After court was dismissed, Leeman shook Walid's hand then gave him a huge hug before turning to his family. Walid himself was struggling with emotion. He gathered up the documents spread out on the table and carefully put them into his briefcase. The courtroom was nearly empty when he walked past where the Arnold's were celebrating and into the hallway.

Outside, scattered among the exiting throng, were Federal Marshals. Walid began to get an uneasy feeling as one of them approached and mentioned that he was being taken into their protection. He didn't mind this, but he felt that something wasn't right about the situation. As he was being escorted down the hallway, he turned back upon hearing a commotion behind him.

There, just outside the courtroom door was Leeman, being handcuffed by the Marshals, while his family began wailing around them.

Walid stopped. They weren't taking him into protective custody. They were arresting him!

The Marshal walking next to him grabbed his arm to keep him moving, but Walid angrily tore it out of his grasp. "What are they doing?"

"He's being charged with the Federal crime of violating the civil rights of Nidal Phad," said the Marshal.

The look on Leeman's face was heart wrenching and still haunted Walid two days later. He turned away from the tranquil scene outside the window and back to the television, where pictures were alternating between burning buildings and bloody victims. GNN was currently interviewing Senator Fish, who apparently spearheaded the pressure on the Justice Department to deny Leeman his freedom. He was still smiling about it, even as the cities burned around him.

Those fools in Washington, he thought. They created this outrage by undermining the authority of their own legal system. Bringing the same charges against Leeman in Federal court merely encouraged others to disregard the verdict of a fair trial as well, and act as if the meticulous presentation of witnesses and evidence over the course of the past six months was nothing more than a travesty.

Why should anyone have faith in the system anymore? Perhaps he should travel up to Maine or back down to South Carolina and join those Third World malcontents and their sanctimonious handlers. Why not help them trash the very country that had taken them in? It wasn't like other Americans really gave a damn about what they had to lose anyway.

Friday, May 7ᵗʰ, 2038
Los Angeles, California

Documentaries were rare in America, but rarer still was one that dealt with the Alberta exodus. Other films had been made that documented the plight of refugees, homosexuals, American Muslims, Latinos and even several that focused on the difficulties of the socially conscious unfortunately residing in the Red States." In each of these, the subjects were sympathetic, thus making it easier to dramatize their struggle against elements of society that the audience would already feel antagonism toward.

It was a far more challenging task to present the objectors (as some called them) or those leaving America for Alberta, because they were very unpopular in cultured circles. Noel Sterling had decided that the best strategy would be to take a comedic approach that would keep the audience entertained.

With a square jaw and handsome features, the young son of Starr Sterling had his mother's movie star looks, but wanted to try his hand at documentaries before crossing over into acting. Thanks to his mother's name, there was an inordinate amount of media attention surrounding his film, although he wanted to believe that part of it was the unusual subject matter being tackled. The premiere at the Chinese Theatre in Los Angeles was a genuine red carpet affair, with many of his mother's friends already inside by the time they stepped out of the limo and into the glare and glitter.

Ahead of them, was one of his mother's old costars in "The Advocate," who had a long history of political activism. He was a stock, gruff-looking man that played a grouchy character with a heart of gold on the series that shone through at crucial moments in many episodes. He was being interviewed by a celebrity reporter, with makeup that probably looked decent to the television audience, but pasty to the point of ghoulish up close.

"This is becoming a problem for all of us," the actor was saying. "Twenty years ago it felt good to be getting rid of a few anti-choice bozos and intolerant types, but in the years since, we're seeing a lot of our nation's wealth taken out of the country. This isn't good for the people who need that money; such as the poor, the homeless, the unemployed..."

"Thank you Ed, and good luck," said the reporter, whose producer was making her aware of the new arrival. "I see that the guests of honor are finally with us now. Let's talk to them."

In response to the frantic prompting from the producer, Noel and his mother sauntered over to the celebrity reporter, waving to the adoring throng of people that packed the bleachers erected on each side of the walkway.

"Oh goodness," said the reporter, trying to keep the light-hearted banter afloat, "What's with the brown suit? Are you trying to hurt my mother?"

"Uh, yes... yes I am..." Noel knew he wasn't sounding terribly witty at the moment, but he wasn't used to the attention he was receiving.

"Well, tell us about the movie. It's certainly a controversial subject, isn't it?"

"That's why I picked it." Noel nervously cleared his throat. "I wanted the challenge, first of all. Secondly, I thought that those of us who see America changing for the better should want to know why it is that anyone thinks they need to leave."

"Now," said the reporter, with an exaggerated concerned expression, "as you know, there have been a number of attacks by terrorists across America over the last few years, who take offense at the content of some movies. The great Michael Moore, of course, was slain in broad daylight by such an extremist. Given that many of the people poked fun of in this film are right-wing Christians, do you fear for your life as well?"

"Hardly," laughed Noel. "The terrorists are all Muslims and these..."

"Yes, of course he fears for his life," interjected his mother, swiftly and loudly, with a powerful clench of her hand on his arm that made him wonder if his bicep might pop. The reporter's face had gone two shades whiter, even under the thick layers of makeup. He realized that he had just goofed.

"My son has received death threats, but has chosen to not to be intimidated by the right-wing nuts who are far more of a threat to our freedom than all of the world's worst terrorists put together," insisted his mother, half-truthfully. In fact, the studio did receive a couple of death threats, but he was assured that this always happens, and that he would be perfectly safe as long as he didn't "mishandle" the Qur'an or offend Muslims in some other way.

As the interview concluded and he was ushered into the theater, he wondered if he had said something that might make him the target of radical Islamists, eager to defend their peaceful religion by hurting anyone who implies otherwise. His concern gradually receded, as they took their seats in time to see the lights go down and the opening credits roll. This was his opportunity to gauge how well his film would do with a live audience.

It opened with a quick historical lesson of the changes in America over the last forty-five years, beginning with how the Clinton and Gore Administrations managed to reverse the Reagan revolution. Particular attention was focused on the cuts in military spending and the build-up of social programs, showing the positive impact that these bold initiatives had on the lives of average Americans.

The changing face of America was profiled, with attention given to the influx of Hispanic and Muslim immigrants. Church spires were being supplanted by minarets in small towns and suburbs, and mosques were even starting in unused houses of worship. Arabic was vying with Spanish and English for recognition as an official language. The fastest growing religion was projected to include one in four Americans within ten years. 31% of the population was Latino and 19% of African descent, including recent immigrants escaping the violence in Nigeria and the poverty in South Africa.

"Now, who do you suppose that leaves out?" asked the narrator, in a droll tone. The picture then switched to a still-shot of a red-faced, overweight woman holding an American flag with a group of other whites. The group had been captured by the camera at a moment when their mouths were hanging open in a ridiculous pose, although the viewer might have guessed that they were in song. "That's right," said the voice-over, "Whitey!"

The audience roared, and the narrator went on. "You see, after white folks stole their land from the Indians... the Mexicans... and... well, you get the picture. They didn't want to let anyone else have it, particularly people who don't look like them."

The pictures on screen alternated between various shots of angry whites holding anti-immigration signs on street corners. Some were opposed to lax security along the Mexican border, while others were against the Pillar project. The celebrities around Noel, who were as white as he, booed and hissed when the messages on the protest signs were shown.

"It seems that white folks had a real problem getting along with people of color," continued the narration. Pictures of lynching, segregated restaurants, dead Indians, mosques and even dead buffalo flashed across the screen in rapid succession. "What to do? What to do? Well, you can't just kill the Negro anymore, although thanks to one man [picture of Hawking] you could take it out on those who worship a different god, but only if they live overseas." Pictures followed of the victims of suicide bombings and roadside blasts that Noel had used because he couldn't find actual images of Iraqis killed directly by American bombs, even though CTV claimed there were 10,000 and other groups put the number as high as 200,000.

The film then offered up the prospect of Alberta as a haven for the intolerant and bigoted. The rest of his work focused on interviews with people who were making the trip across the border. He wanted very much to cross over and document life in Alberta, but the authorities there wouldn't let him. He hoped to gain permission at a later date, as the American imagination was piqued by the scant and often contradictory information coming out of that dark country.

The audience roared with laughter at certain moments and sighed with mild amusement or groaned and hissed at others. There were gasps of astonishment and light mummers whenever a minority was interviewed. Noel knew that this appeared to controvert the popular assumption borne out in his premise that Alberta was for whites only, but he felt somewhat obligated to include these people as well, since they comprised a surprisingly significant number of emigrants. It was supposed to be a documentary, after all.

In fact, he thought he did a pretty good job of capturing the pilgrim spirit and true sentiment of those who were willing to give up life in their country of birth and start over. Many of them were older, some were retired. Spending time with them impressed on him the sacrifice they were making, and he realized a sense of obligation to tell their story in between the comedy.

There was the young mother, who said that she wanted her children to learn the history of achievement and accomplishment in school, without multicultural distortion and omission. Neither did she want the educational system undermining the values she instilled at home.

An African-American woman said that she didn't want her kids taught by teachers who validated the street slang they were picking up from friends, and preferred that they be taught proper English. She also wanted her children raised in an environment where social mobility was encouraged and people were not assumed to be stuck in the circumstances in which they were born.

A business owner said he wanted the ability to fire employees if they underperformed.

A retired couple talked about how they were chased out of the neighborhood they had lived in for forty years by children from a newly-constructed public housing project, who vandalized their house and destroyed their prized garden.

A divorced woman in her 30s said she wanted her son to learn that women were not the sex objects that they were made out to be in modern music.

A professor was denied tenure when it was revealed that he questioned the orthodoxy of life's spontaneous origin.

A young man with a buzz cut said that he was leaving to join the military of a country that appreciated, rather than demeaned, those who served.

An older Hispanic couple said that they wanted to be able to leave the assets that they had worked for their entire lives to their children.

The widow of an African immigrant, gunned down in his taxi in a neighborhood that he was forced by law to travel, said that she wanted to be in a place where people could live and do business on their own terms.

During this portion of the film, Noel noticed a distinct restlessness among the audience. Perhaps there was room for improvement before the general release.

Monday, September 6th, 2038
New York, New York

The gentile aristocrats seated at the Hope Auditorium held their breath in anticipation, as the naked man on stage strained and shook. He was squatting over a piece of poster board set beneath him on the floor, with an image on it that was not yet known to the audience.

As the bald, white man progressed in his efforts, they were summarily rewarded with the appearance of a long turd, slowly emerging from his bowels. The people gasped with excitement, as if they were watching a golf ball rolling toward the final hole in a Master's playoff round.

An adulating crescendo erupted as the excrement slid free and fell with smack against the paper beneath him. The Artist wiped the sweat from his body with a towel, then donned his robe and faced the adoring audience. From the side of the stage, assistants emerged with a pane of glass, which they then preceded to place carefully on the Artist's masterpiece, with his guidance.

From where he sat on the third row, Danforth struggled to hold back a yawn. He did not share the unbridled enthusiasm of those around him, particularly Phyllis Hughes, who always got tears in her eyes when she saw her friend perform.

Once or twice a year, the pale little man would put on such a performance, which was all the rage among the Manhattan elite. They would marvel at the discipline that the Artist endured in regulating his diet prior to a presentation in order to achieve the perfect bowel movement in front of the crowd.

There was more to the performance than theater however. Each art show produced a product, much like a sculpture or a painting. A picture of a notable person was chosen by the Artist to be the honoree of his offering. It would be placed face-up on the stage, on top of a piece of glass. After the intestinal contribution was made, the picture would then be covered with an additional plate of glass, welded and sealed to the first, to create a self-contained piece of political art.

Past honorees included Former President Hawking, Dennis Paterski, the Bible, Leeman Arnold, and even the Fire Chief of New York City, who received the honor after trying unsuccessfully to prevent women from working as firemen. Earlier in the year, it was the unpopular widow of a slain police officer, who was working to keep the convicted Willie Powell behind bars. Such works fetched huge sums of money from trendy New Yorkers and other American art-lovers, who also paid heavenly sums to watch the Artist perform. Between the gate receipts and tax dollars from the NEA, it was little wonder that the man could space his workdays six to twelve months apart.

Danforth had been to see the Artist before, but the coveted tickets this Labor Day were provided free of charge from a particular corporate client, which no doubt considered it part of a small price to pay for a favorable rating in CSR's annual endorsement report, relied on by Wall Street fund managers to make CSR-approved investment decisions. Danforth was finding that his attendance at such ostentatious events enhanced his profile in the establishment. Other than that, he had little interest in the performance, other than a mild curiosity over just who the Artist chose to take a dump on this time.

As the glass was slowly raised before the eager audience, Danforth was one of the first to see that it was the new President of Alberta, framed there with dark stain of excrement mashed into the lower part of her face. The enamored around him burst out in applause at this culmination of the performance. Danforth stood with those around him and went through the motions of banging his hands together enthusiastically.

Out in the lobby, there were local news media conducting interviews with audience members. The Landaus were in front of one camera, with

Beth gushing about the "spiritual" experience and Nigel spouting some
drivel about how "the ambiguity invites the viewer to be a participant."

Danforth himself was caught by the arm as a local reporter swung
him into the cameras and introduced him to viewers.

"How did you like the performance?" she asked.

"It was a spiritual experience," said Danforth soberly. "The ambiguity invites the viewer to be a participant…"

Tuesday, September 7th, 2038
New York, New York

At his desk the next morning, Danforth got a call from Darnell
Massey, who was currently in Montana, climbing the judicial ladder
through the Federal Court system.

"Did you know Maria got married?"

"No, I didn't," replied Danforth. "Who's the lucky gal?"

"She married Kerry Conner."

"What?"

Danforth was stunned. He even went about confirming it independently on the Internet, while still on the phone.

Surely this wasn't a serious move for her. He remembered their times
together in college. She was even more radical than he was then. She
honestly advocated the return of most of the American Southwest to Mexico and ardently supported the eradication of global capitalism.

Yet, here she was marrying an industrialist, one at least as evil as
Dennis Paterski, whom she helped the ACLU defeat in court years ago.
Danforth had heard rumors that Maria changed after the death of her father, but no one could expect this. He wondered if something wasn't going on behind the scenes. Perhaps she was playing the man for his
money, or looking to destroy the airline company from within.

Then Danforth remembered something that he had pushed down deep
inside his brain. Something that embarrassed him; that he wanted to forget, but couldn't. It was the time in Tucson, the day before the drunken
woman died, when Robert went to bat for the ringer at the polls by lying
on his behalf.

He was never able to forget that look of disgust on Maria's face.

Danforth picked up the phone and told his assistant to start a new project. They were going to find out everything they could about Airtana
Airlines.

PART THREE

———

THE MORNING AFTER

2044

Thursday, January 7th, 2044

Kalispell, Montana

For a former millionaire officially more than $100 million in debt now, Dennis Paterski was no doubt feeling pretty good for himself, as he raised his glass with the four other men in the dimly-lighted formal room of the massive mountain home set on a 60-acre estate.

This moment had been more than fifteen years in the making. It was something that he had faith would happen, to the extent that he gambled everything that he possibly could on it. The initial $20 million in assets that comprised his actual net worth those many years ago was gone – used as leverage for loans. His hospital chain had been sold. His property mortgaged. And gradually, over the years, he had accumulated a debt that could do nothing but grow, if this project was to be successful.

At any time during the last twelve years, all they worked for might have been destroyed by a loss of nerve. There were some scary moments, of course. Paterski skillfully managed the business finances with a passion, while the others in the room with him concentrated on research. He was the only one fully aware of the tremendous risks that had been taken.

He carefully cultivated relationships with lenders, from local banks to individually-owned companies as far south as Utah, always exercising the most scrupulous caution before taking loans. He wanted to be sure that the lenders were on board with his vision, and understood the risk they were taking. He didn't want to have to deal with untimely panic as they were racing down the homestretch.

It required a tenacious effort and constant shifting of financial liabilities to keep the project afloat. Occasionally, he would have to pay off a nervous creditor by going deeper in debt with another. At other times, he would have to fly a lender to Kalispell and show him around the mountain campus, explaining anew why their institution was gambling on a company that had never shown a dime of revenue.

Of course, that had all changed shortly after New Years day, as Paterski just signed a deal worth $400 million with Cooper-Redmond Pharmaceuticals. He may not have cared much for the organization's politics, but they were large enough to back up their offer, and even provide an advance that would satisfy every one of Paterski's creditors. The entire enterprise would be out of debt in four weeks and floating in a nearly limitless sea of cash thereafter.

In the room with him that evening, were three men for whom he had the utmost respect, and who believed in him and each other enough to devote thirteen years of their life to the ambitious project. They were gathered around a large picture of their late software engineer, Yong, the grandson of a South Vietnamese Army Captain who spent five years in a Communist reeducation camp following the war. His grandfather promptly fled with his family the day after being released, following his adamant insistence that the tiger cages were no longer necessary to convince him of the truth and virtue of such an ideal philosophy.

Yong was killed in a Fedayeen suicide bombing two years earlier, while on a business trip to Boston. He had been with the project long enough to know that it would be successful and that his wife and children would have financial security even without him.

The two scientists raising their glasses with Paterski were Sanjay Guptapara and Greg Dijkstra, both brilliant geneticists specializing in epidemiology. Sanjay had been fired from a research firm that subsequently went out of business. Greg lost his position at the University of California following a political play by jealous colleagues. He was the nicest, seemingly naïve person that you could ever meet, and the only one of the group that was openly religious and a Democrat, which drove the others nuts.

The fourth member of the research team came recommended to Paterski by a fellow Montana businessman named Kerry Conner, who had employed the MIT grad and former military chopper pilot to fly planes for him many years ago, after serving out a court-martial. Paterski was skeptical at first, but after the first interview, he realized that Aaron Bernstein was a perfect fit.

Like the others, Bernstein was a bit of a reject, having lost his job as a lead electronics engineer after a fallout with his company over technology that he had built on his own time. The company disagreed and fired him, but kept the technology for its own purposes. A year after Bernstein gave up on his lawsuit and joined Paterski's staff, his old firm suffered a debilitating hacking attack that destroyed critical data and set the company back so far that it never fully recovered.

Paterski noticed that it was about that time that the team's software engineer, Yong (and Bernstein's good friend) developed a curious grin that took months to wear off. No information was offered, and no questions were asked.

For more than a dozen years, the five toiled in the research lab on Paterski's estate, which they referred to as a campus. Their families lived with them, elsewhere on the same heavily-wooded land. Children grew up before everyone's eyes, some leaving for college and beyond. They all worked through health problems and death like one big family.

Others joined them for very controlled mini-projects over the years, as the team occasionally required help. So well-disciplined were the five, that no one else in the world really knew what was being developed in that small corner of the state, not even those who worked with them peri-

odically. Some thought it was a software program, others a new supercomputer, and still others a vaccine. In fact, all of these guesses were
partially correct, but no one thought to put it all together. Since Paterski's
was a privately owned company, no one really cared.

Six months earlier, Dennis Paterski had walked into the offices of
Cooper-Redmond Pharmaceuticals and offered to sell them an AIDs vaccine for the most common strain of the virus. He had a hard time finding
an audience at first, but the industry giant eventually did its homework
and realized that Paterski was the real deal. It now stood to make billions
from the manufacture of a product that this mysterious businessman told
them exactly how to build.

Wind howled outside the windows as the four completed their toast,
some of them fighting back tears, all of them dealing with powerful emotion. It was going to be a cold walk home for most of them, but no one
cared at that moment.

January 22ⁿᵈ, 2044
Rothberg, California

The Professor sat on his knees on the aisle of the theater with rubber
gloves on his hands and a scrub bucket by his side. He wished that he had
thought to bring something to protect his nose against the stench of the
stomach contents that he was scraping and sponging off of the floor in
front of him.

It had probably been about three weeks ago that one of the teenagers
vomited during a show. No one wanted to clean it up, so it sat there while
the building went unused.

There used to be a system of responsibilities within the community,
whereby those without jobs made themselves useful and performed such
duties while the rest were out working. That had gone by the wayside
pretty quickly and now the community was losing its best members, those
who would come home at the end of the day from work and spend the
early evenings cleaning the streets, tending the yards, painting the buildings and doing the many other tasks that should have been the responsibility of the unemployed. These valuable members were being cut down by
attrition, as they began to lose faith in the others.

The "others" had started out being those who did not have much employment experience, usually those that were habitual welfare recipients
prior to their invitation to join the community. Not a single one of them
lifted a hand anymore to help, or spent any time looking for ways to bring
income in, yet they were always at the general meetings with ready complaints about how the community was failing to take care of their needs.
Gradually the group got larger as the malaise spread. Rothermel admitted
that there was a certain appeal to it. Why work if all of your needs will

be met anyway? Since all income went into the community fund, there was no personal incentive to be had from additional effort.

Yet, they had to be wrong about it, because it contradicted everything that Rothermel believed, and everything into which he had invested his entire savings. All people were basically the same, once they were removed from the exploitative clutches of capitalism, which warped society into artificial classes. Eradicate the class barriers and the concept of personal possession and property rights, and you will find that equality results in cooperation toward common goals.

So intent was Rothermel on his thoughts that he didn't notice the footsteps behind him until it was too late.

Saturday, February 20th, 2044
Hartford, Connecticut

The mother of three knew the warnings about going out on February 20th; the anniversary of something that happened long ago, which the media didn't talk about anymore, but must have been very bad considering how upset Muslims still were forty years later. Hundreds of people just like her had been killed since then, in revenge attacks on this date.

Yet, the odds of something happening that day were quite remote, according to the man being interviewed on GNN that morning. He was the director for BAIR, the wonderful group that worked so hard to build bridges between the Muslim and non-Muslim communities in America. If she had any actual hesitation about doing her usual Saturday shopping, they were completely dispelled by the indignation that Mr. Sahil expressed over people like him being made to feel that they were under suspicion in their own country.

He even stood in front of an American flag as he talked.

The image haunted the woman as she bundled up her children and scooted them out into the minivan. On the way to the Coop-Mart, she thought about how sad it was that Americans were so intolerant. As she pulled into the parking lot, she noticed another van with an empty space next to it. It looked as if the bearded men getting out were Arabs, although she had been taught not to make such assumptions.

She took the adjacent space and was deliberate in smiling broadly at them as she got out. They looked startled to see her, but eventually three out of the four returned her smile. She thought it was odd that they were sweating in such weather, but figured that it had to do with strain from the tremendous social pressures that Muslims in America were evidently under, according to their spokespersons. She quickly turned her attention to getting her children unloaded and then bustled down the parking lot toward the Coop-Mart.

This was easier to do these days with the help of the medication, although she needed to take the kids to the doctor each month to have their dosages adjusted, as they had a way of breaking out of their lethargy and becoming unmanageable if she waited too long between visits. With their father out of work and unable to send child support payments, the woman, who was unemployed herself after having made the decision to stay home with her children, was finding out just how essential government health care can be.

As she crossed the road toward the automatic doors in the front of the building, she could see a security guard approaching the four men from the van with his hands out in front of him, motioning them to stop. He did not seem concerned about the other people streaming in to the store behind his back, nor did he give the woman and her children a second look.

Racial profiling was occurring right in front of her eyes!

The woman began to pass, but as she did, she thought about whether she would have done the same thing in Nazi Germany. What sort of world did she want her children to grow up in? One in which (as the man from BAIR had said) Muslim-Americans are discriminated against everyday, or one in which all people are made to feel as if they belong? If she was willing to let what was happening there in the street continue, then she was no different than those who drove Jews to the gas chambers.

She stopped and turned. The Arab men looked frightened and nervous, as she expected, but so did the guard. Was he reaching for his side-arm?

"You, there!" she yelled. Everyone stopped and looked at her. She went up to the guard, a young man who was probably barely into his 20s. "Do you know that what you're doing is illegal?"

"Stay out of this," he instructed, but there was a detectable lack of confidence to his voice.

"You are racially profiling these men," she continued, gesturing toward the confused Arabs. "You're in current violation of multiple civil rights statutes. If you continue harassing these men, I'll make sure that you not only lose your job, but wind up in jail!"

The guard swallowed hard. The look of determination that a mother of three was capable of, apparently impelled him to back down. He motioned the men past.

The woman shot him a last look of righteous indignation, before strolling into the store with her kids in tow.

"I saw what you did back there. I was impressed."

It was not one of the Middle Eastern men, but rather a complete stranger, another white woman with a baby of her own in her arms.

"Well thank you," she responded, watching her children take off down the store aisles. Neither of them noticed that the four men had split up and were heading to opposite corners of the store, with eyes darting about nervously. The two women stood talking for a few more minutes, about their common commitment to see the world become a better place, with or without the volition of dangerous throwbacks like the security guard.

What sounded like chanting interrupted their conversation. One of the Arabs, standing closest to them, was uttering what sounded like a very loud prayer in Arabic. This was answered by other distant voices, presumably his companions in other parts of the store. The buzz around them came to a sudden halt, as people stopped talking and turned to listen.

They didn't have long to be curious. Within seconds the men had synchronized. The last thing that the mother saw before the explosion was her 6-year-old boy running past the nearest bomber.

Nashville, Tennessee

Senator Jill Hudson, known to her constituents as "Hudson Jill," for her family's home in the Hudson Valley in New York (and of course, the clever interplay with her name) was just coming back to her hotel from a fund-raising brunch when she got the news from her campaign manager about the Coop-Mart blast.

The candidate for the Democratic nomination for President was glad to see that the man had recovered from the previous evening, when they celebrated the South Carolina primary win with an overabundance of alcohol. Fortunately, they were in the suite of Jill's hotel room when this occurred, because she wouldn't have wanted the things said under the influence of fine bourbon to find their way into print.

The campaign manager was very good at what he did, but he tended to be cocky about it and sometimes spoke more frankly than he should have, particularly when he was as drunk as he had been the night before. "It's one big game, Senator," he had said while teetering on the edge of the bed.

"Pardon?"

"You know… this whole business of mingling with the voters every few years or so and trying to pretend like someone that we're not."

He took another swallow from his glass. "We have to kiss a few babies, wave the flag and package ourselves as committed to family values. We convince these people that we're tough on crime and all for lowering their taxes. That we want strong economic growth and balanced budgets, more police and less porn. We tell these fools that we care about their security and want to crack down on terrorism. Hell, we might as well campaign as Nationalists…"

Draining his glass, he reached over to pour another from the bottle. "And what do we do once we've won? We come back and vote exactly the opposite from the way they think we do. We're stealing their country out from under them and they're too stupid to know... or care. It's a big game, you know..."

Now, the morning after, the same man was earnestly briefing her on the developing situation in Connecticut, with only a trace of bloodshot in his eyes to betray the evening before.

"Can we assume that this is related to Maine?" she asked.

"Of course, but that's not how we're going to play it," he answered quickly. "As with the other attacks, there will be a video released on a Web site somewhere that will show these men – we believe there to be more than one – standing in front of an Islamic banner quoting from the Qur'an."

He sounded confident, and Jill knew that he would be proven right within a matter of hours. Most states in the country allowed for a civil form of *Sharia* (Qur'anic law) in their courts, whereby Muslims had the option of taking matters that usually involved family law before a parallel religious court. However, this was not enough for areas with a high concentration of Muslims, such as in Maine and South Carolina, where activists were demanding that *Sharia* be extended to criminal matters and made compulsory. State referendums proved that they had the support of the people.

Jill's friend, Rahim Sahil, had helped her see the merit in this. "It was not meant for the Qur'an to acquiesce to an infidel system of laws," he told her. "The Islamic tradition is perfectly compatible with freedom and democracy, to think otherwise is the highest form of ignorance."

Even though she may have sympathized with the cause these groups advocated, there was no excusing the increasing violence. Even Rahim was quick to disassociate the two. He would vacillate between insisting that the attacks had "nothing to do with Islam" while maintaining that they were indicative of the "desperation" that Muslim-Americans were under.

She got out of the limo as it pulled underneath the hotel and went directly up the elevator to her room, where she switched on GNN. She knew that she didn't have much time before a statement was expected of her, but she wanted to first gather as much information as she could.

The scene was devastating. A helicopter shot showed the familiar Coop-Mart marquee collapsed along with the rest of the building, in a pile of rubble. Rescue workers were crawling like ants through the debris, looking for survivors. Apparently, cameras were not allowed any closer because of the gruesomeness on the ground. According to the reports, over 500 people were thought to have been in the store at the time. Only a handful were found alive.

Just then, the scene switched to an interview with Senator Fish, in Arizona, who was expected to be the Progressive Party nominee in November, as he had been for the last six straight general elections. By his side was Rahim Sahil.

"That bastard!" Jill couldn't help herself. It was no secret that the Muslim Coalition Party had jumped the Democratic ship for the Progressives several years ago. They were now deemed friendlier to the Muslim agenda, which involved Federal support for the Islamic school system and expansion of the Hate Crimes act to protect against any published material that was deemed offensive to the community.

To ignore these interests was very nearly political suicide as the 'Muslim Machine' was extremely effective at voter registration drives and Election Day mobilization. The effects of the Pillar project and internal growth factors, such as a higher birthrate and rules concerning marriage (only men could marry outside the faith, and the children had to be raised Muslim) meant that one in five voters usually followed the Muslim Coalition Party.

The African-American vote was expected to favor her opponents as well, since the Progressives were promising to force the reparations issue with a November win. Of course, this was helping the Democrats retain seniors, who could still be manipulated easily by Democratic scare tactics over Social Security, although at least there was some merit to them now that the Federal budget was under the imposing threat from the tremendous cost of reparations. The whisper campaign was that the money would have to come from Social Security cutbacks, although Senator Fish adamantly denied it. Of course, he didn't say where the money would come from, other than vague allusions to "those that can afford it."

Senator Fish was being asked about the attacks.

"It's too early to draw conclusions," he responded, with an expression that was almost comically serious, "but we can be certain that these bombers were not true Muslims, as my friend Mr. Sahil can easily confirm. They may have been of Middle Eastern descent, and perhaps this was a factor in this desperate act. According to some preliminary reports, the men may have been harassed by a security guard there at the store that morning, perhaps leading to their decision to make this sort of sacrifice a few minutes later. We just hope that the government is taking adequate measures to protect the Muslim community from any violence or intimidation that may result from…"

Did he think that these people were in the habit of walking around with explosives belts, waiting to be offended, Jill wondered?

Rahim spoke up. "It is tragic that Muslims today live under fear and intimidation. A greater understanding of Islam on the part of Americans is clearly necessary. Although we appreciate the progress that has been made in our public classrooms, it is clear that more must be done to educate our youth on the peaceful religion of Islam. Let's hope that…"

There was a knock at the door. "Senator, it's your daughter on the phone."

She turned the sound down on the television and went over to the phone, already putting together in her head the statement that would be given to the press within the hour.

Friday, August 12*th*, 2044
Tivoli, New York

The Catskills were visible through the window from where Walid sat in the living room of his home of five years, which overlooked the Hudson River near the state capital. He was remarkably relaxed, considering that he was about to be seen by millions on the GNN morning show. Not so for the production crew that was scurrying around the room, trying to get both the set and the subject looking just right.

According to the producer, he should expect a "hostile" interview from the host, a woman that he was told to call by her first name, Katie. This did not surprise him, since the main audience for the show was "stay-at-home" moms and, of course, the unemployed. Both groups were sure to be less than appreciative of his latest legal success, which had the potential to end a form of subsistence that enabled many of them to enjoy daytime television.

The producer dropped to her knees in front of him and shooed away the make-up artist who had been trying to get in a few last-second touches. Walid could see the commercial on the monitor coming to an end. The producer began a countdown with her fingers then gave the "thumbs-up" sign.

"Welcome back this Friday morning. As promised we have established a satellite interview with Mr. Walid al-Rahahti – I hope I'm pronouncing that right…"

"Yes," said Walid.

"Mr. al-Rahahti, thank you for being with us. Now, you recently won a case that had been appealed by the State of New York for a client, which involved child support. Please tell us about it."

"As you said," responded Walid, "the U.S. Court of Appeals upheld the original jury verdict. My client is no longer obligated to pay child support."

"Now this will probably alarm many of our viewers," said Katie, who could be seen shifting in her chair. "In this case, your client was clearly the father of the child in question, wasn't he? Why did he feel that he shouldn't pay child support?"

"Yes, he is the father of the boy. This was not in dispute. He also signed a legal document when his wife was pregnant in which he declined to support the child."

"Did he ask the woman to have an abortion?" Katie asked.

"It wasn't in his place to ask that. He simply declined responsibility for the child and left the choice to her."

Katie scratched her head, as if puzzled by what she was hearing.

"How is it that he thought he had the right to, as you put it, 'decline responsibility'?"

"In the same way that the woman has that right," responded Walid evenly. "If the woman has the choice to abort responsibility, then so should the man. Wouldn't you agree?"

"Well, no I wouldn't agree," said Katie, with a sarcastic laugh that was almost a sneer. "There's a big difference between a woman choosing to have an abortion and a man deciding not to pay child support."

"Is there?" asked Walid. "What would that be?"

"Well, for one thing, the woman's decision is made when she's pregnant. The baby is…"

"And when is the man's made?" interrupted Walid.

"Well, when he decides to have sex, I guess."

"Then isn't the woman's decision made when she decides to have sex as well?"

"Yes… I mean no." The host was getting a bit flustered. "It's different for the woman because the baby… the fetus, rather, is inside of her. It belongs to her, since it is a part of her body and she therefore has the choice alone on whether to have it or not."

"Then the man is not responsible for her choice," responded Walid. "If there's nothing in the woman's body that is his, then how can something that is his be produced from her body at a later date? Are we talking *ex nilhilo*?"

"Let's stop this unconstructive argument for a minute, Mr. al-Rahahti, and look at the practical implications here. If the Supreme Court decides not to hear your case, then it could effectively overturn the system of child support as we know it. Many women would be left without a means of raising their children. Is this what you want?"

"No."

Katie was clearly frustrated by his refusal to engage her in what he considered to be the superficial elements of the argument. She decided to play her full hand.

"For those of our viewers who may be unfamiliar with you," she said with a smirk, "you were the lawyer that represented the well-known racist, Leeman Arnold, who was convicted of killing a Muslim teenager. This was an Islamophobic hate crime that shocked the nation, particularly Muslim-Americans. Mr. al-Rahahti, how do you live…?"

"I did not represent Mr. Arnold when he was convicted five years ago," said Walid smoothly. "I was barred from doing so by the Federal judge in the case. And just so your viewers know, Mr. Arnold killed a 20-year-old man who had broken into his garage at night, armed with a handgun."

"Mr. Arnold is a racist and a bigot, is he not, Mr. al-Rahahti?" said the host, with no small measure of indignation.

"He may have been, yes, but is neither now. He was killed in the Federal prison at Marion two years ago, beaten to death with a pipe."

Katie looked taken aback. She had apparently not done her homework very well.

Walid gave a dry laugh that belied underlying bitterness. "I guess he paid the price for being a racist and a bigot, didn't he Katie? Would you like to see the pictures?"

"No… uh, well I…"

"Too bad for him that he wasn't a Muslim like *you and me*, then he would never have been convicted of defending his property and family, right Katie?"

"Well, I'm not actually a Muslim, although I have a deep respect…"

"Oh that's right," said Walid with mock seriousness. "I'm the only Muslim in our conversation. I think I forgot that when you began lecturing me on Islamophobia."

In a grace-saving attempt, the red-faced morning diva held a finger up to her ear, as if to keep her head from exploding. "Mr. al-Rahahti, thank you for joining us."

Walid smiled. "It's been a pleasure."

It could have been Walid's imagination, but it seemed that the "thumbs-up" signs from smiling crew members were held a little longer than necessary as the lights on the set went down. Walid also got several firm handshakes after the producer finally left.

He waved goodbye to the last of the crew just as the phone rang.

"Mr. al-Rahahti?"

"Yes," he said, bracing for the worst.

"My name is Maria Posada. Do you have plans for the weekend?"

Wednesday, August 17th, 2044
Bozeman, Montana

Walid had never been anywhere near Montana. He was stunned by the beauty of the land, with its green jagged mountains and rolling brooks. Every bend in the road brought a picturesque scene that looked right out of a painting. He was told that the drive up to Butte and Helena that time of year was even more stunning.

Airtana was unlike any other airlines that he had flown. For one thing, he had to drive to New Hampshire to catch the flight, since it was the only state in the Northeast that still allowed Airtana to fly into it. They had a huge presence there, and were apparently one of the state's top employers.

Maria also told him point-blank that he would probably receive extra scrutiny at the company's security checkpoint. He could either bear it, or they would arrange to have a concierge meet him ahead of time. She did not seem the least surprised when he quickly informed her that, as a man, he was not going to be brought to tears by attention that was perfectly natural given the reality of the times.

Even so, he was unprepared for the level of examination that a traveler of Middle Eastern descent would be subject to at Airtana Airlines. He went through a process that was much like what he heard *El Al*, the Israeli airlines, put passengers through. He was held up for about fifteen minutes while a background check was run. He didn't tell them that he was flying in at the request of the owner, but rather that he had business in Montana, since he wanted to see what the process was like for an ordinary Arab customer.

It was all done quite courteously, almost apologetically. After being searched, questioned and even finger-printed, he was offered a first-class seat by the smiling agents. He informed them that he was already sitting in first class, at which point they told him that his card would be credited by 20% of the ticket price. Apparently it was standard procedure for this airline.

On the flight, he studied what he'd been able to pull on the company. They were very profitable and, not surprisingly, the only major carrier never to have had a terrorist incident in their entire history. Some American airlines had suffered as many as five catastrophic mid-air attacks in the last forty years. They all wanted to avoid fines from the DCA, which monitored public discrimination affairs.

Not Airtana, apparently. They paid the fines, but did not alter their security routine. The fares they charged were not much higher than other carriers. Given that they flew to select markets and sold out nearly every flight, it wasn't hard to see how they could afford the fines. Travelers evidently felt that the extra security was certainly worth the slightly higher cost of flying with Airtana.

The company was killing its competitors, but they couldn't shake the government, which had been waging an escalating battle with them over the last seven years, perhaps earlier than that if the Labor Department's unsuccessful fight over hiring discrimination claims was counted. Apparently there was a heck of a story there, because the owner of the Airlines married the Assistant Secretary of Labor not long after the case was decided.

Of course, these were the two people that invited him, and he found both Maria and Kerry to be quite down-to-earth, yet with a certain poise that seemed characteristic of their surroundings. Maria was a beautiful mother of three from a Mexican family (that included the sheriff from his old hometown, as he found out). Kerry was a solid man with steady grey eyes and an unflappable composure. They were very much in love. He noticed that the two of them alternated between Spanish and English around their children, who grew up learning both. They also insisted that Walid teach the youngsters some Arabic words, which the little ones seemed have a tough time pronouncing, much to everyone's amusement.

After spending most of Sunday getting to know one another in a friendly, relaxed environment, they all got down to business that evening over dinner preparations. The company was in trouble with the government. Not because they had cheated vendors or customers out of money, or reneged on their debts or any of the other things that companies in America were more likely to get away with, but rather because they wanted to choose their employees and their customers. This made them a very large target for both the DCA and activist groups, such as CSR.

They had spent the last seven years as a company on the run. When they were blocked from doing business in one city (by the council or mayor) they would move to a different airport in the same area. Eventually entire states began banning them, with California and New York leading the way, followed by Massachusetts. It didn't seem to matter to these legislatures and councils that they were costing their communities jobs or tax revenue. The members considered it more prudent, politically, to cater to special interests.

Kerry's company had tried to make the best of it, but it was slowly being chipped away, market by market, as the powerful CSR actively lobbied politicians with (they suspected) the help of industry competitors.

"There was a time when I thought this whale had found its Ahab," said Kerry with a look toward Maria, who blushed as they were chopping onions together, "but it turned out to be one of her friends instead. And I can't buy him off with marriage, like I could..."

A chunk of onion bounced off his shirt. "Next time it'll be this knife," said Maria, waving it at him in a light-hearted way. She turned to Walid. "This guy, Robert Danforth, is relentless. He called my husband seven years ago and basically tried to extort money."

Kerry took over. "He honestly sounded like some mafia don, telling me that he was concerned about things he was hearing about Airtana, and how he wanted to work with me to ensure that we were protected. I

looked the guy up afterwards. He apparently plays this game with everyone and they all cave eventually."

He reached behind him to stir the chili as he talked. "The corporations are scared of him, because he can alarm the shareholders just by
coughing. All he has to do is hint at a boycott or demonstration, and they
immediately want to start paying him off to avoid bad publicity. The
guy's got a great racket going."

"Kerry told him to go to hell," Maria interjected proudly, "and has refused to talk to him since."

"I'm familiar with CSR," said Walid, "although I haven't had any
professional dealings with them. They're like most organizations of that
type, which refuse to divulge where their money comes from, yet they
demand the highest form of open financial accounting from other businesses. They even get away without having to provide details of their
interrelationships with one another, although what they do is clearly rack-
eteering. They're above the law, and this makes them an impossible opponent."

Walid paused. He wasn't sure how much he should share with these
two. He wanted to tell them about his own decisions over the last couple
of years, but decided against it.

"What's the hardest problem that you're dealing with right now?" he
asked. "Where can I be of service?"

Kerry answered. "We're reaching the breaking point over the Non-
Discrimination Act. Congress not only put extra teeth into it this year, but
they also gave the power of enforcement entirely to the DCA. No more
juries; no more judges. If an interstate company doesn't hire in demographic proportions to the country, then it'll be assessed escalating fines
that are now in proportion to the company's size."

"In other words, they can easily break you if you don't toe the line
and hire, say 30% Hispanic, 25% Muslim, or 39% white," said Walid.

Kerry laughed, "They're not too concerned about that last group, as
you know. It's the only acceptable form of racism. We could have an all
African-American staff and they wouldn't say anything about it."

"Then do it," said Walid quietly.

He got confused looks from both of them.

"How do you define an African-American?" he asked.

"We know about your case involving the Algerian," said Maria, "but
I'm afraid that we can't find enough qualified people that have any asso-
ciation with the continent to fill the mandated 17% of our staff."

"Let me tell you what the problem is." Walid sat back in his chair.
"You're thinking like they want you to think. You're thinking like they
are. And by accepting their preconceptions, you may as well hand them
the battle."

They both stopped what they were doing and stared at him.

"They're the ones that want to divide America into groups. They're the ones that want to put us all into neat little boxes that are tagged according to our presumed ethnicity or religious beliefs... who we want to have sex with even, and then assign instructions and privileges. Have they clearly rationalized these axioms or provided an adequate description of the ground rules they want the rest of us to obey?"

Maria and Kerry looked almost hypnotized.

"Make them justify and define their rules," Walid continued, "before you agree to play their game."

From the look that the two gave each other, Walid knew they now considered the first-class ticket from Manchester a good investment, if they hadn't already.

The next three days were very busy.

Saturday, August 20th, 2044
New York, NY

"We are the Beautiful People!" gushed Beth Landau, to the twenty-five or so gathered in the large room of the oversized Manhattan apartment. Most responded by looking down in embarrassment. It wasn't that they disagreed with her. They were just shy about advertising it.

One person in the room stuck out, however, and it wasn't just because he was the only minority among them. As an ex-felon, Willie Powell appeared out of place in a room full of "beautiful people," although this was his third visit since his release from prison two years ago. The lawyer who helped secure the pardon was Beth Landau's ex-husband, Nigel. The people around him were typical of the sort of supporters that he had amassed over the years since being convicted of gunning down a police officer one night in front of several eyewitnesses.

He found that despite the evidence, certain people were unwilling to believe that an articulate black man could commit such a crime, particularly if he wrote a book denying the fact and attributing his conviction to institutional racism. They were eager to take up his cause with a sort of ardor that belied their internalized guilt as members of the power class. Their naiveté was amazing to him, as was the pardon that he finally received from the governor, who finally bowed to pubic pressure.

He noticed, however, that these same people who passionately defended his innocence and demanded his release from prison were somewhat less than comfortable with his presence. It was unlikely they ever considered that he would seek their company. Perhaps they believed that he would slink back to the old neighborhood in Camden and live a quiet life with his "homies," never to intrude on their white-bread world of social theory and moral superiority.

The mindset of these people was a mystery to him. They railed against the police for protecting the social order while they sat at the very top of it. They used the most brutal terms to describe those who disagreed with their political and social views, even as they congratulated themselves on matters of tolerance and multiculturalism. They even, as he noticed, disparaged privilege and wealth when they, themselves, were the very picture of it.

Beyond these fundamental contradictions, there was a weird peculiarity to these people to which they seemed perfectly oblivious. An animal-rights proponent in the group, for example, spoke of her angst over an operation to remove a tapeworm, which she had formed an emotional bond with after the doctors explained the cause of her acute diarrhea. She even named it and did her best to preserve the "little fellow."

The star of the group was a strange looking man who made his living by publicly defecating on the pictures of unpopular politicians or other notables.

Even Willie got into the act by speaking bluntly of his hatred for white people. He would tell the group about the violent things that he felt like doing to Caucasians, such as gouging eyes and burning extremities. It never ceased to amaze him that these bluebloods would nod with delight and even applaud his darkest expressions of racism.

Several even encouraged him to write a book.

Thursday, September 8th, 2044
Rothberg, California

The Professor had sufficiently recovered from the blow to the head and the subsequent infection from lying near vomit with an open wound. One would think that the new television series based on their community (appropriately called "The Community") would bring everyone together in the theater for the production, but this wouldn't be the case.

In the first place, the theater wasn't fit for gathering. Since the Professor had gotten mugged there eight months ago, no one took it upon themselves to clean it. As far as he knew, his scrub bucket was still sitting there on the floor next to the vomit. No one was there to operate the projector and someone had even tried to burn the place down, which prompted a few brave souls to board up the building as best they could. Like all of the other public buildings, and even some of the houses, it was coated in vulgar graffiti.

Of course, the main reason that there wasn't a gathering was that it wasn't very safe to venture out at night anymore. The council was starting to lose track of just who lived in the community. It was thought that there were some homes that had been taken over by drug dealers after their occupants signed over the tenant rights for meth or crack. Gang activity had started up as well, although it was not nearly as bad as it was in the cities. The Professor felt that the real problem was a lack of resources, particularly funding. If they could get more money, then they might be able to put more computers in the classrooms, as well as other tools of education, which would surely solve their crime problem.

He had finally tapped out the good will of the Cooper-Redmond Foundation. The corporate giant was losing billions each year because of the tough economy, and they had to cut back on their donations. It was the same with the other corporations which had helped out in the past in order to garner good publicity.

There were two bright spots on the horizon, however. One was the anticipation over Reparations. About 20% of the community was African-American, and if Senator Fish was elected next month, as seemed certain, then it would mean an influx of cash into the community fund.

The second reason for slight optimism was the new TV series from which the community would be receiving some royalties. If the series generated enough interest, then it could also mean that donations from the general public might return to the levels they were at ten years ago, when there was so much excitement across the country for Rothermel's project.

The movie that came out six years ago had done poorly, even though it had Starr Sterling in the lead role. Rothermel privately resented that a woman was picked to play his part, because he felt it drew credit away from him – people would still call the community occasionally and ask to speak to "Hannah."

In the TV series, the lead role was played by Sterling's son, Noel. His character, based on Rothermel of course, was named "Noah." The Professor did not mind being portrayed by a younger and much more handsome actor. He only hoped that the series would do better than the movie.

In the movie, "Hannah" had battled greedy corporations and unscrupulous Nationalist politicians to forge the community almost literally out of rock with her bare hands. In the TV pilot, the community was already built and resembled how Rothberg looked on Dedication Day. The producers had developed episode plots around real-life occurrences.

In the pilot, for example, "Noah," who was a well-intentioned character with a square jaw, got sick and vomited in the community's theater. Rather than clean it up, however, he seemed to expect others to do the work, based on the fact that he had "given" them the community. The others obliged to do the work for him, but through the course of the episode, "Noah" learned that his arrogant demeanor was unconstructive to their collective spirit. He offered an apology and promised to do better in the future.

By the end of the program, the Professor was quivering with rage.

Tuesday October 27ᵗʰ, 2044
Eugene, Oregon

"You would be the father of our country. We are your symbolic children. How will you meet our needs?"

The question was posed by a young man in a ponytail at the Town
Hall style debate that was sandwiched between the other two during the
two weeks leading up to the November 8ᵗʰ election. Jill had lost the nomination earlier in the year, but was present in the auditorium as a favor to
her party's nominee.

The Democrats were a party in transition, and fighting for their political lives against the resurgent Progressives led by Senator Fish. The Nationalists had chosen Senator Hawking, the son of the former President, to
represent them. He was as articulate as his father, and every bit as clueless. It was rumored that this would be the last year that the Nationalists
would be invited to the debates, as they were not a serious contender anymore at the national level. The Muslim Coalition Party could easily win
twice as many votes just from running a candidate, but they were throwing their support to the Progressives this year, virtually assuring them of
victory.

The question from the young man in the ponytail had been directed to
Senator Hawking, who seemed unsure about what was being asked. "I'm
sorry, what is your question again?" he prompted.

"What will you do for me?" summarized the young member of the
audience of "undecided" voters.

The Senator stepped forward and held the microphone to his mouth,
looking the other in the eye. "First, can you tell me what it is that you're
unable to do for yourself?"

Jill couldn't help a smile, and dropped her head quickly to hide it. At
least they weren't going to have to worry about competition from the Nationalists his year.

2045

Friday, January 20th, 2045
Washington, DC

The wind wasn't the only bitter element on the blustery day of the inauguration of the first Progressive President in the nation's history, particularly for Democrats like "Hudson Jill." The campaign had been a hard-fought affair, even though the outcome had been all but assured for Fish from the moment the MCP announced its allegiance to his candidacy.

Rahim Sahil sat not far from her on the stand set up behind the speaker's platform, on the west side of the Capitol building. She had shaken his hand politely, but did not care to renew their friendship at that particular time. He had hurt her by attacking the Democrats for "betraying Muslims" when they tried to cut a measly $20 million piece of the budget that went to the Bonan community.

Democrats had been the ones that originally allocated the money, back when sympathy for the tiny group of 2,000 peaked at the height of the Edina scare. Jill knew that it was nothing more than a political measure, designed to curry favor with Muslims, but now it appeared entirely unnecessary, given that the virus was no longer an issue, thanks to that infamous research paper. There was a fight against a new health threat in America now called ARS (Acute Respiratory Syndrome) which Jill felt would be a more appropriate use of the funds.

Not so, argued the activists, who accused the Democrats of 'mean-spiritedness' and 'cultural insensitivity.' This was all that was needed to bring down the enormous pressure of media attention. Underlying facts were irrelevant in America, where public opinion was controlled by spin. The Nationalists found that out when they tried to reform Social Security. Democrats deftly played on the public's insecurities, drowning out the debate and actually getting people to beg the government not to give them any decision-making ability over their own retirement accounts.

Now the Democrats were being victimized by their own game. The Progressives knew how to buy bloc votes. They weren't about to debate facts and figures, nor would they be appealing to anything less than insecurity and group identity. Other than the military, Jill couldn't think of a single spending program that had been cut in the last sixteen years.

Nor was it possible to lower taxes, even the regressive fast-food tax was fiercely protected by its advocates, who feared that removing it would be a license for Americans to buy more fatty food at the counter. Both parties were forced to raise taxes substantially, yet the more they did this, the more overall government revenues declined and the economy suffered. It was a real mystery.

At least the Democrats maintained control of the Senate, even if they didn't have the House or the Presidency. She was confident that at some point the Progressives would be forced to negotiate, and the public would realize that there was a practical limit to government expenditures and promises.

'Hail to the Chief' started up and Jill rose with the rest of the contingent, as the nation's new leader descended the steps to take the podium. After the swearing-in, Fish gave a speech that sounded much like those he had given on the trail.

"Thank you my friends and fellow countrymen," the 59-year-old said to the crowd and cameras, "it is an honor to serve you, the people of this great nation.

"For the first time in our history, full power is truly in the hands of the people, rather than in those of the rich and powerful. We have waited a long time for this, but fortunately we are inheriting our country at its most critical hour. Poverty and unemployment have never been higher.

"There are those among us, or to be more precise, in the mansions on the hills above us, that want to maintain the status quo, because, of course, it works so well for them. They're the ones who horde their wealth in banks, to keep it out of the hands of the poor and needy. How is it that there are millions in this country who go to bed hungry at night when there are trillions of dollars sitting in dusty bank accounts, unused and unneeded?

"The ones who call this money their own have obtained it through exploiting the masses with unfair leverage in a harsh economic system that they defend with euphemisms such as 'free enterprise' and 'capitalism.' They manage to keep this money in their families through inheritance and other loopholes of this 'good ole boy' network of rules that they've designed to their own advantage.

"Likewise, big businesses, when they aren't polluting our air and water, are quite accustomed to pulling the strings in Washington. They've skirted the law whenever they thought they could get away with it. They think they can hire who they want and run their businesses as they please, regardless of who gets left out.

"There will be no more groups excluded from the table under my watch. The NDA will be strictly enforced. No one will be allowed to do business in this country if they discriminate in any way.

"I will press for expansion of the Labor Relations Act of 2032. If an employee disputes termination for any reason, the employer will pay 70% of their salary while the matter is being appealed to the Department of Labor.

"Likewise, I will push for the extension of the Benefits Act to require that employers to pay 50% of salary to unemployed workers for the first twenty-four months following a layoff, before government benefits take effect. This will push the cost of unemployment from the hands of tax-payers and into those of employers, where it rightly belongs.

"If these greedy corporations start associating failure of social obliga-tion with a hit to the bottom-line, then they will begin to take an interest in the community. How much have these businesses really devoted to the education of minorities, for example? Yet, they're the first to complain that there aren't enough minorities who are qualified job candidates. They can't have it both ways anymore.

"Like all Americans, I value our national defense, but as President Al Gore and President Hawking proved in very different ways, true security comes from diversity at home and cooperation abroad. We have learned that it no longer serves our interest to exert control beyond our borders. We have shown the world that we are not a threat and, in the process, learned that they are not a threat to us.

"We can take advantage of this peace by building on the military downsizing efforts of previous administrations. How much sense does it make to retain such a large fighting force when there is nothing else com-parable in the world? Why are we training people to kill, when there are others among us who don't have enough to eat? Don't we value life more than death?

"The theme of my campaign last year was 'No Labels.' What this means is that our nation should come together as one people and resist those who seek to divide us through intolerance. Labels are used for noth-ing more than justification of bigotry and irrational fear. A nation without labels is my vision for America. With your help, we can achieve it. Thank you."

Jill applauded politely, as did the rest, with the notable exception of Senator Hawking, who stood with his mouth open, looking absolutely aghast.

She noticed that there was no mention of Maine in his speech, even though it was on everyone's mind. The outgoing President had ordered troops into the state to protect government buildings from bombings and drive-by shooting attacks by the independence groups, who called their uprising an *Intifada*. Ostensibly, the soldiers were also there to discover and neutralize the terror cells that had put the Northeast into a state of fear following the Coop-Mart bombing the previous year. Jill knew, however, that they wouldn't be putting their full effort into this until they learned the direction of the new Administration.

She hoped that Fish would decide something soon. Deploying the military on U.S. soil wasn't making anyone comfortable, even if it was necessary.

February 19ᵗʰ, 2045
Washington, DC

It had been eight years since Maria Posada fell off the radar screen, at least from Jill Hudson's perspective. The two became friends after meeting in college and stayed as such through their years together in Washington, even as their professional relationship became testy at times, due to the pressures of conflicting political interests.

Then it all changed when Maria quit her job suddenly and moved to Montana, where she began working for Airtana and eventually married the owner, whom Jill knew of, but had never met. Not once during that time did Maria ever call to pull strings for the airlines, even though Jill knew the strain it was under. Not that she would have helped anyway, since she had a clear favorite in the company's battle with the government, but she wanted to at least keep up with her friend.

That's why she was delighted when Maria called to say that she would be in town and wanted to have lunch. They met at a trendy salad bar not far from Jill's Crystal City apartment.

Maria was as gorgeous as ever, even after giving birth to three kids. The blue jeans seemed to fit as well as Jill remembered from college, although they looked out of place in urban Washington. There was none of the passion for the old social justice interests that so dominated their past conversations, however. Maria talked more about her husband and his company, and did so with a sort of pride that was alien to Jill.

It was like a whole new person had taken over Maria's body, albeit one who seemed a lot happier and relaxed. At least she kept her last name. For her part, Jill didn't say much about her own marriage eight years earlier to the son of a friend of her father's, although she was quite proud of her 12-year-old daughter, adopted at the age of three. They shared pictures and talked a little about the old times. Memories were about all they had left in common.

Finally, Jill became a bit bolder with her questions. Maria told her that she was in town with her lawyer to appear before a DCA investigating panel. This was no secret, of course, as it was the talk of Washington and GNN was planning to devote live coverage to the televised session.

"Are you really going to argue in favor of racial discrimination?" asked Jill, a little insensitively.

Maria smiled, "As a minority, I could hardly be in favor of that form of discrimination, but I am in favor of people having the freedom to live as they want and make their own investment choices."

"Does this include freedom from harassment by airline personnel?"

It was a pregnant question, but Maria wasn't at all fazed. "Rights sometimes conflict. We feel that the right not to be blown up over a cornfield trumps the right not to be offended," she responded.

"You are harassing innocent people, though."

"I suspect that they'd be more upset about not getting to their destination in one piece, but if not, then they're always free to switch to another carrier."

"But profiling can lead to the sort of resentment that causes the violence in the first place," insisted Jill.

"Don't be naïve," Maria said bluntly, "only a weak-minded person would kill for such reasons. Do you believe that Muslims are weaker-minded than the rest of us?"

"Of course not, but Islam is the religion of peace, and if peaceful people resort to violence, then there must be legitimate grievance."

"Such as being detained by security at an airport for ten minutes?"

"Well, added to the other things…"

"Jill, 3,000 families lost innocent members to Islamic terror on 9/11. How many of them killed Muslim-Americans in revenge?"

"Well, none I guess, but…" Jill's voice tapered as she remembered watching the bodies pulled out of Parker's church.

Maria drove her point home. "If the violent death of a family member at the hands of a Muslim fanatic isn't enough to inspire violence, then why should anything less? Isn't it time that we stop coddling our enemies and start demanding the same consideration and maturity that we do of ourselves? What is it about Islam that lowers our moral expectations?"

It was an impossible question to answer. Jill opted to change the subject.

"How is it that Airtana survives, given that the company is constantly breaking the law?" she asked, not bothering to disguise the insolence.

"Because of the market, Jill. Just like it's supposed to be. People vote with their dollars. If they disagree with our policies, then they fly a different airline. If enough people do this, then we'll have to adjust to their preferences if we want to stay in business, plain and simple. If government has to force its will on the business community, then it reveals itself to be out of touch with the democratic will of the people, which is what guides a free market economy."

"My God Maria, you sound like a Nationalist! Has it really come to this?"

Maria set her fork down and leaned closer to her old friend. In a low voice she asked, "Who do you want to be, Jill, the maker or the taker? The one who builds successfully with his own two hands or the one who sees what is built and wants to control it by no virtue beyond the power simply to do so?"

"What are you talking about, Maria? What the hell are you talking about?" Jill was aware that her voice was high enough to attract attention from those around them, but it didn't matter to her at the moment. "You used to care about helping people, not wasting your talents on defending some bigoted millionaire! I remember when you and Jean came with me that day to the 'March against Hate' on the mall. We had a great time. You were so sincere then. What changed?"

There was a flicker in Maria's eyes at the mention of her partner from ten years ago. She dropped her gaze for a moment and stirred her salad. They both knew that Jill's question implied more than what was on the surface.

Jill was suddenly hit with remorse. "Geez, I'm sorry, Maria," she said in a much lower tone. "I was out of line. I just... it's just that no one knows what happened to you. You used to have so much in common with us. Did you become religious or something? It's like you joined a cult and emerged as a completely different person."

After a few seconds, Maria raised her head with a gracious smile. "I'm sorry that I chose to lose touch with the old group, Jill. It's a hard thing to explain. When we were in college, we used to glory in our open-mindedness, but were we really? It's true that we were good at shouting down conservative speakers, pushing pies in their faces, and using slurs, but why did we feel it necessary to do those things if the facts were on our side? Why didn't we engage those we disagreed with in rational debate or logical discourse?"

Now Jill looked down, half-heartedly stirring her salad.

"Being open-minded," said Maria quietly, "means being open to the true possibility that you can be wrong. It means listening to those who disagree with you and examining the facts objectively. It took time, Jill, but once I did this, I realized why it was really necessary for us to drown out our opponents with volume and smear. Have you?"

Jill didn't answer.

Monday, February 20th, 2045
Tarrant County, Texas

Felipe was caught between flights in Dallas when he got news of the suicide bombing in Ila. The sheriff would not normally have been away from his post that day, which historically brought trouble of some sort to the small South Carolina community (usually a church burning or two) but he had been obliged to attend the funeral of a former partner from his days on the force in El Paso.

The man had been a good cop, which was almost unheard of in the Border States these days, where the police departments were hardly any different now from their Mexican counterparts. This shouldn't have been a surprise to anyone traveling through the area, because the Third World sprawl reached far across the Rio Grande.

The magnitude of change came as a shock even to Felipe, who had not visited back very much in the seventeen years since he left. When he was a boy it was easy to see where the border ended, even without the river. Now there was virtually no distinguishing the torn-up streets and shabby huts on one side from the other. El Paso had been absorbed into Mexico, as had most of the other areas across the American Southwest. Harsh living conditions, overburdened public infrastructures and a bureaucracy that was riddled with corruption were the natural consequences of unchecked immigration. Kidnappings and drug killings underscored a crime problem that was quite literally out of control.

The once-mighty state budgets of Texas and California were strained well past the breaking point, as a massive influx of Federal funds were necessary to cater to the social security of both legal and alien residents. Local politicians who advocated fiscal conservatism didn't last long, if they were elected at all, since it meant cutting back on welfare programs that served the largest constituency bloc almost exclusively.

Even the urban areas further north were experiencing a rapid decay due to the so-called 'transipolitan effect,' whereby entire sections of cities were swallowed up by refugees from south of the border attempting to climb out of the temporary camps that were originally established in remote areas.

As the tide of immigration pulled the nation down into the Third World, to the delight of America's foes, it also dried up funding for foreign aid and international humanitarian relief efforts, both from government budgets and private sources. With its own problems to deal with, the shining city on the hill was becoming no different than those around it, without the ability to provide assistance even for the harshest African and Asian famines.

Open borders was an irreversible experiment, as Felipe could see in parts of Dallas-Fort Worth, when he stopped over to see his sister. The airlines never ran on February 20th, due to the threat of terror attacks, so he had hoped to spend the day relaxing with his sister's family. Instead he found himself racing out of the city in a rental car, in an effort to make it back to Ila that night.

From what he understood, the incident had occurred at the peace rally that was held each year on the Nidal Phad state holiday. It was jointly sponsored by Christian churches and moderate Muslims within the community, although there were not many of the later, since they faced harsh ostracism from the radicals, who did not believe in befriending infidels.

According to one of his officers, the event was in full force with about 300 people, many of whom were counter-protesters, when the bomber wandered into the crowd and detonated his explosives. Sixteen people, including children, were killed, and about seventy were injured.

From listening to the radio, Felipe learned that this was not the worst that the day had to offer; in fact, it was barely mentioned amidst reports of other attacks across the country. The backlash was particularly bad this year because of the *Intifada* in Maine, where the new President had not yet withdrawn troops sent in by his predecessor.

The issue of Maine independence was a *cause celeb* in America these days, where it was taken up in many corners of the country, from college campuses to the airwaves. The fervor of the debate had been turned up exponentially by the "occupation," as the activists called it, and there was growing demand for the withdrawal of the military presence.

Felipe took a particular interest in the situation because, according to the new variant of the old phrase, "as Maine goes, so goes South Carolina."

Tuesday, February 21st, 2045
Washington DC

Walid sat in front of a bank of microphones, spread out on the long table with dark green cloth draped over it. On the floor in front of him was an open expanse, filled with cameramen and lights. Next to him sat Maria Posada, so relaxed that he thought she might burst out laughing. In front of them was a three-person panel that comprised the DCA committee looking into allegations that Airtana Airlines had violated the Non-Discrimination Act by not hiring in proportion to what the Department had established as appropriate racial and religious composites.

They were in their first day of testimony and possibly their last, as it wasn't clear whether they were going to get beyond the current impasse. The lead panelist was sweating like the sow that knows she's dinner (as they would say back in Ila).

"What do you mean by that?" she asked incredulously.

"It's a question, not a statement," responded Walid. "You are using the term 'African-American,' and I asked you to define it."

A soft buzz was sweeping through the room. The woman's face was getting redder. "Someone who is of African descent, I suppose. Does this clear it up for you?"

"Not really, but perhaps you're referring to someone like my friend Karl. Karl, are you here? Could you stand up please?"

A blond-haired white man stood up shyly on the second row and waved to the chairwoman.

"Karl is a seventh-generation South African," noted Walid. "I assume that this is what you mean?"

There was laughter in the room. Karl took his seat.

"Of course not, Mr. al-Rahahti. He isn't black."

"Ah," said Walid, "then perhaps my friend William will suffice. William, are you here?"

A black man sitting next to Karl stood up, then immediately sat down. The chairwoman smiled. "Yes, that's what I mean."

"This is your definition of an African-American?" asked Walid. "But William is from Barbados. He is not American."

"Obviously I mean someone who has dark skin, but is an American citizen as well," snapped the chairwoman.

"Oh, then someone like Amu here then," said Walid, gesturing to the man sitting next to William. "Is his skin dark enough?"

The tension in the room was almost visible. There was a collective sucking-in of breath. Amu stood there with a smile on his face, but he may have been the only one laughing. He could have been mixed race, as it was very difficult to tell from looking at him. Depending on the circumstances he could probably pass as either black, Mexican, Arab or a variety of races including his native Sri Lankan.

The chairwoman looked as if she was going to explode. Walid knew he had taken everyone by surprise. "Damn it, I am not going to play these games with you, Mr. al-Rahahti!"

"Oh but you must," said Walid calmly. "You see, Amu is an employee of Airtana, which you are accusing of being understaffed with regard to African-Americans. In order to defend ourselves, we need to know how to categorize our own staff. Wouldn't you agree?"

The woman cast a look at Walid that made him glad there were plenty of witnesses around. She turned to Amu. "Please approach the microphone. Now, tell us where were you born?"

"Hartford, Connecticut," he answered somewhat shyly.

"Where were your parents born?"

"Which one?"

"Both."

"San Francisco and Brooklyn, New York," he answered.

"Ok then. What about your grandparents? Where were they born?"

"Which one?"

"Oh for God's sake! Tell us, are you African-American or not?"

Without giving him a chance to answer, Walid pulled the microphone back toward himself. "How is that you define an African-American? It's getting confusing in our new 'No Labels' nation."

The chairwoman bit her lip. "I guess by whether an individual thinks they are one."

Walid turned around, "Karl, are you African-American?"

The South African nodded his head enthusiastically. The chairwoman issued an involuntary, audible sigh.

"He isn't black. Therefore he doesn't qualify!" she shouted. "Only a dark-skinned person who thinks they are African-American can be a real African-American."

"How dark does a person's skin need to be?" asked Walid. "Is my skin dark enough?"

"Of course not."

"But, my skin is darker than William's," the Jordanian-born lawyer truthfully objected. "Yet you said that he would qualify as an African-American if he were a U.S. citizen. Did I hear you correctly?"

"Are you African-American?" asked the chairwoman in exasperation, "because you look like an Arab to me. That's a long way from Africa, you know."

Her sarcasm was hardly enough to deter Walid, although those watching had probably noticed that her tone did not reflect the political correct decorum that was normal for such proceedings.

"Does my friend Kamel look like an Arab or an African to you?" asked Walid, who gestured to his former client. The Algerian that he helped make a multi-millionaire proudly stood, while the chairwoman, who apparently recognized him immediately, dropped her head in her hands and massaged her forehead for a full minute. The room buzzed.

Slowly the woman reached for her gavel. Those in the room came to a hush as she struck it on the desk.

"We will adjourn until tomorrow morning," she said weakly.

Washington DC

It was certainly not the Senator's first time back in the White House since her father left eight years earlier, but the late night session in the Oval Office brought back fun memories for her. Jill certainly enjoyed working with her father more than President Fish, but so did a lot of people it seemed.

As if to emphasize this point, the President brought his fist down on the desk in front of him, startling the others in the room. "Damn it, this is a full-blown crisis. Don't you people understand that?"

With them were the DCA chairwoman who presided over the Airtana hearing, the DCA Secretary, and a whole host of advisors. Everyone knew the gravity of the situation without having to be reminded. Affirmative Action was on the line, as were reparations.

The President was in a particularly bad mood because the Airtana lawyer had made allusions to the Progressive's own campaign slogan during the remarks. Indeed, it seemed a bit odd that those promising "No Labels" should be working so hard to try and assign them, but it was nothing that concerned Jill.

Every time they thought they had a solution to the problem, an enterprising individual would earn their pay by pointing out how it could be circumvented. Even the idea of allowing self-surveys within companies was flawed, because it left open the possibility that employees would lie in order to protect their employer (another Marxist precept biting the dust, although no one seemed to notice).

One aide suggested the "pencil test" whereby a pencil would be placed in the hair of a subject. If it stayed, rather than fell to the floor, then it would be assumed that they were African-American. This seemed to make sense to the others, and there was a palpable sense of relief and even giddiness, but then the aide happened to mention that it was "how they used to do it in South Africa," which brought groans.

But neither could anyone else come up with an objective standard that the lawyer would not find some way around. From watching the evening news programs, they realized that they needed to act quickly. At least a few people around the country were obviously beginning to question long-held fundamentals of group identity. If left to grow, then it would jeopardize the political system to which both the Democrats and Progressives owed their success.

The worst thing that could happen, as it turned out, would be for President Fish's public dream to be realized. It was politically convenient to accuse others of using labels, but, in fact, their threatened absence was terrifying to the very people who mocked them the loudest.

Wednesday, February 22nd, 2045
Richmond, Virginia

The airport outside Richmond was the only presence that Airtana still had in the Washington, DC area, yet people drove from as far away as Philadelphia to catch flights there. As with all of their "oasis" terminals, the company did phenomenal business at the airport. Now, as Maria walked glumly down the long corridor that evening, she wondered if that were about to change, and not just in Richmond, where they had over 1,000 employees, but all across America.

She and Walid had a conference call with Kerry and his executive staff that concluded a few minutes ago. He was remarkably optimistic, but then, he always was. Walid was absolutely beside himself, although he had done a decent job of containing his temper before the panel and cameras, as a good lawyer should.

He also made the best of the bad situation by pointing out that the panel's proposed solution to the problem posed the day before was entirely arbitrary. Even the chairwoman looked embarrassed when he pointed out, as well, the coincidence of the executive order materializing on just that very day with the President's signature.

Walid was able to buy the airline a 36-month extension to comply with the NDA under the government's failsafe method of enforcement. True to his campaign promise, the government was making sure that Airtana would be unable to operate beyond that date if they did not receive DCA authorization.

It was with a heavy heart that Maria boarded the plane for the flight to Bozeman.

Tuesday, August 1ˢᵗ, 2045
Washington, DC

The Imam Rastaban entered the offices of his mosque to see Parker Whitehead there waiting for him. He hoped that his irritation on seeing the other didn't show, but from the look on the Reverend's face, he realized that it must have. He decided to compensate by forcing a broad smile and hearty handshake.

"Reverend, it's good to see you. I'm afraid I don't have much time, however."

Parker returned the smile. "It'll just take a moment, if you don't mind."

The Imam showed him into his office. It was true that he was busy that day. In fact he was returning from an interview with GNN, over the problems in Maine, where he was asked about the violence. He had done a careful job of condemning the tactics, while validating the motives of the insurgents. "As long as there is occupation, there will be resistance," he repeated several times during the interview. He even quoted a few Bible verses, such as "eye for an eye," to try and broaden the appeal to the American masses, which were growing weary of the operation. He knew that they would wear down over time.

He had not seen much of Parker Whitehead since the dedication ceremony nine years earlier. Occasionally he asked the Christian to appear with him and speak on behalf of various causes that were important to the Muslim community, such as changing local noise ordinances to permit the call to prayer, allowing Muslims to wear beards and avoid strip-searches that were religiously offensive, beefing up the religious vilification laws that protected the Qur'an, and even allowing Muslim-only fighting units in the armed forces so that his people would be free to serve without sacrificing the tenets of their faith, which did not permit bathing with infidels.

The Reverend obliged each time, happy to contribute to their "shared values of religious tolerance," even though the favor was rarely returned. As of late, Whitehead had been bringing up annoyances that his parishioners were having with Muslims in the community. This occasion was no exception.

"I'm sorry to have to ask this," he began hesitantly, "but it seems that there are a number of people complaining that they are harassed as they're walking to the Cathedral on Sundays and Wednesdays."

"What makes this my responsibility?" asked the Imam quickly.

"Well, we've noticed that the problems seem to be caused by those in your mosque. In fact, we often catch some on their way to your services urinating in the doorways of our Cathedral. Women complain that they are harassed by men in *galabiyyas*…"

"I guess we Arabs make for convenient scapegoats, eh?" said the Imam.

Parker raised his eyebrows. "Now you know it isn't like that. I supported…"

"Then explain why a Christian army is currently subjugating the Muslims in this country," demanded the Imam. "Why is it that we live as second-class citizens, unable to practice our religious faith according to *Sharia*? Don't you remember what they did to Nidal Phad?"

"Of course, Sir, of course," Parker was clearly on the defensive. "I understand that Muslims have suffered grave injustices in this country. I support you on every issue, you know that. All I'm asking is for some consideration for the sensibilities of my parishioners. Is this too much?"

Even the Imam conceded that he had a good point. Their neighborhood was turning over rapidly, and he didn't doubt that every one of Whitehead's complaints was true. The Cathedral had to maintain a security staff and cameras to protect the building against vandals and arsonists, so they probably had clear evidence of who the perpetrators of the distasteful behavior were.

Soon, perhaps, neither would need to worry about it. He had already sent out feelers to the church, asking if they would consider selling the property. The symbolism of the National Cathedral becoming a mosque would draw enough money from Muslim businessmen to produce a very attractive offer. The daily harassment that the parishioners were experiencing certainly wouldn't hurt their chances either, although he would honor his word to the Reverend and speak to his community about that.

As Parker Whitehead was leaving, the Imam gave him a smile and said, "Hope to see you at the Mall on the third, eh Reverend?" He was referring to the Nidal Phad rally for religious tolerance, which had taken the place of the semi-annual commemoration of the burning of the al-Raz mosque nearly forty years earlier. As the most visible Christian leader in America, Whitehead was nearly always a featured speaker at the event.

He turned and gave a smile and a nod. "Absolutely, I'll be there!"

Sunday, August 6ᵗʰ, 2045
Hiroshima, Japan

"Hudson" Jill's trip to Hiroshima for the 100ᵗʰ anniversary of the atomic bomb detonation had begun with dropping her daughter off at Parker Whitehead's. Relations between the two were awkward the first few years after her marriage. He knew that she had given up on him, and they both knew why.

The pain was mitigated considerably by her adopted daughter, Merica. Parker would probably always be single, but like many childless adults around their age, he had begun to realize a certain void that went beyond simple companionship. The girl was a joy to him, and Jill appreciated the way she delighted in the man she knew as "Uncle Parker." She had practically grown up on his knee and their special bond had not diminished, even as the girl was now moving into her early-teen "grown-up" years, with music, make-up, and talk of boys.

Watching her bounce up the steps and into the arms of the smiling, white-haired man at his parsonage was always bittersweet for Jill. Not only was the girl closer to Parker than her own father, but so was Jill. Her husband was distant and delicate – not exactly the sort to bring out the woman in her.

Now that her daughter was spending the week with Parker while she was away, Jill figured that the two were probably having a better time than she was.

The trip had begun with a stop in Hawaii for the ceremony marking the decommission of Peace Harbor – what used to be called Pearl Harbor before the name was changed in deference Japanese-Americans, who complained of the connotation. It had been forty years since the Navy built its last vessel. There were no longer enough operational ships and submarines to justify maintaining the bases scattered throughout the globe. It was the same with the Air Force. Only about 25% of the air fleet at the turn of the century was still in use. The rest had been disassembled or sold to other countries, such as Poland and the Baltic States, as America desperately needed the money for battling poverty and unemployment – to say nothing of the $2 trillion to support the Reparations Act.

Alberta offered to buy much of the decommissioned military equipment, but Americans were developing a healthy fear of their neighbor to the North, which stood out starkly in a world of Socialist States, Islamic theocracies and benign dictatorships that were all appreciative of the U.S. policy of non-intervention. It wasn't clear what sort of threat the Albertans truly posed to America, or if the fear was simply a convenient distraction from the spiraling economy, but they were the primary reason that the country felt compelled to maintain military readiness, even if it made no sense to fund a force of people trained to kill, when the resources could be used for employing welfare agents, doctors and job training programs for refugees.

There was no question that Alberta was partially responsible for America's economic woes, since so much American wealth had moved up into that rogue U.S. Protectorate, as well as the other "countries" in their so-called Western Alliance, which included Alaska and the Yukon among others. No one in government really understood how the loss of 40 million people could have such an impact on the U.S. economy, especially when they were more than replaced by plenty of others from south of the border and overseas who *wanted* to be here. The country had experienced a net gain of more than 120 million people over the last four decades and mirrored the world's population better than the Pillar project designers could even have hoped.

In an effort to stem the tide of emigration to the north, Congress passed legislation that prevented seniors from receiving Social Security benefits if they lived "abroad" (meaning in Alberta). Restrictions were also placed on personal assets that could leave the country. This had gone through several different versions over the years, from "exit taxes" based on percentages and fixed amounts, to the current rule that simply set a $200,000 ceiling on what could be transferred out of the country.

Still, this didn't stop people from leaving. Even business owners, who theoretically lost nearly everything by shutting their doors and starting over, continued to do so. The U.S. was forced to build a wall around the border to ensure that the rules were being followed, yet whatever wealth was left behind never seemed to make much difference. All the while, Alberta was getting richer, to the embarrassment of the U.S. They had oil, as well as some sort of voodoo economy that stimulated development and employment without the regulatory oversight that the United States employed to ensured fairness. Edmonton was actually beginning to have more influence in the Red States than Washington.

Just thinking about the disparity between the countries was almost enough to send Jill into a tantrum. It wasn't fair that her country should be lagging when they were doing so much to keep anyone in society from being left behind by scrupulously holding corporations to the meticulous system of rules and regulations that assured safety, inclusion, and sensitivity in the workplace down to the smallest detail. By contrast, Alberta didn't even have a minimum wage law or Affirmative Action.

Noise from outside the window broke her thoughts and penetrated some of the jet lag that she was struggling with in the back of the limo, as it whisked her to the ceremony in Hiroshima. The President was in Japan to formally apologize on the 100th anniversary. Though they couldn't bring back the 150,000 people senselessly killed in those two blasts, or afford immediate reparations, the apology would be an acknowledgement of culpability and a symbol of a new America that was no longer subject to the sort of arrogance and imperialism behind such barbaric acts.

Jill sat back in the cool leather seat and enjoyed as much as she could of the Japanese countryside while trying to stay awake. The route was lined with protestors, most expressing their anger at what the U.S. had done a century before, but, as they rounded a bend, Jill noticed two lone individuals with different sorts of signs that said something about "Nanking" and "300,000." These were quickly torn out their hands by Japanese police, but not before they piqued her curiosity.

What was it Jill had been told one time? There was some sort of massacre by Japanese troops on a Chinese city at the start of World War II that left a large number of civilians dead. Was it really 300,000? Perhaps she had misread the sign. If there was really such an atrocity then certainly it would be receiving more attention than Hiroshima… wouldn't it?

Saturday, August 19th, 2045
New York, New York

Phyllis Hughes knew that there was something wrong by the sight of the police cars in the street, even before she rushed into the lobby of Beth Landau's building to find the group standing there with embarrassed expressions.

She had been excited about the upcoming release of her first true box-office production, "Pretend that we're Dead." The premise of the futuristic movie was a society controlled by a right-wing Christian theocracy, which stifles freedom and individuality, and turns the population into mindless drones and women into sex slaves. Creativity and freedom of speech are effectively outlawed by the fascists. At one climactic point in the movie, a heroic opposition figure attempts to speak his mind publicly, but is pelted with food.

The presence of the police cars outside the building disturbed her. She and her friends privately feared something that they referred to cryptically as the "shrinkage." It mainly pertained to Manhattan, but could have described most of America, where the rising tide of crime and poverty was slowly enveloping entire communities, including neighborhoods that had once been buffered by wealth. The safe areas around the Upper West Side were being encroached by the Caribbean and African gangs that lived much closer now than Harlem or the Bronx. They were changing the face of the community and putting residents in fear.

From the faces of those in the lobby, Phyllis knew that a crime of some sort had occurred. She was relieved to find out that it was only a mugging and that no one had been physically hurt, although it was humiliating to be held at knifepoint while having to hand over jewelry and wallets. The victims were very angry at the police for allowing it to happen. "Are we not paying you with our taxes to keep us safe?" Beth demanded.

"You're lucky," responded the officer, who had seen surveillance video, "this is the same guy that knifed a social worker to death on the other side of town three nights ago. He must be on some sort of drug binge."

"But I thought that the suspect in that case was white," responded Beth, somewhat perplexed.

"No, you heard wrong," interjected her friend. "They only gave the height and weight on the news, not the race. That means he was black."

"Yes that's right," Phyllis affirmed, "it was a white social worker killed by an African-American; obviously the effect of rational distrust caused by institutional racism. There was a memorial service last night that I was reading about this morning. The woman's co-workers are using her death to try and draw attention to the plight of the disenfranchised. It's all very thrilling! Perhaps you can use this experience as a platform as well?"

Beth gave her a cold look and started to say something but stopped herself. The group turned its ire back on the police.

"We know who this guy is," protested one of the officers, "we'll catch him soon. He has a criminal record. In fact he was serving life without parole upstate when it was declared unconstitutional by the Court."

"Well," stammered Beth, "I guess... I guess you guys obviously made a mistake then and let the wrong guy out! This merely undermines public confidence."

"Not as badly as the Willie Powell episode did," responded a different policeman, somewhat coyly. "It's always best for us to err on the side of caution now, eh?"

Wednesday, September 6th, 2045
New York, NY

Bernice Greenly watched the televised press conference from her corner office in Manhattan. She wondered how much her news organization should be crediting itself for the President's expected announcement of U.S. troop withdrawal from Maine.

The presence of the Army there was controversial from the moment that it was sent in by the lame duck President following the November elections, ostensibly for the purpose of rooting out the terror groups that made life difficult not only for those in Maine, but in other parts of the country as well, such as the shoppers who were blown to bits in Hartford.

Bernice quickly sensed that Muslims felt alienated by the operation. After all, there were no troops patrolling other American states.

GNN quickly applied the more neutral label of "insurgents" to the terrorists (some interviewees used the term "freedom fighters") and referred to the military operation as an "occupation." Naturally, they kept a body count of each death that could be attributed to the military presence, even those that were direct victims of the very terrorists that the "occupation" force was trying to stop, including local police officers. The numbers weren't that dramatic so far, but it was enough to feed the anti-war movement on college campuses and draw the attention of the United Nations, which had passed several resolutions calling for withdrawal.

Now it appeared that the President was ready to do just that. Bernice watched as he stood behind the "blue goose" in the White House Press Room, along with Rahim Sahil, whom she hadn't been expecting. She hoped that her main correspondent was in position on the front row.

"Thank you for coming," opened the President. "As most of you know, my predecessor sent U.S. troops into Maine ten months ago to protect the civic infrastructure from what was thought at the time to be a security threat. Indeed, several bombings did occur, mostly at police stations, although civilians were targeted as well, in some cases.

"Though not the best solution, as I told my predecessor when he consulted me, I'm happy to announce that the operation has been a success. Insurgency cells have been disrupted and their leaders arrested. There is no further basis for maintaining the state of emergency that required a military presence. The last troops will be withdrawn by the end of the week.

"To ensure that such drastic military measures are never again necessary, and that future problems are always handled by constructive dialogue instead, I have appointed the head of BAIR, Rahim Sahil, to a special task force commissioned for the purpose of finding common ground between the people involved. I've asked Rahim to say a few words, but we will not be taking any questions at this time." The President motioned to Bernice's old college friend, and he stepped up to the podium.

"Thank you, Mr. President. It is an honor to serve the country that I love so dear. America is a great nation, but it will be even greater once all people feel comfortable practicing their own religion. Although the violence is regrettable and, of course, has nothing to do with Islam, it is still an expression of the terrible frustration that Muslims in America must live with each day, as we are forced to choose between following our faith or following our country.

"We appreciate that some token *Sharia* is allowed us in civil matters, but Americans should understand that Islam is a wonderful religion with much broader requirements than what Christians and Jews are apparently comfortable permitting us. Muslims will never have full rights of citizenship in this country, until they have full *Sharia*."

Rahim paused for effect then looked into the camera. "Is devaluing our faith the only way that America can accept us?"

It was a great note to end on, Bernice thought, as she turned down the sound and leaned back in the chair, even if it sounded as if the dialogue would be a bit one-sided. But, it would be a small price to pay for peace.

Tivoli, New York

The words "nothing to do with Islam" were still ringing in Walid's head as he flipped off the TV and prepared to leave the house on one of his late-night walks.

Someone apparently forgot to tell the terrorists that their activities had nothing to do with Islam, since they could not be any blunter about it. They were constantly quoting from the Qur'an in their statements and video releases. They basically operated out of mosques. And they had the support or sympathy of the vast majority of Muslims in the country.

As he stepped out into the cool night air, closing the door behind him, the former FBI agent wondered just when it was that Americans lost their will to think.

2046

Sunday, March 4th, 2046
Kalispell, Montana

Pat Ridley had known many good times in the last thirty years, but two of the best weeks in his life were coming to a close that morning. Never before did he think it possible that he would enjoy himself in Montana, even though he had started voting Nationalist a few years back, much to his sister's consternation.

"What are you doing voting for those Nationalists?" she asked. "They won't give you anything."

Her attitude wasn't much different than that of most others in America, he had to admit. But that didn't mean that he had to follow suit and hold out his hand along with everyone else.

He had read a magazine article a few months earlier about the Paterski project in northwestern Montana. The company had signed several contracts over the last several years and was swimming in money. One of the four people behind the success had a familiar name, Aaron Bernstein.

It turned out that his old helicopter buddy was now sixty-one and very comfortably retired in Kalispell. He had started a new life there after the court-martial, when a local businessman hired him to fly planes. After a time, when his name was no longer as recognizable, he went to work for other companies, and eventually wound up devoting over a dozen years of his life to the brainchild of a remarkable man named Dennis Paterski.

Pat wasn't sure what to expect when he got off the plane in Montana with his 25-year-old son, Matthew, who was on leave from the Air Force, where he was an officer and pilot. Thirteen years earlier he had purposely avoided the Red States on his trip out to California with young Matt. Now he wondered how he could have been so foolish as to believe all those scare tactics that the intelligentsia use to cloud the judgment of those living within their domain.

The quality of life was amazing and the people were quite friendly. No one was wearing hoods or seemed the least bit bothered by the presence of two African-American men. He quickly found out that the region was not nearly as "lily-white" as it was portrayed in the media, and the economy was booming. There was a certain "can-do" attitude reflected in the communities. The people were necessarily rich, but neither was there poverty, as it seemed that everyone knew to take responsibility for their lives.

One thing that did amuse him was that his friend, who was an engineer and a keen intellectual, had somehow become a redneck as well – a Jewish redneck at that. He always carried a gun, usually had his dogs with him, and even drove a four-wheel-drive pickup truck (as did plenty of other residents).   Bernstein hated the government with a passion, which, knowing what they did to him, Pat could perfectly understand.

On the flight from New York, Pat explained to his son about how this former cobra pilot had taken off against orders and flown a gunship solo into the teeth of a Fedayeen ambush to die fighting for the lives of people he had never met. It was hard for Pat to even talk about it without emotion, but his son, being a military man now as well, could understand.

Bernstein had sacrificed his military career at the age of thirty-one, but he met the right man in Dennis Paterski, and with the help of others he had built quite a life for himself. He may have acted like a recluse, but his wife Sharon seemed to belie his anti-social behavior. Such a remarkably well-grounded, gregarious woman would never have been attracted to the sort of fringe extremist that her husband seemed to be on the surface. Pat could tell that they adored each other.

Dennis Paterski was an interesting man himself. He lived alone and was not very social. Bernstein told his friend that Paterski would often stop going to a restaurant if a waiter began to greet him with any familiarity. He seemed to shun friendly people, oddly enough, although he made a point of inviting Pat and his son to supper, along with Bernstein.

It was a good evening. Paterski knew the story of Highway 455, but prompted the two men with questions. Pat could tell that his son was fascinated by all of the new details. They laughed about how Pat had signed his 'confession' to the Army with the three words, "Kiss My Ass." The four men stayed up late into the morning, smoking cigars and sipping drinks. The enjoyable evening was repeated a few days later when they were joined by two others, Sanjay Guptapara and Greg Dijkstra.

Pat learned more about the two biotech inventions that had now brought in over a billion dollars in revenue, with the recent signing of a second AIDs vaccine for another common strain of the virus. Both systems worked together to produce a genetic code that would be specifically tailored either as a vaccine or a cure against a particular virus or bacteria. The first was a device that could analyze nucleotide sequences at an amazing rate. This allowed the team to quickly map out the properties of a virus or bacteria. The second invention was a supercomputer and database software program that could compute chemical combinations that would be effective in killing the pathogen. Together, the integrated system could generate the code for a drug manufacturer to produce the antibiotics that would either eliminate or protect against a pathogen such as the AIDs virus.

"What about ARS?" asked Ridley, referring to the new disease that had been receiving a lot of attention as of late.

Paterski smiled and looked at the others. "We're currently working on that one, although this is classified of course. We hope to begin trials sometime next year. It's a tricky process. Usually there are several possible combinations that will work against a virus, but some of them may be harmful to the subject. Although we can produce a solution on paper in a matter of days, it sometimes takes a year or so before we're confident enough to sell it to a pharmaceutical company."

There was a certain confidence and poise to this group of individuals that had risked so much to pursue a dream. Pat appreciated that his son was able to be in the presence of successful men. He wondered how many problems in life could be avoided if younger people were taught to respect accomplished businessmen, rather than fed a constant diet of corporate villainy.

They spent the rest of their time skiing, snowmobiling, and enjoying western Montana.

Sunday, April 8th, 2046
Rothberg, California

Sunday mornings were one of the few times that the Professor felt any lingering sense of satisfaction with his community. He may have had to jump over piles of garbage and cut his way through some of the overgrown yards that now resembled jungles, to get across the complex, but at least he didn't have to put up with church bells or that annoying traffic from freshly scrubbed families in suits and dresses clogging the arteries of his little town.

Sundays were no different from any other day in Rothberg, and it was perfectly appropriate for him to visit the woman who officially served as the director of community projects to inquire about a business matter.

Letitia Ridley was someone with whom he had a long history of tense relations. She was one of the low-income members of the community, whose immediate promotion from chronic welfare to a directorship was meant to refute the anti-egalitarian idea that people were a product of their own choices rather than the system. If a woman, who was forced by society into the humiliation of welfare dependency, were to be elevated to a position of opportunity, then her success would prove that capitalism, itself, was responsible for her condition.

Rothermel had to admit, however, that Letitia was straining his faith in social equality. She may have started out with the same enthusiasm as others in the community who realized their sense of duty, based on the opportunity to participate in the ideal, planned society, but her commitment eroded rapidly.

Her responsibility was to coordinate the various projects, such as grounds keeping and maintenance. This seemed to go as planned for the first year, but Rothermel noticed that her workday quickly declined to about half of the seven hours at which it started. By the end of the first

year she was getting in around 10:30, working for an hour, and then taking a long lunch, after which she might return for a couple of hours before
leaving the office around 3:00. Soon she stopped coming back from
lunch. When Rothermel inquired, he learned that she suffered from "fa-
tigue syndrome" caused by "historical oppression" and would probably
need to telecommute. The council obliged, of course, but Rothermel
knew in his heart that she was spending her entire time watching TV,
since she was nearly always the first to complain of a disruption in cable
service, no matter the time of day.

   Still, there was nothing that could be done about it, or about the many
others that shirked their responsibilities. Their duties fell to those who
would do them; then eventually they went undone altogether. As Rothermel turned the corner onto Letitia's street that morning, he realized that he
finally understood why the Soviets found the Gulag necessary.

   The topic of conversation would be reparations. The community was
in dire need of funds, and it was estimated that about 200 households were
eligible for some form of compensation from the government, for the
slavery that their ancestors endured. Conservatively, this put estimates of
combined reparations revenue at about $50 million or more.

   It was hard to know for sure because the government had devised a
complicated system of qualification for the program that was hailed as a
"glorious redistribution" and a "permanent leveling of the playing field."
Each African-American would receive full compensation, except for
mixed-race individuals, who would receive no more than half. Birth cer-
tificates and DCA "race review boards" would determine eligibility.

   The latter method was somewhat controversial and would be used
only in disputes. It was sometimes called the "Airtana" rule, since it was
the means by which the airline was being forced to comply with the NDA.
It put the power for determining race within the hands of a DCA committee constructed for that purpose. These were members of the race as determined by Presidential appointment. They, in turn, could deputize other
race review boards to handle the caseloads for reparations. For that reason, it was occasionally referred to by critics as the "friends and family
plan" who contended that there would be widespread fraud.

   Rothermel didn't care at that point. Nor was he greatly concerned
about the disincentives for marriage and the strong impetus for a single
woman to have at least three children in order to receive the maximum
payout from the sliding scale plan that could pay up to $500,000 per
household. A divorce could mean an additional $100,000 for the right
couple, and the rumors alone were enough to finish off the black family,
which, as the critics put it, had survived slavery and segregation, but not
welfare.

Rothermel didn't believe in family anyway, at least not the traditionally defined version that served the purposes of patriarchic oppression. It takes a village to raise a child, as former President Rodham used to say, and the world was a family, whether everyone realized it yet or not.

As he made his way up the walkway toward Letitia's door, he considered strategy. He wanted to convince her that they should not fall victim to the "fast cash" option, in which unscrupulous companies were swooping in to bypass the mandated system of Federal payouts over a ten-year period. These middlemen would offer eligible households half of the full amount up front in return for the rights to their government payments. It was perfectly legal, and highly tempting to most, apparently, but Rothermel knew that it would not be in the long-term interests of their community, which needed the full amount as it was paid out over the next ten years.

This was going to be a true shot in the arm for Rothberg, and the Professor's mood was high as he knocked on the door.

Tuesday, April 17th, 2046
New York, New York

Robert Danforth knew immediately when his computer screen went blank what had happened, but it didn't stop him from throwing a tantrum anyway. Others in the office tried to stay out of his way, although one newer person had the temerity to answer his rhetorical question by suggesting that the rolling blackouts had been expanded.

"You think?" he yelled at her.

The city was supposed to inform them of any changes in the power schedule, which was currently set at six hours "savings time," meaning that the power was cut three times a day for two hours at a time. There had been talk that the energy conservation window was going to be expanded that week, but no one announced any changes to CSR.

It came at an inopportune time for the office. They were working furiously on a project to lobby against proposed development in Uganda, specifically the country's plans to build an additional nuclear power plant. The African nation had already exhausted the goodwill of the developed world by building its economic infrastructure in defiance of environmental concerns. Not only did they build power plants, but they actually used DDT to eliminate malaria deaths, much to the horror of the socially conscious.

The development of other nations in Africa could still be controlled through foreign aid. African leaders were quite happy lining their own pockets, even if it meant keeping industrial growth and economic opportunity out of their people's reach in order to satisfy Western donors' concern that expansion would have a detrimental effect on the planet's ecosystem. It was all for the cause of sustainable development – which was much easier to enforce in the Third World.

No so with Uganda, however. That country had leaders who boldly claimed that self-sufficiency and the pursuit of wealth was not only good for Ugandans, but good for the planet as well. They pointed out that developed nations generated far less pollution per capita and that the more wealth a country had, the more likely it was to adopt environmental protection policies.

Danforth and others scoffed at such sophistry. The statistics may have been true, but the risk wasn't worth taking.

At least his cappuccino was still warm – his only consolation as he sat in a huff, waiting for the power to come back on.

Wednesday, July 4th, 2046
New York, New York

Bernice didn't need to watch the GNN monitors behind her to see what was going on in America; all she had to do was look outside her window, where thick smoke from the cars burning in the street rose past. Through it, she could see the mob down below, throwing bricks and pulling unfortunate drivers out of their cars for the purposes of beating them to a pulp.

The GNN chief knew that it was happening in other major cities, particularly in the Northeast and South Carolina. Muslims were rioting on the news that troops had been sent back into Maine to quell the unrest. For once, Bernice sympathized with the decision to use force. GNN had covered the aftermath of bombings in the last several days. People were leaving the state in droves, some probably for good.

It had not yet been a full year since she watched Fish announce the withdrawal, with Rahim at the press conference. Things seemed promising then, but the optimism faded over time. Churches in Maine were periodically burned to the ground. The non-Muslims complained of intimidation and harassment, although GNN refused to carry this on fears that it might lead to Islamophobia on the part of the general public. Now, there was no denying the violence.

The recent trouble in Maine started when it became known that a Jewish man was serving on the jury of a Muslim defendant, accused of rape. This provoked a harsh reaction from the populace, which was 70% Muslim following the waves of immigration and years of asymmetrical assimilation. Over the last couple of weeks, there had been escalating violence and terrorist attacks on government buildings and public places. About sixty-five people had been killed so far.

As the Muslim ghettos erupted, their politicians vacillated between calls for calm and expressions of outrage. One frustrated New Yorker said it would be better if they just "shut up altogether" given that they did not have the political maturity for spacing their contradictory positions apart over time, as other American politicians had learned to do.

At least it was looking as if the worst of the rioting was over, not withstanding what was happening on the street beneath her. Bernice still knew that it would be days before she would see the inside of her apartment again. By that time, GNN would have the whole affair neatly defined in terms of disenfranchisement and oppression; something for the cultured class to mull on over the morning cappuccino.

From where she stood at the moment, however, it was a little difficult sorting out the victims of oppression from the bodies that they were leaving bloody and broken on the pavement.

Thursday, November 15th, 2046
Nashville, Tennessee

Danforth was waiting in a van, parked as close as possible to the airport. It frustrated him to be so close to where the action taking place, yet unable to participate.

He desperately wanted to be known as the man who destroyed Airtana Airlines. He was getting a lot of competition, however, from many in Washington, including Jill Hudson and the President himself. Together, they were all beginning to tighten the noose around the airline. It was only a matter of time before the company went under, with CSR leading the charge and hoping for the credit. So far, they had cost the airline millions over its refusal to pay domestic partners benefits; and they sued on a variety of other issues related to discrimination, costing millions more in fines. Airtana had been forced to change airports on a fairly steady basis, as CSR waged successful campaigns with city councils to deny the carrier a local presence.

There were bumps along the way, most noticeably the ill-timed protest in Birmingham three months earlier, where Danforth showed up to protest the airline's plans to expand operations, along with a half-dozen other CSR activists, who carried signs and handed out brochures attesting to the company's abysmal treatment of employees. The media was somewhat distracted, however, by the presence of nineteen thousand job applicants standing in line for hours behind them, hoping for one of the forty open positions announced by the carrier.

Now Congress had given CSR a new tool, the Non-Discrimination in Transportation Act (NDTA). Though written in neutral language and promising very hefty fines for any transportation company that discriminated for any reason, it was mainly written to force the airlines, particularly Airtana, into applying the same security standards to everyone, regardless of whether they looked Middle-Eastern. Five verifiable complaints could shut a provider down.

CSR was trying the old "ringer" routine that Danforth had learned 20 years earlier from the Chicano Civil Rights organization in Tucson. The plan was to buy a ticket for a suspicious looking Arab man, then wait to see whether he is harassed by Airtana security. The "ringers" were briefed on how to act and what to say, in order to draw attention. Meanwhile, the encounter would be secretly filmed by CSR and BAIR operatives planted strategically at the gate.

Danforth's face was too well known for him to be on the floor, but he was monitoring the live footage from a bank of monitors that were in the back of the van. There were three "ringers," two of whom were in Middle-Eastern clothing over prominent "Free Maine" T-shirts, while the other had on a very bulky leisure suit. All of them looked as if they could be carrying a belt of explosives under their clothes. All had been sprayed with water to simulate sweat and, of course, each would chant in Arabic while darting their eyes quickly about the room.

Sure enough, the team nailed it. All three men were detained for fifteen minutes each, and two were denied boarding when they became agitated. Danforth couldn't help chuckling with glee. It had been an expensive gamble, but it looked like it might pay off as well as they'd hoped.

2047

Thursday, February 14th, 2047

Lewiston, Maine

The lieutenant had been told that this was where it all began. Back in the 1990's, Lewiston had taken in a large number of Somali refugees, who were attracted by the state's generous welfare programs. In time, Maine ran out of money and had to depend on Federal assistance, particularly as it became a favorite spot for Pillar project immigrants. Unlike past waves of immigrants, however, these people refused to assimilate to their host country. They retained their language, their customs and particularly their religion, which made life difficult for the native New Englanders.

Now they wanted *Sharia*, the Islamic law, extended beyond simple civil matters and established as a parallel legal system. The lieutenant didn't think that this was the best choice (nor did the non-Muslims residents of the state) but neither did he think it was worth going to war over.

Officially, of course, they weren't at war; they were simply there to quell the *Intifada*. This meant trying to "liberate" the citizens from the terror network that the same good citizens worked to protect. Even when they did make arrests, the militants were released by the courts, although sometimes it took groups like BAIR to pressure them into doing so. 'Human rights' attorneys made it impossible to effectively interrogate subjects, and the terrorists knew that. Their every whim was catered to in detention and any misstep was rapidly publicized and condemned by disingenuous lawyers, eager to use the nation's laws to facilitate its own demise.

This was a doomed effort, not just because the *Intifada* was free from the constraints of moral war that hamstrung the military, but rather that the rest of the country allowed it. There was barely a yawn when the enemy put bombs into baby carriages or blew up restaurants, but if a military interrogator so much as dropped a Qur'an on the floor, then all hell broke loose in the mosques across the nation. It was pretty obvious which side would be winning when only one was bound by rules.

This was what made the young officer somewhat nervous about getting his patrol past the elementary school in that narrow section of the street. There was a mosque on the other side of the school, and he wouldn't put it past the enemy to direct fire from it, even if stray bullets wound up in classrooms. Their adversaries had such little regard for human life that they would even kill themselves in suicide bombings.

That the first two patrols ahead of him passed without incident gave the lieutenant a small measure of comfort as he directed his platoon across. He was responsible for the lives of twenty-two men and women under his command, and he got less sleep than they did at night, worrying for their safety.

The first bullets were perfectly timed. One of them caught the young officer in the neck. He slapped his hand to it, fearing the worst. There was a lot of blood, but it must have been a vein and not an artery, because he was still conscious. He took note of the situation. Three dead soldiers lay on the road. The rest of his troops were trying to take cover as best they could, but the trap had been perfectly laid. Although there were snipers in the mosque, the majority of fire was actually coming from the school.

As he stood there with the life seeping out of him, three more soldiers went down. Another four were clutching some part of their bodies and screaming in agony. He felt his leg shatter beneath him from another bullet. The pain was so great that he was forced to take his hand away from his neck. Before the world went permanently black, he uttered a simple command to his remaining troops.

"Shoot back!"

Washington D.C.

Jill got the call to the emergency White House session within minutes of the Al-Jazeera broadcast. The network was the second-rated cable news network behind GNN, and there was always a TV tuned to it in her Senate offices.

The pictures looked awful. It was already being called the "Saint Valentine's Day Massacre," with the word 'Saint' specifically included by the Arab network to project a not-so-subtle emphasis on the purportedly Christian origins of the holiday, as if religious affiliation was what had led American troops to fire into an elementary school and mosque.

Al-Jazeera's cameras were the only ones at the scene. The producers claimed that they just happened to be on site after having been invited by the principal of the school to record an innocuous student activity which, on the surface, did not appear at all worthy of the news giant's attention. Their footage was obviously edited, but it did show U.S. troops firing into both a school and mosque. Of course, someone must have been shooting back at them, since there were dead soldiers lying about, but Jill knew that this wasn't how the world would be judging it.

By the time she got checked into the West Wing and into the Oval Office, the President was beside himself. The final numbers showed that four children had been killed, along with sixteen troops, two teachers and six "civilians." Leaders from the Arab world and Europe were demanding answers. "This is the end," Fish kept saying.

He was right, as it turned out. By the end of that day, the UN had passed a resolution condemning the slaughter of innocents and calling for the immediate withdrawal of troops from Maine. There were rumblings that the International Criminal Court would be pressing for an investigation. Most overseas embassies were forced to close, in the face of mass demonstrations and riots. There was word that the unrest was starting up again in American cities as well, with some neighborhoods expected to be in flames by nightfall.

Appeasement was the only sanctioned way to quell the outrage. That evening, the President announced that all troops in Maine would be taken off the streets pending investigation, but it did not stop mobs from lynching sixteen people over a twenty-four hour period, including the chief of police in Brunswick, who was pulled from his car and burned alive.

Thursday March 7th, 2047
Washington D.C.

Three weeks to the day after the 'Saint Valentines Day Massacre' the President announced that Maine voters would decide whether to live under *Sharia*, which was a near certainty, given that previous referendums had passed by better than two to one margins. This was the nation's first experiment with a parallel religious legal system, and there was some anxiety over how it would progress.

Bernice thought it best to focus directly on the issue and called in a favor with an old college friend, Parker Whitehead, who eagerly agreed to appear on GNN with his counterpart, Imam Rastaban, to perhaps set the nation at ease over the changes in New England. Bernice thought that it would also calm the public's nerves to have the popular Bahira al-Zubayi do the interview. During the two hour session, the three of them appeared quite relaxed, as they sat on the plush "morning show" set in casual clothes to discuss the changes among themselves and with concerned callers.

Parker was especially reassuring. When asked by an angry caller why he didn't "stand up for Jesus" the Reverend gave a gentle chuckle and insisted that he was. "Christ commands us to be merciful to others," he said. "This means accepting a stranger as you would yourself and turning the other cheek. Showing religious tolerance is our way of honoring God."

Another caller asked what would become of the "infidels" living in Maine. The Imam took that question. "No one has anything to fear," he told the caller, with Parker nodding earnestly behind him. "*Sharia* only applies to Muslims. The *dhimmis*, or non-Muslims will be allowed to keep their religion and their legal system, and would not be subject to *Sharia* unless a dispute arises with a Muslim."

At that point, Parker stopped nodding and Bahira looked nervous. "Actually," she corrected him, "the secular law would apply in disputes between unequal parties."

The Imam shook his head in plain annoyance, but the conversation continued. "I think," said Parker, "that the caller is simply expressing a natural fear that a lot of us have when it comes to change. People have a resistance to change, as well as a fear of the unknown. Together, the two can combine to create an irrational fear, such as the case with the Europeans, trying so desperately to emigrate out of their own countries after the balance of power shifted, or the xenophobia that we struggled to overcome in our own nation during the early years of the Pillar project."

"The United States has such an awful history of rejecting people of other cultures and faith," interjected Bahira. "It's little wonder that Muslims have never felt completely comfortable here. Let's hope that the sacrifice of those four beautiful children in Lewiston leads to a softening of the nation's heart toward those of a different faith."

The Imam spoke up. "With all due respect to my good friend, Reverend Whitehead, I think that America is experiencing a spiritual crisis. Since it is no longer a Christian nation, there are many who realize a void that can only be filled with the peace of Islam. As it says in the Qur'an…"

Bahira quickly cut him off, much to his apparent consternation. "It is certainly true that there is a high level of ignorance in America when it comes to Islam. I, myself, have faced such harassment when I wear the *hijab* and people don't recognize me, so I can imagine how it must be for others."

A caller was hastily put through. "My question is for the Imam. Mr. Rastaban, my mother was killed in one of the Starbuck's bombings by the Hizbul' Mujahideen…"

"I'm sorry to hear that," said the Imam dryly, "but you know that this has nothing to do with Islam, of course."

"That's not what the defendants are claiming."

"Well," the Imam replied, "any religion can be hijacked by…"

"They claim that people like you are the ones that have hijacked Islam, and they have more verses from the Qur'an and Sunnah than you do to prove it."

From the audible click, it appeared that the caller had been unceremoniously disconnected. There was an awkward silence on the set until Parker spoke up. "I think that perhaps Americans should be reminded that Islam is a religion, and should therefore be respected as a religion. For those who are Christians, ask yourselves: does your religion make you want to kill? Of course it doesn't. So why would Islam be any different.

In fact, the more devoted to their faith that Muslims are, the more likely they are to be peaceful and tolerant. Isn't that right, Imam?"

"Of course, Reverend, of course. Islam is the religion of peace, and it is my hope that anyone who doesn't understand that will someday be resting in peace."

Watching from her eastside Manhattan office, Bernice was breathing easier. The dialogue was going well. Perhaps peace was truly at hand for the nation.

Wednesday, May 1st, 2047
Washington, DC

Behind Walid al-Rahahti were two large posters, each with a different image. They might have been the most unholy items ever unveiled in the hallowed chamber of the Supreme Court building. Even the Justices, who knew what to expect from the arguments, were visibly disturbed. One showed a grown man performing oral sex on a young girl. The other showed another young girl posing with her legs open on a bed. Both girls were nude.

"Which one is legal and which isn't?" asked Walid rhetorically to the nine men and women seated before him. "If you can't tell, then, how is it that one is Constitutional and the other isn't?"

"I would hope that the image on the right is computer-generated," ventured one of the older Justices, referring to the picture with just a single child in the frame, perhaps hoping that the other, harsher image was illegal to possess.

"It's impossible to tell, isn't it," Walid practically shouted, "yet the possession of one will earn a prison sentence, while the other will result in a lawsuit for unlawful arrest if an individual is taken into custody."

He paused and gave a relaxed look, almost like a preacher reaching a critical point in the sermon. "Let's not play games with people's lives here. Let's stop the hypocrisy. If you've determined that this..." he pointed to the image of the two figures, "is a form of free speech, protected under the U.S. Constitution, because technically it came from a computer rather than a camera, then why shouldn't this?" Here he pointed to the more benign photograph, indicating that the Justice had been wrong.

Walid had forcefully argued every legal point that could be gleaned from the ACLU handbook on the protection of pornography under the First Amendment. There is a clear difference between the possession or distribution of an image and the physical manipulation of human subjects. There was absolutely no reason for the court to deny First Amendment protection to certain types of pornography and not others, particularly when they were unable to distinguish between the two with their very own eyes.

"We rest our case."

Thursday, August 8th, 2047
Bryce Canyon, Utah

Dennis Paterski was on a rafting trip, relaxing before the start of ARS clinical trials, when he got the news that Cooper-Redmond had missed the quarterly payment that was due a few days earlier. The company still owed them about $300 million of the nearly $1 billion agreed to in their contracts, mostly related to a second AIDs vaccine and a few other peripherals.

Cooper-Redmond had brushed off his accountant's inquiry with a reference to the "changing landscape." Paterski wondered if they were either angry that he had signed with other companies, or if they were simply nervous about Congress reducing the patent cycle from four years to two (presumably in order to make drugs more affordable, sooner).

When he reached the VP that he always dealt with at the company, however, he learned that at least one of their pharmaceutical rivals was in the process of making and brazenly marketing generic drugs illegally, including the AIDs vaccine. To top it off, Cooper-Redmond decided not to sue, because it calculated that it stood to gain financially if it, in turn, produced generics for its rivals.

Paterski was beside himself. There had always been something about that company that made him uncomfortable. Though it was the darling of left-wing interest groups, which lauded its "commitment to social responsibility" (generally meaning that the company was a big donor of theirs) it was always in favor of concessions that its competitors found more difficult to afford. Head-to-head competition was one thing, but paying blackmailers like CSR to stir up bad publicity against rivals was repugnant.

He knew, however, that the large corporation spread too much money around Washington to have any worry of being called to account.

Thursday, September 14th, 2047
Rothberg, California

The Professor sat on his living room sofa, clutching a pillow and trembling with rage. His eye was twitching – a nervous tic that developed several years ago.

He had just finished watching "The Community," which was doing well enough to generate a trickle of income to its real-life model. He wasn't sure why he watched anymore, however, given that the TV program usually enraged him. The producers had some way of getting information about the internal affairs of Rothberg and using the material to base episodes around, but they always put the real events through a sort of political correctness filter that massaged them into something that may have played well to the viewers, but not to the community's founder.

This particular episode was loosely based on what had happened last year when Rothermel discovered that those in Rothberg, who were eligible for government reparations, had absolutely no intention of putting the money into the community fund, not even a single dollar. This was shocking to Rothermel, who had invested his life savings in the community and assumed that others were equally committed to the principle of shared ownership.

They needed the money. The donations were not coming in from corporations, who were using the new regulations, such as the Benefits Act, as an excuse to reduce their civic sponsorships (Rothermel was sure they had the money, but just wanted to keep it for their own profit). Likewise, as the country's median income dropped, so too did the donations from private individuals.

The turnover in the community had been rapid and unconstructive, as nearly all of his ideological comrades had moved away to start anew under the old system. These were the ones with jobs, who brought in income, yet tired of doing double-duty in the community, as those they were supporting simply took advantage of the system. They were replaced by slackers and shady elements who contributed to the rising crime and disharmony.

Yet, the idyllic town in the TV series hardly changed, except for getting better over time. In the episode that was currently prompting Rothermel's facial twitches, his counter-part, square-jawed "Noah," was trying to persuade the African-American members of the community to donate all of their reparations income to the community fund instead of just *the three-fourths they volunteered*.

The chief antagonist was a woman who bore a curiously strong resemblance to Letitia Ridley, except that this character virtually supported the community on her back – while "Noah" sometimes unwittingly took advantage of her. In the episode, the female character reminded the fictional "Noah" that he had received an inheritance some years earlier and kept the full amount for himself.

She also pointed out how generous the reparations recipients had already been in their contributions to the fund. The moral of the story was that "Noah" was taking for granted the difficulties that African-Americans faced in life and how they had earned what little money they chose to keep.

As was the case with most episodes, this one ended with "Noah" biting his lower lip and nodding his head, as he thanked his gracious neighbors for teaching him a valuable lesson on tolerance.

Rothermel's fingernails finally bit through the pillow, forcing the stuffing to seep out around the edges.

He didn't notice.

Tuesday, October 15th, 2047
Washington, DC

Jill remembered that open-mouthed stare from somewhere. It was from the Fish Inaugural Speech nearly three years earlier. Now Senator Hawking was looking at her with complete astonishment on his face. "What will it do to industry in this country when the government refuses to enforce contractual obligations between businesses?" asked the son of the former President.

"Oh, don't blow this out of proportion," said Jill. "It only applies to the drug companies. They've been using this patent system to get rich off the backs of ailing Americans. Now let them see what happens when we remove this artificial barrier against competition. We can always set price controls if we have to."

Hawking looked as if he were trying to explain things to a child. "If you remove individual incentive, then you've turned them into simple manufacturers. There won't be any research or development."

"Of course there will be," scoffed Jill, "It will just be done cooperatively instead of competitively, which is how it should be."

"What in the hell are you talking about!"

"Calm down. I'm talking about the companies pooling their resources and becoming stronger. Competition between companies leads to wasted effort, as they're often conducting the same steps toward the same goal – which only one of them will reach. It's far more efficient and sensible to collectivize their effort. The patent system stands in the way of this, which is why it needs to go. We may be able to afford such redundancy when it comes to building a better washing machine, but we can't play games with the nation's medical interests any longer."

She continued. "Cooper-Redmond doesn't mind the sacrifice. I'm sorry about your constituent however, Senator. Perhaps Mr. Paterski should console himself by thinking of all those people left without health care when he decided to close his hospitals."

"He closed his hospitals only in areas that were losing money for him. Should he have kept them open instead?"

"Of course," said Jill, "a good citizen goes the extra mile for others, particularly when he can afford it, although it's a moot point, now that we've nationalized the industry and…"

"And broken the budget to do it," complained Hawking.

Jill kept her composure. "The people have needs, Senator. It's our job to meet them. This was something that your father never understood. Look where it got him."

Monday, October 28th, 2047
Washington, D.C.

Danforth found that he was strangely shy around Maria, almost as if nothing had changed in twenty years. He felt like that same awkward kid who never had much luck with the ladies, particularly the ones that he was deeply attracted to, as he had been to Maria at Berkeley. In the ten years that he waged war against her husband's company, he had never once run into her or even spoken to her.

He thought that she might at least call him and beg him to stop, but the phone never rang. On one occasion, he screwed up the courage to dial her office in Bozeman, but she refused to take the call. He never tried again.

Now, here she was waiting in line ahead of him at a sandwich shop on Constitution Avenue, where they met quite by accident. He knew that she would be in town for the Airtana hearings, but he didn't see her in the large room, despite nearly giving himself neck spasms searching for her. He had politely tapped her on the shoulder, after seeing her ahead of him in line. Her dark eyes started to flash when she saw him, but her smile was quite confident.

"Hello, Robert," she said.

She was looking about as hot as he had ever seen a 42-year-old woman look – not much different than how she did in college, but with a sort of maturity that added to the appeal. He hoped that he exuded the same, although he doubted that it was the case. He was glad that her husband was nowhere to be seen.

"Maria, how are you these days?"

"Very wealthy, Robert," she said bluntly, "how about you?"

He was taken a little by surprise, but did as he always did when given the opportunity – he bragged.

"Oh, doing well also. I guess you've heard that CSR has been pulling in a lot of revenue lately. It's a very successful company that I'm running." He knew that he was overdoing it.

"Well it should be," said Maria, without missing a beat, "you've taken 4,000 employees off of our payroll. I assume you've found jobs for them?"

Any illusions that he may have had about the civility of the conversation beneath the veneer were neatly stripped in one smooth motion. He decided to drop the gloves as well. "I'm sorry to hear about the problems that you and your uh… *man*… have been having with your airline. CSR has been doing very well, perhaps because we obey the law."

"You've been doing well because you're not a real company," she replied evenly, "you're an extortion racket."

The calm assurance in her voice annoyed him more than the words themselves. At that moment they both knew that she was right. He felt the blood rushing to his face.

She finished him off in the same calm voice that seemed to echo in his head. "You're a small person, Robert, you always have been and you always will be. You do what small people do, which is to take what others create and pretend as if it's your own."

Danforth wasn't used to being talked to this way. His sycophantic staff scurried around him each day, enduring his occasional wrath and lavishing compliments to the point that he almost believed them. Yet, here was a woman who saw into his soul, as she had that day in Tucson twenty-one years ago, and reminded him of what little he was really made.

He almost flew into a rage, but managed to control himself. Attempting to hide his bitterness beneath a trembling, phony smile he said, "When I knew you, Maria, you were a dyke."

The conversation around them stopped and Robert knew that people were staring.

Instead of the barrage of profanity that the old Maria would have launched at him, she leaned closer to him, as if about to share a secret. Instinctively, he did the same, immediately regretting it.

"That's because I didn't know any real men then, Robert," she said, loud enough to amuse the people around them.

The laughter pushed Danforth over the edge. He didn't hit her, but he did the only thing left that he could think of and spit at her. It missed, which was fortunate given that his hand was immediately grasped by someone behind him and bent backwards in a way that practically drove him to his knees.

Maria looked up, "Hello Kerry, have you met Robert Danforth?"

"Goodbye, Robert Danforth," said the man in the denim jacket, who immediately escorted Danforth to the door before releasing the painful grip in a move that also propelled him out and into the street.

Danforth didn't bother turning around, even as he heard the applause from the patrons behind him. It was all that he could do not to break into a run.

Tuesday, October 29th, 2047
Washington D.C.

The next day, Danforth sat cooling his heels for four hours, waiting for his turn to speak in front of the committee. He was preceded by a variety of witnesses, who testified to the seven Senators on the panel about their experiences with Airtana. Two were denied jobs with the company. Two others were ex-employees who felt passed over for promotions. Another ex-employee openly cried, as he claimed that the airline wouldn't pay benefits to his unemployed domestic partner, who later died of AIDs "thanks to Airtana."

Two others were passengers who claimed to have been harassed by Airtana security, one of whom was the CSR "ringer" from Nashville. He tearfully recalled the frustration and humiliation from being accosted and detained illegally at the gate while on his way to an interfaith dialogue conference to "build bridges" between Christians and Muslims. He told the Senators that he just returned from a "pro-America rally" in Denver the week before on a rival carrier, with no such treatment.

"Airtana pulled me out of line," he sobbed, "as if I were different from the rest. They questioned me for thirty minutes then prevented me from boarding. Now I know how my Jewish brothers felt under the Nazis."

The Senators wore grim expressions and occasionally shook their heads during the testimony. Danforth's "ringer" (who was actually the president of a local BAIR chapter) finished by telling the panel about the extensive counseling that he had to undergo in order to cope with his ordeal.

Finally it was Danforth's turn. His hand was still bruised from the day before, as was his ego, but here was his chance to exact revenge.

He began by reminding the Senators of Airtana's record of "exclusion," meaning that they did not hire minorities in proportion to the community. The company was also hostile to gays (since it didn't provide benefits to domestic partners) as well as Spanish-only speakers (since it excluded non-English speakers for customer service positions). Neither did the airline contribute to environmental or social causes. They did not seem to have a policy of properly distributing their purchasing among vendors with ownership in proportion to national demographics. Even their employees did not enjoy the same benefits that they should have according to Federal mandates.

For these reasons, the airline had been excluded from doing business in more than half the country. Cities, and sometimes entire states, blocked the carrier from flying into their airports. Yet, the company had been able to get away with all of it so far, even rolling up consecutive quarters of profit as their competitors struggled.

Danforth chided Congress for this. "You are tasked with protecting the public from predators like Kerry Conner," he told them, "yet you have not acted as aggressively as you should. Could it be because the rich and powerful have more liberty than the rest of us in this country?"

After several hours that he knew tested the patience of some there, Danforth read the final lines of his carefully-scripted remarks to the Senators. "Corporate Social Responsibility, Inc. represents the people of this planet against greedy corporations that would pollute our air, poison our water, work our children to death, rob us of our vitality and deny equal opportunity. As the proud president of this successful organization, I can tell you truthfully that I have never seen a more belligerent and arrogant company than Airtana Airlines.

"In the nearly ten years since CSR has been attempting to make its concerns known to the ownership of Airtana, not once has anyone in management expressed the slightest indication that they share our social vision. On the contrary, we have had the door slammed in our face time and again. This is a company that wants to make money, and money appears to be their only motivation.

"If money is all that Mr. Kerry Conner understands, then that is what you must take away from him. Only you have the power to stop him. The people pray that you have the courage to make the right decision."

Miami, Florida

The call-in radio show helped calm her nerves as Phyllis Hughes drove cautiously down 27th Avenue, hoping that the dotted line would soon lead her out of Miami. The line was painted on the roads by the city to help guide tourists, and keep them from straying into dangerous areas. It was something that most cities around the country had to do now, as out-of-towners were frequently gunned down in their cars by gangs.

Phyllis occasionally wondered how it was that these criminals had guns, when firearms possession was now a Federal crime. There were a lot of things that didn't make sense anymore, but right now all she worried about was hugging the painted line and finding the way to her hotel on the beach.

There was never a good time for taking a vacation, but the television producer wondered if this week was particularly ill-timed due to the fuss in Washington. Surely the other networks would be working furiously to capitalize on the attention. She had long ago copyrighted titles for possible movies, "The Kerry Conner Story", as well as "The Airtana Story" and even "The Red State Crook", which was generic enough to apply to any of the powerful businessmen in that part of the country.

Although the network didn't have any programming specific to Airtana, they had found several old movies that Phyllis felt would do well in the ratings. Most followed the same plot: a young, handsome cop and equally young, beautiful reporter bringing their suspicions about a specific corporation to fruition, and eventually bringing down the nefarious CEO. The movie scheduled for that night was particularly well-chosen in that it was about a fictional airline executive, who improves his company's bottom-line by putting a computer chip into his competitors' planes that causes them to lose power in midair.

The call-in radio show returned from a commercial break about the time that Phyllis was relieved to see the dotted line turn in the direction she needed. "We're back with 'EJ in the Evening' – talking about the Conner pig who's about to get eaten in D.C. tomorrow. Caller, what say you?"

It was a female caller. "Well, I think the things this man has done with his company are awful, and I have no problem believing that they're true. I applied for a job with Airtana at Fort Lauderdale Executive and I didn't get hired. There was no concern for my situation at all. I've got two children to support by two men I barely knew and aren't around anymore. What about my needs? Who's going to take care of me?"

"Right you are, caller. I have to agree with you..."

Wednesday, October 30th, 2047
Washington D.C.

Kerry Conner sat at the table facing the seven Senators, with a bank of microphones spread out in front of him. Flashbulbs were popping earlier as he took the oath, but now there was only the movement of the cameramen in front of him, as they quietly swung back and forth, trying to catch each Senator speaking from the lofty panel.

Kerry had nothing on the table and there was no one sitting with him; no lawyers or advisors, not even a fellow executive or officer from his company. It was completely unheard of, and editors were already salivating at the photos they would be running in the morning newspapers to personify the tycoon's isolation and unpopularity.

For six hours, the solitary man in blue jeans sat quietly, listening to each Senator attempt to outdo the other with sound bites. Some of them were quite clever.

"You robbed the bank, while your lawyers drove the getaway car..."

"You run a feudal machine, oiled by the blood of your workers..."

"Your long reign of error and terror is coming to an end, as the people reject your effort to embezzle their future..."

Others were more predictable. In just the first hour alone, he was accused of being aggressive, chauvinistic, racist, homophobic, bigoted, regressive, greedy and intolerant.

"I've waited a long time for this," said Senator Hudson, speaking for all of them. By Senate rules, seats on the panel were limited to seven, which set off a fierce competition between the two parties to place their most prestigious members in the coveted position of standing in televised judgment over the last of the Robber Barons.

Each Senator delivered lengthy opening statements, full of wit and indignation. Some worked themselves up into full-blown tantrums, as if their argument could be justified by mere force of anger. Each one played to the cameras, often waiting until the light and positioning were just right before launching into controlled outbursts.

"You cause unemployment by refusing to hire!" yelled one, to the business owner who created 15,000 jobs.

"People like you don't pay their fair share," sniffed another, to the taxpayer who personally sent millions to the Treasury each year.

"You're financially irresponsible," said another, to the company owner whose books were always balanced – in sharp contrast to the Federal budgets signed each year by his accuser.

"You belong in prison!" exclaimed another, to the citizen who never had so much as a traffic ticket in his life.

"Racists like you make me sick!" snapped another, to the man who woke his Mexican-American wife that morning with a Spanish poem and breakfast in bed.

Through it all, Kerry Conner sat patiently, without expression. He neither cringed at the insults nor laughed at what others in the chamber found humorous. Finally, they finished and he was told that he could speak. Even the Senators leaned forward in anticipation. There were over three hundred people in the room, but a drop of a pin could be heard when he opened his mouth.

Without notes, he spoke directly to the Senators, looking each one firmly in the eye as he alternated between them.

"When I was young, my father told me about a large American city where the Democratic Party came to full power in the 1940s and dominated politically to the point that every single elected office in the city, from the local school board to the mayor's office, was filled by a Democrat. It remained that way for decade after decade, throughout the 20th century and into the next.

"And while Democrats held every possible position in the city, every possible quality of life indicator for the people declined, until the city ranked dead last. The educational system was the worst in the country, despite the fact that few states spent more money per student. Test scores were dead last. The crime rate soared to the highest in the nation. The cost of living was so high that few could afford a house. Unemployment hovered around twice the national average.

"Yet, all during this time, the people of the city kept electing the same party to power. These weren't close elections either. Democrats typically enjoyed 90% of the vote. The worse things got, the more the same destructive policies, with no give and take between experience and ideas, became more entrenched.

"That never made much sense to me and probably not to a lot of other people as well. But as I sit in that very city right now, I have no trouble believing that people really can be fooled into thinking that their problems are best be solved by the very government that creates them."

Jill and the other three Democratic Senators sat quite rigid, while the Progressives leaned back a bit in the tall, padded chairs.

"Two days ago, I met a man named Robert Danforth, who has a phony company that he enjoys pretending is real. But his con game is child's play compared to what you've got going. You've actually convinced people that the worse you make it for them, the more they need you and the more they should hate people like me. You cynically play classes against each other, until the majority finally demands that you punish the successful, as if it makes the rest better off.

"Do you really think it's these idle masses that pay your salary with their votes, rather than the very taxpayers that you demonize? Where do you think wealth comes from? Don't you know that it's produced by people like me? People like you can only take it away. Where do you think jobs come from? I create jobs. You create rules that destroy them by raising the cost of employment.

"You appeal to the worst in people, whether it's indolence, jealousy or greed. Yes, that's right – I said greed! The man who wants to live off another man's paycheck is a gluttonous parasite. The politicians, who abet such a felony by making rules that ravenously steal from the producers of society to give to the leeches, are the true Robber Barons. Not only are you robbing the rich, but you're robbing the poor as well, by paying them to stay poor. You reward sloth with subsistence checks, and punish hard work with taxes at every opportunity. What did you think would happen?

"Yet all the while, you make the people think they need you to solve the very problems that you cause. You promise more for less until you finally run out of 'haves' to steal from, and are forced to define 'the rich' as those who, yesterday, you were calling middle-class – when you needed their votes. You've done the math, however, and you know there are less of them in proportion to the growing poor, so you bring the dividing line of redistribution lower and lower, destroying not just the ability to maintain wealth, but the incentive to reach it. For good measure, you even stigmatize success as a product of ruthlessness, rather than ambition."

Kerry pushed his chair back from the table, as if he were preparing to stand.

"For ten years I've fought to keep my company and the nearly 15,000 jobs that it used to support. I watched as governments made rules that hammered away over half my market and a third of my employees, even though it was devastating to the local economies when Airtana was thrown out. Yet, as soon as one city would shrivel and die, the activists would begin lobbying the next, leaving economic blight behind them as if they were an organic disease.

"My company pays hundreds of millions in taxes at a time when the government is running record deficits. We employ people at a time when unemployment is over 20%. We pump money into local economies when your rules have forced other businesses into bankruptcy. Yet somehow, you feel compelled to convince your electorate that I'm evil because I choose to run my business according to my own free moral will. Well let's see how much better off the country is without big business."

He stood up straight and looked the Senators directly in the eye, as a murmuring began in the room. The flashbulbs began popping again, in contradiction to the rules, but no one noticed.

"You can go to hell," said Kerry Conner, "I'm going to Alberta."

Washington, D.C.

As the hearings were coming to an abrupt end, a small group of protesters were gathering across the Mall, in front of the Lincoln Memorial. They had petitioned the city council for a permit to hold a rally in support of Airtana, but had been repeatedly denied. They were first told that they needed to sign a one million dollar insurance bond, guaranteeing against any damage caused by counter demonstrators. When they produced the money several months later, however, the council found other reasons to deny them the permit.

So finally they gathered as citizens in their nation's capital for a cause in which they believed. Hundreds stood shoulder-to-shoulder with signs that advocated property rights and free enterprise. They were quickly surrounded by a menacing mob of thousands that denounced them as 'narrow-minded fascists' and 'bigots'. "This is for being intolerant," said one young man, heaving a bottle into the small knot of protestors, to the applause of his companions, "just be glad it's not a bomb!"

Eventually the police converged to break up the protest, politely making their way through the surrounding mob to apply night sticks and water hoses to the band of demonstrators, as the crowd roared its approval.

A picture in the Montana Gazette the next morning showed an old man sitting bloody and dazed with his glasses knocked down below his nose and his clothes torn, yet still holding up a sign that asked, "Are you a Maker or a Taker?"

Friday, November 11ᵗʰ, 2047
Bozeman, Montana

Having to fly Airtana Airlines into and out of Bozeman added insult to injury for Jill Hudson, but it was the only carrier left in Montana. The humiliation of having to depend on the very company that she had just vilified was quite real. The perception that she was trying to shut the airlines down was not lost on the employees either. When she flew in four days earlier, the stewardesses did not give her any of the friendly smiles that were directed at other passengers, and at one point the captain got on the intercom to announce that they had a "special guest on board, who's been working very hard in Washington, to put us out of business." This was followed by hissing, and the Senate Majority Leader sank further back into her first-class seat with a newspaper over her head.

They didn't sound like people who were grateful for the protective hand of government against their employer. Neither did the other employees, who placed angry calls to her office, her colleagues', and media outlets around the country. They were joined by thousands of others, including family members, vendors, retirees who needed low fares, entrepreneurs who depended on the airlines, and even those who didn't travel but were very concerned about the exercise of government power to run a legitimate businessman out of the country.

At one point, Jill asked Senator Hawking, whom she had invited to a special committee tasked with addressing the problem, why these people didn't make their voices heard sooner, the way that other segments of the community always did. "Why didn't they come to Washington to march in huge rallies with protest signs, or form demonstrations in their own communities like Democrats and Progressives?"

"Because they have jobs," replied the Nationalist blandly.

She arrived in Bozeman on Monday, after a panic-filled weekend in which her colleagues appeared on news programs, sweating before the cameras and trying to downplay the significance of Conner's threat to dissolve his company and the economic impact it would have. Behind closed doors, the same politicians directed a barrage of angry threats and whining at the Majority Leader.

Kerry Conner kept one of the most powerful persons in Washington waiting for six hours on Tuesday before he allowed her in to see him, just as she had done to him nearly a week earlier. It could not have been any more obvious that the balance of power had completely shifted, nor was there any point in trying to pretend otherwise.

He was completely comfortable during the negotiations, as was Maria, who sat in the office with them, much to Jill's embarrassment. There was nothing that the government could do to him except prevent his personal wealth from being moved out of the country. The Alberta Emigration Act placed a limitation of $200,000 for each of the five members of his family. She knew that he was worth far more than that.

After three humiliating days, in which the Senator practically begged him to find a way to keep his company in business, he proposed a shockingly favorable offer, better than she could possibly have imagined.

As the plane taking her back to Richmond accelerated down the Bozeman runway, the closer objects out the window began to blur and she focused her view on the mountains in the distance, which were beginning to darken against the fading twilight. Her lawyers assured her that the signed contract was bulletproof. Kerry Conner no longer owned any part of Airtana. The company belonged to CSR, Inc.

She smiled and allowed herself to imagine the press conference that would be waiting for her in Richmond that evening, as she made the stunning announcement to the people that their government had saved the airline.

2048

It didn't take long for Lucian to regret taking the shortcut. The path, through an unpaved sparse area of Central Park, shaved about ten minutes off the walk between his apartment and his favorite bookshop, but he would never again be lured into saving such a measly amount of time, when it could cost him his life.

The black man in the hooded sweatshirt appeared from out of no-where. Lucian had fallen over backward with surprise. As the man leaned over him, Lucian found himself babbling for his life in a high-pitched screech. "Don't hurt me! Please don't hurt me! Here, you can take anything I have. Just don't hurt me."

The man drew back with a quizzical expression on his face.

Lucian continued. "Affirmative action!" he announced, as if it were a complete sentence. "Affirmative action! Reparations! Racial prefer-ences! Hiring quotas…" And on he went, down the list of items that he championed over the years, which he hoped would indulge the man stand-ing over him.

Rather than looking appeased, the other seemed more disgusted. He drew further back, and then turned to continue jogging in the direction that he had apparently been heading before the encounter.

Lucian picked himself up and hurried on, with his heart beating fast in his ears. He had never been so close to death.

The feeling of relief that he soon felt on being back in a crowd of people was exceeded as he entered the doors of the familiar bookshop. He knew the owner and the patrons that frequented the establishment. There was a coffee bar in the back and tables out front where they would sit and talk about the politics of the day.

Lucian ordered a cappuccino for himself and then sat down on the couch with a sort of exhilarated liberation. It's not everyday that one sur-vives a life and death experience. Around him were the beautiful people of Manhattan. Like the Landau group, these were young to middle-aged, trendy professionals with the same social and political interests. They were all alarmed at the dangerous strain of right-wing zealotry in the country and delighted at the military's "defeat" in Maine and the "libera-tion" of Muslims there to fully practice *Sharia*.

Lucian was explaining his recent ordeal to a young man with black curly hair and thick-rimmed glasses, when he noticed another man walk into the shop that he recognized from a few weeks earlier. The gentleman had caused a scene when he loudly demanded to speak to the owner, and then indicated his displeasure that the shop was selling a certain book that was offensive to Muslims.

The shop responded by pulling the book from the shelves for a couple of weeks, but Lucian noticed that the owner had recently put it out again; this time in the 'bargain bin' to reduce inventory. So did the disgruntled guest apparently. He gave a loud yell on seeing the book on the shelf.

Distracted, Lucian stopped in mid-sentence and turned his full attention to the spectacle, just in time to see the row of explosives revealed on the man's chest, as he pulled his coat back far enough to reach the trigger.

New York, New York

Pat Ridley probably could have heard the explosion from his apartment, had he not been in the shower following his morning run. He was still thinking about the funny little man, who fell over backwards and mumbled gibberish until Pat finally stopped trying to help him and continued on his jog.

He had it put out of his mind by the time he toweled off and began dressing in the bedroom while watching the GNN morning show. His timing was perfect, and there on the screen was Walid al-Rahahti, being savaged by Senator Jill Hudson, the Majority Leader who seemed to be in constant campaign mode. She was on a satellite feed from D.C. and was juxtaposed next to the image of Walid, who was probably in a local GNN affiliate studio in upstate New York.

Hudson was normally more composed. There was clear anger in her voice as she castigated Walid over his recent legal successes. "Do you think child pornography is healthy for society?" she blasted.

"Do you think virtual child pornography is healthy? Who is it supposed to benefit? What purpose does it serve?"

"That's beside the point," she snapped back. "Thanks to you, images of naked children are now legal to possess. You should be ashamed of yourself."

"Thanks to me?" he asked. "Don't you know that I don't have the power to decide anything? It's the Justices that ruled on this case. Who appointed these judges?"

Hudson hesitated. Walid continued. "Are these not your judges? Every one of the appointments was made by a Democratic Administration, including two by your own father. Would you like to know how those two voted in this decision?"

The Senator looked like she was going to explode. "You know that's not why they were appointed!" she yelled at him.

"On the contrary," said Walid comfortably, "when he nominated them, your father directly compared them to the very Justices that ruled in favor of virtual child pornography in 2002. Would you like the quote?"

Hudson did explode, in a verbal barrage. "You little…" Her next word caused Ridley to do a double-take. He never thought he would hear a public official use that word on GNN. "It's not what the public wants and you know it! I…"

"Since when does it matter what the public wants?" asked Walid. "Do they want strip clubs in their neighborhoods or virtual child pornography? Was this part of the original intent of the authors of the Constitution? Hasn't it been your contention that a judge's whim counts more than either original intent or the will of the people?"

"But it will feed the appetite of sexual predators! Hundreds of children will be victimized…"

"We're liberals," claimed Walid bluntly, "we don't believe in consequences. If we did, then we might be concerned about the thousands of women who fall victim to men wanting to act out dark passions aroused by pornography. You've defended porn in the past, haven't you?"

"Banning pornography scares me more than pornography itself," said Hudson mechanically and dispassionately, as if it were something that she was too used to saying. "But I'm speaking about…"

"Why?" asked the lawyer.

"Because if you start limiting freedom of expression in one area then… then…" The Senator faltered, evidently realizing that she was making her opponent's argument.

"You see, pornography is never defended on its own merit," said Walid, "it's always carefully hidden behind legitimate expressions of free speech, political or social, which are never at issue. This is anti-intellectual. If pornography cannot be examined in its own right to determine whether it is healthy or corruptive, then neither can any form of it. Don't forget, *if you start limiting freedom of expression in one area…*"

The lawyer was mocking her words, flustering the Senator so badly that she could barely respond. "Thanks to you, I can't walk my 15-year-old daughter down the street without having to go past some man publicly masturbating on the sidewalk. I…"

"Aren't you in favor of free speech?" asked Walid. "If a lap dance is a protected form of free expression, then certainly a man has the same right to his own body."

"It's indecent!" roared the Senator. "It's immoral and outrageous!"

"Well," said Walid, who seemed perfectly at ease, "I'm sorry that someone else's behavior offends you, but standards concerning decency are private matters and they shouldn't be imposed on anyone else. Isn't this a wonderful society that your judges are making for us, where pornography is public and morality is private? The judge in the appellate case you just alluded to is Darnell Massey who said – and I quote – 'As a black man I could never be in favor of restricting the freedoms of others to do…'"

"No one I know wants to see that!" Hudson stated incredulously.

"No one I know in Washington says they want to see the American flag burned or children exposed to hard-core porn on the Internet, yet somehow they both remain protected. How is that?"

Hudson ignored him. "It's indecent! It's against our values!"

"Decency and values are matters of personal preference," said Walid calmly. "You said that yourself ten years ago when arguing with a Nationalist over a court ruling. As I recall, you told him that if he didn't like it, he could just move to Alberta. I have the quote here, would you like me to read it?"

Walid seemed to be making a valiant effort to hide the smile on his face, as Hudson repeated the same word she used earlier, ripped off her microphone and rose, effectively ending the segment.

Ridley watched it all with amusement. He sympathized with the Democratic Senator, of course, but he had to admit that Walid had a point. Once the community is stripped of the right to determine its own standards, then there really is no basis for arbitrarily determining where the line should be drawn.

The child pornography issue had bothered Pat to the extent that he called his friend a couple of years earlier to express sharp concern. Walid had known that it would strain their relationship, but he carefully explained his motives in such a way that it almost made sense to Pat. He understood the anger that Walid was feeling over what the government had done to Leeman Arnold, but he didn't share his passion… yet.

Wednesday, January 8th, 2048
Cut Bank, Montana

"…colder than a well-digger's ankles…" went the song, and Sanjay could really feel it out in the main tent that was set up on the high, windy plains. The thermometer showed five degrees outside and the wind chill made it feel about 25 degrees colder than that. It was a long way from his native West India.

Paterski had purposely picked a location for his clinical trials that was extremely hostile to infiltration at that time of the year. They needed to maintain the utmost control over the process for two reasons. First, there was the danger to the community posed by hundreds, perhaps thousands of people with a potentially deadly virus congregating on their doorstep. Paterski had paid a lot of money to the handful of winter residents to stay indoors during the trials, which was easy money in temperatures like these.

Secondly, the entire world knew that a simple secret, potentially worth hundreds of millions, could be discovered from the analysis of just one drop of the substance that would be administered to those on site that week. The chemical sequence, much like a long sentence of letters, was all that was needed for a pharmaceutical company to manufacture a drug that was lethal to the virus that was causing panic across the country. Up until last September, this would have been worth a king's ransom. Now, no one was so sure.

Paterski was taking no chances. A carefully chosen security force patrolled the series of tents set out in the middle of nowhere, making sure that no one breached the perimeter fence that was established about 70 yards away from the group. Normally, there would have been protesters outside the gates, given that they were under constant pressure from "concerned social activists," who questioned their methods and "abominations against nature." Leading the pack was CSR, Sanjay's old nemesis that had single-handedly destroyed his former employer, which was too cowardly to stand up to the puling and threats.

Not so with Dennis Paterski. Sanjay enjoyed recalling their first encounter that day, when the victory celebration at the end of his Vermont driveway was spoiled by a drenching of muddy water. There was a man who didn't let anyone intimidate him. They wouldn't be standing here if he had.

Even if they didn't see another dime from the project, Sanjay and the others were wealthy beyond their wildest dreams. Paterski made sure of it. They could have quit three years ago, but they didn't work for twelve years just to see their inventions used a handful of times. Like Sanjay's prior research into parasitic-resistant wheat, he wanted to feel that his life's work had meaning. He knew the others felt that way as well.

There was a remarkable satisfaction in standing there and watching the line of people go through processing, whereby they were given the trial formula under close supervision, then monitored to ensure that a glass of water was consumed afterwards, so that no trace of the medicine could be stolen. He had seen others with the virus completely healed of it in preliminary runs, and he knew that these people would be as well.

He just wondered if it would ever reach a manufacturer.

Thursday, March 5th, 2048
Washington, DC

Jill Hudson let her hand rest on the phone, as she pondered the stakes.

Acute Respiratory Syndrome, or ARS, had consumed the lives of nearly 9,000 people in the last three years. This was a number that the government kept classified to the extent that even the press didn't yet know about it. Most of the deaths were in the refugee camps or the transipolitan urban areas, where overcrowding and sanitation problems meant increased vulnerability. Such victims were also of a lower profile, and it was easy for the rest of America to believe that the problem was endemic. The public was much more skeptical about medical threats, after the Bonan hype was exposed. The press was far more cautious as well.

This was all starting to change, of course, but even with the surge in publicity, the drug companies were refusing to do any significant research into ARS. Jill's belief, that the elimination of drug patents would spur cooperation, was not met with any corresponding action on their part. It was becoming obvious to her that big business had neither the desire nor the ability for coordination and innovation. Government was clearly needed to fill the gap between need and fulfillment.

Everyone knew by now that Dennis Paterski's clinical trials, conducted two months earlier, were successful, and that he had the cure for ARS. This was part of what was driving the recent publicity, and Washington knew that it was living on borrowed time. The number of reported cases of the disease was climbing, and the public was beginning to demand that the government either buy or develop the anti-viral medication. Jill had been put in charge of a task force to find a solution to the crisis.

As she picked up the phone to dial Paterski, the Senator knew that she held all the cards. The shrewd decisions that were made the year before, to eliminate the patent cycle, meant that not only were drugs cheap, but individual companies such as Paterski's could no longer hold the rest of the industry hostage while they amassed huge personal profits. Without the ability to obtain a contract, his invention was nearly worthless to him. No pharmaceutical company would pay for information that others would benefit from almost immediately as well.

There was a slight smugness in her voice as she greeted him, after being put through by his secretary.

"Hello Senator," he replied, blandly dismissing formalities. "What can I do for you?"

Jill sounded somewhat perfunctory as she stated, "Mr. Paterski, I have been tasked by the President to analyze the potential threat that ARS could pose to the people of our great nation. One of the persons that I want on my team is you. I'm sure that as a proud American, you would accept the opportunity to help…"

"I'm not giving you the formula," interrupted Paterski. "I invested my own money in the project to find the cure, and I intend on receiving a return from it. The formula is for sale."

"At what price?"

"One billion dollars up front," said Paterski, "plus the $300 million that I lost last year after you effectively nullified my business agreement with Cooper-Redmond."

Jill was stunned. "This is not a joke, Mr. Paterski. People are dying."

"I'm serious. I invested my own money and took enormous risk. That's my price."

"You're one of the richest men in America. Surely you've been compensated for whatever you invested."

"I was the poorest man in America five years ago," responded Paterski, "with a negative balance of nearly $100 million. Would you have paid off my debts for me?"

"Of course not."

"Then why take my profit, if you don't share my risk? Thanks to your arbitrary rule change, my invention is nearly worthless. If you'd done this five years ago, then I would have been ruined and there never would have been an AIDs vaccine."

"As the President's representative," said Jill flatly, "and in appreciation for your service to your country, I'm prepared to offer you $2 million from the U.S. Treasury for the rights to your invention. All mankind should be able to benefit from…"

Paterski's laughter made it impossible for her to continue. "What is the tax rate for a reported income of $2 million?" he asked, once he was able.

"I… uh… don't know exactly."

"I do," snapped Paterski, "and so do you, because your signature is on the budget. I won't bore you with the details, but what you're really offering me is $500,000 for a device that I put $120 million into. Does this seem right to you?"

"But you've already made nearly a billion dollars so far. You're one of the richest men in America. Surely you can find it in your heart to help those who haven't been as lucky as …"

"Lucky?" Paterski sounded incredulous. "You think this was a matter of luck?"

Jill hesitated. "I realize that some effort may have gone into…"

"*Some effort*?" mimicked Paterski. "Well, my dear, I guess you can try your hand at 'some effort' and see what it nets you. I've given you my price. Now I'm going to swim a few laps. Good luck with your legislating, Senator."

He was still laughing as he hung up the phone.

Wednesday, March 18th, 2048
Norwalk, Connecticut

"I am a victim of society," said Willie Powell.

The man in front of the ex-felon was begging for his life. Tears, nasal mucus, and even drool were running down his face. His wide eyes were bloodshot and he held his hands in front of him in a pleading gesture.

Normally Willie would simply have killed anyone unfortunate enough to be in their own home as it was being robbed, but he felt that he owed Nigel Landau an explanation as to why he had to do it. After all, the man had worked hard to gain his release from prison seven years earlier.

As they sat on the bed, with Willie holding the knife in his hand and Nigel flattened against his pillow in fear, the career criminal first wanted the other to know that it was an accident. He had no idea that Nigel lived so far away from his socialite ex-wife, and thought he was targeting a stranger. He also didn't know that anyone would be home, since the lights had not come on that evening.

Most of all, however, he wanted Nigel to understand that fate governed more than just that evening's series of events, but rather it was in control of a person's very life. Prison psychologists had helped Willie understand that he did the things he did because he was programmed that way by his environment. It was not his fault that he committed crime, but rather the society that denied from him the things he desired. His only means of achieving them was through "unlawful" means.

Since Nigel knew Willie's background, he didn't waste much time going over it. He simply explained the mechanics of their situation and assured him that there would be nothing personal about the murder, but that is was simply a consequence of social injustice.

Through it all, the lawyer nodded furiously, agreeing with Willie, but insisting at the same time that there was a "third alternative" that deserved consideration. Rather than Willie going back to jail, or Nigel winding up dead, they could enter a "gentleman's agreement" whereby the former client could take what he wanted from the house and Nigel would promise not to report the crime.

The lawyer was very persuasive, using all of the courtroom skills that won Willie his pardon, even against the eyewitnesses and forensic evidence of his guilt. The cop-killer had to admit that he made a good argument and... deep inside, he felt that he owed him something – even if his instinct was telling him otherwise.

Forty minutes later, he found himself sitting in his car, with the glow from his dashboard pierced several times a second by flashing blue strobe from the police vehicle behind him. He held up the hand that had shaken the lawyer's only a short time before, which he could have chosen to kill him with instead. He knew that the nervous officer was currently calling for backup, and that he would soon be commanded to exit his car with his arms out and forced to kneel on the pavement for the arrest.

It wasn't true what they said, he thought. It really was possible to con a con.

Sunday, June 28ᵗʰ, 2048
Atlanta, Georgia

Assembling the ARS Research Team was not as easy as Jill had thought it would be. For one thing, the drug companies were managing to hang on to the best scientists, as well as the coveted "qualifiers' (those who were either female or could qualify as a minority). Since the NDA had been expanded into the corporate hierarchy, a double minority with a science degree was easily worth more than a brilliant scientist with the misfortune of being a white male.

The Senator, of course, was under the strictest letter of the NDA, with no room to spare. At least 51% of her researchers had to be female and the overall racial composite of the team had to match or exceed national demographics – with 'exceed' being the preferred choice. Although the easiest to fill, only one out of five positions was open to white males. She was having so much trouble with the rest that she petitioned the President to have the NDA restrictions lifted in her case, on the grounds that it was a national emergency.

He stared at her as if she had just grown blue hair. "This makes no sense, Senator. Diversity broadens the talent pool. It's what makes this country great. What sort of message does it send – in an election year, no less – when the government declares that it is excluding broad sections of the population from such a critical project?"

"We aren't excluding anyone," protested Jill. "There aren't any 'do not apply' signs being put up. I just want the freedom to choose the most talented individuals regardless of who they are. There's a lot at stake here and…"

"You're damn right there's a lot at stake," snapped the President, visibly upset, "and this is no time for sounding like a damn Nationalist. Are you listening to yourself?"

Jill admitted that he had a point, but it just wasn't that easy to find good scientists proportionate to the general population, despite the tremendous amount of resources and regulation expended over the past five decades. Public universities, for example, were denied funding unless they admitted an equal number of men and women to each science discipline, even if the pool of male applicants was twenty times larger. Now the government was trying to require that graduation rates also reflect the general proportions of the population.

That's what made someone like Jin Xu so valuable. Not only was she one of the country's top scientists, but as a Chinese-American female, she counted in a lot of categories that were at least as important. She volunteered for the project, after having grown bored collecting what amounted to a retainer from Cooper-Redmond, which had discontinued most R&D the previous year.

In fact, Jin Xu was the only one working that Sunday on the CDC campus in Atlanta when Jill walked through, in advance of a week-long visit with the team. They were both surprised to see each other.

"Senator Hudson! It's an honor," said Jin, taking off her goggles and removing her gloves before shaking hands.

"Likewise," Jill responded. "Are you authorized by the union to work overtime?" Her question belied apprehension. There had been severe friction with the union over the attempt to suspend the 35-hour workweek rule on the grounds of national emergency. The union refused to budge.

"Just volunteering, I guess," responded Jin.

"It's appreciated, but please be sure to sign a waiver," asked Jill, referring to the release form that indicated that an employee was putting in additional hours "entirely free of duress."

"I already have." Jin changed subjects. "I didn't know you were coming in this week."

"No one else does either. I just want to do some observation and take notes. You know, find out if there's anything you need."

Jin raised her eyebrows a bit. "Next week the team is going to be in a Cultural Awareness seminar. There won't be any lab work to observe; which is one of the reasons that I'm here this weekend."

Jill couldn't tell if she was feeling dread, annoyance or a combination of both upon hearing that her team would be out of action for another week. At least 300 new cases of ARS would be reported during that time, and the numbers were only getting worse. With a death rate of between 10% and 15%, even under the best care, there was no hiding the scope of the threat anymore, although it helped that Paterski was now the scapegoat.

"I thought the seminar was last week."

"No," said Jin, "that was the Gender Sensitivity seminar, and the week before that was Cultural Sensitivity."

Jill decided to keep her frustration to herself. She was beginning to see why no progress had been reported. She had argued last month against allotting time for sensitivity and awareness training, but had been told that it fostered group cohesion and would therefore enhance productivity. "Sometimes you have to spend money to make money," was the line she remembered.

So far they had spent a lot of money.

Friday, September 11th, 2048
Selma, Alabama

Airtana Airlines officially became Progressive Airlines at a ceremony on a warm day in Selma, Alabama. Danforth chose the location to symbolize the transfer of ownership, as the last large privately-owned company became a publicly-owned corporation, even though Conner naturally refused to play along and was nowhere to be found. His executives had also fled in droves; some went to Alberta, while others joined to form their own Red States airline.

This was fortunate for Robert Danforth, who didn't need any internal resistance to his "Hate-Free Air" campaign that would be starting when the airline resumed operations at the beginning of the year. Employees would be hired with the strictest regard for race and ethnicity, in accordance with DCA regulations, and there would no longer be security teams singling out Middle Easterners. The motto for the new airline would be "Progressive Air, Where Diversity is Job One."

He only felt slightly more confident than he had ten months earlier when Jill called to inform him that he would be buying a major airline for the price of $1. He was too speechless to act on his first inclination and reject the proposal. When Jill then told him that both Conner and Maria made the offer contingent on CSR being the buyer, he realized that his pride was at stake.

Kerry Conner had publicly accused him of having a "phony company" that day in the Senate hearings. Maria had been even harsher in her criticism. He knew that this was their challenge to him to prove that he could actually run a real company… and the publicity would kill him if he turned it down.

If it became known that he refused the opportunity to save 9,000 jobs with just one measly dollar, then it would be the end of both Danforth and CSR. Already, some of his larger donors were letting him know that future contributions were being scaled back. The economic downturn was the official reason, but Danforth knew they were really just waiting to see if his reputation recovered from the damage suffered during the hearings.

In just ten minutes before the cameras, Conner had destroyed Danforth's ten year dream of being known as the man who took down Airtana. Now, Conner and his millions were laughing all the way to Calgary, and Danforth was stuck with the responsibility of proving to everyone that it was possible to operate a real-world business according to the idealistic standards he set for others. The microscope was on him, and there was no CSR available to sell him protection.

As he stood squinting in the sun, he hoped that he didn't look as pale as he feared.

Wednesday, December 23rd, 2048
Kalispell, Montana

The most recent call came in the middle of the night, as was the pattern. With a daughter away at college, Sanjay wasn't able to disconnect the phone overnight. He had been through several unlisted numbers in the last ten months, yet they always found him in short order, which heightened his suspicion that the government was involved.

He called the others to a mid-week meeting two days before Christmas, without Paterski present. There were only two entities that knew the project inside and out. One was the boss himself and the other was the collective minds assembled in the conference room that morning.

A series of large window panes on the outer wall provided a stunning view of the snowy Montana landscape. It wasn't unusual to see wildlife on the campus at any time of the year, which was an excuse for Aaron Bernstein to carry a firearm, although the others usually declined. They all knew he was more paranoid about people than grizzlies.

Still, there was something to the pattern of harassing calls that they had all been receiving. Even Greg Dijkstra was rattled by it, and he was usually so oblivious that it was a source of amusement for the others. Once, a few years back, some radicals found a vantage point on one of the mountains and tried shooting into the lab. One bullet penetrated the glass next to where Greg was eating and working. So deep in thought was he at the time that he responded by taking his sandwich over to the same window, where he stood looking out and munching absent-mindedly.

The three of them had been responsible for different areas of the project, along with their late software engineer, but they had all gradually picked up on what the others were doing, as is often the case with intelligent people who work together, even if they didn't fully share specialized skills. Paterski himself knew the details as well as any of them, and he didn't even have a college degree.

Between rounds of coffee and hot chocolate (for Greg) they renewed their loyalty to the boss. He had hired each one of them more than seventeen years earlier under a clause of confidentiality, on which they gave their word. He had also gone well beyond the contract by providing each with profit sharing and financial independence. They knew that if something happened to them, he would take care of their family, as he had that of their late colleague.

Certainly no amount of money could entice them to betray Paterski. The phone calls, however, were playing on their sympathies by suggesting that people were dying because the company would not release the information that could cure them. To resist this sort of appeal seemed coldhearted and it required the shared resolve of all three, even if some prayed independently that Paterski would agree to reasonable terms.

2049

Friday January 1ˢᵗ, 2049

JFK Airport, New York

Plenty of cameras and reporters were at the terminal where Progressive Air was set to begin its maiden flight from the only operational airport left in New York City, but not many passengers were showing that morning for the trip to L.A. The "Hate-Free Air" campaign, which all but promised a bare minimum of security, had caught the nation's interest and Danforth was able to get several celebrities and political figures to agree to buy tickets even if, they explained, they might not be able to make the flight.

Starr Sterling, for example, had a scheduling conflict. Rahim Sahil suddenly needed cosmetic surgery, as did Phyllis Hughes coincidently. Bernice Greenly, the GNN tycoon, bought a ticket, but then realized at the last minute that she had promised to attend a friend's niece's birthday party. Even Senator Jill Hudson, who architected the deal that resulted in a gleaming fleet of planes painted over with the rainbow colors of Progressive Airlines in airports all across the country, had something come up at the last minute.

The airline had been having a lot of trouble finding pilots. The only two who didn't back down were both Egyptian. A cursory glance at the manifest showed that half the tickets were bought by people with Arab names. As the date and hour of departure approached, Danforth was thoroughly regretting letting it be known that he would be a passenger as well.

All of the cameras seemed focused on him after the call to board was made, and he slowly moved with the rest of the herd in double rows to have tickets scanned. True to the company's word, everyone was passing by without any offense to their sensibilities or right to privacy. The only face he recognized was Parker Whitehead's, who smiled back at Danforth and waved before heading down the jet-way to the plane. His sublime faith in mankind was hardly contagious. Danforth's hands were wet with perspiration and his shirt was beginning to stick to his back.

As he edged closer to the counter, his nerve finally failed him and he stepped out of line.

The look on the face of the ticket clerk reminded him vaguely of the way Maria Posada had looked at him that day twenty-two years ago.

Los Angeles, California

Parker stepped off the jet-way at LAX and said goodbye to the two Saudi businessmen who shared his row on the flight from New York. They were both decent fellows, with wives and families back in the kingdom. Talking with them made the four-hour flight pass much faster.

Flashbulbs were popping in the terminal. There were almost as many journalists there as back in New York, he noticed. A monitor in the waiting area, tuned to GNN, seemed to be the next focal point of interest after the last of the passengers had disembarked and been interviewed. It turned out that Robert Danforth had scheduled a press conference to begin right after the flight landed in L.A. Parker saw his former college classmate take the podium and look into the cameras.

"I'm happy to announce that our maiden flight from New York to Los Angeles has landed safely. I wish I could have been there with them, but as it was I felt compelled to donate my seat to a needy child, suffering from cancer... an African-American child. After all, as the president of this airline, there will be plenty of opportunities for me to fly in the future.

"Although our Hate-Free Air campaign has now proven to America that our fears are misplaced, it is with regret that I have to inform the public that there were numerous threats against this flight from right-wing hate groups in the previous weeks. Though we believe them to be benign, we owe it to our passengers to take all precautions, since these groups can be so dangerous.

"In the future, Progressive Airlines will be adopting the same security measures that other carriers employ. It is regretful that we still have the intolerant living among us, even if they have learned to hide their 'white power' salutes and conceal their skinheads." Danforth paused and looked into the camera. "I want to emphasize, however, that no one will be discriminated against for any reason. At Progressive Airlines, diversity is job one."

Saturday, January 30th, 2049
New York, New York

There was a pall over the group that Bernice immediately took note of when she arrived at Beth Landau's apartment that afternoon. She was not a frequent attendee, since she worked most Saturdays.

The size of the group had depreciated noticeably in the last fifteen years, even though it was still talked about in exclusive circles. Part of this was due to the natural obstacles that were posed to travel in Manhattan. Most of the roads were closed to non-mass transit traffic, to protect the buildings against further truck bombings, but neither was it safe to walk. With the Dominican and Arab drug gangs controlling much of Upper Manhattan, violence was constantly spilling over into other areas of the city. The crime made it impossible to travel at night, and a large number of muggings and assaults were even occurring in broad daylight. The buses weren't safe either, thanks to the suicide bombers.

The group was also suffering attrition of a different sort. Lucian had finally passed away nine months after the bookstore bombing, after hanging on as a blob of scarred flesh that made the others uncomfortable. In fact, it was somewhat of a relief to get the news that he had perished in an apartment fire, after a female firefighter was unable to lift him from his bed. At least he lived long enough to see the Religious Vilification Act signed into law, which made it a crime to publish or sell material that was offensive to Islam, including critical academic works.

Nigel, Beth's ex-husband, was banned from the group after pressing charges against Willie Powell. Another member was expelled after admitting that he had obtained a handgun – illegally, of course – for protection. There was also a spectacular fallout a few years earlier, between animal rights activists, who opposed using animals for medical research, and AIDS activists, who supported the research and accused the others of "homophobia." The conflict was irreconcilable to the point that several members chose not to return, even after an AIDS vaccine rendered the issue moot.

The two people who were always present were Phyllis and "the Artist". They had an odd, interdependent relationship, Bernice noticed, where the pale, bald man was almost completely reliant on her for social interaction and protection. Phyllis took a sort of dominant, motherly role and the Artist rarely went anywhere without her.

The present topic of discussion was ARS. Many of the members, in fact, wore surgical masks and gloves, which was not at all uncommon. The virus was infecting nearly a thousand people a week across the poorer sections of America, particularly the transipolitan areas and refugee camps established for Mexican immigrants. It was now known that the outbreak and dissemination of the virus were greatly facilitated by the flat refusal of the medical unions to accept any form of mandated testing after the Edina fiasco, in which the government had continued to make unnecessary requirements of the broader community for fear of offending the Bonans.

Of course, the real villain in America these days was Dennis Paterski, the 'Monster from Montana' (rumored to be an admirer of Hitler) who claimed to have the cure for ARS, yet refused to make it public unless he received an enormous amount of money. The consensus of the group was that government should enforce Eminent Domain, which was cheaper than paying the 'ransom'. Some said it never should have come to that. Private research should have been banned long ago, with the money channeled into public research programs that worked cooperatively.

Monday, February 1st, 2049
Atlanta, Georgia

Jin Xu lay back on the couch in the break room of the CDC lab, utterly exhausted. Eleven o'clock was not a late hour of the night for her, but when combined with thirty-one straight days of 18-plus hours in the lab, it was certainly catching up to her. Only two other researchers were as dedicated, despite the increasing urgency of their work, as the death toll from ARS mounted. Most of the others held to the union's rules and clocked out after seven hours.

Jin was upset that they had lost one of their best immunologists in December, a victim of the "gender sensitivity" surveys that were mandated in the department, where women were asked to rate the men they worked with to ensure that no one held "repressive" attitudes that could disrupt the harmony of the team. It was her opinion that the friction generated from the constant focus on distinctions and "awareness" was undermining the high-profile project.

She had little patience for the hostility to "vertical thinking" that was now deeply ingrained in the female team members. Many complained that the curriculum was "too masculine," with its emphasis on hard science and rigid methodology. Last year, an entire week was devoted to a seminar that was designed to help women cope with the militaristic language of immunology, which included terms such as "invasion, "domination," and "destruction" – all necessary to the basic understanding of germ warfare at the cellular level.

This week, nearly all of the female team members were at a seminar to discuss the application of "female epistemology" to "workplace cohesion," where one of the topics would be menstruation. Jin estimated that one-hundred and thirty people would die of ARS that week, although it wasn't as if those at the seminar were contributing much anyway, even when they were on site. Many of the men chose to work odd hours just to avoid interaction – and the potential for bad reviews on the sensitivity surveys.

Jin drew the crook of her elbow over her eyes to block out the fluorescent lights, and attempted to relax. The noise from the television was making it difficult for her and eventually she rose to turn it off. As she did, she noticed that Senator Hudson was making a public service announcement, one in a series that was intended to offset the growing anxiety over ARS. They were all well-produced and this was no exception.

The first scene was a shot of the Senator standing outside the CDC and saying, "Many of you are concerned about the spread of Acute Respiratory Syndrome and would like to know what the government is doing to control the outbreak. Well…"

Here she proceeded to walk into the building and appeared to emerge in an impressive looking laboratory that resembled nothing like what Jin and the others worked in each day. It looked more like the set of a science-fiction movie, with robotics and equipment that was far sexier than the test tubes and refrigerators right outside the break room door. The actors behind the Senator were even more diverse than the actual team, with wise-looking African-Americans in evident positions of authority while those of other races worked cohesively around them in horn-rimmed spectacles. There were no white males to be seen, and the only white female, other than the Senator, appeared to be in a subservient role to the rest of the team.

"Our scientists," said the Senator, who paused then reemphasized the words with a confident twinkle in her eyes, "*our scientists* are hard at work on a solution. We have faith in technology and faith in…"

Jin finally found the power switch and cut off the TV. She wondered if the Senator knew that half of her scientists were currently at a conference trying to work up the courage to talk about their vaginas.

Tuesday, March 2nd, 2049
Norwalk, Connecticut

It would be one of the worst days of Nigel Landau's life, and it was all because of the little fink standing six yards away, cross-examining the police officer that arrested Willie Powell nearly a year earlier. Cross-examination was just another word for interrogation.

Nigel should know, of course, since he had been in those shoes himself for twenty years as a defense attorney and civil lawyer. He had two claims to fame. One was the civil trial on behalf of the relatives of Nidal Phad against the estate of Leeman Arnold, which wound up bankrupting the racist's family, much to the delight of people all across the country. The other was winning the release of the man now sitting at the defense table, Willie Powell.

Willie had somehow gotten a very good lawyer to represent him for next to nothing. Walid al-Rahahti had single-handedly destroyed the introduction of Willie's past criminal record by using Nigel's own words against him. In fact, he used the lawyer's former praise of Willie as evidence of his character.

"How can a man who was referred to by Mr. Landau as a 'wonderful citizen', 'political prisoner', and 'sensitive poet' be the dangerous character that the same Mr. Landau is now accusing him of being?" he asked. "Mr. Landau has known my client for over sixteen years and worked very hard to win his release from prison. Now he wants to send him back. What sense does that make?"

That little bastard knew damn well that Nigel had just been saying what he had to say to get Willie Powell released from prison. The evidence could not have been any plainer that his former client was a cop-killer, but it didn't stop crowds of supporters from showing up each day at the courthouse to berate and taunt the widow as she went past.

Now he knew a little of how she felt, having to endure the same crowd himself, which even included his ex-wife, still desperate to assuage her white guilt by championing the case of a man who just "couldn't be a killer," since he was an articulate minority.

Screw 'em, he thought to himself, as he listened to al-Rahahti inquire about the officer's compliance with the state's 'Anti-Profiling' law.

"According to the videotape from your own car, Mr. Powell was the third consecutive African-American driver that you stopped that night, is that correct?"

"Yes," replied the officer, who was clearly nervous.

"And you were already over your weekly quota for stopping African-American drivers as established by the law, am I correct?"

"He fit the victim's reported description of the suspect," insisted the officer.

"Don't you mean that he fit the profile?" asked al-Rahahti.

"I suppose…"

"Your honor," said the lawyer, crisply turning his attention to the judge, "we move for dismissal based on the unlawful arrest of Mr. Powell in violation of the Civil Rights Act of 2019, intended to protect minority drivers from racial discrimination."

The courtroom immediately drew silent as the judge sat back in his chair and looked at the ceiling for a few seconds in deep contemplation. "Let me see both sides up front," he finally commanded.

Nigel's heart was in his throat for the next several minutes, as he could see the attorneys arguing passionately before the bench, but couldn't make out all of the words. Finally they turned. The look on his lawyer's face told him as much as the judge's next words. "Case dismissed."

He looked over at Willie Powell, who was smiling back at him and drawing his fingers into a gesture that looked like a pistol. "Bang" went the thumb on the index finger pointed right at him.

He knew that his life would never be the same.

Thursday, September 30th, 2049
Kalispell, Montana

Dennis Paterski woke that morning, on the last day of September, to the rumble of heavy machinery, which sounded quite unnatural in the quiet Montana wilderness. On getting dressed and looking down toward the gate with his binoculars, he could see tanks and soldiers massing outside of his property in some sort of defensive position.

He picked up the phone and asked his secretary to reach Senator Jill Hudson.

Washington, D.C.

Jill had spoken a few times with Paterski since they first talked nearly a year and a half earlier. He was always happy to take her calls, but he hadn't budged from his original ridiculous price of $1.3 billion for the ARS antibody formula. As the government research dragged on without significant progress, the Senator had gotten more desperate. They had spent far more so far than it would have cost to buy the formula, but that only made it more difficult to pay the amount now. Neither was the government eager to project the image of giving in to a citizen to the tune of so much money.

Their recent endeavor was entirely clandestine. They had obtained the patent documents that Paterski filed for his two inventions in an effort to determine whether they could be replicated. What they found was that the patent information was incomplete. In fact, when the software program was loaded, it actually launched a sophisticated virus instead that they feared notified Paterski of their efforts – in addition to disabling key government information systems for a period of time. The engineers informed her that they would need the actual devices in order to recreate the inventions.

The government was running out of time. She was feeling the heat from the President, who was not shy about pushing public attention back on her, since his party had lost ground in Congress last November despite his narrow reelection.

The call from Paterski was expected. "Why are there U.S. Army tanks outside my gates?" he demanded.

"It's for your own protection. There's a lot of animosity toward you in the country and it's likely that a great many people want to do you harm."

"I'll take my chances," he snapped, "but that's not really what it's about is it?"

She did not reply.

He continued. "I know that you stole the patents. If it's come to that, then why not purchase my research?"

"Congress isn't about to allocate that much money to one individual... although they might authorize Eminent Domain." Jill emphasized the words firmly, although not certain about whether she should have played that card just yet. For one thing, she wasn't certain that Congress would actually approve such a measure. For another, she wondered if Paterski might do something foolish. The man was a wildcard.

After a pause, which told her that her words had finally gotten beneath the other's seemingly unflappable facade, Paterski said with conviction, "You'll have to kill me first."

"Perhaps we will," answered Jill. "Any single life is certainly worth less than the two-hundred others that we're losing every week to ARS."

There was a click, and she knew he had hung up on her.

Friday, October 15th, 2049
Kalispell, Montana

Two weeks went by before Paterski received his first visit from government agents. It was a crisp, sunny day with wonderfully cool weather in the middle of the afternoon, which signaled the approaching winter. Normally, he would be out hiking through the woods or hunting, but he no longer felt comfortable leaving his compound.

His secretary showed the two gentlemen into his office. They were wearing black outer coats that would have gone well with the sunglasses he suspected were carried in their front pockets. They removed their coats in a manner that suggested they were trying to be conspicuous about the guns strapped beneath the jackets. Paterski was not intimidated.

They identified themselves as Treasury agents and got right to the point. "We would like you to know that there is a problem with one of your employees, Aaron Bernstein. It appears that he neglected to report a source of income three years ago having to do with a speaking engagement in Minneapolis."

"How much are we talking about?" asked Paterski.

"Well," chuckled the agent, "that's classified, of course. We just wanted you to know that we're on your property to make the arrest."

Paterski shot up, knocking over his chair and startling the agents.

"I'll walk down to his home and get him," he said.

"Oh that won't be necessary. We've already sent agents down there to make the arrest. It seems…"

"You thugs!" cried Paterski, much to their astonishment, as he immediately picked up the phone to dial Bernstein's number. "You can't come onto my property without notifying me!"

On the second ring, Paterski heard the sound of a shot ringing out in the distance. He dropped the phone and raced out of the office, with the two agents following behind, careening down the stairs and bolting out of the building just in time to hear at least three other gunshots.

Running through the woods as hard as he could toward the noise, he emerged after a few minutes on the dirt road leading up to the Bernstein residence. He didn't have to go far before he saw Aaron lying on the ground with blood pooling up underneath him. A Federal agent, wrapped completely in black stood over him pointing a shotgun into his face. Yards away lay Aaron's dog, in obvious agony from a gunshot wound. Some fifty yards from them was another agent, evidently dead and lying in a heap.

Aaron was screaming for someone to put the dog out of his misery when Paterski knelt beside him, cradled his head and attempted to stop the bleeding. The dog was making an awful sound. Paterski looked up at the agent. "For God's sake do it!"

The agent finally obliged and Paterski looked down at his friend. He was losing a lot of blood from multiple wounds and was completely pale. His lips were blue and trembling. "They just stepped out from behind a tree and shot my dog," he said through chattering teeth. "I just shot back instinctively." He looked Paterski in the eye, as blood began foaming down the corner of his mouth. "I want you to take care of Sharon."

"Take care of her yourself!" snapped Paterski.

Through his pain, the other man gave a slight smile. "These guys have been trying to get me for thirty-five years. I have no regrets. Take care of her..."

Just after he slipped away, Paterski heard the scream behind him. He got up and turned in time to catch Sharon, who was in rubber boots and work clothes from some sort of cleaning project. She broke out of his grasp and bent down over her husband, wailing worse than the dog just had.

Paterski stood and looked up at the sky for a few seconds, breathing heavily. The two agents from his office finally caught up to them, quickly holstering the weapons that they had drawn while running. Paterski looked at them with utter disgust.

"Get the hell off my property!"

Sunday, October 17th, 2049
New York, New York

The color on the trees was spectacular that fall, even in the city, but Pat Ridley couldn't have cared less since he got the news that his friend had been gunned down by Federal agents two days ago on his own property. Aaron had been about a month shy of his sixty-fifth birthday. It was one thing for the country to choose not to honor him as the hero he was, but to kill him?

His wife told Ridley that $1000 went unreported to the government by accident three years earlier, but the couple didn't know. Obviously they would have paid the tax if they had. The government was more concerned with arresting him so they could apply the screws and pressure him to give up information about the project.

Ridley went into the bathroom and vomited after the call. He sat alone for a few hours, and then went jogging in the park. He was still shaking with anger when he got back to the apartment. Without bothering to take off his sweat-soaked clothes, he picked up the phone and called Walid to apologize.

He finally understood where his friend was coming from all these years.

Thursday, November 25th, 2049
Kalispell, Montana

Sharon organized the Thanksgiving Day evacuation. Sanjay and his family went first, followed by her and then Greg Dijkstra. It took a long time for their moving vans to be adequately searched by the soldiers at the gate. No one tried removing any of the lab equipment, since they knew it would immediately be confiscated by military personnel, who were under orders not to allow any such equipment to leave the compound.

The rest of the staff had been released.

The lone figure in the window of the laboratory, watching them all leave, was Dennis Paterski.

Thursday, December 2nd, 2049
Washington, D.C.

By evacuating the compound the week before, Paterski had played right into her hands. Jill knew the public was squeamish about shedding more blood, even if it was for the cause of eradicating ARS. Having the children there on the grounds in Kalispell meant the potential for another Waco or Lewiston, but with everyone now out of the way, she was free to make her move.

It began with a phone call, recorded, of course.

"Mr. Paterski, I would like to offer my apologies again for the loss of your colleague. You understand that his death was unintentional, I assume?"

"Go to hell! I know why he died. So do you."

She continued. "I am authorized by executive order, approved by Congress, to give you your asking price of 1.3 billion dollars for the formula and your inventions. I'm sure that you will find this to…"

"My inventions were never for sale," reminded Paterski, "and my asking price went up after you killed my friend. I want his widow to receive the same amount of money."

Jill sighed. In her heart she knew it would come to this. "Would it make any difference to you to know that Eminent Domain has been approved and that the government is authorized to seize your property in the interest of public welfare?"

There was a pause on the other end. "What I created is what I own. What I own is mine to do with as I please. If you feel that government is no longer obligated to respect property rights, then it will take more than mere government to authenticate its own decision, if this is still America."

Jill nodded her head at an aide holding a phone, who immediately began whispering into it. She needed to keep Paterski on the line as long as possible. "I don't think you're going to find much sympathy on the part of the public these days. For one thing, you're being offered over a billion dollars, which is more than adequate compensation. For another, a lot of people are dying and a lot of others…"

"How much have you spent so far, down at the CDC?" asked Paterski.

Jill was caught somewhat off-guard. "That's not for me to say…"

"Well, say it anyway or I'm getting off the phone, and I assume that you want to keep me on as long as possible until your military squad has a chance to take the building."

Jill's blood went cold. She glanced at her aide who was shaking his head furiously with a perplexed look.

"Yes, I know about that," continued Paterski. "I've got motion detectors set up in the woods. If it's not too late, then I suggest…"

There was a click and the line went dead.

Kalispell, Montana

The team leader was first to emerge from the snowy woods and force his way into the building, entering just as the doorway shook from the force of an internal explosion. The orders were coming fast and furious over his headset. He was told to find Paterski and neutralize him without regard for anything else, including their personal safety. Such orders were much easier to issue from a plush Washington office, than they were to follow on the ground. No one on his team, including himself, had any intention of dying that day, or of being put on trial for crimes against civilians like their comrades in Maine.

He made his way cautiously down the corridor through the haze of pungent smoke, the team following close behind. The only sound was the echo of their wet boots squeaking along the tile floor. There were no further explosions, but they weren't taking any chances. He just hoped that the bastard didn't have the whole building wired.

"Down here, Fellas!" came the call from below, just as they were approaching the open stairwell in the center of the building.

They carefully descended, with red lasers in the center of the circles of light emanating from the scopes on their weapons. There was a smaller hallway below, with immediate double doors on the right that led into a lab. This was obviously the source of the smoke, since it was still seeping through the cracks around and between the doors.

Opening the panels, they found Dennis Paterski standing in the middle of piles of debris, looking down at the mess and sipping a cup of coffee. Shards of metal and electronic components were scattered everywhere. They raised their weapons at him, training the red dots right on his forehead, as he looked up and smiled.

"Who wants coffee?" he asked.

2050

"You disgusting, filthy, little man!"

Both the language and decorum were beneath the Senate Majority Leader, but she was having a very bad day and wasn't afraid to let it show. After two months of effort, the engineers at NSF told her on Monday that nothing could possibly be gleaned from the twisted metal and splintered debris that was formerly Paterski's nucleotide sequence analyzer. All of the parts were generic, and without the instructions or software, it was just a pile of common parts.

Her scientists in Atlanta were making little progress against ARS. The government was starting to lose control of the epidemic, despite extra precautions that the public was taking against the virus. At one point they had started to implement a quarantine plan, which would certainly have saved lives and perhaps even eradicated the disease, but it was struck down by the courts as unconstitutional. Even the mere hint of quarantine was enough to provoke rioting in San Francisco, where the homosexual population was reminded of such suggestions in the early 1980s to contain AIDs. People all across the country were upset at the government, and a general panic was beginning to set in to the national psyche. Many people were now wearing masks and gloves on the street.

None of this would have been happening, of course, if the man sitting in front of her in that small grey room had simply done the right thing. Dennis Paterski was wearing manacles and a jumpsuit, as he had each day for the last three months of his incarceration at the military prison. Other than that, he looked remarkably relaxed, even under the withering barrage of profanity and verbal abuse that the Senator was launching at him.

"You stupid asshole! Why destroy something that could have saved the lives of so many? Are you some sort of sadist? Thousands, perhaps millions, will die because of you. How can a person be so selfish?"

After a period of silence, which she gathered was sufficient to convince him that it was his turn to speak, he finally said quietly, "If I wanted people to die, I wouldn't have created a device to save them."

"You destroyed it… completely from what I hear!"

"It wasn't for sale, and it wasn't for stealing. It was mine."

"You used other people to create it."

"Yes," said Paterski. "I used your rejects: a brilliant researcher who was driven out of his job because he dared create a modified food product that would have saved millions, another who should have been planting rice in a Communist utopia, another who was one of the brightest minds in science, but disagreed with the definitive orthodoxy of Evolution, as was his prerogative, and yet another who was spurned for, of all things, daring to save more than a thousand people from slaughter. Each of these men that you rejected entered into a voluntary agreement with me to invent a product that I funded. That's what made it mine."

"No, it wasn't yours. That's why you're going to be in prison for the rest of your life. Eminent Domain has always been an accepted part of our country's history and law."

"Accepted by whom – certainly not the people having their property stolen?"

"Was this meager political point worth your freedom?"

"What is freedom without property rights?"

Jill thought for a few seconds before replying. "It's a lot better than what you're going to get in here, Mr. Paterski."

"Are you threatening me with torture?"

"If that's what it takes." Jill never thought she would ever hear herself say something like that, but, if torturing a disgustingly selfish individual kept the country from collapsing into social and financial ruin, then she would have no problem asking the court to approve the measure. "Why don't you tell me, can it be rebuilt?"

With a demoralizing smile, Paterski said, "The man who built it is dead. You killed him as I recall."

Jill couldn't help holding a hand up to her forehead and looking away. "Can it be rebuilt?"

"What was it over now? Five hundred dollars in taxes?"

"Yes or no?" she screamed, slamming her hand down on the table. "Can it be rebuilt?"

His look held more disgust in it than her previous torrent of verbal insults. After holding it a few seconds he asked evenly, "What has the four billion dollars that you've spent thus far taught you about the virus?"

Jill cringed a bit at the figure offered, even though it was uncannily accurate. "It produces a hemorrhagic sickness that causes the body to…"

"No, I mean what do you know about its origins? Have you sequenced it?"

"Of course we have. I'm not familiar with the origins, necessarily. I just want to know how to combat it"

"Well, before *you* put *me* on a torture rack, you may want to call Atlanta and ask some questions. I believe you have a Ms. Jin Xu down there? She's a heck of a scientist. I would have recruited her myself, but she was still working on her doctorate at the time."

Atlanta, GA

After disposing of the gloves, Jin Xu washed her hands before heading down to her office and picking up the phone. There was no excuse for carelessness, even if it kept a U.S. Senator waiting. She had also developed a solid standing relationship with the Majority Leader over the last two years based on their mutual admiration for the other's work ethic.

The question was an odd one. What were the origins of ARS?

Well, from medical research, they knew that it had been around for nearly sixteen years, mostly in a sort of low-profile capacity – up until the last five. The virus appeared to be a recombinant, meaning that it was the result of two RNA fragments that fused to create a lethal strain.

The Senator asked a more probing question.

Jin replied that as far as they could tell, the recombinant probably developed on a North Carolina pig farm sixteen years earlier, which was, in turn, related to a break-in at a local research center seven years before that.

The line went dead.

Jin put the phone down, wondering whether she should wait for a possible callback, or if she was free to make her way back down to the lab.

Friday, April 8th, 2050
Portland, Maine

Ordinarily, Walid would not have cared much for traveling to Maine. He was less than a year away from turning sixty, and intended on retiring after securing this final act of vengeance. Not a day went by that he didn't find himself having to resolve doubts about the sanctity of his own choices. Clearly he championed causes in which he did not believe, but after seeing Leeman lynched by the edict of public opinion, he thought it quite appropriate to kick out the hollow artifice that prevented the social system from collapsing under its own weight.

The lawyers that traveled with him up to Lewiston to obtain evidence against the President were much younger than he was (and thinner, he noted) although none of them spoke Arabic. Second-generation Muslims often spoke English, however, which was usually the extent of their assimilation. Each of the people with him worked for a so-called 'human rights group of some sort, organizations that, in Walid's opinion, had proven quite effective in thwarting America's ability to defend herself from terrorism and crime. It was to their credit that the country was far more concerned about the squeaking of a guard's shoe around a prisoner who might be praying toward Mecca, than for the shattered bodies of the same "holy warrior's" bombing victims.

These sanctimonious lawyers were a strange sort, Walid decided. They seemed to have been brought up with very low opinions of themselves, which they attempted to recompense by championing the rights of terrorists, reasoning that if they could possess sympathy for the least deserving, then it was evidence of their true moral superiority. That their behavior was ultimately self-defeating never seemed to occur to them.

They respected him, since they confused his recent quests with their own constant crusade for the sort of unpopularity that was vital to self-righteous egos. On the van ride up from Boston, he watched their faces as he would periodically point out the charred shells of churches and "Christian-owned" businesses. There was little reaction to that, but there did seem to be a slight discomfort when he told them about the bombings and arson related to bookstores, women's shelters, homosexual nightclubs, and movie theaters, although they still seemed incapable of understanding these to be the consequences of their own success.

To a man, they blamed the United States government for everything they found distasteful. The actions of "insurgents," no matter how violent, were legitimate responses to excess of authoritarianism, which consequently placed the blame for the victims in hands other than those setting the bombs or starting fires. In some cases, they even implicated the government for not providing "adequate protection" to the targeted facilities, not realizing the contradiction of the very mission they were on, which was to provide evidence for prosecution against the President for sending troops to secure the region.

Like the others with him in the van, he knew that the soldiers in Lewiston had merely returned fire from an ambush by militant Islamists. They had no intention of killing anyone who wasn't trying to kill them, but it had been a very effective trap, designed to produce civilian casualties and public sympathy. It was just the sort of strategy that manipulated Americans into defeat and retreat where the lives of those outside their borders were concerned. It was easy for political demagogues to deny, for example, that even the lives of millions overseas were worth a single drop of American blood. As the dark cloak of tyranny enveloped the rest of the world, swallowing up the lives and dreams of the expendable, the good people in America would click their tongues, shake their heads, and go about their lives, never believing that someday their children or grandchildren might pay a price for such callousness.

Monday, April 11th, 2050

Westchester, New York

It was fortunate that her mother didn't have to die in a public hospital, like the others did, since the rolling blackouts made it impossible for terminally ill people to live out their last days at home, as they may have wanted, rather than a shared hospice room. That might have been her fate, if she were anything less than an ex-President's wife.

Jill hated the drive up to Westchester from JFK because of how badly it contrasted with what she remembered as a small girl. There were bad sections back then, but nothing like the squalid conditions that existed on the outskirts of the city now, where the wood fires that supplemented the power outages contributed to a permanent haze. Still, the environmentalists were pressing to shut down more nuclear plants, even as energy demand surged.

Past the rundown areas, the larger homes up the pike were beginning to decay as well. They were inhabited by people who could still afford the taxes, but not the repairs, apparently. Feral yards were pandemic. Some blamed it on the watering ban, but Jill knew that there was also fear that a well-maintained yard made a better target for burglars and tax commissioners. Larger problems in America, such as crime and poverty, shifted social priorities, so that the condition of a neighbor's lawn was no longer grounds for straining a relationship that might be called upon in the event of a home invasion.

One of the first demonstrations that Jill led back at Berkeley was a bitter protest over the scheduled termination of the Pillar project twenty years after it began – one of the few issues on which the Nationalists actually had modest support. At the time, she and her friends waved signs reading, "There are No Illegal People" and "We are All Citizens of the World." Knowing now what she didn't twenty-five years ago, Jill wondered what it was that led her to think that the United States had an unlimited capacity to absorb the Third World without coming to resemble it.

Passing through the various security checkpoints and barbed wire at her parent's neighborhood was a relief, even if it evoked a sort of siege mentality. Other than that, the upscale neighborhood looked about the same.

Through the front door was a blown-up picture of "the photograph" taken at the pro-choice rally so long ago, when her mother was a teenager. It was a famous picture that had graced the walls of many other progressive households at the time, with the inscription at the bottom from a magazine article: *"The rally featured women marching side by side with their mothers, who were helping their daughters retain rights that had been denied to them...."* Jill wondered if her mother might finally pass down the secret that she kept with her own mother about what was whispered in her ear that day.

She took her mother's hand in hers, after the usual inquires over that day's bout with the virus. "Tell me about that time with Grandma… the picture," she asked softly.

Her mother had her eyes closed, but smiled as she recalled how her own mother had been so proud of the way she had denounced those hateful people that hot day in 1988. She had used the story of her mother's unplanned pregnancy and inability to get an abortion sixteen years earlier to shame those IQ-challenged jackasses.

"What did Grandma tell you? You know, when the picture was taken?" There was a delicate implication to the question, because Jill's mother had said that such secrets would only be divulged on the deathbed.

Her mother opened her eyes, so that they were pointed sightlessly at the ceiling. "It wasn't important, really. She was just so full of pride at that moment that she told me she was glad abortion wasn't legal back when she had me."

Thursday, June 9th, 2050
Quantico, Virginia

The voice that Senator Jill Hudson heard on the tape was hardly recognizable as the arrogant tycoon, sitting in a Fort Dix prison cell, effectively raising his middle finger at the rest of the world. He was revealing a softer, more human side on the recorded phone conversation between himself and the woman in Alberta.

"I… I just wanted to say how sorry I am for what happened to…"

"I know you are," said the voice of Sharon Bernstein, "but you don't have anything to apologize for."

"We both know that he wouldn't be dead right now if I hadn't…"

"Given in to them?" she asked. "Do you think that's what Aaron would have wanted? He had the opportunity to give in to them also, but he chose to make a stand, and he was proud to be shoulder to shoulder with you and the others. He never stopped being a soldier, you know, even if the country turned its back on him."

She continued, even as it seemed he was softly sobbing, "Those years were the happiest of his life, Dennis. He wouldn't have traded them for anything, even if he'd known the cost. A man stops being a man when he no longer stands up for what is right. Aaron died a man, and that's how he wanted it."

Jill frowned. They weren't getting what they wanted this time, even though they had nearly hit the jackpot a few weeks ago, when Paterski let something slip before Sharon reminded him that the conversation might be monitored. There was also something about the way that the two seemed to interact which raised some interesting possibilities in the Senator's mind.

They were running out of patience. They needed to get Sharon Bernstein back in the country.

Thursday, December 1st, 2050
Philadelphia, PA

The meeting had been a disaster. Danforth pounded the seat in front of him with his fist, briefly drawing the attention of the stewardesses, who knew better than to ask. To top it off, the flight was delayed due to another bomb threat at the airport.

It had been a very rough time for Danforth since that hopeful moment when 'Hate-Free Air' debuted two years ago. He kept the slogan for a few more months before swallowing his pride and admitting that it was depressing business. People wanted to feel safe when they flew. That was all they wanted – to get to their destination in one piece. He had to practically get on his knees and convince them that his airline was as safe as any other.

Then came the crash of flight 555 in March, with 71 people on board a plane that could have held over 300. He quickly discovered and announced that it was due to pilot error, which didn't sit well with minorities, since a black female was piloting the plane. By law, approximately 8% of the pilots needed to be in that demographic, and the airline had to cut corners to make the numbers balance, since there weren't many African-American women with flying experience.

He still remembered the look on the face of the reporter from Black Enterprise Magazine when she buttonholed him at the press conference. "Are you implying that this was caused by a black woman?" she demanded, in a tone that suggested that he might want to consider other options.

But what could he say? The black box data clearly showed that bad decisions had been made on landing. There was no mechanical error. To pretend otherwise would undermine public confidence even further. Eventually they squirmed out of it by pinning the blame on "psychological stress caused by the failure of society to eradicate racism" and promised to invest $100 million in minority education programs.

In fact, his airline was losing money at a rate of a half-billion dollars a year. He was in desperate need, and so, he did what he always did in situations like that and called a board meeting with major donors. Half of them didn't bother to show, however, and those that did were looking at him quite skeptically as he gave the pitch for new donations to keep the progressive company afloat.

"You bought this airline for a dollar," said one executive, who was chewing gum as he watched Danforth's face, "how come you're over a billion in debt?"

"The airline was only worth a dollar when I purchased it," said Danforth, which was true. The previous owners had used the company's assets to transition its employees during the "reorganization," leaving a balance of exactly one dollar on the books when Danforth took over two years ago.

"Your nearest competitor was $3 billion in debt at the time," responded the gum chewer. "You had the most profitable airline in the business, and now it's down for the count. Doesn't sound like you know much about running a business. Maybe you shouldn't be telling us how to run ours." The others nodded and Danforth broke into a sweat. What he feared most was now coming to pass. They were banding against him. His power to intimidate each of these CEOs individually, with implicit threats of bad publicity and shareholder panic, was all but depleted.

Of course, they didn't tell him that outright, but the contempt was visible on their faces, as they used the bad economy and fears of nationalization to excuse their parsimony. The numbers were down across the board, they claimed, and without profit there could be no further sponsorship.

Not only was he losing the airlines, which he never really cared about, but it was taking his beloved CSR down with it as well.

He lay back in the seat and closed his eyes, but Kerry Conner's face still hovered above him.

Saturday, December 3rd, 2050
Fort Dix, New Jersey

Senator Jill Hudson walked down the dull, gray hallway, absent-mindedly studying the pattern of floor tiles while trying to collect her thoughts. She had spoken with the prisoner several times in the last year, but never with the hand of cards that she currently held. Short of torture, this would be their last best effort to get the information from him that they needed to stop the virus.

The last gate rolled shut behind her with a metallic clang and she approached the small interrogation room where she knew Paterski was waiting. After a deep breath, she opened the door to find him staring at her impassively. In the room with them was a monitor, the only indication to him that there might be something different about this session. She sat down and returned his stare with a studious expression of her own for a few long seconds before speaking.

"Mr. Paterski, we know that you memorized the formula before you destroyed it. We know that we could probably get it out of you under torture, but we are a nation of law. Deep inside, you're a decent man who wants to do the right thing, I think. Perhaps you simply need the proper motivation."

He did not respond. She turned and looked up at the camera above them, a signal for them to provide the video feed to the monitor on the table. After giving it a few seconds, she turned on the monitor. As planned, there was the live image of a woman being held in a cell.

Paterski's face registered immediate concern. Jill continued. "Now, I realize that there will be a few more complications to work out, but…"

"Sharon Bernstein is a citizen of Alberta," said the man, with a look bordering on outrage.

Jill smiled, even if it didn't reflect how she was feeling. "Well, in that case, they wouldn't have any problem at all with what we're doing, since I understand that they quarantine victims of disease in that backward little country. Oh yes, that's right. It seems that Mrs. Bernstein is suffering from Acute Respiratory Syndrome. Something she must have picked up when she came down to visit a friend in prison last month."

She could almost see the impact of each word on him. His upper lip trembled slightly as he responded. "You infected her."

"You don't know that to be the case, Mr. Paterski, but it seems that we now have a common interest."

"Let me talk to her."

"It's not possible."

Paterski slammed his fist down on the table, almost knocking over the flat-screen monitor, which he started to reach out for to keep from falling before the chains snapped tight against his wrists. He stared at the image of the woman coughing in bed. "What is your offer," he asked.

Her heart was in her throat as she answered, "We just want the formula – and your confidentiality. Give us that and you can both walk across the border."

"Confidentiality? About what you've done to me and…" he gestured to the monitor, "…to her? Or about a young idealist who participated in an illegal break-in at a research facility in Denton…"

"That's enough," she snapped. "I don't know where you get your information, but I had nothing to do with that break-in!"

"Well, that's interesting," he said calmly, "I never once mentioned your name."

2051

Sunday, January 15th, 2051
Atlanta, Georgia

It was fitting that she was packing her office on a Sunday. Jin Xu had spent so many weekends in the building over the last three years that she couldn't recall even a single casual conversation that she'd had outside the office in all that time. She was kind of a loner anyway, but was finally looking forward to getting a life again, even if it was in a new country.

She had been offered a directorship with the CDC, but was not tempted in the slightest. It was heartbreaking to watch such enormous expenditures and resources wasted in the manner that they had been – so much bureaucracy and so little to show for it. In the end, their success boiled down to a string of letters read across the telephone line to her late last year by Senator Hudson, a combination of chemical instructions for building a substance that was lethal to ARS.

In the three weeks since the CDC had verified its validity, the recipe had been rushed to the pharmaceutical manufacturers where it was being mass-produced for distribution. The crisis was over.

Jin wondered, of course, about the origin of the mysterious code. Only the Senator seemed to know, and she made it clear that no answers would be forthcoming. The researcher decided to make a new start for herself in Alberta at the invitation of her old professor, Greg Dijkstra, who was starting a private project there with his partners.

Several laws had been enacted over the last several years to discourage emigration, including the limitation of wealth transfer and the renunciation of U.S. citizenship, but that didn't bother her as much as the rumors about Alberta – and how non-whites were said to be treated. Surprisingly however, Greg's supreme confidence was more than enough to overcome her inhibitions. She was also flattered that he wanted her there, given the personal and professional respect that she had for him.

She put the lid on the last box, gave a final look around the room then slipped out the door, box in hand. On her way down the hall she heard Senator Jill Hudson's voice coming from the television in the break room – evidently another public service announcement.

Glancing in, she saw the Senator standing in the same "laboratory" with the same actors behind her; some were peering into test tubes while others were shaking hands with each other in an apparent state of self-congratulation.

"…your concerns. Well, I'm happy to announce that our scientists," the Senator paused as usual to reemphasize the words with a proud twinkle in her eye, *"our scientists* have discovered the breakthrough that will

finally defeat ARS and free us from fear. Our faith in technology and
mankind has been rewarded. We are…"

Jin shut the door with her foot, so that she wouldn't have to hear the
rest of it while waiting for the elevator.

Monday, February 20th, 2051
Ila, South Carolina

The picture of the woman was in his hands when the blast occurred.
Felipe had been looking at it in much the way that he found himself staring at corpses by the Rio Grande after a few years. He knew that he was
nearing the end of his ability to tolerate the violence. It would be moot
anyway; the sheriff knew that he would be voted out of office by the
heavily-Muslim population later in the year, if he decided to run.

When he first arrived in Ila more than 20 years earlier, it was a welcome change of pace from dealing with the handiwork of the Mexican
mafia each week. There were a lot of problems in the small town, but the
immigrant population was not quite as set in its ways as it later became.
America was new to most of the people and there was the expectation on
the part of their hosts that they would assimilate and become successful,
as previous waves of immigrants had.

When it became evident that there was no requirement to do so, and
that their needs would be taken care of regardless of whether they
adapted, learned English or worked, then there was no incentive for doing
any of these. The immigrant communities degenerated into slums, conditions made worse by a government that found it increasingly difficult to
maintain the level of entitlement spending. Crime gained momentum,
which only placed further strain on public resources.

Gradually, as group identity hardened and polarized, the Muslims began to win the numbers game. Within the community were radical elements, identified as Islamists, who encouraged policies of social and religious segregation. They were not a majority of Muslims, but it didn't
matter, because they dominated general attitudes and controlled the debate.

Ila recognized all of the Muslim holidays. The government and the
few local businesses that remained gave enormous privileges to Islamic
employees, including prayer rooms, dress-code concessions and even
separate bathrooms.

Pressure sometimes mounted on Felipe's department to enforce the
religious vilification laws by arresting the local pastors who were pur-
ported to speak unflatteringly about the Qur'an or the prophet Muhammad
from the pulpit. He refused to do this. Neither did he act in other such
cases to "preserve civil liberties" by denying the freedom of dissidents to

express themselves. He knew that his successor, whoever he might be, would not be as lax.

What he did enforce, however, was the law against murder, which applied in the case of the woman whose picture he was holding. She was a former school teacher who had converted to Islam upon marrying a Jordanian immigrant. Unlike the other victims of apostate killings, she was not murdered because she left Islam for another faith, but rather because she did not want to submit her case of domestic abuse to the *Sharia* courts, in which her testimony would count only half as much as her husband's.

By law and theory, she didn't have to do this. The religious courts were optional for Muslims. In practice, however, to refuse *Sharia* and force another Muslim to submit to a government court was an act of blasphemy, punishable by death. This was apparently her husband's reasoning when he cut her throat.

The call to prayer echoed through town from the loudspeakers mounted atop the minarets, causing him to look up at the clock for a second. He returned his gaze briefly back to the picture then started to put it back into the folder, just as the wall behind his desk blew apart and instantly took the rest of the room with it.

Hartford, Connecticut

The memorial of the seventh anniversary of the Coop-Mart supermarket explosion was actually more of an excuse for Jill and her daughter to share a trip with Parker. They had flown up two days earlier to do some skiing over the weekend. It was not the first time they had all been on a trip without her husband, but it always felt special.

Merica was growing up fast. She would be graduating high school in a few months and heading off to Berkeley in the fall. Jill wondered how many more of these times they would share in the future. The girl was far closer to Parker than to her own father, so it felt more like a family when it was just the three of them. Jill had gotten over her anger at Parker a few years after her marriage and then began to lean on him again as she once had, as her relationship with her husband drifted into mere formality.

Her daughter stood next to her, as they each held candles in their hands. The Senator was a little nervous in the crowd. There were plenty of cases when radicals bombed the very memorial services held for their victims. She was assured that security was excellent, however.

Parker was speaking on the platform in front of them, as the ceremony was winding down. "The candles that we are holding symbolize our hope and our unity with one another. Our hope is that love will triumph over hate. Our unity is the common bond that people of all faiths

have with one another, as manifested in our common desire for understanding and peace…"

Listening to Parker's voice always had a reassuring effect on Jill. She
could believe him when he expressed his faith in the human spirit and the
goodness in each person. The past three years had been rough for her, but
having the burden of ARS finally lifted was euphoric, even if it wasn't in
time to save her mother.

It was after the ceremony that she learned that Darnell Massey had
been gunned down outside his home in Billings, Montana.

Tuesday, February 21st, 2051
GNN Studios

The segment's intro was a video clip of Darnell Massey, speaking in
favor of the Reparations Act several years before: "As a black man in
America, I can tell you that having to live each day with the effects of
slavery is debilitating. My people have suffered, and compensation is
therefore demanded…" The scene then returned to the GNN studio where
Jill sat across a table from Bahira al-Zubayi.

"Welcome back to 'GNN Tonight'," said the host. "Our guest is
Senator Jill Hudson, who is sharing with us her memories of Judge
Darnell Massey. Senator, where were you when you heard the news?"

Jill gave a sad smile. "I was at a memorial for peace and tolerance,
Bahira. The contrast could not have been any plainer. After enjoying the
spirit of compassion and acceptance of the people around me – many of
whom were Muslim, I might add – it was discouraging to be pulled back
into the reality that there are many in America who don't share our broad-
minded vision of humanity. I'm speaking of the right-wing hate groups
that are most likely behind the assassination. These people constitute a
much greater threat to our freedom than the Muslims that they enjoy using
as scapegoats. If anything good comes of this tragedy, it's that it may
remind us of just who is the real enemy in America."

"Tell me about Judge Massey."

"Well," said Jill gently, "I knew him as just plain Darnell. He was a
warm and loving man, who only wanted the best for the people. He was a
champion of their rights against cold-hearted corporate America, as well
as some of the insensitive elements in government. He was a man who
cared. I think that was evident when he denied the challenge to the Hum-
phrey Act, which places a tax on businesses in proportion to the unemployment rate – part of Congress's plan to keep Americans working."

"You mentioned that hate groups are probably responsible for the
shocking assassination. The judge himself voiced concern early in his
career that he would be the target of such groups. We have a clip of him
speaking to this, I believe."

The video clip showed the judge speaking with the front steps of the court building in the background. "Of course I fear for my life," he was saying, "Federal judges aren't popular in these parts. As a black man in America, I know that I face additional risk, but we've got to stand up to these bigots just the way we stood up to them in Selma..."

Thursday, February 23rd, 2051
Rothberg, California

Pat wasn't sure what possessed him to visit his sister in California. He had never been that close to her, although he appreciated her invitation to the community's dedication ceremony nearly twenty years ago. She was the only member of his old family left.

Lately, family and friends had taken on a new importance for Pat, though he didn't know why. He always placed a high priority on relationships, but he had developed an odd yearning over the last several months to put his affairs in order, as if he were suffering from terminal cancer – which, his doctor assured him, he was not. He wondered if it was a delayed reaction to the death of his friend, Aaron Bernstein.

He planned on taking a long two-week vacation that summer to visit his son in Poland. Matt had just spent two weeks with him in New York over Christmas, but he wanted to see more of the young man whom he was so proud to still call his boy.

The trip out to San Francisco cost an arm and a leg. The price of air travel had skyrocketed since Airtana was effectively driven out of business in the name of progressivism three or four years ago, which was ironic given that only those with moderate wealth could now afford to travel. Fortunately this included Pat, who was staring a comfortable retirement in the face, though he would never see a dime of his Social Security payments, as the new rules effectively allowed payments only to those who were entirely negligent in saving for their future.

He flew into the only operating terminal left at the airport in San Francisco, and rented a car for the drive up to Rothberg. He would never have recognized the community, were it not for the familiar gate with the town's name on it – although some of the letters were missing.

For one thing, there were no real natural landmarks anymore. The beautiful mountains that he remembered, which were only starting to show signs of commercialism, were now completely taken over with shacks, trailers and satellite dishes. There were few trees left on them anymore, but the highest peak had what looked like a statue of an Indian carved into it.

Likewise, the community was a disaster area. Trash littered the roads and yards. Bottles and beer cans were tossed everywhere, even dangling from the bushes along with food wrappers and what looked like condoms.

Used syringes were scattered along the curbs. Graffiti covered everything; vulgar words and pictures painted in various colors that made the place look worse than even the south Bronx.

Broken glass, in piles along the curbs, attested to risk of leaving a car in the street. The ones that were there were either up on blocks or so heavily vandalized that he doubted they even ran anymore. The odor of urine was overpowering. He thought he found the right house at one point, but a grubby white couple was ascending the porch steps, with the man holding his girlfriend over his back, as she was trying unsuccessfully to avoid vomiting on his legs.

Pat retraced his steps and eventually found his sister's home. Like all the others, it was coated with spray paint. The yard looked as if it hadn't been tended to since the day the expensive sod was carefully laid. Half of it was a jungle and the other half was bare sandy dirt. His sister came out and raised her garage door so that he could pull his car in, which gave him some peace of mind.

They gave each other a hug in the foyer. Pat looked around with a sinking heart. The once elegant house had been completely trashed. Holes were knocked in the sheetrock, the carpet was chewed up, and the wood floor was so warped that the beautiful oak planks had been replaced by plywood. Most of the windows were blocked with plastic and boards, the glass long having been knocked out. Tile in the kitchen was broken, as was the wonderful black granite counter that was clearly beyond repair.

The house stank, which Letitia explained, was due to two of the toilets having been backed up beyond the point of being operational anymore. She was almost crying when she talked about how "they don't take care of us anymore" and railed against "that white man that stopped doing things," apparently referring to the Professor, who had become a recluse.

Pat asked about the reparations money that he knew his sister received five years earlier. She had proudly told him that she was eligible for the full $500,000 back when they argued over it a few years ago (he declined to apply).

She explained that she really only received about $250,000 because she had taken the "fast cash" option and gotten half of the full amount in one lump-sum payment from a middleman. She immediately bought a top-of-the-line luxury car that she had to sell in two years for one-tenth of the original six-figure price after the money ran out and she could not afford maintenance and insurance.

Pat gathered that this was generally the case all across the country, where the windfall had created a mini-boom for the economy over the last few years. It hadn't taken long, however, for the wealth to find its way out of the hands of those who "won it" and back into the pockets of those who knew how to earn it.

So much for "permanently leveling the playing field," although eve-ryone was now equally affected by the crippling inflation from the sudden influx of $3 trillion – not to mention the black hole in the national debt.

In the end, he was glad that he only scheduled a few nights to stay over with her. She spent her entire time watching television and eating, even when he had traveled so far to be with her. She explained that she needed to keep up with her shows.

He spent some time walking around the community a bit, which rein-forced his first impressions. It was utterly depressing; nothing like he remembered – and certainly nothing like its television namesake, even though his sister loved the show. "I'm famous," she told him, while brushing food crumbs off her large blouse and into the natty couch.

Pat waved his hand in front of his face to clear the cloud of fruit flies.

He was quite relieved to eventually leave that awful place in his rear-view mirror.

Friday, February 24th, 2051
New York, New York

Bernice was having a very bad day, made all the worse by her angry friend on the other end of the phone line.

The week started out so hopefully. The killing of a Federal judge out-side his own home in Montana was enough to fill the 24-hour news chan-nel with running commentary from pundits warning of the dangers posed by Red State "backwaters" and the "Neanderthals" that coalesced there. Some said the solution to such obvious cultural inferiority was education. Others advocated sending in the troops, pointing out that it was hypocriti-cal not to do this, given what happened in Maine.

Then Bernice woke up that morning to the news that local authorities had an arrest and a confession. The suspect was the father of a little girl raped and killed by a man, whose conviction the judge overturned on a quota technicality. Suddenly GNN lost both its story and a measure of credibility, since it had spent the previous week all but insisting that those ubiquitous (yet oddly invisible) 'hate groups' were to blame. The story was quickly buried and the network tried to move on.

A story they were now relying on was the car bombing in South Carolina that took the life of a local sheriff and several passersby. GNN learned that the police chief was not popular in the local Muslim commu-nity, which was presumed to have produced the bomber. The network cautiously suggested that this was because of his refusal to enforce ele-ments of the hate crimes and religious vilification acts, as community spokesmen seemed to confirm.

It was not until ten minutes ago that Bernice made the connection be-tween the late Sheriff Posada and her friend from college – and then only when Maria called from Alberta to light into her over the network's implication that her brother failed to uphold the law.

"Are you saying that he had it coming?" demanded Maria.

"Of course not, but you know the anger that festers in a minority community when there is the perception that its needs are not... are not..." Bernice faltered.

"Given priority over others?"

"Well, I wasn't going to say that," stammered Bernice. Maria had really changed from the girl that she remembered.

"Bernice, what you ought to be asking on your news programs is whether these laws make any sense. How did it get to the point where the government establishes agencies to analyze what people say, and determine how they should be punished?"

"It's to protect the civil liberties of others, including Muslims in this case, from being offended and having to practice their religion in a climate of fear and intimidation," responded Bernice. "That's not what America is about."

"So you believe that the way to preserve civil liberties is by forcing critics to conform and stay silent?"

"I suppose. I..." Bernice was taken aback by this challenge to the very foundation of hate crime. She had been raised to accept the speech codes on college campuses and in workplaces, prior to their inevitable advance into criminal law. It was necessary to mandate sensitivity in a multicultural society.

She remembered Jill telling her a few years ago that Maria had become quite active in her Catholic faith. Perhaps this would be useful. "How would you feel," she finally asked, "if every time you turned on the television, you saw Christians being lampooned as rubes, ignorant bigots or even mentally unstable characters?"

Maria laughed so hard that it took her a while to answer. "Have you gone your entire life without watching television, Bernice?"

Thursday, June 29th, 2051
Kshesin, Poland

Pat Ridley's heart was swelling with pride as he walked along the tarmac next to the 30-year-old man, standing straight and tall in an olive-green Air Force flight uniform. Major Matthew Ridley had a disciplined bearing that seemed to command respect from the maintenance crew and junior officers they passed. Pat hoped that it was easy to tell that they were father and son.

It was the last day of a 10-day visit – the first time that he had ever been to Europe, other than a very brief stopover on his way to Israel nearly four decades earlier. The Islamic revolutions in France and the

Netherlands were boiling over into other countries there, with civil strife consuming many of America's old allies. The only countries that were open to U.S. military bases were Poland and the Baltics, which was somewhat ironic given that they were all more closely aligned ideologically with Alberta and the Western Alliance. They had long ago pulled out of the deteriorating EU and formed their own 'Free Europe' pact. Despite pressure from the United States, they recently signed treaties with Alberta as well.

There wasn't much left of the U.S. Air Force anyway. Matt joined as a pilot seven years ago, after college and just in time to see the last several military cuts take effect. He was lucky to still have a plane. There were only about a thousand left, evenly divided between bombers, fighters and reconnaissance. The rest had been retired, mothballed or sold to countries like Poland, which needed protection against the instability of Western Europe and Turkey. Along with their Free Europe allies, they were gaining military superiority over their neighbors, which had been downsizing in the face of domestic pressures.

Matt told him that Europe was splitting into two factions, the Islamists and the Christians. Countries like France had lost the battle even before it began, when they chose to disassociate from the Western religious foundation for European law and civilization. Drowned under the tide of Muslim immigration, they allowed the Mullahs to take power in order to appease the radical terror elements that wanted to dominate in a far less generous manner. *Sharia* was also a good buffer against crime and violence, which was wearying the non-Muslim populations.

Countries like Poland and Latvia were holding the line by resisting would-be immigrants, which included the same liberal Europeans who looked down on them as intolerant not long before, but were now trying to escape their own unbearable leftist utopias.

Pat could easily understand, because he saw the same struggle in America, a nation that was unraveling under the strain of opposing cultures. There were the same Islamists looking to dominate the areas where they had the numbers, Hispanic states in the Southwest that sucked the life from the rest, and the Northeast, mid-Atlantic and West Coast progressive elements that wanted to continue handing over the country. The Red States in the West were becoming distinct, isolated and under siege from secular fundamentalists in Washington, who were continually crusading to fulfill a sort of bizarre manifest destiny by cleansing traditional values from these final American outposts.

It was a struggle just to raise his boy right in a culture that was hostile to the values that instilled character. He remembered when Matt was fourteen and brought home an educational brochure from school administrators entitled, "How to Have Safe Sex." Such literature would be burned in places like Idaho and Utah before it made its way into the hands of children. Parents there had a much lower tolerance for watching government actively undermine their moral teachings.

Yet, he had managed to raise a good kid, against the odds. He stepped back and watched as Matt interacted with the maintenance crew of his bomber, going over critical details before stepping up and into the cockpit. After a few seconds he donned his helmet, climbed the ladder and waved at his father.

Pat took a step back, preparing to make his way back to the observation building where he would watch his son take off for a 45-minute training flight. After that, he would be getting on a plane himself for the multi-leg journey back to the States.

Before he turned, however, he felt compelled to catch his son's eye again then raise his arm slowly in a salute.

Friday, June 30th, 2051
Los Angeles, California

His daughter's eyes were bloodshot and vacant. Dirty blond hair hung in stringy, oily clumps over her face. One of her teeth was missing and her skin was cratered with acne. She looked far older than 25 – and nothing like the "porn queen" that she was six years earlier.

He had traveled a long way to see her, but he wasn't sure why. He had never been close to his daughter. She cut off contact six years ago when she left home to become an "adult film actress" which was, Danforth finally admitted, just a woman who sells her self-respect, one john after another. He angrily confronted her at the time, demanding that she leave the industry.

"Why would you ever do this to yourself?" he challenged her, back when she was beautiful

She looked confused. "Ever since I was young I wanted to be like all those women in your magazines and on your videotapes. I saw how much you wanted them, and I wanted to be just like them."

He hadn't known how to respond then and he still didn't. Exploiting someone else's daughter, which is what a man does when he funds the porn industry, is far easier than accepting your own daughter as an object of the lust of others. It made him sick. Sick enough to purge his home of every trace of the perverse hobby that dominated his life for more than thirty years, not that there was much thrill left in it anymore.

But it wasn't in time to save his daughter. She bounced along for a few years in the industry, aging considerably during that time, as one might expect. Her looks soon grew too hard to command the sort of money needed to support the occupational drug habit acquired, so she turned to more direct methods of prostitution (legal throughout America now) slowly winding her way down a spiral toward the drain at the bottom that would soon suck her through for good.

Danforth sat across the table from her at a cheap fast-food restaurant and wondered why the hell he cared.

Monday, September 4th, 2051
Boston, Massachusetts

With the tough economy and threat of terror, only two daily flights remained between Boston and Los Angeles. Each of the Americans who boarded the Progressive Airlines jet at Logan airport that morning would have only a short time to gauge their choices and priorities in life against existential reality, but it is likely that they were able to reach remarkably similar conclusions.

There was a television producer in seat 2A, who did his best to keep his own children from seeing the violent and sexually explicit programming that his network carefully cultivated in other impressionable young minds.

Sitting next to him was a corporate marketing executive whose commercials funded the debauchery.

A former anti-war protestor was sitting in 45C, basking in the sanctimonious glow of success and sipping coffee without the least bit of remorse for the lives of millions crushed under despots that did not seem to share his appreciation for ethical niceties.

An African-American professor of law was sitting in 16C, on his way to receive an award for teaching that black violence was justified by white oppression.

In 19B was a social worker, whose life's work was to employ a variety of government welfare programs for the cause of insulating pregnant teens, single mothers, drug addicts and high-school dropouts from the consequences of their decisions.

In 21A was a lawyer who successfully fought to deny intelligence agencies the ability to implement effective anti-terrorism measures.

A teacher was sitting in 39B, who taught her students nothing about Western civilization except that it was malicious.

A young woman in 24D hadn't slept well the night before, because she was concerned about the possible extinction of a particular species of sand flea near a proposed shopping mall in California.

Her companion, a young activist sitting next to her, was working furiously on a project to eliminate the motto, 'one nation under God' from the nation's currency, proving, perhaps, that there are no atheists, since every man has his god.

There was a nurse and mother of two sitting in 27A, who was always too busy with her family to worry about the decisions that her political representatives made on her behalf or the judges that were appointed to determine her children's future.

Then there was the priest in 11B, who had long believed in the irrelevancy of the Christian faith, but appreciated the usefulness of the vocabulary. God was too big for one religion and could therefore be approached equally from all, which only made sense given that he was in all persons... although, by definition, that would have to include the man currently stabbing a flight attendant to death just three rows in front of him.

New York, New York

It was impossible to get onto the roof, but people were trying anyway. Everyone knew that the Hope Tower was about to collapse as surely as the World Trade Center had fifty years ago, though only a few of them were old enough to remember the footage on television, since it was deemed too "insensitive" to replay in the years sense.

"I hope they play this one forever," said Danforth softly, sitting at the back of the large restaurant on the top floor, which was now packed with bodies. "I hope they broadcast the hell out of it, so no one ever forgets what those people did to us."

A woman sitting next to him got up and walked away, obviously put off by his pessimism. Danforth knew, of course, that they wouldn't be replaying footage beyond the next few weeks, nor would they show the video that was sure to be released on the Internet, with the hijackers reading from the Qur'an in front of a banner that said something like "death to infidels," for fear of offending Islamic sensibilities.

People on the floors under them were jumping out of windows; he heard them as they shouted prayers or screamed warnings to anyone below. Some of the people sitting around him were badly burned. There was a lot of coughing, but no one was worried about catching a cold. Danforth was coughing as well, not from the fumes and smoke that were slowly seeping up the elevator shafts and stairwells, but rather from the damage that his lungs had taken in the last forty minutes.

He looked over at Pat Ridley, who seemed to be leading a series of prayer services, although he couldn't hear much. There was a group of people around him, mostly white, well-dressed and holding hands as they waited earnestly to talk with him. They obviously held him in high esteem. Ridley was smiling contagiously as he moved gently from one to the next. Each would bow their head with him for a few seconds then offer a tearful hug. Some would actually laugh.

Religion was something that normally disgusted Danforth, but knowing that you're about to die has a way of clarifying priorities. No longer did the quest to scrape the last crumb of Western religion from the deepest corners of the country and into the trash seem so important, particularly when it only meant setting the table for a religion with little regard for unbelievers. Nor did he have much awareness of his scorched hands and broken feet – which had swelled to the point of numbness.

He could hear a little of the radio from a few tables down. The low murmur of the broadcasters' voices made it sound as if they were discussing a round of golf rather than a mass murder in progress. He caught vague snatches about a "Progressive Airlines flight from Boston." It was his plane….

Damn the man that forced that airline on him! The company had been a disaster in the hands of CSR, which was bound by contract not to sell it for ten years. It was running a multi-billion dollar debt when he begged to be rescued by the appointment to the SEC. By then he had already lost CSR, along with his credibility within the business community.

"Hate-Free Air" never worked because people knew in their hearts that it was never their own hatred that was the problem. *They* were not the reason that billions were spent each year to prevent planes from being knocked out of the sky or shopping malls from exploding.

Now, as he enjoyed the sort of mental clarity that only a doomed mind can command, he recognized the social farce of political correctness for what it was.

Being politically correct means denying what is factually or historically correct when it happens to be offensive. It means pretending, for example that the elderly black grandfather standing in line at the airport represents the same potential threat to other passengers as the heavily-perspiring Middle-Eastern man behind him, who grips a holy book in his damp hands that blatantly encourages him to kill unbelievers.

It means pretending that the culture which hacks off a young girl's clitoris to ensure that she never enjoys sex is somehow equal to the culture that condemns it. How? Well, it takes faith, you see; faith in some sort of mystical equilibrium, where you find a distasteful element in the history of your own culture and then build an impressive exaggeration around this kernel of truth until you have a bogeyman that looks equally as monstrous. Then you step back and congratulate yourself on the ability to transcend such malignancy with self-critique, basking in the personal glow of moral superiority.

If you're lucky, of course, then you never have to suffer the consequences of such a self-defeating philosophy. Instead it becomes a problem for your children to deal with, while you spend the rest of your life living in the ridiculous little wonderland you've built, never noticing that those whom you've worked so hard to accommodate have no intention of accommodating you…. until finally your artificial world collapses under the strain of its own weight.

At that moment Danforth got up and screamed as loud and as long as he could until he ran out of air. Then he took a deep breath and screamed again… and again.

Kshesin, Poland

Major Matthew Ridley was in a base hanger, working late that afternoon on a sticky situation with two subordinates that would certainly involve disciplinary action of some sort, when he got word that there was an important call being routed to the floor. Calmly, he walked over and picked up the phone on the wall of the giant structure, well out of the earshot of others.

It was his father. "Hello, Son. I just wanted to tell you that I love you."

Matt had a close relationship with his father, but, like most men, they rarely expressed their feelings so bluntly. "Is anything wrong?"

"Yes. My building has been hit by a plane. I'm OK right now, but it doesn't look like they'll be able to put out the fire."

Matt reeled. "What?"

"This may be the last time we talk, Matt. I want you to know that I'm at peace."

"Dad, no…"

"You know I've always been proud of you. You are my greatest accomplishment."

"Can't you get out of there? Isn't there a stairwell or something?"

"Not any that won't turn me into barbecue. There's no way out."

Matt gave an involuntary sob.

His dad continued. "Don't feel bad for me. I've had a great life – all sixty-two years of it. I know it's been kind of ordinary, but God calls us to do the best we can in our given circumstances, so that we can enter His house in righteousness. I'm dying with my head high. I hope you will too."

There was a rumbling in the background.

"It's starting," said his father.

"What? What is?"

The line went dead.

Washington D.C.

"…these horrible attacks. Our nation has suffered a great loss. We assure Americans that we will do our best to find out who is responsible and determine what their demands are. The safety of our citizens is our greatest priority…"

Jill Hudson turned off the television and got out of the limo in the underground parking lot beneath the city streets. Only authorized traffic was allowed in Washington D.C. Employees and residents were forced to leave their vehicles in the huge parking centers on the outskirts and take special transportation into the district. It was the first American city to be off-limits to the general public; a precaution arrived at in stages over the last thirty-five years.

She was under no such restrictions as a Senator, of course, and this was one of the reasons that she made the drive from Baltimore in under an hour. She watched the devastation on the satellite hookup in the back of her limo, strangely indifferent to the presumed death of Robert Danforth. The last leg of her journey was the underground shuttle to the White House to attend the emergency session.

On the way, she thought about the recollections her father shared with her from when he attended similar sessions with President Gore as a young Senator following the 9/11 attacks. That was a pivotal time for America. Many of the domestic and foreign policy reforms that followed shaped the nation and the world; and it wouldn't have happened had a man like Al Gore not been there to humble the country in its hour of crisis and win the respect of nations…. the Commonwealth of Equals.

Now she would be a witness to history, as her father was. Perhaps her future held a two-term Presidency as well. Right now, however, she was just hoping that the Progressive President was up to the task in the way that Al Gore had been fifty years earlier.

After going through the multitude of security checkpoints, she was finally on the elevator that led down to the underground bunker beneath the White House. When the doors opened, she could see the meeting underway in the large conference room behind shatter-proof glass doors toward the back of the level. There was President Fish with his security advisors and military staff, along with the Vice President, whom she knew quite well.

Rahim Sahil was following in his grandfather's steps when he accepted the President's offer three years ago to join the ticket. No one was fooled by the invitation. The Muslim Coalition Party was upset by the military incursions in Maine and was openly running their own candidate. Fish needed to keep as many of the Muslim votes that propelled him to victory four years earlier as possible. His free spending ways had already won over the unemployed, some seniors, and the majority of African-Americans, who appreciated the reparations payouts. The Democrats were also seen as more resistant to raising taxes on the "rich", even though the Progressives now defined that group as practically anyone with a white-collar income. The truly wealthy had nearly been taxed out of existence, along with their supply of golden eggs.

Still, it was a surprise victory that wouldn't have been possible without the former BAIR chief as his running mate. In spite of this, relations had quickly soured between the two, and Jill could hear them arguing even before she walked in the room.

"It doesn't matter how I got it, or how BAIR got it," Rahim was saying. "The point is that we have the hijackers' statement."

"Well, I don't understand how it is that our own intelligence agencies aren't able to come up with this," complained the President, who then turned to his FBI Director. "Why didn't we have a clue about what was being planned?"

The director looked nervous. "We can't put agents undercover anymore, since their identities are likely to be compromised. It's also virtually impossible to use informants, since they find themselves quickly exposed as well. We've got too many leaks in the Bureau and there's not much we can do about it."

"Why not?" snapped the President. It was a rhetorical statement, since they all knew the answer. "Well, what are the details, Mr. Vice President?"

Rahim looked down at the paper in his hands and began reading, "All praise be to Allah, who helped us glorify Islam. There is no doubt that He commands us to strike the unbelievers, kill them, and fight them by any means necessary to achieve…"

"Not that part of it," interrupted the President impatiently, "we don't have time to listen to all that preaching, particularly since we're going to be pretending like this has nothing to do with Islam, right Rahim?"

His sarcasm was uncharacteristic and took the Vice President by surprise. He looked down in mild embarrassment, which Jill had never before seen him do. After a couple of seconds he said, "There are three basic demands. They want *Sharia* extended to other states, Maine independence, and…" He hesitated.

"And?" asked the President.

"They want the President put on trial for war crimes," finished Rahim.

This shouldn't have been a surprise to anyone in the room. All of these demands had been made before, usually following acts of violence. The collapse of the Hope tower alone, however, had probably killed over 5,000 people according to preliminary estimates, including the new SEC chairman. Their demands had to be taken seriously.

"How would you feel about that?" the President suddenly asked of Rahim, with distinct suspicion in his voice.

"If you're implying that I had anything to do with…"

"No, of course not, but you have to admit that it's mighty convenient for you. You've been undermining this Administration for the last four years by implying that we should submit to the ICC over Lewiston."

"I have never come out and said that publicly," insisted his Vice President, "at least not since I left BAIR."

"Did you leave BAIR?" asked Fish sardonically. "It's hard to tell, because you don't act like you've broadened your advocacy beyond the Muslim community."

"It's difficult when the rights of Muslims are constantly trampled on. There is no group in America that is viewed with more suspicion."

"I can't imagine why." The President's tone shocked many in the room. It was evident that he was under tremendous stress. "I've committed no war crime, Mr. Vice President. If you would publicly support me on this, then perhaps it would make a difference in the…"

"There were M-16 rounds in the bodies of those children that came from the guns carried by soldiers ordered into their community by the President," Rahim maintained. "Lawyers have worked very hard to establish these facts. By the international treaties that *we* have signed, we are legally obligated to turn… to turn the President over to the ICC for trial."

Jill tried to defuse the tension. "What about the other demands?" she asked the President. "Can we make concessions there?"

The President did not appear to mind changing the topic, although his tone had not mellowed. "You know that we can't allow Maine independence, even if we've lost control of the entire state. My fear is that if we did, then we can say goodbye to Idaho, Montana and those other Red States that would jump at the chance to join Alberta. Besides," he turned back to Rahim with a cold stare, "where would it end?"

"A Muslim homeland is hardly unreasonable," said the Vice President quietly, "and neither is allowing *Sharia* for Muslims living in other areas of the country. It doesn't affect anyone else and it's optional for believers."

"Optional if you don't mind dying, you mean," corrected the President, clearly referring to the apostate killings.

"With all due respect, Mr. President, you should not be so small-minded as to judge an entire religion by the actions of a handful of people operating outside its teachings. Islam is the religion of peace to…"

"Does that look like peace to you?" asked the President, jerking his finger behind him at the images of aftermath at the Hope tower site.

"Is dead schoolchildren in Maine something that you're proud of?"

"Put it in perspective!" yelled the President.

"Mr. President," broke in Jill, "if I may, Sir, do we know who the hijackers are?"

The President gave a sarcastic glance back at Rahim. "Why don't you tell us, Mr. Vice President? Your intelligence sources are apparently better than ours, since we've got Islamists in our Bureau that we can't get rid of because of the MIWU." He referred to the Muslim Intelligence

Workers Union, a powerful force within the FBI, which did indeed prevent the government from eliminating those who were openly disloyal.

"Perhaps if your policies were not so offensive to people within your own government, then you wouldn't have such a problem," Rahim practically sneered.

"Well, who are they?" asked the President again.

"The information I have is that they are Allah's Holy Army. There were supposed to be five hijackers on board the plane, all members of the military..."

"Our military? Are they U.S. citizens? No wonder they're celebrating these attacks up in Maine and down in..."

"Yes. And they each complained of discrimination because of their beliefs while in uniform."

"Why, are they Presbyterian?"

Rahim ignored him. "Although I don't agree with their methodology, of course, I can sympathize with their grievance. The creation of separate units for Muslims in our armed forces – optional of course – is hardly asking too much, given that nearly half of all new recruits are Muslim."

"I thought Segregation went out of fashion a hundred years ago," responded President Fish.

Jill broke in, "I think the Vice President may be right. This is different in that it's voluntary, sort of like one's choice of church. Our armed forces have stabilized at about 200,000 personnel, most of whom are Muslim anyway, so this doesn't affect very many people."

"And *Sharia*?" asked the President. "That would affect a lot of people."

"Only those that choose to submit – and only in states that approve it in referendums. I realize that it isn't a perfect system, but there's obviously a lot of anger among Muslims, and allowing them to practice their religion is far greater than the cost of disallowing it... as we've seen today"

Jill paused and then emphasized the next words carefully. "Our highest priority has to be stopping the terror."

Finally there was a pause in the conversation, as the tension in the room began to ease. After a few moments of silence, Rahim added softly, "The response to these acts of desperation must be a greater understanding of Islam on the part of Americans, Mr. President, as my grandfather once told his President at a time very much like this."

The President took off his glasses and rubbed his eyelids for a while with his fingers, obviously deep in thought. He may have been no Al Gore, and "Hudson" Jill knew they had a long night and week ahead of them, but at least they were making progress.

Sunday, December 24ᵗʰ, 2051
Bangor, Maine

The brown Second Lieutenant's bar on Sadiq Yassin's overcoat trembled slightly in the bitter wind as he stood in his uniform on the steps of the small Episcopal church in Bangor, trying to convince the tiny group of people standing in front of him to join his unit on the Christmas Eve convoy out of the city. Some of them seemed more reluctant to leave than others, but all of them were following the lead of the grey-haired Bishop, who stood in front of the rest, angrily denouncing the evacuation effort with fire in his aged eyes.

The young soldier had been commissioned as part of the convoy to escort willing residents out of Maine prior to the independence that would officially be granted at a ceremony the following weekend. Even though he was traveling with the Green brigades (newly formed Muslim Army units) it didn't stop the other good Muslims of the state from throwing bottles, rocks and eventually bullets at them – especially when it became apparent that there would be no retaliation.

Their mission was simply to provide a protective presence for the non-Muslim residents of Maine who wanted to leave. Unlike some in his unit, Sadiq did not harbor any private enthusiasm for the changes. What was happening to these people was unfair, even if many were as oblivious to it as those on the church steps in front of him.

From others in the community, he had been told that the church was once the scene of an interfaith dialogue meeting that received national attention shortly after 9/11. Though no one was really old enough to remember it, there was still an amiable feeling on the part of local Muslims toward the "people of the book" who attended the church. It didn't hurt that the bishop was outspoken in his condemnation of the "occupation" of U.S. troops and the culpability of the government in the "Saint Valentines Day Massacre."

The largely Arab neighbors felt that the dwindling group of parishioners was not a threat and would probably make excellent *dhimmis* (his men referred to future *dhimmis* who facilitated their own subjugation as "dhimwits"). They were deferential, typically obsequious and non-evangelical. It was doubtful that there would be any trouble when the time came to inform them that they would not be able to build new churches, ring church bells, or bear full testimony in Islamic courts. In any case, by the time their daughters or granddaughters were required to take the veil, it would be far too late to object.

At the moment, however, the old bishop stood among the handful of people and berated the young officer. "This is America! You can't make us leave!"

"Next week it won't be America, and you may be wishing you had," replied Sadiq. His calm manner only seemed to further anger the bishop.

"We'll all be better off after you get those tanks out of the state and stop pointing your guns at us! That's when things will finally start to calm down around here."

"We aren't pointing our guns at you," corrected Sadiq.

"No, just at little Muslim schoolchildren," sneered the old man. "They make for better targets, since they can't shoot back."

"Do any of you want to come?" asked the officer, to the six or seven others.

"No, they don't want to come," answered the Bishop for them. "This is our home, and we're committed to making our community a place that is respectful of peace and love. I have a feeling we can do that under our own flag a lot better than we can under that filthy symbol of genocide and oppression." He jerked a finger at the patch on the officer's shoulder.

Sadiq's felt his face warm and he had to wrestle with himself to keep from giving the old man his unvarnished opinion in the presence of his troops. Patriotism was a very unpopular sentiment in the Green Brigades, and candidly expressing his feelings would probably kill his career.

It was beginning to grow dark in the late afternoon. Gusts of wind carrying tiny ice pellets beat against the dilapidated doors of the sanctuary behind them. Most of those in the group were elderly, although there was an idealistic-looking younger couple with them. They were all shivering, presumably from the cold.

Sadiq turned away and walked back down the steps toward the caravan of military vehicles on the road, wondering what the story of those who chose to stay would be in a few years.

2052

Friday, April 5th, 2052
New York, New York

Not many people in the city appreciated the man at the corner of 66th and Freedom nearly as much as he enjoyed his First Amendment right to expose and massage himself in public fashion. In fact, Darryl may have been the only one to find some advantage in the situation. Not that he cared to watch such a lewd act, which even he found disgusting, but rather because it occasionally detoured foot traffic down the alley where he strategically positioned himself between the dumpsters to prey on the unsuspecting.

He found that whoever had the scruples to avoid such distasteful behavior to the point of walking down a dark alley invariably had money for the taking. But Darryl had more on his mind that night, thanks to the collection of hard-core rape simulation videos that he kept back in the apartment, which artificially heightened his appetite in a way that he was sure most men understood, even if they exercised more restraint than was his personal choice.

It had been a dry night thus far – not even a purse snatching – when he heard footsteps approach. Both sets were quick and light, as if belonging to two females. As they passed the opening, however, he could see that one was a very pale bald man.

Slowly he crept out and cast a quick look in the other direction to make sure no one else was following. Satisfied that it was just the three of them, he rapidly caught up to the others as quietly as possible and decked the man's head with a brick.

The woman screamed as her companion fell dazed into a filthy puddle. He offered no further resistance, so Darryl didn't bother to finish him off before turning his attention back to the woman. He expected to have to catch up to her fleeing down the alley, but she hadn't moved. In fact, she was trying to reach down to help the man, who sat with his mouth open, paralyzed with fear. "Don't you touch him!" she shrieked at Darryl.

He got a bit of a kick out of raping the woman in front of her dazed companion. She seemed to believe that submission would improve their chances of surviving the experience. She was wrong.

After he killed her, Darryl stood over the bald white man, who was shaking and sobbing. He started to raise the brick in his hand when shouting was heard behind him. It startled him into turning away and immediately running off in the opposite direction.

Saturday, May 4th, 2052
New York, New York

Bernice had debated going to work that day. She was usually at GNN a full day on Saturday and then some on Sundays, but she decided to go by Beth Landau's apartment this morning to spend some time with the group before making her way into the office.

The past month had tested Bernice's faith in her principles as much as anyone else gathered there, but she had no doubt what Phyllis would have wanted. Her late friend was proud of her movie, "Pretend that we're Dead," which postulated a sort of right-wing future where the right to privacy was ignored and everyone's genetic profile was stored in a huge database. It was a relief to all of them, six years ago, when the DNA crime database was declared an unconstitutional violation of the freedom from illegal search and seizure.

The Artist, of course, was having a tough time knowing that the police could simply unseal the DNA records to easily discover and arrest the killer. The ghastly bandage on his head seemed to pulsate to the throbbing of his falsetto voice as he whined about their refusal to comply with his pleadings.

There were not many from the once mighty Landau group left. They lived in little islands now, as criminal gangs began to take control of the areas between them. Those who hadn't fled the city for God knows where had no desire to risk the streets on foot, even before the incident with Phyllis. She wasn't the first to lose her life in such circumstances, anyway. Another woman had been knifed to death while on her way to a large protest march against police brutality.

"Maybe if we all join together and go down to the station, we can get them to take us seriously," muttered the Artist.

Bernice had had enough. "Maybe you should honor her memory by shutting the hell up," she snapped. The others around her caught their breath. They were tired of the whining as well, but the Artist had always been treated with venerable awe since joining the group more than twenty years ago.

"But they've got to catch this animal," the Artist protested.

"He's not an animal," Bernice responded evenly. "Phyllis wouldn't have wanted us to call him that. I'm sure she would prefer that we refer to him as 'one whom our system has failed.' Stigmatizing the criminal is not a solution, in fact, it's self-defeating."

But the Artist continued, in high-pitched sniveling that wore thin on her nerves. After giving him a chance to bellyache, she finally got up and shouted, "You were there! How come you didn't do anything? How come you didn't protect her like she protected you?"

Her exasperation was getting the best of her and she knew it was best to leave. On her way to the door, however, she had one last word for him. She turned to look him in the eye.

"You're not even a man."

New York, New York

Having to drive everywhere was ridiculous, but there wasn't an alternative, as Bernice had to remind herself when pulling into the underground parking deck a few minutes after leaving the meeting in a huff. It was too dangerous for a single woman to walk anywhere, and the subway was absolutely out of the question. No one went underground anymore, except the homeless, who lived there now, after the mayor relented to the demands of civil rights activists.

As Bernice started to make her way to the elevators, which would take her all the way up into the lobby, she decided to defy her circumstances by walking out of the deck, onto the street and around the block to the front entrance. If she couldn't at least do that then what was the point of keeping GNN headquartered in Manhattan? Why not do as many of the smaller businesses had done and relocate to the Northwest? Not to Montana or any of the Red States, of course, since that would be too strange, nor to the Southwest, since the quality of life indicators were terrible, but perhaps up to Seattle or B.C., where true progressivism was alive and well. Many of her like-minded friends in other parts of the country, who were adamant supporters of the Sanctuary process in their local areas, were starting to relocate to the Northwest.

It felt odd to walk in sunlight again, and to feel a natural spring breeze against her body. Bernice enjoyed as much of it as she could, trying to let her temper ebb from the encounter with the Artist. She trudged up the slope then around the corner and onto the main street, Martin Luther King Jr. Avenue. There in front of her was a sight that warmed her heart. Three little girls in *hijabs* were standing outside the lobby of GNN, handing out brochures. Bernice felt slightly ashamed to be so afraid of the city streets, when here were such tiny, innocent creatures on the sidewalk – with their father standing not far way, of course.

She went up to them, admiring their cherubic faces, and started to walk past and into the lobby of her office building, when they saw her. One of them slipped a brochure into her hand and the three girls began to chant in harmony, *"Don't read the news, it's controlled by Jews."*

She was too stunned to read what was in her hand, but the father hurried up to her and began insisting, "It's true! We are demanding that GNN apologize for its racist propaganda."

Racism? At GNN? Bernice looked at the brochure. It skewered her news network for an editorial that criticized the World Forum on Racism for holding their annual conference in Tehran, in a country, not unlike others in the Middle East, where Jews were not allowed. GNN accurately reported that Iran refused to budge on their anti-Semitic policy.

"Do you believe that a country which doesn't allow Jews is an appropriate choice for an anti-racism conference?" she asked incredulously.

The man's eyes narrowed suspiciously as his little girls' eyes widened. They began to shrink away from her, as if she were diseased. "It isn't true. Iran allows Jews. They are the People of the Book, according to Islam. They are welcomed there. They own businesses and enjoy religious freedom."

Bernice knew that nothing could be further from the truth, but she turned without argument and walked into the building, even as the chanting started up behind her. The man was too determined to believe what he wanted, regardless of the facts, and they already had enough bomb threats dictating their news policy as it was.

Friday, May 17th, 2052
New York, New York

The bright lights of New York City were a long way from the bamboo fields along the base of Mount Kenya, but Mutii carried a *panga* knife under his robes nonetheless. The African machete was the only protection he dared carry in a country that had a strict ban on firearms. Those rules may have prevented some criminals from owning guns, but the rest could pick fights to their advantage with other sorts of weapons.

The first-generation Muslim immigrant did not enjoy being cooped up in an apartment, and he would thus occasionally go for walks with his family, staying with crowds in the safer areas. Times Square was much too seedy for his tastes, so he would often head to the Upper West Side with his wives in tow.

On this occasion, he crossed the street at the corner of 66th and Freedom to find a man standing in front of him, holding his bare penis in his hands and leering at Mutii's women. This was a highly inappropriate thing to do! Mutii quickly shepherded his wives a few doorways down the block, before leaving them in front of a brightly lighted shop and briefly excusing himself. He returned to the corner, where the offensive party was now leering at others, who were trying to pay him no attention.

A quick and professional downward slash of the *panga* cleanly detached the erect member from its owner, where it bounced along the pavement a few times like a short cut of bamboo, before rolling into the sewer.

"You'll want to apply direct pressure to this area here," instructed Mutii politely, before turning back to join his family.

The next evening, there were no men to be found on the street corners of any city enjoying Constitutional freedom in a way the Founders never intended, as the unholy alliance, the odd marriage of convenience between Islam and the radical Left was symbolically severed – with the master determined in clear-cut fashion.

Thursday, August 29th, 2052
Montpelier, Vermont

Beslan was the name of a civil rights icon; a man who claimed to have held the head of Martin Luther King Jr. as he lay dying on the balcony of a Memphis hotel, though eyewitnesses told a different story. He appeared on a televised talk show the next morning, still wearing a bloody shirt from the day before. There had been no time for the presumptive heir to change overnight, apparently. He would spend the next five decades of his life in a relentless quest for personal publicity, exhibiting a charlatanism that even his supporters found discomforting, as the legacy of the civil rights era was evoked so casually that it gradually lost meaning.

It was fortunate that Reverand Beslan wasn't alive to see what was becoming of the Ila, South Carolina elementary school that bore his name, although it's likely that he would have made his way to the school entrance and knelt in prayer, once assured that it was safe and that the news cameras had a clear line of sight to his sublime act of righteous supplication.

As Senate Majority Leader, and her party's nominee for Vice President, Jill Hudson was not at liberty to ignore the horrible images being flashed across the al-Jazeera channel of the only television in the quaint bed and breakfast outside the tiny Vermont capital. The inn, which was tucked in the trees about a hundred yards from the main road, was completely commandeered by her campaign staff, as Secret Service kept the public well away. Jill was opting to meet with her advisors before phoning into the emergency session at the White House.

The situation at the school was grim. About five hundred students and teachers were being held hostage by two dozen masked gunmen with bombs strapped to their chests. They had been herded into the gymnasium, where the captors were actually standing on trigger bombs scattered among the children and set to explode if they were knocked off. About a dozen people were dead already.

The only good news was that three hundred Muslim hostages had been released and there was a chance that others would be as well once the gunmen were able to sort them by religion. They were apparently qualifying reprieves based on the ability to quote a particular prayer or Qur'anic verse from memory.

According to al-Jazeera, there were only three demands, two of which were nearly identical to the Hope hijackers a year earlier. South Carolinian independence had taken the place of Maine, but there was still the demand for national *Sharia*, and an insistence that President Fish step down to face the ICC for the Lewiston incident. "Let's see if America thumbs her nose at international law after her own children are massacred," read their statement.

The Senator's advisors were united in agreeing that the demands should be met. There was no other way to avoid bloodshed. Most of the children left in the school were minorities, African-American and Latino. The terrorists were prepared to die (although it was imperative that they not be described as terrorists, since it might offend the Islamic community).

Within the hour, she was on the phone with the President, making her argument as respectfully as possible. He immediately protested, as she expected he would, saying that it made no sense to follow rules that their enemies had no obligation toward themselves. "We can't win an asymmetrical war," Fish insisted. He also pointed out that most of the countries that would be standing in judgment of him perpetrated far greater abuses within their own borders. Some were even exporters of global terrorism.

"That was the case when we signed the treaty fifty years ago," she answered. "If it didn't stop us then, why should it now?"

"It's gotten worse," fumed the President. "Democracies have been falling like… like dominos since then. Dictatorships have gotten more brutal. They don't fear outside intervention. There's even totalitarianism in Europe now for God's sake. It's obscene for these people to use our own terminology and standards against us when they don't even have a human rights record of their own."

"The example starts with us, Mr. President, just like it has in every conflict since Vietnam…"

"We've lost every conflict since Vietnam!" Fish interjected angrily. "Playing this fool's game is one thing when it's someone else's country or family on the line, but now it's ours, and we can't afford to keep appeasing these barbarians just because they want us to feel guilty about something that's relatively insignificant compared to their own atrocities!"

"With all due respect, Sir, you're sounding just like a Nationalist. I remember during the debates back in '28 when you said that as long as there is even a grain of truth in what our adversaries say, then we have no business pointing fingers. There were four children killed by American bullets in Lewiston…"

"My God," Fish exploded, "you know damn well that they were killed by accident! We don't have people in uniform looking to use children for target practice. Those troops were ambushed and they returned fire. The whole thing's been spun out of proportion. How can you possibly compare that to what those terrorists are doing down there at Beslan?"

It was hopeless trying to get through to him. The man just wouldn't listen to reason. Jill decided to try a different tack. "Mr. President, if you at least step down, then it will put a Muslim into the highest office in our land for the first time in history. Think of what this will do for our international standing. Would you put your own ambition above the nation's interests?"

It was a bold question, and a bold gamble. There were only five months left in the term, and only two until the Democrats almost certainly won in November, with Jill on the ticket.

The sigh on the other end of the line suggested that he would at least be thinking about it in the days to come.

Wednesday, September 4th, 2052
Ila, South Carolina

Sadiq Yassin was now a first lieutenant serving in a Green brigade, although he was attached to a different unit from the one that he had been with for the evacuations in Maine the year before. It was an honor to serve under Colonel Aziz Rastaban, one of the most respected Muslim officers in the ranks. The oldest son of the long-serving Imam of the National Mosque in Washington had pressed for many reforms on behalf of fellow Muslims in uniform, including separate eating and training facilities. He was also rumored to be on the brink of becoming one of the youngest generals that the armed forces had seen in peacetime.

Right now, the units were assigned to Beslan Elementary, where the nation's attention was riveted. They were draped around the playground, woods and entrances of the sprawling complex and had even taken one of the unused wings of the school, where they were holding steady, trying not to provoke a shootout, which would undoubtedly leave scores of innocents dead. Behind each unit, however, was another, with the job of guarding against the distinct possibility of a rear attack by extremist elements in the community.

The population of South Carolina was about 60% Muslim, but none of the remaining four hundred hostages inside the school were thought to be, since the last release four days earlier. The private sympathies of many in the community were therefore with the "insurgents'" who made it quite clear that they were willing to die for an independent Muslim State. A Green brigade had been assigned to the crisis for that reason, but they still needed to watch their backs.

As a Sufi Muslim, Sadiq could hardly be more disgusted with the tactics of the terrorists, although he was careful to avoid that term around the others, whom he did not know very well. He was new to the unit, but he assumed that ambivalence lurked in the hearts of many of his fellow soldiers, as they did in many citizens across the country.

For the last six days, there had been no change in their situation. The hostages were kept in a gymnasium around the corner from where Sadiq and his men lay partially hidden in the tall grass. Occasionally, food and bottled water would be sent into the school at prearranged intervals.

That afternoon however, there was an enormous explosion that caught everyone by surprise. Sadiq would later learn that one of the bombs in the gym went off by accident, killing several people, but also blowing a hole in the wall, through which many others tried to escape.

At that moment, Sadiq was startled to see about a dozen children fleeing around the corner, straight to where he was lying about fifty yards away. The young lieutenant sat up to get a better view. Quickly he saw that the hostages were not being given their freedom, but were instead trying to escape. After a couple of seconds, several masked men came into view, chasing after the children and firing into their backs.

Like the others, Lt. Yassin was under strict orders not to fire unless fired upon, but the sight of grown men mowing down children from behind is not something that a good man can tolerate. He was somewhat proud to see that the men in his squad did not need his command to inspire their intercession either. Together they began taking out the terrorists, who had apparently overextended themselves unwittingly in the heat of their pursuit.

Just then, there was hot flash of pain in his back, like he had been jabbed with a spear. He lost control of his weapon and fell forward, helpless as the men around him cried out in pain, as they were cut apart by a surprise ambush from the rear. One of his sergeants collapsed dead on top of him, inadvertently sparing his life.

Just before he blacked out, he saw plainly that the fire was coming from Rastaban's personal bodyguards… directed by the colonel himself.

Thursday September 5ᵗʰ, 2052
New York, New York

She was right of course – that friend of Phyllis's from GNN, who only showed up about once a year at their gatherings. The Artist was reminded of her statement again while watching news footage of the hostage disaster.

He was hardly a man, he thought, as he turned to look at his pale, hairless image in the mirror. It wasn't so much that he was soft and delicate on the outside – since that isn't what truly defines a man – but rather that he was that way on the inside.

He had depended so heavily on Phyllis. She was the one to fend off the strangers who would bother him with their questions or adulation. She managed his business negotiations and financial arrangements with a tough persona that he could never manage. When he had to travel, which was rare, she made sure that the correct brand of bottled water was waiting in the hotel room along with sheets that had a thread-count of at least 250. She did everything short of cutting his meat for him.

Yet, he couldn't lift a finger to save her life as a man would be expected to do for a female friend at such a time.

Where was such a person supposed to fit on the Evolutionary tree? According to Darwin it is the fittest who survive, yet he survived by the mere chance of others happening into an alley at the right time. His genes didn't deserve to be passed down, not that there was much chance of that happening anyway. He was an Evolutionary dead-end, with no purpose beyond wasting the planet's limited resources.

His only contribution was his art, which (when it boiled down to it) was literally crap.

The images of slaughter in South Carolina, however, were giving him ideas about how he could perhaps make his own suicide a form of art...

Saturday, September 6th, 2052
Arlington, Virginia

Parker watched the horrible scenes again that morning on GNN, even though he had personally petitioned the news channel not to replay them. Ostensibly, it was out of respect for the families of the schoolchildren and other victims of the hostage standoff that ended two days earlier in a bloodbath, but he also feared that such images might cause Americans to think badly of the Muslims living among them. He was very concerned about anything that might give bigotry a foothold in America. The rising number of complaints from Muslims, even as the legal protection of religious minorities expanded, was disconcerting to the Reverand.

He had not heard from the Imam in over a year – not since Parker was recruited to support the prosecution of a young Christian radical, arrested on a Boston street corner after violating the law against religious vilification by reading passages from the Hadiths and Qur'an that endorsed the rape of women captured in battle. The Reverand lent his image to a TV spot at the time, in which he spoke of the importance of "non-judgmental acceptance" and "sensitivity." The radiant ad featured shiny, cultured Americans in a park, reaching to shake the hands of dignified, smiling Muslims in Middle Eastern garb, as the chorus of the song "Share the Land" played poignantly in the background.

It was odd that the Imam had not yet returned his call following the Beslan massacre. Parker had been quite explicit in his message about the need for interfaith dialogue and prayer in the time of crisis, the very things needed to soothe the tension over the incident and assure Americans that the terrorists represented no one but themselves.

Friday, October 4th, 2052
New York, New York

It had been five years since the Artist last performed. The object of "honor" then was a poster of Kerry Conner, detested by the Manhattan crowd at the Hope Theater as an uncouth throwback. The theatre, of course, had been crushed beneath the tower in last year's attack, probably never to be rebuilt, but there were plenty of other venues left in the city, even if they were closed most of the time due to security concerns.

The security at the Cooper Theater that night was extremely tight, and the audience was understandably small. There was no official law against presenting theatrical material that some might find offensive, but fear of violence made such productions impractical and therefore rare. Everyone privately knew where the threat to free expression now came from, but it was only acceptable to blame "Conservatism," in a general sort of way.

Starr Sterling hoped her presence on the front row that night would inspire the cause of artistic freedom. She also wanted to live down the generally held understanding that she had been too craven too fly on "Hate-Free Air" four years ago. If not for losing her nerve at the last moment, she would no doubt be hailed as a genuine hero, much like that white-haired preacher.

Her friends warned her against attending the memorial to Beslan Elementary, particularly with the Artist performing. His art was offensive enough, they said, and there was no telling who he would be "honoring" this time… it might even be the *Islamic* terrorists themselves.

Starr doubted very much that this would be the case; in fact, she guessed that the honoree was more likely to be President Fish, since he had not only ordered troops to surround the school, but had created the very conditions that fostered the acts of desperation by the insurgents, according to their demands. He had resigned in the days following the fiasco, and the nation was excited about having its first Muslim in office, if only symbolically, given that a new President would be elected next month.

Like other people there (as well as the angry protestors outside the building) she was uncomfortable with the possibility that the Artist's memorial might be politically incorrect, but she was familiar enough with his work to feel more at ease than she ever would have been flying the now defunct Progressive Airlines. She had mentally rehearsed a statement to the press, in which she would draw moral equivalence between Lewiston and Beslan.

The lights dimmed, as the small knot of aristocrats and celebrities huddled near the front of the mostly empty theater in respectful silence. The curtains on stage drew back, revealing a screen. For the next thirty minutes, pictures of Beslan victims appeared one after the other, apparently beginning with the oldest and moving to the youngest. Then, after the bulk of the 344 victims had gone by, a shocking thing happened. Pictures of the victims were interpolated with violent passages from the Qur'an.

The audience began to stir and a few people got up and left. The pictures continued. Shots of children in various stages of play were punctuated with verses like "slay the unbeliever wherever you find him." Under a dress that was slightly more scintillating than her 66-year-old body merited, Starr was breaking into a cold sweat.

The last scene on the screen was a video that the hostage takers had apparently produced, showing them standing in front of an Arabic banner and praising Allah. Then the lights dimmed again. When they came back on, the screen was gone and the Artist was standing naked with his back to the audience, hovering over an object on the floor.

A portion of the spectators was gone at that point, but Starr was one of those remaining to watch the little man on stage strain to produce a bowel movement that would fall on a picture of who knew what. She clutched the arm of her chair in frozen anticipation, digging her nails into the varnished wood and hoping that this could not get any worse.

No one in the room applauded or sighed as they usually did when the mass of excrement fell with an audible smack. There was nothing to indicate that they were blissfully having a "spiritual" experience or any talk of "the ambiguity inviting the viewer to be a participant." There was only excruciating tension, as the Artist's two assistants (both trembling visibly) came over to lower the glass and the little man guided it down, then worked the knobs on the corners to seal the art. The assistants each edged further away in opposite directions until they finally turned and left the stage in an undignified sprint.

The Artist looked up with a grin on his pasty face and slowly lifted his new masterpiece into view. The audience erupted in a frenzy of groans and anger. "Oh God," was all Starr could say, and she repeated herself several times. It was worse than she could possibly have imagined.

Under the pane of glass was an open Qur'an, with the excrement stain fully visible on one side.

The audience rose in a panic, pushing and stumbling to exit the auditorium, as Starr sat paralyzed in her seat, unable to join them. They scrambled up the aisles, leaving the trampled bodies of tuxedoed gents and full-feathered socialites crushed and squirming in their wake.

Coming down the aisle now was an Arab security guard, with his gun drawn and his face glistening with sweat. The Artist simply stood there leering as his executioner approached, obviously having anticipated that someone would find a way to kill him that night, even without knowing who or how it would happen. Starr felt her bladder empty through her dress and into the seat, but she still couldn't move.

The gunshot was extremely loud, even in the open space of the large auditorium. She watched the Artist drop the glass and fall backward. Two more shots were presented for good measure, each spitting out chunks of flesh from the man's body in a very unnatural spectacle.

Starr looked up to see the guard's attention turned to her. "Are you a believer?" he asked placidly.

She nodded, thinking that it might save her.

"Allah has prepared a place for both of us then," the man said, as he leveled his weapon, smiling.

Saturday, October 5th, 2052
Arlington, Virginia

Parker couldn't help but feel excited by the conversation, even though the Imam was beside himself with anger over the desecration of the Qur'an in New York. The Reverand certainly didn't approve of what the Artist had done, but he was grateful to finally hear from the religious leader after so many months of unsuccessful effort.

"Yes, yes, I understand your anger, Imam. I remember many years ago when the same man defecated on the Bible. There was a disappointment among believers that…"

The Imam cut him off, too upset to engage in dialogue at that moment. Parker listened patiently to his haranguing, and pledged his public support, including an agreement to appear with the Imam at an "anti-bigotry" rally hastily planned for the following weekend to protest the desecration.

2057

Tuesday January 16th, 2057
Washington, D.C.

Meeting with her daughter was a welcome respite from the events that were pressuring the Administration, even before their second term officially began later that week. With the rest of the political field fractured between weakened Progressives, the Muslim Coalition Party, La Vida Nueva (the dangerous Christian party that was becoming a major force in the Southwest) and the archaic Nationalists, winning elections was much easier for the Democrats than dealing with the unprecedented problems facing the country.

As if extreme poverty, egregious crime, and hints of domestic insurgency weren't enough, the United States was now being dictated to by other nations. The Iranians, in particular, had allied with the Arab League and other Muslim counties in Africa, Europe and Asia to demand that the U.S. pull its "imperial fleet from international waters" – meaning simply that all overseas military bases should be closed, including Air and Army installations.

The Muslim countries had been demanding this for some time. It was no secret that they wanted to march Turkish and French armies into Poland and the rest of Free Europe as they had already into Spain and Italy (with the help of sizable North African immigrant populations) completing the Jihad that was stopped centuries ago at Tours and Vienna. America's military presence was an impediment to this vision.

The latest threats needed to be taken seriously. Not only were they bolder and more assuming, but the FBI claimed to have credible evidence that Iranian agents had been able to place at least one "dirty" radiological bomb in a major metropolitan area. It was hard to trust what came out of the Bureau, however, since it had long been compromised by Islamist sympathizers protected by the rules of religious tolerance. It was quite probable that the Iranians were simply bluffing – and using America's own intelligence resources to do so.

Against these issues, it was a relief to find her daughter waiting for her that morning on the first floor of the official residence on the grounds of the U.S. Naval Observatory, which had been occupied by Vice Presidents since the time of Walter Mondale. Merica was wearing a *hijab*, the Muslim headscarf, as she had the last time they saw each other, when she told her mother about her new boyfriend. Jill believed that it was just a phase at the time, but that was several months ago and, from her conversations since, it was evident that Merica was becoming more involved in religion – much to her own chagrin.

"Faraj and I are getting married next month," her daughter announced.

It came as a shock. Jill had not even met the young man. "I… uh… don't know what to say," she stammered. "Shouldn't we talk about this first?"

"How do you mean?"

"Well, it's a big step. Are you sure you're ready?"

"I'm twenty-four."

"Are there no other men at Berkeley?"

Merica laughed. "By 'men', I assume you're speaking metaphorically?"

Jill understood. From her own days there, she recalled the sensitive, effeminate males on campus, who were always deferential to feminists to the point of utter docility. Watching them occasionally trying to impress the female students with their self-hatred and glorification of women was entertaining, to say the least.

"Why convert to Islam?"

"What am I converting from?" asked her daughter. "We had no religion growing up. You always told me not to listen to Uncle Parker's 'nonsense,' and I assume you told him the same thing, since he never answered my questions about his beliefs."

Jill cringed a bit on hearing confirmation that the ground rules she established with Parker, when Merica was young, had been respected to the fullest intent. Her disagreement with Parker over religion in the lives of their prospective children doomed the relationship they both desperately wanted so many years ago.

"Why do you need religion at all?" she asked her daughter.

"We've talked about this before," Merica answered. "It just makes sense. It's quite obvious that the world didn't create itself. Matter, design, and intelligence are not entities that spring up out of empty space. I also believe that there is an absolute standard of right and wrong that validates our innate opinions of morality and ethics. They have no meaning without God."

"But why Islam?" protested Jill. "It's based on the teachings of a violent man, who slept with children and condoned rape…"

Her daughter's expression stopped her from advancing the critique any further. "There is a lot that I don't yet know," she responded, "particularly about the Prophet, but when I look around this country I see worse coming from those outside the faith rather than within. Muslims are not the ones printing pornography or pushing the envelope of filth and vulgarity on television just for the sake of doing so.

"It impresses me, also, that Muslims believe in their faith enough to die for it, while Christians are too weak even to fight for theirs. Why would a true religion allow itself to be cannibalized by another?

At that moment, Jill wished that Parker were there to explain his confidence in the ultimate triumph of peace through mercy and tolerance. He channeled his Christian faith in positive ways, by accepting and trusting others, while making sure that no one was offended by his word or deeds. This was the example her daughter should be following, rather than someone "willing to die for their faith" by flying a plane full of terrified people into an office building. Such fervency may prove conviction, but not truth. If anything, it should inspire skepticism on the part of the open-minded.

As she was trying to put her next words together, they were interrupted by a Secret Service agent, who informed her that "there's been an incident that requires evacuation."

Tuesday, January 23rd, 2057
New York, New York

It had been a full week since the bomb went off in Lower Manhattan. They were calling it a dirty bomb, but the damage to the buildings on the Lower East Side, some of which were reduced to bare girders, seemed too extensive for a homemade explosive. The sea of buildings stopped the conventional effects of the blast, but Bernice and the rest of the staff in close proximity to ground zero had been fully exposed to the radiation.

There was no leaving now even if she wanted to, what with the mobs controlling the streets below. Over the last week, she watched from her window as people she worked with for years were torn apart as they emerged from the building, attempting to make a run for it during the day. Some met with greater success at night, under the cover of darkness. Slowly, the building was emptying, as family concerns managed to prevail over the instinct of self-preservation. The GNN monitors were long dead, although she could still watch the al-Jazeera broadcast channel thanks to the building's generators. They shut the power off at night so as not to attract the attention of the people below.

Bernice Greenly stood at her window again and looked down on the scene in the street, where shouting and screams occasionally drifted up along with the smoke and stench. She glanced back at her office door. It was old, but solid – picked by her grandfather many years ago to block out noise from the newsroom.

Wednesday, January 24ᵗʰ, 2057
Kshesin, Poland

America was reeling from its first nuclear attack and facing a crisis of confidence that reached deep into her soul. Panic ensued on the streets of metropolitan areas that were directly unaffected by the blast in New York, followed by looting and rioting. Most of the country sat at home, watching the mayhem from their living rooms, huddling in fear behind locked doors and wondering how many days the once great nation had left.

While her leaders debated the structure of aid packages to the Arab League and other conciliatory gestures, a leader of a different sort emerged from an empty hanger during a cold, dark morning on an airbase in Kshesin, Poland. There, only a handful of planes remained after the recent orders to return all equipment and personnel home-side according to Iranian demands. Three of them were on the tarmac, fully fueled for the long trip back to the States. There were two fighters and one long-range bomber barely visible through the misty, early-morning shadows at the end of the runway, past the series of hangers and shops.

The door to one of the bays rolled up slowly and six men in uniform emerged from the shaft of light, walking crisply in formation through the empty darkness. The only sound was that of their footsteps echoing back to them from the vacant structures around them as they marched past. Their breath was visible against the icy chill, as they moved into and out of the shadows.

Three of the men left children behind, two others left only their wives. There had been tearful goodbyes, as they knew they would probably never see each other again. If they survived, they would face a firing squad for what they were about to attempt, but none held any illusions about seeing that day's dawn. In spite of this, or perhaps because of it, they held their heads high on that long march through the freezing night air.

The leader of the group, slightly ahead of the tiny formation was Colonel Matthew Ridley. As they passed the two Nighthawk fighters, four of the other pilots broke off in pairs to prepare their aircraft. The colonel saluted each of them, as his father had once done on a distant highway many years earlier. He proceeded with his mission navigator to the B-2 Spirit bomber and climbed up into the plane. All of the craft had been checked and loaded under the cover of darkness several hours before. All that remained was to power them up and establish secured communications with one another.

Ten minutes later the planes shot up into the cold, black sky and became tiny forlorn objects against the massive expanse around them.

Washington D.C.

When the people elect a President nearly eighty years of age and in ill health, they are certainly expressing supreme confidence in his choice of Vice President. Although the Administration had not fully disclosed the extent to which the President was incapacitated from an illness in the weeks following the election, it would not have been a source of public concern to know that the Vice President was acting fully in his role. "Hudson" Jill had more presence in American politics than anyone else. Her years of leadership in the Senate and common-sense approach to issue resolution exuded the sort of confidence that America needed in her most desperate hour.

The membership of the Cabinet was virtually of her own choice. They were a progressive's "Dream Team." The Secretary of Labor was a former union boss, the Secretary of State was Muslim, as was the head of the DCA; the Secretary of Education formerly headed the teacher's union, the Energy Secretary was a former Greenpeace activist, as was the DOT head, the Attorney General had an excellent career as a criminal defense lawyer, and so the list went. Jill was confident that all were experts in their field. Over the years they had worked to find solutions to problems that had long plagued the nation, even if success was oddly elusive.

The problems of unemployment and corporate disparity were being countered through industry nationalization, continuing what began with health care under Al Gore.

Personal debt, which affected 85% of Americans, with four in ten unable to make anything beyond minimum credit card payments, was being relieved with caps on interest rates, an easing of bankruptcy consequences, and severe penalties against lending institutions for forcing ordinary Americans into debt by giving them credit cards. Banks were also being taken to task over the practice of using looser standards to qualify minority loan applicants, which resulted in a higher rate of default.

The high crime rate was attacked with laws and quotas that prohibited police from disproportionately targeting minorities and the poor, thus spreading law enforcement resources evenly across all demographic categories, which would undoubtedly result in more criminals being caught.

The only thing they didn't have a solution for were the budget deficits, which supplemented a national debt that was now more than five times the GDP – not that anyone cared anymore.

The Cabinet member that Jill was most interested in at the moment, as she sat in the bunker deep beneath the White House that had long supplanted the West Wing, was the Secretary of Defense, a Berkeley classmate of hers who formed a student protest group against the Iraqi war that later evolved into a think-tank that provided alternatives to military action. As she sat pondering the new crisis, the woman entered the office, pale as a ghost. They had already spoken briefly about the situation, which involved a rogue squadron of jets that had taken off from a base in Poland an hour earlier and was streaking toward the Middle East.

Jill was alarmed by her Defense Secretary's condition. "What's wrong? Did I miss an update?"

"No," said the woman, slumping into the chair across from the desk with a sort of resignation that indicated it might be a while before she got back up. She was visibly trembling. "My God, they've got nukes on board that bomber. What if they use them?"

Jill frowned. The woman may have been a good administrator, but she wasn't doing well in the clutch. The Pentagon brass had begged her to reconsider her choice for the top spot last year, but she was convinced that she needed someone to balance whatever testosterone was left in the military. Now she was beginning to share their doubts.

"Do you think they could be defecting?"

"Not a chance," replied the Secretary. "They're patriots… if you'll pardon the expression."

Normally Jill would have been revolted by the word. It harkened up images of trailer-trash nuts and red-faced flag-wavers, breeding their dangerous strain of right-wing religious zealotry against the progressive tide. Now it merely terrified her. Although still disapproving, she could at least sympathize with her friend's panicked condition. The fact that these might be the sort of people who wouldn't mind starting World War III made it all the more critical to keep a level head.

"Do we know where they're going? Can we shoot them down?"

"We barely know where they are right now. Obviously they disabled the tracking and, of course, the stealth is difficult to find on radar. We believe the whole group is somewhere over the Black Sea or Turkey. Our nearest aircraft are in the Mediterranean, but we certainly won't get permission from Turkey to fly into their air space."

"We might," said Jill, picking up the phone.

Black Sea, Asia

As his bomber hurtled under the stars against the cold, black night, Matt Ridley instinctively checked their position against the time, which he had been doing each minute. They were still about an hour away from the first target, but he expected that Turkey would be coming up underneath them at any moment. The area they would be crossing over was the location of the Armenian Massacre, where well over a million ordinary Christians were butchered by Turkish Muslims just prior to World War I as the world stood idly by.

He hoped those souls were cheering him on, because they were going to need a lot more than luck to make their target.

Washington D.C

The Vice President was unable to secure permission from the Turkish Prime Minister, but she had been able to give him the projected location of the squadron in the hopes that their fighter might be able to reach it in time. She was also trying to get the Pentagon to establish voice contact with the treasonous crew.

Armenian Air Space

The colonel's gamble paid off. The Turkish jets opted not to chase them into Armenian air space once it became apparent that they posed no threat to Turkey. They would be over Iran in a matter of minutes, however, and there lay their toughest challenge.

The radio in his helmet came to life and he knew that they had finally been found out.

Edmonton, Alberta

The newly elected President of Alberta stood in his office overlooking Highway 2, which, much to the horror of Old Canada, had been dubbed the Reagan Expressway several years ago in honor of an American President. It was a gleaming high-tech corridor that ran 150 miles between the capital and Calgary, which was still the largest city. The Rocky Mountains were framed to the west, pristine and untouched, whereas the residences and farms stretched across the eastern plains. It was a wonderful, booming country with an optimistic entrepreneurial spirit.

One of the things realized early on, however, was that Alberta needed to form international relationships. Without America's leadership, the free world was rapidly dissolving and then solidifying into the authoritarian faction. Nations that hung in the balance were making downward progress, which was natural given that democracy's antagonists were always more ruthless than its defenders.

It was easy to pull neighbors like Saskatchewan and Alaska into the Western Alliance, but most Albertans felt that they had an obligation toward freedom-loving people in places that weren't as accessible, such as Poland, Latvia and other former Soviet States that feared totalitarianism more than the scorn of world opinion. It was disappointing that the United States chose to abandon Free Europe to the Islamic armies that would surely be knocking at the door once they were gone. As usual, the Americans chose the path of appeasement.

Kerry Conner did not. The former Montana businessman had found his place in the country that adopted him, opting to get involved in politics almost immediately. One of the sayings he had when running for President the year before was that it was "a terrific country when an immigrant with a mere $95 million to his name can one day run for the nation's highest office."

In fact, he loved the people of Alberta. Nearly all of them had roots across the border, being part of the sea of nearly 50 million Americans that had crossed over in the last forty-five years, but there were starting to be many second and third-generation Albertans that only knew the new country and were fiercely loyal to their homeland. The spirit was contagious, as similar populations dominated in Alaska, the Yukon and other territories that were also experiencing heavy growth.

Now, the country was united in a desire to fill the international void created by America's departure and defend freedom abroad. There had long been a clandestine agreement with the leaders of Free Europe that they could depend on Alberta if necessary. Now it looked as if that time had arrived.

Naturally, they were taking an interest in the situation that was now developing over northern Iran. With the help of the Polish Air Force and their own intelligence, they were able to pick up on the attempt by various commanders at the Pentagon to establish contact with the rogue squadron. It was not until the voice of the American Vice President filled the office, however, that one of the pilots did respond.

"This is Colonel Matthew Ridley of the United States Air Force, how may I help you, Madame Vice President?"

"Who is giving you orders, Colonel?"

"I am."

"Well, as your acting Commander in Chief, I am ordering you to stand down. Return to base!"

"Negative."

"You are over Iranian air space, Colonel. What are your intentions?"

"We're about to rock the casbah. Care to join us?"

Kerry raised his eyebrows. The pilot must be pretty close to his destination to sound that cocky.

"You'll die if you don't turn around right now. Do you know that?"

"Yes."

There was a long pause.

"I know why you're doing this, Colonel. The Iranians have assured us, however, that they did not intend for that dirty bomb to go off in New York. We believe them."

"That wasn't a dirty bomb, Madame Vice President. That was a nuclear weapon with a signature traced straight to Tabriz."

"Good God! Is that where you're going... to bomb the reactor there? If you do that thousands, perhaps millions will die!"

"That's doubtful, but we're past Tabriz now as it is."

"Are you going to bomb Tehran? Dear God, Colonel, what will that accomplish? We don't solve problems by dropping bombs on people any- more. We're civilized. We try to understand the culture of others and adapt to them. Surely there is another way."

"There is."

"Good. Good." There was obvious relief in the Vice President's voice. "Please tell me a better solution, Colonel"

"Expect them to do the same for us and punish them when they don't. Goodbye, Madame Vice President."

Kerry turned away from the window with a smile. He was beginning to really like that Ridley fellow.

Iranian Air Space

Matt had not been entirely truthful with the Vice President. He had no intention of bombing a populated area. He just wanted to take out the two nuclear plants north of Tehran and then the other reactor outside of Tabriz. The Iranian jets had been quick to intercept them a few hundred miles inside the border, but his Nighthawk pilots were quite skilled, and they managed to survive long enough to reach the outskirts of Tehran, where they then curved north, dodging SAMs and taking out the first re- actor with a couple of 2,000-pound bombs.

One of his fighters went up in a ball of flame just off their wing, as the second target came into range. Matt and his navigator were well- steeled against emotion by then, and only hoped that they would be able to accomplish the mission before meeting their own fate. The other fighter immediately replaced the wingman, keeping the pursuing jets oc- cupied as the bomber positioned itself.

They had not bought quite as much time as they thought they would be by hitting the deepest target first and then fleeing north. Apparently the Iranians were on to their game, particularly after the second reactor was destroyed. There was only one more remaining, and it was going to be a desperate race to reach it.

Washington D.C.

The Vice President sat in the President's chair, feeling very much alone, as she tried to calm the Iranian Ambassador over the phone. Her Defense Secretary had passed out after the bombing started, and was be- ing treated for shock in the adjoining room. So far, the Iranians had been able to take out at least one of the planes, but two of their reactors were obliterated and the bomber was still in the air. She kept an eye on the monitor mounted on the wall behind her desk, which spit out the latest updates in a ticker-tape ribbon across the bottom of the screen.

"This is an outrage!" the ambassador exclaimed, for what must have been the eighth time in the brief conversation.

"We are outraged as well," she responded. "Please be assured that we would have done everything to prevent this... this act of treason, had we any foreknowledge."

"How convenient that this is happening only days after you accuse Iran of complicity in the dirty bomb."

"It wasn't a dirty bomb," Jill was surprised to find herself saying. "It was a tactical warhead with nuclear material from your reactor, there in Tabriz."

The ambassador exploded in a frenzy of words. "Lies, all lies! You are merely trying to justify your hostile action against the peaceful citizens of Iran! Do you know what Tabriz will look like if your bomber gets through?"

"Probably a lot like New York, only with fewer bodies."

The ambassador could only spew a few unintelligible grunts. Jill leaned forward and rested her elbows on the desk. "We know the nuclear material came from you. We can also prove that we had no foreknowledge of the raid and that we did all we could to stop it."

There was a long pause on the other end of the line. When the ambassador finally did speak, she could imagine the sneer on this face. "Facts may matter to certain Americans, but not to the rest of the world. The people will believe that you personally ordered these attacks if that's what we tell them, just as surely as they believe the Jews were responsible for 9/11 and Hope Tower."

Jill leaned back in her chair. She was shocked by his bluntness, but she also knew that he was right. She glanced back at the screen. Another plane had been taken out... so had the last reactor.

Iranian Air Space

A few minutes earlier, Matt and his navigator were pumping their fists after scoring a direct hit on the nuclear power plant outside Tabriz. They were now trying to gain altitude, with several Iranian fighter jets right on their tail. They had no real plan beyond what they had been able to accomplish so far, thanks to the sacrifice of their comrades. Nor did they have any hope of outrunning the faster jets behind them if they tried to turn north to Armenia. With Lake Urmia behind them, and Turkey just a few miles ahead, their best hope was to continue due east to the border, where they hoped the Iranians wouldn't follow.

Matt expected his plane to disintegrate at any moment. Just as it seemed they wouldn't make it, his navigator told him that the pursuit had peeled away. Another squadron was approaching them from Turkey, however, so they needed to work their way down into Iraq. Four different countries were clustered around the northern Tigris region, but none of them were friendly. The United States did not have a single ally in the region, as the tide of Islamic fundamentalism washed unchecked into every nook and cranny, destroying intellectual and critical opposition with brutal force.

The Iraqis were evidently unprepared for aerial warfare over the northern part of their country, given that there was no resistance during the grueling fifteen minute overpass. They could see the Turkish fighters keeping pace just across the border, however, stalking them like an angry dog on the other side of a picket fence.

They would have to take their chances over Syria.

Thursday, January 26th, 2057
Washington D.C.

It had been a relief to learn that the last plane had finally been downed over northern Syria two days earlier, but Jill Hudson and her Secretary of State faced the monumental task of repairing the damage done to international relations. The UN had declared that it was moving its headquarters to Brasilia, ostensibly in outrage over the bombing of Iran, but Jill knew that they really just wanted an excuse to leave New York after so many of their staff were either killed in the Lower Manhattan blast or debilitated and dying from the effects of fallout. With radiation levels so high, she could not order troops into all parts of the city, so there were portions where absolute anarchy reigned, with people trapped in office or apartment buildings while the mobs raged below.

Their more pressing concern at the moment, however, was world opinion. They had to find a way to convince the UN that the raid had been unsanctioned; otherwise they might lose the international respect so carefully cultivated since Al Gore's courageous speech before Congress following 9/11. The Iranians were pressing for war crimes prosecution at the highest levels of the United States government, while al-Jazeera was continuously broadcasting images of the destroyed facilities and the worst cases of trauma to be found in the local hospitals. Anti-American mobs were rampaging through European capitals. No one was buying the story that the retaliatory raid was unapproved, as true as it was.

Jill got the impression that her own Secretary of State, whose family was from Turkey, had his doubts as well. There was an uncharacteristic tension between them. His responses were terse to the point of insolent, as if he suspected her of misleading him.

Saturday, January 28ᵗʰ, 2057
New York, New York

They couldn't even watch al-Jazeera anymore, since the generators had finally run out of fuel two nights earlier. Most of the others were gone now, although some were still scattered in pockets throughout the upper levels of the GNN building, hiding in offices and under desks. Some were barricaded in closets. They all knew that the lobby had long since been compromised and that the floors below were being taken in succession, even in the middle of the night. All of the fire doors opened into the stairwells, so there was no way to block them from the inside, but they had thrown as much junk and debris as they could into the wells themselves during the days, in an effort to stave off the inevitable advance.

The air was putrid with vomit and bodily waste in the still night air, but nothing was as horrible as the awful sound of crunching wood and cursing coming from the stairwell down the hall, as the obstacles were gradually circumvented over a period of hours. Then all went quiet for about fifteen minutes. It was an odd sort of silence; somewhat like the calm before the storm that each knew was coming, as they hid in fearful isolation from one another. Some had literally sealed themselves in large filing cabinets, others climbed up into the plenum, sitting atop the air ducts, but knowing full well that they would be discovered and pulled down.

The eerie calm was suddenly broken by a horrific wrenching of metal and loud yelling, as the stairwell door was breached and bodies spilled into the final floor of the cable news headquarters. They gradually made their ways down hallways lined with posters celebrating gun control, criminal rights, and the struggle against industry and intolerance. The décor in the main hallway was arranged chronologically and hailed the history of appeasement in an Age of Tolerance, first in Iran, then Palestine, then Iraq, then Central Asia, then Europe, then Maine, then South Carolina… It's doubtful that anyone in the horde noticed, as they surged past, easily breaching the barricaded offices along the way.

From where she stood, alone in the middle of her own large office, Bernice Greenly heard the shouts of excitement, immediately followed by screams and awful moans, then crying and more screams. She took a long last look around the room, catching her image in the mirror, where she could clearly see pink scalp beneath missing clumps of hair, which confirmed the numbness in her extremities. The radiation was shutting down her body.

The tumultuous clamor could be heard advancing up the hallway like a rush of floodwater through a dry gully, drawing closer to her door. Soon the handle began to move and she could hear them congregating on the other side. The couch and desk that had been pulled against it would not be holding. She walked over to the window, opening it to look down. Her eyes were accustomed to the darkness, so she could easily make out the lines of people many floors below, moving like soldier ants to and from the building. In the distance was an orange glow from the flames that were consuming Lower Manhattan.

Behind her was the sound of wood giving way, followed by the scraping of heavy furniture being pushed across the floor. She waited until she heard the footsteps fervently reach the edge of the rug before stepping off the ledge.

Monday, January 29th, 2057
Washington D.C.

It was a bit of a gamble, holding a press conference when they weren't sure of what their strategy would be. The President looked very frail as he deferred to Vice President Hudson for the question and answer session that followed a brief statement, which spoke of the hope for peace and reconciliation. By contrast, Hudson was smart, peppy and combative, which was what the country needed to see.

"Do you admit that the government knew of Iran's involvement in the New York City explosion?" asked a reporter.

"Yes, we traced the nuclear signature back to the Tabriz facility in the hours following the blast. We also accept responsibility for last Wednesday's raid, although it was not ordered by anyone at a higher level than the officers involved."

"Were all of the pilots in the raid killed?"

"Yes."

"There are many in America who say that the raid was good for morale, that the image of retaliation is appreciated by a large section of the populace, and that it's responsible for a general improvement in attitude and a conviction that things will eventually return to normal. Do you share their optimism?"

After a noticeable pause, Jill answered cautiously. "Of course I share their optimism, and I can understand how people feel about the raid, even if I don't personally agree with them. There isn't anything we can do to change what happened. If any good comes of it, then so be it. However, there are far more people in this country who understand that such acts only perpetuate the cycle of violence. The only way to stop the cycle and avoid war is to exercise restraint. Nothing is worth war."

Tuesday, January 30ᵗʰ, 2057
New York, New York

While APCs and other armored vehicles patrolled the Upper West Side, buffering the affluent from the mobs controlling the rest of the city, a small group of people sat close together in Beth Landau's apartment for the final meeting. Their numbers were limited only to about a half-dozen like-minded residents of the building, but this had been the case for some time, as it had ceased being safe to travel for more than a few blocks, even on the Upper West Side. Most had plans to leave the city once they could make arrangements to places like Washington State, Oregon or other precious islands of progressive prosperity that were broad-minded, yet livable.

They wanted to be around people who thought as they did and relished "hate-free zones," where immigrants and the poor were always welcome, and the police and government were under the tightest scrutiny to respect the broad civil liberties of criminals and non-citizens. This ruled out the Red States, where even the Army couldn't keep the roads open for very long against a hostile force of rebellious locals, but the quality of life was miserable in much of the rest of the country.

Had they wanted to open the French doors leading to the balcony that evening, there might have been a distant glimpse of Lower Manhattan burning, along with the remote sounds of gunfire and sirens. Instead, they were huddled around the radio, listening to their favorite program on National Public Radio. Over the airwaves came the soft, mellow voice of a narrator, speaking about the idyllic and innocent days of his youth in a whimsical tone that was soothing to these cultured aristocrats.

He was followed by an equally subdued voice that presented a report on Alberta as if it were a National Geographic piece on a remote aboriginal tribe practicing strange and arcane customs. The group was amused by the befuddlement in his tone, as he spoke of identification cards, decency standards and the absence of public welfare programs. They could appreciate the implied inability of the refined narrator to understand these boorish, uncouth Albertans with intellectual capacities far below the NPR audience.

The members of the small group were still shaking their heads and smiling sadly at the ignorance of others, as they began to bid each other goodbye and bring their thirty-five year tradition of gathering together in Beth Landau's apartment to an end.

Fortunately for Beth, no one noticed the application for Albertan immigration that she had carelessly left open on her desk.

Wednesday, February 7th, 2057
Fajami, Syria

It had been exactly two weeks since Matt Ridley and his co-pilot tried bailing out of their B-2 Spirit, as the broken bomber was going down in flames from a Syrian missile. Apparently there had been some damage to the ejection system because his crewman failed to eject with him. Matt watched the plane spiral down below, knowing that his friend would almost certainly be facing a quicker death than he would. On reaching the ground, he disconnected the chute and let the wind drag it away, just as he caught sight of trucks rolling straight toward him on the flat, dry desert floor.

He tossed aside the handgun, smoothed out his olive flight suit and stood rigidly at attention, waiting for them. They were not his enemy, so there was no point in shooting at them. He could never fight his way out of the country anyway, so capture was his only choice.

Two weeks later, he found himself lying with his head and stomach against the filthy cement floor of a prison cell, floating in and out of consciousness; a far cry from the tall soldier in the meticulously groomed uniform that had proudly stood as the first Syrian soldiers walked up cautiously, then knocked him violently to the ground with the butt of their weapons.

Blood crusted around open wounds on his head. It also drooled from his mouth and onto the floor of the wretched cell. The bones in his hand were broken, as was his spirit.

Saturday, February 10th, 2057
Washington D.C.

Jill had spoken honestly at the press conference. The survival of the pilot was a surprise to her when she found out about it from the Syrians a few days later. They apparently believed that the United States already knew the man's status, and would eagerly bargain for his release. Of course, rather than coming out and saying that, they began making private demands that were outrageous, while hinting that the pilot might be sent to Iran to face trial and certain execution. Neither did Jill come out and say that she only hoped they would do it quickly, before the myopic public found out and began making a hero out of him

"He's not our pilot anymore," she told the disappointed diplomats, "not since he stopped following our orders."

The country had far greater things to worry about than a traitor and mass murderer who jeopardized their foreign policy, even if it did improve the mood of the country in some quarters.

The people rarely knew what was good for them anyway.

Friday, March 9th, 2057
Rothberg, California

The Professor wasn't sure who was living in his house when he left, nor did he care about the woman relieving herself in the bushes along his side yard, as he made his way over piles of garbage and out into the filthy street early that morning.

Three years ago, he woke to find strangers sleeping in his living room. They never spoke to him, even as they continued to make his house their own, acting as if he was invisible, as they took over bedrooms, cooked food, and used drugs. Eventually, he retreated to his own bedroom, locking the door and venturing out only on rare occasions to get supplies in the early morning, while the others were sleeping off hangovers.

He believed that different people rotated in and out over the years. Occasionally there was yelling and screaming. Walls were punched in and furniture was ripped up. None of it was repaired, of course. Several times he saw his door knob move in the middle of the night, and he had taken to jamming the bookshelves against it, forming a line all the way across to the opposite wall so that it couldn't be opened. Sometimes, following an evening of loud arguments, he would see pools of blood on the floor downstairs in the early-morning hours. They would dry and solidify into stains that gradually dissolved over time under the wear of foot traffic.

It pained him to leave his books behind. They were a lifetime accumulation of works by academics just like he had once been, idealists who knew what was best for society from the vantage point afforded by ivory towers, buffered by tenure and affluence from the consequences of the world they designed through deliberate omission and colorful misrepresentation.

Then again, perhaps it wasn't such a great loss after all.

At sixty-nine, the Professor stood on the side of the road with a duffel bag over his arm that represented his entire worldly possessions, and a thumb out toward passing traffic, leaving the world he knew behind him, and feeling better than he had in a long time.

Tuesday, March 27th, 2057
PBC Network

In this week's episode of the "The Community," a crisis brews when the leader, square-jawed "Noah," is asked to share the basement of his home with a needy family. The others in the community help him to understand that the children of these hard-working parents have to sleep in the streets of the clean, sparkling town while he sleeps alone in a large house. Noah bites his lower lip during the moment of realization, and

515

then welcomes the family into his home, as the community cheers and the character based on Letitia Ridley nods wisely. His spirit will be all the richer through this experience.

Sunday, April 15th, 2057
Syrian Desert

The two soldiers sitting across from him in the back of the truck watched him in silence with dark, beady eyes, as the three of them rocked back and forth to the tossing and lurching of the vehicle. There was no lamp or windows in the enclosed cargo area, but light made its way through the cracks and openings around the door and sides of the truck. Visibility wasn't a problem, but breathing was difficult in the stifling heat.

Matt was told quite plainly that he was being transported to Iran, to face the "people's justice." He figured it couldn't get any worse than the sort of justice he had faced a couple of months earlier, although conditions improved after he told the Syrians what they wanted to hear – namely that his government had ordered the raid. There was no shame in breaking under torture, and he figured that there were far worse things for other countries to believe, than that they might be punished for detonating a nuclear bomb in the heart of an American city.

The bones in his hand would probably never heal, not that he expected to live much longer anyway. His captors had enjoyed taunting him with the fact that his government refused to negotiate his release. They also told him about their vision of America's submission to Islam, as promised to the Taliban by an American Vice President. According to the story, Aziz Sahil had traveled to Afghanistan to negotiate Osama Bin Laden's extradition to the ICC. In the *galabiyya*, he bent his knee before the Mullahs and promised that if they complied, then there would come a day when the Great Satan would be humbled before Allah. Jihad wasn't won on the battlefield anymore, but rather in the hearts of soft-headed Westerners, who would do anything to win the approval of other nations, even if it meant selling out their grandchildren's future.

Matt wasn't so sure about the truth of the story, but it was hard to argue with anyone disparaging a country that would turn its back on the five good men that had given their lives in her service. Their sacrifice would always be greater than his, since each left a widow at the very least. These were the sort of people with religious values and political beliefs that America lampooned and ridiculed, yet they formed the moral backbone of the nation during its two greatest centuries. Now the social fabric of the country was coming apart without them.

As his father had once done in a hospital room forty years earlier, Matt used his free time to evaluate his own priorities against those of his country, coming to similar conclusions.

This was fortunate, in fact, because he wouldn't have much time for putting his thoughts together on this particular journey, as two enormous explosions on either side of the vehicle brought it to a sudden stop. Gunfire erupted around them as Matt threw himself to the floor of the truck. The thumping of helicopter blades could be heard, as his two guards began banging and struggling with the door, which could only be unlocked from the outside. They were now sweating profusely.

There was less than two minutes of battle before an ominous calm settled around them. One of his guards began mumbling some sort of prayer. They were both oblivious to Matt, who hugged the floor, hoping they would forget about him. Suddenly the lock on the door blew off and it was pulled wide, allowing blinding sunlight into the cargo hold, which the three of them had to shield their eyes from. He heard his guards drop their weapons and the shouting in Arabic, as the truck dipped from the weight of others climbing into the back.

He was hauled roughly to his feet by men wrapped completely in black, and dragged out of the truck and into the bay of a waiting chopper that was kicking up sand and dirt. Dark smoke poured out from what was left of the convoy vehicles, and he could see bodies strewn around them as the bird lifted into the air.

Edmonton, Alberta

Kerry Conner's nerves were stretched about as tight as they could possibly be, as he sat at his desk staring at the phone. Several others were in the room with the President, but no one dared make a sound. Each dealt with the tension in their own way. Some gazed out the windows, others scratched notes on pads of paper, and still others were shamelessly emptying the candy jar at the end of the desk, hardly aware of what they were doing.

Finally the phone rang. Kerry picked it up as quickly as he might have cut the head off a rattlesnake on his father's West Texas ranch. Everyone in the room was holding their breath.

The smile that appeared on his face was all the others needed to break into a series of whoops and handshakes.

Over Syria

The chopper hung low to the ground as the desert raced by beneath them. The men around him had pulled off their masks, revealing grim faces, but none of them spoke to him. The heavy tension was finally broken after they passed over a mountain range at a certain point that Matt guessed was the Syrian border. The other men then became all smiles.

"How did you find me?" asked Matt, having to raise his voice over the noise.

"It wasn't hard. You were the only black man in Syria," said the man sitting across from him in a thick accent.

Matt laughed with the rest then ventured, "I hope I'm not in Syria anymore."

"Welcome to Israel," smiled the other. "Our boss is really looking forward to meeting you."

They each shook hands with him and introduced themselves by only their first names, but wouldn't give him more information. Matt gathered that this was not a military operation, but he was told that a "Mr. Ohayon" would answer his questions once they landed. Matt watched the roads and towns pass underneath him. "I didn't think there was much left of Israel," he offered.

"Well," said the man across from him, "we were told that if we only pulled out of the West Bank and Gaza, the Palestinians would have their own State and would cease the terror attacks. That didn't happen. Then we were told that if we tore down the security fence, we would have peace…"

"And that certainly didn't happen," finished another. "So we knew then that our very existence was what they really had a problem with. We put the fence back up and stopped feeling guilty about our right to live peaceably. After that grand experiment, even the leftists among us recognized what the Palestinian intentions really were, so they've been pretty quiet since."

"I think it's too late for my country," said Matt ruefully. "The barbarians are well within the gates and it's just a matter of time before it splits apart."

The other man gave a wink. "I have a feeling that won't be much of an issue for you anymore."

Matt knew better than to ask what he meant, but it looked as if they would soon be landing anyway. He could see a chopper pad below, outside of a large building in a sparse area of the country without much around – save a conspicuous fleet of cars parked in a line down the only road.

As they disembarked, the noisy engine was cut off and the blades came to a stop. Matt stood with the rest at the end of the pad as the pilot got out, pulled off his helmet, and then shut the door behind him. He was a trim man who looked to be in his fifties, with graying hair around the temples.

He walked up to Matt, who realized that he was now standing alone, as the others were making their way inside, and gave him a salute, with an arm that seemed to be trembling slightly with emotion. "Matan Ohayon," he introduced himself. Dropping his salute, he shook Matt's good hand with a firm grip. "I own the security company that performed this extraction."

"Thank you," said Matt, who was perplexed by this celebrity treatment. "Who paid you?"

Mr. Ohayon smiled and held out his arm, indicating that they were to proceed to the building. "There's no amount of money that would cause me to conduct this sort of operation so deep into Syria. In fact, I'm not making a dime, although I could have become rich several times over. I financed it myself, and would have paid every cent I had to bring you back. You see," he said in response to Matt's confused look, "you don't know me, and neither did your father, at least not personally, but I knew him.

"When I was fifteen, my family lived in a West Bank settlement called Bet El that was evacuated by your father's unit. We ran into dire circumstances on the way out and many people were killed. It was feared that your father might abandon us, but I remember seeing his face as he walked by our car on a road with the mortars falling around us, and I knew that he was a great man who was prepared to give his life on our behalf. I would easily do the same thing now to save his son."

Matt had to turn his head, presumably to brush something out of his eye. When he turned back, he could see that the other man's eyes were watery as well. "How do you feel right now, Matthew?" he asked.

"Grateful."

Mr. Ohayon smiled, "What I mean is do you need to rest or see a doctor immediately? I have a physician waiting for you, but I would also like you to meet some other people as well, afterwards."

Matt briefly saw the doctor, who took x-rays of his hand, but pronounced the rest of him to be repairable. He then took a quick shower and changed clothes before Mr. Ohayon led him down a hall and through a door that led into a very large room with hundreds of ordinary Israelis waiting for them, perhaps over a thousand. There were older people there, but also some younger ones with children. Everyone stopped talking when they entered.

"Matt Ridley!" shouted Mr. Ohayon. The room burst into wild applause.

These were the people of Highway 455 that his father spoke about only a few times in his life. Some in the room were too young to remember, but most wanted very much to tell Matt about what they saw that day, about a man who later told Matt that he lived an ordinary life. For the next several hours, speaker after speaker took the microphone at the front of the room to tell him their memories of a calm black Army Captain with courage and honor, who walked taller than anyone that day, even under a barrage of shells and bullets, to become their protector. People spoke of how his rectitude and strength inspired them long after he saved their lives.

And to a person, they each wanted to shake hands with his son.

There was not a dry eye in the building.

2067

Wednesday, March 9th, 2067
Seattle, Washington

The Biomedical conference was letting out after a third day of the week-long session, when Greg and Jin Dijkstra decided to take the kids for a walk along 9th Avenue toward Freeway Park. This suited the two teenagers, who had exhausted about all of the secrets that a large hotel convention center has to offer and were running out of books to read. The two parents, however, were somewhat apprehensive.

The Seattle area was one of the last great outposts of progressivism in America, where people still held egalitarian illusions, untempered by the reality of human nature that had destroyed other cities. In a sense, it benefited from the buffer that the Red States provided against the rest of the country, while at the same time holding itself above such uncouth individualism. While the homeless congregated and roamed the streets virtually in mobs, the intelligentsia would sip their cappuccinos in trendy coffee bars and glory in their cultural superiority.

Yet, it was the same homeless people that Greg was most wary about as he walked with his family toward the park. This was a different sort of city than their beloved Edmonton, where those without means were required to prove their earnestness to private charities before receiving handouts. In Seattle, such programming was deemed "harsh" and "mean-spirited." The homeless were allowed to roam wherever they wanted, fed and sheltered by the taxpayers, with their rights ensured by the police. Naturally the numbers swelled.

The father of two was now in his sixties, with the same befuddled appearance that served him well in his career, and even better when he managed to sneak two particular inventions out of a Montana compound twenty years earlier under the nose of the U.S. Army, although he no longer sported mismatched socks, thanks to the former Jin Xu. As he stepped over bums and directed his family through the mass of panhandlers, one particular man caught his attention. He was sitting in rags against the wall of a brick building about ten yards away, wearing a despondent expression that did not change, even when a well-dressed African-American bent over to drop a dollar into his cup.

Greg recognized Rothermel immediately, even through the disheveled hair, mangy beard and thirty years of age. On one level, he was glad to see him, after having heard that Rothberg burned to the ground several years earlier in a meth lab explosion and rioting. Of course this contrasted with the finale of "The Community" series, in which square-jawed "Noah" leads his people out after an unsuccessful fight with an evil corporation wanting to take over the town and turn it into a toxic waste dump.

He stopped and stared surreptitiously for a few seconds, while his family paused with him, wondering what drew his attention. Greg then led the way across to the other side of the street, before his old colleague could catch sight of him. He didn't want to embarrass the Professor.

Perhaps Greg would have felt better, however, had he known that the old man, now in his late seventies, and with only a few months left, was not as unhappy as he looked there on the street, although his chapped, sunburned hands and face had been exposed to the elements for more than ten years now. He may have been living on public handouts, as had been the case his entire adult life, but no longer was he being paid by the tax-payers to mold the political and social values of their children, free of critical debate. He had learned that it was not possible for such liberals to live in a world of their own design, as they depended on the very moral fabric they sought to destroy.

The Professor was seeing the world for the first time in his life.

Tuesday, March 15th, 2067
Great Falls, Montana

Walid al-Rahahti stood listening to the rumble of tanks in the upper floor of his two-story law office on the east side of Great Falls. Armored columns had been periodically advancing through the center of town for the last several days, as the Blue Army met no opposition in its mission to establish a new base of operations against the insurgents. Walid knew they would not get much further than that, since the Red State rebels, as they were called, had long since melted back into the mountains, as was the case up and down the Rockies. It was a lot easier for the technologi-cally superior army to chew up vast sections of open real estate than it was to compete in the rugged wilderness.

The problems had started a little over ten years ago, when the locals began blocking roads to keep out the refugees fleeing from other states and to prevent the Federals from establishing the parallel system of *Sharia*. The people in the red sections of the country were very protective of their quality of life, which they felt was threatened by an influx of those who once ridiculed them. Although unemployment, high crime, and moral decay could chase the elites from their socially tolerant and cultur-ally diverse paradises, it was not enough to prevent them from seeking to impose the very processes that nurtured such corrosion on those who wanted nothing of it.

Tensions flared and the Blue Army had been called in several times to restore order and keep the roads open. The rebellion was started when it became evident that the people did not have the democratic power at the national level to prevent their communities from falling victim to the same forces of social degeneracy that were destroying other parts of the country. Their guerilla tactics appeared to be holding well against the more powerful force, but the battle had only been fought half-heartedly by a President who believed that nothing was worth war.

That was all about to change.

Monday, May 30th, 2067
Washington D.C.

Colonel Sadiq Yassin sat in the deep, cool cushions of the black leather chair that Memorial Day, sipping coffee from a white china cup with the White House logo printed on the side, as the battle of wills raged around him. He had come a long way from that grass field outside Beslan fifteen years ago, where he lay twisting in agony until medics rushed in to begin the long process of recovery from the bullet to the back. The first step had been to unexpectedly lend support to the cover story – that he and his men were victimized by the hostage-takers at the school, who discovered their position and opened fire. As he explained to Colonel Rastaban, who came by his bed to apologize for the "misunderstanding," Allah works in mysterious ways. If it took a bullet to awaken religious enlightenment, then it was certainly worth it. Any doubts about his earnestness were answered when he personally led the only successful ridgeline assault at Monteagle.

The man to whom he had pledged his loyalty was now a full General in command of the Green Army, which was technically one of two self-contained, identical field armies, composed of infantry, armored and airborne divisions with 100,000 troops. It was an all-Muslim unit, unlike the Blue Army, which had few Muslim soldiers. The separation of strength played well in contemporary America, where the Green Army could be used in Muslim areas and the Blue in others, so as not to further arouse the passions of the agitators.

Such was not the case in Tennessee, however, and that was part of the issue of contention between General Rastaban and President Jill Hudson in the small conference room. Six months earlier, a ragtag group of black and white rednecks, calling themselves the "Bama Boys" blew the pass at Monteagle and declared independence. Their claimed domain ran from the formidable heights of the mountain ridge back down Highway 24 to Lookout Mountain. For a time, they even held Chattanooga before being pushed out.

Since the Blue Army was occupied with the Red State rebels in the Northwest, it was Rastaban who was tasked with putting down the Monteagle insurrection. Unfortunately, he could not bring his full force to bear on the Bama Boys, since he was ordered to keep part of his troops in New England, as a check against the Islamic Republic of Maine. As a result, the campaign in the South was unsuccessful against expectations.

They were also limited as to the type of warfare they could engage in, since the President made it clear that she would not tolerate any deviation from the rules of "sensitive war" that had been put in place following the unsuccessful military action in Maine twenty years ago.

Fortunately for the Green Army, the Bama Boys did not wage terror-ist attacks against civilians, as had the Islamic insurgents. This reduced broader public sympathy, which was trained to blame the government for any civilian casualties, although it also meant that the Bama Boys re-ceived a great deal of help from the local population, which did not care much for the Federal taxes and bureaucracy which prompted the rebellion. The Green operation was heavily compromised by intelligence leaks, as was the Blue in the North.

The President was a strong woman in her mid-sixties, smart and ener-getic. Sadiq knew that it bothered the General to have to answer to a fe-male, which may have explained the slightly insolent tone with which he addressed her, as he tried to make the case for redeploying his forces in support of the Red State campaign. "The threat that the Montana rebels pose is far greater than Monteagle," said the General. "If they succeed, then you'll be fighting to keep most of the West – and I don't have to tell you what sort of problems you may face from La Vida Nueva."

He said the last part grimly, playing on the President's well-known fears of the powerful Christian political group that was gradually becom-ing a major force in the Hispanic states. The unity coalition, comprised of Catholic and Protestant Latinos, was battling the Mexican mafia with re-ligion, and was actually beginning to take back many of the communities. It was feared that they might press for independence, particularly if the Red States went first.

Rastaban was making an argument that was hard for the President to refute. His suggestion was that they draw on international troops to put down Monteagle, while the Green Army supported the Blue's push into Western Montana. Of course, the only nations that the General could promise would help were the Islamic Republics of Maine and Carolina, which had their own standing armies. The President seemed highly reluc-tant to extend the same respect to these former American states that she did to overseas countries, however; perhaps a lingering antipathy over the tactics by which independence had been won.

"I don't want Maine brought in at all," she stated firmly. "As for South Caro... the Islamic Republic of Carolina, well, I'll just have to talk with the Prime Minister."

"I've already talked with the Prime Minister and..."

Anger flashed in the President's eyes. "You'd better not have!" she snapped. "Foreign policy is not your responsibility!"

"Of course," said the General meekly. Sadiq could see that it pained him to be dressed down by a woman. "What I meant to say was that I have a friendship with him from my youth that may come in useful, should you wish to seek his favor. He's called me on occasion to express his discomfort with a Christian State forming on his doorstep, and I know that he has expressed the same fears to you as well."

The President softened a bit. "I'll be glad to talk with him again, General, but please remember that all inquiries from foreign parties are to be directed to the State Department. This is not a military State yet, thank God."

Fortunately she did not notice the look of contempt in General Rastaban's eyes at that moment.

Thursday, September 1ˢᵗ, 2067
Cut Bank, Montana

Paranoid Pete was a low-level intelligence officer in the United States Army, which spoke volumes about the abysmal quality of America's fighting man. This was especially true in the Blue Army, which was known to be far more lax than its Green cousin, since they were stuck with just about anyone who applied, given the unpopularity of military service. He got his name from the obvious effects of what those around him figured to be a near constant assault of marijuana on his senses. His peers did not take him seriously, even when they joined him for late-night pot sessions, where he would expound on his fears while glancing furtively around him, as if spies were watching. They even had a song for him: "*Paranoid Pete, Paranoid Pete – He'll hide your reefer in his sleep!*"

Some of his ideas were crazier than others, such as those involving government conspiracies and UFOs. Others had more truth to them, such as the enemy's capabilities or proposed offensives against its positions. The others would often correct him, if they could, although this would usually occur late into the sessions, after the pot-induced haze loosened a bit of the discipline to which intelligence officers were obligated, as they began to struggle a bit with paranoia themselves.

Tension in the camp had been rising over the last couple of months as the ranks of the Green Army began assembling beside their own. Though officially the Greens were referred to as "an auxiliary force," it was tacitly understood that Washington was disappointed with the Blue Army's lack of progress against the Red State rebels, and certain operations were already being transferred.

Paranoid Pete was not on duty in the early morning hours of September 1st, but he was awakened by the sound of bombers screaming low overhead, as were others in the camp outside Cut Bank, Montana, given the length of the flyover. Unlike the others however, he didn't go back to sleep, but dressed quickly and went outside to take a look. They were heading due north, into Alberta, which surprised him immensely.

Alberta

The 1967 Arab-Israeli War was called the 'Six Day War', but it was really decided in the first ninety minutes when a massive and well-planned Israeli bombardment destroyed the formidable Egyptian air force as it sat on the ground. Without air support, and with Israel controlling the skies, the Arabs had no chance of avoiding defeat. The Israelis could have taken all five Arab capitals had it not yielded to the will of the United States and the UN.

In the same way, the war between Alberta and America was over, literally before it started, when the U.S. Air Force staged a devastating and coordinated surprise attack on the military installations of its young neighbor to the north in the early morning hours; first destroying the runways so the planes would be trapped, then the military bases, where troops were literally killed in their sleep, then a third pass for the grounded air fleet.

The only resistance came from audacious anti-aircraft batteries, where courageous individuals stayed to the bitter end, faithfully pumping out lethal missiles and flak into the black sky before being obliterated. Even as one would explode in a massive fireball, the loyal men in the adjoining stations would stare unflinchingly into the night as their big guns hammered away, before they were eventually silenced as well.

It was the most stunning battlefield success since the Nazi Blitzkrieg hammered through the Soviet defenses on the Eastern Front. Literally overnight, the Albertans were left almost without a military to defend them.

Of course, it helped that the two nations were not really at war, so there was no expectation of such an attack. Not even the American Army commanders had any warning, which was intentional, given the alarming flow of intelligence leaks. Even the 150 pilots who flew the sorties were in the air over Alberta before learning of their mission. Ten turned back rather than bomb; another thirteen flew past their targets and landed in small airfields in the Yukon, defecting to an enemy that was already defeated for reasons no one knew. Even more puzzling were the two that actually turned and destroyed American targets before they were shot down. A staggering thirty percent of the others were lost overnight to the devoted defenders manning the anti-aircraft guns.

Most Albertans were roused shortly after the bombing started, with news traveling along a communications infrastructure that was largely undamaged. Flashes of light were seen in the distance, followed by the deep echo of explosions. Sirens wailed through the dark, as did some of those finding out that their loved ones in uniform were dead. About half of the country's 200,000 soldiers were serving overseas, mostly in Free Europe along with their commander. Casualty rates were well over 50% for the rest. Most military equipment, including armored vehicles, had been destroyed by morning.

When the early light of dawn finally broke across the nation, American jets roamed the skies, and occasional bombing sorties could still be heard. Rising columns of smoke were seen in every direction. The people were still reeling, as word came that American armor was thundering across the border, completely flattening the few defense units that survived the bombing. The Army was on Albertan soil and organizing a broad advance up the mid-section of the hapless nation.

Edmonton, Alberta

It was the American President who called first, before the darkness lifted. Kerry Conner was being driven to a bunker outside Edmonton when he was told that Jill Hudson was trying to reach him. The 72-year-old Albertan President first directed his driver into an underground garage, just in case it was a ruse, before picking up the phone and demanding, "What do you want?"

President Hudson sounded taken aback by his tone. "I... I just wanted you to know that the orders for the attack came directly from the President. I'm also sincerely sorry that it came to this. We felt that we had to act in our own self-interest."

"You didn't have to do this. Do you have any idea how many innocent people have lost their lives?"

There was a sound on the other end that may have been a hard swallow. "Only military installations were attacked..."

"You sound like a damn Fedayeen talking that way, Hudson," said Conner, not bothering with diplomatic formality. His voice steadily rose to a shout. "These were 18 and 19-year-old teenagers... innocent because they didn't mean you any harm. We weren't at war!"

"Your support of the Montana insurrection makes you a..."

"Is that what this is about? Well, thanks for telling me..."

"We warned you not to interfere with the internal affairs of the United States. You..."

Conner cut her off again. "They want their independence as badly as the folks in Maine or South Carolina wanted theirs, Hudson. They just aren't willing to stoop to killing indiscriminately for it like the Jihadis do. It doesn't make their cause any less legitimate. In fact, we wouldn't recognize them if they fought that way."

"Our sources also indicated that you were planning to attack our army in Montana."

"Are you serious? Don't you know that half our defense forces were overseas?" Conner didn't wait for an answer. He dropped his voice to a low growl. "Get your planes out of my airspace, Madame President. Get your troops off my ground!"

"You have nothing left, Mr. President," said Hudson. "As you said, the only forces you have are overseas and our allies have promised to make sure they stay there. You chose to overextend yourself with foreign intervention."

"No," said Conner, "we recognize that people beyond our borders are just as deserving of human rights and political freedom as we are."

She brushed him aside. "Nevertheless, we are asking for your unconditional surrender. The people of Alberta will not be harmed. America will be happy to have them as U.S. citizens again…"

Conner laughed, "Then you do intend to harm them… by taking away their property, controlling their businesses, telling them how and where they can pray, and then taxing the holy hell out of them again. I think they'll prefer freedom."

Hudson sighed. "Again, Mr. President, you have nothing left. You have no choice. Do the right thing and spare your people the suffering."

"We may not have much of an army, thanks to your sucker punch," said Conner, quietly, "but we've got something that you don't have anymore. We have men."

"This isn't a boxing match," Hudson laughed. "We'll accept your unconditional surrender. How much time…"

"You started negotiating the terms of your own surrender shortly after 9/11," said the Albertan President, with the growl back in his voice. "We will choose to die fighting instead."

Before she could answer, he hung up on her.

Edmonton, Alberta

Maria was waiting for him when Kerry finally arrived, haggard and shaking slightly with anger. She gave him a quick hug, whispering in his ear that the base where their youngest son was stationed had not yet reported. He nodded then continued to the conference room, where some of the Cabinet members were arriving as well. She was proud of him, knowing that his concerns at the moment were not for their son. She was able to worry enough for the both of them as it was.

After communications with the full Cabinet was established, he relayed the conversation he had with the American President, evidently struggling to contain his temper as he talked. Following a quick discussion, a formal vote was held among the members to advise war or surrender. The vote was six to nothing for war.

It took about thirty minutes to create a secured channel with the Commander of the Armed Forces, but it was a relief when his calm, confident voice was finally heard. Kerry apprised him of the situation, including the obvious fact that they had been compromised by American spies. "Should we make our stand at Medicine Hat or fall back to Lethbridge?" he asked.

"Neither," was the firm reply. "Pull back immediately to Calgary, blocking the roads as you go. We can't defend the far ends of both major routes to the city. There are two strategic priorities at this point: keeping the mountain roads open and defending the highway to Edmonton. If the Civil Defense Forces are organized correctly, then we can probably hold out for several months."

Maria didn't know about the rest of them, but she breathed a little easier on hearing that it might not be over in a matter of hours after all, even as the basement trembled slightly from distant shelling. She hoped that they could find a way to bring the Commander back from Poland.

Glacier National Park, Montana

Rumors of the Army's steady advance into southern Alberta were not entirely accurate, as the intelligence officer dubbed Paranoid Pete understood; even as he was busy fleeing into the dark mountains along an obscure trail that he seemed to know surprisingly well. Most of those who knew he was missing would laugh at first when they heard about it, with visions of a wide-eyed crank, clutching his reefer to his chest, and scampering through the woods in the middle of the night while glancing over his shoulder, thoroughly unglued over the thought of war with Alberta, even though the back of the enemy was already broken.

Others would not be laughing, however. The ones charged with investigating the sabotaged armor and communications equipment that was discovered that morning, for example, would think it rather suspicious that an ivy-league educated intelligence officer would be stoned most of the time, even if he was the child of hippie parents in Sun Valley, Idaho. They would find on closer examination, though, that his mother was a physician and the daughter of a research scientist named Sanjay Guptapara, one of the wealthiest men in Alberta.

Peter Allen had known for some time that his days with the Blue Army were numbered. He discovered several weeks earlier that he was under investigation, as efforts were made to plug the many leaks that were partly responsible for the Blue's failure to root out the rebels. He wished that he had known of the aerial attack on Alberta, not that he personally had any intelligence contacts there, but he would have done all he could to warn them.

With the Blue Army poised to take Alberta, the Green Army would presumably take its place against the Montana rebels, meaning that there was no point in remaining on the inside of a force that was no longer an immediate threat to his Red State homeland. His hand at been forced at the right time.

At that moment, he was crossing through an area between two boulders, where the path narrowed and darkened, when loud rustling broke the silence and figures covered with leaves rose up out of the ground behind him, with two others emerging suddenly from the shadows ahead. They didn't shout at him, but their unexpected appearance startled him.

"Red Zombie," grunted the man directly in front of him, who was wrapped in black.

Peter's mind was racing, trying to recall the critical partner in the complicated challenge-response system that was based in part on mathematics. "Uh… total eclipse." He winced as soon as the words stumbled out of his mouth, knowing that he had calculated incorrectly.

He could feel the men behind him tense up, and he drew himself up, expecting the worse. The one who challenged him, however, dropped his weapon and pulled back the black hood, revealing a bright smile against the dark grease paint.

"You were off by a factor of ten, but it's understandable given the amount of weed we've been sending you. Welcome back to free territory, Captain. It's good to see you again."

Voice of Alberta Radio

The President's statement was brief.

> "As most of you know, our defense forces suffered a grave attack this morning from the United States of America. Many of you have lost family members, and many of you are still waiting for word. Our prayers are with you.
>
> "Our great nation has been blessed by God, and we are fearless in acknowledging it. Through His mercy, we have been fortunate in never having to fight for our freedom… until now. Earlier today, the option of surrendering to the United States was categorically rejected. We have chosen to protect our liberty, our country, and our way of life with our blood. We will not bend our knee.
>
> "We stand and fight together as patriots, dying if need be. May God be with us."

Washington, D.C.

Jill listened to Kerry Conner's address while sitting alone in her office, as she had requested of her staff. It was a lot shorter than she anticipated – and far more belligerent. She had hoped that common sense would eventually set in on him after he hung up on her, but that apparently was not the case. He was an old man, serving his last year in office. Perhaps he didn't mind dying, but she knew that there had to be others in the country, with their lives ahead of them, who felt differently. Even after listening to his lunacy, she was still confident that it would be over in a matter of days as the Albertans realized their predicament.

The military analysts were plotting strategy in the next room. Both field armies were close to full strength, although the Blue had taken casualties in the Montana conflict each time they tried to advance into the mountains. The Green Army had been pulled away from New England and Tennessee, and was in full support of the Blue as it crossed into Alberta. Back at Monteagle, Islamic troops from Carolina were massing in the valleys primarily to the north, poised to strike once they were satisfied with their preparations and tactics.

Jill had to admit that General Rastaban's strategy was working. Accepting international cooperation not only helped the military, but it made good diplomatic sense as well, as other countries would be less prone to think of America as an arrogant nation. She hoped that this would finally prompt OPEC to drop its embargo against the U.S., but if it didn't, then the acquisition of Alberta's oilfields, along with the other Western Allies would certainly ease the energy crisis.

Her advisors foresaw a quick and decisive victory, with the beleaguered Blue Army pushing up quickly to Edmonton, while the Green filled the breach in Montana – and southern Alberta, if needed. It was against the President's nature to fight aggressively, after all, she was fond of saying that "nothing was worth war," but this was not an actual war. Since America had never recognized Alberta's independence, it was still technically a U.S. Protectorate – and this was an internal police action, intended to close the pipeline by which the Albertan industrialists were supplying the Red State rebels.

Rastaban was extremely adamant about neutralizing Alberta, although Jill purposefully excluded him from the decision making process. Even so, the general's logic was influential. They were already drawn into the Red State rebellion, and he said that it made no sense not to challenge the Albertans when they were clearly involved as well.

The Albertans frightened her. Their military had been nearly equal to the Americans, and the leaders were dangerous conservative kooks. A nation without affirmative action or other programs that provided special recognition to minorities was clearly one with deeply entrenched racial hatred. Nor were there gay rights or other allowances that legitimized homosexuality, which meant that the government plainly endorsed hate crime. When Rastaban insisted that Alberta was planning to attack America it was the final straw, and Jill quickly authorized a limited strike on military targets within the rogue protectorate. Over two-thirds of Americans were minority, and the President had an obligation to protect them from fascist threats. She regretted the loss of life, but it would have been greater had they not acted.

Conner's address was discouraging. He seemed determined to go down with the ship. She still felt that it was best to give the people a few days to consider their position, while the Blue Army massed and prepared for the final assault. Surely internal dissention would develop, breaking morale and making it easier for the people to be defeated psychologically.

After all, most were former Americans.

Friday, September 2nd, 2067
North Sea, Europe

Amari was born in France, but his parents were originally from Algeria, which is where their loyalties remained. They were part of the great Muslim tide that washed into the country through immigration, then eventually gained enough political power to wrest control from the acquiescent natives, whose political parties busied themselves with infighting over which was more tolerant. The immigrants had used terror attacks to control foreign policy for decades, but a hard series of new attacks, aimed at securing domestic power, easily brought the French to their knees.

The scene played out in the Netherlands, then in Spain and Italy, with assistance from France, along with ample credit given to America's policy of toothless diplomacy. Finally, there was the battle for Germany, which was far more difficult and only successful in part, as the Germans realized that there was nowhere else to flee. People fought harder with their backs against the wall.

But the Jihad had to eventually continue against Free Europe – although these countries weren't like the rest. There was no fifth column within, working to soften the borders with moralistic overtures for immigration and appeasement. These people knew how to stand and fight, and if Jihad was to succeed, it had to exit the shadows and engage the enemy on the battlefield. This was much easier, of course, now that Allah had somehow prompted the European infidels to provide its enemy with the very technology needed to bring about their own demise.

Amari was patrolling the skies over the North Sea with his squadron of Mirages when he was delighted to hear that the Albertans were trying to airlift a planeload of soldiers home from Poland in a C-130. It was confirmed to be fully loaded, with about a hundred troops on board. They were foolish to think that they would make it back, given that the Islamic Alliance of Europe controlled the skies, even over Great Britain (which maintained public neutrality in order to avoid domestic unrest). Amari and his crew would have the privilege of engaging the plane.

Three fighters against one cargo jet meant that the C-130 was quickly destroyed in the waters off of Denmark. Amari allowed one of his wingmen to take the kill, not because he was squeamish about the slaughter, but rather for morale purposes.

It was then, that he received word of an F-18 Hornet that had taken off from the same Polish airbase, piloted by the Commander of the Armed Forces of Alberta. Amari could barely contain his excitement as he rushed to intercept the jet over the North Sea. Within fifteen minutes, however, he was feeling apprehensive on hearing that the fighter had fought its way through a different squadron, downing all three of the Mirages. This was good confirmation that it was indeed the Commander, who had a reputation for being quite a pilot in his day. Still, the F-18 did not carry an unlimited supply of weapons, so Amari liked his chances.

On receiving visual sight of the low-streaking jet, the French pilot followed textbook engagement procedures, losing a wingman in the process, but finally bringing down the Hornet after it ran out of missiles. Amari circled the water over the wreckage of the disintegrated F-18 after the kill until nothing was visible on the surface. Allah had truly blessed him that day with the opportunity to kill a great unbeliever.

Friday, September 16th, 2067
Great Falls, Montana

The Blue Army pushed as far west as Butte only once in the six months that they battled the rebels of Montana. Any attempts to go further, toward Missoula, had been met with rocket attacks and ambushes that left the wrecks of helicopters and armored vehicles smoldering along Interstate 90. By the time General Rastaban's troops took their place, the Blue was lucky to have hung on to Helena after such a miserable summer. He wanted to push quickly to Missoula, with visions of mounting an offensive up the heart of rebel territory, north through the Swan Valley before the snow hit in early November. This would have tightened the noose around the enemy, even if they couldn't move in for the kill until spring.

Sadiq Yassin had his doubts about how successful such an operation would be. The rebels loved the mountains, where even the best trained troops usually bogged down. They enjoyed a sympathetic local community and were very well-armed. The Montana rebels were also skilled at thwarting gunships with rockets carried by forward scouts, who buried themselves under the snow or rock along ridgelines to escape thermal detection. Only a massive ground offensive would root them out. Certainly the Green Army, with its discipline and caliber of troops would fare much better than the Blue, although success would have to be well-earned.

Rastaban was fuming about the way the war was being run from Washington. The President did not want the Green to mount an offensive against the Red State rebels until Alberta was taken. Naturally, the Blue Army was bogged down outside of Calgary, where the heavily-armed locals were putting up impressive resistance with makeshift blockades, landmines, and guerrilla attacks. The war still could have been over in a matter of days if the President would authorize the Air Force to use bombs against the civilians-turned-soldiers, but she was reluctant to violate rules that even the countries of Western Europe – under their new Islamic leadership – no longer observed in practice. He could understand his General's frustration.

Taking out a nation's military was an excellent first step toward neutralizing its offensive capabilities, but no foreign army was going to make much progress against a land where most of the 19 million households had firearms. The people who left America for Alberta over the years were fiercely determined to regain their perceived right to bear arms. Upon arriving, they generally loaded up on weapons and ammunition, almost as if they anticipated the present invasion. These people were not suicidal extremists, but they did not mind sacrifice for the cause of freedom. In an odd sort of way, they thought of themselves as the rightful heirs of the American Revolutionaries, carrying the same resolve to pay the cost of liberty with blood.

By contrast, the Blue Army was composed largely of society's dropouts and drug addicts, many of whom joined merely to escape jail. They knew well that their countrymen either ridiculed the military or made soldiers out to be black-hearted automatons. They had no stomach for battle and certainly did not want to give their lives for a country that they had been taught to loathe. Sadiq knew from his sources that many had simply allowed themselves to be captured, once the extent of the enemy's civil strength was realized.

Such would not be case with the Green Army, should they be allowed to fight – and fight they way that the General wanted. His patience with Washington was growing thin, even though his field army had taken no casualties. If given approval, he would send his tanks right over the Ford pickups and Toyota sedans that clogged the highway from Calgary to Edmonton. He would take the capital in a matter of days and hang the leaders, with the green crescent and star of Islam flying atop the city's flagpoles. Any civilians who stood in the way would be crushed.

That was how a war should be fought.

Saturday, September 17th, 2067
High Level, Alberta

General Rastaban would have been far less pleased to know about the passenger in a dusty green pickup truck that was pulling into the driveway of a remote cabin, after a long drive across the Yukon and Northwest Territories, then down the northern part of Alberta along the Mackenzie Highway. This was the last leg of a journey that began in Poland and extended across Siberia and Alaska, involving a series of vehicles, including a train, several ATVs, a tiny plane, and even a dogsled. Two and a half weeks after the bombing began, and nearly that much time since he was presumed dead over the cold waters of the North Sea, the Commander had finally arrived in Alberta.

Though Kerry Conner could not leave the capital to meet him, Maria was there to see the door to the mud-covered truck open and out step Matt Ridley, who returned a crisp salute to the two officers by her side before shaking her hand and making his way directly into the cabin to avoid any overhead surveillance. The 46-year-old had become a close friend of her husband's over the last ten years, as there had instantly been a strong mutual admiration. He had a sharp military mind, but more than that, he was a leader with the immense respect of his troops and his countrymen.

After showering, the haggard-looking man listened to the grim assessment of the nation's broken defenses from the other officers, as he picked at the food on his plate. The Americans had been very determined to wipe out all military capability, and very nearly succeeded. Only a handful of units survived the bombing intact, about 20,000 troops in all. Based on the Commander's original direction, most were positioned defensively around the capital, with a few having been dispersed down to the Southern mountains, in an effort to keep the supply routes open, which, ironically, had been used to send materials in the opposite direction just a few weeks earlier.

Alberta's most prominent citizens had pledged their entire wealth in defense of the country, including Dennis Paterski and his wife, Sharon. Alaska and the other allies were told to keep their smaller forces at home and on full alert. Even so, several thousand volunteers had broken through the lines in handfuls to make their way down and aid the defense, just as others from around the world were managing to do as well. "Who's holding the mountains?" asked Matt.

"Mostly the Poles," replied Maria, referring to the 1,500 troops that had been sent for training prior to the bombing. "They've been fighting like demons to keep those passes open," she added. The Polish troops knew the price that the Albertans were paying for helping to defend Free Europe. Along with a few hundred Latvians, they had done a magnificent job of keeping the Blue Army out of key Rocky Mountain valleys.

"How's B.C. taking all this?" asked Matt, referring to independent British Columbia, which was normally hostile to Alberta's conservatism, being closer in sympathies to their progressive neighbors across the border in Washington State.

"They've half-heartedly given the Americans permission to close off the pipeline," said an officer, referring to the mountainous southeastern corner of B.C. that was used to ferry supplies between Alberta and Montana, "but the Blue Army has its hands full with Calgary. That'll change when the Green is brought up."

"Is that going to happen?"

The officer nodded his head. "Yes. Half their force is already on our soil and it's doubtful that we can prevent them from rolling right up into Edmonton once they get started. The Islamic leadership is not as… well, concerned with public relations."

"Why should they?" said Matt, absent-mindedly rubbing his left hand. "The Muslim countries have always felt that Western standards of human rights should apply only to Western nations… those ivory-towered idiots were just too determined not to believe them."

"The people will be elated to finally learn that you're alive," said Maria. "They haven't had good news in some time."

"Our chances depend on mobilizing them," Matt insisted. "We've got enough guns and guts. It's just a matter of using them correctly. We don't want to have to wage guerilla war from the mountains, like they do in the Red States. We need to make our stand here and now."

He stood up, as if to emphasize the point. "I need to get back down there, but I'm too damn tired to drive the rest of the way. Anyone want to take me?"

Maria stood up with the rest. "It may be better if you remain up here, Commander. No one knows that you're back yet, and we really need to find the spies that compromised our defenses. Otherwise we might be risking another assassination attempt."

"Nonsense," said Ridley. "This is war and war is about risk. A lot of good men didn't give up their lives over the North Sea so that I could hide out in a remote cabin, waiting until the war is over. Now, who's driving?"

Sunday, September 18th, 2067
Voice of Alberta Radio

…Our foe is not the United States of America; it is only a shell of that once mighty nation. At one time, America knew what duty, honor and sacrifice meant, but this is not the country that we face tonight. Their people have lived gratuitously from the blood of ancestral benefactors, who are long since dead. They spend their time pursuing idle *entertainment and wonder why their lives have no meaning. They criti-cize those who would make hard choices then wonder no one dares takes action.*

Though America is no more, the spirit of a great nation is alive in your hearts because you have chosen not to live like cows, at the whim of others, but rather to fight for your country. You know that no nation will become great unless good men are willing to sacrifice their lives to protect their families, their countrymen, and their freedom, and you have chosen to stand tall together, fighting and dying as proud men should.

It's time to stand and deliver…

Mission Range, Montana

The Commander's address was coming over a weak signal on Captain Peter Allen's radio, which he was listening to through an earplug, elated to learn that he was still alive. His fellow rebels always had the greatest respect for Matt Ridley, a fighting man's man. They celebrated as well that Alberta had officially recognized Montana's independence and welcomed them into the Western Alliance, although there would not be much left of any of the allies if things continued the way they were going.

There was a distant crunching of leaves underfoot and the captain tensed up, motioning his squad into hiding. A column of men was finally seen advancing up the slope in the dark. As they broke the treeline, Allen held his weapon above his head to get their attention. The leader caught sight of him and yelled a greeting in a heavy accent. The two cautiously approached each other. The night before, about 1500 others had filed qui-etly past on their way up the pipeline. Most were Ugandan troops, carry-ing heavy packs and walking silently in the pitch black, on their way to support a fellow Alliance member in what most of the world considered a lost cause. They were joined by several hundred Israeli commandos. Ap-parently the Israelis found a way to penetrate air defenses and make it all the way to Missoula. No one wanted to challenge the American Air Force over Alberta, however.

Captain Allen was amazed at the number of Americans making their way north, volunteering for a virtual suicide mission. In addition to fel-low Red State rebels, there were some boys from Texas that broke through the lines to make it up the Rockies before the winter set in. Now it appeared that these new men were from the Southwest as well. After establishing identity, the captain found out that they were *La Vida Nueva*, from New Mexico.

"I didn't think that folks down there cared much for white people," he said bluntly.

"On the contrary," smiled the leader, "it's our state motto: 'Welcome to New Mexico, where we love white people.'"

"Actually," said another, "the only *gringos* we don't care for are the *Federales* and their ACLU lawyers that are always siding with the gangs over the people."

"Who do you think we're trying to keep out of Montana?" asked the captain rhetorically.

He watched them move away toward the north, where the distant peaks were silhouetted by flashes of light and the dull rumble of shelling could be heard. There were only about fifty of them, but they were following thousands of others.

Still, he wondered how much difference they would really make.

Saturday, October 1st, 2067
Great Falls, Montana

The bomber had been waiting all night for the sound of the office door downstairs. He had not fallen asleep during that time, because he was far too excited about what he was within a few hours of achieving. Footsteps made their way upstairs, and then past the closet where he was hiding. He waited until he heard the door to the office open before putting his hand on the handle.

There was no sound of the other door closing, however. The bomber waited a few more minutes, until the aroma of burning tobacco wafted beneath the closet door. Carefully, he turned the knob and stepped out into the corridor. It was not warm in the office, but he was sweating profusely as he looked down the hallway and saw the open door. Smoke was slowly floating out of the room, visible only in the shaft of light coming from within. The bomber slowly crept down the carpet, not aware that his shadow was visible across the threshold.

"Come in!" yelled a hearty voice, nearly paralyzing him in his tracks. When he regained his senses he stood and walked with a determined stride through the doorway. His hand was under his coat, fingering the trigger for the explosives belt.

The lawyer looked surprised to see him, but then recovered quickly. He did not make a move for the desk drawer, perhaps knowing that his handgun had been removed anyway when they searched the office overnight. The bomber was reasonably confident that he would not be armed either, as the Army had conducted house-to-house searches for illegal firearms much earlier in the year. Anyone in possession faced a prison sentence, and it did not look as if the 76-year-old lawyer had many years left. His hair was gray and his wrinkled face was drawn around bright, coal-black eyes.

"Walid al-Rahahti?" the bomber asked.

"Yes," said the other, looking more relaxed. "So, they've sent you to kill me, have they?" He took a deep puff from the cigar in his hand as he talked. "Oh, don't worry," he said, on seeing the bomber's expression, "I won't try and stop you. Let's see those explosives you've got under your coat there."

He motioned with his hand, and the bomber dutifully opened the coat, revealing the sticks of C4 explosive packed with ball-bearings that would be tearing him in half in just a few seconds and most certainly killing anyone within twenty-five feet.

The lawyer took another drag from the cigar. "Ah, I see," he said, "you're all set to send yourself to Allah. Perhaps someone told you that Islam is about achieving glory by killing others?" The bomber did not respond. "Or is it the virgins?" asked Walid. "Perhaps it never occurred to you just how sick is the religious teaching that promises you an orgy for an act of mass murder."

There was a cold glint in the lawyer's eyes. The bomber wanted to pull the trigger right then and there, but something caused him to hesitate. The man standing before him was a traitor. He was also an infidel, by virtue of his having given information to other infidels, the Albertans. Apparently he had also run a very effective insurgent network against both the Blue and Green Armies, on behalf of the local rebels. The General desperately wanted to find out where he was getting the information, but the government lawyers had already gotten wind of the case and would never allow them to use the sort of tactics that would gain them what they needed.

"When did you decide to betray Islam?" asked the bomber.

"What you're calling Islam is what I call death," said the lawyer, motioning again to the explosives. "What is the point of life if it is only to kill others and yourself? Why would Allah put us here in the first place? Why not skip life altogether, given that it's so unnecessary?"

The bomber started to answer, but at that moment they both heard a knock downstairs. Through the fog of a sleepless night, and the natural haze of euphoria over being on the doorstep of Paradise, the bomber began to realize that the lawyer was expecting someone else when he called down the hall... so early on a Saturday. Perhaps it was the traitor! From the expression on al-Rahahti's face, he knew that he guessed correctly.

But now the old man was charging him, and moving surprisingly fast for his age. The lawyer was forcing his hand, martyring himself for his own cause. The bomber had no choice but to pull the switch. He lived for a few more seconds, long enough to see the old man disintegrate in a cloud of pink. He also saw what was left of his own legs, still standing in place as his torso slid past to the floor.

Saturday, October 15th, 2067
Edmonton, Alberta

It was to be Sandoval's last assignment. They were getting quite close to him and he knew it would only be a matter of time before he was found out. The last communiqué contained information that would certainly expose him if acted on – and it sounded as if it were about to be. He wanted to destroy as much data and equipment as he possibly could before he left, but his nerves were failing him. He walked quickly down the empty corridor to the door at the back of the building, but not too quickly to draw the attention of the cameras, he hoped.

Sandoval's journey began as the child of bourgeois middle-class parents in Ann Arbor, Michigan. His delve into radicalism began twenty years earlier, on the campus of the University of Michigan where, as a freshman, he got caught up in the anti-war movement. He listened to speakers and professors talk about the brutal occupation of Maine and the desire of the residents simply to live free. He even traveled there, shortly before independence and met the people, who told him how much they loved peace, freedom and tolerance. He supported their cause and even began to practice their religion, finding that it filled a void.

After independence, he was at first confused by the things that were happening in the new Republic of Maine, such as the eviction of homosexuals and the establishment of a parallel justice system that worked to the advantage of Muslims, and then favored men over women. These seemed to contradict the liberal principles that he embraced growing up, but it was nothing that couldn't be explained within the context of the Qur'an. He had already been trained to overlook far more brutal acts of terror by the anti-war movement. The urge, not just to belong but to belong to something bigger than himself, was quite powerful. Eventually the world around him was filtered through blind devotion to Allah. Only phenomena which confirmed the Qur'an was real. Anything that contradicted it was false and evil.

He became a Jihad Joe, the name given to men who look all-American on the outside, but are ready to sacrifice themselves for Allah at the slightest encouragement. There were thousands like him now, which made for security nightmares in the States. Air travel in America was no longer possible, and much of the population passed through elaborate systems of screening checkpoints and substance analyzers for the most ordinary public functions.

He was destined to be something greater than a mere Fedayeen, however, particularly after he worked his way into Alberta at the urging of his mentor, Rastaban, and into that country's military. The General now in command of the Green Army had long known that there might come a time when a personal source on the inside would be more useful than the other spies, who reported to civilian intelligence agencies.

That time had now come, and Sandoval was literally on his way out the door after having delivered for the General.

Innisfail, Alberta

Matt Ridley was sitting in the back of an unassuming SUV with dark tinted windows when the black helicopters came down.

After spending several weeks organizing the Civilian Defense Forces and watching the Blue Army stopped, pushed back, and even routed in places, he insisted on getting out and meeting the people who were defending their country.

The first stop was in the mountains, since they knew the visit to Calgary was bound to cause a stir that might not go unnoticed by the Americans. High in the Rockies, where the snow already coated the peaks and was advancing steadily downward, he met the Poles and Lats, who knew him by reputation and were greatly cheered by his visit. These tenacious fighters along with experienced Montana advisors were keeping the routes open for the Albertans, as they successfully repelled the half-hearted penetration attempts by dispirited, but better equipped forces. The wreckage from U.S. choppers dotted the landscape in places, joining the burned-out shells of armored vehicles along the road, as they were all slowly disappearing under drifts of snow.

So effective were the defenders there, that Matt was able to pull many of the other volunteers away from the mountains and use them strategically along the Calgary-Edmonton line. He was amazed by the thousands of young men (and even women) pouring into the country from as far away as Uganda to join the cause.

There were even four Bama Boys, who joined the Latvian units, rednecks from Monteagle, two black and two white, who were quite pleased to meet the Commander as well. They knew a little something about holding mountain passes and they had even faced down the Green Army in Tennessee. Matt knew that their presence, though symbolic, was still quite a sacrifice considering that the Carolina army that was massing around their homeland, readying for a final brutal assault over the Monteagle ridgeline. "Your battle is our battle now," said one, explaining why they were sent.

Calgary was also inspiring. From the truck window, Matt could see ordinary civilians, men and women alike, standing grim-faced behind makeshift barriers of old cars and burning tires, with heavy-gauge shotguns. From the windows of the office buildings were white-collar workers, now manning sniper nests in their former workplaces, with long-range rifles trained down along the streets and highways. It wasn't hard to see why the Blue Army had been unable to take the city.

The drive up the Reagan Expressway to Edmonton revealed more of the same. Gritty citizens patrolled along the edges of the highway and underpasses with large-caliber handguns and sawn-off weapons. The same was seen at the various checkpoints along the way, where the only form of identification the convoy needed to pass was to roll down the window on Matt's side, where his familiar face would evoke immediate salutes and stiffened postures from the resolute defenders.

It was right as they were making the turn to bypass Red Deer that the helicopters swooped down. There were two of them, and they immediately fired missiles to take out the security checkpoint at the exit and the front and lead cars, which were spaced generously apart so as not to give the appearance of a convoy. Even as the ground was still shaking, the ropes dropped and armor-clad, commandos in black followed, immediately surrounding the vehicle before its occupants could even open the door.

They broke the windows with their weapons and Matt was horrified to see them shoot the other occupants at point-blank range, once they got a quick look at everyone. It was obvious that they knew exactly who they were looking for – the only black man in the vehicle. He was quickly disarmed and dragged out, kicking and clawing, until four of them managed to subdue him with plastic restraints. Matt felt a prick in his arm and that was the last thing he remembered before waking up in the cell.

Friday, October 21ˢᵗ, 2067
Washington, D.C.

President Jill Hudson sat at her desk beneath the White House, tapping her fingers against it deep in thought. She felt like she was losing control of the war, despite the fact that it was theoretically being planned only yards away, in the War Room. There had been unauthorized troop movements, military offensives that she was informed of after the fact, and she was even getting rumors that General Rastaban was planning to execute the Commander of the Armed Forces of Alberta, whom she had not known was in custody until just a few days ago.

Minutes earlier, she had snatched up the phone and ordered an aide to get Rastaban on the line. Now he was waiting for her. Carefully, she picked up the handset, turning to look at the monitor behind her, which showed troop movement in the southern part of Alberta. The Green Army was positioning itself behind the Blue, eager to join the battle, although they had not yet been ordered to do so.

"General, I hope you're doing well."

"Yes. Thank you, Madame President." There was a certain coldness to his voice, but she realized that she probably sounded the same way to him.

"I'll get right to the point. There's a rumor that perhaps you may be planning to execute the Albertan Commander. Is that the case?"

"Yes." His bluntness surprised her.

"That is unauthorized, General. I am not approving you to do that."

"It's already done," he replied calmly. "He was given a wartime tribunal and found guilty. The punishment…"

"No, no, no!" Jill yelled. "You can't do that!"

"Yes ma'am, we can. Our legal adjunct carefully examined the military code. According to the…"

"I am the Commander-in-Chief!" shouted Jill.

"Absolutely," said the General, "but not every decision has to cross your desk. We're trying to fight a war. You don't have military training and many of the restrictions that are being placed on us are simply preventing us from winning this war. I have an obligation to my men…"

"No, you have an obligation to your Commander-in-Chief," stated Jill firmly.

"I think I understand what this is about, Madame President. I remember the resistance to Muslim units twenty years ago, and the bigotry and hatred that we had to endure for being different."

"This is not about Islamophobia," said Jill, with resignation in her voice.

"Isn't it though?" asked the General. "I don't see you treating the Blue Commander with this sort of disrespect. Do you believe, as others apparently do, that a Muslim officer is less capable of defending your white, Christian country?"

"Of course not," said Jill, "I mean… no, that isn't an accurate description of America…"

"You seemed to be resistant to the idea of troops from Muslim nations assisting our defense efforts here."

"Yes, well I… I was bothered by what happened… what they did after taking control of…"

"I see. You believe that the only way that we Muslims can be acceptable to you is if we devalue our faith, is that it?"

"No, no, of course not, but…" Jill closed her eyes and saw the images of burning buildings and bodies hanging from trees in Maine and South Carolina – thought to be collaborators, apostates, homosexuals, Jews or others deserving of death under Qur'anic law. She couldn't bring that up now, of course, since she didn't want to offend the man.

"I've got a meeting to get to, General. In the future, any such decisions should be run by me first. Is that clear?"

"Of course," he said – even though they both knew he would not.

After hanging up, Jill rested her elbows on the desk and put her hands over her face in frustration. She had been about to sack the General, but had to hold back for fear of appearing Islamophobic. The country had enough crises to deal with already, without raising the immediate ire of Muslim-Americans, a sizable third of the population that always seemed to be in a perpetual state of disgruntlement anyway, thanks to groups like BAIR.

After a few seconds, she slowly raised her head, with a horrific thought that had not occurred to her.

What if she couldn't fire the General? What if his men were more loyal to him, than to their own country?

She turned back to look at the monitor.

Great Falls, Montana

Matt Ridley was very much alive, for the moment, as he stared at the mountains beyond the town through the window of his tiny cell. They reminded him of the trip he once took with his father as a boy, in a rented a van traveling all the way across the country to see Aunt Letitia in California. The Western scenery was jaw-dropping for a 12-year-old raised in New York. More important was the time that he spent with his father, which he never forgot. His hero and role model was intrepid, self-assured, and easily resembled the tall Army Captain described by the Israeli survivors, even though Matt never saw him tackle anything more dangerous than an overgrown yard. Now that he knew he was about to die, he recalled how his father had died, and the quiet dignity displayed in his last moments.

The cell door behind him opened, startling him slightly, as he had not heard the main door on the block, given that he was lost in thought. He turned and smiled, which seemed to put off the four men quickly entering his cell expecting a fight. He went peaceably with his hands tied behind his back. They marched down the long row of cells filled with Red State fighters, who saluted him with tears in their eyes as he walked by, knowing that he would not be coming back.

They went down a flight of stairs and out into an open area behind the prison. A few hundred yards later, they were in a courtyard with small walls. Only the treetops and distant mountains were visible. At one end was a pole buried in the ground; at the other was a line of soldiers with rifles. Each wore the green star and crescent of Islam on their shoulders. Apparently they were hand-picked for the job, because there was not a hint of mercy in any of their eyes.

Matt was tied to the wooden pole. He shrugged off the mask that they tried to place over his head. He wanted to look his killers in the eye and see the last few seconds of what the world had to offer him. In the distance, he heard gunfire, followed by shouting from over the wall. He knew the rebels were trying to stage a rescue – or perhaps it was a contingent of Albertans, disobeying orders that he specifically laid down in the event of capture. It made no difference, since they would not be in time anyway.

Setting his gaze on the distant mountains, he held his head high before the men around him, even as he humbled his heart in preparation for meeting his Lord.

Saturday, October 22nd, 2067
Gibson Dam, Montana

The cargo plane went by low overhead just as expected, but Captain Peter Allen could see two dots to the north that he believed were probably American jets coming in to intercept the craft. They angled west as they got closer, obviously following the route of the plane. *Go down, go down,* he thought to himself, hoping that whoever was piloting the plane that had risen off a Great Falls tarmac a few minutes earlier would notice the pursuit before it was too late. If they could find a way of landing the plane somewhere in the thick woods, then they would have a much better chance of making it on the ground.

The captain had been having a bad day after the rumors of the Commander's execution began filtering into his forward observation position on the eastern slope of the Rockies, about seventy miles west of Great Falls. Initially, there was hope that a rogue Albertan raid on the American prison would successfully rescue the man so well respected on both sides of the border. That hope faded through the night, but then he received word that a plane might be coming down near them and that they were to make all attempts to extract the party on board safely to Kalispell. The code word given was "*taqiyyah*," which the captain recognized as the Qur'anic principle that encouraged the deception of non-believers.

He and his five men saw the plane streaking up out of Great Falls and hugging the tree line in a desperate attempt to get as much ground between the passengers and the pursuers before being forced down. There was a private hope that sprang in their hearts at that moment that the Commander might just have made it after all. They knew that the road they were on continued for a few more miles into very remote wilderness before narrowing into a dirt trail that picked its way through the spruce. All five were equipped with ATVs, which they set off in immediately on losing sight of the three planes.

The distant missile explosions were heard a few seconds later, as they raced down the road. Based on the planes' trajectories, the captain guessed that it might be happening about fifteen miles ahead. It would take forty minutes to cover that distance, even on a clear road. About twenty minutes later, however, the thumping of a gunship was heard above the roar of their engines. They took cover in time to see the 50-foot-long Chinook pass over, with its blades beating the air and forcing it down into the trees. They knew that there would be at least twenty troops on board, more than they could take on with what they were carrying. Another Chinook followed a few minutes later, brushing them off the road again.

They proceeded more cautiously now, standing high on the footrests of the four-wheelers, with an eye out for anything ahead of them. A horrific roaring sound soon thundered through the valley, followed by another just a few minutes later. The spruce were too thick to get a glimpse of what was happening, but black smoke began rising over the trees in the direction they were heading. After a few minutes, they could see the metal from the plane reflecting through the trees in a clearing on the right side of the road. They proceeded into the woods on the opposite side to hide their vehicles. With their weapons in hand, they crept cautiously back across the road and down to the crash site.

Through the trees they could see the hull of the cargo plane, which was largely intact, although one of the wings had been sheared. The pilot had made a good landing. The cargo hold was open in the back and the five moved cautiously down toward it. On the other side of the plane lay the wreck of the Chinook, evidently downed with a shoulder-fired rocket. Black smoke rising beyond the trees to the west told them that the other Chinook had met the same fate. Two spent rocket shells lay on the ground nearby.

The captain was impressed.

The cargo hold of the plane was almost empty, but they could see from the empty boxes and tire tracks that whoever flew in had come very well prepared for doing business.

The distant roar of truck engines chased them out of the area and back across the road, where they barely managed to conceal themselves before three 2-ton cargo trucks, loaded with Green Army troops, appeared on the road. Only the men from one of the trucks jumped out to examine the wreck of the plane and confirm that no one was there. They quickly loaded themselves back in the truck and all three vehicles set off down the road in pursuit.

After a time, the captain and his men crept out of the trees and cautiously tailed the sound of the trucks, staying well out of sight. It wasn't long before an explosion was heard, followed by another. Instinctively, they drew back into the trees. Additional explosions sounded different from the first two. They were followed by small-arms fire, which faded after a few minutes. Starting up the four-wheelers again, the men decided to cover about half the distance, and then proceed on foot. After hiding the ATVs in the trees again, they crept warily down the trail until they came around a bend and saw the wreckage of the three trucks, still burning.

Bodies were scattered everywhere, all with the green star and crescent patch. Some had been killed in the explosion, others in the brief firefight following the ambush. There were nearly two-hundred of them. Whoever had done this certainly knew what they were doing. Before they could examine the scene further, the distant sound of truck engines was heard yet again and they had to take to the woods, doubling back to the ATVs through the brush as they caught sight of a convoy that was about twice as large as the first. It pained them not to be able to help, but they were equipped more for reconnaissance, than for combating a force that was many times larger.

"Do you think it's him?" asked his sergeant.

They both knew who he meant. "I don't know," said the captain, "but I don't know who else could do that kind of damage."

They were in the position of having to follow cautiously, in case one of the trucks doubled back on them. It was a weird kind of chase, with the five Montanans in pursuit of an enemy convoy that was in pursuit of an unknown party that they presumed to be friendly. Soon, they passed the remains of the first three trucks. Some of the bodies had literally been driven over by the second convoy of heavy trucks, although they apparently had to stop to move two of the vehicles out of the way. The men soon entered the snowline, with the tracks of those who passed before clearly outlined. They stopped to slip on the white coveralls that helped them blend into the snow.

It wasn't long before a new series of explosions was heard. Cautiously they advanced, hearing the sound of shooting echoing in the distance, followed by another blast. After abandoning the vehicles yet again, they walked until they came out on much the same scene. Cargo trucks lay upended, with bodies crushed underneath. There must have been 300 more dead soldiers scattered about. Only two were moving, and the captain had his men put them out of their misery on request. The party from the plane had been absolutely meticulous about killing their pursuers. They buried claymore mines in tandem by the side of the road, hidden in snow banks, and set them off in succession after the last truck was in position. There was no other sign of them, however.

As they were making their way back down the road, another helicopter passed over, with the green star and crescent underneath. At that point, the men firmly believed that it would meet the fate of the first two. More trucks went by as they left the road to retrieve their four-wheelers. Some of the vehicles were armored and would probably withstand the claymores down the road. Just as they were about to start the ATVs, there was a heavy rumble, followed by a slow-moving Bradley M2 Fighting Vehicle passing by. This was followed by more troop carriers.

The men looked at each other. The captain knew what they were all thinking. There was a very high-value target in the woods ahead of them. The trucks that had passed before fell into ambushes because they were chasing, rather than hunting. An army that sends its men with such recklessness must be extremely desperate to recapture whatever had gotten away. Could it be Commander Ridley?

They knew that the road wound its way into a valley, very near the continental divide in the Marshall Wilderness area. Not many people would be able to find their way through this area without some sort of assistance. The captain decided that they might do well to leave the road and cut directly over the ridge to the southwest on their ATVs, provided the snow wasn't too deep. This would not only help them gain ground on the people ahead of them, but it would also give them a better vantage on what was happening below.

As they were tracking through the snow, the captain received word that rebel units were being brought up from the south to try and seal the road behind them, meaning that no one else would be getting in, provided that General Rastaban didn't send the whole Green Army, although that wouldn't have surprised the captain at that point.

As they finally broke over the ridgeline, the sound of gunfire and explosions echoed up to them. Down below, the road came out on a clearing, where the crew from the plane was evidently holed up in a series of cabins that lined the far end against a rocky knoll. It was an old camp that had been abandoned decades earlier.

It was quite a scene, as they made their way down, not caring anymore about the sound of their vehicles. Cargo trucks were barreling their way across the meadow as they were met with fierce fire from the cabins, barely making it halfway across the expanse before rumbling to a stop, sometimes in flames. Fedayeen fighters were pouring over the sides and charging the cabins like mad fire ants, where they were cut down by a barrage of bullets. There were scores of them, shooting as they ran, with their shots picking apart the brittle sides of the cabins, which offered concealment but not protection. The captain wasn't sure what caused the crew to have to stop, but it was obvious that they were making a desperate last stand.

A lethal wave of weapons fire emanated from the old structures, mowing down the attackers and hurling chunks out of their bodies. "What guns!" yelled his sergeant, admiringly.

The trucks had all stopped well short of the line of cabins by the time the Montanans were halfway down the ridge, trying hard to maintain con-

trol of their vehicles in the heavy snow. At the same time they were try-
ing to keep an eye on what was happening below, as wave after wave of
Holy Warriors were picked up and thrown backwards by the big guns.
Still they came.

So did the Bradley, which was undaunted by the volley of lead, as it
made its way around the wreckage of the trucks and into position for
point-blank shelling of the flimsy cabins. The captain noticed that some
of the Fedayeen were scampering off into the woods, not noticing that the
tank was about to decisively turn the tide.

The ATVs finally broke out onto the road. Captain Peter Allen pulled
out his sidearm, exhorting his men to stand and deliver. He took aim at
the first Fedayeen that noticed them, picking him off in a single shot. His
sergeant barreled past and literally ran over another, who was carrying a
shoulder-fired rocket, which Peter then bent down to retrieve from the
mud. He hoisted the tube between the handlebars of his four-wheeler and
carried it about fifty yards further, where there was an overturned cargo
truck at the edge of the clearing, with a couple of Fedayeen in the process
of being dispatched by two of his men.

A crack of fire from the Bradley reverberated through his rib cage as
he dismounted from the ATV. One of the five cabins was instantly turned
into a hail of toothpicks. He checked the rocket then hoisted it to his
shoulder as he stepped away from the vehicle and out into the open where
he had a clear shot. Ignoring everything else around him, he bit down
hard while holding his breath, took aim and pulled the trigger.

It wasn't an impressive looking shot, but it was enough to damage the
big gun on top of the vehicle and stop its rotation. The fire from the four
remaining cabins immediately ceased and his men regrouped to make a
pass at them, dodging bodies and occasional sniper fire as they shot across
the meadow, firing wildly behind them. The armada of four-wheelers
came to a stop just on the other side of an upended cargo truck that provided shelter right outside one of the cabins.

The captain looked up right as the door opened. "Commander?" he
yelled.

Out from the cabin and the one next to it, however, came five Arab
soldiers, soaked with perspiration and armed to the teeth, all with the
green star and crescent of Islam clearly visible on their dark uniforms.
Most carried heavy-caliber machine guns, and were draped in belts of
brass ammunition. What was this?

The captain and the others quickly raised their weapons and were
about a split-second away from wiping out these hated Green warriors
when the man closest to them yelled "taqiyya!"

"Stand down!" ordered the captain to his men, who had no trouble
obliging, particularly after the grim-faced Green soldiers fired past them

and into the bodies of advancing Fedayeen. They all turned to do battle, with their new comrades in green exhibiting particular tenacity and skill in bringing down those still foolish enough to press the charge. Brass casings flew everywhere, and smoke rose from the heavy guns, along with the acrid smell of singed barrels. It was a fierce fight, with the defenders standing shoulder-to-shoulder, blazing away until they finally scattered the survivors into the hills.

When it was over, they took a minute to catch their breath and make sure there was no one else left.

"I admire your handiwork," said the captain sincerely, to the leader of the group, who identified himself as Colonel Sadiq Yassin. "Where's the Commander?"

"Dead, I'm afraid," replied the man bluntly. "He was executed by Rastaban yesterday."

The captain's heart sank. Yassin continued. "What I'm carrying with me, however, needs to get to get to Edmonton. There are probably more than a hundred Fedayeen spread out in the woods. Do you think we can make it to Kalispell?"

Peter grunted. "Don't worry about that," he said with a wry smile. "My mountain boys will make pretty quick work of them." At that moment, shooting was heard in the distance, which they all knew wasn't directed at them.

"Good," said Yassin, "because I think that things are about to change."

Sunday, October 23rd, 2067
Edmonton, Alberta

Religion was an important part of life in Alberta, especially with the country under siege. Kerry Conner was a man who came to religious faith late in life, sometime after he became a father. His wife had been deeply involved in the small Catholic church at Bozeman, particularly after the children came along, but she began worshipping with an Evangelical congregation after they moved to Alberta. This prompted him to think deeply about life and the universe. He was even getting to the point that he could hold his own in arguments with his dear friend, Dennis Paterski, who had always been agnostic.

Maria had seen her husband alone in prayer several times during the last two months, which wasn't unusual, considering the circumstances. Such was the case now, when she surprised him in his provisional office at two in the morning. The door had been closed and the light off, so she assumed that he was sleeping, but as she quietly entered, she caught sight of the man who would bow to no other man there on his knees before God. Just as she was about to retreat back into the hallway, he called for her and switched on the desk light. The soft incandescent glow exaggerated the wrinkles on his weathered face, making him appear to have aged even faster than he really had since the bombing began seven weeks earlier.

Behind him was an odd sight. Although the window normally offered a stunning view of the vibrant city lights, the area was now under blackout restrictions. Distant flashes could be seen to the south, along with low thunder from shelling along the expressway, which was hit hard each night. The people were fighting their hearts out.

"The Green Army is flooding across the border," Kerry said. She nodded.

"They're bringing artillery, armor, and gunships, in addition to 100,000 troops." He rubbed his eyes with his hand. "I can't send our people up against that, with revolvers and 12-gauge shotguns. Even if we do triumph eventually, the human cost would be horrific. Matt himself said that these Green troops play by different rules. Even if he were around…"

His voice choked and she went over to put her hands on his shoulders. She didn't want to make his decisions for him, since the people didn't elect her, but she deeply believed that they were prepared to pay the cost of freedom. She'd been able to travel far more extensively than her husband since the war began, and talked with many who were not as fortunate as they were to hear from missing loved ones. Yet, there was no resignation in their hearts. They wanted to believe that their sons died for a cause that would not be betrayed.

"If we don't make our stand here," she asked quietly, "then where else will we?"

She could tell that he understood. They were both old and had good lives behind them. It would have been easy to give up. But there were younger generations to think of, that deserved a chance for freedom. If Alberta went under, then the Red States would follow with Free Europe close behind. The Left would finally see the fruits of its victory, as the shadow of totalitarianism fell across the entire planet, and Western civilization was relegated to memory.

"We're going to need a miracle," said the President.

Just then, the phone rang.

Great Falls, Montana

General Rastaban finally picked up the line in his office, located in the same complex of buildings where the Albertan Commander met his fate the day before. Continuing to put off the Blue Army commander would only further arouse her suspicions.

The woman on the other end lit into him immediately. "Why are you pushing past Lethbridge and Medicine Hat? You know that your orders are to stay put!"

"You've had your chance," replied the General. "Your troops have only gained ground that the enemy's given you. There are morale problems within your ranks and we know that it's leading to a high number of defections, which are further compromising both of our field armies. I intend to win this war. I will win it quickly and I will win it decisively. There's nothing more to talk about." With that, he hung up the phone, knowing very well that she would be soon be talking directly with the President.

Absent-mindedly, he stared out the window toward the west, where only a day earlier he had seen a cargo plane disappear over the horizon, carrying his best laid plans with it. His hand had been forced and he had to act quickly, before he was entirely ready.

Damn that Sadiq Yassin! The man had played the game so patiently since Beslan. Rastaban was sure that he was a true believer and had even tested him, slowly developing a confidence in the young officer with each success. Yet, Yassin had only been planning his revenge – for fifteen years – right under the General's nose, and he could not have done worse to him if he had walked into the room with explosives tied around his waist. Rastaban quivered with frustration just thinking about it.

He shook his head forcefully, as if to physically cast the thought from his mind. He needed to collect himself, because he still had time to act – even if it was much sooner than he intended.

Washington D.C.

It had been nearly an hour since President Jill Hudson had gotten off the phone with the Blue commander, who was upset over the unauthorized maneuvers of Rastaban's Green Army to the south of her position. The commander was taking it as a slap in the face, an affront to her abilities as the highest ranking female officer in the nation's history.

Jill had tried several times to reach the Green General, but Rastaban was "indisposed." Now she was getting worried. The green triangles on her monitor were almost perfectly positioned to overtake the blue triangles and head straight into the teeth of the Albertan defenses. Jill knew that this was not the way that a military should operate. A chain of command had to be followed; and in this case it began with her.

Just as she made the personal decision to relieve the General of his command, there was a muffled crack, almost like a gunshot from the War Room next door. The screaming that ensued confirmed that it was indeed a gunshot. Several others followed. Two men rushed past the glass wall of her office, not even bothering to glance in her direction. They were followed by a woman who was screaming. She was an assistant to the Secretary of Defense. As Jill stood up, a chunk of bloody flesh came spitting out of the young woman's head and lodged on the glass door to the President's office. She fell to the ground immediately, completely motionless as blood oozed under the door.

Jill rushed over and was about to open the door when a man in the uniform of the green star and crescent came striding up, with a wild look in his eyes. He was holding a handgun. She immediately dropped to her knees and bolted the lock at the bottom of the door, then reached up to catch the top lock as the man caught sight of her and heaved his weight against it.

She hoped that it would hold him. The glass was supposed to be bulletproof. She didn't wait to find out, but instead dove behind her desk as the thumping from bullets sounded behind her.

The glass was holding.

Something caused her to look up at the monitor behind her desk – just in time to see the blue triangles slowly disappearing, one by one, all down the line from Calgary to Medicine Hat.

Edmonton, Alberta

It was a very weary Kerry Conner who gathered with his Cabinet in the War Room that Sunday morning as the reports began coming in from Calgary. Artillery shells were blasting chunks out of the Blue Army. Gunships were raking the Blue lines with withering fire. Caught from behind by the Green Army, the doomed soldiers were trying to flee, but there was nowhere to run.

Yet, through it all, neither the Blue commander nor the U.S. President appeared to be authorizing any effort to return fire.

The ability to stomach what he was seeing and hearing was wearing thin. Finally he had enough. "Let's try and get President Hudson on the line," he ordered.

Washington D.C.

The thumping had stopped for a few seconds, and Jill poked her head over the desk to take a look. The uniformed man who had been trying to break in was dead, but his place had been taken by one of her Secret Service agents. Another agent lay dead behind him, so it wasn't hard to guess what had happened.

The agent who was now trying desperately to break the lock and gain entry was someone that she knew by name. She would always greet him cordially, "Hello, Muhammad, how is the family?" Now he was trying to kill her.

Jill's senses returned. The thick office glass was holding against the bullets and there was no point in staying under her desk anymore. At that moment, her switchboard buzzed to say that the DCA Secretary was on the line to discuss strategy for dealing with a dangerous display of the Ten Commandments in a Texas courthouse. Jill cut her off to order a security detail down to the room. As she hung up, another operator buzzed to tell her that both the Blue commander and the Albertan President were on the line. Jill took the commander's call first.

The poor woman was wailing, "They're killing us… they're killing us."

No kidding, thought Jill, as she looked into the dark eyes of the cold-blooded killer on the other side of her office glass. "I have reason to believe that this might be some sort of coup. Are you able to defend yourselves?"

"No…" came the whining reply.

"Well do your best!" snapped Jill. "I'll try and get you air support."

She disconnected the call, and then had her switchboard try and reach the Air Force Commander at the Pentagon. She did not want to talk to the Albertan President until she was sure of her situation. Her operator came back on to tell her that apparently there was some accident and the commander was unavailable. "The new commander in succession was a General Muhammad…"

"Never mind," Jill snapped. The man outside her door had been shooting the metal lock at the bottom and making progress from the sound of it. The echoes were graduating from muffled thumps to sharper cracks, indicating that part of the barrier was giving way. She decided to ignore it for the moment. The switchboard operator called to say that the elevator had been sabotaged, but a security team was making its way down the shaft.

Jill finally picked up the line from Alberta.

"Madame President, you are aware that you are under attack from your own forces?"

"Yes, I believe I am aware of that," said Jill calmly, with an eye toward the door, where the lower lock had now given way under pressure from the agent's catapulting body slams. The lower part of the door was flapping open a few inches on impact.

"May I assume that we have a truce?"

Even her personal predicament could not induce a quick answer to the question. Jill had to think for a few seconds. "Yes," she finally said, through gritted teeth.

"Good. You need to bomb the daylights out of those Green Army positions – right now, while they're exposed!"

Jill turned back to look at the monitor. Hardly any American planes were in the air over Alberta. She knew why. "Our military command structure has been compromised," she stated bluntly. "We... I don't have the ability to call in air strikes. I also don't have any control over what the Green Army is doing right now, of course. I'm afraid that their intention is to drive right through the heart of Alberta and take the capital." Her voice faltered a bit. "Rastaban complained about the way we were fighting the war. I'm afraid that the tactics he'll be using on your people are..."

"Oh," interrupted Conner, "I'm afraid that you don't have the information we do. It's not us that he's after. It's you."

At that moment, a horrible wrenching sound reverberated through the office as the door finally gave way.

Jill dropped the phone.

Tuesday, October 25th, 2067
Washington, D.C.

The last time Parker Whitehead had seen the Cathedral that full was thirty years ago, for the rededication ceremony after the bombing. Of course, there were no dignitaries to be seen now. The pews and aisles were filled with ordinary people, desperately praying for God's help in that critical hour. It was tempting to stay, but he felt the Lord directing him to talk to the Imam again. The man wasn't returning his calls, however, and so he decided to walk the ten blocks to see him at his office.

The way over was unpleasant. The city was in a state of panic. Sirens were wailing everywhere as the social order was breaking down. Cars jammed the roads and exit ramps, loaded with people and what little they could carry out of the city with them. Shooting was heard in the distance as tempers flared. Looting was rampant, since the few police who remained had far more serious matters to deal with than theft.

It had been two days since the news that surviving remnants of the Green Army were slowly making their way across the Upper Midwest. They were currently rumored to be in either Minnesota or Iowa. The Carolinian Army, which had been massing in the Tennessee Valley for a presumed assault on Monteagle, had simply turned around instead, and was now moving toward the nation's capital from the southwest. There were also horrible reports coming in from New England, as the armies from Maine moved down to take Boston, on their way to New York.

There were probably a few Americans left who defied the ban on firearms, but they were a dying breed over the last six decades, particularly outside of the Red States. The people were largely defenseless.

But Parker had hope that if he could just talk to the Imam, then they might be able to resolve the crisis with unity. No doubt the men marching in those Muslim armies were angry about a lack of understanding and compassion on the part of Americans, even though the Reverend was almost at a loss to think of what more they could do to prove their good intentions.

Perhaps if he and the Imam could establish a public dialogue to address their concerns and show that the differences between the two cultures were not really so great, then it would bridge the divide and bring the two sides together... to begin a new age of peace and tolerance.

Armed guards outside the mosque frowned at Parker as he approached. He identified himself and told them of his business with the Imam. One of them went inside briefly then returned.

"The Imam is unable to see you."

Parker's jaw dropped. "He has to! There's a crisis brewing in America right now. We must talk with each other... we must establish interfaith dialogue to..."

Impatience flashed in the guard's eyes. He stepped back and raised his weapon. "Islam isn't in America to be equal to other religions. The only crisis right now is that there are too many *dhimmis* who don't understand that."

Parker's face went white, but it wasn't from fear.

Washington D.C.

"Congratulations on surviving your assassination attempt."

Rahim's words were flat, almost as if it would have made no difference to him if the White House security team had not arrived to take down the rogue agent, just as he finally managed to force his way into the President's office two days ago. Jill stared back at him for several seconds before answering; wondering what was really going on in that head of his.

She had invited the former President and current head of BAIR, the Board on American-Islamic Relations, to the meeting with other government leaders to try and address the concerns that the nation was having over the current state of affairs. It appeared that a military coup was taking place, and that the Islamic Republics in the two former American states were working in cooperation with the Green Army. Just as disheartening, were the reports of armed bands of Muslim citizens, who were taking over local communities and declaring them to be "hate-free zones" while terrorizing the non-Islamic residents.

Rahim seemed remarkably unfazed by the events, even though they clearly threatened "American-Islamic relations." He opened by expressing concern about a feared backlash against Muslim-Americans by "vigilantes" and right-wing Christian hate groups.

No one was really buying it anymore.

The conversation quickly moved to the concerns of other members, who assumed that Rahim would play a critical role in the presumed transition.

"Will this affect Social Security payments?" asked an older woman from the agency.

"Not at all," answered Rahim. "Entitlements will continue to be extended… if there is a leadership change, that is."

"What about Affirmative Action?" asked an African-American Cabinet member.

"Islam respects all people."

"And the unions?" asked the Labor Secretary. "How will they fare?"

"Very well," answered Rahim. "The Middle East has a history of labor-friendly governments."

"What about transgender restrooms?"

This was getting to be a bit too surreal for Jill. "Good lord! Are you people accepting defeat already? It sounds like you're planning a new government."

"We're just concerned about our constituents," insisted the head of Social Security. "We want to make sure that the entitlements will still be there, even under a… a new system."

"No one wants this to happen, Madame President," said Rahim, with the same unconvincingly bland tone, "but, if it does, we want the people to have assurance that Islam provides special protection to *dhimmis*."

"Yes, we can see how special it is when homosexuals are strung up in Maine and priests are machine-gunned to death as they are chased out of the Vatican…" The flash of anger in Rahim's eyes caused her to hesitate. She had never expressed this sort of exasperation to him before.

He spoke slowly. "It is this sort of attitude toward Muslims that is responsible for the anger and violence. We are tired of being treated like second-class citizens. We haven't forgotten 9/11, you know, when we had to live in a climate of fear and suspicion."

"I'm sorry, Rahim." Jill spoke the words apologetically, with her eyes down on the table in front of her. As she pondered what to say, a lunch conversation with Maria Posada from more than twenty years ago came back to her. After a moment she raised her head with an odd look of defiance. "Yes, I'm sorry, Rahim, but it's time that Americans began acting as if their right to safety exceeds your right not to be offended."

"It's too late," he responded, with surprising bluntness.

"We'll see about that," she said, standing up. "This meeting is over."

Washington D.C.

That evening, the President addressed the nation on the al-Jazeera network (which promptly offered a rebuttal). She spoke about the need for Americans to embrace "duty, honor and sacrifice," and take up arms and defend the country.

"What arms?" asked a woman in Ohio, who didn't know anyone who dared disobey the strict gun control laws.

"Did she say 'doody'?" asked an older, pot-bellied dropout across the street, who picked up the phone to share the joke with a friend.

A 22-year-old man in Boston enjoyed video games too much to worry about sacrifice.

The man living downstairs from him avoided anything that involved delayed gratification.

A mother of teenagers in Minneapolis wanted to keep her boys out of a war, at any cost.

Another woman, living near Detroit, knew that, like most Americans, she was too morbidly obese to fight for anything other than another Jumbo Burger.

A former police officer in Cleveland hoped that the Muslims might bring law and order back to the nation.

A florist-shop employee in Milwaukee didn't know much about Islam, except that it was the religion of peace.

A college student was far more concerned about the destructive effects that war might have on the environment. The death of a culture that gloried in consumption and waste was nothing to cry over, anyway.

His friends believed that nothing was worth war.

A middle-aged woman in Westchester closed her eyes and visualized world peace.

In Trenton, a 35-year-old postal worker was very upset that the President's address preempted one of her favorite TV shows.

A Methodist parishioner in New Jersey saw no need for violence, since he knew that his faith in God would keep him safe. His district's gay bishop was several hundred miles away, speeding toward the Red States in a loaded-down Buick.

A graduating senior in Illinois had been taught that America was an imperialist, racist, and insensitive nation, hardly worth sacrifice. Millions of others agreed with him.

An atheist celebrated what he hoped would be the end of Christian civilization. His wife, a college professor, hoped it would be the end of Western civilization as well.

Leftists across the country cheerfully burned American flags.

Wednesday, October 26ᵗʰ, 2067
Edmonton, Alberta

Kerry Conner sat in a darkened room, watching a video with his wife and members of the Cabinet. With them as well, was a former Green Army Colonel, who had risked his life to bring them the intelligence information that turned the war, along with the videotape. Thanks to Sadiq Yassin, the Albertans now knew the identities of each of the spies that had compromised their early-warning systems and left them vulnerable to the devastating attack. It would never happen again.

The picture on the screen was of a man in a prison cell, being recorded through a horizontal slit in the door. He was in good condition, but knew that he would be executed within a few hours. He looked at peace.

Each man sat with his own thoughts, watching as their close friend of ten years exhorted them to carry the battle to the enemy and never stop fighting for freedom. He looked every bit the mirror of rectitude and dignity that they remembered.

Kerry spoke softly when it was over, "Give me a minute or two before we turn the lights back up."

Friday, October 28ᵗʰ, 2067
West Virginia Airspace

Her Vice President had been eager to prove her broad-mindedness, by staying at the White House when Marine One, as the Presidential helicopter was still called, lifted off from the White House lawn an hour earlier for the quick ride to Andrews Air Force base. "Arabs and Muslims are just like us," she told Jill two days ago. "We have nothing to fear, particularly if we welcome the changes, rather than succumb to intolerance or aggression."

The same woman was shaking like a leaf on a tree, as the chopper pulled away. The image was still fresh in Jill's mind an hour later, as she was safely aboard Air Force One on her way to Seattle. She wondered if it would be the last time that a truly American President would see the White House.

From the air, she saw that parts of the city were burning, as the two Muslim armies camped on the outskirts of the District – the Green near Bethesda, and the Carolinians across the river in Arlington, near the cemetery, where the Mujahideen amused themselves by defecating on graves and knocking over markers shaped like crosses.

Vaguely, she wondered what would happen to the loyal military personnel that had stayed faithfully to the end to keep the air base open. Would they be evacuated as well, or fall prisoner… or worse?

No other countries cared to help. Alberta had no air force, anymore, and they had turned their back on Free Europe ten years ago. The UN was absolutely useless. Rahim suggested that Syria and Iran might be persuaded to send military contingents. Jill laughed at him.

It had been three full days since she made her plea to the American people, but there was almost no response.

Where were the patriots?
Where were the men?

2078

Thursday, September 15th, 2078

Quiñones Ranch, West Tejas

The large helicopter was sitting a hundred yards behind them, with engines completely cut off, as it had been for the last two hours on the grounds of the old Conner ranch. The only sound was the light breeze rustling the leaves of the tall oak tree above them on the grassy hill, as the woman gazed out over the flat peaceful valley that led to magnificent mountains framed beyond. Her husband's head, with gray hair and hearing aid, had slumped several minutes earlier, but she still held his hand in hers.

Down the knoll behind them were children and grandchildren, standing at a respectful distance, watching the scene while dealing with their own emotions. Among the group, which clearly favored their matriarch's Mexican heritage, were the Governor of Montana and the Vice Chairman of the Western Alliance.

They had no difficulty securing permission from *El Norte*, the Southwestern nation, or the current owners of the old ranch, to allow the old man to die peacefully under the spectacular sunset, as he wished.

With the sunlight fading around her, Maria placed her husband's hand over his body and turned to walk back down the hill, where her family came forward to embrace her.

2098

Thursday, December 25ᵗʰ, 2098
New York, New York

A young boy in a *keffiyah* stood relieving himself against the wall of a burned-out cathedral a few blocks from where the old man sat looking out the third-floor window, with his snow-white hair swaying softly in the heavy air. The structure was an eyesore, soon to be replaced with a new mosque, from what he heard. It certainly wasn't legal to build churches in this part of the city. Even over in the Christian quarter, it required permission from the Council just to make repairs.

The former 51ˢᵗ Street in Queens looked like any other day. Women in veils moved in and out of the crowd, on their way to market while their men traveled to work or to the mosque with *kufis* covering their heads. There were no colored lights, decorated trees or other signs of the Winter Holiday anywhere. There wasn't even a Santa image in sight. Thick haze hung over the city, perhaps from the wood fires that were used for cooking and heat by millions of households to the west, or perhaps from other sources of pollution. The sky was a dull yellow.

The scent of open cooking floated up to him, along with a mixture of English and Arabic. He had the window open for a few minutes, to enjoy a last look around before they came for him. He knew that they would be when he put his name on the essay published in the underground newspaper. He may have been spry for 95, with a mental acumen undiminished by age, but he had nothing left to lose by openly criticizing the Mullahs the latest round of crackdowns in the White ghettos

The only woman he ever loved had died ten years earlier, on the other side of the continent, where some could still afford the luxury of egalitarian thinking – sheltered in shrinking pockets of inherited wealth. The other social elites had fled along with her, or turned to the cyanide capsule as a means of painlessly escaping the natural consequences of cultural suicide, even as the changes were just beginning, so many years ago.

Most of the common people simply adapted, usually by taking the religion and professing the Prophet. Having already been tamed by long decades of self-indulgence, they were willing to make whatever deal they needed to ensure survival and feasible pleasure. Others, like the white-haired man, accepted *dhimmitude*, being careful not to evangelize or make trouble. They kept to themselves, either growing their own food or offering skilled services for food grown by others.

Down the street he saw the government car and van. He closed the window as they pulled to the curb, and walked around the apartment one last time to make sure that everything he needed was packed in the two bags by the dilapidated wooden door. The noise of boots on the stairs grew louder, finally culminating with a loud knocking.

He pulled open the door to find not the jack-booted thugs that he was expecting, but rather a solitary man standing with his hat in his hand. He had horn-rimmed glasses and a studious, pedantic look about him, almost as if he should have been an academic. "Parker Whitehead?" he asked.

Parker nodded. "I know why you're here," he said, pointing to his bags then stepping back in an inviting way. "Would you mind coming in and having a cup of tea with me?"

The man surprised him by agreeing to this. He seemed apologetic about the situation, and Parker knew that this was not something that he enjoyed doing. They sat at the table for a few minutes, waiting for the water to boil and exchanging formalities, which seemed out-of-place with the circumstances. The man's name was Hamzi. He was in his mid-40s and of Iraqi descent. Parker mentioned his time in the country back in 2026 and asked if perhaps the other knew of the Assyrian Christian community in Baghdad that he had visited at the time.

"Yes, my father spoke of them," said Hamzi, with a sad smile. "They were good people, always helping others in hard times. I'm afraid they didn't survive the purges, but I assume you knew that?"

Actually Parker didn't. Like other Christian communities across the Islamic world, and then parts of his own country, he had simply stopped hearing from them after a time.

Time was short, so Parker quickly got to the point. "Why? Why is this happening?" he asked.

By the way the other man blushed, it was clear that he knew what was being asked. He nervously pulled out a pack of cigarettes. "May I?" he asked.

"It's not really my apartment anymore, is it?"

Hamzi answered the question by putting a cigarette to his lips and lighting it. He took a few deep drags, and then spoke slowly, in an almost philosophical tone.

"Sometimes it is a mystery to me as well, I have to admit. I've studied history. America was a better country than any other at one point, with more freedom and prosperity than to be found anywhere else at the time. There was even a power that was unmatched, yet never used for conquest or subjugation." He took another drag, looking down at the table as he talked. "Certainly it was to our shame that this happened, since America succeeded by following a different political and economic model than the rest of us – even worshipping a different God. You can imagine our jealousy and frustration. When the strange practice of self-flagellation began to erode America's moral self-confidence, it was something that her enemies eagerly encouraged."

Parker stirred his tea absent-mindedly. "But didn't our desire to better ourselves with self-critique serve as an example?"

Hamzi raised his eyes and laughed, "Did you see the rest of us doing it? No, we merely enjoyed repeating the bad things you said about yourselves, feeling all the more superior for it."

"Our acceptance of others didn't win us respect?"

"Perhaps," Hamzi replied, "but it is a strange country that brings in immigrants, only to teach their children what a horrible history it has; that mocks its patriots and seeks sympathy with its own enemies. What other conclusions did you think we would draw?"

"That we wanted to build a better nation together, with unity and understanding. We trusted you...."

"And we appreciate it," said Hamzi.

"...we trusted you to want the same," finished Parker.

"I don't mean to sound trite, but did you not see what was happening in other countries? Did you not read the Qur'an?" He leaned over to knock a bit of ash onto the saucer. "Islam is not designed to co-exist with other religions, unless it is in complete domination. What sort of egoism made you think that you would be the exception?"

"Because groups... spokesmen... they all said they shared our concern for tolerance and that we were bigots to think we had anything to fear."

"Have you never heard of *taqiyyah*, the Muslim principle of deceiving enemies in order to divide them and gain trust for the purpose of achieving power?" asked Hamzi.

"Of course, but..." Parker's voice faltered.

"But what?"

"The Islamic groups assured us that they were not deceiving us."

Hamzi gave a deep, genuine laugh. "And you still don't know how it came to this?"

The old man realized how foolish it sounded.

Hamzi leaned forward to look the other in the eye. "You wanted so badly to believe that others were just like you, to fit this ideal model of harmony and equality, that any evidence to the contrary was spontaneously disregarded. Critical thinking is a necessary element of defense, you know. Once it is lost, then so is the battle... the jihad."

"Jihad?" asked Parker.

"As the Prophet said, there are many ways to wage war," replied Hamzi, "even against an enemy that can't be defeated on the battlefield. The best way is to have your opponent deny that it is at war, and turn it against itself. Even a superpower can be defeated, particularly if it provides its enemies with the very tools to do so. How does a nation get to the point that it has sympathy for those seeking its destruction, but only ridicule for those wanting to preserve the culture that made it successful?

"Well, in this case, we simply adopted your language of human rights and tolerance – although not the practice, of course – and used your ego to our advantage. Once you became self-obsessive and unwilling to critically evaluate others, moral perspective was easily lost and you began to demand the strictest conformity to impractical standards that your own enemies had not the slightest intention of observing. Violent attacks against you merely resulted in calls for internal change – greater tolerance and understanding – rather than punishing your enemy and boldly demanding the same respect. How could you not lose?"

Before Parker could answer, a knock sounded at the door. Hamzi quickly stubbed out his cigarette and reassumed an apologetic demeanor. "I'm sorry, but it's time to leave."

The old man nodded and stood up to get his bags, not worrying about the dishes, as he knew that he would not be coming back, although he made sure the light switch was turned off, in case the electricity someday returned.

Outside, the high-pitched *adhan* called the faithful to prayer, with the chant wailing from the heights of minarets and echoing down through the domed mosques and crowded bazaars that lined the streets of the hazy city.